THE ERIC SYKES
COMPENDIUM

UFOs Are Coming Wednesday
The Great Crime of Grapplewick
Smelling of Roses

Eric Sykes

This compendium edition first published
in Great Britain in 2006 by
Virgin Books Ltd
Thames Wharf Studios
Rainville Road
London
W6 9HA

The Great Crime of Grapplewick first published in
Great Britain in 1984 by Macmillan London Limited.
First published by Virgin Publishing in 1997.

UFOs Are Coming Wednesday first published in
Great Britain in 1995 by Virgin Publishing.

Smelling of Roses first published in Great Britain in 1997
by Virgin Publishing.

A catalogue record for this book is available from
the British Library.

ISBN (10) 0 7535 1193 2
ISBN (13) 978 0 7535 1193 0

The paper used in this book is a natural, recyclable product
made from wood grown in sustainable forests. The
manufacturing process conforms to the regulations of the
country of origin.

Typeset by TW Typesetting, Plymouth, Devon
Printed and bound in Great Britain by
Mackays of Chatham PLC

CONTENTS

UFOs Are Coming Wednesday   1

The Great Crime of Grapplewick   217

Smelling of Roses   395

UFOs ARE COMING WEDNESDAY

Part I

SWINEGAP, NEAR BIRMINGHAM

ONE

Apart from the people who are born or die on the 4th of May, there is nothing significant for anyone in the date itself. It is not a bank holiday, nor a Saint's day, it isn't even the longest or shortest day, it's simply the 4th of May. It was, however, an auspicious day for the people of Birmingham, or to be more exact, Swinegap, a thriving new town a few miles to the west.

Before dawn letters were delivered to the homes of four prominent citizens. The envelopes were properly addressed and marked *Strictly Private and Confidential*.

Councillor Blackstone OBE, leader of the Tory Council, was the first of the four to discover the letter on his doormat. He was halfway through his breakfast before he slit open the envelope. He was not only a councillor but also the town's leading solicitor and accustomed to scanning quickly through long and complicated documents – but before he had reached the bottom of page one of the letter he started it again, reading slowly and more carefully. The message was so world-shattering that his first reaction was that it could only be an elaborate hoax. But suppose it were to prove genuine? His mind flashed along several paths and he began to feel the cold awakenings of panic. Ashen faced, he rose unsteadily to his feet. His wife popped her head in from the kitchen and, regarding her husband's general demeanour, thought it must be the egg again. As he walked stiff legged to the bathroom clutching the letter, she assumed it was.

At the home of the Opposition leader, Councillor Sharp, results were just as devastating, except that Sharp was slightly more fortunate in that he read the letter whilst still in bed which, if you're going to pass out, is the best place to be. His aged mother was unable to prise the letter from his grasp, but by laying her head sideways on the eiderdown she tried to read what she could. Fortunately, before she could start making sense of the piece that was visible her son revived, puzzled as to why his mother was apparently listening to his knee.

Three streets away the mayor, unable to find his own glasses, asked his wife to read it out to him. The fact the letter was marked *Strictly Private and Confidential* was irrelevant as he considered his wife barely able to understand 'wish you were here' on a holiday postcard, so whatever secrets the letter contained would be beyond her comprehension. She was a slow reader and at first he wondered idly whether she would be finished by lunchtime, but as he listened to her stumbling dissertation his interest and pulse quickened. If the letter was genuine, it would without a doubt be the most stupendous happening in the history of the town, even in the history of the world. His palms began to sweat. Frantically, he snatched the glasses from her face in order to read the letter for himself. Unfortunately he had underrated his wife's capacity for understanding and only half noticed her sliding sideways out of her chair and on to the floor with what later turned out to be a mild heart attack.

The mayor's thoughts were racing incoherently through his head too fast for him to keep up. Was the letter genuine, and what action should he take? With some relief, he saw on his second reading that copies of the letter had also been sent to three of his colleagues. That eased the burden a little, and being a Class 1 bureaucrat he immediately came to a decision – 'See what the others think first.' That was his standard ploy: to nod wisely through the debate, then always vote with the majority. It was the surest way to attain high office, an index-linked pension and, in all probability, a knighthood. Striding over the prostrate figure of his wife he made for the phone. It wasn't that he was an uncaring man, but he knew where his priorities lay, and that pathetic bundle on the floor came way down the list.

The last man to receive the letter was the local police inspector. Being a professional he read the letter in a detached, unemotional way. In the past he'd had many things pushed through his letterbox: petrol followed by a match which fortunately went out before hitting the floor; threatening and obscene letters practically every week; and of course dog droppings, or what he assumed to be dog droppings – he had never had them analysed. So this latest *Strictly Private and Confidential* load of bumph was just par for the course – the sooner they brought back hanging the better. He only had to read the first few lines to realise that it was a load of codswallop. Crumpling the letter, he was just about to sling it into the fireplace when the phone rang. He picked up the receiver and barked 'Yes?' (He used to give his full title but criminals, cranks and members of the public phoning to complain about rising crime figures had led him to become more secretive.) He was relieved to hear the mayor's voice asking him if he had received an anonymous letter. The inspector's initial reaction was to deny all knowledge of any such letter but something in the mayor's voice intrigued him. He replied that he had received one but that he hadn't had time to digest its contents. As he spoke he hunched his shoulder to hold the phone against his ear while he desperately tried to straighten out the letter. It was only then he became aware that copies had also been sent to the other officials. He listened to the mayor with half his mind but picked up enough to know that a meeting was arranged in the town hall in twenty minutes' time when all four of them would discuss the missive and its implications. He was about to ask 'What implications?' but the mayor had already broken the connection. He fumed all the way to the town hall at this disruption of his day and half an hour later he was seated, with ill grace, in the mayor's parlour.

They were all seated at a round table to avoid the risk of a breach of protocol, but in spite of this Councillor Blackstone OBE was quick to assume the chair.

'We've all read the letter, I assume,' he began.

The inspector nodded, although he hadn't had time to read it all. In any case, it was difficult to follow the letter while he ironed it, a wise precaution as it turned out because Councillor Blackstone OBE suggested that they place the letters before them to ascertain that they were all identical. He cleared his throat.

'I think it is safe to say that this morning we have all received a shock, to put it mildly. It's not every day that four prominent citizens receive notice that a spacecraft from an alien planet will be landing on Wednesday, with even the location of its landing site – Tenkly Common, not two miles from where we sit.'

The inspector was not listening, he was reading the letter quickly to try to find out what all this fuss was about. The letter purported to come from a planet called Androm, headquarters of the Inter-Galactic Peacekeeping Force. This force had been initiated to monitor the delicate mathematical structure of the Inner Galaxies and the Supreme Powers were gravely concerned about the way in which Earth people were conducting their affairs. The inspector pushed the letter away.

'We're not going to take this seriously are we? This is *Boy's Own Paper* stuff. It's a joke,' he sneered. 'Inter-Galactic Peace-keeping Force? Concerned for us, are they? Well, I'm sure we're all concerned about the state of things nowadays, but what motive would *they* have for coming here?'

Councillor Blackstone OBE eyed him coldly. 'It's quite obvious to me that you have only given the letter a cursory glance. Paragraph four states quite clearly their motives. May I read it to you?'

' "The Supreme Council on Androm are deeply concerned by the proliferation of nuclear weapons on planet Earth. In fact, the situation has gone from merely grave to critical and Earth is in danger of being utterly destroyed sooner rather than later." '

Councillor Sharp decided that it was time he put his fourpence worth in. 'We all know that,' he said testily, 'but that's up to us, isn't it? It's nothing to do with anyone else.'

'In any case,' broke in the inspector, 'if this did come from outer space, somebody human on this planet must have typed the letters and shoved them through our letterboxes.'

Councillor Blackstone OBE sighed and looked at the ceiling. 'Not necessarily,' he said. 'May I draw your attention to paragraph eight?'

They all turned over their top sheets.

'Paragraph eight,' continued Blackstone OBE, 'states categori-cally that men from Androm, having assumed human form, have been infiltrating every country on this planet for thousands of years, in which case the delivery could have been made by a citizen of Androm.'

This last observation intrigued the mayor. If such was the case, any one of his colleagues could be from Androm, he mused idly. His thoughts were broken by a discreet tap on the door and a young girl pushed it open with her back, edging in carrying a tray on which were four cups of coffee, a jug of milk and a sugar bowl. They suspended their discussion whilst she placed a cup of coffee in front of each of them. The mayor, watching her covertly, continued his train of thought. Was she one of the aliens? No, he smiled to himself. If she had assumed human form she would have done a lot better than a spotty face and a king-sized hooter. And look at those legs. Oh, dear Lord, if he had a pair like that he wouldn't be wearing a mini-skirt, he would be hopping around in a sack. She couldn't be an alien in a million years, but then again it could be a perfect disguise.

He looked up to see that the inspector was staring at him, in fact they were all staring at him.

'Well,' snapped Councillor Sharp, 'do you or don't you?'

The mayor hadn't the foggiest idea what he was on about, but he nodded and said, 'I would have to give it some thought. It's not as simple as it sounds.'

They all looked at each other with baffled expressions. Sharp sighed and jerked his thumb towards the young girl. 'This young lady would like to know if you want milk.'

'Oh, er, no thanks.' He recovered himself. 'I was miles away thinking about this document.' He tapped the letter in front of him. 'Yes,' he said as an afterthought, 'I will have some milk,' but by that time the girl had gone.

The inspector took a quick sip of his lukewarm coffee and pushed it aside with disgust.

'Let's collate the facts,' he began. 'We each get a letter marked "Strictly Private and Confidential". It claims to come from an unknown planet called Androm and we are informed that one of their space modules will be landing on Tenkly Common on Wednesday.' He paused. 'Right so far?'

They nodded.

'We are then told,' he continued, 'that the four of us are to wait, maintaining the strictest confidence, for the alleged landing whereupon we will be taken aboard for instruction.'

'Instruction for what?' blurted Councillor Sharp. 'Fretwork, clog dancing, the theory of relativity?'

Councillor Blackstone OBE stopped his flow. 'As long as it's not Marxism.'

'Now then, now then,' soothed the mayor. This was his domain and there would be no political in-fighting in his office. He made his contribution to the discussion.

'What happens if we get on board and the spacecraft takes off?' As soon as he'd said it he wished he hadn't.

The inspector chuckled and said drily, 'We'd better remember to take our passports.'

Councillor Blackstone OBE sighed once again. 'They give their reason for their anxiety on page two.' He read once more:

'"Although the self-destruction of planet Earth is of no consequence in itself, the great fear is that this very action of self-destruction will affect the planets of the solar system and the consequences of this are too horrific to contemplate."' He took off his glasses and sat back in his chair.

The inspector had had enough. 'If you want my opinion,' he said slowly, 'I think it's a load of codswallop.'

Councillor Blackstone OBE steepled his fingers. He was a solicitor and viewed most things from a legal standpoint. 'It's all very well to dismiss this as codswallop,' he said gravely, 'but do you realise that we would be shirking our duties in ignoring this situation?'

He glared at the inspector as though he were a hostile witness.

'All I am saying,' said the inspector, 'is that we should wait and see what happens.'

'That's a very slipshod attitude, if I may say so,' interposed Councillor Sharp. 'If we all adopted that philosophy this town would still have horse-drawn trams.'

Councillor Blackstone OBE went on as if there had been no interruption. 'We can, of course, sit back and keep silent in the hope that this is all a gigantic hoax. But on the other hand, have you considered the possibility that if this Peacekeeping Force, or whatever it calls itself, does land on Tenkly Common next Wednesday the consequences are liable to be disastrous for each one of us?'

There was silence around the table. They looked at each other uneasily, not quite understanding. Blackstone OBE now had his audience and continued: 'Think about it – aliens from another planet land in our country and we, having had prior knowledge of their arrival, did nothing about it.'

Still their faces remained blank. Councillor Blackstone OBE shook his head.

'Don't you see? England would be invaded and because we withheld the information we could become accessories after the fact. In effect, we could be guilty of treason.'

There was yet more silence around the table as they all digested this seemingly simple truth. Treason was an ugly word. After only a few moments the mayor's face brightened. He had the answer.

'Ah, well, that's taking it a step further. If I read you right, this isn't a local problem at all; it's of national importance and as such it is our bounden duty to override the confidentiality of this document and pass it on to a higher authority.'

They all nodded vigorously. That was the obvious solution. It was the right and proper course to take. Councillor Blackstone OBE, as senior member, was unanimously appointed to place the whole matter in the hands of their local Member of Parliament, and that was when the snowball really started to roll down the slippery slope.

TWO

Charles Tupping was a rookie back-bencher. Due to the death of his predecessor, he'd retained the seat in a by-election. It was a safe Tory stronghold and from a majority of 25,000 he managed to scrape home by 800 votes. He was now a Parliamentarian of some eight weeks' standing and although he hadn't yet made his maiden speech he felt that already he was being noticed. On one or two occasions the Prime Minister had nodded to him as they had passed in the corridors of Westminster and once he'd sat at the next table in the tea room. Oh, yes, it was only a matter of time before they were exchanging Christmas cards and from there the path to the Cabinet lay open, and perhaps eventually – why not? – the door to Number 10. But in the meantime there was work to be done.

Tupping was dictating a letter to a shared secretary when his train of thought was interrupted by the telephone. It was Security at the Main Gate to tell him that a Councillor Blackstone OBE wished to see him most urgently on a matter of extreme importance. Tupping said he'd be right down and, dismissing the secretary, he hurried outside to the gate. He could easily have obtained a pass for the town councillor to come inside, but he was deeply embarrassed by the little cubby hole he had been given as an office.

Outside it was bitterly cold and Tupping wished he'd worn his overcoat, but then he remembered that very few MPs wore overcoats outside when being interviewed on television, whatever the weather.

'Hello, Blackstone,' he said; 'sorry I can't take you in. I'm in a meeting of the Back-Bench Committee and I'd have to get security clearance for you and all that rigmarole, so if it's not going to take too long, I thought we might have our little discussion out here.'

Councillor Blackstone OBE shrugged and silently handed over the letter. He had never liked the pompous little twit and had voted against his adoption as the Parliamentary candidate. Tupping hurriedly scanned the pages. God, that wind was cold. He could barely read the printed pages for the tears in his eyes. Finally he lowered the letter and stared at the councillor.

'It couldn't be a joke, could it?'

Blackstone groaned inwardly. He wouldn't have been down in London freezing to death outside the Houses of Parliament if he thought it was a joke.

'That was our first impression,' he said, 'but we felt we couldn't dismiss it outright, and if it is genuine then the consequences don't bear thinking about.'

'Hmmm,' said Tupping. He felt his nose beginning to run but he was reluctant to use the nicely folded silk handkerchief in his top pocket. He turned away and sniffled.

'I see. Well, let me sleep on it and I'll let you know in the morning.'

Blackstone was exasperated.

'With due respect, Mr Tupping, I feel that time is not on our side. After all, if they're coming, they'll be here next Wednesday.'

'Yes, I realise that. It's just that we have a rather heavy schedule what with the Health Service cuts and everything. Still, leave it with me, I'll see to it. Got a meeting with the Minister for Ag and Fish and I can't keep him waiting. George here will get you a cab.' He nodded towards the commissionaire, who immediately turned away. He had better things to do with his time and he wasn't even called George.

Blackstone watched the disappearing back of his MP. Pompous prat, he'd run him around the next time he came up for his weekly surgery.

Tupping was glad to be back in the warmth of his small office. Outside he'd been too cold to give the letter much attention so he read it again and with a sickening lurch of his stomach he suddenly realised why Councillor Blackstone OBE had travelled all the way down from Birmingham to hand it to him personally. It was called 'passing the buck'. After all, the town council, the mayor and the police inspector were mature people, older and presumably wiser than he was, so why had they dumped this on him? Was it a test of some sort? Was it a trick to measure his aptitude as an MP ... or did they really believe that spaceships would be landing next week? He stared unseeing at the letter.

Suddenly a cheery voice bellowed, 'Bad news, old boy?'

Tupping jerked upright like a badly manipulated puppet. He didn't actually lose control of his bowels, but it was a close thing. Thankfully, it was his cousin Gerald, a Parliamentary figure of high esteem. Indeed, he was respected enough to be Parliamentary Private Secretary to the Prime Minister. Tupping sighed with relief. Since entering the House his cousin, some twenty years his senior, had taken him under his wing and his intervention at this precise moment seemed like a monumental slice of good fortune. Without a word he handed over the letter. If the Prime Minister's PPS couldn't advise him on this one, then who could? He wiped his sweaty palms down the sides of his trousers as his cousin read through the letter before throwing it down on the desk.

'Good grief, Charles,' he said, 'is that all that's bothering you? You'll be getting more outrageous letters than that in this job, I can tell you.'

Tupping smiled shakily. 'I wasn't really worried, Gerald. As a matter of fact, I think it's rather funny.' He was immensely relieved by his cousin's reaction and admiration shone from his face in a dazzling beam of hero worship.

Gerald patted him on the shoulder. 'Don't give it another thought. Put it in the shredder where it belongs,' and with that he swept out of Tupping's office in a cloud of expensive aftershave. Almost immediately the door opened again and Gerald reappeared. 'On second thoughts, let me have the letter. I'll show it to God; he needs a laugh. Hasn't had much to cheer him up lately!'

Alone again, Tupping smiled shamefacedly at his momentary panic. Little did he realise that he had just handed over the stick which would be waggled about in a gigantic hornets' nest.

A few hundred yards away in the Cabinet Room at Number 10 the daily briefing had passed off without incident. The PM was in a lighthearted mood, cheered by the opinion polls that morning. He wasn't too far behind the Opposition leader. More importantly, in five days' time it had been arranged that he attend a top-level summit meeting in the Bahamas – which couldn't be bad. He was looking forward to the trip – sunshine, white private beaches, banquets and fine wines. Of course, there would be talks as well, but he didn't anticipate these being too taxing. And when he stepped off the plane on his return he would cheerfully announce that the discussions had gone exceedingly well, etc., etc. His homecoming speech was already written, in fact he had memorised most of it already. So today was one of the few occasions on which the PM felt he could relax and enjoy the perks of power.

His Cabinet went along with his euphoric frame of mind. Secretly they would be glad to see the back of him. He'd had a rough passage over the past few months and they feared he was close to a breakdown. Perhaps six days in the sun would be just the break he needed to top up his batteries.

The PM smiled benignly as he imagined his wife, Mary, in some of the light dresses she had purchased for the trip. He was relaxed and content. It was a mistake. He, of all people, should have known never to drop his guard – it's the quickest way of inviting a sucker punch and, sure enough, it was about to be unleashed.

Sensing the almost boyish exuberance of his master, Gerald deemed it an opportune moment to broach the subject of the letter. He began with a soft chuckle. The PM looked across at him.

'Well, Gerald,' he said, 'whatever it is let's all share it.'

'Oh, it's nothing really, Prime Minister. My cousin has received a letter and it was rather amusing to see his reaction.'

'Is it a funny letter?' prompted the PM, smiling.

Gerald ventured a grin. 'No, as a matter of fact it's rather serious. I was enjoying more the expression on my cousin's face when I burst in on him.'

He handed the letter to the Prime Minister, silently congratulating himself on his skilful passing of the buck. He watched the PM's face covertly while pretending to rummage in his briefcase, ready to burst out laughing or look statesmanlike, depending on the reaction of his leader. But things didn't seem to be going according to plan. The PM should have dismissed the letter with a smile by now, but instead his expression was becoming increasingly grave and it was obvious that he was giving it his utmost attention. The letter was read and re-read in an icy silence; the drop in temperature was almost tangible and Gerald wondered for a moment whether he had handed over the right letter. He hoped to God it wasn't the one he'd received that morning accusing him of being a 'poofter'.

As the PM continued his reading, the PPS began clipping pens in his inside pocket and coughed discreetly. 'I'm sorry to rush you, Prime Minister, but we're due at the House in thirty minutes and the press and TV are outside.'

The PM looked at him blankly. 'Press?' he echoed.

'Yes, sir. You said you'd have a statement for them concerning the Child Allowance Bill.'

The PM rose and, scowling, thrust the letter back at his PPS.

'I haven't time to read it now,' he snapped and strode towards the door.

Gerald's heart sank. He knew that the PM had read enough to be perturbed and by handing the letter back he had cleverly returned the buck. But why was this such a hot potato? Good grief, UFOs had been spotted for years – saucer shape, round, elliptical, static, moving at the speed of light, little green men with three heads – so what was all the panic about? He cursed his cousin for dropping him in it but was appalled by his own stupidity. He should have learned by now that it was always the messenger who took the bullet.

THREE

It was true that the letter had affected the Prime Minister and with each step as he slowly descended the staircase to the hall in No. 10 his gloom deepened. Only himself, the Foreign Secretary and a handful of senior civil servants were privy to the secret agenda of the Bahamas Summit headed 'UFOs'. He had not attached too much importance to this until now. Over the years every major government in the world had assembled mountains of information concerning Unidentified Flying Objects. All these sightings came from reputable witnesses: airline pilots reporting near misses, police alarmed at strange lights too powerful to be earthly, skimming at roof-top height over main roads. The CIA had only recently submitted a dossier presenting evidence that aliens from outer space had already infiltrated several countries on Earth. Even more immediate, two unidentified spacecraft had crashed in the Andes. This sighting had been verified by unimpeachable sources but inspection of the crash site was impossible for the moment due to the high levels of radiation. On his own patch, the Government had received notice from GCHQ Cheltenham of the increased volume of radio traffic in outer space.

The fear now amongst world leaders was that the likelihood of extraterrestrial intervention in Earth's business was now at a critical stage and, therefore, was it not his duty to inform his colleagues at the Bahamas Summit of the contents of that letter? He groaned softly. He hadn't really taken the Bahamas trip seriously; for him it was a junket, a week in the sun, but if the letter was authentic, his duty was plain. He would have to be in Britain with his own people on Wednesday, not swanning about in the Caribbean. Mary was going to be bitterly disappointed about cancelling the trip. Damn the letter and damn Gerald for showing it to him. Then, just as suddenly as the gloom had descended, he brightened. What letter? He hadn't read any letter. No such letter existed. That was the answer! Having convinced himself, he was greatly cheered. He squared his shoulders and stepped out of the famous front door to meet the press and was greeted by a barrage of flashbulbs.

'Good afternoon, ladies and gentlemen,' he said.

There was a murmured reply from the assembled '*News at 10 Downing Street*' mob. The Prime Minister pointed to a bespectacled harridan from one of the tabloids.

'Yes, Miss Curshaw,' he politely solicited a question.

He was proud of his name-dropping. He was under the impression that it made him more approachable, a man of the people, one of the lads.

But the woman reporter flared at him, 'It's Ms Jackson, actually.'

There was a ripple of laughter and the PM smiled with them. 'Clever bitch,' he thought. Did they expect him to remember all their names? He was the Prime Minister, for God's sake, not a telephone directory.

Ms Jackson continued. 'Can the Prime Minister assure us that there will be no cut in child allowance for single-parent families?'

The PM answered easily. He had been well briefed for such a question and spoke with a confident evasion. He did not like Ms Jackson, he knew her of old, a rabid left-winger. He could imagine her bedroom full of pictures of Harold Wilson and a lock of Denis Healey's eyebrow under her pillow. Before Ms Jackson could nail him with a follow-up question, he pointed to a man at the back.

'Yes, sir?'

The man at the back spoke loudly and clearly.

'Prime Minister,' he began, 'is there any truth in the rumour that on Wednesday next a spacecraft will be landing near Birmingham?'

There was a stunned silence as all the media people turned to stare at the man. He was a stranger in that tight clique. This was an entirely new departure from the agreed line of questioning but it was infinitely more interesting than single-parent allowances. There was a rustle as pages were flipped over in notebooks. They waited eagerly for the reply. Those with microphones thrust them forwards and television lenses zoomed in on the PM's face. It bore the look of a man struck violently over the back of the head with a sock full of cold porridge. In fact, for the moment he was brain dead, but with the skill of the consummate politician that he was, his mouth switched to automatic pilot.

'I'm sorry,' he blurted. 'I didn't hear the question. Can you repeat it please?'

It was a standard retort to give himself time to get up off the ropes. The assembled reporters turned round again but the stranger was nowhere to be seen. The damage, however, was done. In millions of homes viewers would be able to watch a badly shaken Prime Minister floundering in front of the cameras. His stricken face would appear on millions of TV screens at six o'clock and pictures would be plastered all over the morning editions of every newspaper. The fan was already beginning to revolve and the Prime Minister sensed that something really nasty would hit it when he reached the House of Commons.

FOUR

Q uestion Time began with the usual exchanges of traditional
platitudes. A Conservative member con-   gratulated the
Prime Minister on last month's trade figures. A Labour member
posed a question that was deftly fielded by the Prime Minister
although it was only realised later that he had answered a question
that had not yet been asked. It was a normal Question Time . . .
but the bomb had been primed and was about to explode.

There was a question from a Labour back-bencher.

'Mr Speaker,' he began. 'I was about to ask the Prime Minister
a question relating to car manufacture in Birmingham but in the
light of recent information to the effect that a landing vehicle
from outer space seems imminent in the area, would the Prime
Minister . . .'

The rest of his words were drowned by cries from the
Government benches – 'Disgraceful', 'What landing vehicle?',
'Out of order', etc., etc., and from the Opposition came cries of
'Explain', 'Resign', 'Take more water with it'.

The uproar was unprecedented and the Speaker was inaudible
as he frantically sought to gain control. The Prime Minister was
rattled; this wasn't just a leak, it was Niagara Falls. How had the
contents of the letter fallen into Opposition hands?

The answer was simple. Unknown to the PM, Councillor Sharp,
niggled by the way in which Councillor Blackstone OBE had
taken over their conference, had decided that if the document had

any relevance as a matter of National Importance, it should be an all-party matter. Before Councillor Blackstone OBE had even boarded the train for London, Sharp had faxed his copy of the letter to a prominent Labour back-bencher. He knew the man slightly, having scraped an acquaintance at the Party Conference in Blackpool.

The Labour MP had read the fax, more amused than anything else, with half his attention on his portable television. Hearing the reporter's question and seeing a close-up of the PM's face, he'd read the faxed letter again. His pulse quickened and in less than an hour he'd advised a great many of his Labour colleagues of the strange letter. It was a little gold mine. At the very least it would embarrass the Government if it could somehow be worked into the afternoon questions. The Labour benches could not have hoped in their wildest dreams for the effect it was now having on the Prime Minister.

The PM appeared to be in a coma. It was momentary, however, and he soon sprang to his feet.

'Will the honourable member . . .' He tried again. 'Will the honourable member . . .' but it was no good. The cacophony was now at such a level that had Concorde flown through the chamber, no one would have heard it. Spittle flecked the corners of his mouth and his eyes were wild. The question had not been tabled and he should have left it to the Speaker to censure the man – but the Prime Minister was beyond reason.

The Opposition were out for blood. Cries of 'Androm' and 'Take me to your leader' were thrown across the floor of the House. The Speaker was no help – he had collapsed, but there were plenty of doctors in the Commons so nobody was particularly perturbed.

'Will the honourable gentleman,' the Prime Minister yelled again, but the noise was still too great. The Foreign Secretary took the back of the PM's jacket and tried to pull him down, but the leader slapped his hand away.

'We have been aware of the impending landing for some weeks now,' he ranted and the baying subsided to normal levels. The Opposition sensed they were about to hear something momentous and the Government benches were eager to hear what they were supposed to have been aware of for weeks.

'Oh, yes,' the PM went on hysterically. 'My colleagues and I have had constant discussions along with the Joint Chiefs of Staff.'

His Cabinet colleagues stared at him aghast. What was he on about? Discussions about what, for God's sake? As for the Joint Chiefs of Staff, they'd not been seen in the Cabinet Room since the Falklands. The PM babbled on manically, committing the cardinal sin of making policy on the hoof. On the bench behind him, Gerald groaned as he listened to the PM digging himself deeper and deeper into a dark and friendless pit. Gerald was under no illusion as to his own future. That stupid letter! And, worse, he'd even chuckled as he'd handed it across the desk. He looked over his shoulder to his cousin on the back benches, his face shining with patriotic fervour as he drank in the words of his Prime Minister. Gerald's teeth ground together, panic turned to anger. If he was about to get the boot he wouldn't go down alone. No, by God, he'd take that prat of a cousin with him even if it came to murder.

Mercifully, Question Time came to an end and the Government front bench couldn't wait to leave the chamber. They hustled their spluttering Prime Minister out before he could break into 'Mary Had A Little Lamb'. Most of them were totally ignorant of the existence of the letter and were totally mystified by the taunts about Androm and spacemen from the Opposition benches. Of one thing they were certain, especially when the whips informed them there was to be a full Cabinet meeting at eight o'clock: they were all on the verge of a major crisis.

That evening lights burned in the Cabinet Room at No. 10. The first hour had been tempestuous, to put it mildly. As the Prime Minister apprised them of the facts, his ministerial colleagues listened with growing incredulity and alarm. After all, the letter was anonymous. Why hadn't the PM ignored it, laughed it off for goodness' sake? Aliens from an unknown planet landing on Wednesday, and near Birmingham of all places! Why not Hyde Park or the Champs Élysées? With mounting terror they realised how deep was the hole the PM had dug for himself and in order to save his face they had no option but to jump in after him. Wild thoughts of revolt flashed around the Cabinet table, but they were only thoughts. They were too astute and wily to speak out and there might come a time when their words would be remembered and used against them.

Openly, they had no option but to back the PM's actions and a damage limitation conference ensued. After Wednesday, the knives would be out. There would be time before the next General

Election to have the PM certified. The Chiefs of Staff from the Air Force and the Army were ushered in and some of the Cabinet Ministers were ushered out.

Amongst those who remained, a war council was established. The Prime Minister was in an impossible situation. He could apprise the military of the letter, but not his concerns about the Bahamas Summit. The summit agenda was too secret, so all he had to justify his performance in the Commons was the letter.

It was no wonder that the military men were aghast. They were expected to come up with a plan to counter a full-scale alien invasion on the basis of an anonymous letter. Various plans and stratagems were discussed and it was finally agreed that from 24.00 hours on Tuesday the surveillance wing of the Royal Air Force would monitor air space over Birmingham. Traffic control at Birmingham Airport would not be involved, and would be told that the increased RAF presence was due to a large-scale routine exercise. The RAF planes would fly thousands of feet above the commercial lanes and would be in contact with an elite force of ground troops. On landing, the aliens would be apprehended by the ground force and taken to a secret rendezvous where they would be interrogated. It was a hastily cobbled-up plan but it was the best they could do in the short time available. It wasn't exactly 'Overlord' but then Churchill, Eisenhower and their top brass had had nearly a year to prepare for that show. Good grief, if they had had less than a week, we would all be speaking German. As dawn took over the burden from the Downing Street lights, the military hurried away to set the wheels in motion. Secretly they were convinced that the man running their country was definitely losing his marbles.

The PM had time for a shower and a change of suit whilst a TV crew set up cameras and lights in the Cabinet Room. At ten o'clock that morning, the Prime Minister was to appear in a special news flash on all channels. It was now almost thirty hours since he had slept and he was full of black coffee and benzedrine, heavily made up to hide the dark patches under his eyes. It was through this grotesque mask that he smiled at the nation. He appealed to the British people to stay calm and carry on as normal. The likelihood of a spacecraft actually landing was extremely remote. It was all a storm in a teacup and he urged that Wednesday be treated as a normal working day. There was much more of this, all in the same vein, and in view of the circumstances it was a creditable performance – he sounded quite sane and statesmanlike. Any fears that the people may have had regarding invasion should now be dispelled – but he had greatly under-estimated the man in the street.

FIVE

On Monday the traffic roared up and down the M1. It was a normal, average, horrendous day on the motorway but very few people noticed that the turn-off slip roads to Birmingham were taking an above-average volume of traffic. As a result, by midnight Birmingham was at a standstill.

It was now obvious to the Birmingham traffic police that the main bulk of the vehicles were making tracks to Tenkly Common, so cars were diverted – down side streets, up alleyways – anywhere to get the damn things out of the centre of the city. Anywhere would do as long as it cleared the main streets. The Automobile Association was out in force and yellow signs marked 'Tenkly Common' were displayed all round Birmingham.

At this point the mood of the crowd was orderly. Some were apprehensive and others reverent but mainly there was a happy holiday atmosphere. There were exceptions: for instance, when two traffic control police returned to their parked car they found it jacked up and the wheels missing.

On Tuesday, however, on D minus one, the good humour of over 100,000 motorists had evaporated. By midday all vehicles heading for Tenkly Common had come to a standstill. Cars, buses and lorries continued to pull up behind the stationary traffic, and before long there was a tailback as far as Watford. On the southbound lane the jam stretched as far north as Carlisle. Desperate appeals were made by radio and television for people to avoid the motorways unless in an absolute emergency; but they were bolting the stable door when the horse was long gone.

Airports ground to a halt as the foreign media arrived along with the thousands of sightseers. Many planes from overseas were diverted to France, Holland and Belgium. The railways suffered the same fate. The platforms were now so jammed with people that passengers arriving at Birmingham New Street were unable to alight and had no option but to stay on to London. Eventually, in the interests of public safety, the trains stopped running altogether.

Inevitably some people managed to get through to the landing site but they had arrived on foot and so tightly were they packed, the majority had to sleep standing up. Oddly enough there were few locals present. With so many strangers in town they felt it best to stay put and keep an eye on their possessions. In any case, the restaurants, garages and hotels were enjoying the biggest boom since any of them could remember. Most of the ordinary householders had put bed and breakfast signs in their front windows, and weary travellers who couldn't afford the £100-plus per night spent three or four days in the open air. Oh yes, the locals welcomed the strangers with open arms all right. Nothing was too much trouble and nothing was cheap; even water was expensive and luckily it didn't rain. A bonanza of tax-free money was finding its way under floorboards and mattresses were growing lumpy. By next week many of the local inhabitants would be buying time-share villas in more exotic places.

However, for the rest of the country the outlook was bleak. By Wednesday afternoon business in England was practically nonexistent. Factories closed due to widespread absenteeism and industry was unable to move its products. Inevitably shares on the Stock Exchange fell dramatically; the pound was pathetic beside the dollar and the Deutschmark, and to all intents and purposes Britain had ceased to function as a trading nation. Millions of people were totally unaware of this as they waited for the arrival of the beings from outer space.

From the onset of darkness on Wednesday a tense feeling of expectancy pervaded the atmosphere. People began to converse in whispers, eyes scanned the blackness for some visible sign of the arrival, and speculation was rife as to where the aliens would actually land. The designated site, being so densely packed, was now out of the question. In fact, the whole area for miles around was now jammed into a solid phalanx and a landing was impossible.

Throughout the night millions of eyes searched the heavens but it was a fruitless vigil. Low cloud blotted out the stars, even the navigation lights of commercial aircraft would have been a welcome diversion; but, alas, the airport had been closed since mid-afternoon. It was a long night.

With the dawn the skies lightened promising a fine Thursday, but there was still no sign of any alien spaceships. The monitoring aircraft circling miles above the cloud base had no information to beam down to the special forces, which was just as well because the elite ground troops weren't even in position. Owing to the tremendous press of people, there had been no place for the military helicopters to land. The backup plan, considering the situation, was simply fatuous. The helicopters would make height sufficient for the special forces to descend by parachute. Fortunately the major in charge of the operation was a realist and countermanded the order. He only had to look down on the white mass of upturned faces to visualise the carnage below as two sticks of paratroopers in full battle gear landed feet first amongst them. So, on his own initiative, he ordered the choppers to land in a farmyard some twelve miles short of Tenkly Common. It was the nearest point but then a forced march of twelve miles was merely a constitutional for a seasoned force of combat troops, and they swung out of the farmyard in fine fettle.

From then on their troubles began. The crowds thickened and in four hours they had only covered half a mile and were trapped in a seething mass of sightseers. Some of them took off their balaclavas. These masks were supposed to provide anonymity, but what did that matter now? They had become separated from each other and in any case the balaclavas were frightening the children.

For the whole of Thursday nothing moved. None of the crowd could have gone home even had they wanted to and after suffering for the last three days, they were loath to miss anything now. Rumours floated around like the evening midges: 'The spaceships have landed in Manchester', 'The spaceships are orbiting Earth waiting for the crowd to disperse', and some people had heard on their car radio that two flying saucers had crashed in the Channel. As the hours went by children became fractious. Many were desperately hungry and to cap it all it started to rain – that was the last straw. As the rain got heavier, people turned round and tried to move in all directions to where they'd left their cars. But it was hopeless. The cries of the young and the admonitions of their parents were augmented by engine noise as cars were started up. The exodus seemed to have begun, but it was to be many hours before they would begin to disperse.

The police, the AA , the RAC, in fact all the authorities connected with transport were pressed into service to unsnarl the biggest jam in road history. The whole operation was overseen, literally, by the Minister of Transport fluttering up and down the motorways in a helicopter to the extent of its fuel load, a quick filling of the tanks and up again. It was very impressive, except that the Minister slept most of the time. Finally his chopper alighted and he leaped down, refreshed, announcing to the waiting media that the motorways were now running normally, and any hold-ups were now due to the usual roadworks.

Inevitably there was a heavy price to pay for the last week, both financially and politically. The centre of England was littered with discarded beer cans, coke cans, containers of every description, papers, articles of clothing and three bodies. In fact it was a forty-odd square mile rubbish tip, and the compensation claims on the Government were horrendous although the army of cleaners off- set this to some extent by causing a drop in the unemployment figures.

The real battle in the House of Commons became a no contest as the Opposition brought their 16-inch guns to bear against the sticks wielded by the Government front benches. It was carnival night, birthday and Christmas as political points were scored one after another. It was too easy, it was trawling in a fish hatchery, but the Opposition party was relentless. 'Would the Prime Minister deny that the whole disgraceful episode had been manufactured in order to divert attention from the shambles of the Health Service?' 'Was he aware of the widespread damage both at home and abroad this mischievous malicious hoax had caused?' 'Did the Prime Minister realise the enormity of the danger in leaving the country virtually defenceless during the last week?' There was more, and the Government's responses were pathetically defensive.

In the event, by some miracle, the Government survived. This was largely due to the prompt and decisive action taken by the Prime Minister: he sacked most of his Cabinet. It wasn't a pretty sight. The corridors of power resembled a bowling alley, so many heads were rolling. It wasn't just a reshuffle, it was breaking open a whole new deck.

Surprisingly, outside Parliament the whole affair died a quick death. People seemed reluctant to discuss it and, of course, nobody would admit to being on the motorways – they'd watched the whole thing on television. Everybody knew it was a joke from the start, and most of the people who had besieged Birmingham were obviously foreigners ... Ah well, what can you expect? What's the weather forecast for tomorrow? And what are the chances of Spurs winning the Cup? And did you see *Neighbours* yesterday? The country slipped into its normal lethargic routine – and that was fatal. The bell was about to ring for round two.

SIX

In a small Welsh town a few miles north of Cardiff, the two leading councillors, the mayor and chief constable received letters marked *Strictly Private and Confidential*. The contents were identical in every respect to the Swinegap letters, except that the location of the landing site would not now be on grassland but in the playground of a children's school. This small target would require pinpoint navigational skill and, in the interests of public safety, it was imperative the area be isolated. There must be no recurrence of the shameful behaviour of sightseers on Tenkly Common. And, as before, the time of arrival would be Wednesday next.

The dignitaries, on receiving the letters, not unmindful of the prosperity that worldwide notoriety had brought upon their predecessors, ignored the strictly private and confidential nature of the missives and immediately despatched them to the Government. And to make doubly sure of their windfall, they also leaked the letter to the dailies before they could be issued a 'D-notice' forbidding them to print the story. The townspeople were excitedly discussing the contents of the letters even before the Government received them. Of course the aliens wouldn't land in a little town near Birmingham. That was a try-on. This was different, this was Wales, boyo. Oh yes, there'd be a welcome in the valleys for the little green men. Since the pit closure some years ago they hadn't had much to sing about but they hadn't let it bring them down. They were, to a man, God-fearing chapel-goers and here was their just reward. Never mind a week in Swansea for a holiday, it would be the Costa del Sol from now on. Anxiously they awaited the morning papers, but they needn't have worried. News of the spacemen was headlined on every front page, perhaps not as enthusiastically as the first time, but nevertheless the front pages carried it: *Daily Mail* – WAS TENKLY A REHEARSAL?; *Daily Express* – HERE WE GO AGAIN; *Daily Mirror* – A WELSH WELCOME FOR SPACEMEN; and from *The Times* – TROUBLE IN ZIMBABWE.

It was enough to inspire the little Welsh town to drooling point in their preparations to reap the riches. Hotel charges were trebled, the two restaurants vied with each other to see how high they could raise their prices. It was ludicrous: £2.50 for a bread roll and in case customers came in just for the bread, each establishment now had a £10.00 cover charge. Extra tables were crammed in to the extent that some customers would have to eat in the kitchen. Spare rooms in private cottages were scrubbed out and bed and breakfast signs sprouted like mushrooms in a damp bedsit. Ordinary sightseers would not be able to afford the prices, but there was always the expense account media personnel, many of whom had already arrived and were doubled up some three or four to a small back room. Cardiff wasn't too far away, with much better accommodation, but they had learned from the Birmingham fiasco that if you weren't right on the spot it was a wasted journey. The foreign press arrived only to find the little town already booked out and resigned themselves to spending a week in the open. But the astute council gave the delighted children two weeks' holiday and turned their school into a hostel. Hospital patients were also sent home and their beds commandeered for the makeshift hostel, with the price of a bed at £500.00 per night, breakfast not included. No one complained. After all, as the mayor lightheartedly mentioned in his welcome speech, when the spaceships landed they couldn't be better placed. School desks which had been turfed out were placed in a circle round the school yard, and would be used to give the town dignitaries a ringside seat on the night.

Not surprisingly, ordinary sightseers with traumatic memories of the horrendous three or four days at the last lot, stayed home and traffic was comparatively light. In any event the police acted quickly and road blocks were installed every twenty miles or so on the main highways leading to Wales. Motorists who could not produce a specific reason to cross the border were turned back. Naturally some got through to arrive at the little Welsh town, and wished they hadn't. Every small space that could hold a bed was already booked although sleeping bags were available for hire at £50.00 per night. Alternatively, if one decided to spend the night in the car, it was just as expensive in parking fees.

The Government decided to stay out of this one but the Bahamas high-level conference was once again postponed. The Prime Minister declared during Question Time they were keeping a watchful eye on the proceedings, and more than that he could not say as it would not be in the national interest. It was a political answer that meant nothing in Parliament but satisfied the electorate. This time no military aircraft would be circling the airspace over Wales, and special forces would not be on the ground. It was just as well because Wednesday passed without incident, and when Thursday came and went so did most of the media, leaving the inhabitants of the little Welsh town counting considerably more than just their blessings.

SEVEN

Perhaps the Joker or whoever was sending the letters was over-playing his hand, or maybe the letters were genuine. Whichever the case, exactly two weeks later in a little town not far from Scarborough the by now familiar letters were received by the four leading citizens. This time, however, there were no headlines, although most dailies printed the information in the middle pages. The inhabitants of the little town, being hard-headed Yorkshire folk, were thankful not to be splashed all over the media. They had had enough with foreigners tramping over their patch with expensive cameras clicking at everything. 'Excuse pliss, did Emiry Blonte live here?' 'Say buddy, how far is Ilkley Moor?' and 'Was this the place they made *All Creatures Great and Small*?'

Outwardly the locals appeared to treat the arrival of the spacemen with indifference, but this was merely a facade. They knew in their hardhearted Yorkshire way that if the spacemen did land they would be treated like any other visitors, with courtesy and plain honest-to-God Yorkshire hospitality. In any case, if they came they came, and if they didn't there was always the football pools.

On the Wednesday the media drifted into town. They were bored, blasé, and had seen it all before. Nor were they the top names in the media; in fact the newspaper reporters were way down the pecking order – the ones who usually covered weddings, anniversaries and local obituaries. For television, the occasion was used as a test for new, aspiring directors. The overseas correspondents didn't turn up at all.

The Government chose to ignore the whole thing, and very wisely too, because again it was a non-starter. And as the media circus packed its equipment, the consensus of opinion was that spaceship news was box-office poison and the next time they dashed off to some little town in the middle of nowhere, it would be after the aliens landed and not before.

Over the next ten months several other small towns received letters marked *Strictly Private and Confidential*, but in most cases they found the waste-paper basket. The whole thing was becoming a bore, although on the occasions when it was made public there were still the inevitable sightseers, extraterrestrial societies, wandering layabouts and the usual people who appear on the scene whenever there's a chance of a television camera being present. In fact, one old-age pensioner became a celebrity merely by holding up a placard which read 'Hello Mother'.

EIGHT

Chief Inspector James, one of the most experienced investigative officers in Scotland Yard, had been assigned the task of finding the Joker and after nearly a year was still completely baffled. He had had several meetings with the Prime Minister, each one more uncomfortable than the last. He remembered the last encounter which took place in Downing Street. It was horrendous to say the least. The Prime Minister's paranoia was evident.

'I want him, chief inspector,' ranted the Prime Minister. 'I want the miserable bastard who perpetrated this nonsense, and I want him not now but yesterday!'

He thumped the desk and a picture of his wife and children crashed to the floor. The chief inspector bent to retrieve it.

'Leave that rubbish where it is!' yelled the Prime Minister. 'You're a high-ranking police officer, not a dustman!'

It was a painful interview. His anger flared as he recalled the meeting. He was one of the Met's most respected policemen, after all, and he had been taken off a multi-million-pound drugs bust for this – finding some Joker who wrote anonymous letters. It was a Noddy job, for God's sake, one for PC Plod. All he'd done so far was ordinary 'Bobby on the beat' stuff. He'd interviewed the original recipients of the letter, Blackstone OBE and his cronies. He'd examined their medical histories for signs of instability, malicious or violent tendencies, but apart from the fact that Sharp was homosexual and the mayor a reformed alcoholic, there was nothing to suggest they had any part in the original hoax.

The chief inspector had done all he could and he was still no closer to an arrest. He'd even had the PM relate to a police artist a description of the man who had posed the question at the Downing Street press conference. An Identikit picture was drawn up and excitedly the Prime Minister yelled, 'That's him! That's him to a T!'

The chief inspector groaned. In front of him on the desk he had twelve more Identikit pictures of the man from his interviews with the press people who were present at the time. He looked despairingly at the line of faces in front of him. It looked like the band of Dr Crock and His Crackpots. Each face was different: one wore glasses, another a beard, protruding ears, then ears that were hidden under white, lank hair.

Chief Inspector James was coming to the end of a long and illustrious career and his retirement was inexorably creeping up on him – in eight months to be exact. Pray to God this was not to be his last case. He wanted to go out in a blaze of glory. This was more like a slow canter to the knacker's yard. In a fit of rage he brushed the Identikit pictures to the floor. The only chance of apprehending the pimply faced git was to nab him red-handed actually posting the letters. He wondered where the next location would be and as if to answer his question the phone rang. He picked it up.

'Chief Inspector James,' he rasped. Then he sighed, 'Where's that?' Glancing at a map of the British Isles on the wall, 'Yes, I know it, near Norwich. Yes, OK, send the letters over and do the usual interviews. Thanks.'

He put the phone down, took a blackheaded pin from a box on his desk, then moved towards the map and stuck it in a little town two miles to the north of Norwich. It was the twentieth black pin sticking like fungus to the large map. He stared at it for a moment, then in a sudden fit of anger and frustration tore the whole thing off the wall, punched it into a ball, black pins and all, and slung it into the metal waste bin.

He lifted the telephone receiver and jabbed at the buttons.

'Hello Miss Dawson. Is the governor in yet? This is Chief Inspector James.'

He waited a moment. Miss Dawson's voice was replaced by that of the head of Scotland Yard. James didn't waste time on preliminaries.

'Four more letters from a little town outside Norwich called Hampdown. The local bobbies are sending on any pertinent information. Look sir, can you spare me a few minutes if I come up?' He listened, then he broke in, 'I know that this has become a personal vendetta between the Prime Minister and whoever we are after but quite frankly, we haven't a cat in hell's chance of catching this Joker.' He listened again. 'Yes sir, that is exactly what I'm suggesting, close the file – unsolved, and let's get back to real police work. The local lads have enough on their plates without . . . Hello? . . .'

He jiggled the receiver but the head man had already terminated the interview. He slammed down the receiver and slumped back in his chair. He couldn't blame the governor, he knew that the Prime Minister was breathing down his neck. The latest stroke of genius to come out of 10 Downing Street was that local police keep an all-night surveillance on their mayors' houses. The inspector wondered seriously if the PM knew what was going on. Didn't he realise that the cost to the police bill would be astronomical?

'Sergeant Thompson!' he yelled.

There was a scuffle of footsteps and Sergeant Thompson entered the room.

'Yes sir?'

He stopped in his tracks and stared at the lighter part of the wall behind the chief inspector.

'The map, sir,' he pointed, 'it's gone.'

'It hasn't gone,' said the inspector in a tight voice. 'It's in the waste-paper bin.'

Sergeant Thompson raised his eyebrows.

'You heard me,' he said. 'It's in the bloody bin.' He went on, 'God knows how many people have been shot, strangled, murdered, houses burgled, tons of drugs smuggled into the country, and for the best part of a year all we've done is receive a file full of identical letters, stick pins in a bloody map and polish our fat backsides.'

'Yes sir,' said Sergeant Thompson. 'What else can we do?'

Suddenly the inspector reached for his hat.

'I'll tell you what we're going to do,' he said, 'I'm taking you to the pub and you, sergeant, are going to buy me a pint.'

'Yes sir,' replied Sergeant Thompson and hurried after him.

Two months later, the next little town to be targeted was called Grapplewick, eight miles north of Manchester, and although no one was aware of it at the time, it was destined to be almost the last. Unlike all the other small towns, however, the local dignitaries were not forewarned by letter, they were to receive the ultimate accolade: they were visited instead . . . by an Alien from Outer Space.

Part II

GRAPPLEWICK, NEAR MANCHESTER

NINE

E ven in Lancashire Grapplewick was a joke. Every stand-up comedian in the north featured the town in his act. It was generally agreed that Grapplewick folk were thick, but this is rather unkind; to be charitable, the townspeople had better things to do than think.

At the turn of the century Grapplewick flourished with the import of raw cotton, but that was in the golden age of the British Empire. Now the two empty mills which had once so proudly dominated and blackened the town were mute evidence of the slump of the thirties. The Second World War brought a timely reprieve, leaving a legacy of small businesses, component parts for this or that, surviving only because they were cheaper than other more notable rivals. A small influx of Asians added to the life support, and Grapplewick was breathing although, according to other Lancastrians, brain dead.

Some of its past glories remained – the town hall with worn stone steps, brave flaking pillars, and masonry so beloved of Victorian architects; two churches; a synagogue; and now a mosque, shining like a cat's eye in the dark. It certainly did better business than the other denominations. For other forms of escape there were two cinemas, one of which had been a music hall and still bore peeling, faded old bills featuring G. H. Elliot, and Mushy the forest bred lion; numerous pubs, and one or two amusement arcades. Dirty little houses built for the workers in the halcyon days of full employment led off the high street in identical poverty-stricken ranks. It was a tired town, cowering in the folds of the moors as if ashamed of its ugliness.

To be philosophical, however, 'In every dustbin there's a daffodil'. Unfortunately, most of the lowly people who rummage around in these receptacles are neither botanists nor philosophers, but the seed of Grapplewick's flower was planted in a small barber's shop on Coldhurst Street.

The owner was Albert Waterhouse and apart from the plate glass window and a striped pole, it was exactly the same as all the other dwellings that propped each other up on either side of the cobbled thoroughfare. Councillor Albert Waterhouse no longer operated in the shop. He'd had to share his haircutting activities with his civic duties, but now, having been next on the list, he was enjoying his one-year tenure as mayor. Naturally, with his newly exalted status it wasn't fitting that he should be seen in such a dump. Indeed, he even went somewhere else for his short back and sides. The running of the business was left solely in the hands of his nephew, Norman.

Having worked in the shop since leaving school, Norman now had seven years' experience behind him, and to be left in charge of the whole shebang pleased him immensely. He was a good-looking young man, proud of being the best barber in Coldhurst Street. It never once crossed his mind that he was the only barber in Coldhurst Street.

'You can't beat Benidorm,' he shouted into his customer's ear, snip-snipping all the time.

The man looked at himself in the flyspecked mirror.

'Who?' he asked.

'Benidorm,' said Norman, looking at the man's reflection.

Everything had to be shouted to overcome the utter mindless cacophony of pop music that blared from a transistor radio on a shelf by the door from the moment the shop was opened to closing time.

'Topless birds,' he blew away some loose hair, 'never got to the hotel till dawn,' snip, snip. 'Bars open all night, English beer and all.'

There was more dialogue in the same vein – topless, beer, and all-night parties. It's amazing what a week's package tour will do for a young man's education.

On the bench a young lad awaiting his turn tried desperately to follow the conversation. He got the odd words interspersed with 'boom, boom, boom, Ah lurves ya bybee'. He tugged at his mother's sleeve. Mrs Dobson was miles away looking idly towards the window, seeing nothing. A bus stopped outside and some people on the top deck peered down into the shop incuriously. Then the bus moved off and it's doubtful if she even noticed it.

'Mam,' hissed the boy tugging her sleeve more urgently.

'What is it?' she mouthed. She wasn't going to compete with the radio. Her son strained up to her to avoid the off-chance of being overheard by the barber.

'What's topless?' he asked.

'What are you on about?' she replied, puzzled.

'He said "topless birds in Benidorm".'

He nodded towards Norman. The penny dropped and, turning on her son, she clouted the back of his head.

'I told you to bring a comic,' she hissed.

His cap fell off and he bent down to pick it up, thankful for the chance to hide his embarrassment as the tears welled up in his eyes. There was a further distraction as the shop bell tinkled. Nobody actually heard it above the continuous assault from the latest hit single, but they all felt the draught from the open door. All heads turned to see who it was but all that could be seen was a tall dark shape, backlit from the sunlight outside. It stood very still.

Mrs Dobson looked enquiringly at Norman, who smiled weakly at the stranger in the doorway. Men often came in the door, looked around the shop and then went out again, but this man just stood there, neither coming nor going. Mrs Dobson's son peeked fearfully from behind his mother and the customer in the barber's chair gulped noisily, never taking his eyes off the stranger. Everyone in the shop remained motionless. It could have been Madame Tussaud's apart from the noise blasting from the radio, which continued to assault everyone's eardrums. In fact no one had noticed the noise, but they certainly did when the stranger reached out and switched it off. The resulting silence was almost tangible, as if one had run through a raging storm into a church.

The people in the barber's were unaccustomed to the quiet and were now gripped by fear. Mrs Dobson was the first to move. Grabbing her little boy's hand she scurried towards the door, averting her eyes lest she looked into the man's face. She could not explain her feeling of dread; it sprang from a long-buried superstition like throwing salt over your shoulder or crossing your fingers when you pass a squint-eyed woman. She dragged her son through the door into the safety of the street. He turned back for a final furtive look, and she clouted him again.

Mrs Dobson's departure was too much for the man in the barber's chair. He snatched the cloth from his neck, and jamming his cap over his half-finished short back and sides he edged quickly past the stranger to the door. 'I'll not be going in there again' he muttered to himself in the sanctuary of the street, not realising at the time the prophecy of his words.

Norman would have given anything to be able to follow his departed customer but he was stuck in the shop, alone and helpless without the caterwauling of the transistor radio backing him up. The stranger now closed the door and to his relief Norman could see that he was just an ordinary well-dressed man – which in itself was odd, as well-dressed men didn't usually come down Coldhurst Street, and they certainly never stopped off at his shop.

'You're closed.' It was a flat statement and Norman was confused.

'No we're not – we're usually open while eight o'clock!'

The man turned over the 'open/closed' sign on the door and took off his hat. Norman pointed hopelessly to the card. 'I can't close the shop just yet,' he said. 'You see, it's not my shop. It belongs to my uncle and . . .' The man appeared not to have heard and simply went over to one of the barber's chairs and sat in it, his hat in his lap. Norman tried desperately to continue. Moving alongside the chair he started to explain: 'Tuesdays and Wednesdays are our busy times . . . I mean, I can't close now as there'll be an early evening rush and I'm short-handed as it is.' He stopped there, quite proud of his last remark. It gave the shop the status of a *salon* – the type you got in a big city. Suddenly another thought occured to him and he smirked knowingly at the man's reflection.

'Oh, I get it. It's privacy that you want, isn't it? You're wearing a wig, aren't you?'

The man didn't react and so with a degree of confidence Norman leaned towards him. 'I've got another customer who wears a wig; it's so obvious as the glue runs down his forehead but he never lets on and I have to trim the fringe and the bits of his own hair that grow around the edges. He knows I know but he won't let . . .'

The man slowly turned his head to face him and Norman stopped speaking. It hadn't been that important anyway.

'Do you believe in UFOs?' the man asked quietly.

The sudden change of topic bewildered Norman; he had to unscramble his brain from wigs and haircuts and start again from scratch.

'Aaah,' he replied – he hoped in a knowledgeable way. 'Flying saucers and all that, well, I don't know. Some people have seen them – but not round here!' he chuckled. 'If we get an aeroplane over Grapplewick then we know the pilot's lost!' Norman had hoped that the man would laugh or at least smile, anything, in fact, other than that intense stare. He turned away and pretended to tidy away his clippers and the rest of his paraphernalia.

'I'm from another planet.'

Norman froze and his mind suddenly blanked. There weren't too many answers to that and he couldn't think of one of them, so he turned back and smiled tentatively.

'Is this for a bet?' he asked.

'Naturally you are sceptical.'

'No, no, it's not that, it's just that, er . . .' he floundered. He didn't want to upset the man and thought it would be best to keep on the right side of him and keep him talking until someone came into the shop. The door wasn't actually locked and nobody took any notice of the sign anyway, so maybe somebody would come – then he could make a run for it.

'I am from the planet Androm,' the stranger continued, 'and at present am attached to the Inter-Galactic Peacekeeping Force.'

A small worm of recollection began to turn in Norman's memory and he snapped his fingers.

'Wait a minute! Wasn't there a lot about this on the box, oh, er, a few months ago – I remember now – "UFOs are coming Wednesday" or something like that.' Norman was extremely pleased with himself. He never read the newspapers and so all his worldly knowledge came from the TV, yet it enabled him to pontificate on most subjects as he snip-snipped. Only yesterday he had been discussing the plight of lemurs in South America.

'That's right,' he continued, 'then another town got a letter – yes, I remember now, some lads went from here but only got as far as Cheadle because of the traffic. I watched it on the telly – well, we all did – but the flying saucer never came. I think three towns got this letter and then the whole thing fizzled out.'

The man nodded slowly.

'Not quite true, but close enough. Thirty-two towns received letters; they didn't keep quiet about them as we had asked, so now there will be no more correspondence. Instead, I have been despatched with our message.'

By now Norman was terrified. The man was obviously raving mad, and although he seemed quite quiet and controlled at the moment, the slightest wrong move could set him off.

'I was just going to make some tea. Would you like a cup?' It was an inspired question. Once in the back room where the kettle was, he'd be through the lavatory window and across the moors like a whippet. It was as if the man had read his thoughts.

'I am neither mad nor am I of this planet. This earthly human form I have assumed enables me to pass freely amongst your kind. To all intents and purposes I look human, except for my eyes.'

Norman's curiosity overcame his fear.

'Your eyes.'

He leaned forward to look more closely, they seemed to be quite ordinary. There was nothing thaaaaaat waaaaaa . . . he felt light-headed and relaxed. The man was slowly dissolving before him; no, not dissolving, changing shape, the face filling out and getting darker. His overcoat was now a brightly coloured poncho and the hat on his lap was now a small brown monkey. The man had gone and in his place was this large, jolly, black African. But no, it wasn't somebody else, it was still the man. His voice hadn't changed.

He spoke. 'Supposing my mission was to some destination in Central Africa, this is the form I would assume.'

Norman gaped, he wasn't mentally equipped to take all this in. It was one thing for some nutter to say he was a spaceman, but this was something else. The monkey regarded him solemnly.

'You like to play with him,' said the man tossing the animal over.

Norman caught the monkey, or rather it grabbed on to him and nestled in the crook of his arm, head jerking up, down and sideways, big, black, round eyes flickering, taking everything in – photos of the models on the wall, the cracks in the ceiling – then bending its head right back to examine itself in the mirror. Norman laughed and the startled monkey shot on to his shoulder and made its way round the back of his neck. He reached for it but it wasn't there, it wasn't on the bench either. He turned a complete circle but there was no sign of it. He looked quickly to the man's lap but no, just a trilby hat. He was about to look under the wash basin when the thought struck him – *a trilby hat!* He peered fearfully over his shoulder at the man sitting there, dressed as before, and the enormity of the last five minutes hit him like a runaway bus. The man had actually changed himself to a black African and back again, and in full view. He hadn't nipped behind a screen or anything. And what about the monkey? Was he a spaceman too?

'Are you convinced now that I possess extraordinary powers, or must I subject you to further demonstrations?'

'No, no thanks,' stammered Norman, although if this man could change into anything, he wouldn't have minded a few minutes with Dolly Parton.

The fact that he had been subjected to a sophisticated form of hypnotism never crossed his mind, indeed very few thoughts had ever made the journey and hypnosis was way down the list.

'Good,' said the man. 'Having got this far, questions about why I am here on your planet, and how, will have to be postponed for a further meeting, but everything will be explained to you in due course.'

They were interrupted by the tinkle of the shop doorbell, but Norman had forgotten all his earlier fears, and this was an intrusion. He whirled around.

'I'm sorry, sir, we're closed. What's the matter with you, can't you read?'

He pointed to the sign. It was only then he noticed the man had a white stick and he was staring vaguely at the ceiling.

'Oh, I'm sorry,' said Norman acutely embarrassed.

'That's all right,' said the blind man. 'I'd like two pounds of streaky bacon and a small brown loaf.'

Norman frowned, then smiled kindly. 'You're in the wrong place mister, this is a barber's shop.'

'It's not Smith's then?'

'No, this is Albert Waterhouse's Gents' Hairdressing.'

He didn't realise that he was now talking to the man as if he were not only blind, but four years old and deaf with it.

'Smith's is down by the traffic lights, next door to the tandoori . . .' He could have bitten off his tongue. 'I'm sorry, you won't be able to see it, but you'll be able to smell it,' he added in a sudden flash of brilliance. 'Tell you what, I'll walk you down there,' but before Norman could take the blind man's arm the alien visitor had risen from his chair and stood in front of the man, putting the palms of his hands over the man's eyes.

Norman watched with his mouth hanging open. He had a feeling he knew what was going to happen but he wasn't sure whether he'd believe it. The spaceman took his hands away and walked back a step. For a moment the blind man remained motionless, then he started to blink hard, looking around the room with growing wonder. He staggered back into a chair then bent forwards to look at himself in a mirror. Slowly turning to the spaceman he dropped to his knees, whispering, 'I can see, I can see,' in an increasingly louder voice. He took the spaceman's hand and kissed it. 'Thank you . . . thank you' was all that he could say. The spaceman raised him gently to his feet and turned him towards the door.

'Smith's,' he said, 'I believe it's next to the tandoori restaurant.' Norman didn't see the man go; he was too busy staring, awestruck, at the spaceman. If he had had any remaining doubts about him five minutes ago they had been instantly swept away, and if the spaceman were to tell him to jump off the roof, well, he'd be halfway up the stairs without a second thought.

The man put on his hat and a wave of panic hit Norman. He didn't want him to go; he might never see him again and he wanted to take him home and introduce him to his aunt and uncle. For years his Aunt Florrie had staggered around on bad legs and Norman was convinced that if the spaceman could restore a man's vision, five minutes with him and his aunt would be ready to compete in the Commonwealth Games. Again the man seemed to be reading his thoughts.

'Your uncle is the present mayor of Grapplewick,' he said.

'Yes, sir,' Norman replied with a slight bow.

The man handed him a small business card. 'You will bring him to this address at eight o'clock this evening.'

Norman looked at the neat print on the card. All it said was 'Kershaw's Croft'. He turned the card over, but there was nothing on the other side. Kershaw's Croft . . . slowly he remembered – it was a tumble-down old place on Windy Moor. 'Is this the . . .' he began, and looked around the shop. The man had gone, the shop door banging shut in the breeze.

Norman dashed into the street, looking up and then down, and although there were one or two people about, there was no sign of the tall, mysterious stranger. He shook his head and slowly walked back into the shop. The first thing he had to do was to contact his uncle. He dialled his number but it wasn't until the phone was ringing that the scale of what he was about to divulge hit him. He slammed the phone down in a panic. What could he say? A spaceman had just dropped in and wanted to see the two of them up at Kershaw's Croft. No; he couldn't come out with the news just like that. His uncle wasn't the most receptive person at the best of times and he seldom took a statement at face value. If you told him it was raining, he would go outside to check for himself. Somehow Norman had to convince his uncle of the incredible, miraculous, fantastic happenings of the last half-hour, but at the same time it occurred to him that he and his uncle had never really had a conversation.

Norman had never known his parents, which is hardly surprising as they abandoned him when he was six months old. His mother, sickened by the vision of dullness and monotony that stretched out in front of her for the rest of her life, decided one morning that it was too great a price to pay for one night of fumbling passion in the churchyard. Tucking little Norman into the bottom drawer of a dresser that served as his cot, she wrote out her abdication letter to her husband and decamped without a backward glance. It wasn't that she was heartless, but she was fed up. Marriage hadn't stopped her husband putting it about with other women and for the past three nights he hadn't been home at all, which in retrospect wasn't surprising as he was halfway to Australia on a ten-pound assisted passage.

Thus baby Norman was left in sole charge of himself, which was an enormous responsibility for one whose only qualification in life was sucking his toe. Fortunately for Norman, just as he was beginning to feel hungry his Uncle Albert called round to see whether his brother had finished varnishing the harmonium, and that was the start of his new life with his adoptive parents. They didn't even have to change his surname, he was well looked after and, possibly because he was adopted, not much was expected of him; indeed his main achievement to date was in getting older, but now Norman felt that things were about to change. He had been hand-picked by an alien and in his bones he knew that, for him, life was just about to begin. Squaring his shoulders he dialled home again, hoping in his heart of hearts that nobody would be in to take the call. 'Hello?' said a fearful voice at the other end. It was his Aunt Florrie, who still mistrusted the telephone.

'Hello, Auntie, it's me, Norman.'

'Norman,' she replied incredulously – he didn't phone very often. 'Are you all right? Nothing's happened, has it?'

'No, everything's fine. Is me uncle there?'

'No, your uncle's not here, you should know that by now. It's Wednesday afternoon so it's his dancing lesson.'

Norman clucked his tongue. Of course, it was Wednesday and his uncle would be at Madame Lesley's. 'I forgot it was Wednesday, Auntie. Have you got Madame Lesley's number?'

'Well, I don't know, Norman. Can't it wait until he gets home?'

'No, I must speak to him now. It's urgent!'

'Well, you know best,' he heard her say as she put the phone down while she rummaged around for the number, and he wondered again what was so special about Madame Lesley's phone number that it couldn't be entered into the little address book on the hall table.

'Hello, Norman. Are you there?'

'Yes, Auntie.' He clicked the top of the pen to take down the number.

'It's Grapplewick . . .' uselessly she waited for him to write that down and, even worse, he did.

'Got that, thanks, Auntie.'

'Grapplewick 0423.'

'0423, thanks, Auntie.'

'Now, are you sure, Norman? Your uncle said he was only to be rung there if it was something very important.'

'Don't worry, Auntie. It is important, believe me.'

'It had better be, because . . . Hello? Hello?' but Norman was already dialling 0423.

Madame Lesley's Dancing Academy was originally built as a tabernacle. It was well constructed and on the outside it didn't look that different from the local library or town baths. Inside, however, it was derelict and worm-eaten and so, with a small legacy and savings scraped from years performing at music halls around the country, Madame Eunice Lesley was able to secure the freehold at a giveaway price. Turning the building into a dancing academy swallowed her remaining capital and so it was with great relief when she opened for business that she found Britain was undergoing a renaissance in ballroom dancing and everybody wanted to take classes. Soon the money would come pouring in and she wouldn't have to pass the bank on the other side of the street.

That was the theory, anyway. In actual fact Grapplewick turned out to be the only place in the country that wasn't interested in the passion of the tango or the exuberance of the quickstep. Sadly she had just one pupil, and that was a small, portly, middle-aged man. He was, however, a town councillor and so would be a useful connection for her. Unfortunately for Madame Eunice Lesley, Albert Waterhouse was the last person on earth she should have relied upon to spread the word about ballroom dancing. No way was he ever going to blab it abroad that he had a dancing lesson every Wednesday afternoon. Secretly it had always been a cherished ambition of his to be able to glide effortlessly over a ballroom floor in top hat and tails with a number on his back, but it was an ambition doomed from the start. Not only was Eunice six inches taller than him, but when they danced he held her in his arms like a guardsman presenting arms, his eyes staring fixedly at her chin as they lumbered around the hall. Eunice suffered bruised toes after every session, and even worse, she developed a rash under her chin from his brillantine.

She did, however, have a flat above the academy and on every Wednesday after the dancing lesson she would invite him upstairs for tea and cakes. Very soon this had become a regular routine and eventually the dancing was dispensed with altogether, Albert Waterhouse coming around on every Wednesday just for his tea. One thing led to another and after a few weeks they would hop into bed first and then have their tea and cakes. As he was now the mayor Albert considered it imperative that no one should find out about this enjoyable liaison. Florrie was certainly unaware of it; every week she wrapped his dancing pumps in brown paper and off he went to his lesson. It never occurred to her that after all these years at Madame Lesley's his pumps were still as good as new. Perhaps he was particularly light on his feet?

On this particular Wednesday the mayor was propped up in the large soft bed, making out his racing selections in the newspaper. Eunice, overflowing her stool, sat at her dressing table, dabbing at her eyes with a mascara brush. 'Big Jessie,' muttered the mayor almost to himself. Eunice didn't seem to hear; fastidiously she selected a chocolate from the box in front of her and popped it in her mouth. 'You what?' she said, although with her mouth crammed full of chocolate it sounded like 'Ott?'

The mayor looked over his half-moon glasses at her. Every week he bought her a half-pound box of chocolates and they never lasted more than twenty minutes. Silently the mayor thanked God that she was a dancer and not a sweet manufacturer, otherwise she'd be bankrupt within a month. Even now, with a fresh hazelnut whip in her mouth she was peering into the box, fingers wriggling, ready to pounce on the next one. 'Big Jessie,' he repeated, louder this time, 'I reckon she's worth a pound each way in the 3.30 tomorrow.' Eunice was now leaning towards her reflection in the mirror, jaws on hold while she concentrated on applying her eye makeup. Satisfied, she leaned back and dabbed the corners of her mouth with a Kleenex.

'Oh, racing,' she said, 'I thought you were still on about that traffic warden.'

The strident ring of the telephone interrupted their pleasant domestic exchange. This was not unusual as people often rang to talk to Eunice, so the mayor just ignored it, turning back to his racing paper. Eunice ambled over to the bedside phone. 'Hello,' she answered uninterestedly, and then stiffened, putting her hand over the mouthpiece. 'It's for you!' she hissed. Albert stared at her with a look of incomprehension in his eyes. 'It's your nephew!'

The mayor's stomach lurched – nobody phoned him here; obviously something was wrong, something had happened to Florrie or there was some trouble at the shop. He nodded to Eunice and she took her hand away from the mouthpiece saying, 'If you want Mr Waterhouse he'll be in the ballroom. Hang on a minute and I'll put you through.' Dropping the receiver on the bed she then hurried over to put a record on to the turntable. By the time she picked up the phone again the room was filled with the sound of *La Cumparsita*. In a very posh voice she then said, 'To whom do you wish to speak to?' She listened for a moment and then replied, 'I'll get him for you.' Holding the phone at arm's length she called out, 'Mr Waterhouse, Mr Waterhouse, telephone. It's your nephew!' Albert waited a couple of seconds and then took the phone.

'Hello, Norman, what's the matter?' He stuck a finger into his ear and tried to listen, but it was hopeless. 'Hang on a minute, lad, I can't hear you – will somebody switch that damn thing off!' he yelled. Eunice, anticipating his reaction, whipped the needle off the record and in a loud voice shouted at the wall, 'Take five, everybody!' Albert winced. It sounded patently false to him, but then again, it was only Norman at the other end of the phone.

'Right, lad, now what are you ringing me here for?' He listened for a bit. 'Tonight.' He glanced over his shoulder at his pocket watch hanging on the headboard. Eunice was back at her dressing table and she seemed to be concentrating on her eyes again, but she wasn't missing a trick.

'Listen, Norman, can't it wait until tomorrow . . . what do you mean, no? Who is this Mr High and Mighty? No, don't tell me over the phone. I'll see you at home in about half an hour, all right,' and with that he put the phone down and took his trousers from under the mattress.

'Trouble?' asked Eunice as he slipped his arms through his braces and reached under the bed for his boots.

'Now, Eunice lass, you should know better than to ask a question like that.' She shrugged her shoulders. It would have to wait until next Wednesday, but she would find out.

At home Florrie was agonising over her decision to give Norman the telephone number. She understood the need for secrecy; after all, to be taking dancing lessons at Albert's age was ludicrous anyway, but if this knowledge fell into the wrong hands it could be political dynamite. Albert had often stressed that point and Norman was daft enough to ring up just to tell him they were low on shampoo. She wished to God that she'd never given him that phone number. Florrie crossed over to the window and looked up and down the street. She noted that on the other side of the road the coal lorry was still parked at number 26. She sniffed. He must have been over at that house for about two hours now, and they hadn't even got a fireplace. She was about to drop the curtain when the bus pulled up at the stop and Albert got off. Panic fluttered in her breast – in all the years he'd been going to dancing lessons he'd never come back this early. Whatever Norman had said to him it wasn't about shampoo, so taking a deep breath she waddled over to the front door and jerked it open to let him in, but his key was already in the lock, and as it was attached to his braces she ended up hauling him indoors and they crashed down on top of each other. It was the closest they'd been in years.

'What the hell do you think you're playing at?' Albert snarled as he snatched the key out of the lock and examined his trousers to see whether there was any obvious damage.

'Did our Norman contact you?' Florrie said in reply as she picked up his brown paper parcel.

'Give us a chance to get me things off,' he said, hanging his hat and then his overcoat behind the door. It seemed to take him hours to do this and he still had his scarf on. Florrie hovered around impatiently as he took his hat down again and brushed it. The suspense was killing her; she couldn't bear it any longer.

'Well, did he ring you?'

Albert handed her his jacket. 'Yes,' he grunted, making his way straight over to the television set and switching it on. As he flopped into the high-backed chair opposite, Florrie hesitated for a moment, then flounced out into the kitchen. She realised this was the end of the conversation with her husband, but she'd get the full story from Norman when he got in.

Albert stared at the TV screen. An American police car, lights flashing, sirens blaring, gunshots, but Albert wasn't really watching. His mind was elsewhere. Florrie came out of the kitchen, drying a plate.

'He said it was important so I gave him the number. I mean, what else could I do? – he said it was urgent.' She waited for Albert's response but all she could see was the back of his chair. 'I couldn't very well say no, could I?' More sirens, screeching tyres and the splintering of glass. Suddenly the chair back spoke: 'And we pay good licence money for this rubbish!'

'Well, you don't have to watch it, do you?' Florrie replied, still wiping the same plate – it was a wonder there was any pattern still left on it. 'Any road, I've got more things to do than to wait on you hand and foot and I'm going down to our Emmie's before I . . .' Her voice faded as she went back into the kitchen but Albert had every confidence that she was still talking to him. He leaned forward and changed the channel. A burst of inane studio laughter filled the room as some idiot staggered through a yard balancing a bucket on his head. Albert clucked his tongue in disgust. Outside the 6.30 pm train thundered past. Albert didn't hear it; he could feel the vibrations through his chair. Automatically he pulled out his watch and looked at it. At the same time a cold draught swept through the room followed by the sound of the front door slamming, and Norman hurried in. Again Albert lugged out his watch.

'Who's looking after the shop then?' He tapped the timepiece, mute testimony to the fact that there was still an hour and a half to go before closing time.

'Something cropped up, Uncle,' Norman said, addressing the back of the chair, although his eyes were straying sideways to the TV set. A shriek of laughter greeted him and he smiled.

'It had better be important or I'll be advertising for a new apprentice hairdresser tomorrow.'

Norman didn't hear this as he was too busy looking at the man with the bucket on his head staggering towards a large hole in the road. The mayor exploded. 'Never mind all that rubbish,' he bellowed, indicating the TV set. 'What was that phone call about?'

'Phone call?' echoed Norman vaguely. His uncle shook his head in despair.

'You rang me at Madame Lesley's.'

'Ah yes,' said Norman, television instantly forgotten. 'There's been a visitor at the shop.' Albert looked at him quizzically.

'It wasn't the health department again, was it?'

'Er, no, Uncle, he, well, he wasn't an ordinary visitor, he, er . . .' Norman was floundering so the mayor waited a second or two before losing his patience.

'Well come on, lad, you said it was important. Who was it?'

'He was a spaceman!' Norman blurted, blushing like a Barbara Cartland virgin. His uncle looked at him directly for a moment and then crouched forward to turn the sound up on the television. Whatever Norman was about to divulge wasn't going to be for Florrie's ears.

'What did you say?' he asked incredulously.

Norman gulped. 'He said he was from another planet.' This time the mayor put on his glasses and peered at Norman closely.

'Have you been at the conditioner again?' he asked quietly.

'It's true, Uncle, honestly!'

The lad was tremendously sincere but that didn't necessarily mean he was tremendously sane. He wondered whether there was any history of lunacy on the lad's mother's side of the family. He took off his glasses.

'I'm telling you this, Norman, so think on. If that shop isn't open in half an hour then you'll be signing on at the DSS tomorrow morning.'

Norman was desperate. 'It's no joke, Uncle. I'm telling you the truth. I saw him with my own eyes!' The mayor was silent for a moment.

'Was he collecting for anything?'

'No, nothing like that. He told me to bring you to a meeting tonight.'

Albert's eyebrows shot up. 'Oh, he did, did he? This Mr High and Mighty, who does he think he is?' He was gathering steam now. 'I'm the mayor of this town and I don't come running at anybody's beck and call. Number one in Grapplewick, that's me; I'm not a pile of horse droppings, you know.'

Norman tried to placate him. 'He knows you're the mayor, Uncle, that's why he wants to talk to you. Maybe they've been watching you for years.'

Albert was suddenly wary. As far as he could remember he had kept his nose clean, but there was always something that he could be trapped over.

'He wasn't a little fat fellow with glasses, was he?'

'No, Uncle, he's tall and there's something about him; well, you won't believe this but . . .'

'Did he have a briefcase with him?' the mayor broke in sharply.

'He didn't have anything with him – listen, he just came into the shop and sat in the chair, and with me not two feet away from him, he changed into an African Chief.'

'A blackie in my shop?' asked Albert, affronted.

Yes, and he had a –' Norman stopped suddenly. A sudden flash of insight warned him not to mention the monkey; he had just remembered his uncle's aversion to all pets. 'Then he changed back and a blind man came into the shop.'

'How do you know he was blind?'

Norman snorted. 'Because he had a white stick with him.'

It was the mayor's turn to snort. 'Well, that's nothing, is it? You can buy a white stick at a novelty shop; anybody can walk around with a white stick and get people to see 'em across the road.'

'Let me finish, Uncle, *please*!'

His uncle nodded.

'The man got up and put his hands over the blind man's eyes and he could see, I'm telling you, I've never seen anything like it!'

Albert was impressed. 'And this man wants you to bring me to a meeting tonight?'

'Yes, at eight o'clock tonight.'

Albert wasn't entirely convinced by Norman's argument. 'It sounds like a load of old cobblers to me.'

Norman was desperate – he knew he had to persuade his uncle but shifting him was like trying to empty the bath with a sieve. Then for the first time in his life he had a brainwave, and although he didn't realise it at the time, Norman was about to deliver his trump card.

'Look, Uncle,' he said, resting his hands on the arm of the chair, 'has it occurred to you that if this man has the power to bring back a man's sight, he may also have the power to take it away, so don't expect me to see you across the road when he does.' Albert looked at him sharply. 'Well, Uncle, if we upset him there's no telling what he may do.'

The mayor slumped forward with his chin in his hands, his mind racing back to the days when he was a young man working at Hobday's cotton mill. Making his way home one night he'd realised he had left his money in the back pocket of his overalls. Immediately he dashed back to the mill and just made it through the gates before they were closed for the night. He ran past the lodge and along the long passage into the card room, zig-zagging between the cotton skips and machinery, when suddenly all the lights went out. He stood stock-still in the middle of the floor, paralysed. The blackness was almost physical; there hadn't been a chink of light anywhere as, being wartime, the blackout boards had been placed over the windows. For a minute or two he didn't move, panic creeping slowly and insidiously into his mind. He tried to orientate himself but he was hemmed in by the still-warm machinery, so he closed his eyes. When he reopened them it seemed even blacker than before; the darkness was so absolute he wasn't even sure whether his eyes were open or not. He heard his heart thumping and a scuffling noise that could have been mice or rats. He desperately tried to remain calm and logical, and with hands outstretched before him he inched forward only to fall into a skip half-full of cotton waste. Something ran over his hand and that was the point when he started screaming. He yelled and yelled at the top of his voice and then, by the grace of God, the lights came on. Two of the fire-watchers appeared at the far end of the hall to see what all the commotion was about. Albert had almost fainted with relief on seeing the two men; five minutes more and he would have been a total gibbering wreck. But as a result of that incident he had developed a pathological terror of losing his sight.

Albert shuddered at the recollection. 'All right, Norman, best be off; it's after seven now.' As he shrugged on his overcoat some of his old spirit returned. 'If you're wasting my time, I'll have you open all Sunday.' Norman didn't care about Sunday; once he had delivered his uncle to Kershaw's Croft it would be up to the spaceman to decide what would happen next.

'Where is this place then?' asked Albert, winding on his scarf. Norman proffered the business card the alien had left with him.

'Kershaw's Croft? But I know where that is!' he said in disbelief. 'That place has been derelict for years; it's falling down!' Suddenly another thought struck him. 'If this man is so special, why isn't he staying at the Metropole?'

'You won't listen, will you, Uncle? He's not like us!'

'Aye, and if this thing turns out to be a joke, you won't be like us neither!' his uncle retorted, and they let themselves out.

Not two minutes after they had left the house, Florrie came downstairs in her street clothes. With shrieks of canned laughter still blaring from the television, she was unaware that Norman had come in and gone out again with his uncle, leaving the house empty. 'So anyway, I'm just popping down to our Emmie's like I said, and I'll make your supper when I get back ... Oh, and tell Norman where I've gone and tell him I'll not be long – and ring Alec about that pot of paint.' She lumbered over to the front door without looking back, and let herself out. 'Well, ta-ra then,' and she was gone also.

TEN

Norman and his uncle sat side by side on the otherwise empty bus. Not a word passed between them, and when they arrived at the last stop at Windy Moor they were loath to get off. The Lancashire moors can be forbidding enough during the day, but at night, anyone crossing the moors by foot is extremely uneasy – and those are the stout-hearted ones. The mayor and his nephew could hardly be put into that category. They had, however, come all this distance on a weekday, so they thought they'd best get their ordeal over and done with.

The bus driver jumped out of his cab, taking half a fag out from behind his ear. 'Camping out, are you?' he asked, cupping his hands while he lit what was left of a Woodbine.

The mayor buttoned his overcoat and tightened his scarf. A cold wind was blowing and he didn't like the driver's remark, but equally he was in no hurry to leave the friendly lights of the bus. 'Just paying a social call,' he said.

'Oh, aye. Well, there's nowt between here and Bradford.'

The mayor chuckled grimly. 'It'll be a long walk, then.' He was pleased with this comment as he prided himself on his repartee. 'Come on, Norman, let's make tracks,' and both men strode out towards a tiny pinprick of light in the dark lane. It didn't take them long to reach the streetlight, and Kershaw's Croft was another half mile or so from that point. As they looked back down the lane they saw that the bus had already left for its return journey into town. They were now well and truly marooned on the moors. As Norman turned to walk further down the lane the mayor surreptitiously picked a large stone from the wall and slipped it into his pocket. If there was going to be any trouble up at the croft he wasn't going to abide by Queensberry rules.

There were only a couple of stars twinkling in the wintry sky and when Norman and Albert reached Kershaw's Croft they could only vaguely make out its shape. 'I told you it was derelict,' wheezed Albert. The walk had left him breathless but he wasn't afraid – the stone lying heavily in his pocket gave him courage. Norman knocked hesitantly on the door but there was no response; the low keening of the wind was the only sound to break the night's silence. The noise of the wind was somehow malevolent and both men were feeling increasingly unhappy about being stranded on the moor in the middle of the night. Norman knocked again and they waited.

'I told you you were wasting your time,' said the mayor uneasily and turned to leave.

A well-modulated voice spoke.

'Please enter, gentlemen.'

Norman and Albert stood stock-still, frozen to the spot. It was Norman who recovered first. He cautiously stepped forward and was about to push the door when he noticed that it was already open. Inside, the croft appeared even darker than the moor and Norman hesitated before entering, but his uncle behind him shoved him in. 'Don't be so bloody soft, Norman,' he said. With a clomp, the croft door swung shut behind them. At the same time the place was flooded by brilliant powerful lights, and in front of them appeared a tall man.

Norman immediately recognised the man, but he was not dressed in the earthly gear that he had worn earlier that afternoon. He was now wearing a close-fitting garment made of some silvery metallic substance, the sort Norman would have expected a spaceman to wear. In fact, the man no longer looked human but more like a robot. He sat in what appeared to be a command chair. On each arm rest there were scores of different coloured buttons. Apart from the chair – or throne, to be more precise – the croft was empty and everything was white; the floor, walls and in all probability the ceiling too, only Norman found it impossible to look up into the glare of the bright lights overhead.

The man spoke. It was the same voice that had bade them enter.

'Welcome, gentlemen,' he said, 'welcome aboard Space Vehicle Limbo Two.'

The bright lights restored the mayor's confidence and now he was convinced that this was all one big joke; probably some kind of *Candid Camera* set-up. This man looked like he was part of a carnival, dressed up to look like something out of *Star Trek*.

'Never mind all that,' he started. 'I don't know what your game is, or what it is you hope to gain by it, but I'll have you know . . . have you know . . . haaaaa . . .' His voice trailed off and he stared mutely at the spaceman. Norman looked on in amazement; he'd only seen that expression on his uncle's face once, and that was on the day that Norman had come home from school to tell him he'd passed his O-levels. The spaceman stared calmly back at his uncle for a few moments and then repeated, 'Welcome aboard Space Vehicle Limbo Two.' In return the mayor beamed. He took off his hat.

'Welcome to Earth,' he replied, looking around him, 'and may I say with all humility what a great example of technicalogical gadgetry your spacecraft is.' He moved over to the wall and, bending forward, pointed at nothing, saying, 'Can you get BBC2 on that?' Norman wandered over to see what it was that his uncle was looking at, but his uncle pulled him back. 'Don't touch any of them switches.' Norman couldn't guess what his uncle was on about; to him it just looked like a blank wall. The mayor shook his head vigorously. 'And I thought this place was derelict!'

'Naturally you did,' replied the stranger. 'From the outside it is just a derelict croft, thus avoiding any suspicion that the place is anything else but that. Even you, born and bred in Grapplewick, would not have thought otherwise had you not entered at my invitation. You can see now that a space vehicle can take many different forms.'

The mayor laughed. 'I've passed this place many times. If I'd known then what I know now I would have popped in for a cup of tea!'

'Then you would have been no wiser,' replied the man; 'you would have found the inside as derelict as the exterior. Our space vehicle would have been elsewhere.'

'Of course,' nodded the mayor sagely. Norman looked on, perplexed. He knew the man was different – he'd seen that for himself – and if truth be told he even believed that the man was an alien, but he found it a little hard to swallow that Kershaw's

Croft was really a space vehicle. Again, uncannily, the man seemed able to read his thoughts.

'Your face expresses doubts, my young friend.'

'No, no,' protested Norman, 'it's just that, well, they look like bare walls to me,' he finished lamely. He was surprised at his own temerity, but he'd been brought up to be honest and straightforward, and he couldn't understand why his uncle was bowing and scraping to this stranger.

The man smiled. 'I appreciate your scepticism. It's actually one of the reasons you were selected, but I must tell you that we only allow humans to see what is absolutely necessary. I have granted that power to your uncle the mayor in order that he will truly appreciate the reason for my visit. In your case it's superfluous as you have already witnessed demonstrations of my power. However, to convince you further,' he pressed several buttons on the arms of his chair, 'come.' He went over to the wall. 'Do not be alarmed at what you are about to see. You are perfectly safe.' He slid back a small panel and in the blackness beyond it Norman saw a myriad of twinkling lights. He turned to the spaceman for enlightenment. 'Don't you recognise Grapplewick from three thousand feet?' asked the alien as he slid back the panel. 'Have no fear,' he added, 'I will return you to *terra firma* in a moment and once more this ship will become Kershaw's Croft.'

Norman was staggered; he now wouldn't have minded a closer look to see whether he could spot Coldhurst Street, but a new thought pushed all others aside. 'Can you go anywhere in this?' he asked eagerly.

The man spread his arms. 'Where is anywhere? Venus, the outer galaxy, the sixteenth century, tomorrow?' Norman stared at him, aghast, and was suddenly very glad that he hadn't actually mentioned Benidorm.

'Oh, it's nothing,' he said weakly. 'It's just hard to imagine Kershaw's Croft whizzing around the world.'

'Don't be embarrassed, Norman,' said the man kindly, 'a space vehicle can take on many forms, too many for an Earth mind to comprehend. Really, though, it's very simple. Do you remember a TV series called *Doctor Who*? His space vehicle was a blue police box. We thought that was very imaginative – in fact you had us worried for a time!'

A door at the rear of the room opened and a girl stepped through. She was clad in the same material as the spaceman, only there wasn't so much of it. She actually reminded Norman of the principal boy in last year's pantomime, although this pantomime character didn't smile – she just looked straight through the two Earthlings as if they weren't there. She moved behind the spaceman's chair and put her hands on his head. He closed his eyes and a burst of indecipherable radio static filled the room. It stopped as quickly as it had begun, then the man opened his eyes and the girl stepped away from the chair.

'Good news,' he said, 'our forward party is already orbiting the sun.' Norman and the mayor looked suitably impressed. 'That was my assistant Oomi,' continued the spaceman. 'You will be meeting her again over the next few days as she will be acting on my behalf in Grapplewick.'

'Of course,' the mayor replied with a half bow, 'of course.'

The spaceman stood up. 'Now – to business!'

'Grapplewick is at your disposal,' said the mayor and Norman couldn't help but feel that his uncle was overdoing it a bit.

'Mr Mayor,' said the spaceman, ignoring the sycophancy, 'you will convene a meeting at the town hall tomorrow morning at ten o'clock. Those present will form the emergency committee; that is yourself and Councillor Butterworth, the Superintendent of Police, Mr Smith and, of course, your nephew.'

The mayor was slightly disconcerted by the inclusion of Norman; after all he was just the messenger. Why did he have to be present? He cleared his throat. 'It will be as you say, but why him?' He gestured at Norman. 'I mean, he closed early tonight and he'll be up to his eyes tomorrow, what with half term and everything, and then there's the . . .'

The alien cut him short. 'If it is so important then you will be at the shop tomorrow, not Norman. I have specific instructions for him.' The tone was hard, commanding.

'Of course,' said the mayor meekly. 'We can always say we're closed for alterations.'

'Thank you,' said the alien, his voice gentle again. 'I will see you both tomorrow at ten o'clock. In the meantime I have a small gift for you both.' Oomi came in again carrying a silver tray on which were two small round badges. The mayor took one and studied it with reverence. They looked just like ordinary badges to Norman, and on the front of them were embossed the words 'Beautiful Grapplewick'.

'Thank you, sir,' gushed the mayor. 'This town needs something like this.' He nudged Norman, who mumbled his thanks. In fact he would rather have had a spacesuit – or the console.

The alien shook his head, sensing Norman's disappointment. 'You will wear these at all times, for they are not as dull as they appear.' Norman perked up on hearing this. 'They are in fact anti-module badges and will offer you protection should our vehicles contaminate the earth on arrival. This is highly unlikely, I might add, but it's better to err on the side of caution.' Norman and his uncle couldn't get their badges on quickly enough. 'I shall look forward to seeing you tomorrow, when my mission shall be explained to you in full. Then you will learn what is expected of you.'

The mayor was about to make a farewell speech when a gust of wind blew open the door of the croft – how or why was a mystery – and once he and Norman had stepped back into the night, it slammed unaided behind them.

They stood for a moment, looking back at the dark silent shape of the croft and then set off for home, slowly at first, then gradually quickening their pace until they were both running at full speed for the sanctuary of the bus shelter. As they staggered to a stop under its welcoming roof, Norman was bending forward with his hands on his knees, trying to catch his breath. His uncle was in a worse state, hugging the lamp post for support and struggling to breathe. He rasped and retched in a desperate effort to fill his lungs with sweet cold air.

'Are you OK, Uncle?' gasped Norman. The mayor didn't reply; he couldn't, he just waved his hand and pointed to his chest to signify that as soon as he'd sorted out his respiratory system and had recovered enough to stand upright, he'd speak.

'Now do you believe me?' cried Norman, wiping his nose with the back of his hand.

The mayor reached out and patted the boy's shoulder. 'Norman,' he began, 'we've seen some things tonight.' He stopped and gathered his breath for the rest of the sentence. 'We've seen things tonight that are beyond human comprehension.' Norman nodded and looked back fearfully in the direction of the croft, but he could see nothing in the darkness. Anyway, maybe the croft was no longer there – it could be hovering over Grapplewick again, or it may have even gone back to the sixteenth century. He shuddered.

Simultaneously, Norman and the mayor saw the bobbing headlights of the bus as it made its way up the hill and juddered to a halt by the stop. They boarded it in silence.

During the return journey Norman imagined himself in control of Space Vehicle Limbo Two. He'd spend a week or so in Spain and then on the way back he'd press a button for a week ago and nobody would even know that he'd been away. His uncle, meanwhile, pondered on more down-to-earth matters: how was he going to convene a meeting at such short notice? How could he impress upon such cretins as Councillor Butterworth and the unimaginative Police Superintendent the importance of the meeting, and what on earth could he tell them over the phone? In the end he decided that the less that was said, the better. He'd leave it up to the spaceman to explain it all tomorrow. In fact he wouldn't mention the word 'spaceman' at all on the phone; he'd say that a Very Important Person had come a long way with the express purpose of divulging information which could be of benefit to them all – yes, that was it, that was the clincher. If he mentioned the word 'benefit' then wild horses wouldn't keep them away . . . and he was right.

ELEVEN

Councillor Arnold Butterworth was the leader of the opposition in Grapplewick, staunch Labour, somewhere to the left of Stalin. He believed passionately that all workers were downtrodden and that the sooner they all united and marched forward, the better the world would be – as long as he was in charge. It came, therefore, as a complete surprise to him to receive a phone call from the mayor who, being a right-wing fascist, had never spoken a word to him outside the line of duty. Butterworth's first reaction on being called to the meeting was to tell the mayor to get stuffed but, on reflection, he was intrigued by the fact that the Conservative leader would not be present and that the superintendent would. Perhaps the matter was a criminal one, involving the leader of the council.

Butterworth's mind was working overtime as he dodged in and out of the pedestrians ambling, grey-faced, up and down the high street. Suddenly he paused. Maybe the criminal matter involved himself; what about that free fact-finding mission to Romania? After two weeks living the life of Riley, he had come back eulogising the Romanian regime. Six weeks later they had executed his host together with his wife. No, it couldn't be that. He hadn't signed anything, and Romania was now old news, but all the same he doubled his pace, holding on to his trilby when a strong gust of wind tried to tear it from his head. He bounded up the town hall steps into the quiet sanctuary of the main hall.

'Morning, Councillor Butterworth,' said the town clerk. Grapplewick was an urban parish council and still retained some of the old titles. Butterworth, as he always did, ignored the clerk – another right-wing lackey – but his scowl faded as he spotted Mrs Dobson, one of the council cleaners, on her knees scrubbing the floor. He felt an overwhelming urge to give that ample behind a playful smack – why shouldn't he? Other people did, but he had never really had the courage. In any case, on hearing his footsteps she straightened up and moved her bucket so that he could pass.

'Morning, Mrs Dobson.' He smiled and raised his hat.

'Morning, Mr Butterworth, a right procession passing through here today.'

'Oh, yes,' he replied, a touch smugly. 'Important meetings you know, no rest for the wicked.' He allowed himself a sideways glance at her. Big she might be, but well formed, and although she was married with a young son she still dispensed her favours when her old man was on nights.

Mrs Dobson nodded up the stairs. 'They're in the mayor's office, been there half an hour I reckon!'

'Half an hour!' he repeated, annoyed. Trust them, he thought, the meeting had been called for ten and it was only five to now so they must have come in early to discuss something privately, without him being there. And why was Norman present? Maybe he was an independent witness to whatever it was the council was going to charge him with. He nodded at Mrs Dobson and ran up the marble steps.

The town clerk sauntered over to Mrs Dobson. 'He looks like someone in a hurry,' he said.

Mrs Dobson wrung out her cloth into a bucket. 'He always is,' she said enigmatically and the town clerk felt a twinge of jealousy as he looked at the retreating form of the Labour councillor. He looked again at Mrs Dobson. She couldn't be having it off with him as well, could she? He dismissed the thought instantly. She wasn't that hard up.

Butterworth strode into the mayor's office. 'I'm not late, am I?' he said as he took off his overcoat. Everybody looked at him but no one said a word. 'What's all this about then?' he continued as he took off his hat and scarf. The superintendent was busily writing in his notebook but he broke off long enough to say, 'Not now, we're busy.'

Butterworth was mortified; he was, after all, leader of the opposition and not some snotty-nosed kid from Northmoor Street.

'Go on, lad,' the superintendent was saying to Norman, 'describe him.'

Norman shrugged. 'Well, he was in and out like, and he asked for a pound of streaky bacon, and when we found out he couldn't see, the man put his hands over his face and that was it, he had his sight back.'

The superintendent stared at the ceiling in exasperation. 'Yes, yes, you've told us all that,' he said. 'He was blind, OK, I've got that. Now, what did he look like?'

Norman screwed up his face in concentration. 'Well, he was, er ... I'm sorry, I wasn't paying much attention to him. I was watching the spaceman.'

'Spaceman,' Butterworth interrupted sharply but the superintendent waved at him to keep silent and leaned towards Norman, struggling to keep his temper.

'How tall was he, was he white, short, fat, thin, medium?'

'Yes, I think so,' said Norman unhappily and the superintendent slammed his notebook on to the table, muttering through clenched teeth, 'It's like talking to a cushion!'

'What's all this about a spaceman?' Butterworth persisted.

In response, the mayor began to recount the remarkable events of the previous day, but as he spoke the town hall clock boomed out the hour of ten o'clock and they all moved across to the window overlooking the high street to watch the arrival – all, that is, except Norman whose eyes were fixed firmly on the grey skies. The superintendent spotted this and shook his head in disgust – was the lad really expecting to see Kershaw's Croft circling the town prior to landing in the town hall car park? The others were eagerly craning forward as a bus pulled up, but only two people got off, and unless he'd transformed himself into a geriatric, the spaceman wasn't one of them.

The last stroke of ten passed unnoticed but behind them came a voice: 'Good morning, gentlemen.'

They whirled round and stared at the man, slack jawed. It was uncanny, they hadn't even heard him close the door.

'Good morning,' said the mayor, finding his voice. 'Ha, ha, bang on time.' He nervously 'ha-ha'd' again.

Superintendent Smith pulled himself together and looked at the man with a policeman's eye: about six foot, mid-fifties, white,

Caucasian, or perhaps not; a man who would fit into any of the major capitals of the world, but here in Grapplewick he stuck out like a twenty-carat diamond in a Nubian's belly button.

The man spoke as he was taking off his hat and gloves. 'Please be seated, gentlemen.'

They scrabbled for seats. 'Just like musical chairs,' thought the policeman wryly. He remained standing; nobody was going to tell him when to sit down on his own manor. The man regarded him coolly, and the superintendent sat, knowing he'd lost the first round.

'I will be as brief as I can,' said the man. 'Unfortunately, I have a luncheon appointment on the other side of the world – Brazil to be exact.'

The mayor glanced at the superintendent who winked back at him: he could easily check the airports. Norman stared at the man incredulously. He didn't doubt for a moment that the man was having lunch in South America. He was visualising Kershaw's Croft hurtling across the Atlantic. In the distance a train whistled and as the mayor automatically reached for his watch the man spoke again.

'No need for introductions, I know who you are. As for myself, I am at present a member of the Inter-Galactic Peacekeeping Force, representing many planets in the solar system, or to put it crudely in your language, I am a spaceman.'

The superintendent raised an eyebrow and studied the man with that particular policeman's look that would have made George Washington wonder if he really had chopped down a tree. Butterworth, however, not having been fully briefed on the previous day's events, threw down his pencil on his doodle pad and cleared his throat. The man only held up his hand and whatever objections the councillor had been about to raise remained unspoken.

'Yes,' continued the spaceman, 'I am from the planet Androm. This you will believe in due course, but as time is short I'll get straight to the point.' Norman and his uncle leaned forward eagerly but Superintendent Smith lolled back in his chair, waiting to be presented with the evidence.

'I have to warn you, gentlemen, that although your planet Earth is but a speck in the cosmos, it is important in its strategic position.' The mayor nodded wisely as if astronomy was an open book to him. 'Many thousands of years ago you Earth people dabbled with nuclear fission, and with catastrophic results. Your illustrious ancestors succeeded in destroying each other, along with all other life forms on your planet. Not a tree, not a river or ocean remained. You were, in effect, a ball of dust, and may I say, in all modesty, that it was due only to our swift actions that we were able to maintain the rotation of this galaxy.'

'How do you know all this?' quizzed the superintendent.

'I know because I was in charge of that particular operation,' replied the man coolly.

There was stunned silence around the room, broken finally by the superintendent, who now felt he had enough evidence at least to have this nutter certified. 'You must be getting on a bit,' he sniffed.

The man appeared not to notice the sarcasm. 'Our intellect does not wither; we merely change the casing when necessary.' The mayor was impressed; he wouldn't mind a body transplant although he was pretty sure Eunice would get a shock.

'To continue,' said the man, 'it was essential to maintain life forms on earth. A repeat of the fate which befell the planet Mars would have been disastrous. Therefore, after carefully monitoring radiation levels across your world, we were able to drain off the excess and create new life on the planet.'

This was proving to be too much for Councillor Butterworth's socialist philosophy. 'All right then,' he challenged; 'if you recreated humans, why did you make them black, white, yellow, red? Why did you give them different lifestyles, different languages, why did you make a few rich, them that feed off the workers . . .'

The man suddenly slapped his hand on the table and Butterworth stopped in mid-sentence as if someone had cut out his tongue. 'I'm not here to defend our motives,' replied the man curtly, 'but in order to satisfy your curiosity, it was an experiment which unfortunately didn't turn out as we had hoped. It might have gone better had we not, in our generosity, granted you free will.'

'Free will!' spluttered Butterworth. 'Who d'you think you are, God?'

The man smiled for the first time. 'Ah yes, God. He was one of our better ideas.' The gathering around the table stared at him in stunned amazement – even Butterworth, who was a staunch atheist, was taken aback by such blasphemy, especially coming from an alien. The man sighed as if he'd just asked them to add up two plus two.

ERIC SYKES

'Yes, God,' he mused. 'Brilliant in its conception, a God with no shape or form, God, the ultimate deterrent, the guider and provider. Sadly, as with all good ideas, the concept of God was plagiarised by intellectuals in order to assume their dominance over more simple minds. Swayed by the powerful, you created your own gods of the elements and when they proved insufficient you built idols of stone and wood. Even now in some parts of the world there are people who worship beasts. You, in your enlightened state, ridicule these fetishes of backward nations when you yourselves have created new, less worthy gods – the gods of money, possession and pleasure, which in themselves are evil when pursued to the detriment of others!'

There was an uncomfortable silence around the table as they accepted the truth of his words, but equally they hadn't gathered here in the early morning to be lectured; they were busy people and he hadn't told them anything that they couldn't have read in a church magazine. The superintendent cleared his throat.

'Forgive us misguided mortals,' he began, 'but if I read you right, your presence here seems to be of great importance, not just to our small town but to the whole world, so why are you telling us all this, and what do you want from us?'

'I will explain in due course,' said the man, 'but first I must make clear to you all the urgency of our mission. You Earth people have again reached the same dangerously high level of nuclear development. I'm not talking just about the superpowers but the smaller Middle Eastern nations as well. Nuclear arsenals are being stockpiled and unless we intervene, humans may once again unleash a holocaust that even we wouldn't have the resources to repair.'

The superintendent shifted uneasily in his seat. 'With all due respect, Mr ... whatever your name is ... we're not entirely ignorant of the situation. Great Britain, Russia, the USA and others are all monitoring each other's nuclear capabilities as well as those of the Third World nations. What I want to know is why you're not talking to those countries' leaders. Why us here in Grapplewick?' The mayor nodded in agreement and the committee turned as one to face the spaceman.

'We already have,' he replied, 'and not just once but many times. Yes, even with Stalin in his day as well as Churchill, Truman, Kennedy, Thatcher and many others.'

'And they didn't believe you?'

'Oh yes, they believed us and wholeheartedly agreed with us, but then – as is the case now – no one wants to be the first to make a move. Ironically, they trust us but are deeply suspicious of each other.'

Norman felt that it was now time that he spoke. He had never been to a grown-up meeting before, but he didn't want the others to know that. 'Excuse me,' he started, 'but why are you telling us all this?'

'Because,' answered the alien slowly, 'one of our space vehicles will be landing here next Wednesday.'

They were dumbstruck. Four mouths fell open like a choir on television with the sound off. A trickle of saliva rolled down the mayor's chin and he wiped it away with his hand.

'Here?' he gasped.

'Just outside the town on a site you call Sagbottom's Acres.'

Enlightenment dawned on the superintendent's face.

'Wait a minute, aren't you the nutcase who's been sending letters every fortnight to various town councils?'

Butterworth nodded eagerly. 'That's right, UFOs have been threatening to come for about a year now, and always on a Wednesday, too.'

The man studied him for a moment.

'I did not write the letters personally, but yes they were sanctioned by my department. Sadly, on each occasion the letters marked "Strictly Private and Confidential" were leaked to the press and higher authority, resulting in devastating public curiosity. In the circumstances, it was therefore impossible to permit our vehicles to land to a pop star's reception. The success of our mission depends on absolute secrecy.'

Superintendent Smith had heard enough and felt a warm feeling of elation. Any information regarding the letters was to be forwarded immediately to Scotland Yard, and he not only had information, he had the squire responsible, game, set and match. He began to develop his case.

'Let's look at a few facts, shall we?' he said, leaning his hands on the table. 'You sit there and tell us you're a spaceman, no papers or identification. That's just for openers. Secondly, we're expected to believe that a spaceship will be coming here next Wednesday.'

He strolled over to the window and looked out.

'Take yesterday for instance. You walk into a barber's shop and hypnotise *him*,' he turned and pointed dramatically at Norman.

'Just look at him, I ask you, anybody could put him under. He walks around in a trance most of the time anyway.'

Norman blushed. 'Oh yes,' he blurted, 'and what about the blind man then?'

'Oh, the blind man,' retorted the superintendent. 'Well, we've only got your word for that, haven't we?' He turned triumphantly to the man. 'And now, sir, I think you have a bit of explaining to do and I must ask you to accompany . . .'

The mayor interrupted him.

'Hang on a minute, Wilfred, why don't we hear what he's got to say first? After all, the other towns only got letters but we've been honoured by a personal visit.'

The superintendent turned and surveyed him with raised eyebrow. The mayor fidgeted uncomfortably.

'All right, all right, so he hypnotised me in Kershaw's Croft . . . I was tired,' he added lamely.

Norman sprang to his defence. 'He didn't hypnotise me, and I saw Grapplewick through the window.'

Superintendent Smith snorted, 'If he'd said it was Father Christmas's workshop you'd have believed him.'

The spaceman was unperturbed. 'Superintendent,' he said softly, 'would you do me the courtesy of going back to the window?'

The policeman stared at him quizzically, then did as he was asked.

'Fifty yards down the high street a woman is looking into a bicycle repair shop window.'

The superintendent searched for a moment. 'I see her, an Indian woman.'

'She is actually from Hyderabad, but no matter.'

The others, unable to contain their curiosity, joined the superintendent at the window.

'You will also notice that she is pregnant.'

'Well gone,' added the mayor, craning his neck over Norman's shoulder.

'Either that or she's been doing a fair bit of shoplifting,' smirked the superintendent. Then a sudden realisation hit him. He whirled around to face the spaceman and confirmed that from where he was sitting there was no way he could see even the rooftops opposite, let alone down into the street.

'Watch her carefully,' said the man. 'She appears to be healthy, but observe now how she staggers and clutches the wall for support. She's now collapsed.'

They stared down, fascinated, as the colourful sari crumpled into a heap on the pavement. A young woman rushed across to help; she was followed by an elderly man and very soon a knot of people had gathered around the fallen woman. Together they carried her into the bicycle shop.

'Call an ambulance,' ordered the superintendent.

'It's not necessary. The people in the shop are already calling the hospital.'

'Is she having the baby?' asked Norman.

'Alas, no,' replied the man quietly. 'In five minutes she will be dead.'

Horrified, they all turned towards him.

'Dead?' repeated Butterworth incredulously.

The man spread his hands. 'You are the judges. Shall she live, or will she die?'

'Us,' whispered Norman through dry lips. 'What can we do?'

'I have the power of life and death,' said the man, 'but her fate depends on your verdict.'

Uncomprehending, they stared at each other.

'You have three minutes left, gentlemen.'

'Live,' shrieked Norman and the others nodded hurriedly in agreement.

'So be it,' said the man. 'Please continue to watch the shop.'

They all turned back to the window. A few seconds later the sari-clad woman walked out of the shop into the street, obviously reassuring the people around her, and a policeman who had now arrived, that she was all right. The policeman spoke into his radio, perhaps to cancel the ambulance. Superintendent Smith made a mental note to quiz the constable later when he returned to the station.

'As you have just witnessed,' said the man, 'the woman is now as healthy as she was before she took that turn, and her son will be born in six weeks' time.'

Totally impressed, the committee returned slowly to the table and sat down again. They were beginning to believe in the awesome power of the man in front of them.

Outside the mayor's office in the body of the town hall there were the usual queues of people, mainly elderly folk enquiring about the rates, disability allowances and old-age pensions but there were also one or two younger people there, worried about housing. Mrs Dobson, along with Cissie, another cleaner, was now scrubbing away at the corridor not too far away from the mayor's office. Anybody watching them would have surely noticed that they had been scrubbing and polishing the same small area of corridor for the past twenty minutes. The town clerk paced the same corridor with a piece of paper in his hand, ostensibly for the mayor. He paused every so often outside the mayor's office door, desperate to know what the meeting was about. He'd tried going into the office next door and putting a glass against the wall but that was a pointless exercise; the Victorians had built their town halls to last and a cheap glass was no match for the thick stone walls holding the rooms up. The investigation as to what was going on in the mayor's office was therefore left to the cleaners.

Cissie leaned over to her friend. 'Are you positive that's the same man?'

Mrs Dobson nodded. 'I am that, it's the same one all right. I'd recognise his shoes anywhere – you won't find another pair like that in Grapplewick.'

Cissie was convinced. Mrs Dobson was something of an expert on footwear as she spent so much of her time on her knees. Scrubbing the floors all day she had the opportunity to study many pairs of shoes as they walked in and out of the town hall.

Mrs Dobson continued, 'I'd know that man anywhere; like I said, I was in the barber's with our Jack when he came in. I never saw his face but I noticed his shoes when I run out!'

'What's he doing in here then?'

Mrs Dobson leaned on her bucket and shrugged, then she looked over to where the town clerk was pretending to pick up his piece of paper outside the mayor's door. She winked at Cissie. 'I'll soon find out,' she promised. Tiptoeing up to the unsuspecting clerk, she quickly goosed him.

'Oh!' he shrieked and immediately clasped his hand over his mouth. Cissie giggled into her bucket as he whirled around to face Mrs Dobson. OK, so he'd been to bed with her a couple of times, but that didn't entitle her to that sort of familiarity, and certainly not in the town hall. He really didn't know what attitude to take. If he smiled and passed it off as a joke then he would be undermining his authority, but on the other hand if he was stern and rebuked her, it could be the end of his carnal pleasures. Before he could decide on which course to take, Mrs Dobson spoke.

'Tom's on nights again,' she said in a little girl voice. The clerk gulped. Under that floral pinny and those thick stockings, she was all woman.

'Same time?' he croaked and she nodded.

'I'll leave the door on the latch. By the way, what are they talking about in there?' she added as an afterthought. 'You're the town clerk. You should be in there with them.'

She was right. As he was virtually the chief executive of this place it was his duty to know what was going on in every meeting and he was dying to know what was going on in this one. 'I can't just barge in,' he said, 'it's a private meeting.' Mrs Dobson sniffed, and the way she sniffed somehow affronted the clerk's manhood and pride. 'Tell you what,' he went on, 'you keep your eyes open and see that nobody comes up the stairs or around that corner. If they do, then cough loudly.'

Mrs Dobson scuttled back to Cissie.

'What's going on in there then?' asked Cissie.

Mrs Dobson leaned over and whispered in her ear. 'I'll tell you tomorrow,' she promised. 'Now take your bucket over there and keep your eyes peeled on the corridor. If anyone comes, cough.'

Cissie gave a practice cough and carrying her cleaning accoutrements she ambled down to the far end of the corridor. Taking up her new position she glanced over at the town clerk, who was standing rather undecidedly outside the mayor's office. She hissed and when he turned to look at her she put her index finger and thumb together and peered through them. He nodded eagerly, taking the hint, and bent down to the keyhole. He couldn't see very much as the man talking had his back to him, so he put his ear to the keyhole instead, and listened.

'When our space vehicle lands on Wednesday, you will be introduced to your teachers.'

Norman immediately visualised a teacher coming down a ramp from the spaceship, wearing a tweed jacket with leather patches at the elbows and smoking a pipe. He blinked rapidly and turned his attention back to what the man was saying.

'Four vehicles will land throughout the world. They won't land in the capital cities of the world but in humble locations such as yours. Once they have landed, the teachers will train the future governments, which will consist of ordinary people selected much as you have been selected.' He paused. 'Is that clear so far?'

Everybody nodded in assent, although if truth be told, what the alien was saying was well beyond their comprehension.

The mayor took the opportunity to speak out loud. 'On behalf of Grapplewick Council, may I say how honoured we are by this undoubted faith you place in our stumbling abilities. Please rest assured that we will do all in our power to assist you in your endeavours.' Butterworth patted the table in agreement and the superintendent nodded.

The man continued. 'So far so good. Planet Earth will be divided into four sections, which means that you will be responsible for one quarter of the world and its population.'

A shockwave ran through the room and at the keyhole the town clerk paled.

'One quarter of the world and its population,' repeated the man. They looked at each other in dismay.

'But that's just not possible!' blurted the mayor. 'I mean, we don't mind helping out but, er, with all due respect we haven't got the office space or the staff; we're up to our eyes in administration as it is!'

Butterworth nodded gravely in agreement. 'We've a housing list that's as long as your arm, and that's just here in this small town. We certainly couldn't cope with a few more hundred million homeless.'

The man shook his head slowly. 'Your agitation is natural but you need have no fear. Your positions in the new government will depend entirely on the good sense of your President, who will guide and educate you.'

'You will be our President?' asked the superintendent.

'Alas, no,' replied the man, 'after Wednesday my work here will be done. Your new President, however, is sitting here at this table.'

They gaped at him, each one hoping beyond hope that they were not to be the chosen one, the scale of the responsibility being way beyond even their combined abilities. Grapplewick was one thing but this was a whole new international ball game.

Finally, after surveying them all silently, the man spoke. 'Norman Waterhouse will be our representative here on Earth. I give you . . . your President!'

This announcement was greeted with stunned silence. This lasted just a second and then Butterworth exploded.

'Now I know this is a joke,' he snarled. He was so angry with himself for being taken in by this man. All thoughts of the pregnant Indian woman had vanished from his mind. '*Him*,' he said scornfully. 'President of one quarter of the world, yet he's as thick as two planks. He hasn't even got the brains of a two-year-old!'

Norman shot back without thinking, 'I have!'

The mayor pulled Norman back on to his seat. 'I have to agree with Councillor Butterworth,' he said. 'I've brought Norman up so I know. He's a good lad but he's not really fitted for high office, or even office come to that.'

The man continued as if there had been no interruption. 'All frontiers, all country boundaries will be dismantled. There will be one common language throughout the world, and all the people will be governed by one law!'

The superintendent, whose enthusiasm for the new Jerusalem had slightly waned once he had learned that Norman was to be its President, decided to add his fourpence-worth. 'It's a sensible philosophy, and one – I may add – which would make my job much easier. But there's one thing that bothers me – why him?' He nodded his head at Norman. 'He's only a lad and all he knows is hairdressing, and quite frankly, I wouldn't trust him to mow my lawn.'

Norman was quick to defend himself. 'How would you know? You don't come into my shop any more!'

'Not since I had that rash!' replied the policeman hotly.

The spaceman held up his hands and the argument subsided with ill grace.

'Since the barber's shop seems to have become a bone of contention I shall remove it.' He put his fingers to his temples and closed his eyes. They waited apprehensively but after thirty seconds he relaxed and a collective sigh went around the room. They hadn't realised they had all been holding their breath in anticipation. They waited for an explanation but none was forthcoming. The man simply sat in silence. The mayor made a move to speak but the man shook his head. Again they waited, and then, faintly, from somewhere down the high street, they heard a siren. In a body they rushed to the window just in time to see a fire appliance approaching erratically through the traffic. The noise of the siren reached a crescendo and then receded rapidly as it turned sharp left into a side road.

'It's going up Coldhurst Street!' cried Norman. The mayor nodded sickly in agreement. He had a feeling he knew exactly where it was going.

The superintendent commented drily, 'That wasn't one of our fire tenders. That one was from Manchester.' All heads swivelled as they heard the tinny *clamballang* of a bell getting louder as it fussed past a cyclist before grinding round a corner in the wake of its big brother.

'That's ours,' confirmed the superintendent. He turned to look at the man with a new regard. If the fire was where he thought it was, then this man obviously did possess powers that were beyond the understanding of mere mortals.

The strident ring of the telephone broke the silence and they all jumped as if some puppeteer had jerked all their strings at the same time. They stared at the instrument for a moment, ring ring . . . ring ring. The mayor pulled himself together, walked slowly towards it and lifted the receiver. It could have been Neville Chamberlain expecting a call from Hitler. He nodded a couple of times and then said sadly, 'Gutted . . . you mean gutted completely. Yes, yes, I see. Well, thank you, Mervyn.' He put down the receiver and looked at the man in awe. 'My shop has been gutted,' he said with wonder.

The superintendent put a hand on his shoulder. 'Easy, lad. Come on, Albert, sit down.' The mayor did as he was told in an obvious state of shock.

The man, however, was relentless. 'Your shop is nothing compared to the safety of the solar system, and having to listen to your petty wrangling, my patience is rapidly becoming exhausted. Now, do I continue or do I bestow the fate of your shop upon the whole of Grapplewick? It's of no concern to me to raze this place to the ground and all the people with it.'

They stared at the man, aghast. 'Eighty thousand people,' whispered the mayor.

'As with the lady from Hyderabad, their fate is in your hands. Our space vehicle would encounter no difficulty in landing in the blackened hole that once was Grapplewick.'

They were appalled. The mayor's shop was one thing and the death of the lady from Hyderabad would not have been cataclysmic, but the whole of Grapplewick and its people? What sort of man could do something like this? He was certainly not of this world – they had all witnessed demonstrations of his awesome power – and all lingering doubts had been swept away. Nobody was prepared to speak. There wasn't a coherent thought between the four of them.

The man surveyed them contemptuously. 'Well, gentlemen,' he said, 'do I have your full cooperation?' Nobody moved. They were all shell-shocked. The man sighed. 'Please remember, if it does become necessary to erase Grapplewick, you four will be spared, not out of generosity on our part but so that you can live out the rest of your days with the deaths of eighty thousand people on your consciences.'

By now the committee of four was very afraid, and totally convinced of the spaceman's omnipotence.

'We are your humble servants,' whispered the mayor, looking down on the table top. 'You have only to command.'

The man nodded briefly. 'In order to ease your minds as to Norman's suitability to carry out the presidential tasks ahead of him, I will ask one question. Can any of you tell me the correct definition of "geopotential"?' The mayor, councillor and policeman shrugged their shoulders, utterly baffled. 'Geopotential' was not a word frequently bandied about in Grapplewick, and in any case their minds were still caught up in the events of the past few minutes. They couldn't think straight. The man waited, and when he was satisfied that no answer was forthcoming, he turned to Norman. 'Geopotential?' he asked.

Without hesitation Norman rapidly replied, 'The geopotential is the potential energy of a unit mass with reference to sea level.' He paused to see whether his answer would suffice.

'Go on,' urged the man.

Norman smiled as if further elucidation was unnecessary, then continued. 'Surfaces of constant geopotential, or level surfaces, are fixed in space and may therefore be used as a scale to measure height, and the common unit of measure is the dynamic metre.' Finished, he slowly looked around at his audience.

'By jingo, Norman,' said the mayor, 'you're a bit of a dark horse.'

His nephew smiled shyly. 'By the way, for an average value of the gravitational constant, the dynamic metre is equal to approximately 1.02 metric metres.'

The man spread his hands. 'You have given the correct answer. Alas, I am clumsy, but when the teachers arrive they will educate the extremely fertile mind of this boy.'

Butterworth raised his hand to be allowed to speak. 'Excuse me, sir, but how many years will this education take?'

'One hour,' replied the man calmly. Butterworth whistled silently and they all looked at Norman with a new respect in their eyes. Norman was embarrassed; for the life of him he couldn't understand their change of attitude towards him. They were all staring at him with undisguised admiration. Was it something he had said, or was it something he had done? He couldn't recollect having said anything startling at all.

'You may well be wondering how we will effect these world changes,' said the man, and their attention was turned from Norman back to him. They all nodded, although the thought hadn't occurred to any of them. 'Firstly, on the arrival of our space vehicle, your planet will be bombarded with hypergalactic rays which will immediately suspend all life.'

This was greeted by unanimous incomprehension. The man sighed again. 'To make it easier for all of you to understand the new regime, all thoughts will be blotted out and all minds erased, to accommodate the new thinking. Whatever people were before exposure to the rays will be expunged, and incidentally, this time around everybody will be the same colour.'

'Thank heavens for that,' sighed the superintendent, 'I've got used to being white.'

'On the contrary,' said the man. 'You will all be black.'

Again they were fearful.

'Do not be afraid. When the effects of the rays have worn off it will be as if nothing had ever happened. You will not remember that once there were different coloured people, and as I said before, there will also be only one language. In effect, gentlemen, the new history of Earth will begin on Wednesday!' He pushed back his chair and rose. 'For your final instructions, the arrival of the space vehicle will be heralded by two sonic booms. These will alert you on Wednesday evening that the space vehicle's arrival is imminent, and the four of you should make your way to Sagbottom's Acres to greet your teachers. I repeat, only the four of you will assemble. Should there be any more present then I will know at once that secrecy has not been maintained, as I've demanded. Do I have your word, gentlemen, that what has been discussed in this room will remain locked in your hearts?'

They readily agreed, but all they really understood of the meeting was that on Wednesday evening a spacecraft would be landing in Sagbottom's Acres, and that wild horses wouldn't drag this information out of them.

As he stood up to leave, the man turned to Norman. 'I see you are not wearing your badge,' he admonished. Norman smiled and turned over his lapel to show that it was pinned to the underside of his jacket. The mayor showed that he had done likewise. The man shook his head. 'It is necessary to display these badges for all to see as they have no power whilst hidden.' Both Norman and his uncle hurriedly pinned them to the front of their jackets. The man continued, 'And I have badges for the two of you.' He handed them to the superintendent and Councillor Butterworth.

The superintendent took his badge over to the window in order to study it in greater detail. '"Beautiful Grapplewick,"' he muttered. The mayor joined him by the window and explained the badges' unusual properties. Superintendent Smith was impressed. An hour ago he would have tossed the badge into the bin without a second thought, but not now. Had he been given a pair of flippers he would have put them on over his shoes before flapping his way back to the station.

'Thank you, sir . . .' he turned to say, but the man was no longer there. They looked at one another in amazement. 'I didn't hear him close the door, did you?'

They walked slowly back to the table, totally drained, stripped of reason. If someone had walked in and announced that they were all to be shot immediately, they would have meekly lined up against the wall. Minutes ticked by and still nobody spoke. The superintendent lowered himself into a chair and stared unseeingly at his anti-module badge. Norman, with the resilience of the young, was the first to break the silence. 'Why the secrecy?'

They all stared at him as though he were mad. They didn't want to discuss the matter any further. In fact they didn't even want to leave the room and the security of each other – ever. Still Norman persisted. 'Everything that man said seems logical, although upsetting in its own way, but why keep it a secret? Surely the people of Earth have a right to know what's going to happen; what harm would it do to tell them?'

The superintendent's eyes widened. Could this be the same lad who was fully conversant with the intricacies of geopotential? He rose and placed his hands on the table in order to lean over so that his face was close to Norman's. 'I'll tell you why it has to be a secret, sunshine. If what we've just heard in this room went public, then there would be panic in the streets; mayhem.' He pointed to the window. 'What would happen out there would make the war in Bosnia look like a vicars' picnic; cars overturned, looting and . . . Gordon Bennett . . . it would be no good looking at me to sort things out as I don't have enough men under my command to contain it. By the time the military got here, well . . .' He left the sentence unfinished.

Norman remained unimpressed. 'Well, that's just your opinion, isn't it? Why should people panic? We're not panicking, are we?'

He looked around for support but there was none. The mayor smiled sadly, shaking his head at the naivety of youth. 'We're not panicking, Norman,' he said in a calm, reasonable voice, 'because we're all mature people who can be told these things and as rational human beings we can accept them for what they are.'

Butterworth nodded. 'The mayor's right, Norman. That's why we're the elders of the town council. We're not your average Herbert walking the streets out there.' He nodded out the window to the great beyond. 'Out there, lad, it's a jungle, or a tinderbox. One spark like this and we're all gone. Oh yes, lad, make no mistake about it. If they had an inkling that civilisation as we know it will be finished on Wednesday, why, there'd be a bloodbath . . . It'd be . . . well . . . Goodnight, Vienna!'

Superintendent Smith moved away from the table. 'So you see now why it's imperative that we keep the secret.'

Norman nodded submissively. This little exchange had expelled from their minds some of the horror of the past hour just as a toffee will pacify a bawling infant. In reality, the man had asked nothing of them other than to keep a secret, and the more they thought about it the more relieved they felt. Really, there was no difficulty in keeping the knowledge to themselves. If the aliens did arrive on Wednesday, then no doubt the alien teachers would congratulate them on having kept the secret safe. If on the other hand it turned out to be some gigantic hoax then nobody would be any the wiser. Oh yes, the sun was definitely out again. Indeed they were well on the way to dismissing the awe-inspiring events of the morning as a bad dream.

Their complacency, however, would have gone straight out of the window had they known that already there was a leak. The town clerk had heard enough at the keyhole to tighten his bowels. He would have stayed for more if he hadn't had to scuttle stiff-legged to the toilet, so unfortunately he didn't see the man leave. Nor did he hear the pledge to total secrecy, and tonight when he kept his assignation with Mrs Dobson, she would also be privy to the startling events of the morning. And apart from her other attributes, she had the biggest mouth in Grapplewick.

TWELVE

For the purists, town clerks now bear the title of Chief Executive, but there are still some urban parish councils preferring to retain the old values, and town clerk has a grand traditional ring to it. However, chief executives are mainly chartered accountants and here again Grapplewick differed. Sidney not only had difficulty in checking his weekly salary, he hadn't even had to apply for the job. He simply inherited it from his father along with the chauffeur's uniform and all the regalia of the mace-bearer. The yearly balance sheets for the council affairs were drawn up by a distant cousin, a chartered accountant in Manchester, who was competent enough to add authenticity to the yearly figures. So everything in the garden was decidedly rosy. Sidney was content – a job for life, unmarried, and the clout of his position to grant small favours in return for high jinks in the bedrooms and meadows of Grapplewick.

Tonight was Sidney's snooker night, and awaiting his turn at the table he smiled to himself, ashamed of his panic a few hours ago. The mayor and superintendent, in fact all four of them, had left the office together and they didn't seem unduly perturbed. He must have misinterpreted what he'd heard through the keyhole. It could have been something to do with a TV commercial, or better still, they were probably planning a town pageant. That would explain Norman's presence. Being young he would very likely be leading the procession as the spirit of the future or some such nonsense. Yes, that must be it. They'd all been wearing badges when they came out; it must be a pageant of some sort.

In the afternoon, news reached him that the mayor's shop had gone up in flames but he was hardly surprised. Waterhouse's Barber's had always been a fire hazard with a couple of dozen electrical appliances on one adaptor. It could have blown the street up any time. He cleared his mind as he bent forward to smash the white ball into the red triangle; purely by chance one of the reds shot into the corner, and he was left with an easy black. In fact, due to phenomenal luck he fluked his way into the semi-finals. He hadn't bargained for this and it was late when he left the British Legion, too late to catch the last bus, and he had to walk three miles or so to the Dobsons' house.

By the time he let himself in through the Dobsons' front door it was well after one o'clock in the morning. Creeping silently up the stairs, he eased himself softly into the bedroom. In the half light of a street lamp, he could just discern her dark head on the pillow, turned away from him, feigning sleep. With scarcely a rustle he took off his clothes and slipped in beside her.

'Oh!' she said, whipping around to face him. 'I nearly had a heart attack – I were fast asleep!' She wasn't a bad actress and Sidney even half believed her.

'Oh, yes,' he said, fumbling with her nightie and at the same time trying to get his underpants off.

'My God, you're like a block of ice,' she whispered. His hand, flinging off his pants, caught the bedside lamp and it crashed to the floor. She jerked upright into a sitting position, holding her breath while he lay with his face in the pillow. After a moment she relaxed.

'It's a wonder you didn't wake our Jack,' she hissed, lying back.

'I'm sorry,' mumbled Sidney. He started to fondle her breasts and kiss her, but she turned her face away. He knew then something was wrong. Normally by this stage they'd be groping and giggling like teenagers, and she would have got hold of it by now and be saying things like, 'Ooooh, who's a big boy then?' Tonight, however, she was lying there like prime beef on a butcher's slab.

'What's to do?' he whispered, sliding his hand down her belly and into the thatch of pubic hair. She grabbed his wrist and moved it back. He struggled up on one elbow. 'What's the matter?' he hissed.

She was silent for a while and then spoke. 'You just dashed past me this morning, not a word, not a gesture!'

Sidney had to cast his mind back. 'Oh that,' he remembered, 'I couldn't help it. I had to go to the toilet and when I'd come out you'd gone.'

'Well, I couldn't hang around on my knees all day, could I now?' She was angry now, and he thought it best to say nothing. Eventually she turned her head to him. 'Well, what did happen in the mayor's office this morning then?'

Sidney relaxed sulkily. He knew he wouldn't get his reward until he'd told her all the facts. He started to put together all the snippets he had heard; something about a woman in the street looking into a shop window, the fire bells and 'Beautiful Grapplewick' badges, but Mrs Dobson wasn't satisfied with his casual descriptions. She questioned him on every point, especially the bits concerning the spaceman – did the man actually say he was a spaceman? What was the reaction of the superintendent and everybody else in the room to his statements and where would the spaceship be landing on Wednesday?

By now all Sidney's desire for her had gone, and as the interrogation progressed he became increasingly uneasy as all his fears and uncertainties of that morning came flooding back to him. He began to remember things that his mind had mercifully blotted out, and he realised that his conclusion that the meeting was just a preparation for a pageant was simply his brain's way of hiding under the sheets.

On the moors outside, a cock observing the coming of day fluttered importantly on to a fence and, checking again that it really was getting lighter, puffed out his chest, crowing loud and long. It was a totally unnecessary reveille. People were programmed to their alarm clocks and no longer relied upon mangy old cockerels, but in the distance Mrs Dobson caught the sound of its final crows and quickly sat up in bed. It was indeed getting light; she could now see articles of bedroom furniture and discarded clothes on the floor. Nosy neighbours with incontinent habits would soon be able to recognise a man other than her husband creeping out the back door.

'Hey,' she hissed; 'it's daylight, you'd best be off before anybody sees you.'

Sidney was out in five minutes. He had a reputation to keep up as well and as it turned out his timing was spot on. He spotted

Mr Dobson at the end of the street coming home early from his night shift. Luckily it was a blustery morning and both men passed each other with heads down against the wind, so Mr Dobson did not recognise Sidney, although he did wonder afterwards who was the silly bugger hurrying along in his stockinged feet with a pair of boots under his arm.

However, the secret details of the meeting were well and truly blown. By the time Mrs Dobson arrived at the town hall, the milkman had a potted version of the advent of the men from space and the bus conductor was already regaling his passengers with tales of UFOs. Quicker than radio or television, the jungle drums of Grapplewick were being tuned.

THIRTEEN

O ver two hundred miles to the south-east of Grapplewick, Chief Inspector James sat in his office at Scotland Yard, morosely surveying a bottle of champagne on the desk before him.

A cargo of high-quality cocaine and lesser drugs had been seized yesterday, drugs with a street value of over £80 million. And, more importantly, several big dealers and pushers had gone in the bag to await trial. It was a good result after months of patient police work – a very satisfactory outcome – and he, Chief Inspector James, had set the whole works in motion. For eight months he'd masterminded the operation and now, though he'd tilled the land and planted the trees, someone else was eating the fruit. He smiled ruefully. It was kind of the lads to send him a bottle of bubbly along with an invitation to join them later on for a bit of a do in the Dog and Partridge. He wouldn't go, though . . . he felt deeply ashamed of his present assignment. The drugs bust was in the Premier League and he was piddling about in the fourth division.

The Drugs Squad had lost a good man in the dawn arrests, and another young detective had been shot through the leg. James shook his head sadly: he should have been with them. On his present job the only injury he might sustain would be if his chair collapsed. His phone rang. He decided to ignore it but then he overrode his decision. It would pass a bit of time.

'Chief Inspector James,' he barked.

He listened uninterestedly, taking up a pencil so he could doodle during the conversation. There was a peremptory knock on the door and Sergeant Thompson poked his head in.

'Oh, sorry,' he blurted and made to withdraw.

But the chief inspector motioned him to stay. He still doodled and listened. Suddenly he became alert, and the point of his pencil snapped. He barked urgently into the phone. He reached across for another pencil, but this time he was scribbling hurried notes, punctuated by 'yes' down the phone. Finally he put the thing on its cradle. There was a new light in his eyes.

Sergeant Thompson watched him curiously and wondered if the chief's retirement had come through, or perhaps he'd been offered the Freedom of the City. He knew better than to ask.

The chief rose quickly.

'Sergeant,' he said crisply, 'arrange for two seats on the Manchester shuttle a.s.a.p. tomorrow morning.'

'Yessir,' replied the sergeant, then added tentatively, 'More letters, sir, from the phantom postman?'

James smiled. 'No letters this time, sergeant. This time I think we have *the man*!'

Sergeant Thompson was flabbergasted. 'You mean the Joker, sir?'

The chief inspector slowly nodded, rubbing his hands together in anticipation. A premonitory shiver ran up the sergeant's back. If they should come face to face with the Joker he hoped fervently that his chief would not jeopardise the end of a glowing career by battering the man to death with his bare hands.

'Get two mugs, sergeant,' ordered the chief inspector. 'We'd best drink this before it goes off.'

He began to untwist the wire from the cork, as if it was somebody's head.

FOURTEEN

Bernard Whittaker, just turned sixty, was editor of the *Grapplewick Bugle*. Most of his working life had been on newspapers, and he had no regrets that this undistinguished tabloid was where he would end his career. Interspersed with the national news, he desperately tried to fill his paper with fascinating items of interest, but it was an uphill struggle. Very little happened in this backwater and when it did he beefed it up to make it sound exciting. 'Bus swerved on Featherstall Road narrowly missing parking meter' ... 'Local boy rushed to hospital after falling off bike.' These gems of journalism were always accompanied by a picture – 'Bus driver standing by his vehicle'. '"It could have been fatal had there been anybody about," said driver Barnshaw' ... 'Smiling boy holding up bandaged finger.' '"There should be cycle paths," said his mother.'

The editor did his best but it was like trying to make a ballroom dress with a Meccano set. He looked through the glass partition that separated his office from the main one, and smiled wryly at the frenzied activity of his staff. He shook his head. One week on a real daily and they'd be screaming for a holiday.

The big news of the week had been yesterday when Waterhouse's Barber's caught fire, and he wondered if it was worth carrying over for another splash. It was pathetic. He flung down his pencil and swivelled his chair to face the window. He couldn't see the street from where he was sitting and was, therefore, unable to watch the arrival of Billy Grout, one of his reporters, who was about to hand him the biggest scoop in Grapplewick's history. Better than that, it would be the highlight of his long journalistic career.

This hot potato of news was being rushed to him by bike, Billy's legs going like piston rods as he cycled furiously down the high street. Twenty-three years old, he was one of two reporters on the staff. His colleague, if one had the temerity to call him that, was a grizzled, disillusioned old man. Only the editor appreciated the talent of Aaron Brandwood, a one-time magical name in journalism. Unfortunately, with the occupational hazard of irregular hours, slow booze and fast food, he had descended steadily towards his current position on the *Bugle*. He rarely set foot out of the office, and when he did he could be found slumped over the bar at the Gaping Goose.

So Billy Grout was the leg man. He covered all the outside interviews and, be it a wedding or a death or Saturday at the football ground, he attacked the assignment with keenness and enthusiasm. And now as he hurtled down Churchill Close, he knew he had a winner, his short cut to Fleet Street. He skidded sideways in front of the *Bugle* office, rushing in to take the stairs two at a time. Normally he would have hauled his bike inside, but today he was too excited for caution. He dashed straight through the main office, raincoat tails flying, scattering papers in his wake. Any other time he would have knocked on the editor's door, but today he barged straight in slamming it behind him. For a moment there was an awkward silence, all eyes on the editor's office. They waited, but seeing that Billy was not immediately ejected, they returned to their work. Papers were picked up from the floor and typewriters clacked again. (Modern technology in the form of word processors had not yet reached the *Bugle*.)

A wag in a cod American voice said, 'Hold the front page, scoop's arrived.'

Nobody spoke, and the typewriters were spasmodic and desultory as furtive glances were directed to the glass partition separating them from the big chief. They couldn't hear what was being said but Billy was obviously fired up, throwing his arms about and striding up and down. Whatever the subject it wasn't the usual run-of-the-mill banality. Perhaps this was the big one, or it could be that Billy was just asking for a rise. No, it couldn't be that, he'd be out of the office by now clearing his desk.

'Now calm down, Billy, and stop marching about.'

The editor had listened but he hadn't stopped marking and crossing out bits from the copy in front of him.

Billy stood in front of the desk, flushed, eyes bright as he waited.

'All right,' said the editor finally, 'so the Martians have landed.'

'No, no, Mr Whittaker, I didn't say that,' replied Billy eagerly. 'Just give me the word and I'll check it out.'

The editor flung down his pencil and leaned back.

'A spaceship will be landing next Wednesday, and one of them is already here.' He shook his head. 'If it was Aaron I'd send him back to the Gaping Goose to sober up.'

Billy was embarrassed. He realised now that Aaron, with years of experience behind him, would never have barged into the editor's office without absolute, cast-iron proof, and all he had was tittle tattle. He rallied. It might only be gossip, but quite a few people were discussing it.

'Let me have a word with Mrs Dobson, she actually saw the . . .'

He stopped at the look on the editor's face.

'She *claims* she actually saw the spaceman,' he ended lamely.

The editor smiled sadly and resumed his work, drawing a square around a piece in front of him.

'Mrs Dobson, eh?' he said, almost to himself.

He put the paper into the wire basket and started on another clipping. He quickly perused it then jammed it on to a spike.

'Mrs Dobson,' he repeated. 'And she's going out with a spaceman?'

By now Billy was convinced that he'd made himself look like a right Charlie and was wishing passionately that he'd taken some statements, or asked a few more questions.

'Still here?' asked the editor without looking up. Billy turned dejectedly towards the door. 'Oh, by the way,' the older man called out just as Billy was turning the handle on the office door, 'any news of Spot?'

Billy stopped, mystified. 'Spot?'

Mr Whittaker peered at him over his half-moon glasses. 'The wire-haired terrier that's been missing since Monday.'

Billy shrugged. 'I don't know,' he said miserably.

'Well, find out, dammit. Our job is to sell newspapers and that's the sort of thing our readers like to read.'

'Yes, sir,' mumbled Billy as he walked out of the office, closing the door softly behind him.

As soon as he had gone the editor leaned back in his chair, chewing his pencil thoughtfully. He found it helped him to think. He knew Billy to be honest and open, and he knew the lad hadn't made the story up. There could be something in this, a humorous half-column in the 'Round and About the Town' section of the paper. He reached towards his phone and contacted the switchboard.

'Ah, Doris. Get me the town clerk, will you?'

'Right away, sir.'

He leaned back again, putting into shape the conversation he would have with Sidney, but before his mind had formed more than 'Hello, Sidney, this is Mr Whittaker from the *Bugle*,' his door opened and Billy stuck his head in.

'Excuse me, sir, but there's nothing on file about a missing dog called Spot.'

The editor certainly didn't want Billy overhearing his imminent telephone conversation. 'Well, find a dog called Spot and lose him,' he snarled, waving his hand in dismissal just as the telephone on his desk rang. He waited a second or two to make sure that Billy was well out of earshot before he answered it. 'Mr Whittaker here, the *Bugle* ... ah yes, Sidney, I'm fine ... no, no, it's nothing important; it's just something about one of your cleaners – a Mrs Dobson, I believe ... Hello ... Sidney, hello? Oh, I thought we'd been cut off ... No, it's not important but apparently she's been seeing little green men ... No, it's just that one of my lads came up with something. According to her there's going to be some sort of invasion from outer space ... Hello? Hello?'

This time the line really was dead. Whittaker slammed the receiver down and flipped the intercom.

'Yes, Mr Whittaker?'

'I've just been cut off, try him again will you, Doris? On second thoughts, get me the mayor.'

Within a minute he was listening to the effusive greetings of Albert Waterhouse. The *Bugle* may have only been a provincial newspaper but still, a call from its editor was important and intriguing, especially as Bernard Whittaker was not given to idle chit-chat. 'And what can I do for you, Bernard?'

'Just doing a bit of checking and ringing round, Albert. According to one of my lads, you had a bit of an unusual visitor yesterday.' He paused, waiting for an answer but instead all he heard was heavy breathing. 'Can you hear me, Albert?'

There was a click and the connection was broken. Whittaker was fast becoming exasperated. Slamming the receiver down, he asked Doris to redial the mayor. As he waited he ran his fingers through his hair, thinking how outrageous it was that British Telecom spent a fortune on advertising immediate communication to all parts of the globe while he couldn't even hold a decent conversation with a subscriber who was only 300 yards away. His phone rang and he snatched the receiver. 'Sorry, Albert, we were cut off,' he started but it was Doris who was on the other end.

'He's not in,' was all she said.

Whittaker was staggered. 'Of course he's in, I was speaking with him ten seconds ago.' He drummed his fingers on the desktop. 'OK, Doris, keep trying.'

Looking thoughtful, he replaced the receiver. First the town clerk and then the mayor ... it didn't need a great intellect to realise that both men were avoiding him, but why? Perhaps his young reporter wasn't quite as mad as he had thought he was. Opening his office door he yelled out, 'Billy!'

'Just on my way, Mr Whittaker.'

The editor stared at him uncomprehendingly, then after a moment said, 'Never mind the bloody dog, get in here.' Billy did so apprehensively, closing the door behind him.

Whittaker sat back in his chair and steepled his fingers, indicating that he was deep in thought. Billy's anxiety grew; he was sure the editor was trying to find the right words to sack him. After what seemed a lifetime, the great man spoke.

'Billy, I want you to go up to Coldhurst Street and see if you can find out the cause of the fire that destroyed Waterhouse's Barber's the other morning.'

Billy's relief was so immediate that he spoke before his brain had given him the command to do so. 'It's OK, sir, I covered that last night. The fire brigade said that it was probably an electrical fault.'

The editor humphed and shook his head. 'I know that, Billy, I printed the article. Listen, lad, I want you to go up there and ferret around for yourself. You might find a box of matches, you might find a petrol can. You may even find a lost dog called Spot.'

'I'm on my way,' said Billy, once more taking on the role of ace reporter. He hurried to the door, then stopped and turned slowly around, his brow furrowed. 'Spot?'

'Get out!' bawled the editor.

FIFTEEN

The mayor stared ashen faced at the phone in his hand. Norman, standing by the window with his own problems, turned to face his uncle. 'What's up?' he asked, but there was no reply from the hunched, shattered hulk in the chair. Undeterred, Norman moved over to him. 'Who was that on the phone?'

The mayor stirred himself. 'That was Bernard Whittaker,' he said, and slumped back into his torpor. Norman knew who Bernard Whittaker was, but in the past his uncle had always taken pride in their relationship; after all, not everyone in Grapplewick was important enough to be on first-name terms with the editor of the *Bugle*. Norman didn't want to ask what it was all about – that would be presumptuous and he wasn't the President yet; but the expression on his uncle's face was one of absolute shock. Had the call been from Dr Baines he would easily have assumed his uncle had been given three months to live. Perhaps he hadn't insured his shop, but whatever it was, this boded no good. He was fidgeting with the paperclips on the desk when the phone rang again, so sudden and strident he scattered the lot over the floor. Both stared at the instrument as it commanded them to action.

'You answer it, Norman,' hissed the mayor as if the place was bugged, 'and whoever it is I'm not in.'

He scurried to the hat stand and took down his overcoat. Norman looked at him unhappily and the mayor nodded to the phone urgently. Norman picked it up gingerly.

'Hello?' He looked quickly at his uncle who was now ready for off. 'No, I'm sorry, he's gone out. No, I don't know when he'll be back ... yes, I'll leave a message, 'bye.'

He put down the phone and the mayor looked at him inquiringly.

'That was Superintendent Smith.'

'Good grief,' expostulated the mayor. 'Why did you have to hang up? I wanted to speak to him.'

'I'm sorry, Uncle, but you said ...'

The mayor waved him to silence.

'I know what I said, but you must learn to use your head, see if there's any life in that grey matter of yours.' He tapped Norman's forehead to emphasise his meaning. 'Now pick up them paperclips and stop larkin' about.'

Norman knelt on the floor, aggrieved by the unfairness of it all. 'Don't worry,' he thought, 'there'll be some changes when I'm in the big chair.'

The mayor was about to lift the phone when the door burst open and Councillor Butterworth stood for a moment taking in the scene, then with a backward glance up and down the corridor he closed the door behind him.

'Hello, Arnold,' said the mayor automatically.

'Never mind all that, somebody's been talking.'

Norman scrambled to his feet from behind the desk with a handful of paperclips.

'Oh, you're here as well, are you?' sneered the councillor. 'And who have you been blabbin' to? Been flashin' your badge in the Amusement Arcade, have you?'

Norman looked at his uncle, puzzled.

'Oh, don't come the lily white innocent with me,' Butterworth went on. 'It'll be "Beautiful Grapplewick" all right if it's a great black smoking hole on the moors, won't it?'

The mayor rose out of his chair.

'Now hold on a minute, Arnold. Don't go casting aspersions like that. Norman hasn't been out of my sight since the meeting.'

The councillor calmed down somewhat, but he wasn't actually convinced.

'Well, somebody's let the cat out of the bag. Everybody's been asking me questions – what's the badge for, and does it turn blue if there's acid rain, and is it true about a spaceship? A spaceship – I ask you, how did they get on to that?'

The mayor shrugged and spread his hands. 'Don't ask me. The editor of the *Bugle* was on to me five minutes ago, but I didn't say anything, did I?'

He looked to Norman for back-up. Arnold thew up his hands and looked at the ceiling.

'Well, that's it then, isn't it? If all this gets printed in the paper, we're finished. There's no telling what he might do.'

'Oh, Bernie's all right, he won't print any . . .'

'I'm not talking about him,' broke in Butterworth, 'I'm talking about that other feller, the one who was in here yesterday.' Even now, he couldn't bring himself to say the word 'spaceman'. In fact he had begun to wonder whether the previous day had all been a bad dream, but his little badge pinned on to the lapel of his jacket told a different story. 'Any road, if you want me, I'll be back at my house. I have a lot of things to attend to,' and with that he was gone.

Norman looked at his uncle apprehensively. His uncle stared back at him with the same expression. They would have been even more uneasy if they had known what things Councillor Butterworth found so urgent. They involved timetables, planes to distant places, cross-Channel ferries, even a couple of weeks at his sister's in Bradford, anything to get him out of the area until after next Wednesday. Wrapped up in their own miserable thoughts Norman and his uncle remained silent. The atmosphere in the mayor's office strongly resembled a pre-war dentist's waiting room, until at last Norman spoke.

'Well, we haven't spoken with anyone, and Councillor Butterworth hasn't either, so it must be Superintendent Smith!'

The mayor had reached the same conclusion himself but was loath to accept it. 'No, not him. I can't believe that. I've known him for years and he wouldn't let on.'

'What's going to happen, then?' asked Norman.

The mayor shook his head. 'Your guess is as good as mine; in any case, why are you asking me? You're supposed to be the genius, the chosen one, President of quarter of the world. I'm just the simple alderman.' For a second the mayor's spirits rose as he thought this simple truth might extricate him from the trouble which lay ahead, but in his heart of hearts he knew that this was a delusion. All of them were implicated; all of them had solemnly sworn to keep the secret, yet now it might just as well be broadcast on the six o'clock news. So immersed were they in shared misery and despair that they didn't hear the timid knock on the door. It was repeated a second time, only louder.

'Who is it?' shouted the mayor. His secretary, a mousy fifty-year-old spinster, poked her head in. 'It's a lady to see you, Mr Mayor.'

'A lady?' he repeated, puzzled. He was about to say he didn't know any ladies, but just stopped himself in time.

'Yes,' she simpered. 'She wouldn't give her name, but –' She stopped, flustered, as Oomi walked around her into the room. For a moment they didn't recognise her, but then Norman remembered where he had seen her last.

'It's Oomi, isn't it?' He turned eagerly to his uncle. 'We met last night at Kershaw's . . .'

'Shut up, Norman!' hissed the mayor, and putting on his nice, public face he turned to his secretary. 'That's all right, Edna. This lady is a friend of . . . of Norman's.'

The secretary smiled as if she were sucking a lemon, and let herself out. Norman was busy staring at the girl. He hadn't given her a moment's thought since leaving Kershaw's Croft, but now that he was looking at her in more familiar surroundings he could see that she was beautiful, with long blonde hair and very little make-up. He had already seen her in the spacesuit, but he far preferred her in what she was wearing now – a smart two-piece navy costume under a camel overcoat worn casually over her shoulders.

Norman gazed at the girl with open-mouthed admiration. He'd never come across anybody like her in real life before, and certainly not in Grapplewick. The mayor looked at him with annoyance; for heaven's sake, hadn't he ever seen a woman before? He turned to Oomi.

'Good morning, my dear. Won't you have a seat?' He gestured at the armchair but she ignored him and remained standing, cold and aloof.

'The Master is displeased,' she began, speaking without expression.

'Displeased?' smiled the mayor, all raised eyebrows and total innocence. 'With us?' he said, indicating Norman.

'The Master is concerned by the lack of security and has instructed me to impress upon you the importance of our mission. He is angry that the secret arrival of the teachers is already being discussed in the streets of your town.'

'How can this be?' asked the mayor, turning to Norman in surprise. 'If I may say so, I think your Master has been misinformed. I can assure you that no one apart from those present at the meeting has any inkling of what will happen next Wednesday. Wouldn't you say so, Norman?' Norman was about to reply, but the mayor hurried on. 'Believe me, young lady, your Master's secret is safe with us.'

Norman frowned. How could the secret be safe if half of Grapplewick had already ditched the subject of last night's television in favour of the arrival of UFOs next week? Too green to recognise the dubious skill of the successful politician, he was about to speak when Oomi took a step back, and closing her eyes she stood rigidly to attention. Puzzled, Norman looked at his uncle who put a finger to his lips, shaking his head quickly in the universal 'do not disturb' sign. Norman took advantage of her closed eyes to give her the once-over, then the twice-over. She really was quite perfect. His heart sank a little when he remembered who she really was, an alien from outer space – the body was from 'wardrobe'. Well, he thought, if she had been trying to pass herself off as an ordinary young woman then she'd overdone it. No woman in Grapplewick looked like that. Norman was just admiring her shoes when they moved. Slowly, Oomi came out of her trance.

'Feeling better, love?' asked the mayor.

'The Master is angry with your lies and deceit. He instructs me to say that you are fully aware that the landing at Sagbottom's Acres is common knowledge, and he informs you that your fate now lies in the hands of the Overlords of Androm.'

The mayor paled. A smile was etched on to his face but it could have been an attack of wind. 'Forgive me, young lady, the man, er, Master, is quite correct in his assumptions. I admit that there are one or two people who may have stumbled upon the truth – inadvertently, I hasten to add.' By now the mayor was wringing his hands and forgetting to smile. 'I can assure you that by now the gossip and rumours will have died down. I know my Grapplewick. You only have to get three of its leading citizens in a room together and the balloon goes up. Suddenly the pound is being devalued. They're like little children, but there's no malice in them. Tell your Master to rest assured.'

Oomi remained unmoved. 'The Master hears what you are saying.'

The mayor looked up at the ceiling. 'Thank you, Master. Look kindly upon your humble servant. Knowing all things you will be aware that my nephew and I have honoured our pledge of secrecy.' He bowed his head and Norman half-expected him to say 'Amen.'

At that moment they became aware of a commotion outside in the corridor; angry voices were being raised and they were getting louder.

'What the dickens is going on out there?' the mayor asked. He stepped forward but just as he reached the door it burst open and the town clerk stumbled in, hustled by an angry mob. The mayor scurried behind his desk for safety while Sidney, now arched over the front of it, turned his head. 'I'm sorry, I couldn't hold them back. They're all over the town hall!'

The noise of the crowd was subsiding now that they'd reached their objective, but there was still a fair amount of babble from those outside in the corridor and on the staircase. The mayor banged on his desk for silence. Following the events of the last couple of days, this rabble was easy to handle. They were, after all, only human.

'All right, all right!' he shouted. 'Calm down. You've had your fun.' He waited until all the muttering had died away. 'That's more like it. Now, what's this all about then?' The people at the front of the crowd avoided his eyes, glancing instead at one another and waiting for someone else to speak.

'Well, come on,' said the mayor. 'You haven't all come up here on a mystery tour.'

'Where's ours, then?' piped up a voice from the crowd. Norman thought he recognised the voice, and being taller than his uncle he spotted the man near the door. He knew the face too but couldn't bring the name to mind. Most probably he'd been a customer of his in the shop.

'Who said that?' asked the mayor, on tiptoe now to look over the crowd. A burly man with two days' growth of stubble suddenly leaned over the desk and grabbed hold of the mayor's tie so that their faces were only inches apart.

'Never mind who said that,' he snarled. 'Where's ours?'

The mayor snatched back his tie and tucked it back into the top of his waistcoat. 'What are you talking about?' he squeaked as he eased the knot in the tie, which was now choking him. 'What do you want?' he asked in a more normal tone of voice.

The man jabbed his finger at the badge on the mayor's lapel. 'That's what we're talking about, them badges. Where's ours then?' He turned to the people behind him. ' "Beautiful Grapple-wick",' he said in a poncy voice.

'Oh, that,' said the mayor uneasily. 'But that's just a badge, you know, like the ones that say "I'm Backing Britain".'

A big ugly woman suddenly spoke up from the back of the crowd. 'Aye, and I'm Madonna.'

'Why have only a few of the high-ups got them, then?' growled another.

'I'll tell you why,' said the tie-grabber. 'When the saucer lands we're likely to be incinerated while they hand out bunches of flowers to them aliens.'

That got the crowd going again. 'Where's ours, then?', 'What about the children?' and 'One law for the rich' were favourite chants. The mayor had to bluff it out, play for time; after all, he reckoned, somebody in the town hall must have called the police by now. Norman was mortified that Oomi should have witnessed this. He turned to say something to her but just caught a glimpse of her as she pushed her way through the crowd. He tried to follow but the mob surged forward, flattening him against a wall. Through the jostling figures he saw his uncle flailing about with a wooden ruler, but there was no doubt that he was vastly outnumbered. Oh God, thought Norman as he struggled to help, they're going to kill him.

Suddenly a piercing whistle shrilled. All action was suspended and everybody froze as if the film had broken down. Really, apart from a few hotheads at the front of the crowd, they were all normal law-abiding citizens who had turned up at the town hall to voice a legitimate grievance. Most of them had only the vaguest idea of what it was all about, while almost none of them had anticipated the violence the demonstration would entail. The arrival of a posse of police was just the last straw. They struggled to get back to the anonymity of the street, but it was impossible in the crush. Heads turned fearfully towards the door, expecting to see the plastic shields and stout batons of the riot squad. When, after a few moments, nothing had happened, fear turned to curiosity. There were no cries of pain, no panic-stricken wailing, thuds or the sound of heavy boots on the marble stairs, which wasn't really surprising as the police were nowhere in sight. Instead, a wiry little man with a William Powell moustache and heavily Brylcreemed hair was pushing his way towards the office blowing a whistle. The crowd parted like the Red Sea as he made his way towards the mayor. He was obviously someone in authority – why else would he have a whistle? 'Gangway please, make way,' he called, and the crowd did as he asked, squeezing up against each other to allow him passage to the desk.

Norman gaped in astonishment. It was Jimmy Jackson, who owned Sutton's Iron Foundry. He was a local villain, known to the authorities as Oily Jack, but at that moment Norman didn't particularly care. As far as he was concerned, this man had saved his uncle from a very nasty going-over; possibly he had even saved him from being killed.

Jackson edged his way around the desk, took the mayor's limp hand and shook it. 'Got your message, governor, and I came as quick as I could.'

The mayor stared at him through one puffy eye. He was in no fit state to comprehend what was going on – his hair was all over the place and there was a large cut on his cheek.

'You phoned me about half an hour back about badges for all,' Jackson continued, pointing at the mayor's badge, which surprisingly was still in place, although his lapel wasn't. The mayor didn't answer. He had suddenly realised that his dentures were on the floor. He hoped no one would step on them, but he was in luck. Norman spotted them under his desk, picked them up and slipped them discreetly into his hand.

Jackson spoke out for the benefit of the now-silent audience. 'Now, just sit down and relax while I attend to these nice people here.' The mayor nodded and, under the pretext of blowing his nose, popped his dentures back in.

Jackson now faced the crowd. There were still some sullen, angry faces there but most of them were ashamed of themselves and extremely grateful that it was he who had been blowing the whistle, and not the police.

'Now listen, the lot of you,' he started in a voice that carried to the bus stop outside. 'Half an hour ago, his Worship the Mayor phoned me with a specific order that "Beautiful Grapplewick" badges should be made available to you all. He knew you'd all be worried and that's why he rang me.' A slight murmur ran through the crowd, who now felt even more ashamed of themselves.

'So all them as wants badges, call in at Sutton's Iron Foundry on Waterloo Street and place your order. The badges will be ready in a day or two, OK?'

The crowd nodded, some said thank you, and they turned and shuffled in orderly fashion out of the office, slowly at first, then with more urgency until there was a mad stampede out of the main door and up towards Waterloo Street and Sutton's Iron Foundry.

Norman was looking at Jimmy with undisguised admiration at the way he'd handled the mob. 'There's a job for him in my future administration,' he thought. But he was puzzled too: the mayor hadn't phoned anybody that morning, and somebody like Jimmy Jackson was definitely not on his calling list. Not only that, how could he possibly supply the badges? They weren't your everday trash, they'd been forged in the outer Galaxy.

Jimmy had taken the mayor's badge and he was measuring it carefully, making notes in a little black notebook. Norman approached him.

'Where are you going to get the badges from?' he asked.

Jimmy gave him a knowing look and returned to his notes. Norman pointed to his own badge, then to the one Jimmy was examining.

'These aren't just ordinary badges, you know, they're specially treated.'

Jimmy snapped his notebook shut and winked. 'Don't worry son, I'll treat 'em special.' And he strode out whistling.

Their troubles, however, were far from over. As Norman closed the door he became aware of someone leaning casually against the wall. 'Oh no, not him,' he thought. The last person they wanted to meet at that moment was Mr Whittaker, editor of the *Bugle*, the eyes and ears of Grapplewick.

'Hello, Norman,' he said. 'Quite a morning.'

He strolled over to the desk and stubbed out the soggy end of his cigarette. He nodded to the mayor. 'Your cheek's bleeding again.'

The mayor whipped out his already soiled hankie and attended to it.

'Thanks, Bernie,' he said. 'Saw all that, did you?'

The editor didn't reply. He walked over to Norman and bent slightly forward so he could read the lettering on his badge.

' "Beautiful Grapplewick",' he muttered, cocking his head to one side in appreciation.

'It's just a badge,' explained the mayor. 'I don't know what all the fuss is about.'

Again the editor ignored him, addressing himself to Norman. 'Well, well,' he said, 'I hope you know what you're doing.'

Norman was baffled. He looked to his uncle who shrugged helplessly.

'You *are* taking over the whole administration, aren't you?'

Norman opened his mouth to reply but his uncle pulled him hastily to one side.

'No comment,' he blurted.

He recognised the ploy, snip away at the weak link in the chain, Norman being the dodgy one in this case. The editor surveyed them both for a moment, then nodded as if it was of no consequence and turned away. Quickly the mayor flashed a 'leave it to me' sign to his nephew, and watched the editor warily as he strolled round the desk. Norman took half a pace forward and the mayor dug him in the ribs with his elbow, shaking his head vigorously. The editor seemed unaware of all this and picked up a framed photo of the mayor with his arm around Florrie at Blackpool Tower. With his eyes fastened on the photo he said softly, 'Do you really believe in all this visitors-from-outer-space crap?'

The mayor cleared his throat, but he wasn't about to speak. He'd been in local government long enough to recognise a loaded question, and this one was a floating blockbuster. A straight yes or no either way would have enormous repercussions. The walls wouldn't just be splattered, the fan would get clogged as well. Whittaker appeared to be in no hurry for an answer; in fact he looked as if he might have forgotton the question, but the mayor wasn't fooled. Political clichés and evasions clattered through his brain like a changing destination board at Waterloo Station until finally he decided that the best course of action was to draw a cheque on a long-standing friendship. He worked his face into an ingratiating smile. 'Look, Bernie, we've known each other a long time. I can trust you and I know that anything that is said within these four walls is strictly off the record, so I'll say this . . .' He leaned forward over the desk and lowered his voice. 'Me and Norman have seen and heard things in the past twenty-four hours that are beyond the comprehension of the human mind.'

The editor's eyebrows rose and he put down the framed photo. After a moment he nodded. 'I believe you. Has this anything to do with your shop catching fire?'

'No comment.'

'I see.' The editor stared at Norman. 'And Sagbottom's Acres is to be terminal three for interplanetary flights, with little green men checking the tickets?'

The mayor snorted and waved his hand derisively, mainly to prevent Norman from speaking, but he was too late. 'He's not green; he's just like us, and Oomi is . . .' He stopped suddenly, realising that he had already said too much. His uncle clucked and looked away in disgust.

'And they're landing on Monday?' continued the editor.

'No, Wednesday,' Norman replied again, without thinking. This time his uncle rounded on him.

'You know, Norman, just when I think you're the biggest idiot in Grapplewick, you go one better.'

The editor took pity on him. 'Don't let it worry you, lad. You haven't told me anything I didn't already know. It seems as if the whole town's talking about the spacemen and Kershaw's Croft, and the landing next Wednesday.' He moved towards the office door but the mayor headed him off.

'Listen, Bernard,' he gushed, 'we go back a long time, you and me, and we've done each other some favours.' By now he was dry-washing his hands. 'I've never refused you an interview, have I?' Whittaker looked at him sharply – as far as he could remember he'd never asked the mayor for one.

'What I'm trying to say, Bernard, is that, well, as a friend . . . You won't print any of that in your paper, will you?'

Whittaker smiled and patted his shoulder. 'No need to worry, Albert, there'll be nothing in the paper. Good grief, if I printed all that, they'd have me certified.' The mayor nodded, vastly relieved. 'Mind you,' he went on, 'a year ago the story of UFOs coming on a Wednesday was big news, but now it's a dead duck. It's not even a good joke any more.' Again he turned for the door but still the mayor wasn't fully satisfied. He darted around and pressed himself against the door to prevent Whittaker from going.

'The, er, slight disturbance you witnessed earlier this morning. You can, er, ignore that, can't you?'

Whittaker buttoned his raincoat. 'Oh, that'll have to go in the paper. I've got a photographer downstairs taking pictures, but don't worry. I'll steer clear of science fiction.'

The mayor nodded gratefully. 'Thanks, Bernie. I owe you one,' he said and ushered him out. He almost closed the door but his secretary was quicker, poking her head in the opening. She was about to speak, but changed her mind when she saw his dishevelled appearance.

'Well, what is it now?' he snapped peevishly.

She glared at him through her thick spectacles. 'Just to let you know the police are on their way.'

The mayor sighed and looked at his nephew. 'Well, that's a relief. Thank you very much, Edna,' he grated sarcastically. 'It's nice to know that help is at hand.'

She was about to withdraw when he called her back. 'Oh, and Edna, you can deal with them when they get here. Tell them the problem's all been taken care of; you know, it was a storm in a teacup. Something about school meals . . . you know.' He flapped his hands and dismissed her.

SIXTEEN

There seemed to be more traffic in the high street than was usual at that time of day, thought Bernard Whittaker as he made his way back to the *Bugle* office. Even more unusual was the knot of people gathered outside the town hall, looking up at the building as if the mayor was on the roof threatening to jump off. Whittaker looked up to check, but there was nothing to be seen; the only signs of life up there were the pigeons, strutting importantly up and down the ledges and window sills. He entered his office deep in thought and slumped behind his desk, not even bothering to take off his hat and coat. He felt a stirring in his bowels and recognised the signs. There was more to this story. Whittaker knew it wasn't a mere hoax.

In all the other towns, letters had been delivered to the mayors, top policemen and other big-wigs, informing them that UFOs would be coming Wednesday, but here in Grapplewick the message had been conveyed in person, by a man claiming to be an alien from outer space. He drummed his fingers on the desk. Deep in his bones he felt that something quite extraordinary would happen next Wednesday, but he was equally certain that whatever it was, it would have very little to do with flying saucers. Frustrated, he banged the arms of his chair and rose to walk over to the window. Whoever this man was, he wasn't to be underestimated. Obviously he was clever; he had managed to scare the living daylights out of three of the town's leading citizens and had convinced them that they were dealing with an eighteen-carat, genuine alien from a distant planet.

Whittaker snorted derisively. Why then were these leading citizens pathetically trying to hold on to the secret when throughout the town it was common gossip . . . The phone rang and he snatched it up impatiently.

'Yes . . . a bus conductor? What's he want? No, no, put him on, will you?' He nodded and grunted as he listened. 'I see, and after you dropped them they just set off walking?' There was another pause. 'And what makes you so sure they were going to Kershaw's Croft?' Again he listened and nodded. 'Well, thanks for telling me . . . yes, if I do print anything I'll be sure to mention your name.'

In the main press room uneasy glances were thrown at the glass partition. Furtively they watched the editor thoughtfully replacing the phone. Billy was busy one-finger typing a negative report on his fruitless investigation of the charred remains of Waterhouse's Barber's Shop. Search as he might, he hadn't uncovered any signs of arson. In any case, what *were* the signs? Heads came up as the editor's door jerked open and he swept through the office.

'Billy,' he barked, 'come with me.'

'Yessir,' squeaked the lad, scrabbling hastily out of the chair to catch up with his boss.

As soon as the door closed, typewriters ceased their frenetic clattering and telephone bells were ignored as the staff eagerly congregated to discuss the unsettling events of the last two days, and in particular next Wednesday. Aaron was the exception: he didn't join the excited jabberings of his colleagues, but put on his coat and decided to go home. No point in going to the Gaping Goose, the topic of conversation would be the same.

Billy eased himself into the passenger seat of the editor's decrepit old Ford. He didn't strap himself in; there weren't any straps. Gingerly he eased the door shut, trying to be gentle in case it fell off, but the editor leaned across him and slammed it fiercely. There was a tinkle on the pavement which could have been the door handle, but Mr Whittaker seemed unperturbed. He switched on the engine and after three protesting screeches from the gear box, he managed to find first, and they were mobile.

'We're just going to have a look at Kershaw's Croft.' The editor had to shout to combat the noise of the engine.

'Oh, Kershaw's Croft,' replied Billy.

He hadn't the foggiest idea why they should want to visit that place, and thinking of the hill up to Windy Ridge, he wasn't sure the car would make it. A few minutes later they turned left down Linney Lane and from there on to the moors. Once they were out of the traffic and free to clank and judder laboriously between the dry stone walls, the editor seemed to relax. With a series of jerks and squeaks he wound his window down. Immediately this doubled the racket of the straining engine, discouraging any further conversation, but worse, a gust of wind joyously rushed in, frolicking with some papers on the back seat. Billy snuggled down and pointedly turned up the collar of his coat. He's enjoying this, he thought, but he didn't know his boss. The editor screwed up his eyes against the cold, but it helped him to think. The icy blasts cleansed his mind, which was cluttered with an endless stream of unanswered questions. For instance, the fire at the barber's. Fortuitously the place was empty, but then why had Norman been given the day off? Normally his uncle worked him from nine to eight, six days a week, with a fortnight's annual holiday and Christmas. And even stranger, why was he invited to attend the meeting at the town hall?

He shook his head trying to put his thoughts into some sort of sequence. Firstly, the bus conductor had taken Norman and the mayor to Windy Ridge on Wednesday night and they had set off walking in the direction of Kershaw's Croft, so the first encounter had to be there. It was the only building within a five-mile range; it couldn't be anywhere else unless they all met under the lamp. More importantly, whatever had transpired between them was shattering enough to induce Norman to change from wearing his usual pair of old jeans to a collar and tie, and shocking enough to turn the mayor into a frightened old man. He remembered a phone call to the police station earlier. As soon as he announced his name he was greeted with a terse 'No comment' and a dead line. As for Councillor Butterworth, he'd vanished altogether. So what the hell was going on?

That angry mob at the town hall this morning rampaging into the mayor's office, that was definitely out of character for the slow-thinking people of Grapplewick. It certainly wasn't spontaneous, so who was behind this carefully orchestrated disturbance? Not Jimmy Jackson, that was for sure. He was too thick, but bright enough to climb on the bandwagon when he saw the opportunity to make a few bob out of the badges. And, incidentally, what about those badges? What was all the fuss about a small piece of enamel with 'Beautiful Grapplewick' stamped on it? Billy interrupted his train of thought.

'I think you've passed the turning, Mr Whittaker!' he yelled.

'What? . . . Oh yes.'

He stopped and, looking over his shoulder, began the erratic process of reversing until they were level with the lane. He shook his head ruefully. If Billy hadn't been with him he might well have ended up in Huddersfield.

A few minutes later they arrived at Kershaw's Croft. Billy eased himself out of the car, thankful he hadn't had to push it. He stretched luxuriously – the journey back would be a doddle, it was mainly downhill. His euphoria evaporated when he turned to look at Kershaw's Croft. Without the noise of the engine, the keening of the wind was more pronounced and malevolent. A cloud passed over the sun and the derelict hulk was thrown into deep shadow. He shuddered and was glad the editor hadn't sent him on his own. Gently Mr Whittaker pushed the heavy wooden door open. He paused, head cocked to one side.

'Did you hear that?' he asked in a quiet voice.

'No, Mr Whittaker, I didn't hear a thing.'

'Exactly . . . these hinges have been oiled,' the editor replied, and carefully he went inside.

Billy followed him, at first fearful and then relaxed. It wasn't as dark as he'd imagined. Two dirt-encrusted windows on opposite walls gave the room light which dramatically brightened as the sun came out. He smiled at his earlier forebodings; it was only a pathetic little one-roomed cottage. Confidence restored, he strolled over to the window and bent forward to peer out. As he did so something glinted between his feet. He stooped and picked it up.

'What have you got there, Billy?' asked the editor, joining him. Billy held it in the palm of his hand.

'It looks like a sequin,' he said. Mr Whittaker took it from him.

'You're right, Billy lad, it is a sequin.'

'Hang on,' said Billy quickly, 'here's another one,' and he handed it over.

The editor looked at the two sequins for a moment, then gazed out of the window for quite a time. Finally he turned to Billy.

'Odd place to find 'em, wouldn't you say?'

Billy shrugged. He hadn't a thought in his head, but he was fascinated when the editor popped the two sequins in an envelope, sealed it and slid it into his inside pocket. Taking his cue from this, Billy scanned the floor eagerly for more. Perhaps Mr Whittaker was just a sequin-collector, but whatever the reason, he was pleased with his discoveries, and at least they wouldn't come away empty-handed.

'Never mind that, lad, nip out the back and see what you can come up with.'

Billy was about to go when he turned, a puzzled look on his face.

'What am I looking for, Mr Whittaker?'

The editor looked at him in surprise.

'How should I know . . . anything unusual. If there's a dustbin, tip it out and sift through it.'

Billy nodded and went into the overgrown yard. The editor called after him.

'And if it barks, you've found Spot.'

Billy nodded again and looked helplessly round the great piles of knee-high rubbish, wondering where to start. He wasn't too despondent, however. The yard was sheltered from the wind and quite pleasant in the sun. Unfortunately myriads of flies thought so too, and they weren't particularly happy about being disturbed. A mass of them rose to investigate the bandit at twelve o'clock high. Billy flailed his arms to ward them off but it was hopeless. He lost his footing amongst the rotting debris and fell back, disturbing more flies. It was too much for him, Spot couldn't have been here, they'd have had him for breakfast. He struggled to his feet and scrabbled to the wall wiping his hands on the sides of his raincoat. What a mess! He tied his handkerchief round his mouth and looked round for a stick with which to sift through the stinking piles of garbage, and then his eye lit on something odd, something definitely out of place here. It was the smashed remains of a light bulb, but not your ordinary 60-watt domestic type. This was much larger: the bulb holder was as thick as his wrist. He picked it up gingerly and took it inside.

The editor was on one knee trying to prise something from between the floorboards. He looked up when Billy entered.

'Good lad,' he said after examining the shattered light bulb. 'We might be able to trace where this came from. It hasn't been outside long either . . . it'd be rusted.'

Billy took the handkerchief from his face. Some of the flies had come in with him but they soon left to get back to their breeding ground.

'See if you can get this out, Billy.'

The editor pointed to a small object wedged in a crack on the floor. Billy took out his penknife, and after a short struggle flipped something out. It was a round, plastic badge bearing the words 'Beautiful Grapplewick'.

'That's it, Billy,' said the editor triumphantly. 'That's what I've been looking for.' His smile faded as he caught the pitying look on his young reporter's face. 'Something the matter, lad?' he asked.

Billy pointed at the badge. 'I could have saved you a journey if I'd known.'

'Known what?'

Billy shrugged. 'Just before you came in this morning Jimmy Jackson phoned for an ad to be put in tonight's edition. He's manufacturing these at the foundry. You could have ordered one from him.'

'Is that so?' asked Whittaker, feigning ignorance. 'Has he put a price on 'em?'

'Five pounds ninety-nine,' replied Billy promptly.

Whittaker stared at him aghast. 'Each?' he asked incredulously.

Billy nodded. 'Bit steep, isn't it?'

'I should say so,' chuckled Whittaker. 'Now you know why we came up here.' He stuffed the badge into his pocket and looked around the room. 'You know, Billy,' he said, 'over the years many people have used this croft . . . tramps, courting couples, hikers seeking shelter from the rain . . . they've all been here.'

Billy nodded thoughtfully. 'Gypsies too, I'll bet!'

Whittaker eyed him thoughtfully. 'Well, doesn't it strike you as odd?'

'Doesn't what?' asked Billy, blinking hard in concentration.

'Where's all the muck, the beer cans, plastic bags, newspapers, rags?' The editor spread his arms and turned a full circle. Billy turned around too but didn't have a clue as to what his boss was getting at.

'No dust on the floors, no cobwebs on the ceiling . . . what does that suggest to you, Billy?'

Realisation suddenly dawned and Billy's eyes lit up. 'Somebody's cleaned it out – and if there's no dust around that suggests that it must have been done recently!'

Whittaker smiled benignly. 'That's what I wanted to hear!' he said. 'You know, Billy, there's more to you than meets the eye,' and he slapped him on the back. Billy glowed with pride. 'Now here's what I want you to do. I want you to go round to all the pubs and hotels in the Grapplewick area and ask if they've had a man and a girl booked in within the last week.'

Billy took out his notepad and pencil. 'What do they look like?'

Whittaker sighed. 'That's what I want you to find out, lad. It's not likely there's going to be too many strangers booked in – Grapplewick's hardly a tourist trap.'

'Right,' said Billy, putting his notebook away. 'I'll do the hotels first.'

'Good idea. There's only three. If you had started with the pubs you'd still be making enquiries by Christmas.'

Billy set off along the lane but Whittaker called out after him. 'Hang on, Billy, I'll give you a lift!'

It was always best to have a passenger in case the damned car decided to call it a day.

SEVENTEEN

By Saturday nearly everyone was aware of the facts: a spacecraft would be arriving on Wednesday. Those who didn't know were either very young or very senile. Very few people actually believed that a spaceship would be arriving at Sagbottom's Acres, but no one was brave enough to come right out and say so as there was now a sort of buoyancy in the town. You'd have to be exceedingly unfeeling to tell little children looking forward to Christmas that there's no Santa Claus. People still gathered in groups but no one was fearful now; instead they discussed arrangements for Wednesday night and how they were going to get up to Sagbottom's Acres. They were excited and happy, as if the following week was an unexpected national holiday and the landing of aliens an extravaganza dreamt up by the Leisure and Pleasure Committee.

This was all well and good for the ordinary folk, but the more enthusiastic they became, the deeper grew the pit of despondency and gloom for the mayor. Normally his greatest skill was to be able to sleep, but he hadn't had much of that since Thursday. Breakfast had always been a high spot of his day, but today he just toyed listlessly with half a fried egg and a sausage congealing on the plate in front of him.

'Would you like another cup of tea?' asked Florrie helpfully. In reply the mayor threw down his knife.

'It's supposed to be a secret and yet everybody knows; they know about me and Nigel Smith and Norman!'

'And Arnold Butterworth,' his wife added.

'Aye, and where's he now? If I know him he'll be on a banana boat to South America, leaving us to hold the baby.'

Florrie hovered around behind him with an empty teapot in her hand. Casually she asked, 'Well, what did the man actually say to you?'

The mayor stared hard at her. 'You know I can't tell you that. I've sworn an oath of secrecy!'

'Yes, but everybody . . .'

He cut her off angrily. 'They don't know it all; they think they do, but they wouldn't be so jolly if they knew all the facts . . .' He became silent.

Florrie tried again. 'Our Emmie says . . .'

He silenced her with a look of contempt. 'Your sister is a big mouth, and always has been. My gallstones were all over Grapplewick before even the doctor knew what it was!'

With a sigh Florrie rose to put the kettle on, speaking as she went. 'I was just going to say that our Emmie wanted to know if we were going in the official party on Wednesday, and if not we could go with them.'

The mayor slapped the table in exasperation. 'This is serious!' he shouted over his shoulder. 'It's not the Grapplewick annual gala!' He was about to follow Florrie into the kitchen when Norman came down the stairs, engrossed in a dog-eared atlas. Oblivious of his uncle, he sat down and flipped over a page.

'Well, don't say good morning, will you?' snapped his uncle.

Norman looked up, frowning a little at his uncle as though trying to place him in a foggy memory. 'Sorry, I was miles away,' he offered as an explanation and returned to his studying of one quarter of the world. The mayor was about to make a comment but it died on his lips when he saw the atlas. He moved around to Norman's back and peered over his shoulder.

'Where did you get that?'

'Eh?' grunted Norman, reluctant to be disturbed.

'That's my old school atlas,' continued the mayor, straightening up. 'I didn't know you were interested in geography.'

'I wasn't until I met the spaceman,' replied Norman with all the reverence of a born-again idiot. The mayor snorted and Norman swivelled around in his chair 'You don't believe him, do you?' he said hotly. 'You don't believe that the teachers will arrive on Wednesday. You think this is all a big joke, don't you?'

His uncle backed away, hands half raised in surrender. 'I don't think it's a joke, Norman. If I did I'd be laughing, but quite seriously, lad, I don't think you should put too much faith in all this.'

'In all what, uncle? You've met the man; you've seen what he can do.' The mayor sighed and made to turn away, but Norman grabbed his sleeve. 'And what about Kershaw's Croft? He might have hypnotised you but I had all my faculties and I know I was looking down on Grapplewick from the air. I know I didn't imagine that.'

The mayor shook his head sadly. 'All I'm saying, Norman, is this: if the spaceship lands on Wednesday, then all's well and good – you'll be quids in and President from here to . . .' – he leaned over to look at the atlas – 'from here to Persia, but if it doesn't land, what happens then?'

Norman stared uncomprehendingly at his uncle while the mayor looked at the atlas again. 'Incidentally, lad, I shouldn't rely too much on this if I were you. Persia's gone and you won't find Rhodesia any more, nor Tanganyika, nor British West Africa. It's all a different world now.'

Florrie lumbered in. 'Hark at David Attenborough; you're not so bright yourself, Albert Waterhouse. Do you remember when I told you about the Toxteth riots? You said it would never happen in England.' She picked up the remains of breakfast and lumbered back into the kitchen, full of self-importance.

'I hadn't seen the telly, had I!' yelled Albert to her retreating back, and then, more quietly, 'Bloody women. Always have to put their fourpence worth in.' He looked at Norman. 'Where was I? Oh yes. Suppose all this is some sort of joke; just suppose a spaceship doesn't come. What then?'

Norman was incredulous. 'You don't think it's going to happen, do you?'

'No, no, I didn't say that, but let's suppose that everyone in Grapplewick goes up to Sagbottom's Acres on Wednesday and nothing happens. What then?'

'They *will* land,' insisted Norman fervently.

'Yes, but if they don't, what do you reckon the feeling will be?' Norman shrugged. 'Well, I'll tell you what it'll be. Your life, and mine, and the superintendent's, won't be worth that much.' He clicked his fingers.

Norman stared at him. 'Why?' he asked innocently.

'Because,' said the mayor, tapping his fingers on the table, 'we will be held responsible, that's why!'

Norman digested this slowly, then shrugged again. 'So what? They can't do anything.'

'Oh, can't they?' sneered his uncle. 'Why do you think Superintendent Smith is keeping such a low profile, and where's Councillor Butterworth? We won't see him until all of this has blown over – I'll tell you that for nothing.' He slumped dejectedly back into his chair. 'I wish to God I'd never clapped eyes on your spaceman.'

Norman didn't pick up on the subtle shift in responsibility; he was more concerned with his uncle's heresy. 'Be careful what you say, uncle, he knows what you're thinking.'

The mayor, however, was unrepentant. 'We should have reported this to a higher authority straight away!' He blew his nose vigorously into a red and white spotted handkerchief. 'I blame Superintendent Smith. He should have detained him while he had the chance!' Before Norman could reply, Florrie came through carrying a basket and tying a scarf around her head. She put on her coat and took in the two silent men in front of her.

'Somebody died or what?' There was no reply. 'Oh, well,' she muttered, 'I'm just going to do some shopping. I won't be long.' Norman and the mayor waited for the door to slam, but instead she came running back into the room. 'Quick, come to the window. Have a look at this!'

Norman hurried after her and the mayor followed, curious to know what was important enough to cause his wife to rush around forgetting her bad legs. Before he got to the door he could hear the shrill chanting of young voices, shouting, 'Nor-man! Nor-man!' Outside, a small group of children was bunched around the front gate, some even with their mothers, and all clapping their hands in time to their piping cries of, 'Nor-man! Nor-man!'

Florrie beamed with pride and tried to usher Norman outside to meet his fans, but he wouldn't budge. Red with embarrassment he slunk away from the window, and the chanting tailed off in disappointment. The mayor, however, stuck his head out of the window to tell them to bugger off, but remembered just in time that he was the mayor and their mothers and fathers had votes. Instead he smiled benignly at them and waved as they drifted off down the street. He was about to go back into the house when he noticed that some of the kids were wearing yellow oilskin sou'westers. He looked at the sky but it wasn't raining and neither had it been.

'Must be a club or something,' he muttered to Florrie.

'What?'

'Them sou'wester hats, look.' He pointed down the road. 'Them waterproof fishing hats. Look, there's people across the road wearing them too!'

'Anti-fall-out hats,' Florrie replied, still waving.

'Anti-fall-out hats,' he repeated stupidly.

'In case of radiation next Wednesday.'

He frowned. 'What are you talking about?'

Florrie turned to him, wondering if he was having her on. 'For protection,' she said. 'You know, anti-fall-out.' She smiled at another passer-by. 'There's a queue at Bottomley's, everyone's buying them.'

He pondered for a moment, jingling some loose coins in his pocket. 'Well, where are ours?' he eventually said.

'They're not cheap, you know. Any road, I thought you might be able to wangle us some free ones; I mean, you are in with him, aren't you?'

'In with who?' he asked.

Florrie nudged him. 'You know ... the man,' and she moved away from the window, leaving him to wonder about the headgear.

An old man shuffled past him. 'Morning, Mr Mayor.'

Albert beamed. 'And good morning to you. It's a nice day, isn't it?' His shoulders went back as he watched the old man make his way up the street. Oh yes, he thought, there's still some respect about, some folk know who's number one. Full of self importance, he was about to go in when a new rag-tag of kids dashed breathlessly up to the gate. The smallest of them, with an enormous yellow hat almost covering his eyes, gasped, 'Hey mister, does Norman live here?'

'Bugger off,' said the mayor and slammed the door.

EIGHTEEN

Superintendent Smith wasn't particularly imaginative. He'd risen to his present position by his ability to keep his nose clean, proceeding through his chosen career strictly by the book, and his ability to lead men. This was the official appraisal. In reality he'd 'yes sirred' and 'no sirred' through the ranks, a smart policeman covering up the blunders of his superiors by laying the blame on lesser mortals and modestly taking the credit where it should have been apportioned to others. The major breakthrough, however, came during a particularly vicious strike when his bloodstained features took up most of the front pages of the national dailies. One of the headlines read THE BRAVE FACE OF THE THIN BLUE LINE. They were all in similar vein. The sad truth, however, was that Sergeant Smith, as he then was, had been panic-stricken and desperately trying to get out of the way when he ran face first into a wall. But from then on his rapid promotion was assured.

Today he was off duty, an imposing figure in brown tweed jacket and flannels. The queue outside the sport shop waiting patiently to buy their fishing hats amused him, and the sprinkling of 'Beautiful Grapplewick' badges caused him to shake his head ruefully. Everybody knew about next Wednesday, but they weren't panicking in the streets, the man was wrong about that. On the contrary, it was probably the happiest little town in Britain. And again, although the man, whoever he was, must be well aware by now that the secret was blown, he had not carried out his threat. Grapplewick had not shrivelled in a searing ball of flame.

The superintendent shook his head again at the ease with which they'd all been manipulated at the meeting, for he was sure now that it could only be a confidence trick. After hours of careful consideration, he'd dismissed from his mind the extraordinary happenings two days ago – the Indian woman and the barber's shop. They weren't logical and therefore they didn't exist. There were one or two kids hanging about outside the mayor's house and they drew back to let him through. He pressed the door bell and they regarded him seriously while he waited. A curtain twitched aside as the mayor looked to see who it was, and a few moments later the superintendent was ushered into the front room.

'I've been trying to get you on the phone,' started the mayor without the usual formalities.

'I've been out,' said the superintendent, settling himself into a chair.

The mayor was still on his feet. 'You don't seem bothered at all.'

'Why should I be bothered?' asked the superintendent.

The mayor turned a full circle looking up at the ceiling.

'Good grief, you've been out, you've seen 'em, they're treating it like wakes week. They'll be up at Sagbottom's on Wednesday.'

'There's no harm in it, Albert.'

The mayor leaned forward and rested his hands on the arms of the superintendent's chair. 'Not now, there isn't, but what about next Thursday when they're still up there, waiting, eh?' There was no reply from the chair. The mayor nodded and eased himself upright. 'What happens when the spaceship or whatever it is doesn't come. What'll we say? "Sorry, folks, that's all. Hope you enjoyed it"?'

'Why should we say anything?' asked the superintendent coolly.

'Because,' replied the mayor, 'everybody knows about the meeting and they'll think we've led them up the garden path.'

'Oh, come on, Albert, they'll take it in good part. They'll have had a good week and this will be the culmination. Why don't you put on a show for them; arrange a few fireworks or something.' He smiled. 'They're not kids. They don't really believe that flying saucers are going to let down at Sagbottom's Acres.'

The mayor snorted. 'Oh no? Then what about the mad rush to buy those badges and the fishing hats? That's nearly a week's wages for some of these folk.'

He was interrupted by a timid knock at the front door and he moved irritably over to the window, convinced that it was the kids again. He waved his hand angrily to disperse them and turned from the window. He suddenly stopped in his tracks, and turned to look again. 'Come here,' he beckoned to the superintendent to join him. 'See that? Those kids are wearing T-shirts with "Norman" on the front.'

'Aye, I believe your nephew's becoming a bit of a cult figure around here.'

'And how much has that set them back? I bet those T-shirts cost more than a dress shirt in Manchester!'

'Oh, I admit there's a bit of profiteering going on. I stopped for a pint at the Feathers on my way here and they've got a new drink out called Space Alien. It's only lager with a drop of whisky in it, but the kids are lapping it up.'

The mayor was quick to take the advantage. 'That's my point. They wouldn't be chucking their brass around if they didn't believe.'

The superintendent surveyed him for a moment and then indicated a chair. 'Sit down, Albert, I want to talk to you.' He waited until the mayor was settled and then leaned towards him, elbows on his knees. 'Albert, you have to understand that we're not living in a perfect world. A lot of flash Harrys in Grapplewick have been smart enough to see that there's a lot of honey in the pot, and this space thing's an ideal opportunity to get at it. Many will come out of it a darn sight richer than they were last week. Jimmy Jackson was the first but he won't be the last; not by a long chalk.'

The mayor frowned in concentration. 'What are you getting at?' he asked, feeling in the back of his mind that there was more.

'What I'm getting at is this: you and I – forget Butterworth – you and I have created the scenario for people like Jimmy Jackson to rake it in. They'll be laughing all the way to the bank, and what do we get in return?' The mayor shook his head. 'Well, Albert, you have just put your finger on it. All we can look forward to is a very angry mob who'll want revenge for all the money they've laid out.' He sat back and regarded the mayor.

The mayor was at a loss as to where the conversation was

leading. 'Well,' he finally said, 'what do you propose to do about it?'

Superintendent Smith leaned forward again. 'Sagbottom's Acres,' he began. 'The whole of Grapplewick will be there on Wednesday night, there'll be sideshows, cars, beer stalls, hot dog stands. None of these concessions will be cheap, so whoever owns Sagbottom's Acres is sitting on a gold mine.'

The mayor digested this information, but he wasn't at his best in the mornings. 'Old deaf Crumpshaw owns Sagbottom's,' he said lamely.

The superintendent leaned back and casually examined his nails. 'Not any more, he doesn't.'

Still the penny hadn't dropped and the superintendent sighed. 'I bought it last night.'

This thunderbolt scattered the mayor's wits over a large area. His jaw fell open and he found that he was breathing extremely heavily. 'Just in the nick of time too,' went on the policeman, undeterred. 'Apparently he was earlier approached by somebody else but he said no because he was a stranger and Crump didn't like the look of him. However, when I offered him ten grand he jumped at it.'

'I'm not surprised.' The mayor had found his voice again. 'He must need the cash. He hasn't done a hand's turn at the farm since his brother died.' He thought for a moment. 'He must be the only person in Grapplewick who hasn't heard about the UFO landing.'

The superintendent shrugged. 'Not surprising really. He never comes into town; can't abide it. He has all the groceries and stuff delivered.'

The mayor nodded. Then, in a blinding flash of inspiration, he slapped his forehead. 'Wait a minute! The spaceman – could he be the man who was trying to buy the land in the first place?'

'The spaceman?' asked the superintendent slowly.

'Yes, the main reason we all believed him was that he didn't ask for anything. He was getting nothing out of all this, but if he owned Sagbottom's Acres then that would explain it all.'

The superintendent pondered for a moment. 'You could be right,' he finally conceded, 'but if that was his intention then he's missed the boat.'

The mayor smiled. All his fears dropped from him as he became confident with his appraisal of the situation. The man, for all his clever tricks, was mortal after all, and even more important, he'd met his match in Grapplewick. Oh yes, they weren't the hayseeds that people thought they were. 'I'll just put the kettle on,' he said.

'Wait a minute before you go, Albert. I don't want you thinking I'm just a cheap hustler like the rest of them.' The mayor opened his mouth to protest but the superintendent held up his hand for silence. 'Knowing that you and I are going to carry the can for the whole scam, I can see no reason why we shouldn't make a few bob out of this for ourselves, to heal the wounds, as it were.'

'We?' asked the mayor curiously.

'I'm going to cut you in for half.'

The mayor's wits let him down again. 'Half?' he repeated.

'For five thousand quid we can be the joint owners of Sagbottom's Acres.'

The mayor sprang to his feet. There were a lot of things to think about here. Firstly, £5000 from him would just about drain his bank balance, and secondly, there were ethical considerations to weigh up. After all, he was the mayor and beyond reproach. To enter a questionable deal like the one which was being put forward to him might not exactly be illegal, but it wasn't exactly kosher. The superintendent walked over to the window. 'Car parking alone would be worth, oh, let me see, private cars, buses, coaches at a fiver a time, say seventy-five grand, and that's not counting the concessions, then there's . . .'

'Hang on a minute, I'll get me chequebook.' The mayor hurried over and took it out of a vase on the mantelpiece. 'Who shall I make it out to?'

'Best make it out to cash, don't want the tax people ferreting around, do we?'

The mayor hesitated for a moment, and then the sum of £75,000 flashed in front of his eyes again. He made the cheque out with a flourish and handed it over to the superintendent, and they shook hands, as two honourable gentlemen should. The superintendent then took his leave.

No sooner had the door closed than the mayor gave an exuberant little skip. Not only had he exorcised his fear of the spaceman, he was now a man of means. By next Thursday, come what may, he would have twenty, even thirty thousand pounds. He rubbed his hands together in sheer, breathtaking, intoxicating excitement. It was an invigorating feeling. He wouldn't tell Florrie; he'd just watch her face when the workmen arrived to put in a new bathroom, white tiles and a carpet, with a shower and all. Then perhaps they could go to Scarborough for a week. He raised his arms and pirouetted on one leg. For the first time in his life he was a really happy man.

Superintendent Smith, striding along the high street, didn't feel too bad either. Already some of his policemen were setting up cones and car parking signs around Sagbottom's Acres – all in the line of duty, of course. As superintendent he had impressed upon them all the need for clear signposting to ensure a trouble-free and orderly event. After all, well over 50,000 people were expected to attend and it had to be organised properly. Oh yes, he thought, whatever happened on Wednesday, he didn't plan to come out of this at the bottom of the heap. Perhaps old deaf Crumpshaw had already forgotten that Sagbottom's Acres didn't belong to him any more, or the price that he had been paid. Five thousand pounds. The superintendent shrugged. He hadn't exactly been honest with the mayor but so what? He'd just been taking out insurance; the cheque would cover him in case they were rained off.

NINETEEN

The bells of St Mary's parish church crashed upon an unsuspecting Grapplewick. Those who treated Sunday as a lie-in sat up in bed wondering if the spaceships had landed ahead of schedule, mindful of the old tradition of ringing the church bell as a warning of invasion. Normally the Sunday morning silence was scarcely broken by the mournful tone of a single tenor bell, and that didn't last long, but this Sunday was different. All the bell ringers had surprised each other by turning up for duty and the *clash-clamballang* of the peal embarrassed even them. They were glad when the conductor finally called stand.

Inside the church itself, the congregation whispered and rustled. There was an air of dankness, of mothballs and bad breath. During the bells, the fluting notes of the organ were puny in comparison, but with no competition from the belfry, the organist was inspired, bobbing and weaving, pulling out stops, fingers darting over keys. It was understandable. He'd never had an audience of this magnitude before – usually the choir outnumbered the congregation. Today, however, there was a full house and he was making the most of his recital. It might have been a Bach cantata, or a Bach fugue, the vicar couldn't be sure, but he couldn't help thinking that it was a good job Johann Sebastian died when he did. Mercifully, the organist played a long chord to signify that he had finished and the whispering died down in anticipation, emphasising the squeaks and clacks of shoes as latecomers entered the church.

The congregation rose during the introduction to Hymn 289 and the vicar surveyed the aisles and pews as 'Praise My Soul the King Of Heaven' was joyously bellowed out. He was proud and humbled by the enormous turn-out. 'Praise Him, Praise Him . . .' It was rousing, stirring stuff and he imagined that somewhere in the vast firmament above, beings from another galaxy were looking down on this solid, devout display of worship and congratulating themselves on choosing Grapplewick as a landing site. Their judgement had not been at fault – these were decent and deserving people.

Ninety per cent of the congregation were first-timers, if you don't count christenings, and not all were from Grapplewick. Two tall men at the back of the church were definitely out of place. They were different, big and brawny like rugby players . . . or off-duty policemen. Policemen, in fact, is exactly what they were, but they were far from off duty.

In the front pew, the mayor fidgeted. He wasn't a regular churchgoer and he was nervous. He was about to step up to the lectern to read the lesson. Yesterday he had been flattered when the Reverend Copthorne had invited him to participate in the service, but now it didn't seem like such a good idea. The congregation settled down and the vicar smiled at him encouragingly. He stood up and put on his half-moon glasses, glancing around the mass of faces in the church. He swallowed hard when he saw that nearly everyone was wearing badges. The church looked like a huge dark cotton field. Pulling himself together he began to read from the massive old Bible. 'The Gospel According to St Luke' – he wasn't a bad speaker and the congregation was suitably impressed, but the two tall men at the back hadn't come for the purification of their souls. They just wanted to check out the mayor and long before the end of the lesson they were outside lighting cigarettes in the churchyard.

Later that afternoon, the mayor, as was his custom on Sundays, was snoring gently in his favourite armchair. The *News of the World* slid gently from his lap when his eyes closed and from the kitchen came the clack of plates as Florrie washed up after lunch. This scene of domestic tranquillity was suddenly shattered by the imperative ring of the doorbell. Albert jerked upright out of his sleep, glancing this way and that to establish his whereabouts while Florrie looked in from the kitchen with a frown.

'I wonder who that can be?' she said.

'I don't know, do I?' he snapped. Hastily he stuffed the *News of the World* under a cushion and the doorbell rang again, this time more insistently.

'Well, go and see who it is,' he hissed, smoothing his thinning hair. 'Whoever it is, try and get rid of them.'

But she couldn't have heard him. When she came back into the room she was followed by two large men.

'These gentlemen would like to talk to you, Albert. They're from, er . . .'

'Special Branch, madam.'

The bigger of the visitors proffered his credentials to the mayor.

'I'm Chief Inspector James and this is Detective Sergeant Thompson.'

'Would you like a cup of tea?' asked Florrie.

'That would be nice, thank you,' said one of them.

She looked worriedly at her husband.

'Would you like a fresh pot, Albert?'

He shook his head, he hoped this wouldn't last long and he'd have one later.

'Sit down, will you.'

He motioned to the chairs and they sat. Both held their hats on their knees and the sergeant took out a notebook.

'Sorry to bother you on a Sunday afternoon, but I'm afraid the matter is urgent.'

'That's all right,' said Albert. 'How can I help you?'

The one with the notebook was obviously the spokesman.

'Your nephew Norman lives here, I believe.'

'Yes, he's upstairs. I'll get him.'

'Thank you, sir, it'll save time.'

Albert struggled out of the chair, but Florrie came out of the kitchen.

'I'll get him, you get on with it,' and she began her laborious ascent up the stairs. Any other time she would have stood at the bottom and bellowed 'Normaaaan!' but not when they had company. The mayor slumped back in his chair.

'Been up here long?' he asked.

'A few hours.'

The mayor nodded. 'Well, you won't have had a chance to see much of Grapplewick, then?'

There was no reply. The sergeant was tapping his pencil on his notebook. There was a long, silent pause broken only by the ticking of the clock on the mantelpiece.

'Good grief,' the mayor thought, 'she's no athlete but she should have reached the summit by now.'

'Just got back from church.' He said it as if he was a regular.

He was saved further embarrassment when Norman entered the room, hair brushed and a jacket on. Florrie must have briefed him.

'Ah, this is my nephew Norman. Norman, these gentlemen are from Special Branch.'

Norman nodded and took a chair from the table. He guessed what their business was about and was frightened. These weren't locals, they represented authority with a capital 'A'. He gulped when the bigger one spoke.

'We hope this won't take too long so I'll get straight to the point. You two people, I believe, were the first to make contact with the so-called spaceman.'

The mayor wriggled. 'Well, Norman was the first, and he telephoned me to . . .'

The big man cut him off. 'Yes, I understand, and consequently you two, Superintendent Smith and a Councillor, er . . .' he looked to his colleague.

'Butterworth, sir.'

'Yes, Butterworth, had a meeting with this man in the town hall.'

'That's correct,' said the mayor.

'In this meeting he led you to believe he was an alien from outer space.'

'He's from the planet Androm,' blurted Norman.

There was silence while the big man regarded him. 'Yes, well, be that as it may,' he said.

Norman regretted his outburst, it was childish rather than presidential.

'Now, sir,' the big man addressed the mayor, 'this man had an accomplice, a young lady, I believe.'

'That's right, Oomi she was called.'

He was beginning to relax. It wasn't about the purchase of Sagbottom's after all, and giving away information like this did not constitute a violation of his oath of secrecy. His composure was shattered by the next question.

'Can you describe exactly what happened at that meeting?'

Florrie lumbered in with a large tea tray of cups and saucers, teapot, sugar and milk, and the mayor sighed with relief.

'Thanks, Florrie,' he said fervently. 'Will you be mother?' The longer she was in the room the more time he'd have to think up an answer.

'D'you take milk?' she asked one of them.

The other looked at his watch, and then pointedly at his colleague.

'Yes, thanks, ma'am.'

She poured in the milk and handed over the cup; everyone had to be attended to. The man again looked at his watch.

'Would anybody like a bit of shortbread with that?' she asked, but they all declined and she made her way into the kitchen.

The spokesman was about to continue his questioning when she came into the room again with a plateful of chocolate biscuits.

'One of them won't do you no harm,' she said.

Then the telephone rang and she hauled her aching legs over to see who it was. 'Hello,' she said. 'Oh, hello, Emmie, I was just going to ring you, yes . . . oh did he? . . . Yes, well they don't, do they . . . mmm . . . yes, . . . mmm.'

The big man put his tea cup on the table. He guessed that the phone conversation would go on for some time.

'I think it might be better to continue our discussion on the way to the station.'

Albert spluttered a mouthful of tea across the table and his teeth went with it. Sergeant Thompson looked away in disgust but his superior leaned over and slapped the mayor on the back until he'd put himself together again.

'The police station?' croaked the mayor.

'Just a formality, sir. We've arranged for a police artist to be present, we'd like an Identikit picture of the two.'

'An Identikit picture?' asked the mayor.

'Well, you two must have a pretty accurate idea of what they look like. Also we think it highly unlikely they'll have a police record so it'll be a waste of time for you to sift through the rogues gallery.'

The sergeant snapped his notebook shut and stuffed it in his inside pocket.

'It'll be a great help to us, sir.' He rose to his feet.

'We've asked that Superintendent Smith be present. Between you, you should be able to come up with something resembling the two of 'em.'

The mayor looked across to where his wife was still umming and arring. They might as well have a ride down to the police station, they should be back before she'd finished. In fact, she didn't even see them leave.

The superintendent, however, was not at the police station when they arrived. He had more important things to do. In fact he was up at Sagbottom's Acres supervising crowd control arrangements. Three large fields were being marked off as vehicle parking spaces and there were primitive toilets – 'Elsans' for the ladies and long disinfected trenches for the men – shielded from prying eyes by canvas screens. There weren't too many such facilities, either for the ladies or the gents – they cost money. The superintendent wasn't bothered about that, though. If there was an outbreak of dysentery there was always the moors.

The whole extent of Sagbottom's Acres was quite considerable and at the centre of it all was a natural amphitheatre surrounding a fairly flat circle about the size of half a dozen football pitches. Purple heather and yellow spotted gorse concealed the slight humps and hollows. There wasn't much grass for a landing strip, but good grief, they were expecting a flying saucer, not a Tiger Moth. Presumably it would plonk straight down, not taxi in. As far as the superintendent was concerned, this was the ideal landing site and in order to keep the place clear of inquisitive spectators, he'd had the whole area roped off. As an added deterrent, signs were erected at fifty-yard intervals warning people to keep clear as this area was likely to be contaminated with radioactive particles.

There were enough vantage points on the surrounding hills anyway, so everybody should get a good view of anything that might happen. Workmen were erecting a platform for the dignitaries and the welcoming committee. He watched them hammering and sawing with unaccustomed haste. There wasn't much time. The bunting had to be rigged, and the microphones. He smiled to himself as he thought of Wednesday night. There would be an almighty rush for the toilets if a spacecraft actually did land. With that thought in mind, he called over a sergeant and instructed him to erect one directly behind the platform. The sergeant saluted and was about to carry out the order when the superintendent added, 'Oh, and mark it Decontamination Centre – that should keep the Herberts out.'

He stood there surveying his domain, a commanding figure in his uniform and gumboots. His posse of police was similarly shod. This didn't pass unnoticed by some of the secret watchers from the town; by Monday afternoon, anti-radioactive gumboots would be selling like ice cream in the desert. He gazed around at the frenzied activity and in the distance he took in the tumble-down stone dwelling of Farmer Crumpshaw. Thank God it wasn't built on the landing site or he'd have had to buy that as well. He was about to turn away when he spotted movement. The faraway figure of deaf Crumpshaw had emerged and he was heading in this direction. With a curt 'Carry on, sergeant,' he hurried to his car. He didn't particularly want to meet the farmer at that moment – or at any moment – and in any case, he was already late for a meeting at the police station.

TWENTY

Old deaf Crumpshaw was a recluse, and as his nickname implied, he was totally and utterly deaf. If a land mine exploded in front of him he would only see the flash. He was now well into his eighties, but according to local folklore he was much older; it wouldn't have surprised anybody to learn that he had received the Queen's telegram. Very few people in Grapplewick had actually seen him but he was nevertheless extremely well known. The stories about him were legendary; some said that he had cut off his brother's head with a sabre and buried him in two places on his land; some said that in fact the body was buried but the head was kept in a glass case on his dresser at the farmhouse; others said that it was his parents and not his brother whom he had hacked to pieces.

There were even more lurid tales sufficiently gruesome to deter casual visitors to the farmhouse. In fact, older people would make a detour of miles rather than go past the place. However, like most rumours that circulate in small, suspicious communities, they bore little relation to the truth. Crumpshaw's parents had died peacefully and were respectably buried in St Mary's churchyard, while his brother had been respectably killed on the Somme.

Old deaf Crumpshaw neither knew nor cared what people said about him, being content that they left him alone. Although Sagbottom's Acres had only been part of his holding, he wasn't rich. Miles of dry black stone walls crisscrossed his farm, but he had neglected the land until it had deteriorated into its original wild state. Many years ago he had kept sheep, but again this fact had become subject to legend. One day he had a thriving flock, but come the dawn they were all gone. Some recalled a fleet of lorries groaning on to the moors during the night; others that a German bomber pilot had jettisoned his bombs in his haste to get back to Deutschland, thus wiping out the entire flock. The most accepted – and most implausible – explanation was that old deaf Crumpshaw, sick to death of having to move his sheep from one pasture to another, had simply eaten them all. In any event, he was now a poor man living on social security. He was entitled to meals on wheels as well, but was unaware of this, and the social services didn't enlighten him as they were reluctant to drive the van over to his place. All his food and bits and pieces were obtained from a mobile shop that called every so often, but his store of money was now desperately low; in fact there was enough in the tin under the bed for about five pounds of potatoes and two tins of beans. The arrival of Superintendent Smith had been timely, to say the least.

The deal for Sagbottom's Acres had been negotiated by notes written on scraps of paper: 'Would you be willing to sell Sagbottom's?' Then Crumpshaw had written 'How much?', under which the superintendent had written 'Five thousand pounds.' He was delighted when Crumpshaw wrote back, 'Have you got the money with you?' Pulling out a wad of notes the superintendent had become the new owner; the deeds and receipt were handed over, but not until the farmer had laboriously counted out the money. Satisfied, Crumpshaw nodded and the superintendent saluted, desperately trying to hide his elation. Crumpshaw sucked on his one remaining tooth gleefully as he watched the policemen depart. He, too, had been trying to hide his elation. He knew that particular piece of land was useless, but if somebody with more money than sense wanted to buy it, well, that was their lookout.

He waited until the superintendent was well out of sight before he stuffed the money into his biscuit tin, which he then tied securely with a piece of string before sliding it under his bed. He decided that the next day he'd buy a tin of corned beef to go with his beans and potatoes. He could now afford to splash out a bit.

Early the following morning, three vans arrived at Sagbottom's Acres, disgorging practically the whole of Grapplewick's police force to prepare for the coming of the spacecraft. They were followed by carpenters and builders and a large transporter loaded with planks and scaffolding. They set to work with some urgency in a supremely well-organised manner supervised by Superintendent Smith.

In spite of all the activity it was late afternoon before old deaf Crumpshaw noticed all the activity. Because of his deafness, it wasn't so surprising he hadn't heard the clatter and bustle coming from Sagbottom's Acres – it was only when he shuffled across the yard to the privy that he became aware of the scores of people swarming all over the place. He frowned as a terrible thought occurred to him – was the superintendent going to build new houses on the land? No, it couldn't be. That was illegal. This was farm land in a green belt. Something funny was definitely going on, though, and he didn't like it. Furious, he flung on his cap and loaded both barrels of his shotgun. He left the farmhouse and made his way up the slight rise behind it, followed by Rex, his Welsh border collie. He was old and past his prime, too. He couldn't even remember what a sheep looked like.

The sergeant watched the farmer approach. He knew all about old deaf Crumpshaw. Like many other boys he'd been weaned on the legends but he'd never actually seen him before. He eyed the shotgun with some trepidation and hoped that Crumpshaw wouldn't do anything silly. Wheezing with the effort of the 300-yard journey, the farmer gave himself a moment to recover his breath while the sergeant waited apprehensively. Finally the old man spoke. 'What the bloody hell's going on?'

It was a useless question. He wouldn't be able to hear the answer anyway. The sergeant explained about the spaceship coming Wednesday, and was about to say more when he remembered Crumpshaw was deaf. He tried a second time, loudly and clearly, stretching his mouth around every syllable. Crumpshaw must be able to hear him. Only the dead were that deaf. Everybody else had stopped work and was looking at them, so the officer was glad when the farmer turned and shuffled across to the half-erected platform.

'What's this then!' He gestured with his shotgun.

The sergeant followed him. He didn't like the way the old man was waving the gun around. 'It's a platform!' he bellowed. 'For the VIPs!'

'Well, it looks like a platform to me,' grumbled the old man and again the sergeant tried to explain about Wednesday night and the aliens, except this time he used sign language. He pointed at the sky, then with the flat of his palm he simulated the landing. He then turned to the platform and shook hands with himself to indicate the welcoming committee. All in all it was a creditable performance and some of the carpenters applauded, although Crumpshaw didn't know this as they were behind him. The police officer continued, motioning to all the policemen dotted about the area who were knocking in signs and erecting the canvas shelters for the ladies and gents.

'Is it a missing person?' Crumpshaw eventually asked.

The sergeant shook his head in despair and slapped his hands against his flanks. Leaning forward he put his mouth to Crumpshaw's ear and bellowed, 'You're a stupid old bastard, aren't you!'

The farmer smiled triumphantly: 'I knew it was a platform all along.' And somewhat mollified he whistled for his dog. Rex was right behind him and barked a couple of times to let his master know he was at hand, but Crumpshaw turned in another direction and whistled again. The dog moved to heel and barked furiously.

'Where the dickens has he got to?' Crumpshaw muttered. 'He was here a minute ago.'

He whistled again and the sergeant took pity on him. He grabbed the old man's arm and pointed to the dog. Crumpshaw looked down and nodded.

'Oh, there you are. Took you long enough to get here,' and with that he set off down the hill to check on his biscuit tin.

Monday isn't the best day of the week for most people, but in Grapplewick it was different. The festivities had begun in earnest; absenteeism was the order of the day and the local school was closed for the lack of pupils. Pubs were well patronised but there were no ugly scenes of drunkenness. On the contrary, the streets were full of laughter, and on the few buses that were still running the conductors cheerfully declined to accept fares. 'Beautiful Grapplewick' badges were everywhere and there were still queues for the anti-fall-out hats. There hadn't been such a spirit of goodwill in the town since VE Day.

Bernard Whittaker moved over to the window and gazed down on the high street, shaking his head at the gay scene below. Normally the people in the street would be elderly, wandering aimlessly up and down like inmates in a geriatric open prison, but today throngs of young people in white Norman T-shirts were hanging around in groups, laughing loudly, while all the shopkeepers were standing in their doorways, smiling and waving. It was like Blackpool promenade on a rare hot day.

Aaron joined him at the window and together they surveyed the festivities below. They watched in silence for a moment, then the old reporter shook his head. 'There'll be tears before bedtime,' he said morosely. Whittaker turned away and sat down at his desk.

'I can understand them using it as an excuse for skiving off work, but look at the money they've laid out! They can't believe it, can they?'

Aaron shrugged. 'The special edition should be on the street in an hour or so. Let's see what effect that has.'

Whittaker sighed. 'That's if they have enough money left to buy a copy.' He turned to the old reporter. 'Did you want me for anything?'

'Oh aye . . . That "Beautiful Grapplewick" badge you found up at Kershaw's Croft?'

'Well, any reports on that?'

'Well, yes,' Aaron grinned. 'You'll enjoy this. I phoned the lab in Warrington this morning and they've tested the badge thoroughly; it would seem it's just ordinary plastic; nothing sinister apart from the words "Beautiful Grapplewick". They think that's hilarious!'

Whittaker smiled. 'It's a damn sight better than "Beautiful Warrington",' he observed and began to re-read his leader column for the extra edition. Aaron took this to be his dismissal and went back to his desk.

Before lunchtime the *Grapplewick Bugle* was on the streets, and so successful were the sales that Whittaker had to order a reprint of the edition. The headlines in thick black type screamed IT'S ALL A HOAX, under which there was a full-page warning to the people that the madness had gone far enough and that Grapplewick was in danger of becoming the laughing stock of Britain. It reminded people that over thirty small towns over the past year had received similar messages purporting to have come from outer space, and on each occasion no UFOs, in any shape or form, had made an appearance on Wednesday or indeed any other day.

The article went on to describe how the leading citizens had been duped by means of trickery and hypnotism into believing they were being addressed by a man from outer space who instructed them to prepare for the advent of fellow aliens. The article carried on relentlessly – the preposterous charade had now taken root in the minds of normally level-headed people, and the time had now come to call an end to these ludicrous preparations.

The article was followed by a detailed description of the man and the girl and was illustrated by two large Identikit pictures. The usual statement which said that if anybody knew of their whereabouts they should contact the police, was printed at the bottom of the page.

The article was effective. It was as if someone had thrown a large bucket of cold water over the whole of Grapplewick. Smiles disappeared and gleeful cries were now frowned upon. Yellow hats were furtively stuffed out of sight and the queue for badges outside Sutton's dispersed quietly. Everyone avoided each other's eyes and knots of people gathered on the high street outside the newspaper's office, anxiously awaiting more information on the scam. Shopkeepers whose tills had been pinging joyously now stood anxiously in their doorways. Jimmy Jackson was hurriedly packing a suitcase while the mayor was in a state of panic, wondering if he was now part-owner of several acres of nothing. The superintendent was having troubles of his own. As far back as a year ago a directive had been circulated to all police stations, stating that any information regarding the identity of the sender of the hoax letters was to be forwarded immediately to the Home Office. The superintendent had not only ignored this directive; he had actually spent three hours in close proximity with the man and had had ample opportunity to apprehend him. Whatever the outcome was to be, his career certainly lay in ruins.

Whittaker was astonished by the success of his article. He also felt a pang of guilt, as if he had taken a sweet away from a four-year-old child. This feeling quickly evaporated though, when at around four o'clock that afternoon an amazing incident occurred that completely reversed the balance of opinion in the town. An army convoy trundled down the high street and on to the moors. It wasn't a large convoy, just a jeep followed by six three-tonners crammed with squaddies from an engineering battalion who whistled at everything female under sixty – the prerogative of troops in transit. Their arrival was innocuous, an event which under normal circumstances wouldn't have merited a second glance, but in the present situation the townspeople seized on it as a vindication of their earlier beliefs.

Rumours spread through the town like an epidemic of cholera and this show of military might, witnessed by many people, assumed sinister proportions. In less than an hour it was a well-known fact that those troops were digging in round Sagbottom's Acres, heavy nuclear artillery was on its way to shoot the saucer out of the sky as it circled in preparation for landing, and on the radio the Government had declared Grapplewick an open city. Nobody had actually heard this, but everyone knew several people who knew someone who had. It was the stimulus they needed to shrug off their despondency and embarrassment. They were more than ever convinced of momentous happenings due on Wednesday night.

With regard to the newspaper article, it had obviously been written on the instructions of higher authority in order to dissuade people from going up to Sagbottom's, but they had under-estimated the Grapplewick folk. Fists were shaken at the windows of the *Bugle* and some of the hotheads wanted to form a vigilante group to march on Sagbottom's Acres and engage the troops. But a further rumour soon put a stop to that; the troops had supposedly been ordered to shoot on sight anyone approaching.

The sad truth of the matter was that the convoy, engaged upon a perfectly normal movement from Manchester to Catterick, was lost. The troops neither knew this nor cared, but the green lieutenant in the jeep leading the convoy was having difficulty with his map-reading and the grid references didn't include Grapplewick. It wasn't just a slight error on the lieutenant's part, it was a monumental cock-up, and if they hadn't turned soon they'd have probably ended up in Scotland. But, unwittingly, they had completely negated the effect created by Bernard Whittaker's article. On Tuesday, Jimmy Jackson unpacked his suitcase and opened Sutton's Iron Foundry for business as usual. Queues were already beginning to form for the anti-fall-out hats, and excite-ment was further fuelled by the rumour that Councillor Butter-worth, having disappeared, was being held hostage by the spaceman. For what purposes nobody seemed to know, but it was enough to add to the mystery of the UFOs.

TWENTY-ONE

S uperintendent Smith, the mayor and Norman were seated in the interrogation room at the police station. The policeman was in civvies, having been suspended from duty pending an investigation. Chief Inspector James of the Special Branch was conducting the interrogation with Sergeant Thompson in attendance.

'Are you sure, are you absolutely sure he asked for nothing in return?'

'Positive,' replied Norman. He was the only one present who absolutely believed everything the spaceman had said, and he couldn't wait for Wednesday to assume office.

The Special Branch man ran his fingers through his hair as he paced up and down. 'All right,' he said. 'Let's go back to the beginning . . . the barber's shop.'

His sergeant flipped over the pages of his notebook to the relevant one.

'How many times do I have to tell you?' blurted Norman. 'He sat in the chair and changed into a black fellow with a monkey on his shoulder.'

'Did he wave any sort of object in front of your eyes?'

'No, he didn't, but OK, say he hypnotised me. What about the blind man then?'

The Special Branch officer stared at him for a moment. 'That's easy. He could have been an accomplice.' Norman snorted and the big man raised his eyebrows. 'OK, let me put it to you another way. Grapplewick's a small place and you've lived here all of your life. Isn't it slightly strange that a blind man comes into your shop and you don't recognise him?'

Norman blushed. 'I don't know everybody, do I?' he mumbled.

Superintendent Smith cleared his throat. 'The following day, Thursday, I ran a check with the social services and the person Norman described to me was not registered amongst the blind.'

The big man nodded and for a while there was silence in the room. Suddenly Norman's eyes widened. 'Wait a minute. I think I've seen him again; yes, I thought I recognised him.' He swivelled around to his uncle. 'Do you remember the mob that broke into your office looking for badges?' The mayor looked back at him uncomprehendingly. His spirit was crushed; whatever happened he was a broken man who would probably be removed from office, and if that wasn't enough, his nest egg was gone too.

'The badges?' he asked.

'Yes,' said Norman excitedly. 'The blind man. I spotted him in the crowd. I knew I'd seen him somewhere before.'

The Special Branch men exchanged glances while Norman looked anxiously from one to the other. 'That doesn't prove he's not an accomplice, though, does it?'

DCI James eyed him sympathetically. 'No it doesn't, Sonny Jim, and it's rather odd behaviour for a man who's just been granted the gift of sight.'

Norman pondered this for a moment. 'Ah, yes, but if he was in cahoots with the spaceman he wouldn't have stormed into the town hall, knowing I'd be there and might recognise him!'

The Special Branch man looked at him coolly. 'How was he to know that you would be there? How could anyone have guessed?' Norman's shoulders sagged. His ace had been trumped. 'Kershaw's Croft,' the man went on, 'you were obviously under hypnosis.' He nodded to the mayor who instantly perked up.

'That's right!' It might be quite a good defence plea. 'He must have been good because normally I . . .'

'Yes, yes,' broke in the Special Branch man testily.

'He didn't hypnotise me, though,' said Norman. 'When I looked out of the window I could see the lights of Grapplewick twinkling below.'

'It could have been a photo on a black background.'

Norman shook his head. 'I'm sorry to disappoint you but it couldn't have been a photo. I distinctly remember that the lights were twinkling.'

The superintendent sniggered.

'Something amusing?' asked the interrogating officer, and the superintendent glared back at him. He wasn't used to being interrogated and he objected to being treated like a suspect and being forced to listen to the damn fool answers Norman was coming out with. The lights were twinkling, for God's sake. The next minute he'd be talking about sleigh bells ringing.

'With due respect,' he began, 'we've established that the man is a gifted hypnotist and he used his powers on these two.' He waved his hand in the general direction of the mayor and Norman as if to dissociate himself from them. 'But what rational explanation can be given for the Indian woman and the burning down of his shop?'

'Ah yes, the shop, that's easy. Only a guess, mind you, but we're back to the accomplice. As for the woman, I'm afraid that is still a mystery.'

Again Norman interrupted. 'Yes, somebody could have been there to set light to the shop, but how would he know the exact moment to do it?'

The big man stared at him for a moment. 'What are you getting at?'

Norman was triumphant. 'The spaceman predicted it. Before it happened he put his hands to his forehead and a bit after that we heard the fire engines.'

They sat back to await an explanation, but the big man appeared to have other things on his mind.

'Now this girl Oomi, was there anything odd or different about her?'

The superintendent shrugged. 'I never met her so you can leave me out.'

Norman opened his mouth to speak but was interrupted by a peremptory knock at the door.

'Yes,' growled James.

Sergeant Buckley came in and hurried across to him to whisper in his ear. Norman and the superintendent strained to hear what was being said but with no luck.

Finally James nodded. 'Thank you, sergeant, I'll be right with you.'

He turned to the three of them. 'Well, I don't think there's any need to detain you further. If something crops up I'll let you know.'

Gratefully they all rose and shuffled out. As they were crossing the charge room nobody noticed the lady in conversation with the desk sergeant.

The Special Branch man popped his head out after they'd gone and beckoned to her. 'Would you like to come in here, madam.' He stood to one side while she entered the room. 'Sit down, please,' he said, indicating a chair.

When she was settled he began, 'So you think you recognise the Identikit picture in the paper?'

He wasn't optimistic: there had been a score of claimants in the police station since Bernard Whittaker's article, and up to now all of them had proved to be dead ends. One of them, a stunted bearded man, came to turn himself in insisting he was the spaceman. It was a farce and Chief Inspector James was bored with it all. It was a degrading assignment for Special Branch anyway. It was 'bobby on the beat' stuff, and he had more important things to do than chasing up and down the country like a travelling salesman. However, the instructions were from the Home Office and until the letter writer was apprehended it would continue to supply the Opposition parties in Parliament with ammunition with which to taunt the Government. He was in a no-win situation: if he wasn't successful it would be a black mark on his record, and if he did make an arrest and the sender turned out to be a spotty Herbert he'd be a joke for not having caught him sooner.

The woman seemed composed, almost resigned. 'Oh yes, I recognise him and he's no more a spaceman than you are. His real name is Heinrich Adlon.'

He stared for a moment, realising that he hadn't been paying much attention.

'I'm sorry,' he said. 'What was the name again?'

'Heinrich Adlon.'

'A German?'

'Well, German parents, but he was born just outside Birmingham.'

The chief inspector looked at her, with the first stirrings of excitement coursing through his body. The first letter had been delivered to a small town just outside Birmingham, so there was the faintest of hopes that there just might be a connection. 'Now then, er . . .'

'Lesley, Eunice Lesley.'

'Thank you. Do you live in Grapplewick?'

'I run a dancing academy. Madame Lesley's.' She smiled and dropped her head. 'Not very successfully, I'm afraid.'

Chief Inspector James nodded sympathetically. Deep within his gut he had a feeling about this one, a feeling that he was about to achieve a major breakthrough. 'And you're absolutely certain that you can positively identify this man?'

She looked at him steadily. 'I should hope so ... he's my husband.'

TWENTY-TWO

The wave of optimism that emanated from Grapplewick police station quickly reached Special Branch headquarters in London. At last an ointment had been discovered for the festering sore that had troubled the bureau for nearly a year. To date all they had achieved was to collate an extremely large file of 'Strictly Private and Confidential' marked letters, all similar and all useless, which had been delivered to various towns around the country. But now the hoaxer had made a serious error and Special Branch had a face, a name, an occupation, and most important of all, irrefutable evidence that the man was mortal.

Back in Grapplewick, having questioned Eunice Lesley for over two hours, the officers had learned the full story of their alien hoaxer. Eunice had told them of her younger days. Back then, she had been a dancer in the summer season at Bournemouth. She had been different from all the other girls in that she had inherited £50,000 during the run of the show. This was no secret; in fact on hearing the news she had taken the whole troupe out to dinner. Neither did having the money make any difference to her choice of lifestyle – twice nightly she had still enjoyed bouncing around with the rest of the girls to the tune of 'The Sun Has Got His Hat On.'

Unfortunately for Eunice, topping the bill at Bournemouth had been The Great Firenzi, a hypnotist of great skill and charm. All the girls had fantasised about him; he was cultured, aloof and untouchable, so it was hardly surprising that Eunice, gauche and not especially pretty, had nearly fainted when he had asked her if she wanted to be his assistant. By the end of the season they had married, although it would have been more honest to say that Firenzi had acquired for himself a slave. Eunice had given him her heart, her soul, her body, and sadly, her £50,000 inheritance. On his part, he had been charming, witty, attentive, and, after securing the inheritance, invisible. She had never seen him again.

When the Special Branch officers asked Madame Lesley for photographs of her husband, she refused. In fact, she didn't have any. She had destroyed them all. It didn't really matter to the officers too much; after all they could look through old copies of *Spotlight* and summer season souvenir brochures. Within a couple of hours photocopies of the wanted man would be faxed over to Grapplewick police station.

'What a bastard. Fifty thousand pounds was a lot of money in those days,' commented the junior Special Branch officer.

Chief Inspector James nodded wryly. 'It's a lot of money now.' Outwardly he remained calm, even indifferent to this mass of information coming in about the hoaxer, but this was just a policeman's facade. Inside, more than ever, he was burning to get his hands on the man. He knew now he wasn't a pimply-faced youth from a deprived background, but a cultured, devious and clever con-man. How many other women had he married and left penniless? But the jackpot question was, Why the spaceman masquerade? – *that* was the bottom line. What was he hoping to achieve with this elaborate con? Perhaps this was a job for Special Branch after all.

Wednesday morning dawned bright and clear. The citizens of Grapplewick knew nothing about the advances made by Special Branch, and nor did they care. Even if the true facts had been broadcast on breakfast television they wouldn't have believed them; no one was going to rob them of this day. From very early in the morning the traffic was all one way to Sagbottom's Acres. On a normal day a ten-minute drive would have taken Bernard Whittaker from his home to the office, but on this Wednesday after nearly an hour he was still on the road and he was still in first gear. On a normal day the streets of Grapplewick were never blocked; even during the rush hour the volume of traffic was negligible – like a quiet Sunday morning in the City of London.

Whittaker was astonished by the assortment of vehicles, family cars, mini-buses and even horses and carts bedecked with flowers. Indeed, he was crawling behind one charabanc crammed full of youngsters wearing Norman T-shirts, who shouted goodnaturedly to the pedestrians as they passed by. As he looked out of his car window, Whittaker was even more astonished to see people leaning out of the upstairs windows of their houses, cheering loudly and waving Union Jacks. Union Jacks, for God's sake! Two days back nobody in the town would have been able to lay their hands on one of those little flags but now it seemed that everybody had one. In front of him the charabanc stopped and one of the lads blew tentatively on a hunting horn while the others all cheered. 'Beautiful Grapplewick' badges were everywhere and Whittaker imagined that come the next day, Jimmy Jackson along with many other profiteers would be on their way to the Costa del Sol for a well-earned rest. Deep in thought, Whittaker went past his office but had no difficulty in doing a U-turn across the road. There was nothing at all coming in the other direction.

Once behind his desk he marvelled at the collective hysteria which had gripped Grapplewick. He knew Hitler had managed it in Germany in 1938 but then he had had an objective – world conquest. Here there was nothing, just a euphoric lemming-like rush towards the cliff edge. It was quite remarkable. The town's inhabitants were being drawn to Sagbottom's Acres as people are to the scene of a bad accident.

At this stage Whittaker too had no idea that the identity of the spaceman had been established. His own line of enquiry seemed to be struggling through treacle and he felt that he was running out of time. Wearily he picked up the phone. 'Hello, Doris? Get me the station master at Grapplewick Central.' He waited until she acknowledged, and was about to put the phone down when Billy burst into his office.

'Don't you ever knock?' growled Whittaker but his young reporter didn't appear to have heard.

'I think I'm on to something, chief,' he said eagerly, rummaging through the capacious pockets of his raincoat.

The phone rang and the editor snatched it up. 'Yes?'

'The station master,' said Doris and put him through.

Billy pulled out a wodge of rubbish from one of his pockets and then delved back in to find some more.

'Hello George, yes, Bernard Whittaker here ... yes, I'm well, how are you? Yes ... no ... nothing's bothering me, George, but I was hoping you could help. I'm trying to trace a man between fifty and sixty, and a girl, much younger ... they may have bought tickets in the last few days ... Yes, I know, but these aren't your ordinary everyday people; he's smartly turned out and from all accounts the girl's a bit of a looker. No disrespect George, but they'd stand out on your station like a Chippendale in the waiting room.'

Billy leaned across the desk and tapped his arm. 'The girl,' he hissed, but his boss ignored him.

'I know it's the busy season, George, but try whoever's in the booking office. Ask him if he remembers any strangers.'

Billy shook his arm again.

'Hang on a minute, George.' Whittaker put his hand over the mouthpiece. 'Well, what is it?'

'Nothing on the man, Mr Whittaker, but a girl – and I'm sure it's the one we're looking for – has been staying at the Duke of Wellington for the past six days.'

Whittaker's eyebrows shot up. 'Good, Billy, that's great.' He returned to the phone. 'George,' he started, 'can you hang on a bit longer ... thanks.' He hooded the mouthpiece again and looked at Billy. 'Do you know when she checked out?'

'Early this morning; if I'd got there yesterday ...'

Whittaker shushed him and went back to the phone. 'We're getting there, George. Now, does anyone your end recall seeing a girl at the station this morning, buying a ticket?' He waited a moment or two before replying. 'No, I don't know where to, but there can't have been that many people about. We're talking about Grapplewick Central, not Gare du Nord.'

Billy tried to interrupt again but the editor waved him off whilst continuing his conversation with George. 'Yes, I understand that, but the people off on holiday and commuter folk presumably have bought return tickets. This person certainly won't be coming back ... yes, well, ring me if you hear anything. I'd send someone down but we're pushed for time. Thanks, George, see you soon.' He put the phone down, feeling that he'd just had a wasted conversation.

'Tell you what, Mr Whittaker,' Billy piped up, 'one of my mates is a porter down there. Any talent on the platform and he'd spot it all right!'

Whittaker looked at him thoughtfully. 'OK,' he said, 'get down there and have a talk with him. If he does remember the girl then he may just remember her destination.'

Billy puckered up his forehead. 'You mean the girl who checked out of the Duke of Wellington this morning?'

'Yes,' said Whittaker, inwardly despairing of his young reporter. He flicked down his intercom and got Doris again. 'See if you can find the whereabouts of Norman Waterhouse. If you locate him, I'd like a word.' He looked up to find Billy still standing there. 'What are you waiting for now?'

Billy hesitated. 'Well, the thing is . . . that girl . . . well, she's gone back home.'

Whittaker waited very quietly for Billy to continue.

'Well, the manager gave me her forwarding address.'

Whittaker regarded him for some time then sighed and shook his head. Slowly he reached forward and switched on the intercom again. 'Forget that call,' he instructed, and leaned back in his chair. 'You've got her home address?' he asked incredulously.

'Yes, sir, it's here somewhere.' Billy's hands shot into his raincoat and patiently his editor watched the ever growing mountain of debris from Billy's pockets – chocolate wrappers, bills, Polo mints and receipts – and that was just his raincoat. By the time he'd been through all his pockets there was enough litter on the desk to fill a decent-sized dustbin.

'Ah, here it is!' said Billy triumphantly, and passed over a crumpled piece of paper showing Oomi's address or, to be more exact, Ann Taylor's address, which was Yew Tree Close, Bogsea, Sussex. Remarkably, there was a telephone number there as well. 'Is that what you're looking for?' Billy asked hopefully.

Whittaker smiled, and keeping his voice as noncommittal as possible he replied, 'It's a start, Billy lad, it's a start.' Inside, he could hardly contain his excitement but it wouldn't do to make too much of this information in front of his reporter. Next thing he knew, Billy would be asking for a rise. He looked up to find Billy looking at him as though that might just be what was on his mind. 'Is there anything else, Billy?'

'No, sir, it's just that I thought we should have somebody up at Sagbottom's. You know, human interest and all that.'

'By God, Billy, you're right! Get up there as quickly as possible and circulate.'

'Thank you, sir,' and Billy was gone before anything more specific could be asked of him.

As soon as the door closed Whittaker switched on the intercom, but almost instantly he had second thoughts. It was useless ringing now; the girl wouldn't have got home yet, and that was if she was going direct. She might have stopped off in London for some sightseeing or shopping. He slammed his desk in frustration; he didn't have the resources to check her out and he didn't want to leak the story to his pals on the big dailies. Grapplewick would quickly be confirmed as an open asylum. They would also elbow him out of the biggest story of his career.

Outside, above the noise of the traffic he heard the sound of the hunting horn and realised that the charabanc must have only moved fifty yards or so since he made his U-turn to the office. He frowned. Another sound was missing. There was no noise coming from the outer office. He turned to look through the glass partition. No wonder he hadn't heard the clack of typewriters – the desks were empty, the machines covered, the photocopiers switched off and the phones silent. He walked over to his door and flung it open. Only Aaron was in the office, busy on the telephone. As Whittaker approached he cupped his hand over the receiver. 'Thought it might be a good idea to hire a helicopter to take pictures of the harvest festival.'

Whittaker thought for a moment. 'No, Aaron, cancel it.'

The old reporter looked at him for a second or two then turned back to his desk. 'Forget it, Bob, some other time.' He put the phone down.

'You didn't tell him what it was really for?' enquired Whittaker.

'No, we were just haggling over the price.'

'Good. The fewer people outside Grapplewick that know about this the better.' He looked around the deserted office. 'Where is everybody?' he asked.

'Where else?' replied Aaron. 'Badges, gumboots, the lot.'

The old editor sighed; he shouldn't have asked, he could have guessed. 'Oh, by the way, young Billy managed to trace the girl; she's gone home.'

'To Androm?'

Whittaker smiled. 'She caught a train early this morning to the south coast.'

'A train? I'm surprised our spaceman didn't give her a lift in Kershaw's Croft.' He slapped his thigh. 'Oh, I almost forgot; he can't. Kershaw's Croft isn't there any more; well, most of it's gone.'

Whittaker frowned. 'What are you talking about? It was there on Friday.'

'Well, it isn't now. Some enterprising Johnny has been dismantling it and would you believe, the stones are now for sale as souvenirs.'

Whittaker stared at him. 'I do believe it, and I also believe that the whole town has gone stark staring raving bonkers!'

TWENTY-THREE

The town hall, which was normally bustling with queues of enquirers, was utterly deserted. The only signs of life came from the mayor's office on the first floor, where an emergency meeting was being held, chaired by the head of the Conservatives, Councillor Davies. The only other people present were the mayor and Norman. It should have been a full council assembly but the rest of the members were strangely unavailable, either too ill to attend, or abroad. In other words, nobody wanted a part in this meeting. Councillor Butterworth, one of the original gang of four, was safely tucked away in a nursing home; at least, the nursing home's address was on the notepaper tendering his resignation. Ostensibly Councillor Davies had called the meeting to discuss the present situation and to find out what the hell was going on. He was totally unaware of the events of the last few days, having spent the past two weeks in Marbella on a fact-finding mission. He had returned late on Tuesday night, so the atmosphere in the town had knocked him for six.

The mayor filled him in with an up-to-date appraisal of the facts, cleverly easing the burden of responsibility on to others; Norman had been hypnotised at the barber's, he had accompanied Norman to Kershaw's Croft against his better judgement, and after the meeting in his office – which he had merely organised – rumours started circulating that the man was an alien who was proclaiming that a spacecraft was going to land at Sagbottom's

Acres on Wednesday. The mayor finished his appraisal with a shrug as if to say, 'What could I do?'

It was a masterly whitewash but Norman listened with only half an ear. He was a demasted ship in the doldrums. All his dreams were up the spout; the Utopia of which the man had spoken was a brilliant concept and would have certainly been welcomed by the ordinary people of the world, but if he was being honest with himself he would have to admit that the main reason for his depression was Oomi. Not only was she part of this chicanery, but he'd never see her again.

'It's incredible,' muttered Councillor Davies as he rose and walked over to the window. Outside the traffic was thinner than earlier; presumably most of the spectators had already reached Sagbottom's Acres. 'And do you mean to tell me,' he continued, 'that they all believe a spacecraft will be landing today . . .'

The mayor shrugged again. 'I don't know whether they believe it, but they're all going up to Sagbottom's.'

The councillor looked at him, visualising the crowds packed on every vantage point like an old Biblical depiction of the Sermon on the Mount. Finally he spoke. 'And what happens afterwards?'

'Afterwards?' echoed the mayor.

'Presumably they'll be up there all night. What's going to happen on Thursday morning?'

This was a question that had bothered the mayor for the past five days. 'I don't know,' he said unhappily. Inside the office there was a deep silence, broken only by the distant noises in the high street. Both the mayor and Norman sat staring at the carpet in utter dejection until finally the councillor cleared his throat. 'What time will you be going?' he asked.

The mayor looked at him vacantly. 'I haven't made up my mind whether to go or not.'

The councillor looked aghast. 'You must go.' He looked at them both. 'Don't you see? If you're not there the crowd will assume that you knew all the time that there'll be no UFOs and they'll come storming off the moors like Genghis Khan's mob in search of blood – your blood.'

The mayor could easily imagine this, but he wasn't going to give way to Councillor Davies so easily. 'Yes, but if we do attend, they won't have to come storming off the moors. We'll be there.'

Councillor Davies thought about this for a moment. 'OK, but

it's the lesser of two evils. If you're there they'll think you've been taken in as well and you may even get some sympathy.'

The mayor mulled this over. Inwardly he agreed with the councillor that it was the best course of action. The more he thought about it the better he felt; after all, he was the mayor and a leader of men. Yes, he'd go to Sagbottom's Acre in the full panoply and majesty of his office. To hell with sneaking in like an urchin under a circus tent flap, he'd go in style, with trumpets blaring. All he needed now was to organise this. He rose purposefully to his feet and strode to the door, calling in the town clerk.

By late afternoon most of Grapplewick's citizens were at Sagbottom's Acres, with a three-mile tailback stretching to the outskirts of the town. The area around the assumed landing site was already crowded with the early arrivals – groups of young folk in Norman T-shirts waving scarves above their heads, families with spread blankets littered with half-eaten sandwiches and bits of shell from hard-boiled eggs, and elderly people dozing in light collapsible chairs. Only the very old could sleep through the incredible cacophony of sound that surrounded them: the two carousels on which bobbed fierce horses that clanked around to tinny music and crashing cymbals in desperate competition with several amateur pop groups who had made just enough money to buy mind-blowing sound systems but not enough to pay for music lessons. There were shrieks of laughter and joyful screams from the many side shows surrounding the area, and the mouthwatering smells from numerous fish and chip stands, hot dog vehicles and candy floss stalls permeated the air. It was quite amazing how, within one week, the town's citizens had been transformed from a shambling, listless bunch of no-hopers into a co-ordinated force of goodwill and high spirits.

Billy Grout forced his way between these groups of people. He already had a few interviews in his notebook, but they weren't very meaty. He wished he had a photographer with him. Most of the people surrounding him had cameras but to capture the atmosphere of Sagbottom's Acres called for a wide-angled lens. Even then it would be impossible really to capture the immensity of this carnival. Behind him he heard the tinkling of bells, and on looking around saw donkeys giving donkey rides. He wondered where on earth they had come from. It was really all too much for one reporter. He didn't know where to begin, and hoisting his bike on to his shoulder he struggled through the crush towards the way out. He had to get to a phone: Mr Whittaker wasn't going to believe this. A new sound joined the cacophony and to the right of the official platform the town brass band embarked on a rendition of 'The Dambusters March' in a futile attempt to lend dignity to the proceedings.

Just after dark an unmarked police car swept out of the station yard and up Radcliff Street.

'You still got the brake on?' asked Chief Inspector James.

The local detective constable automatically felt for it before he recognised the sarcasm and he put his foot down. There was no reason why he shouldn't, the streets of Grapplewick were deserted. It was an eerie experience, like driving through a ghost town. Most of the houses showed lights, but this was the customary obvious ploy to persuade marauding villains that the dwellings were occupied. Conversely and even stranger, all the pubs were dark and closed. As they sped up the high street Chief Inspector James suddenly realised it wasn't just the lack of traffic that was noticeable, it was the complete absence of buses. He felt conspicuous as the car drew up behind what appeared to be the only other vehicle in town. He heaved himself out and leaned back into the car.

'Wait here,' he said. 'Put your lights out and keep your eyes skinned. If you see anybody suspicious see what he's up to.' He straightened, looked up and down the street then bent back in again. 'If you see *anybody*, see what he's up to,' he added, and he made his way into the newspaper office.

The constable doused his lights and stepped out of the car. Apart from the switchboard girl, he was the only local police officer left in Grapplewick and he was impatient to get up to Sagbottom's. Turning in that direction he could discern a faint golden glow illuminating the sky. A firework burst into tiny droplets of light. If he didn't get there soon he'd miss all the fun.

Up in his office the editor poured out two glasses of Scotch and handed one to the Special Branch man, who nodded his thanks and drank deep.

'I've been trying to get in touch with you,' started the editor.

James nodded again. 'I've been busy. What's on your mind?'

Mr Whittaker accepted the brusque manner; the policeman had an unenviable task, but then again he himself hadn't exactly been enjoying a week's package holiday either. And he didn't actually enjoy being spoken to as he did to others.

'We're almost certain that the man posing as a space alien is an illusionist who used to do a stage act under the name of "The Great Firenzi".' That should have brought the policeman to heel but it didn't.

'You're right,' he replied. 'He was an illusionist, and his real name is Heinrich Adlon.' He shrugged. 'But he's probably used another dozen aliases since then. Well, is that all you wanted me for?'

The editor was nettled, but he still had a high card to play.

'Not quite,' he said. 'We've traced the girl, his assistant.'

The chief inspector stared at him for a moment.

'Oomi?' he asked, deceptively calm.

'Her name is Ann Taylor.' The editor was in the driving seat and he was tempted to throw in 'but she's probably used another dozen aliases since then', but he resisted the childish impulse.

'Yes,' he went on, 'we have her home address and telephone number.' He paused. 'Unfortunately the number has been reported as being out of order.'

James eyed him with new respect. 'Good work,' he said. His lethargic facade dropped away and he was all business.

'Do me a favour, will you?' He slipped a card across the desk. 'Ring that number and ask for Superintendent Cranleigh. If he's not there have him located, priority one. Tell him you're acting under my orders and to send two of our lads like the clappers of bastardy to this girl's address . . . and tell him, no arrest, just keep the house under observation.'

Mr Whittaker nodded. The Special Branch man strode to the door. 'Oh, and by the way,' he said, turning to the editor, 'thanks for the information, it could be the best lead yet,' and he was gone.

Mr Whittaker, well pleased with himself, winked at the closed door and pulled the phone towards him. After he'd dialled the number he heard the screech of tyres from below as the police car headed fast for Sagbottom's to witness the last act.

Late in the evening, lights were blazing in the mayor's office. At short notice, Sidney, the town clerk, had done a splendid job. A table set up along one wall was loaded with bottles of drink, plates of sandwiches and cake, now sadly depleted, cigarettes and one or two Havana cigars, even two jugs of Tetley Bitter. All this for no more than the expected half dozen dignitaries. It surprised and heartened everyone as they entered the room, and with smiles and much handrubbing they selected their particular fancies. After the initial assault on the hospitality, the mayor, resplendent in his robes of office – black, red and ermine – belched behind his hand as he surveyed the others.

Superintendent Smith was now back in uniform, dress uniform with medal and white gloves; Norman was morose and dejected. Florrie wasn't much better, overdressed and made up but still miffed at not having had time to have her hair done. Sidney came from the table and set down a fresh gin and tonic before her. It was her third and she perked up a little. Two more gins and she'd be in the maudlin stage ... 'having to walk three miles to school barefoot'. Sidney himself added to the splendour in his own medieval town clerk's get-up. His tricorn hat and mace were on another small table in a corner. The Reverend Copthorne had yet to arrive, and unfortunately Councillor Davies, having instigated the get-together, had been unexpectedly called away to Leicester where his brother had been taken ill.

Norman suddenly blurted out, 'Why do we have to go up there if it's all a joke?'

Up to then the conversation had been amicable – football, the weather, the exorbitant price of most things; anything, in fact, that avoided the subjects of aliens and flying saucers. Now the last in the pecking order had had the temerity to throw a large rock into the placid water.

The mayor stared coldly at him. 'It's hardly a joke, Norman, when the whole town is up at Sagbottom's.'

'Oh, no,' replied Norman hotly. 'They're all up there waiting for a spacecraft that won't arrive because he said he was from the planet Androm when all the time he's just an ordinary con-man!'

The mayor smiled. 'That's what we've been told, Norman, but just because somebody looks like him doesn't prove that's the right person.'

Superintendent Smith picked up the drift. Norman had to be up there on the platform with them. If the crowd turned nasty and wanted somebody to point at, Norman was their man. The superintendent still had the remains of his career to think about. 'Oh, yes,' he added aloud, 'we've had numerous cases when a suspect has been positively identified and it's turned out to be somebody else.'

'That's right, Norman,' continued Florrie. 'It's not definite that he's the trickster; we've only been told he is. But if he is, what's he getting out of it, eh? Answer me that! As far as I can see he doesn't stand to gain anything at all; nothing financial any road!'

Norman digested all this information for a second or two. His aunt did have a point. 'Yes, what's he getting out of it?' he repeated. 'There's been a fortune spent on badges, fall-out hats, gumboots and all that, but I can't see him being in cahoots with Jimmy Jackson and all the others.'

The mayor spread his hands: 'Well, there you are then.' But Norman wasn't wholly satisfied.

'It must be something to do with Sagbottom's Acres,' he said. The mayor buried his face in his tankard while the superintendent turned and helped himself to another dying sandwich. The conversation had taken a very embarrassing turn. He had been looking forward to making a tidy little profit from the land, but Sergeant Buckley had told him only two hours ago that the latest figure for car parking alone was £80,000. That wasn't just a tidy little profit; that was big league stuff, and when it came to light – as it undoubtedly would – the Serious Fraud Squad would have a field day.

Florrie giggled. 'Don't tell me the man's in partnership with old Crumpshaw! They would have heard the argy bargying in Blackpool!' She giggled again and the mayor decided that she'd had enough to drink for one function. He was about to steer the subject away from Sagbottom's Acres when there was a discreet knock on the door and Reverend Copthorne sailed in. It would be hard to describe his entrance in any other way; he could have been on a unicycle underneath his cassock, so effortless was his glide to the table of goodies.

'Evening all,' he said, eyeing the remnants. 'I hope I'm not late.' Judging by what was left on the table, he decided that he was.

'No, reverend, we've agreed to make a start at eleven,' said the mayor. He had decided upon that time earlier as, counting fifteen minutes to get there, that would leave them with only three quarters of an hour until Thursday, and what happened then rested in the laps of the gods.

The vicar nodded and smiled at all of them in turn. 'You know,' he started through a mouthful of madeira cake, 'I've got a theory about this spaceman.'

They waited while he tucked the crumbs into his mouth with a very white little finger.

'I don't think he's a spaceman at all.'

Again they waited. His face was glowing with excitement.

'I fervently believe that this is the second coming . . .'

They stared at him in open-mouthed disbelief.

'Yes,' he went on, 'I've given the matter some considerable thought and I feel convinced there is every possibility that tonight we could be witnessing the manifestation of Jesus Christ our Lord . . .'

They were stunned. They'd come a long way from con-man to the Son of God, but on reflection it wasn't too far fetched. The first time round had been a little town in Bethlehem so why not Grapplewick? But before anyone could challenge this theory, something even more dramatic occurred – an incident that shocked them all: a dull boom broke the silence. The mayor half rose to his feet and they stared at each other in puzzlement. The superintendent was halfway to the window when there was another boom – this time louder, bringing a small shower of plaster from the ceiling.

Norman looked up at the slightly swaying chandelier.

'The two sonic booms,' he whispered, hardly able to keep the jubilation out of his voice. 'They're coming,' he gasped joyfully.

Florrie hurriedly gulped down the rest of her gin and the superintendent stared stupidly at the white dust on his sleeve. The vicar was all for a prayer of thanksgiving but there wasn't time. No one knew how soon the spacecraft would be landing. Their only desire was to get up to Sagbottom's as quickly as possible.

There was so much noise and revelry on Sagbottom's Acres that nobody heard the sonic booms. It wouldn't have mattered if they had, as most of the crowd had forgotten the reason they were up there in the first place. Every few yards it seemed there was a bonfire surrounded by red animated faces and silhouettes, the bright flickering flames dominating the sickly white lights of the dozens of stalls where almost anything, from beer and hot dogs to badges and fall-out hats, was still available. The carousels indefatigably made their rounds, more pop groups now adding to the indescribable cacophony, and the night sky was rent with cascades, coloured balls and bangs from a seemingly inexhaustible supply of fireworks. Nearly everyone was partaking in the festivities, the exceptions being the sleeping young, the drunk and the dead. At half-hour intervals huge floodlights were switched on to a loud cheer, and an even louder one when they went out again. The lights were an intrusion: better the blackness in the middle, giving the appearance of a land-locked harbour surrounded by a busy holiday port.

Chief Inspector James surveyed the scene. It was grotesque, and something somewhere didn't quite fit. Circulating amongst the revellers were half a dozen men from the Liverpool Special Branch and some from Manchester. All carried pictures of The Great Firenzi and their job was to find him. They were diligent and at least thirty men between fifty and sixty-five years old had been manhandled to dark spots outside the area of festivities and questioned thoroughly. But it was hopeless, and deep in his bones, James knew it. A nut case might hang around to enjoy his success but Heinrich Adlon most definitely possessed all his marbles and would be miles away by now. But why? ... What was it all about? James shook his head in frustration and decided to get himself a beer. Before he reached the stall the floodlights were switched on again and this time they were pointing to the entrance where a motorcade bearing the official party bumped down the grass to stop in front of the platform. For a moment all the chatter and the singing died down as word sped round that the mayor and the official welcoming committee had arrived.

At least it was a diversion and a derisory cheer went up, thousands of little Union Jacks were waved, and parents held up their offspring to witness the arrival. The Grapplewick brass band drum-rolled into the National Anthem but it was hopeless against the screaming obscenity of a rock band not fifty yards away. Even the bandmaster was having difficulty in hearing his musicians so a steady beat would have to suffice. A few of the town's leading citizens were already on the platform, and a gust of wind blew the strains of 'send her victorious, happy and ...' They rose to their feet but the mayor, unable to hear the band at all, graciously waved them down again, proud that they should stand for his arrival. He was also impressed by the fact that on the seats they were to occupy were badges and anti-fall-out hats, a touching gesture. As he settled himself he, like all the others, was absolutely amazed at the incredible sights around him. He'd also noticed the vast sea of vehicles in the car park as they arrived and at five pounds a time he didn't need a ready reckoner to know his ship had come in. He leaned across Florrie and tapped Norman's knee.

'You all right, Norman?'

Norman frowned at him, missing the words in the general hubbub. The mayor held up his thumb and Norman nodded and smiled back. He was convinced now that the Special Branch had made a mistake. Just look at the extraordinary spectacular extravaganza before him. How could the man from Androm possibly be a mortal, a common confidence trickster? Who else in the world could inspire a gathering such as this? And even if the whole thing turned out to be a gigantic hoax, what did it matter? He felt better and more mature for having met the man in the first place. The barber's shop in Coldhurst Street seemed a million miles away and even Benidorm didn't measure up. For the first time in his life Norman was actually thinking.

Some of the floodlights came on again, directed at the platform, and the dignitaries cringed, screwing up their eyes in the harsh white glare. And amid the general cacophony a chanting was being taken up, 'ee ... ee ... ee ... ee ... ee.' The bandmaster was still waving his baton for the National Anthem although most of the band had finished some time ago. The two carousels slowed to a halt, and the chant taken up by other sections of the crowd increased in volume.

'Speech ... speech ... speech ... speech.' The mayor licked his lips. The small Welsh garrison must have felt like this when confronted by the might of the Zulu hordes. 'Speech ... speech ... speech.' The cry was not accompanied by handclaps. Manfully the rock group tried to compete until somebody pulled the plug leaving them gyrating and striking noiseless guitars. It was several moments before they realised their tasteless mime was no longer backed up by the tape played through the enormous loudspeakers. The chant was louder now and the dignitaries on the platform rose and applauded.

The mayor, still seated, looked round at them and, realising what was expected of him, got to his feet. With an increased heartbeat that would have killed him if he'd noticed, he walked the three paces to the microphone. Thankfully the sheer mass of his audience was invisible behind the lights, but when the chanting died away it felt strangely lonely. He blew into the microphone to satisfy himself it was working, then he began.

'Fellow citizens of Grapplewick, we are all gathered here to welcome some very important people from afar.'

He was desperately trying to avoid words like spacecraft, modules and aliens, he hadn't expected to make a speech, and he realised that this was probably the most important address in his life. Indeed it might actually be *for* his life. He switched to neutral political ground.

'When I was a lad ... many years ago,' he added but nobody laughed. 'Many years ago I lay in this very field and looked up at the sky and thought, what is life, who am I and what am I doing here?'

A wag in the crowd shouted 'Trespassin'!' and a great roar of laughter went up. The mayor beamed at the unseen hordes. That's the ticket, he thought, keep it light and friendly. He turned to where he thought the interruption came from and said, 'You're right and I'm not ashamed to admit it. I *was* trespassing.'

This got a laugh as well from people who hadn't heard the interruption. The mayor was more relaxed now.

'No, but to be serious for a moment ... as I lay in this very field, I never thought I'd live to see the day when the whole of Grapplewick would congregate here in a body ... with such good fellowship and community spirit in your hearts.'

This raised a cheer and he took out his handkerchief to blow his nose. It wasn't an act, he was genuinely moved.

'And I tell you this,' he went on, 'I'm proud ... yes proud and humble to be your mayor.'

Some of the people round him clapped but he didn't hear anything beyond the lights so he went on, which was a mistake – they were getting restless. Faintly from the distance he heard, 'You'll neeeever walk alone' from the football supporters' club, and a rocket swooshed into the air. Behind the stage the heavy metal group and their road manager were frantically scurrying around with torches trying to locate the plug only to find that some bastard had cut the wires as well.

The mayor droned on about what a happy week it had been and this was a day one would be able to relate to one's children and one's children's children. He was waffling and regretted not sitting down when he'd said the proud and humble bit.

Norman fidgeted uncomfortably. 'Sit down, Uncle,' he thought, willing his uncle to do just that. If he'd been doing a turn at the music hall he'd have had the hook around his neck by now. He felt a tug at his sleeve and looking down he saw the editor. 'Oh, hello, Mr Whittaker,' he said.

'I think you'd better come with me, Norman.'

The lad frowned. 'Not now, Mr Whittaker. They could land at any moment. Didn't you hear the sonic booms?'

Whittaker looked away in exasperation, then turned his back to the platform. 'Look, lad,' he hissed, 'I haven't got time for games. I want to show you something before this lot string you up from the nearest lamp post.'

Norman hesitated for a moment, then jumped down while the editor cleaved a path through the crush and led him through to the car park. Meanwhile, the mayor was still struggling, sweat pouring down his face. His mouth was in a rictus of a smile as the crowd began to give him the slow handclap. Another chant began which the crowd soon took up: 'Nor-man, Nor-man, Nor-man.'

Thankfully, Norman didn't hear it; he was jolting back to Grapplewick in Whittaker's old jalopy.

'Yes, Mr Whittaker, just because he looks like the stage hypnotist doesn't necessarily mean that it's him.'

'It's him all right, The Great Firenzi. Oh, and by the way, his real name is Heinrich Adlon.' He glanced over at his passenger but Norman didn't like what he was hearing so had turned away. 'Oh yes, and we now know the identity of the blind man. God, he must have had a busy week!'

'How d'you mean?' asked Norman reluctantly.

'Well, it's my guess he not only set fire to your uncle's shop, but he's been up and down the town like Wee Willy Winkie, spreading all the new rumours and keeping the old ones going.'

Norman stared along the beams of the weak headlights, mulling this new information over, searching for flaws. 'OK then,' he said after some time, 'answer me this. If he was running about, spreading all these rumours, why did the spaceman insist that we all kept the secret?'

Whittaker turned on to the cobbles of Linney Lane. 'Psychology,' he muttered.

Norman frowned. 'I'm sorry? I'm not with you.'

'Clever, I'll admit, but if the mayor and the rest of you told everybody what had transpired at that meeting, they wouldn't have believed you. They would have thought that you'd all gone round the twist. By maintaining your secrecy and even denying that anything unusual had been said, you fuelled the rumours – especially when you went around wearing the badges.' He looked across to see how Norman was taking the news. 'By the way, I also talked to Jimmy Jackson, and somebody – I suspect you'll find it's your blind man – put the idea into his head about manufacturing "Beautiful Grapplewick" badges for the public at large.'

'So you think they were getting a rake off?'

'No ... That was pin money to them, but the badges did have a purpose. They weren't just window dressing but more of a yardstick. The more badges that were on display, the more people would turn up to Sagbottom's.'

This all fitted but Norman didn't want to be convinced. 'What about Kershaw's Croft?'

'Ah yes, Kershaw's Croft.' Whittaker pulled up at a stop sign and looked right and left before entering the high street, although for all the traffic about his could be the only car in the world.

'Tell me, Norman, when you saw the pair of them in Kershaw's, did they sparkle? I mean their space costumes, did they sparkle?'

Norman couldn't see what he was getting at but he remembered last Wednesday distinctly.

'No they didn't, just plain white like plastic, but I'm certain they didn't sparkle ... Why?'

The editor nodded with satisfaction. 'That's it then.'

'What's what?' said Norman, exasperated.

Mr Whittaker looked at him. 'Last week I found a couple of sequins at Kershaw's and I assumed they'd come off their costumes. But now I know I was wrong: you've cleared up another little loose end.'

'What loose end?' asked Norman impatiently.

The editor was in no hurry. He pulled into the kerb almost opposite the town hall and rasped on the handbrake.

'You told Chief Inspector James that when you hovered about in Kershaw's Croft, you looked down on the lights of Grapplewick and they were twinkling.'

'They *were* twinkling,' protested Norman.

The editor shook his head. 'They were twinkling, yes, but they weren't the lights of Grapplewick. They were sequins dangling on a black velvet background.'

Norman just gaped at him. 'Sequins,' he croaked eventually.

'Oh, yes, I spoke to a film director pal of mine and he put me on to it. Apparently it's an old studio trick to simulate distant lights in the background.'

Norman gazed unseeing through the windscreen. On reflection he had to admit to himself that the man hadn't allowed them to get too close, and he'd soon slid the cover back into place.

'But why?' he asked.

'Why what, Norman?'

'Well, if it was all a con trick, what did he get out of it? And why was it necessary to get everybody up on Sagbottom's Acres?'

The editor raised his hands. 'Just look around you, do you see anybody, any cars about?'

Norman shook his head.

'Well, that's it. It was imperative that Grapplewick was deserted.'

Norman looked at him blankly.

'Come with me for a minute, lad.'

He got out of the car and waited for Norman to join him.

'You'll not be fully convinced until you've seen this.'

They walked the two or three paces to the corner into Trafalgar Street, and Norman stopped dead in his tracks. Two cars were standing outside Lloyds Bank. Inside the bank, all the lights were blazing.

'Come on, lad, I want to show you what was in it for your spaceman.'

He took Norman's arm and together they walked through the impressive portals of the bank. The first person they saw was Chief Inspector James.

'Oh, it's you,' he said, lighting a cigarette.

Over his shoulder Norman could just make out other men; one was taking photographs, another dusting the twisted remains of a round steel door with a small brush. A blue fug still clung to the ceiling.

'By the way,' went on the inspector, 'thanks for the tip.'

The editor smiled. 'It was luck. I must have been the only man left in Grapplewick and even then if I hadn't taken the wrong turning getting up to Sagbottom's I'd have missed it.'

The Special Branch man nodded.

'Any leads on where they've gone?' asked the editor.

'Not yet, but it's only a matter of time. Airports are sealed up, road blocks and so forth, but I'm not optimistic, they had too much of a start. Still, at least we now know that all the letters weren't just the product of a diseased mind.'

The editor shook his head in admiration.

'What a build-up though: twelve months of UFOs Are Coming Wednesday until everybody gets fed up with the joke, then ignores it altogether.' He chuckled. 'He must have had his sights set on Grapplewick for a year.'

Whittaker looked at Norman pityingly. 'Come on, son,' he said. 'Let's get you sorted out.'

He was about to leave when he turned to the Special Branch man. 'Oh, by the way, I'd appreciate it if you could let me know how you get on.'

'Of course . . . we owe you one.' And they shook hands.

Out in the street the editor jerked his thumb towards the bank. 'That was the first sonic boom. The second was Barclays just up the road.'

Norman was numb. He returned to the car like a slow programmed robot. At the back of his mind he'd clung to the belief that they were all mistaken and the man was genuine. But after the devastation in the bank he was finally convinced: nothing mattered now. Wrong again – a tight feeling squeezed his stomach.

'What about Oomi?' he asked fearfully. 'Was she . . . er . . . was she part of the gang?'

'No, no,' smiled the editor, 'not in the way you mean. I spoke to her on the phone about an hour ago.'

'Spoke to her?' asked Norman.

'Yes, she's an actress and your spaceman asked her to play the part of his assistant . . . the money was good and as long as she stayed in her hotel room, apart from when she had to play Oomi of course, it was a doddle, money for old rope. She hasn't any idea that the whole thing was a set-up. She's under the impression that it was a documentary programme dealing with the gullibility of a small town, and the effects of mass hysteria.'

Norman's relief was almost audible and the editor glanced quickly at him. 'By the way,' he said, 'time's getting short if you want to pack a few things.'

'Pack?' asked Norman. 'What do I want to pack for?'

The editor put his indicator out unnecessarily and turned left towards where Norman lived. 'Listen, lad, in a few hours there's going to be a lot of very angry people looking for someone to hit, and I've got the feeling that you're the patsy, so your best bet is to make yourself scarce.'

He took one hand off the wheel to delve into his inside pocket, bringing out a wad of notes which he passed over to Norman.

'Take this, you'll need a bit and as everybody else seems to have made money out of it, let's just call it your share.'

Norman stared at the fistful of crispness in his hand. He'd never even seen so much money in his life. He looked at the editor suspiciously.

'What about you? You haven't made any money out of it, have you?'

'Not yet I haven't, but whichever way this story breaks I have an exclusive and that should make the *Bugle* solvent.'

'But I don't need all this,' protested Norman.

'Oh, yes you do. There's your train fare for a start, milk train to Manchester, Manchester to London, change there for Bogsea.' Whittaker put two fingers into his waistcoat pocket and pulled out a card. 'Here's the address. I've written it down.'

'Why on earth should I want to go to Bogsea?' asked Norman, not relishing the thought of travelling the length of England on his own.

'Why?' repeated Whittaker. 'Why? So I'll know where to contact you when the story breaks. The address I've given you is Ann Taylor's address.'

Norman looked at the card, bewildered. 'Who's Ann Taylor?'

'Didn't I mention it?' said Whittaker innocently. 'You probably know her better as Oomi.'

Norman's face brightened and suddenly he felt very good. He wanted to hug Whittaker; he nearly did, but just as they were sweeping into Feathering Road an ambulance bore down on them, racing from the opposite direction. Whittaker swerved to the side of the road to avoid a head-on collision and with a screech of tyres they got away with a side swipe. The ambulance however was not so lucky. It mounted the pavement and crashed into a wall. The two drivers, shaken but otherwise unhurt, got out to ascertain the damage to their vehicles and to themselves. Both were relieved to find that apart from slight shock there was nothing serious, and the ambulance had only superficial denting at the side. Whittaker was missing his rear bumper but this was no great loss. He didn't have a front one anyway.

'You shot out of there without stopping,' said the ambulance driver accusingly.

'I'm sorry, but I didn't expect to meet anyone tonight,' replied Whittaker. He wandered over to the ambulance but apart from the few dents it seemed all right.

The ambulance driver seemed quite unbothered as well. 'Don't worry about that. I've got to get to the hospital as quickly as possible. I've got two heart attacks in there.' His mate jumped down from the back.

'What the bloody hell's going on?' He nodded to the stretchers inside. 'This hasn't done them any good, you know . . .' He was cut short as another ambulance came screaming around the corner.

'Busy tonight,' said Whittaker unnecessarily.

'And then some,' replied the driver as he grated his gears to reverse the wounded ambulance away from the wall. His mate clambered into the back to check on the patients, ignoring the editor. Whittaker's blood was up, though, and he was determined to find out what all the sudden activity was about.

Sitting in the passenger seat, Norman fidgeted impatiently. Already he had forgotten about the near-miss accident for he was floating on a bed of elation. Later on that day he would be meeting Oomi again, only this time she would be a more human Ann Taylor. He thumped the dashboard in frustration as Whittaker, talking outside to the ambulance driver was obviously in no hurry. At last he seemed to finish his conversation, and slowly he strolled back towards the parked car. Come on, come on, Norman urged silently although he still had hours before the train was due to leave. Suddenly he jumped sharply as another ambulance with sirens blaring came hurtling around the corner and careered past at such high speed that the parked car swayed in its backwash. As if reminded of the urgency, the damaged ambulance across the road suddenly shot forward, causing Whittaker to stagger out of its way. He watched the disappearing tail lights thoughtfully as he opened the back door and casually chucked in his back bumper. He then opened the driver's door and flopped into his seat behind the wheel, but he didn't start the engine. Instead he just stared out of the windscreen.

'Trouble?' asked Norman after a time.

Whittaker looked at him strangely. 'You could say that,' he answered enigmatically.

Norman waited and after what seemed like ages the editor shook himself out of his thoughts. 'I don't think you'll be going to Bogsea after all,' he said, turning on the car engine.

Instantly Norman was bewildered; shattered would have been a more appropriate description. 'Not going to Bogsea?' he asked.

Whittaker found first gear and released the handbrake. As they shot forward he continued. 'That's right, Norman, we're going back to the moors.' He paused and his next words hit Norman like a lorry-load of wet fish.

'A flying saucer has just landed on Sagbottom's Acres.'

TWENTY-FOUR

A s the car struggled forward up the hill towards Sagbottom's, Norman craned forward in his seat to look up at the sky. The same golden glow hung over the area, but there were no fireworks now. The last time he had approached the field, a jumbled cacophony of noise had greeted his ears, but now, the straining noise of the clapped-out engine was intrusive in the silence.

Reaching the crest, Whittaker stopped the car and switched off the engine. They got out and apart from the sighing wind there wasn't a sound in the air. Below them in the amphitheatre they saw the same vast crowd as before, stretched out as far as the darkness would allow, but this time it was still and silent, gazing with rapt attention at a round sinister object in the centre of the field. Norman gulped and looked at Whittaker, who was equally overwhelmed. From their vantage point about half a mile away, the UFO looked no bigger than a table mat, but once up close they could imagine that it was very big indeed.

Leaving the car where it was they hurried down the slope towards the flying saucer. Their footsteps were muffled in the grass, but such was the silence surrounding them that many heads turned in their direction. Norman was eager to push his way forward to the platform, but Whittaker stopped him.

'Hang on a bit, lad. Let's see what's happening.'

Norman looked around him and for the first time he noticed that everyone was wearing their anti-fall-out gear. To his left he saw the platform where his uncle in his red robe and the vicar were wearing their yellow plastic hats. Feeling a little conspicuous he dragged his own from under his belt and put it on.

Whittaker, meanwhile, was standing on tiptoe staring at the spacecraft. There was something menacing in the way in which it just squatted there, with slits for windows around the side which glowed faintly in the floodlight beams. He whispered to the man next to him. 'How long has it been there?'

The man eyed him suspiciously. ''Ast thou been asleep or summat?' he hissed, then reluctantly he added, 'About half an hour I reckon.'

Whittaker wasn't satisfied. 'Just landed without warning, did it . . . or did it hover over the field first?'

The man pushed him away. He wanted to watch the saucer, not answer silly bloody questions. Whittaker turned to another man in front of him, who turned his head but his eyes remained on the saucer.

'I've just got here,' whispered Whittaker. 'What happened?' The man stepped back alongside him so that he could talk and look at the same time.

'Fantastic!' he replied. 'Fanbloodytastic! One minute it was dark and the next, whoosh! All of a sudden there were these bright lights in the sky . . . I thought it was fireworks for a minute but it was too bright for that . . . Then the whole of the sky lit up and I've never seen owt like it! When they went out, there it was where you see it now.' He pointed towards the field. 'Bloody creepy, I can tell you. I never believed in flying saucers up to now, but what can't speak can't lie.'

The man was a good foot shorter than Whittaker and he had to tilt his head back and hold on to his yellow hat so he could look into the editor's face.

'Bright lights they were!' he continued, his eyes widening at the memory. 'Bright and white!' He jerked his thumb at the scaffolding holding the arc lamps. 'Makes this lot look like my granny's gas mantle!'

'Are you satisfied now, Mr Whittaker?' The editor looked across at Norman and smiled. In his yellow oilskins he looked as if he was just about to launch a lifeboat.

'Just hang about a bit, lad, until we know what's happening.'

Norman decided that Mr Whittaker was a hard man to convince, but he stayed put and craned his neck to look again at the module.

Most surprisingly the person who lived within fifty yards of the spacecraft was totally unaware of the momentous goings-on at Sagbottom's Acres. Old farmer Crumpshaw, unused to the fresh air and excitement of the previous Sunday, was in bed where he'd been for the past three days. He didn't believe in doctors and so when he felt poorly he just drew all the curtains and hauled himself under the blankets, surfacing spasmodically to help himself to whisky or to use the bucket. Only when he felt better or the bucket was full did he venture out.

It was his dog Rex who awoke him, with forepaws on his bed, licking his face. Blinking his eyes, Crumpshaw grimaced. 'Get off me, you dirty little bugger!' he muttered, pushing Rex away from him. Wagging his tail furiously the dog scampered to his empty food bowl. Old Crumpshaw had no idea how long he'd been in bed but it was obvious that Rex wanted feeding. He swung his legs out on to the cold floor and rubbed his face. He was feeling better now, the sleep must have done him good, and judging by the light streaming in from under the curtains, it looked like being a fine day.

First he staggered to the kitchen and opened a tin of dog food, forking it into Rex's bowl. The dog, not having eaten for about two and a half days, devoured it as it came out of the tin, most of it never even reached the bowl. Crumpshaw wondered whether he should open another, but then decided that the dog could wait. First he would empty the slops and then perhaps have a fried egg. As he went back into the bedroom to pick up the bucket he remembered the biscuit tin and his fortune under the bed. Immediately he cheered up and decided that he would have two fried eggs and possibly some bacon as well. Slipping on his boots he shuffled into the yard and emptied the bucket down a drain.

As he was coming back into the house he stopped, realising that something was very wrong. It couldn't be day as the sky was black, but it was light over at Sagbottom's Acres. He walked over to the wall and his mouth fell open in disbelief. The field was brightly lit up and there were hundreds of people in it, all staring silently at some sort of black object in the middle of it. He shaded his eyes and looked harder. There were people as far as he could see, and they were all wearing yellow oilskin hats. Thousands of 'em. What the hell was going on? He remembered the old tales that his father used to tell him; tales of dark satanic rites where people came on to the moors to dance naked until the cock crowed. But what the dickens was the thing in the field that everybody was worshipping?

Anger now replaced his apprehension. If they wanted to play silly buggers then they could, but let 'em do it elsewhere. Muttering to himself he hurried back into his house and with trembling fingers loaded his double-barrelled shotgun. Some of the crowd nearest to his house had heard him emptying his slops, and the clatter of the bucket, but they were totally unprepared for the furious onslaught of the old man when he reappeared, bulldozing a path through them. A few turned angrily to see what the commotion was all about, but they soon made way on seeing him, a bearded patriarch in shirt and long johns waving a shotgun. He was obviously not a man to be argued with.

Crumpshaw came to the rope bordering the field and, lifting it up, he staggered in. A collective gasp went up but it was lost on him. He looked around at the awe-inspiring scene and all anger left him. He was now frightened. He turned fearfully to the round black object, but facing it gave him a new confidence. It certainly wasn't some devilish creature with horns and cloven hooves. Instead, the thing in the field looked benign and innocuous, like some great fat mushroom without a stalk.

Up on the platform the superintendent watched the little white figure in front of the UFO. Very soon the vicar saw what he was looking at and came over to join him. The two of them in their oilskin hats looked like a comic double act, but the time had passed for any humour.

'Well, do something, superintendent,' wailed the vicar.

Superintendent Smith looked at him. Hell would freeze first before he would set one foot into the field below him. He had his hat and badge on, but was that enough? He picked up a loudhailer and put it to his mouth.

'This is Superintendent ... endent Smith ... ith speaking ... king. For your own safety ... afety, leave the area ... rea ... immediately ... tely.'

The mayor went over to the superintendent. 'He won't hear you; it's old deaf Crumpshaw.'

Word went around the crowd like molten lava: 'It's old deaf Crumpshaw, it's old deaf Crumpshaw ...' Some of the older people genuflected in respect while very young children peered fearfully from behind their mothers' jeans. Crumpshaw indeed couldn't hear a thing but he noticed one or two uniformed policemen dotted around the field, so he guessed that whatever was going on must have had some form of official blessing. However, he was still undecided.

Back on the platform the superintendent, realising that he wasn't getting through to the old man down below, bent down to his sergeant. 'Go in there and get the pillock out!' The young sergeant gulped and turned to his right and left, but the two constables who had been behind him had magically vanished. It looked like he was the muggins.

'And sergeant, better give him one of these.' The superintendent handed him a sou'wester. The sergeant took it with ill grace and sidled slowly into the field, holding the hat before him as if it were a peace offering. The crowd waited expectantly. They weren't experts on neutrons or fall-out, but they all agreed that the sergeant was a brave man. Sweating now, and constantly pushing up his hat, which kept sliding down over his eyes, the young sergeant advanced slowly. If radiation didn't get him then there was always the shotgun.

Crumpshaw watched him approach and was confused. If he was going to be arrested then why didn't the man just get on with it? Why didn't he come straight up instead of crouching and tiptoeing towards him holding out that hat? Involuntarily the farmer took a step back and as he did so he stumbled over a tussock. As he fell his fingers closed on the trigger and a blast erupted from the barrel. People gasped and screamed and the sergeant fell flat on his face. He wasn't hit; it was just a reflex action on his part. In fact the shot hadn't even been discharged in his direction.

Crumpshaw was dazed. Still weak from his three days in bed, it took him a couple of minutes to struggle into a sitting position. In front of him the policeman was kneeling on all fours and gazing, not at him but over his shoulder. With a puzzled expression on his face, Crumpshaw turned and faced the great black mushroom behind him – which was now sagging and crumbling into a shapeless mass. The police sergeant was the first to recover. Rising to his feet he carefully approached the hissing, contracting black blob. The farmer and his shotgun forgotten, he raised his arm slowly to feel the object which was rapidly sinking into the field. With ever-growing confidence he brushed his hand over the surface and smelled his fingers. 'It's rubber,' he muttered. He moved over to one of the slitted windows that had reflected the arc lights and touched that surface. It felt tacky, and when he looked at his fingers they were glowing. Increduously he turned to the distant platform and shouted to his superior, 'It's luminous paint, sir!' He didn't know whether his explanation had been heard so he held up his hand to show his bright fingertips. This acted as a signal. Suddenly one flashbulb went off and soon camera flashes were rippling through the packed assembly like so many fireflies on a black summer's night.

All the dignitaries were on their feet now, and a murmur was stalking through the crowd. They were still unsure about what was happening but convinced that whatever it was, it was definitely not in the script. The superintendent spoke into the microphone, calling for calm and insisting that everybody stayed where they were. He then jumped down and entered the field, warily approaching his sergeant. The town clerk laboriously helped the mayor down from the platform and he followed the superintendent into the field, together with the fire chief and the more inquisitive members of the public. The area seemed harmless enough and soon scores of people were scrambling over the ropes and moving into the field. The police, however, were quicker, and linked arms to form a cordon around the dying rubber space module.

Whittaker jerked Norman's arm. 'I think it really is now time I got you on that train,' he whispered, but Norman remained rooted to the spot, fascinated by the scene before him. Angrily the editor came back and whirled him around. 'Pull that silly bloody hat over your face in case anybody recognises you. You're coming out with me.'

Norman didn't argue and slowly and imperceptibly they backed out of Sagbottom's Acres. When it was safe to do so they turned and ran for the car. Behind them the UFO was now nearly flat on the grass. The superintendent and fire chief circled it cautiously, looking for any clues as to where it might have come from. One of the firemen who had also been examining the saucer called them over, pointing to the ground. Two or three yards away from the rubber mass was a piece of piping that just protruded above the surface of the ground. The fire chief knelt down and sniffed it. 'Well, that explains the lights,' he said.

'Lights?' asked the superintendent.

'The bright lights that preceded this thing.' He kicked the pipe gently. 'When we dig this up, we'll find it's an eight-inch mortar which fires a flare. We used to call 'em Bengal Lights.'

The superintendent looked at him. 'And this was the light in the sky?'

The fire chief shrugged. 'Oh, I think when we search the area we'll find one or two more of these, all set to go off simultaneously.'

'What was the object of that exercise?' asked the mayor, butting in. The fire chief ignored him and knelt again, lifting up a segment of the heavy rubber to scoop the dirt away from another piece of metal. He shone his torch at the exposed piece and examined it carefully. Finally he rose to his feet and dusted the earth from his hands. 'We'll soon have that dug out,' he said. 'But a pound to a pile of goat droppings that'll be one of the cylinders that inflated the damn thing.'

'You think there's more than one?' asked the superintendent.

'I should think so,' replied the fire chief. 'They'd have to be pretty powerful to inflate this thing in under two minutes.' He turned to the mayor. 'In answer to your question, sir, bright lights, everybody looks up, and for a time we're all blinded. By the time we get our vision back this thing has inflated like a bloody great chocolate soufflé.'

The mayor nodded. 'Yes, I was blinded for quite some time.'

'And then to add to that lot,' continued the fire chief, 'each of them flares is equal to a million candle power.'

The mayor turned to the superintendent. 'Your lads have been up here since Sunday. They must have been walking around with their eyes closed!'

Superintendent Smith grabbed his arm and led him a couple of yards away so they wouldn't be overheard. 'The man, smart-arsed Jack, phoned me on Saturday night.' The mayor looked puzzled but the superintendent carried on. 'The spaceman,' he whispered, 'he warned me not to venture inside the landing area as it was already charged with neutrons or something like that. He said that a homing device had already been laid to guide down the module.'

The mayor nodded understanding and turned to Florrie, who by this time had pushed her way through the crowd to be beside her husband. 'How did it come down?' she whispered breathlessly.

The mayor raised his eyes to heaven. 'It didn't,' he hissed, 'it came up.' This left her more confused than ever.

Superintendent Smith gazed around at the sea of confused faces and decided that the moment had come for him to make a tactical withdrawal. At the moment the crowd was in a state of shock and bewilderment, but this moment wouldn't last and he didn't want to be around when it wore off. He turned to his hapless sergeant and whispered in his ear. Within seconds a gangway had been cleared through the spectators and the superintendent strode purposefully through it as if he were off to make further investigations. He didn't fool the mayor, however, who scampered off after him, leaving Florrie to fend for herself.

In fact they needn't have panicked. The crowd was more interested in the pile of black rubber which was lying in the field, and some of the more adventurous ones were already carving it up for souvenirs. As it was, for three or four weeks after the event unscrupulous dealers were selling pieces of rubber from the fake spacecraft at exorbitant prices, although the amount of rubber that changed hands would have been sufficient to have covered at least ten miles of the M1.

The whole extravaganza had been brilliantly orchestrated, from the very first contact in the barber's shop to the carnival at Sagbottom's Acres. Every step had been carefully calculated and carried out with meticulous timing, but it wasn't over yet. The Great Firenzi was still at large with a fortune at his disposal. For him the world was a plateful of Whitstables, but there were forces out to find him. Interpol had already been alerted, but they would be of no use if he was still in Great Britain. Nobody could be sure of where he was; but one thing was for certain. He wasn't on his way back to the planet Androm in Kershaw's Croft.

Part III

BOGSEA – BEACHY HEAD, SUSSEX

TWENTY-FIVE

A s the train pulled out of Manchester, Norman settled back in a window seat and opened his newspaper; *The Times*, no less. He'd no intention of reading it, it was merely to conceal himself from the other passengers and from the way everybody else flipped open their dailies, they weren't too keen to be seen either. He gazed sightlessly at the newsprint, thoughts tumbling in a shapeless, chaotic mess through his already over-taxed brain. Uppermost in his mind was the spaceman, or The Great Firenzi, or whatever. The sheer nerve and effrontery of the man was unbelievable. Had he been on the side of law and order what a great prime minister he would have made. But then again, had he been on the side of law and order he wouldn't have been a politician.

Norman smiled ruefully to himself when he thought of the dangling sequins in Kershaw's Croft. But they *had* looked like lights. Anybody would have been fooled, and even had he seen through the deception, there's no telling what might have happened. There was a ruthless streak to the man – the burning down of his uncle's shop, that wasn't an illusion, that was cold, calculated, wanton destruction. Norman tried to find logical explanations for the man's sequence of trickery but there still remained one or two imponderables. How had he managed the Indian lady? He couldn't have been able to see her, let alone predict her movements precisely. And there again it was never explained how his accomplice had managed to fire the shop at exactly the right moment. His thoughts raced on. Had old, deaf Crumpshaw not accidentally shot the space module, they'd all still be up on Sagbottom's Acres staring at it. And with at least eight hours' start, the man could have been anywhere. As it turned out, he'd been within a hair's breadth of being caught red-handed by the editor. Two unforeseen slices of bad luck, but still he'd managed to evade capture and disappear.

The train jerked into Stockport and Norman blinked out of his reverie. He was still holding his newspaper exactly as when he'd left Manchester and he was overwhelmed with embarrassment. People would think he was a slow reader and had just mastered the headlines. He flapped it open to the centre pages and hid himself again, and as the train eased out of the station his thoughts returned. How had the detective from Special Branch . . . James, that was him . . . how had he managed to identify the man so quickly? But then Norman was unaware of the vital information passed on by Madame Lesley. His weary brain, unused to overtime, shied away from the problems. All in all it had been one helluva week, and probably the most important in his life. Seven days in which he'd emerged from his chrysalis to become an adult. Never again would a package tour to Spain with a bunch of his mates appeal to him. The barber's shop which had been his world was no more, and rather sadly he had to admit to himself that the sun didn't rise and set on Grapplewick. It was a discovery that gave him no comfort.

Norman was genuinely fond of his uncle and aunt, and he had been reasonably happy living with them, just a pleasant empty vessel floating aimlessly from one meal to the next. Part of him wanted to get off at the next station and speed back home to hide his face in the bosom of mediocrity, but his new-found strength resisted the urge. The Great Firenzi had inadvertently pointed him in the direction of a harder, more competitive life, and it scared him a little. A wave of depression engulfed him, but lifted just as suddenly when he thought of Oomi, or to be more exact, Ann Taylor. The new name wasn't as exotic but it didn't matter. She was the same girl and, more important, she was innocent. She had been deceived just the same as everybody else.

Lulled by the mesmeric rhythm of the wheels, Norman dozed against the cool pane of the window, mercifully missing Rugby and Newport Pagnell. He awoke to see the dark, dreary, tall buildings of Euston Station beckoning to him. Immediately he was gripped by panic – he was alone in London! According to his uncle's atlas, London was the hub of the British Empire. He was amazed at the amount of people running, walking and dodging each other as if they all knew exactly where they were going, and all were obviously late for whatever it was they were hurrying to. A tannoy blared incomprehensibly and the tempo of the crowd quickened. Norman found himself swept along the concourse towards the Underground, but he soon figured out that that was where he wanted to go, so he didn't resist. He couldn't understand why everybody was in such a state. They weren't even content to stand still on the escalator and enjoy the adverts but had to push past him and leap down two stairs at a time. Did they know something he didn't? Was there some sort of emergency, or were Londoners like this all the time?

At the bottom of the stairs there were several openings to platforms with destination boards, but the rushing torrent of people didn't give him a chance to read them. Central line, Circle line flashed past, and what the hell was Bakerloo? He began to panic again so when he saw the large 'Way Out' sign he took it.

Back on ground level he breathed deeply to rid himself of his claustrophobia, and looked around. In the street it was just the same as below; thousands of men and women all looking worried and rushing around as if there was a curfew. Suddenly Norman remembered the money Whittaker had given him. He took it out of his back pocket and hailed a taxi, which turned out to be a very good investment. Forgetting his hunger and his tiredness he looked out of the taxi window and began to enjoy himself. He saw many large, impressive buildings that made Grapplewick Town Hall look like a gatehouse. His head swivelled from side to side as they drove over Waterloo Bridge. St Paul's was to the left and Big Ben and the Houses of Parliament were to the right. He was amazed at the width of the Thames; the river Ribble flowed through Grapplewick and he could spit across that.

Owing to the volume of traffic, the taxi never exceeded twenty miles per hour, so for Norman his trip was a wonderful sightseeing tour. On reaching Waterloo he wished his journey could have been longer – that is until the cabbie told him his fare. Good grief, he could have bought a suit for that back home!

After a wash and brush-up and a quick snack at the station, Norman boarded a suburban train for Bogsea. There weren't many passengers at that time in the afternoon and Norman dozed again until the station announcer woke him with an 'All change ... Bogsea, all change ... Bogsea.' His heart beat faster; this was the end of the line in more ways than one. He squared his shoulders and strode to the ticket barrier. He wasn't a hick any more. After all, he'd got here, hadn't he? And under his own steam too.

The big burly man at the gate clipped his ticket and it was only when Norman had passed through that he stopped. There was something familiar about the man. Norman eased back ostensibly to read the destination boards, but he surveyed the railwayman covertly and suddenly he knew what it was. Pinned on his lapel was a *white plastic badge*.

Norman was staggered. He couldn't read the lettering from where he was standing and before he could edge nearer, the man turned his back and hurried through a door marked STAFF. It wasn't just a coincidence, though: other people were wearing badges. The woman in the newspaper kiosk was one of them. He waited until she was attending to a customer then he strolled across and was able to read the lettering: 'Bogsea is bracing.'

'Yes, luv, what can I get for you?'

He stared at her uncomprehendingly for a moment. 'Oh, er, have you got the, er, *Times*?'

'I'm sorry luv, not this late, they've all gone.'

He nodded and was about to walk away when he saw the headlines of the *Evening Standard*: BIG BANK ROBBERY. He took the paper and put the money on the counter.

'Fourteen million they got away with,' said the lady. 'How they could blow open two banks and get away without anybody knowin' is beyond me.'

It wasn't beyond Norman though. Nostalgia flooded his mind as he thought of Lloyds and Barclays banks in Grapplewick, dear little Grapplewick. He frowned at his momentary weakness and went out to the taxi rank. It wasn't far to Ann Taylor's address, just long enough to give him time to read the article. In fact he read it twice, but there was no mention of the spaceman, or Sagbottom's Acres. For some reason or other it was being kept out of the newspapers but why? And were the 'Bogsea is bracing' badges anything to do with UFOs, and if so when were they supposed to land? More than ever he was eager to see Ann Taylor; she would have the answer to that. He swayed forward as the taxi pulled up outside an ordinary semi-detached suburban house.

Ann had obviously been expecting him because just as he entered the front gate she was at the door. She smiled, but it wasn't particularly warm, it was the sort of greeting you'd give to a delivery man.

'Did you have a good journey?' she said, standing to one side so he could come in.

'Yes, thanks.'

He waited till she'd closed the door, then followed her into the lounge. A man with his back to him was talking quietly on the phone. His heart plummeted – was it her husband? Never once had he thought of her being married. But then again, why not? Red juicy apples don't hang on trees for long when some greedy bastard with a ladder comes by. But he needn't have worried. The man turned to look at him and Norman relaxed, then immediately he was uptight again. It was Chief Inspector James of the Special Branch.

'Right sir, I'll keep you informed.' And he put the phone down.

'Ah, so you got here then.'

Norman nodded and they all stood looking at one another like Act Three in a bad provincial theatre. Ann was the first to break out of the deadlock.

'Well,' she said with forced cheerfulness, 'have you had anything to eat, er . . .'

'Norman,' he broke in, amazed at his own temerity. 'No thanks, I had a meal in London.'

It sounded good and cosmopolitan. No way would he admit that his meal was a dead hamburger at the station buffet.

James sighed. 'Look, why don't we all sit down? I have a few things I'd like straightened out.'

Ann sat on the settee against the wall, and the two men in armchairs facing each other, but before the policeman could begin, Norman blurted out the question he'd pondered in the taxi.

'What about the badges "Bogsea is bracing"? Why are they wearing those?'

James shrugged. 'Same reason you had "Beautiful Grapplewick".'

Norman stared at the chief inspector, mouth wide open, then he remembered Ann was present and he shut it.

'You mean they think UFOs are going to land?'

The policeman smiled. 'Grapplewick did.'

Norman ignored this. 'Yes, but when? When are they going to land?'

'Tonight.'

'Tonight?' Norman was flabbergasted. 'Tonight,' he repeated. 'But how – I mean the man was up north yesterday. Well, he couldn't have left Grapplewick much before midnight.'

'Ah yes,' said Ann, 'but immediately after the meeting in the town hall at Grapplewick last Thursday morning, he came down here and set this one up.'

Norman couldn't quite take this all in. 'You mean, do the same thing here?'

Ann nodded. 'I'm afraid so, a carbon copy job except that he didn't burn down a barber's shop, he set fire to the mayor's house instead. The burgling and the banks were news to me. Chief Inspector James told me.'

Norman looked at the policeman who raised his eyebrows as if to say, 'Satisfied now?' but Norman wasn't. It was a bit too rich for his apprentice brain.

'But the blind man – Mr Whittaker told me he was in Grapplewick all the time.'

'He was, the man here was another accomplice, and also ...' she hesitated and lowered her head, 'another Oomi.'

'Well obviously,' said Norman. 'You couldn't be in two places at once.'

Chief Inspector James sighed. 'I'm sorry to interrupt, but I have work to do.' He turned to Ann. 'To continue where we left off, how did you get up to Kershaw's Croft and back again?'

'He had a camper, you know, like a mobile caravan, which he parked round the back, then afterwards he ran me back to the town and dropped me off near the hotel.'

James nodded. 'That figures, we found the tracks out the back and it had to be either a camper or a four-wheel drive. We're checking that out now.'

Norman squirmed with embarrassment when he thought of that night in Kershaw's Croft.

'I'll bet you thought we were a right couple of Herberts,' he muttered bitterly.

Instinctively Ann reached out and touched his knee.

'Oh no,' she said earnestly, 'that's not true ... Well, partly; he thought your uncle was a bit ... well, a bit gullible, but he was impressed with you. As a matter of fact after you'd gone he said we had to go careful with you. He's the one to watch, he said, he's unpredictable.'

Norman looked at her and it was Ann's turn to blush. The chief inspector sniffed. He hadn't missed the exchange but before he could continue his interrogation, a bleeper chirped twice and he took a radio from an inside pocket.

'James,' he said into it, and after listening for a few moments he said, 'OK, I'll be out shortly and we'll tour the banks. Out.' He stuffed it back into his pocket.

Norman's eyes widened. 'Do you think he'll do the banks here?'

'I hope so,' said the policeman, 'but I very much doubt it. Every bank within a five-mile radius is being watched, but I think he's smarter than that.'

'How do you mean?' asked Norman.

'Well, for a start only half of the town have made the pilgrimage up to Beachy Head. There's still too many people about. Apparently they didn't fall for it.'

'And we did,' growled Norman, flagellating himself.

Again Ann shook her head. 'Don't feel too badly about it, Norman. There's an international match on telly tonight at half past seven, live from Wembley, and that's more important to a lot of people than a spacecraft landing. That doesn't say much for the people of Bogsea, does it?'

Norman silently agreed, but he glanced covertly at his watch to see if he'd missed it. Again the bleeper demanded attention. 'James,' said the policeman into his radio. He held it to his ear while he listened, then said, 'Well, he's bottled up here somewhere . . . yes, the minor roads are most important . . . OK, out.'

Norman was impatient with a question.

'How did you know that he'd be pulling the same stunt here?' he asked.

'We didn't until last night,' answered the chief inspector, picking up his hat. 'Your Mr Whittaker gave us Miss Taylor's address, and I assigned two of our lads to keep an eye on the house. Well, they spotted the badges and the activity in the town and it didn't take 'em long to piece two and two together.'

He turned to Ann. 'I'll be off now, but thanks for your help.'

She rose to show him out. 'See you later, Norman,' he said. 'I must ask you not to leave the house. I may be back with more questions.' He hurried down the short drive. It was getting dark.

As he got to the gate he stopped and walked back to the girl. 'Just as a precaution,' he said softly, 'don't draw the curtains.'

Norman was still standing when she returned.

'Sit down, Norman,' she said. 'I appreciate you standing up every time I do, but I think we know each other better than that.'

He blushed and lowered his head. Now the chief inspector had left, all Norman's new-found poise and sophistication seemed to have accompanied him straight out the door.

'Can I get you a cup of tea or something?'

'Tea will be fine,' he mumbled and she went into the kitchen. He was about to sit down again but then changed his mind. In a momentary flash of insight he saw himself through her eyes, a bumbling stumblebum well placed for a gold medal in a prat show. Sternly he straightened his tie and strode in after her. She turned when he came into the kitchen and smiled.

'Do you like it strong?' she asked.

'It doesn't matter,' he replied. He had more important things on his mind than the strength of tea. 'Er, Ann . . . the man, well, you know . . . the spaceman . . . well, when he came to the meeting in the town hall he was suddenly there, and when he went he seemed to disappear. I talked to one or two other people but nobody remembers him. What I mean is, how did he manage to arrive without anybody seeing him?'

She smiled as she spooned the tea into the pot. 'Same way as I did,' she answered. 'An old man walked up the steps and into the toilet on the first floor near your uncle's office. In his carrier bag was a smart suit, and all he had to do was change and walk into the meeting. On the way out he did exactly the same, but in reverse.'

Norman's eyes widened. 'And you did the same?'

'Well, yes . . . except I used the ladies.'

He looked long and hard at her. The man was a genius – he hadn't missed a trick. There was still one burning question to be answered, though.

'What about the Indian woman on the street?' he began.

'That was me,' Ann replied.

'I guessed as much,' Norman replied hotly, 'but why Indian?'

Ann giggled and Norman frowned. Instantly she became contrite. 'Oh, Norman, I'm not laughing at you, I was remembering how I looked and felt when I spent that time traipsing up and down in front of that bike shop before I got the signal.'

'Signal?' he asked, and she put the teapot down and faced him.

'I had a bleeper on me, like Chief Inspector James's, only when mine bleeped I had to stagger to the wall. When I was bleeped again I had to fall down, and that's when they carried me into the shop.' She giggled again. 'I genuinely nearly did have a heart attack when they laid me on the floor. I was so scared that they'd hear the bleeper that I kept moaning to cover the sound of it.'

Norman smiled with her. 'I'll tell you something,' he said, 'it fooled us completely.'

Ann poured the boiling water into the pot. 'Before you ask,' she said, 'I had to be Indian because a long sari would hide my legs and the pregnancy disguised my shape.' She put down the kettle and turned to face him. 'And you realise the brilliance of his thinking? I had to be coloured as no European could faint without first turning deathly pale.' She looked earnestly at Norman. 'Don't you think that's clever?'

He shook his head in wonder. 'He's going to be a hard man to catch.'

Across the street, Detective Chief Inspector James sat in the front of the unmarked police vehicle, receiving information and issuing orders. Not surprisingly a wide search of all the trailer parks and camp sites had drawn a blank. He'd also spoken to all of his surveillance teams positioned outside every bank in Bogsea, but everything was as normal. Suddenly his radio crackled into life. 'Team Three, Lloyds.' He pressed the button on his radio. 'Go ahead, Team Three.'

'A white Ford saloon has just parked about one hundred yards from the target.'

James thumbed his mike. 'Can you see who's in the car?'

There was a slight pause. 'No, the occupants are not visible from here . . . hang on . . .' The chief inspector waited. 'Yes, two men have got out and locked the car doors . . . They're moving in the opposite direction. They're too far away to identify . . . Over.'

'OK, one of you follow them but don't apprehend, just keep them in view. We'll be round there just as quick as we can. Out.' He lowered the radio from his mouth and spoke to the sergeant next to him. 'Where is Team Three?'

'Ashton Street, sir. About five minutes from here.'

'Let's go,' ordered James. 'Don't drive too fast, though, make it look natural.'

The local officer looked into the rearview mirror and eased away from the kerb. After fifty yards or so he turned left into a major road that led directly towards the bank. No sooner had he rounded the corner than a dark blue van pulled into the space vacated by him and two men in raincoats got out. One of them opened the back doors of the van and two uniformed policeman got out, taking their places in the front seats. No words were exchanged, but one of the men in the raincoats raised his hand and spread his fingers to indicate five minutes. Then the two of them walked across the road to Ann Taylor's house.

Norman was beginning to relax. The tea was doing him good and Ann had switched on the electric fire, infusing the lounge with the warm glow of intimacy. 'Any more questions?' she asked mischievously from the armchair opposite.

He smiled. 'Not that I can think of.'

After a moment of silence he put down his teacup and leaned forward earnestly. 'You know, Ann, I think meeting you was the most important day of my life.' She looked at him seriously but before he could continue they were interrupted by the ringing of the doorbell and the spell was broken.

'That's probably Chief Inspector James,' Ann said as she went reluctantly to the door, but she was wrong. The hall light fell upon two men in raincoats.

'Special Branch,' one of them said, and proffered his card for identification. Ann didn't bother examining it.

'You'd better come in then,' she said and they stepped past her, waiting for her to close the front door. They then followed her into the lounge. She gestured towards Norman. 'This is . . .'

The taller of the two broke in. 'Yes, Miss Taylor, we know who he is. Chief Inspector James would like him down at the station to identify a couple of people. It shouldn't take long and Inspector Simpson will wait here with you to keep you company while he's gone.'

Norman rose to his feet and smiled at Ann. 'OK, I'll be as quick as I can.'

She took his hands. 'Quicker than that, I hope,' she said softly.

Norman looked at her, then whirled around, clapping the detective on the back. 'Lead on Macduff,' he said cheerfully, and practically skipped out of the house. Ann hurried over to the window to watch him go, but the police officer with her was quicker; he drew the curtains and faced her.

'Why did you do that?' she asked.

'I think it best if we sit down,' he advised, but she remained where she was.

Something was wrong, she only wanted to see Norman off. It wasn't against the law, was it? The man took her arm, not gently either. 'I think you'd better sit down,' he repeated and shoved her to the armchair.

'Who do you think you're pushing?' she said angrily. 'This is my house, and I'll . . .'

He plonked her down. 'Sit,' he commanded. 'Now don't give me a hard time, just keep your trap shut.'

She stared at him. 'You're not from Special Branch, are you?'

He leaned towards her. 'I won't tell you again, shut it.'

She waited until he was seated opposite, then leaped out of her chair to the door, but again he moved swiftly, deceptively so for his build, and grabbing her arm he pulled her round and back-handed her across the face. Eyes wide she stared at him, despising the tears that rolled down her cheeks. It wasn't so much the pain of the blow, but the desperation of knowing that Norman was in trouble, in deep trouble.

Chief Inspector James walked into the half-empty pub, wincing at the deafening pop music that was almost mandatory in places such as this.

'What are you having?' he asked his companion.

'I'll have a half of bitter, thanks.'

'Two halves of bitter,' he shouted to the landlord, although there was only the width of the bar between them.

The man nodded and as he took two glasses over to the pumps, the chief inspector turned and leaned his elbows on the bar.

'Where are they?' he asked softly.

The detective glanced casually round and as he lit a cigarette he murmured, 'In the corner by the juke box.'

They nodded to each other in silent toast as they took a mouthful of the flat, unexciting brew, carried their glasses casually over to where the two youths were sitting, pulled out a couple of vacant chairs and sat. The young men looked at them warily. There were other empty tables, why did they want to sit here? James took a long swig from his glass, then took his identification quietly from his inside pocket.

'Chief Inspector James, Special Branch,' he said, 'And this is Detective Sergeant McCumber.'

One of the youths looked wildly round but there was no way of escape. They were in the corner and to get out they would have to pass the heavies, and that wasn't a sensible option.

'What's up, then?' asked one of them with transparent bravado.

'Which one of you owns the white Ford?'

'What white Ford? What're you talking about? We don't know nothing about a white Ford.'

Chief Inspector James finished his drink. 'OK, let's continue this at the station. On your feet.'

One of them blustered, 'Hang on a minute, what about our rights? I mean I'm not going anywhere, I've done nothing.'

James leaned over the table. 'I haven't got time to play silly buggers. Now are you going to walk out of here nice and easy, or do I have to drag you out?'

Slowly they rose to their feet and as they did so, strong hands gripped their arms and they were hustled out and round the corner to the white Ford. Once there the detectives pushed them roughly against the car, slapped their hands on to the roof and spread-eagled their legs, searching swiftly until James delved into the side pocket of one of their bomber jackets and produced a set of ignition keys. He tossed them to his colleague whilst he held on to the collars of the two unfortunates.

'Try them for size,' he said.

The detective inserted one of the keys and the door opened smoothly.

'OK, cuff 'em,' and in a few seconds both youths were handcuffed and hustled into the front seats of the car.

Chief Inspector James slammed the door, then climbed into the back seat. 'Now,' he started, 'I haven't got much time so I want some quick answers, OK?' He leaned forward between them. 'Where did you get this car from?'

The two youths stared out of the windscreen, both acutely conscious of the chief inspector's face turning from one to the other.

James sighed. 'OK, you want it the hard way.'

He grabbed the long hair of one of the youths and jerked his head back viciously. The pimply face screamed, more with shock than anything else, and the detective outside the car looked quickly up and down the deserted street. The youth yelped again as James tugged once more until the man's head was arched over the back of the seat.

'It belongs to a mate of ours,' he gasped.

James yanked again. 'Listen, Sonny Jim, we've checked and this car was stolen not ten miles from here this morning.'

'Stolen?' the youth asked apprehensively. 'We didn't know nothing about that, honest, that's the God's truth. If we'd known it was stolen we wouldn't have had no part of it.'

James released the other man's hair and took out a handkerchief to wipe his fingers. 'OK, let's hear it.'

The youth didn't hesitate. 'We were in the pub about half past two and this bloke came up to us and asked if we'd just park the car for him.'

'This afternoon?' asked James quickly.

'No, he asked us this afternoon and said he'd be back this evening, and if we weren't going to Beachy Head to see the Saucer would we park it then – outside the bank.'

The words were tumbling out now and the other had joined in.

'Tall geezer, well spoken, he said not to ask any questions and he gave us a century each.'

The chief inspector looked from one to the other, then apparently satisfied he stepped out of the car slamming the door behind him.

'Book 'em,' he said to the local detective.

'Yes sir, what's the charge?'

Chief Inspector James shrugged. 'I dunno,' he said, 'parking on a double yellow,' and he crossed the road to where his own car waited.

'Any developments?' he asked as he eased into his seat.

'Not a dicky bird, sir.'

James grunted and stared sightlessly through the windscreen. Something was niggling him, some unformed thought at the back of his mind. The two youths were harmless Jack-the-lads overjoyed at the hundred pounds for the easiest job they were likely to get, but why? It had to be his man who'd put them up to it. But for what purpose? And suddenly he knew.

'Back to Ann Taylor's place,' he barked. 'And don't spare the horses.'

The driver screeched away from the kerb and Chief Inspector James thumped his knee impatiently, silently castigating himself. What a dummy, what a thickhead he'd been. Of course, the Ford was a decoy – that's all it was – and it had succeeded brilliantly. They had drawn him away from the house. He clenched his fists

– if anything had happened to Norman or Ann he swore he'd make the man pay. All the frustrations and humiliations of the past twelve months welled up inside him. By God, he'd have the man if it was the last thing he ever did.

James was out of the car before it had stopped. 'Get around the back,' he spat at his driver, 'and are you armed?'

The local officer stared at him. 'No, sir, we weren't issued with any.'

James looked towards the house and tugged a 9 mm automatic pistol from his shoulder holster. He handed it over to the officer. 'Take mine. It's not standard but it's better than most.'

The officer hefted it in his hands. 'I'll manage, sir.'

'Good. I'll give you five minutes to get round the back. If anybody comes charging out, shoot, OK? Forget all that crap about fair play, just shoot first. Do you understand? We're dealing with a high roller!'

The officer hesitated for a moment and then hared for the corner of the street. James looked at his watch and waited.

There was silence in the room. Ann sat stony-faced staring at the glowing bars of the electric fire while the man, still in his raincoat, lounged in the armchair opposite, eyes half-closed, nursing a glass of whisky. He was, however, alert and instantly stiffened as the front doorbell chimed. He immediately jumped to his feet and his hand moved quickly to an inside jacket pocket, retrieving an ugly grey revolver. Ann drew a sharp breath and felt herself trembling. 'See who it is,' he hissed, 'and whoever it is, get rid of them.' Ann hesitated. 'It might be Chief Inspector James,' she said, halfway between hope and panic.

The man thought quickly. 'OK, just tell him your boyfriend's gone to the town to look for him, and I'm your Uncle Jack.'

'What if he doesn't believe me?' she wailed.

In response the man smiled without humour. 'Then it'll be too bad for you both.'

The doorbell chimed again and he thrust her towards the door. 'Don't forget now – don't be clever or I'll blow his head off.'

Ann opened the door slowly and Chief Inspector James smiled down at her. 'Mind if I come in for a minute?' he said. 'I'd like a few words with Norman.'

Ann felt the presence of the man behind her. 'I'm sorry,' she replied, 'but Norman's gone to town looking for you.' Although she was an actress this wasn't a role she relished, and to her ears her voice sounded false and stilted.

James peered over her shoulder and she turned. 'Oh ... That's my Uncle Jack.' If this was an audition, she certainly wouldn't get the part.

Still smiling, James walked past her. 'Chief Inspector James, pleased to meet you.' He held out his hand. For a second the man hesitated, then they shook hands. The gun had been returned to its pocket. Ann was still holding the door open. 'Do you mind if I come in and wait for him then?' asked the policeman. 'I can only spare a couple of minutes so let's hope Norman hurries back quickly.'

Ann glanced at the man who gave a slight nod. 'Of course,' she said, closing the door. 'Come through.'

The three of them walked into the lounge where the policeman remained standing while the other man sat down in his armchair, outwardly relaxed but all spring and steel inside. Ann sat opposite, desperately trying to think of a way in which to warn the policeman, who seemed completely at ease, jingling loose change in his pocket. 'I suppose Ann's told you what the flap's about,' he asked casually. The man nodded and sipped his drink although his eyes never left the chief inspector.

'Ah well,' sighed James, 'I wouldn't have minded a glass of whisky myself but I think I'd better be off before temptation gets the better of me.' He took his hand out of his pocket to look at his watch and as he did so a few coins spilled out and fell on to the carpet. Instinctively the man bent down to retrieve them and James was ready for him. His knee jerked up, crashing into the man's face and sending him hurtling over the arm of the chair. Blood from his broken nose sprayed on to the carpet as James dived after him, pinning him down on the floor. It was an unnecessary precaution. The man lay limp on the ground amongst two of his teeth, gasping for breath through his bleeding mouth. James straddled him, removing the gun from the thug's raincoat pocket. He then bundled him over to go through his other pockets, hoping to find papers, a wallet, any source of possible identification. He spoke over his shoulder. 'Can you bring me some cold water and a rag?'

Ann didn't answer. She just stood in the middle of her lounge, white and shaking, hands over her mouth to suppress a scream. James looked over at her and rose to his feet to put his arm gently around her shoulders.

'Sorry it was a bit rough,' he said gently, 'but you don't mess around when the other feller's got a gun.'

'You knew he had a gun?' she asked, astonished.

'I guessed . . . when I went to shake hands with him he had to let go of something in his pocket before he took his hand out, and I assumed it wasn't a Mars bar.'

She shuddered. This wasn't her world and it frightened her. Up to half an hour ago she had treated the whole affair lightheartedly, and the appearance of Norman was a happy ending to a pleasant dream. But not now. This wasn't part of the pleasant dream. This was real violence, not at all like on television. There was blood all over her lounge; not ketchup, and the gun was real too. She turned away from the sprawled figure on the floor; her only experience of violence had been in her last two plays.

'Have a sip of that.' James was handing her a glass of whisky but her hands were shaking so much that she couldn't hold it. He helped the glass to her lips and as the spirit warmed her insides her trembling eased and she greedily gulped some more.

'You first alerted me that something was wrong before I even entered the house,' he said.

Ann frowned, trying to recall her few banal lines at the door.

'It was smart of you to draw the curtains.'

She stared at him in confusion. 'Oh yes, but I didn't draw them. He did.'

James's eyebrows shot up. 'Well, that was good of him, then.' He saw that she had finished the drink. 'Now be a good girl and fetch me that water.' She hurried into the kitchen and almost immediately she came back, ashen-faced.

'What is it?' he asked quickly.

Ann pointed in the direction of the kitchen. 'When I was in there I noticed something white outside the window and when I put on the light it ducked out of sight. I'm sure there's somebody out there.'

James tensed for a moment and then relaxed. 'It's OK. That'll be my driver. Stand at the window and wave a white cloth or something, but don't open the door until you see him approach or he may shoot you.'

Ann hesitated. 'Go on,' James said, 'I want him in here sharpish.' He looked down at the groaning mass on the carpet struggling weakly to sit up. James watched his feeble attempts for a moment, then bent down, grabbed the man's lapels and dumped him on the chair. There was no fight left in him and not much blood either, judging by the steady trickle coming from his shattered face.

James heard the back door close as the younger detective came in. 'Good. Now get him handcuffed. I don't think he'll be a problem but you never know.' Ann shuffled in with a basin of cold water and set it down on the floor.

'When he's secure,' continued James, 'clean him up a bit. I'm sorry, but I don't have any time.' The young officer drew out his handcuffs and looked with distaste at the ruined face. He'd seen a few traffic accidents in his time but he'd never heard of such goings-on in an average law-abiding semi-detached. 'Well, get on with it,' growled James as he examined the papers he'd taken from the man's pockets. 'I want him bright eyed and bushy tailed.'

Norman had followed the detective into the back of the van. He had wanted to look back at the window but the van doors had been slammed shut and immediately his arms had been pinned behind him and a soft pad slapped over his mouth and nose. The ether had taken effect quickly.

Some time later – Norman had no idea how much later – he opened his eyes and a wave of nausea swept over him. Weakly he closed his eyes again but that only seemed to increase his dizziness, so he took a deep breath and steadied himself to rejig his senses. Wherever he was, it was dark and stank of fish and diesel oil. He tried to move and found that he couldn't because he was tied to a chair. Panic-stricken, he struggled and thrashed with every ounce of his strength, but it was useless. Tears sprang to his eyes, but they were born of frustration; they weren't the mewlings of an adolescent. With a sickening awareness he remembered Ann and groaned as he recalled himself skipping out of the house like a besotted twelve-year-old.

A bright light dazzled him momentarily, then went out. He tensed, mouth open to hear better, and then it dawned on him that the dizziness wasn't the after-effects of the ether but because the room was gently rocking. He was on a boat, but where and more importantly why? Claustrophobia overtook him. Like a frightened child he opened his mouth and screamed for help. He wasn't a seaman so he didn't recognise the sound of a hatch being opened, but he heard footsteps on a steel ladder and a shape suddenly loomed in front of him.

'One more peep and you're dead.'

The voice was strangely familiar but Norman was unable to recognise the speaker in the dimness, until the probing beam of a lighthouse flashed through the porthole, illuminating the man for a brief second. Norman's throat tightened. It was the spaceman.

'I knew we'd have trouble with you,' said the man, almost apologetically, but then he pushed his face close against Norman's and his voice became harsh. 'You should have stayed in Grapplewick where you belong. You're in amongst the big boys now and whether you live or die is immaterial to me. You are my hostage – a little insurance in case the police get too close. By now they must know that I've got their star witness, so you've really served your purpose. You may be of further use, but if you give me any trouble, you're history. Is that clear?'

With that he turned and hoisted himself up the ladder. Norman saw his dark bulk against the starlit night and then the hatch slammed down, leaving him in blackness again. Again panic feathered his insides, but he made himself think of the girl. That seemed to give him strength. Suddenly the silence was shattered by the throb of engines, and from the increased rocking of his tiny cell, Norman knew that they were under way.

Although the pain from his smashed face must have been excruciating, the man was a hard nut to crack and Chief Inspector James wasn't making progress as fast as he would have liked. 'I'll ask you again,' he shouted. 'Where have they taken the boy?'

The man looked at him, hate in his swelling eyes. 'Get stuffed,' he muttered thickly.

James stood back and sighed. 'You know you're a berk. You amaze me, you honestly do. Do you really believe they'll be coming back for you?'

There was a flicker in the man's eyes. He obviously hadn't given it much thought and James was quick to press home his advantage. 'We've got you in the bag. Possession of a firearm, kidnapping, and if anything should happen to Norman, accessory to murder as well.' He ticked off his fingers as he spoke. 'And you really believe they're coming back for you. It's more likely to rain gold sovereigns,' he sneered, and stood back. 'Take him down to the station,' he said to the young officer. 'I don't waste time on pillocks.'

* * *

Up on Beachy Head the crowds were still gathering in anticipation but most of the townspeople had already decided that the whole thing was a practical joke and had started drifting off back to their homes. More sightseers were turning away when it happened: there were several bangs and the skies were lit with a blinding light. Instinctively the watchers looked up – as they were meant to – and, momentarily robbed of their vision, they missed the blimp as it struggled frantically to inflate. The two Special Branch men, however, were not blinded as they were equipped with night-vision glasses: had they not been so prepared they could well have believed that a flying saucer was actually quivering on the grass. Further down on the coast two of their colleagues were only interested in observing the sea, and from the white glare cast by the flares they spotted a boat travelling slowly and without lights in a westerly direction. It was a phenomenal stroke of good fortune. Without the light from the flares they would have missed it.

The harbour master's office was ablaze with lights as Chief Inspector James leaped out of the car and hurried along to the jetty. He was about to mount the steps when his radio bleeped. Quickly he snatched it from his pocket and pressed the switch. 'James,' he said.

'Control, we've got him. Sector Four have a boat in sight, maybe a forty-foot motor launch travelling slowly without lights in a westerly direction. Over.'

Chief Inspector James was wary. 'What makes you sure it's him?'

'Couldn't be anybody else, sir. Drifted out of an inlet on the tide until they were far enough out to start the engines without being heard from the shore.'

'Are you tracking him?'

'Yes, sir, we've notified the coastguard's boat and they have him on radar, following at the same speed, awaiting instructions.'

James thought for a moment. 'Tell the coastguard to intercept and investigate.'

'Will do, sir. Over and out.'

James was about to stuff the radio back into his pocket when he stopped and pressed the switch. 'James, patch me into Sector Four,' he instructed. He waited a second or two. 'Do you have night glasses, over.'

'Yes, sir, but even so we would have missed him had it not been for the flares. They lit up the whole area. Over.'

James nodded to himself. 'Of course. Well done. Out.' He lowered his radio thoughtfully. He'd seen the flares from the car on his way over. It had been a replay of the Grapplewick incident, right down to the inflating flying saucer, and that bothered him. Two and two weren't making four in his calculations. Now, making his way up the stairs to the harbour master's office, he paused. Heinrich Adlon was brilliant. For twelve months he had meticulously planned every step of the operation. It was inconceivable that his own carefully rigged flares should be his downfall. It would have been a beginner's mistake and up to now, he hadn't made any at all. James gazed unseeingly over the black water and excitement suddenly gripped his bowels as a glimmer of understanding grew at the back of his mind. The art of the master illusionist was the art of deception. Flap the right hand about and do the real business with the other one. Adlon's timing was precise – his skill rested on that precision. He had known down to the last second when the flares would be released so it wasn't feasible that he should be sailing close to the coast only to be picked up by his own illumination.

James slapped the rail triumphantly. Another decoy – that boat was meant to be seen. He bounded up the last few steps into the office.

The harbour master, a Captain Fletching, whirled around as James entered. 'Coastguards are closing in on the boat now,' he said.

'Good,' replied James. 'Have the coastguards identify the boat; that's all, then get back here pronto – we haven't got much time.'

Fletching looked at him, not understanding. 'Well, chop chop,' said the detective.

'You don't want us to make an arrest?' asked the captain, puzzled.

'Oh yes, and I've a feeling we're getting close, but our man won't be on that boat.'

The harbour master shrugged and passed on the instructions to his radio operator. He then turned to James. 'What now?' he asked.

'Firstly, have you had any traffic in the last hour?'

Fletching picked up a pad. 'A sloop from Barcelona moored at 21.40 hours.' He flipped over a page, but James interrupted.

'I'm only interested in outgoing traffic.'

Fletching put down the pad. 'Nothing outward bound since this afternoon.'

The radio operator looked across. 'Excuse me, sir, but Jack Sprotly went out about twenty minutes ago.'

James was immediately alert. 'Who's Jack Sprotly?' he barked.

Fletching grunted. 'Oh, Jack's all right. He's one of the local fishermen. He owns the *Molly Neek*, a trawler. We don't log their comings and goings. They tie up just outside the harbour in any case; not our pigeon.'

James looked at him keenly. 'Is it normal for one of these trawlers to go out at this time of night?'

Fletching shrugged. 'They're a law unto themselves that lot, but yes, it is a bit early. They usually leave for the fishing grounds at about two in the morning.'

James looked over at the radio man. 'Did you see him personally?'

'Yes, sir. I was having a drag outside on the jetty when he sailed past. He waved.'

'Waved, did he?' asked James thoughtfully. 'So you know him well?'

'He lives next door to me. I was in the same class as his wife at school.'

'In which direction was he heading?'

'Due east, sir . . .' He stopped, a puzzled frown on his face. 'That's odd.'

'What is?' snapped James.

'They usually sail south or southwest for the fish.'

James snatched the radio and quickly contacted Control.

'Go ahead, sir.'

'Call off the bank surveillance teams in town – I want every man I can get down at the harbour, and I want two of my men round to . . . hang on a minute . . .' He looked at the radio operator. 'What's this trawlerman's . . . er, Jack's address?'

'Thirty-six Crombie Street, just behind the harbour.'

James nodded and repeated the address into his radio, adding, 'There'll be a man in there and he'll be armed and dangerous. As soon as you've got him, let me know. Out.'

He looked at the perplexed faces around him. 'I'm only just beginning to understand how our friend works, and if my hunch is correct, then there's a man in that house holding Jack's wife hostage.'

TWENTY-SIX

Norman tried to rub some life into his wrists as he emerged on deck. In the cold wind a thin suit was no match for the weather and the thought of a thick woollen sweater and gumboots overrode his fear. He staggered and grabbed for the rail as a wave crashed into the bows, but almost immediately he was prodded forward by the man who had just untied him. Norman's vision was just beginning to adjust to the night, and in the faint gleam of the port navigation light he recognised the man who was shepherding him along the deck. He was the man who had walked into the barber's shop in Coldhurst Street, only then he had been blind.

Norman was pushed forward again and he stumbled up the steps to the tiny wheelhouse. The skipper was behind the wheel, standing close to the spaceman. They both looked around as Norman was hustled roughly inside. It was impossible to shut the door; two people in that enclosed space were more than enough and three were definitely a crowd. Norman was just grateful for the warmth.

For a time nobody spoke and Norman was able to observe the skipper's face lit by the light from the binnacle. It was grim and afforded Norman no comfort. The skipper moved easily with the sudden lurches of the deck, dividing his attention between the compass and the clear screen. The boat ducked into a deeper trough and a flurry of white spray lashed against the window of the wheelhouse. Norman flinched at the fury of the sea, but after a couple of swells began to get used to it, learning to anticipate the pitch and yaw of the thrusting bows. It actually wasn't that rough a sea, but the stubby trawler was pushing through it with a fussiness that overdramatised the slight swell.

'How long now?' asked the man.

The skipper looked up to the clock on the bulkhead. 'Twenty-five minutes, roughly.'

Now that he was attuned to his surroundings, Norman began to think. Why had he been brought to the wheelhouse only to be ignored? Surely they would have been less cramped had they left him tied up below deck. He examined their reflections in the glass screen. Was the skipper one of them? The way in which he had answered the spaceman had given Norman a faint surge of hope. As soon as that thought had crossed his mind the skipper spoke again. 'If anything happens to my wife, I'll have you – wherever you run to.' The man ignored the threat but Norman's question had been answered. At least he had one ally.

Ten minutes later the spaceman's accomplice returned and leaned over Norman to tap The Great Firenzi's shoulder. Both men then stepped outside the wheelhouse. Norman observed them as suddenly they tensed. At a shout the skipper closed the throttle and Norman lurched as the boat shot forward. As he steadied himself he could see ahead: some way off the port beam was a small pinprick of flashing white light.

'Spot on,' muttered The Great Firenzi and walked on to the deck.

'I'll give him "spot on" if I ever catch the bugger,' muttered the skipper, busying himself between wheel and throttles so he could lay the trawler alongside a rubber dinghy. Swiftly The Great Firenzi stepped down into it, followed by his accomplice.

'You can go home now,' shouted the spaceman. 'Thanks for the lift.'

The skipper slammed the side window shut and pushed forward the throttle, spinning the wheel to make a wide sweep which caused the dinghy to wallow madly in its wake as he set a course for the harbour. He was impatient to get back to his wife.

In a more spacious bridge area aboard the coastguard boat, Chief Inspector James stood with legs braced as the ship bumped slowly over the oily sea at half speed, two miles behind the labouring trawler. Beside him stood the captain, leaning forward with his hands on the chart table.

'What I don't understand is if you're quite certain your man is on board the trawler, why don't we just catch up and nab him?'

Chief Inspector James shook his head. 'I don't think he's making his get-away in a trawler, even if it's only to France. He doesn't know which ports are being watched, and if it comes to the crunch he couldn't outrun a pedalo in that thing. No, I've got a feeling he's leading us somewhere.'

'Sir,' a signalman at the radar console called to the captain, 'they've turned, sir, heading on a reciprocal course.'

The captain stepped across and looked over the signalman's shoulder at the screen to watch the sweep arm painting a small blip.

'What's happening?' asked the policeman, joining them.

'They've turned, heading for home.'

'Just like that,' mused James.

He rasped the bristles on his chin. He was tired and now wasn't the time. He had to out-think the man but whenever he took a piece off the board, the man had another move up his sleeve. Why was he turning back? What the hell was he playing at? He had to find out and quickly.

'All right,' he said. 'Intercept as quickly as possible.'

'Increase revolutions to full ahead both,' ordered the captain, and the boat surged forward like a dog let off the leash. In less than ten minutes the ship's spotlight picked out the trawler forcing its way in the opposite direction. As they closed within hailing distance, the captain took up the microphone.

'This is the coastguard: heave to and stand by for boarding party.'

Crouching behind the guard rails eight armed policemen of the Special Branch waited tensely for anything that might happen. The trawler's screws whirled frantically in reverse until the boat was wallowing and dead in the water. The coastguard boat, circling warily to keep the trawler in the centre of its searchlight beam, drew alongside, bumping gently against the fenders as they made fast.

James was the first to board, and even though it was only a gentle swell he had to time his jump to meet the rising deck of the trawler. The eight policemen followed in line and scuttled over the deck, guns outstretched, safety catches off. Norman, shielding his eyes from the bright light, picked his way across the deck to where Chief Inspector James was standing.

'Inspector,' he called, 'it's me, Norman.'

Jack Sprotly came out of the wheelhouse. 'What the bloody 'ell's goin' on?' he roared. 'I 'ave to get back . . . my wife . . .'

'First things first,' said James curtly. 'I'm Chief Inspector James, Special Branch. Were you carrying any passengers?'

Norman broke in. 'Yes, the spaceman; well, you know, and the man that was in Grapplewick with him – the blind one!'

'And where are they now?'

'They got into a dinghy with an outboard motor.'

One of the SB team hurried up to James and took him to one side, speaking in a low voice.

'Can't we just dump the lot overboard?' asked James. The officer shook his head and tapped his watch.

James nodded. 'OK, everybody aboard the other boat – *now*!'

Immediately the black-clad officer clambered over the rail and James pushed Norman after him.

'Hang on a minute,' said the trawler skipper; 'I'm not leaving my boat. There's nothing wrong with her!'

'I haven't time to argue,' replied James. 'Your boat will be blown to smithereens any second, so move yourself!'

Sprotly got the message and leaped for the rail. James was close behind him and barely made it to the other boat, which had already begun to pull away. In the captain's small cabin James quizzed Norman and Sprotly and his puzzlement deepened; why should the two criminals transfer to a small dinghy in mid-ocean? Granted, a small rubber dinghy wouldn't be picked up on any radar screen, but they were only ten or so miles from shore, and James was convinced they weren't going to attempt crossing the Channel in it.

He looked at Norman. 'Ask the captain to come in here, will you?'

Norman sprang to his feet; he was getting used to the sea now and was beginning to feel like an old sea dog. James had assured him that Ann was well and he couldn't wait to get back to her.

The captain ducked into the cabin. 'You wanted to see me?'

'Yes,' said James, 'I'm assuming our man isn't planning to spend the next couple of nights in a dinghy, so he has to be making a rendezvous at sea.'

The captain nodded.

'Therefore, it would seem that he's waiting for a ship of some kind,' carried on James. 'Now, did your operator see anything in the vicinity on his radar?'

The captain thought for a moment. 'No. I looked as well but didn't notice anything – mind you, we were only on a five-mile wave and we didn't actually get to the periphery, so there may be something two or three miles out that we missed.' He looked across to the trawler skipper. 'If the transfer position is correct, we can have another sweep from there.' He left and went back to the bridge.

'Are you sure about my boat?' asked Sprotly.

James shrugged. 'No, I'm not, but my man believes there are explosives packed in the locker. The fact that Norman was pushed on to the bridge for no apparent reason makes me think that he was transferred there so he wouldn't see the explosives being set. In any case, if the boat doesn't blow within the next couple of hours, you can pick her up in the morning.'

The skipper snorted. 'That's if something doesn't run into it in the middle of the night.'

Both men left the cabin and, bending double into the wind, made their way along the deck. There were still about three hours left to daybreak but the adrenaline of the chase and the biting wind revived James. He was about to mount the ladder up to the bridge when a brilliant white light lit up the horizon. This was followed a couple of seconds later by a dull rumble. Both men whirled around and watched as a bright red glow illuminated the underbelly of the cloud base.

James patted the skipper's shoulder. 'Sorry about that. At least you won't have to worry about somebody running into her.'

Norman was in the wheelhouse, excited by the thrust of the bows as they bumped over the swell. The sea wasn't lashing at the windows of this boat; it now had more respect. They had all seen the flash of the explosion but Norman had shrugged it off as sheet lightning. It was only when DCI James and the skipper had come in that he learned the truth, and the shock of it was almost palpable. Up to now the whole thing had been an exhilarating chase which would end with the capture of the villain – and he couldn't be far ahead; Norman had last seen him boarding a rubber dinghy, for God's sake. Suddenly, though, the scenario had taken a turn for the worse and it wasn't a *Boy's Own* adventure any more. A trawler had been blown out of the water and it was only the sharp thinking of the chief inspector which had prevented Norman and Sprotly from going up with it.

'Sir!'

Everybody jumped and glared at the signalman.

'A ship coming up now at about six miles, and there's another one, sir. Probably a freighter.'

The captain watched the screen. 'There's another one coming up, a big one. An oil tanker, I think.'

'What is it, an invasion?' asked James, trying to inject a light note into the tense atmosphere.

The captain didn't take his eyes off the radar. 'No, we're coming into a bit of traffic here, but they're moored in the roads, waiting for a berth, I fancy. Either Southampton or Portsmouth.'

'Well, that's it!' exclaimed James. 'It has to be one of them!'

'Another two, sir, about ten thousand tons.'

The captain turned to the policeman. 'You've picked a busy night, inspector.'

James folded his arms and looked at the deck. He knew in his bones that Heinrich Adlon was aboard one of them, but the trick was to find out which one. He looked up. 'Is it possible to talk to the skippers of these ships?'

The captain thought for a moment. 'Yes, but I think it may be advisable to contact Southampton or Portsmouth first. They'll know who's moored and why.'

DCI James nodded. 'And in the meantime let's get in amongst them and have a close look!'

Aboard the *Kendo Maru*, Heinrich Adlon lay on his bunk, hands clasped behind his head, but he wasn't relaxed. He had twelve million pounds in the hold but he wasn't home and dry yet. He wasn't worried about Norman or the skipper – they were old news – but Chief Inspector James bothered him still. He couldn't figure out how the man knew he was at Bogsea – and where was James now? What was he up to? Had he been fooled by the decoy boat? Perhaps he had caught up as far as the Sprotly woman, although that was unlikely. Still, he was dealing with a high-ranking officer in Special Branch, not the lollipop man, so he had to expect changes to his carefully laid plans.

Adlon ran through his mental itinerary – on the following afternoon the ship would sail into Southampton to offload a cargo of iron ore and then proceed to Lisbon where it would load up with olive oil and timber. All in all this was a perfectly normal itinerary for the ship. She was registered with Lloyd's and her bills of lading were all in order. From Lisbon she would sail to the South Atlantic, and only then would he relax. Adlon suddenly jerked to a sitting position as a bright light flashed through the porthole, but then it moved on. He crawled over to the porthole and was now able to observe that the light was a searchlight from another ship. Immediately he was on the alert. Something was terribly wrong.

The coastguard boat circled the *Kendo Maru* slowly, bathing the decks in a harsh white light. The captain had obtained all the information pertaining to the ships entering and leaving the port of Southampton and there was nothing out of the ordinary on any of them. They were all bona fide merchant ships with correct papers, and there was a total of eight of them in the area. Slowly the coastguard boat cruised in and out of the moorings, examining each ship in turn. The *Kendo Maru* was the last one.

'That's the one!' proclaimed James excitedly. 'It has to be!'

The captain stared at him. 'How can you be so sure?'

'I'm sure,' said the policeman. 'It must be. All the ships here, once unloaded, are bound for different ports in the UK – except for the *Kendo Maru*, that is. Her next port of call is Lisbon. After that he's away and that'll be it. We'll have lost him and he'll go somewhere where we can't touch him.'

The captain was still uncertain but James was impatient. 'I'll get a boarding party together.'

He was on his way to the door when the captain stopped him.

'Belay that,' he said. 'You can't just board a ship like that on the high seas, it's piracy. I'm sorry, but as captain of this vessel I refuse to go alongside without the proper authorisation.'

'The trawler didn't bother you.'

'That was different, I knew the skipper. In any case, if we board this ship and it turns out to be what you think it is, there's likely to be bloodshed – and if it doesn't turn out to be what you think it is, I'll be hiring out deck chairs on the promenade.'

James stared at him for a moment, then rooted in his pockets for a card.

'Get me this number and tell whoever answers it's Chief Inspector James, Special Branch.'

The captain hesitated for a second.

'You'll be lucky to get that job with the deck chairs,' muttered James softly.

The captain nodded and hurried away. James sighed. Excitement and anticipation surged through him, but to a casual observer he might have been idly contemplating what to order for breakfast.

'Your call, sir.' A seaman handed him the phone.

'Good morning, sir, James here. I'm sorry to wake you at this hour, but I think we've got our man.'

He spoke quietly for a few minutes then put down the phone.

'Problem solved,' he said to the captain. 'In forty minutes a detachment of Royal Marine Commandos will be choppered here, so we're to stand off until we hear them approach, then put on all your deck lights. Any questions?'

The searchlight went out and the boat picked up speed into the night. But Adlon was uneasy: somebody had been interested in the *Kendo Maru*, curious enough to circle slowly examining the decks with a powerful light. Whoever it was appeared satisfied enough to switch off and move on, but this did nothing to allay his suspicions. More than ever now it was imperative he stayed one jump ahead of the pack. At the back of his mind he knew they were closing in. He was certain he'd covered every angle but apparently so had the opposition. He had to find an alternative escape route.

Swinging his legs over the edge of the bunk, he put on a reefer jacket and made his way along the passage to the deck. The wind hit him, setting him back a pace, and he hunched his way forward to the ladder up to the bridge wing in order to give him a better vantage point. But there was nothing to see, the night was at its darkest and only the faint small navigation lights of the tanker at the next mooring were visible. All was black and silent apart from the busy wind and the occasional slop of the sea. A lesser man would be comforted, discounting the searchlight as a routine inspection, but instinct made Adlon uneasy. Somebody had been nosing around and he knew that he was the centre of attraction. Shivering in the night air, he turned up his collar and made his way back down to the galley for a mug of hot coffee, tea, cocoa, anything that would help him to think. But again his luck turned sour. Wrapping his hands around a mug of stewed coffee as he sat in the warm, humming boiler room, he missed the throb of the rotors as two helicopters passed close by.

The coastguard boat was in position, a freighter and a tanker hiding it from the *Kendo Maru* as the marines abseiled on to the deck. With the ship's lights ablaze, it was a spectacular sight for the few men lining the rails of the rusting freighter moored some fifty yards away. The manoeuvre completed, the helicopters peeled away and all lights were again doused, bringing a smatter of applause from the insomniacs on the ship nearby.

'Slow ahead both,' ordered the captain, and the coastguard boat crept towards the target. They steamed to within three hundred yards and then the telegraphs rang for just enough revolutions to keep her head into the swell. When she stopped, two marines pushed a rubber dinghy over the side and climbed down into it. After adjusting their paddles in the rowlocks they bent their backs and pulled strongly and silently into the darkness towards the *Kendo Maru*.

Aboard the coastguard boat there was no talking. All was silent except for the low rumble of the engine. The strong wind was now carrying all sound away from the target ship. All heads were turned anxiously towards the navigation lights of the *Kendo Maru* in the distance. James gripped the guardrail and leaned out to listen for the splash of oars and the return of the two marines. He listened in vain. Suddenly they were shinning up ropes to board the boat behind him, clambering on to the deck. They weren't a special unit for nothing.

Now that the preliminaries had been taken care of, the game was about to begin in earnest. The marine lieutenant knew what he had to do and ordered his men to move towards the rail and stand ready with grappling lines. Soundlessly they moved over to the side of the boat like a collection of ghosts all in black – black jumpsuits, black balaclavas and blackened faces. They looked sinister enough even without the evil lightweight sub-machine-guns they all carried. Whatever happened, they were going to be a huge shock to somebody's system.

The coastguard boat surged forward, two searchlights illuminating the *Kendo Maru*. With a crunch they were alongside, grappling lines clutching the rail of the bigger vessel. Almost before the captain gave out the order for the engines to be cut, the marines were fanning out on board the deck of the freighter. One marine crept along to the wheelhouse, the rest went below deck.

James boarded the *Kendo Maru* in a more sedate manner – he was no spring chicken any more and not up to the antics of the younger, highly trained men. Once on board he waited a few moments. Very shortly an assortment of crew, clad variously in dirty singlets and shirts, blinked their way up on deck, hands clasped behind their heads. James noted thankfully that he hadn't heard any gunfire, but the smoothness and the success of the operation made him vaguely uneasy. Four marines were still searching the vessel for the proceeds of the bank raids, whilst another emerged from the hatch to report that all crew members were now on deck.

The captain of the *Kendo Maru*, a wizened Oriental, seemed subdued and this gave James fresh heart. If the Oriental had been the captain of an innocent freighter plying an honest trade, he would have been surprised, angry, anything but cowed. James turned his attention to the line of crewmen scrunching their eyes against the harsh glare of the searchlight. 'OK, Norman, let's see if there's anybody you know.'

Norman had been daydreaming; he'd decided that as soon as he stepped back on to dry land he was off to the recruiting office. He wanted to be a marine. He'd been watching the quiet, deadly efficiency with which they went about their business, and now as Chief Inspector James was about to thrust him on to centre stage again, his chest swelled with pride. Norman at last realised that he wasn't just an average Herbert, he was one of *them*, an integral part of the operation. Slowly and carefully he went down the line, unaware that James behind him was holding his breath. As he passed the assortment of men without recognising any of them, his heart began to sink. What if Chief Inspector James was wrong? How was he going to tell him that the spaceman wasn't here? He remembered that the man was a master of disguise and glanced quickly back to the Oriental captain, but his hopes there were dashed. He might have altered his face but there was no way in which he could have shortened his legs.

Then, at the next man, Norman could hardly keep his exultation in check. It was the blind man who had walked into his uncle's shop in Grapplewick. He turned to James. 'That's one of them,' he said casually, surprising even himself; he hadn't meant to sound like Mr Cool. James breathed a huge sigh of relief and stood aside as one of the Special Branch men reached over and snapped a pair of handcuffs on the man, who stood in the line looking dazed. He made no protestations of innocence. James put it down to his being amazed at seeing Norman very much alive and well.

James stepped forward and looked into the man's eyes. 'All right, sunshine, where is he?'

The man craned his neck up and down the line and shrugged. 'I dunno,' he eventually mumbled.

'He should be here, though, shouldn't he?' The man hesitated, avoiding the detective's hard gaze. 'I'll ask you again,' continued James, 'and if I'm not satisfied, you're going over the side with an anchor chain around your ankles.'

Fear sprang into the man's eyes. He wasn't sure that the policeman would carry out his threat but as a betting man he wouldn't touch the odds with a ten-foot pole. 'I dunno,' he repeated, and as James turned away he blurted out, 'He's on the ship somewhere, but I don't know where.'

James nodded. 'OK. So where's the loot?'

The man's mouth snapped shut. For him the money obviously added up to more than his life.

'OK,' said James resignedly. 'Fetch me a length of chain.'

The man hesitated just long enough to realise that he had got his sums wrong, and that his life just had the edge over the money. 'It's in the hold,' he muttered.

James turned to one of his men. 'Take him below and have him point it out.' As the man was hustled out of the line James walked over to the stern and looked down at the oily black waters beneath. He was joined by a marine lieutenant.

'I'm sorry, sir, but there's no sign of anybody else.'

James sighed. 'Ah well. You've done a great job and I'll certainly mention it in my report.'

'Thank you, sir. What's the next move?'

'As soon as it's daylight, get the crew to bring this ship into Southampton, and make sure that nobody goes ashore unless I say so. OK?'

The young lieutenant hesitated. 'Need any help with the big one, sir?'

James shook his head. 'Nah, he's mine, and I've looked forward to this for a long time, but thanks again for all your help. It's good to know we're on the same side.' With that he strode briskly along the deck to clamber back on to the coastguard boat.

Norman scuttled off after him, perplexed as to why the chief inspector seemed so calm. Granted, they had the accomplice and the money, but what about Mr Big? The whole object of the exercise had been to bring him in, but they had missed him yet again. Surely this was a smack in the face, to put it mildly, yet James was behaving as if he was going away for a weekend's fishing. Surely it would have been better to stay aboard the *Kendo Maru* until daylight when they would have a better chance to search the vessel more thoroughly. However, not for the first time Norman had underestimated the Special Branch detective. Underneath that calm exterior bubbled a cauldron of excitement.

The coastguard boat steamed out of the roads in a westerly direction. 'Get a fix?' asked James calmly, sipping a mug of hot, sweet tea.

The captain nodded. 'According to my charts, the tide changes at about five o'clock and it's a riptide coming in from the Solent. That's always a bit tricky in this area.' He ran a slide rule over a chart and pencilled a dot. 'This should do it, as near as dammit,' he said.

James put down his mug and yawned; he hadn't slept for nearly a day and a half now, and that wasn't good. 'OK,' he said, 'I'll leave you to it. I'm going down below to stretch out for a bit. Let me know what transpires.'

'Will do,' replied the captain, and gave orders for the change of course.

Norman hadn't had his full quota of sleep either, but no way was he going to close his eyes now. He sat down on one of the bridge chairs, determined to see out the last act. Within five minutes his head fell forward and he went out like a light.

Four hours later the captain shook Chief Inspector James, who was instantly awake. 'Congratulations, sir, you were right.'

James rubbed his eyes and grunted. 'Well done.' He swung his legs off the bunk and followed the captain on deck, who handed him his binoculars and pointed out to sea. James lifted the binoculars to his eyes and after a moment his face split into a wide grin. 'I don't know who's going to be best pleased on seeing the other; him or me. By the looks of it he's had a long, hard night too.' He handed the glasses back to the captain. 'Just like a fly in a web,' he murmured.

The captain nodded. 'But how could you have been so certain?'

James rested his hands on the rail. 'First thing I noticed when we went round the *Kendo Maru* was the dinghy tied up astern.'

'Yes, I noticed that too.'

'Bit unusual, isn't it?'

The captain thought for a moment. 'Yes, I suppose it is.'

'When those two marines rowed across, they emptied the petrol from the outboard motor on the dinghy and filled it with sea water.' He shrugged. 'Well, you know the rest: when we were on board I looked over the side and the dinghy was gone. He had to drift some distance to be out of earshot before he started the engine, but they don't run very far on sea water. Game, set and match: all we had to do was wait for him to join us.'

They both leaned over the rail to watch as The Great Firenzi was hauled on deck more dead than alive. James stood over him and looked down at the shivering, sodden illusionist. 'Welcome aboard Limbo Two . . . you miserable bastard.'

EPILOGUE

After reporting to his superiors, the chief inspector repaid a debt. He phoned Bernard Whittaker, editor of the *Grapplewick Bugle*, giving him the biggest exclusive of his career. Not only was it taken up by the major British dailies, but newspapers all over the world carried the story. From the sting to the final arrest of the 'spaceman', the story captured the public's imagination, and Norman featured prominently in the incredible saga. It was serialised in several magazines and Norman was interviewed and photographed, even appearing on the cover of *Time*. That was the last straw. He fled to a quiet resort in France until things quietened down. He wasn't alone, though: he took with him his wife, Mrs Ann Waterhouse.

Auntie Florrie died from a surfeit of riches – fridge, washing machine, new carpets and a fur coat. But it was the three weeks in Scarborough that brought about her final collapse. In a typically English summer she died of pneumonia. Her last words were, 'Tell me honestly, Albert, where did you get the money from?' He couldn't tell her the truth – he thought the shock would kill her – but now somebody up there would probably have enlightened her regarding the night on Sagbottom's Acres when her husband and Superintendent Smith became more than solvent.

Albert missed Florrie, he'd nothing to ignore any more, and after a decent interval he married Madame Lesley. It remains an amicable relationship – she doesn't have to give him dancing lessons and he doesn't have to buy her a box of chocolates every week. They now live in Farmer Crumpshaw's house so they can keep an eye on Sagbottom's.

Old deaf Crumpshaw died a week after he'd shot the spacecraft. He'd had enough and couldn't wait to hand in his life membership. Two days later the delivery man found him stretched out on the bed in a clean shirt clutching his will. It was a remarkable few lines, leaving £5000 to his dog.

Eunice Waterhouse, née Lesley, also enjoyed a fair amount of notoriety, being The Great Firenzi's first wife. Appearing on television chat shows she came across so well they gave her a six-week cookery series, which was a mistake. However she had an unexpected windfall when a Sunday newspaper suggested that she had supplied Heinrich Adlon with information regarding the town, and implying she was working hand in glove with him. First she was furious but after weeks of litigation she was somewhat mollified by an out-of-court settlement of £150,000.

Superintendent Smith retired shortly after the big night and took his riches to Marbella in Spain where he moved into a sumptuous villa near San Pedro. He also acquired a popular restaurant called La Lampara Azul, and along with some Spanish businessmen he bought a half share in a hotel. This was in his early days as a resident when he was known among the locals as El Hombre Rico because of his lavish lifestyle. So on a policeman's pay and a dodgy deal to buy Sagbottom's, one wondered if he hadn't any other little earners going before he emigrated. However his luck eventually ran out. He was no match for the Spanish mafia and when a great section of the hotel fell down, he was horrified to learn that it was his half. Now, sadly, his magnum of champagne is reduced to a Campari and soda, and the palatial villa has gone. He is now in a rented room at the back of the village. He doesn't own the restaurant any more, but he still carries a bit of weight with the council and due to his experience as a police superintendent, they have decided to be generous and give him a job as a traffic warden.

Grapplewick itself has prospered. It is now arguably the most famous little town in the world. Hollywood, Lourdes, Salem, Niagara Falls – all trail miserably in its wake. Lancastrians abroad no longer tell people they are from Manchester or Liverpool. They all live on the outskirts of Grapplewick. And every year on the first of May, thousands make a pilgrimage to Sagbottom's Acres

– space societies, interplanetary societies, geographical societies – they all congregate to celebrate the landing. The fact that it was all a scam and the spacecraft was just an inflatable rubber contraption that resembled a saucer doesn't seem to matter. Every year Albert Waterhouse dons the mayor's robes of office, and along with members of the council they re-enact the scene as midnight strikes. All the side shows and refreshment tents are silent while flares are fired into the sky. But there the resemblance ends. Four searchlights shoot out and converge on the spot where the spacecraft was reputed to have landed, and Norman walks across the field and places a wreath in the centre of light. Why is a mystery, but no one is complaining. The tills are pinging, the pubs are full, and most of the houses take in some of the thousands of overseas tourists that flood these shores to visit Sagbottom's, Big Ben, Stratford and St Paul's – in that order.

Every other shop sells mementos, the most popular being stones from Kershaw's Croft, although enough stone has now changed hands to build several pyramids.

It is generally accepted that when UFOs land, it will be on a Wednesday, and the venue has to be Grapplewick.

There is a very interesting footnote, however, and one that is inexplicable to this day. The spaceman or Heinrich Adlon or Firenzi, the great illusionist, was transferred ashore from the coastguard boat, more than half dead. When he opened his eyes some time later he found he was in a prison hospital. But he never did anything by halves, and closing his eyes again he quickly completed the journey. An hour later a doctor wrote out a death certificate and the body was transferred to the mortuary. It was the end of possibly the greatest stage illusionist since Houdini . . . or was it?

Chief Inspector James reflected on the man's brilliance. His thoughts were mixed as he sat in the front pew of the little chapel in the crematorium in order to pay his last respects to his adversary. Certainly his old animosity was gone and he could not help but admire the sheer ingenuity of the man. The patience and planning of a twelve-month scam undoubtedly ranked high in the annals of crime. The illusions and tricks, the split-second timing of each miraculous event were surely the work of a master craftsman.

There were not many people in the congregation. He was the only one as far as he knew with a personal connection to the dead man. The others were extras: gravediggers, the crematorium staff, passers-by, in fact anybody to make up the numbers. They all stood now as the rollers began to revolve, moving the coffin forward. The organ piped out a background of genre music. Everyone craned forward as the little doors opened. Beyond them the fire of the crematorium shone. The inspector was deeply moved. It seemed such a stupid way to end one's days, after mewling into the world at life's outset, only to end up a pathetic pile of ash.

The coffin was about to pass through the furnace doors when a strange thing happened – the rollers ceased to revolve and the coffin stopped. There was a rustle in the congregation and one of the crematorium technicians stepped into the aisle, probably with the intention of giving it a helping hand, but before he could move forward the sides of the coffin fell outwards and the lid collapsed inside with a hollow thud. It was perfectly obvious to everyone in the congregation that the coffin was completely empty. Before anyone could scream or fall back in a dead faint the rollers began to revolve again, the coffin resumed its last journey into the flames and the doors slowly closed, blocking it from sight.

Chief Inspector James remained standing for several minutes. He badly needed a drink.

THE GREAT CRIME OF GRAPPLEWICK

ONE

O n a typical cold damp winter's morning in the middle of August as nine o'clock boomed out over the complex of one of His Majesty's Prisons, the little door in the massive gate opened and 416236 became a person again. Terence was his name, Raffles to his colleagues, and he was known to the police as Pillock Brain.

With casual elegance he fitted a badly made cigarette into an ebony holder and applied a match.

'Be seeing ya,' said the warden behind him.

He raised an eyebrow and turned to make a witty riposte.

Bang! The little door slammed shut, and the badly made cigarette exploded in a shower of sparks. He quickly looked over his shoulder to see if the incident had been observed, but apart from a dog who shied away on hearing the slam of the door, and two spotty urchins, there was nobody to embarrass him. However, even two spotty urchins are an audience to a born actor, as Terence undoubtedly was. A bad actor, but nevertheless a compulsive one, he drew himself up to his full 5 feet 11½ inches on the Beaufort scale and brushed himself down with a pair of old kid gloves. He knew he was an imposing figure – black Homburg, long black overcoat with a half belt at the back and spats, which will give you some idea of how long it had been since he'd had a chance to go shopping.

The two Herberts giggled and nudged each other. There wasn't much entertainment in the immediate post-war years, and suddenly out of the blue here was this tall thin idiot, a brown paper parcel under his arm, and what looked like a smouldering daisy sticking out of his mouth. Even the dog came back to have a look.

Terence winked at the kids and took a match from his pocket, then he flicked his thumbnail against the head. It was a trick he had learned during his stay inside – it was nonchalant and had the effect, especially on new inmates, that here was one cool hombre. However, and perhaps because he was outside his environment, it didn't quite work out. The head of the match ignited and flew onto his Homburg, while some of the phosphorus stuck to his thumbnail. There was a burst of laughter from the audience. Terence dropped his parcel and hopped from one foot to another, sucking his thumb.

'Hey, mister,' gurgled one of the kids, your hat's on lire.'

Quickly he snatched it from his head and the wig came wirh it. This was the end for the spotty urchins. They were holding each other up, tears streaming down their cheeks – it was better than a Laurel and Hardy film. Terence snatched up his parcel and threw it at them. They ran off a few yards and stopped to watch the next hit. They didn't get a treat like this every day. Terence stuffed his wig in his overcoat pocket, then put his hat back on. Without the wig it came right down over his eyes, but at least it hid some of his embarrassment. He bent down to pick up his belongings, and as he did so his braces went. Typical, he thought – if this is freedom I'm going back in. Not only that, the parcel had come adrift, and there were all his worldly goods for everyone to see -shaving gear, carpet slippers and a sock – not a lot to show for the most brilliant criminal brain in the business.

He straightened up and shuffled off down the street, clutching his parcel and his trousers, head well hack so he could see where he was going. In high glee the kids skipped after him, pointing out his braces which were hanging down below the hem of his long black overcoat. The dog enjoyed the braces too, and kept darting in, trying to grab them.

A little way up the street a pavement artist watched him approach from the corner of his eve and continued chalking his picture, which might have been a sunset over the sea, or it could have been a fried egg on a lawn. Whatever it was it didn't enhance the pavement – had he been a dog his owner would have been fined on the spot. However, he was waiting for Terence, and whenever he had time to spare – which meant most of his waking hours – he drew or sketched or doodled. In fact his work was on exhibition on the walls of several County Courts, police cells and public lavatories – thus he was known to anybody in authority and anybody against it as Rembrandt.

Terence stopped by the chalking scruffbag and turned round to the kids, who hovered at a safe distance. Rembrandt didn't look up and continued chalking.

'So dey let you out all right, sorr?' he said, addressing the spats.

Terence looked casually about him and spoke, hardly moving his lips. 'Did you find Helliwell?'

'No sorr, oi did not and dat's a fact.'

'Did you get round to all the old places?'

'Definitely, sorr,' Rembrandt deftly applied a touch of purple chalk and surveyed the effect. 'Oi went round to all de old places, and if he'd been dere oi would have found him.'

He was about to shade the purple hit when the brown paper parcel fell on it, and in a blur he was yanked to his feet by the lapels of his raincoat.

'You've had eight months,' said Terence in a quiet voice.

'Yes, sorr, oi know dat. Oi tink he must have died, sorr. A bomb could have done it in de war.'

'If Helliwell was dead, I would have heard about it.'

The lads looked on silent and wide-eyed. Here was this tall thin idiot with his trousers round his ankles, holding the little man against the wall. It should have been funny, but it didn't seem laughable. The dog growled.

'Eight months, you great steaming Irish bog!'

'Dat's roight and don't you worry, sorr. If he's aloive oi'll foind him, and when oi do, oh yes sorr, oi'll mark him all right.'

Terence, head back so he could see, looked into the dirty, unintelligent face and spoke slowly. 'I don't want him hurt.'

'Oh no, sorr, oi wouldn't hurt him. Oi'll mark him where it doesn't show. De police do dat, and when you come to court you're doubled up in agony and not a mark to show for it.'

A sudden gust of cold wind hit Terence's thin bare legs. He looked down, saw his trousers in a heap round his ankles, and glanced quickly at the kids. 'You managed a car, I trust?'

'Roight behoind you, sorr,' said Rembrandt.

Terence had already seen it, but thought it was derelict. However, he shuffled himself into the passenger seat and the kids moved a little closer, while the dog added a neat touch to

Rembrandt's masterpiece. Terence settled himself in and slung his parcel in the back seat. 'Not exactly a Rolls. is it?'

'No, sorr, a Rolls is much bigger dan dis. Oi did tink of getting a Rolls and dat's de truth, but dey always have somebody watching dem.'

The engine coughed into life and Rembrandt rubbed his hands together. 'Roight, sort, where to first?'

Terence extracted another badly made cigarette from an old tobacco tin. 'Grapplewick,' he said.

'Roight, sorr.' Rembrandt was about to let off the brake when he stopped. 'Grapplewick?' he said. 'Dat's de one place oi've niver heard of, but it sounds a divvil of a long way to me. And why should we be after going to Grapplewick, sorr?' He leered across at Terence. 'Oi know Big Alice wouldn't mind having a look at yez.'

Terence shuddered at the thought of Big Alice – seven years was a long time, and she'd be bigger now. 'Helliwell was born in Grapplewick,' he said.

Rembrandt shook his head. 'Oi wouldn't go back to de place where oi was born – no sorr, if oi had money you wouldn't get me going to dat place. In any case oi tink Helliwell's probably dead.' A new thought struck him. 'Dat's it, why don't you ring de War Office, dey'll be able to tell if he's dead or not.'

Terence wound down the window and flicked the end of his cigarette at the two urchins. They dodged to one side, but the smaller of the two pounced on it and had a couple of quick drags. 'I may have been under lock and key for seven years, but I still maintain my sources of information. Oh yes, Helliwell got himself a nice cushy number in the Ministry of Supply during the war.'

Rembrandt's eyebrows went up. 'Oh, so dat's why de war took so long.' He chuckled at his own witticism. 'Oi'll bet a lot of dose supplies didn't get to de lads at de front.'

Terence sniffed. 'Quite correct. A large percentage went to Ikey the Fixer.'

Rembrandt sucked in his breath. 'Dat's a cliver man, Ikey. Dey'll niver be able to put a finger on him – he's got a chief inspector who runs errands for him.'

'Correct again.' Terence smiled thinly. 'I met them both in the exercise yard a week ago.'

Rembrandt's mouth dropped open. 'He's inside?'

'Snug as a bug in a rug,' he drawled smoothly, 'and incidentally it was our old mate Helliwell who shopped him.'

Rembrandt's mouth fell open again -Terence turned away in disgust. 'Holy Mother! We'd better foind him before Ikev gets his hands on him.'

Terence lit another cigarette. 'There's no rush. Ikey won't be available till about 1965.'

'Dat's all very well, sorr, but he's got influence. Some of his boys'll be looking for him.'

Terence raised an eyebrow. 'I've no doubt of that, but they'll be looking in the wrong place.' He blew a cloud of smoke through the window. 'You see, my little Irish derelict, I took the liberty of telling Ikey that Helliwell's home town was Tunbridge Wells.'

Rembrandt nodded sagely. 'Dat's good tinking, sorr.' But he was uncertain. 'And how far away is de other place – er – what was de name again?'

Terence was arched forward, trying to knot his braces round his waist. 'Grapplewick,' he grunted.

'Dat's de one, sorr. How far is it?'

'About 250 miles as the crow flies, but with your sense of direction, God knows.'

'Dat's a long way, sorr. I'll need to see a mate of mine, he's got some cheap petrol, but it'll cost a bit.' And with that he let off the brake, but before they could move off a new Rover swerved past and squealed to a stop in front of them. The driver leaped out and rushed across the road to disappear down the gents' toilet. Terence and Rembrandt looked at each other, then Terence collected his parcel from the back seat, Rembrandt switched off the engine, and they both made themselves comfortable in the brand-new Rover.

The two urchins watched silently, not understanding, then decided the best place for them was somewhere else, so they ran off. But the dog knew, and, barking furiously, chased the car for a little way towards Grapplewick.

TWO

It is hardly surprising that Rembrandt had never heard of Grapplewick. It is marked on the map as Gwick, because the full name is too long for the dot it represents – a typical northern town splotched on the moors like a handful of goat droppings. Two tall factory chimneys make it a good landmark for pilots, and many a weary traveller on the moors, spotting the two chimneys, knows it is Grapplewick, which gives him a chance to avoid it. It is a town where nobody seems aware of anything, but everybody knows what is going on – in the town, that is, anything over 20 miles away being foreign and suspect. Of course, they bought newspapers – newspapers were useful for lighting fires or wrapping up fish and chips, and most children had the job of cutting it up into neat squares to hang on the nail in the lavatory at the bottom of the yard ... quite a few of the men actually read the newspapers, but only the sports page.

The majority worked in the two cotton mills, married somebody they'd known all their lives, supported Grapplewick Athletic, and took their wives to bed every Sunday afternoon. Their women brought up the results, supported their husbands, generally hated Sunday afternoons, and, once married, gave their brains a long holiday from which most of them never returned. The younger people, learning nothing from their elders, prepared to go the same way, spending Sunday afternoons parading up and down the High Street, known as the chicken run. The girls, arm in arm, followed by the boys, would go up to the Odeon, then back to Burton's, then up to the Odeon again, the girls giggling and glancing over their shoulders, while the boys played football with anything that happened to be loose, or indulged in a little mock wrestling, seemingly oblivious, always keeping their distance from the girls – as the light decreased, so did the distance between them.

The well-to-do and the bosses lived on the Binglewood Estate, situated on high ground and sufficiently wooded to block out the view of Grapplewick. The only workers to set foot in this exclusive area were tradesmen, gardeners, servants and one or two keen ones from the factory who hung about the golf club on Sunday in the hopes of carrying a bag around for sixpence, and to say 'Yes sir, no sir.'

Even as Terence was emptying his last slop bucket prior to his release the streets of Grapplewick were bustling, echoing to the sound of thousands of clogs on their way to the mills, the foggy gloom illuminated by the glowing ends of countless Woodbines, Park Drives, Craven As and dubious concoctions of all brands salvaged from the gutter. Hawking and coughing accompanied the steady clockering of feet, dwindling and then quickening as the factory hooter wailed its mournful note. The last few footfalls became frantic, and then Grapplewick went back to sleep again until it was time for school.

Near the town centre, at the corner of Leslie Street and Featherstall Road, the men of the Fire Brigade turned up for duty at the station. A red brick eyesore, erected in 1882, it was approached across a cobbled yard, swept and hosed down each day – the old stables were still in use, although now tenanted by the two Clydesdales belonging to Hoskins' Brewery, and they ate well. The main building housed the ancient fire engine, more of a collector's piece than functional, which was hardly surprising because, apart from two engine changes, it was the original tender that had replaced the horses – a fond, familiar sight in the streets. The old 'uns still maintained it would get round faster if they'd kept the horses. However, since the inception of the Brigade there had only been one noteworthy fire, a warehouse on Featherstall Road, and to everyone's embarrassment, although it was only 500 yards from the station, the warehouse would have been completely gutted had it not been for the timely arrival of the Blackburn Fire Brigade. Apparently, on hearing the alarm, the Grapplewick lads collected their gear and helmets and flung themselves onto the engine. Unfortunately, however, nobody could fmd the driver, and although he wasn't the only one possessing a licence he'd taken the starting handle home with him for safety, and, to complicate matters, he was keeping two homes going, although neither woman was aware of the other. Unable to locate him, the lads endeavoured to push the great engine, applauded, jeered and urged on by a great crowd of town-folk, and to their everlasting shame everything was under control by the time they arrived.

People still recounted the story, with embellishments, and the present Brigade still bore the brunt of the taunts. Fortuitously from that day Grapplewick seemed fireproof, unfortunately giving the lads no opportunity to vindicate themselves, and Aggie, as the appliance was affectionately known, was as yet unblooded.

Leading Fireman Ned Bladdock entered the station. He was round and pedantic, carrying with him an air of authority. He nodded at Barmy Chronicle, accepting a mug of hot, sweet tea. Night shifts had long since been abandoned, and Barmy, although not now on the official strength, looked after the station at night. But then Barmy was not official on any list – officially he didn't exist, even at Somerset House there was no record of a Mr and Mrs Chronicle having any offspring, but somebody must have had fun, because one summer morning the result was found abandoned in the station yard, wrapped in a copy of the *Grapplewick Chronicle*, and legend has it that the fireman who was cleaning the yard swept the bundle along quite some distance before little Barmy rolled out. The poor fireman was so shocked he promptly dropped down dead. According to the story, in order to make up the numbers the Brigade enrolled the little mite as apprentice Chronicle, and the name stuck – Barmy was added later when it became obvious. He stirred the thick tea, leaning forward at a dangerous angle. The front of his long coat was already steaming from the heat of the great pot-bellied stove, which he kept going winter and summer. He gave Ned a wide, toothless grin and put his thumb up.

'OK?'

'It'll do.'

Barmy nodded and swaggered to the door, with his thumb ready to greet the next arrivals.

Ned smiled affectionately after him. 'Silly sod!' He wondered, not for the first time, if Barmy had ever been outside the gates.

The fire station was his home, in fact his whole world, but he seemed happy enough, and what chance would he have outside – big boots, long johns and an old First World War greatcoat that had originally belonged to someone who was at least a foot taller. No, it was probably better that he didn't set foot in the street – they'd have him in an asylum before he could say 'OK?'

Cyril Chadwick was the next arrival. Ned nodded to him and dragged out his heavy pocket watch. Young Cyril ignored the gesture – it happened every morning but it was merely habit. The mainspring had long gone, and it only had one hand, so it was permanently at quarter to . . . but to what hour was anybody's guess.

One by one the others rolled up and, as usual, Jack Puller was the last to report – a giant of a man with a Kitchener moustache and a black tobacco line etched round his bottom lip. He squirted a stream of brown juice into the yard.

Barmy grinned. 'OK?'

Jack tossed him a warm greasy bacon sandwich wrapped in a sheet of newspaper. 'Get that down you.'

Barmy took the paper off as if it was his twenty-first birthday present. 'Ooooh, bacon,' he said.

They took it in turns to bring Barmy food. Being an unofficial citizen he didn't have a ration book, but then the lads had little need for ration books either. Every Thursday the Brigade made the rounds of the outlying farms, ostensibly to deal with drainage, flooded fields, burning ricks or whatever. And in return for these courtesy visits the farmers supplied them with eggs, meat, butter, sides of bacon etc. It was considered a sound investment – who knows, perhaps one day their fields might well be flooded, their ditches stagnant, or even, God forbid, there might be a fire.

By the time Jack had helped himself from the dixie the sandwich was gone. The only sign that there had ever been a bacon sandwich was the fat glistening on Barmy's chin.

Jack shook his head slowly in admiration. 'Enjoy that, did you?' he said.

Barmy gave him his eternal grin and stuck his thumb up.

Jack winked. 'It'll make you randy, will that.'

Barmy pursed his lips like the neck of a balloon and slapped the back of his neck.

'Did you have droopy Nellie in here last night?'

Barmy spluttered with delight and some of the lads sniggered – although this was a regular exchange.

'Leave him be,' said Ned Bladdock, getting into his overalls. Droopy Nellie'd have him for breakfast, then spit out his braces.'

Nellie, something of a local celebrity, was a big Irish-woman – eighty-six convictions for being drunk and disorderly and didn't mind putting herself out for a couple of pints of Guinness. The lads of Grapplewick said they wouldn't touch her with a bargepole, but all the same she seemed to get through an awful lot of Guinness.

Jack winked again. 'I'll bet you 'ave a different one in 'ere every night and two on Sundays, eh, Barmy?'

Barmy chortled, pleased with everything. He hadn't the foggiest idea what Jack was on about, but it made him feel he was one of the lads.

'Why do you have to keep having a go at him?' spluttered Ned into his Woodbine. Jack hauled himself up into the driving seat of the huge, antique engine.

'He don't know the difference, do he? If Betty Grable walked in here wi' nowt on, he'd think it were a bloke who'd walked into a bacon slicer.'

Everybody laughed except Cyril, who blushed and snatched the starting handle from under the seat. Trust Jack Puller to make a coarse remark about Betty. Betty was an angel and he loved her with a shining white purity. Every Saturday he wrote to her, do Hollywood – he'd even sent her a photo of himself in his fireman's uniform, but so far she hadn't had a chance to reply. His grasp tightened on the starting handle and for one fleeting moment he had a mad urge to clout Jack Puller round the mouth with it. The urge, however, was short-lived as logic asserted itself. In order to defend Betty's honour he would first have to step up onto the running board. Then the handle was unwieldy and weighed a ton. By the time he got into a position to strike, Jack would have killed him.

'Are you going to crank her up or not?' Jack asked patiently. Cyril pulled himself together as he realised Jack was speaking to him.

'Eh?'

Jack leaned down so his face was almost level. Cyril could smell the acrid tobacco juice on his breath.

'I said, are you going to give us a crank, or are you waiting for me to stuff it up your jacksi?'

Cyril looked at the handle as if he'd just realised it was there.

'Oh,' he said. 'Start her up now?'

'Bloody 'ell!' exploded Jack. 'I'm not sitting up here to have my picture took.'

'Give it 'ere, Cyril,' said Ned kindly, and with two strong turns the big engine roared into life.

A flock of pigeons strutting in the yard rose instantly in a solid flap of panic and settled on the roof. The lads in the station watched the throbbing tender anxiously in case something fell off.

'As you are, come on, come on.' Ned guided the engine out into the yard with beckoning arms. Jack eased the choke as it rolled out. He never once glanced at Ned. There were at least two yards to spare on either side, but if Ned wanted to play silly buggers every morning it was up to him. Massive and gleaming, the thundering juggernaut was deafening in the confines of the station, but once outside it seemed to shrink as if fearful of the open air. The pigeons returned to the yard to mock, and some of them pecked arrogantly under the trembling engine. Jack swung himself down and hurried back into the warmth of the station.

'Bloody 'ell,' he shuddered. 'It's enough to freeze t'bloody taters off a polar bear.' Ned joined him at the stove and the yard was left to the pigeons.

''Oo's on the gate?' he said.

Fireman Helliwell slammed his mug down.

'Not yet. He won't be 'ere for hours yet.'

Jack looked at him steadily.

'If it's thy turn on t'gate, then bugger off. Tha knows what t'Chief's like, 'e's unpredictable. 'E might not be 'ere for hours, he might not come at all today, and then again 'e might just now be standing in t'yard, wondering if 'e's on t'*Marie Celeste*.'

Helliwell went.

Ned looked into his steaming mug. ''E's going through a bit of a rough patch at the moment, is Mr Thurk.'

The lads nodded slowly in agreement. Jim Cork spoke up. 'If you ask me, he's not getting all his own way at the Town Hall.'

Ned smiled. 'Don't worry about Mr Thurk. It'll take a bloody landmine to shift him.'

It was another of the vagaries of Grapplewick. The Mayor was not elected annually – in fact he was not elected at all. Mr Thurk's father had been Mayor and his father before him, so, as with Royalty, the Mayoralty was handed down to the eldest son – likewise the position of Fire Chief, and, as the Grapplewick Prize

Band was mainly composed of Brigade personnel, Thurks ascended naturally to the role of Bandmaster. The walls of the station were lined with yellowing pictures of various Grapplewick brass bands – stern moustached faces, smartly turned out in uniform, each man holding an instrument, and sitting front row centre of each photograph was a Mr Thurk. Sadly, there were no records on the walls of Grapplewick bands since 1932. Smart uniforms don't remain in one piece forever, and musical instruments deteriorate, so that now, although the keenness was still there and band practice was conducted every Thursday by Mr Thurk, he was the only one to retain a full uniform – three-quarter-length tunic, red sash, gloves and peaked cap. There was no money in the Band Fund – in fact, they didn't even possess a big drum. In order to practise they had to hire one from the scout troop for half-a-crown a week. This always stuck in Jack's craw. He could never get over it.

''Alf a crown a week for a big drum . . . no wonder they can afford to go to camp every bloody year.'

Fireman Helliwell leaned against the gate. He wasn't thinking about music. He was watching the struggling buttocks of a young woman as she hurried down the street. A medium-sized man in a dark uniform touched the peak of his cap to her as he passed and Helliwell practically swallowed his fag end.

'Bloody 'ell,' he muttered and hurried into the yard, hitting the bell twice with his knuckle. Immediately, hoses were rolled into the yard – four of the lads were polishing the old engine, although the brass plate on the side shone like new and the wording on it had in fact long since been huffed away. Jack Puller had the bonnet open, and was bent deep into the warm engine when Mr Thurk entered the yard. Ned shouted 'Shun!' and everybody stood rigid.

'Morning, Chief,' said Ned.

'Morning, lads. Carry on.'

The lads carried on, pretending to carry on. Barmy hurried out with a mugful of tea. Mr Thurk accepted it gratefully.

'Thank you, Mr Chronicle,' he said, as always one to observe protocol.

'Good practice last night. Especially "Men of Harlech". That was especially good.'

The lads nodded. It was a grand tune, even if it was Welsh.

Ned spoke up. 'It'd sound berter if we 'ad something decent to play it on.'

Mr Thurk nodded sadly. Here we go again. All avenues had been explored in order to raise funds. They'd had door-to-door collections, but the proceeds were frugal, and the operation had resulted more than once in actual bodily harm. The Firemen's Ball was another disaster. They'd started with a Paul Jones, to break the ice – men walking round on the outside, women going the other way – then the band broke into a waltz. Either the break into the dance wasn't obvious, or perhaps the tempo was too similar, but the dancers kept walking round in circles. 'Wings over the Navy' made no difference – it was like the exercise yard in a mixed prison. There was only one thing for it – a loud chord in G followed by a cymbal clash. The marchers dispersed and sat round the hall. After a whispered discussion between Mr Thurk and the organising secretary, which every eye in the hall tried to lip-read, the secretary blew twice into the microphone and asked if there was anybody who could play the piano. There was. And as the band shame-facedly packed up their instruments, the couples were swinging round the floor to something like 'An Apple for the Teacher'.

Open day at the Fire Station, another money-making scheme, had grossed £18 15s. 6d., but on the debit side they'd lost two helmets, four axes and a length of hosepipe. Also practising was thirsty work, so the band fund barely covered the bill from the off-licence.

Jack raised his voice over the noise of the engine. 'Any news from Mr Forsythe?'

Mr Thurk looked into his mug before replying. 'Not very helpful, I'm afraid.'

Jack spat and leaned into the warmth again. Forsythe owned one of the two mills and, as Foden's, Bickershaw Colliery, Black Dyke and all the big brass bands were sponsored, Mr Thurk had agreed to approach Mr Forsythe.

'We had a long discussion, and he wasn't actually against sponsorship in toto, there were economic factors involved, er, import of cotton, labour costs, in fact there was a possibiliry of going on short time, and what with the er . . .'

He trailed off. The lads weren't listening, and being basically an honest man he hated his own words. He hadn't really had a long discussion. When he had entered Mr Forsythe's office the great man had looked up, then gone back to the papers on his desk and said: 'If it's about that band o' thine, tha's wasting my bloody time.'

Mr Thurk had cleared his throat, in fact he had cleared his throat twice. Then he left.

Shamefacedly he handed his mug back to Barmy and rubbed his hands briskly together. 'Well, er ... tempus fugit.' He walked round the bonnet and tapped Jack on the shoulder.

Jack ducked out of the engine.

'Ready to move?' he asked.

Jack wiped his hands on a piece of waste paper. 'As ready as she'll ever be. Where to?'

'Just drop me off at the Town Hall, and pick me up at the usual time.'

The lads scrambled inside the station for helmets and tunics as Mr Thurk swung himself up beside Jack, and in no time at all they were trundling along Featherstall Road – a schoolboy on a bike pedalling furiously to keep up with them.

A keen young policeman watched the brand-new Rover as it passed him. He was about to move on, then stopped. Apart from the fact that it was progressing in a slightly erratic manner, there was something about the car that seemed odd. He turned quickly but it was fast disappearing. Suddenly he realised what had alerted him – there didn't seem to be anybody in it.

Rembrandt straightened up slowly and glanced furtively in his rear view mirror. 'It's OK, sorr, we've passed him, never saw us at all.'

Terence was almost bent double and cursed as he scraped his head from under the dashboard. He quickly swivelled in his seat to look out of the back window, but the policeman was very distant and didn't appear to be agitated. He grunted down again to pick up his hat and wig.

'We're making good time, sorr.'

Terence looked at him in amazement. 'Good time? What are you talking about? We've been on the road three hours now and we're still in London.'

Rembrandt nodded. 'Oh yes, sorr, oi'm laying a false trail so dat nobody can guess where we're goin'.'

'You're bloody well lost, aren't you?'

Rembrandt was vehement. 'Dat oi'm not, sorr. If oi was lost oi wouldn't know where oi was, but you see, sorr, if oi was to go straight up de A1, dey'd know. Oh yes, dey'd know all right.'

Terence shook his head in despair. 'You're a berk, d'you know that?'

'No, sorr, dey'll all be looking for dis car.'

'Exactly, but if you'd gone straight towards Grapplewick we might have been there before it was reported. In fact, we could have been there while the owner was still in the khazi.'

Rembrandt was unmoved.

'Oi know what oi'm doing, sorr. Oi know all de hack doubles in London.'

Terence banged the dashboard in exasperation. 'Fell, for god's sake don't keep driving past the nick. It's bad enough being inside – so just move it. Helliwell could be dead of old age before we get to Grapplewick.'

Rembrandt sniffed. 'You're de guvnor.'

And he turned right into another street, hoping it wouldn't bring them past the prison again.

THREE

The secretary coughed and adjusted his glasses. He was reading the minutes of the last debate which had taken place only two days ago. A Council Meeting was in progress, but then in Grapplewick Town Hall there were plenty of these get-togethers: the regular Council Meetings, and the Extra-ordinary General Meetings (which took place in the Council Chambers), then, apart from all the official meetings, as long as there was a quorum, they gathered in the Mayor's Parlour. Commander Wilson Brown was the newest member to be elected to the Council and he was appalled at the manner in which these affairs were conducted. There seemed to be no division of parties – when canvassing, all the candidates wore large blue rosettes and were all duly elected. It wouldn't have mattered to the electorate if they'd worn false ears and explodable boots. Nevertheless, due to his fine war record the Commander had been elected with a very impressive number of votes, but once in the Town Hall it counted for nothing, and it hurt. He glanced round the table. What a shower. He had only contempt for his fellow Councillors who had allowed this archaic state of affairs to continue. However, with a quiet word here, and a couple of drinks there, he felt he was gaining ground. It appeared to him that he was the only one who was experienced enough, and qualified to hold office. The others as yet couldn't, or wouldn't, grasp the opportunities, but one thing was certain – there was a lot of gravy about, and he was going to be the first to dip his ladle in. The secretary was still on his feet, squinting at something he'd written – owing to the fact that he took the minutes down in longhand it was never a faithful record, merely a gist.

Councillor Wilson Brown tapped the table irritably. Is there much more of this?'

The secretary looked at him over the rim of his glasses. 'I'm doing the best I can.'

Wilson Brown looked at him with distaste. The secretary wasn't a pretty sight – a tall, thin, stoopy man with a huge, beaked, purple-veined nose that overhung his tiny mouth, and no top lip to speak of. Wide-eyed children watched him eat his food, wondering if he was actually stuffing it up his nose.

Mr Thurk nodded to him kindly and he carried on.

'Where was I? Oh, yes. Councillor Wilson Brown pro-posed a motion that a statue of Winston Churchill be erected in the town centre, but the Mayor suggested a bandstand would be a more popular choice. Councillor Wilson Brown then replied ...

He stopped short and looked round the table. Councillor Wilson Brown broke the silence.

'Never mind what I said, just get on with it.'

Lady Dorothy glared at him. 'It should never have been said. It is a word I am not accustomed to hearing, and I cannot protest too strongly.'

'I apologised, didn't I?'

Mr Thurk broke in. 'I think we can delete that from the minutes. Carry on, Wilfred.'

The secretary nodded. 'Well, that's all there is. After the offending remark, the meeting broke up in disorder.'

With this, he sat down heavily and winced, making a mental note to see Dr McBride about his piles. No sooner was he down than Councillor Wilson Brown was on his feet.

'If I had commanded my ship in the way in which the affairs of this town are conducted, Grapplewick would be under German occupation.'

Lady Dorothy glared at him.

'With due respect, Commander,' she said in an icy tone, 'you are not the only man in this room who served his country during the war.'

'Hear, hear,' muttered deaf Crumpshaw. Lady Dorothy than-ked him, although she knew he hadn't heard a word.

Councillor Wilson Brown raised an eyebrow. 'I am well aware of the sacrifices made by the citizens of this town.'

Lady Dorothy blushed. She had presented Wilson Brown with an opening and he'd fired a full salvo. Her husband had been killed in 1944, but his name did not appear on the cenotaph. The Mayor patted her hand as he also remembered. His Lordship had managed to stay out of the war until it became obvious that we were going to win, so in 1944 he obtained a commission in the Honourable Artillery Company where he divided his time between his London clubs, the officers' mess and the occasional hunt. From information gleaned from his driver, he discovered that the Second Front was imminent, so he badgered the War Office with requests to be in the first wave on D-Day. On Winston Churchill's personal intervention, his wish was granted and he was transferred to an infantry regiment along with his valet and head groom. Unfortunately, when the invasion force finally sailed he was in London badgering the War Office for permission to take two of his hunters, and on hearing the news that they'd started without him, he had his gear packed and went home to Grapplewick. His personal valet and head groom leaped into France on D-Day, tragically landing on the same mine. His Lordship was never the same after that. A few weeks later he was jogging over the golf course on his favourite mare – he'd had more than a stirrup cup, in fact he'd had a bootful – and was unaware that a well-hit golf ball struck his mount on the backside. The horse staggered, giving him just enough time to hold on, then the mad gallop began, down the fourth fairway, churning up the green, through the rough, over two stone walls, with his Lordship now hanging round its neck like a long-lost relative.

The horse, with the adrenalin of over-confidence and a belly-full of best-quality oats, did an almighty leap to clear an outhouse. It didn't, but His Lordship did, and even his aristocratic skull was no match for the hard cobblestones on the other side. Thus Lady Dorothy, from being a grass widow, became a fully fledged one, and took his place on the Council. As Councillor Wilson Brown had remarked on more than one occasion, this was highly unorthodox, if not downright illegal. However, as he was the new boy he had to accept the situation – for the time being anyhow. Mr Thurk, on the other hand, enjoyed the company of Lady Dorothy and he found himself, not for the first time, wondering if she harboured such feelings for him. He pulled himself together as he became aware that Councillor Wilson Brown was speaking.

'With regard to the brass band, it is the joke of Grapplewick, and to suggest that we encourage it would be a gross misappropriation of the rates, and most certainly would make this Council the laughing stock of the North of England.'

Mr Thurk was on his feet. 'May I remind you, Councillor, that all the well-known bands – Foden's, Black Dyke and Bickershaw Colliery – only achieved greatness because of the financial encouragement they received.'

Wilson Brown shook his head. 'At least they started with a knowledge of music.'

The Mayor said nothing. The Band Fund was a regular topic at these meetings and a little money had always been allocated before the arrival of Wilson Brown.

The door opened and one of the cleaners stuck her head in. 'Are you goin' to be at it all day?' she said with a long-suffering face.

Councillor Wilson Brown glanced at her. 'How long we carry on is no concern of yours, and the next time I suggest you knock before entering.'

She stared round the table. 'Oh, aye, and what about my 'usband's dinner?'

Mr Thurk turned round in his chair and smiled kindly. 'It's all right, Mrs Macclesfield. You needn't do in here today, thank you.'

And with that she sniffed and closed the door behind her. Immediately Edward Helliwell, one of the younger members, took advantage of the break and was on his feet. 'If I may intercede, at our last meeting we did not establish what we were going to do with the space in the town centre. Now, having heard the proposals – i.e. a statue in honour of Winston Churchill and the Mayor's suggestion for a bandstand, both of which seem highly controversial and emotive – can we consider transforming it into a Garden of Rest?' He looked round the table and coughed into his hand.

Councillor Wilson Brown went on as if Edward was a ghost. He turned towards the Mayor: 'At the risk of being pedantic, don't you think you have enough on your plate with your duties as Mayor and Chief of the Fire Brigade without spending valuable time on that tuppenny ha'penny band?'

Mr Thurk ignored the remark, but drummed his fingers on his order papers. Lady Dorothy came to his rescue.

'The brass band is entirely voluntary and a spare-time job, and as long as I have been privileged to know the Mayor he has not once allowed it to interfere with his official business.'

'Hear, hear,' said deaf Crumpshaw.

'My dear lady,' said Wilson Brown in feigned astonishment, 'what the Mayor does in his spare time matters little to me. As far as I am concerned he is at liberty to indulge himself in plasticine modelling, he can run with his hoop up and down the High Street or go clog dancing in the evenings for all I care. It is the time wasted in Council Meetings holding out his begging bowl for the band that irks me. . . . Band!' he snorted derisively. 'We might as well spend the money taking a party of blind people to a silent movie.'

Councillor Helliwell was still standing. He coughed again, discreetly. 'We could stock it with flowers in season and in November it could be transformed into a sea of poppies.'

He looked round, but everybody was staring fixedly at the table. He heard a bus pass, and somewhere in the building someone dropped a bucket.

'Perhaps we could give it some thought.' He coughed again, and sat down to join the others staring at the table.

At the same time, in Bishop's Stortford, the police received a phone call to the effect that a baker's van had been stolen from the High Street. The desk sergeant made a note of it and put the phone down. It rang again almost immediately. It was a PC Macnamara calling in with the news that a brand-new Rover reported stolen in London was now parked outside Turner's bread shop.

Terence was furious. 'Didn't it get through to your thick Irish brain that a bread van might be conspicuous?'

Rembrandt didn't reply. He was driving with one hand whilst he held a crusty loaf in the other.

Terence tried again. 'Why a bread van, for God's sake?' Rembrandt swallowed a great lump. 'We have to eat, don't we? It's good bread, dis.'

Terence looked out of the side window. 'Brilliant.'

Rembrandt glowed with pride and took another huge bite.

Terence turned to face him. 'If you see a coal cart, we'll switch. Then we can have toast.'

Rembrandt considered this for a moment, then shook his head. 'It's new bread, dis. You never toast new bread and dat's a fact.

Some time later the police found the bread van in Boothby Pagnall, and a little old lady came out of the butcher's shop to find a space where her Ford Prefect had been.

FOUR

Fireman Cyril Chadwick had the original idea. One morning he arrived at the station one hour late. Ned opened his mouth to ask for an explanation when he caught sight of the sack that Cyril was carrying, and the mysterious smile on his face. So he followed him into the station. Cyril put down the sack gently and waited till the lads gathered round. Jack was the first to speak.

''As tha brought tha lunch?'

Cyril winked and delved into the sack. The lads moved back a step in case something sprang out, and with the air of a professional illusionist he brought out a gleaming kettle drum. Twenty-three mouths fell open, and one set of dentures and a wad of tobacco fell out. Ned's eyes widened and he moved forward to touch the skin.

'Bai, that's a grand drum is that.'

Cyril preened and took a pair of drumsticks out of his belt. 'Listen to the tone,' he said, and propping the drum between his stomach and the wall he gave a couple of rolls and a paradiddle. Jack brushed his wad of tobacco on his sleeve and popped it in his mouth.

'Where did you pinch yon bugger from?' he asked.

Cyril put the drum back in the sack. 'I got it from Cowell and Bottisford's.'

The lads looked at each other in wonder. Many's the time they'd all stood, noses pressed to the window of Cowell and

Bottisford's: drums, euphoniums, big drums, trombones – it was one of the best music shops in the North of England.

'I'll bet that set thee back a bit,' said Ned.

'No it didn't,' said Cyril. 'They took my old 'un in exchange for this.'

Jack spat on the stove. 'Go on, pull t'other one. Thy drum was clapped out, only had one skin and that had a plaster on it. That one there's practically new, snares and all. Aye and bloody white ropes 'anging down.'

Cyril shuffled uncomfortably. 'Well, I, er, had to give 'em something else as to sort of make up the difference . . . and it's only lent, mind you. If anything happens I can get it back in five minutes.'

He stroked the sack and the lads waited. Ned spoke first. 'Come on then, what else did you give him besides that drum of yours?'

Cyril blushed and lowered his eyes. 'My 'elmet.'

Every head swivelled to the rack where the helmets hung. 'Tha's given him thy 'elmet?'

'No, not given, only lent. He promised I could redeem it if it was necessary.'

Ned bridled. 'That's all very well, but that 'elmet doesn't belong to thee. It's Corporation property. What're you going to wear on the engine – a beret?'

Cyril came back quickly. 'We only wear them for show, anyway. We nearly always wear our peaked caps.'

'Mr Thurk's not too happy about that either. Always on about a smart turnout.'

Cyril played his trump. 'All right then, which d'you think he'd prefer – us with caps instead of 'elmets or a smart brass band? Go on, I know which he'd prefer.'

Jack thought about his cornet. It was getting harder to play. If he didn't get a new one, he'd be needing a truss.

Ned looked at the sack again. 'I've seen a grand big drum in that there window, a right bobby dazzler. Got battle honours as far back as the Crimean war.'

Jim Cork nodded. 'Aye, it'll be better than the one tha borrows now.'

'It will an' all,' said Jack. 'And we wouldn't have to pay half a bloody crown a week for the loan of it.'

Ned solemnly took a coin out of his pocket. 'We'll toss up,' he said, 'and if it's 'eads it's all right, and if it's tails tha takes it back and we'll say no more about it.'

He spun the coin into the air and they all crowded round to see what it was. Ned had to toss it three times before it came up heads.

The following day Mr Bottisford, pottering in his shop, listened absent-mindedly to the approach of the fire bell. He glanced towards the window and was surprised when the fire engine pulled up outside. He was even more surprised to see the firemen leap off, two of them running to a hydrant with a hosepipe, while several more manhandled a ladder to his bedroom window. He stood aside as three of them entered the shop itself, one going into the back room while two of them dashed upstairs. It was all carried out so quickly that before his brain could get round to forming a question, the large fireman was coming slowly down the stairs, helmet in hand, mopping his brow. His companion brushed past him to the door and said, 'False alarm.'

Ned Bladdock walked in wearily. 'Sorry about that, Mr Bottisford,' he said. 'Bloody kids.'

'False alarm, was it?'

'Aye,' said Ned. 'We can't afford to ignore 'em.' He leaned his elbows on the counter with the air of a man called out on unnecessary alarms every five minutes.

Jack Puller joined him. 'Especially this shop,' he said, looking around him with shining eyes.

'Oh, I don't know,' sighed Mr Bottisford. 'Business is terrible. I sometimes think I'd be better off with the insurance. Then again' – he swept his hand round the brass band instruments – 'this lot 'd take a lot of burning. I should have gone into the timber business.'

Jack nodded, and there was a pause. Then he placed a newspaper bundle on the counter. Mr Bottisford looked on curiously as Jack took out his battered cornet. Enlightenment dawned.

'You've seen Cyril, then?'

'Aye,' said Jack, and pushed the instrument tentatively forward.

Mr Bottisford scowled at it. 'How have you ever managed to play on this?'

'It's not too bad,' said Jack.

Mr Bottisford picked it up carefully. Jack watched him apprehensively.

'Don't turn it upside down! One of the stops £11 fall out.'

While Mr Bottisford was examining the cornet, Jack took off his helmet and placed it deliberately before him.

Mr Bottisford took the hint. 'Not another helmet.'

'Biggest we have in the station,' said Jack, proudly pointing to the '7½' on the head band.

Mr Bottisford shook his head sadly, and walked round the counter to a glass case containing half a dozen cornets. He selected one and handed it over. Jack licked his dry lips and took it as if he was about to baptise a new-born baby. He put it reverently to his lips, but before he could blow Mr Bottisford grabbed his arm.

'Dost a want everybody to know what's goin' on?' he bleated. 'Supposin' somebody comes in?'

'That's all right, Mr Bottisford,' said Ned with authority. 'Street's roped off as far as Woolworth's.'

'Never mind Woolworth's,' snapped Mr Bottisford. 'They'll hear that.'

Ned agreed, and Jack wrapped it quickly in the paper before Bottisford had a change of heart. Jim Cork joined them with a large object wrapped in a tatty blanket, and Mr Bottisford was hardly surprised to find it was a battered old euphonium. He glanced at it scornfully, then suddenly he took it from Jim and examined the bell closely. He pointed to the scratched initials 'J.B.'.

'This belonged to Josh Barlow,' he said.

'That's right, my Uncle Joshua.'

'Well, I'll go to our 'ouse,' said Bottisford in amazement. 'Josh taught me all I know about music.' He held the instrument fondly, then lifted it to his lips and blew tentatively. Again he blew, but it was useless – not a peep. His lips and his wind had gone years ago. He lowered the euphonium, breathing heavily. 'Well, tha's kept it clean any road,' he wheezed. 'Bai, when Josh blew a note on that, all t'visitors used to get off t'*Queen Mary*.' He smiled nostalgically, then frowned. 'I've got enough helmets, though.'

Jim Cork looked over his uniform, then down at his thigh boots. Ned looked up at the ceiling in exasperation.

Mr Bottisford nodded. 'Well, I can use them on t'allotment, I suppose,' and five minutes later curious onlookers observed a fireman walking out of the shop in his stockinged feet carrying a blanket-wrapped bundle. In half an hour rumour swept the town that a child had perished in the fire.

Ned and Jack were about to leave when Mr Bottisford stopped them. 'They're only on loan, you know.'

'Ah know that,' said Ned. 'Them helmets and stuff's only collateral . . . we can reclaim them any time.'

'Aye,' said Mr Bottisford shrewdly. 'On production of my instruments.'

Ned nodded.

'Or,' went on Mr Bottisford, 'tha paid for 'em in cash, and that'd suit me a lot better.'

'Right,' said Ned. 'Oh, and by the way, if you're ever free on a Thursday, you might like to pop in and listen to a band practice.'

Mr Bottisford's eyebrows shot up in delight, then they slowly went down. He'd heard them once, and that was in the open air. God knows what it would be like in a confined space. 'I always listen to the wireless on Thursdays,' he said. 'But I'll tell thee what, I wouldn't mind coming in one day to have a look at the old photos.' He looked from one to the other. 'They're still on t'walls, aren't they?'

Jack nodded. 'Aye, every year till a few years before the war.'

They were proud of the past Grapplewick bands, but embarrassed and somewhat ashamed that they had not attained the standard to join their illustrious forebears.

'We had a good band in them days,' said Mr Bottisford. 'I was second trombone, you know.'

Jack nodded. 'Aye, we've seen you on the photos.' He was eager to be off with his shiny new cornet, but Mr Bottisford hadn't had much chance to reminisce since Cowell died. He leaned across the counter.

'The old Mr Thurk was Bandmaster in them days, and what a Tartar he was. Couldn't read a note, but what an ear for music,' he giggled. 'Once at a band practice Tommy Burton the double B had had a few pints of brown ale, and during a loud piece . . .'

Jack broke in, eager to be off. 'You've told me before.'

Mr Bottisford ignored the interruption. 'I could see old Tommy squirming in his seat, holding it back till we got to a crescendo . . . crash went the cymbals, and Tommy's face relaxed. I was right next to him and never heard it, but at the end of the piece old Mr Thurk put down his baton and looked straight at him.'

'Tha'd be better off playing the double B at t'other end,' he said. Mr Bottisford burst into laughter until a cough took over. 'Wonderful ear for music, old Mr Thurk.' Mr Bottisford was wheezing and dabbing his eyes.

Outside, the fire bell dinged fiercely. Jack heaved a sigh of relief.

'Well, another emergency, I suppose,' and he made his way to the door.

Ned dawdled. 'That's a grand big drum you have in the window.' But before he could pursue the matter the engine burst into life, and he hurried out. Jack didn't wait for stragglers. That was the beginning of the exchange of stock between the two concerns. It was a slippery slope.

Three miles south of Grapplewick, Terence and Rembrandt stepped out of a small MG sports car. Terence stretched himself and surveyed the scene. The Pennine Gorge was a well-known beauty spot, frequented mainly in the summer but hardly ever in the winter when a good snow would make the road impassable. Terence blew into his cold hands and walked to the edge of the plateau. The keen wind made his eyes water and almost took his breath away. A few drops of rain spattered the back of his neck and he pulled his collar up. It suddenly occurred to him that there wasn't a cloud in the sky, and he whirled round to see Rembrandt relieving himself against the wheels of the car with no regard for the direction of the wind. Angrily Terence took out his handkerchief and rubbed the back of his neck.

'You dirty little bugger,' he snarled.

'It's OK, sorr,' said Rembrandt, tucking his pitiful manhood away. 'They can't touch you for it as long as it's against the off-side wheel. It's an old law, you see, sorr, from the days when they had horses.' He was about to elaborate when Terence cut him short.

'Just get the baggage out.'

Rembrandt stared at him, perplexed. 'Get the baggage out, sorr?'

'Out of the car.'

'Out of the car, sorr?'

Terence looked up at the heavens with a sigh and back at Rembrandt. 'You suddenly gone deaf or something?'

Rembrandt was uncertain. But when Terence took a men-acing step towards him he had the boot open in a flash and two newly acquired suitcases and a carrier bag appeared like magic on the ground at Terence's feet.

'Thank you,' he said with a biting sarcasm that only people of breeding could get away with. He strolled casually to the edge of the gorge and looked down. Then he turned his gaze to the left and in the far distance two tall factory chimneys stood out against the bleak moors. Rembrandt followed his gaze.

'Dat must be Grapplewick, sorr.'

Terence didn't reply.

'We can be there in ten minutes. It's all downhill from 'ere, sorr. 'Tis only the first bit that's up.'

Terence went to the side of the plateau where the ground sloped steeply to accommodate a footpath. He swung to face Rembrandt.

'Bring the car here.'

Rembrandt peered over his shoulder at the grassy slope. 'We'll be better off sticking to the road, sorr. Dat's only a path.'

Terence clenched his fists and it was enough. Rembrandt was in the car like a startled ferret, slowly easing it forward to the edge. Terence waved him nonchalantly forward, then casually held up his hand. Rembrandt snatched the brake and leaned out.

'Are you sure this is the quickest way, sorr? Oi don't tink it's a road at all.'

'Out,' said Terence.

Rembrandt couldn't wait. He fumbled with the door handle and shot away from the car. He was about to ask why it was necessary to park so near to the edge, but he was too late. Terence was thirty yards away, scrambling to a piece of high ground in order to survey the road. Satisfied, he held onto his hat and scuttled back down to the plateau. Rembrandt watched him apathetically, hands deep in his pockets, hopping from one foot to the other for warmth – or it could have been a weak bladder. Terence pushed him to one side, leaned into the car and released the brake. Then he strolled round the back, placed his foot on the rear bumper and gave it a contemptuous shove. Nothing happened. In fact the car seemed to bounce back slightly. He frowned and, placing both his hands on the boot, he gave a tentative heave. The car was unyielding. He looked round to see if Rembrandt was watching, but it was OK – Rembrandt was totally absorbed rummaging deep into the litter bin. Checking that the brake was off, Terence went round the back and tried again. This time he was really straining. His face puckered up and reddened, and a vein in his forehead throbbed dangerously. But the bloody car was obstinate. He straightened up, breath rasping in his throat. He didn't have to turn to know that Rembrandt was watching him now. It made him angry – he should have told the little sod in the first place, but it was too late, his pride was at stake. Jamming his hat down, he leaned forward and with a grunt he made an almighty heave. A look of horror crossed his face and he shot upright, clasping the seat of his trousers. Rembrandt clucked sympathetically and shuffled to the back of the car.

You should let me do dat, sorr.' And with a flick of the wrist he had the boot open. ''Tis easy when you know how.'

Terence's agonised look changed to amazement. He forced himself to speak calmly – he was in no position to rant. 'It's nothing to do with the boot. I was trying to push the car over the edge.'

He stopped suddenly as another spasm wracked him. Rembrandt smiled confidently and shook his head. 'You'll not do dat, sorr. No sort, safe as houses is dat little car. Whilst you wuz up de hill, I put two rocks under the front wheels.'

Terence screwed his eyes shut and turned to face the sky, struggling to contain himself. One thing was certain, had he been mobile with both hands free, the little Irish reject would be on his way down to the bottom of the Pennine Gorge. Realisation dawned on Rembrandt. He looked aghast at Terence, then at the car, then leaned forward to peer over the edge.

'Oi'm not wid you, sorr. If we push de car over, how're we going to get to dat town?' He pointed in the direction of the two factory chimneys.

'We take a bus.'

Rembrandt took a smart step back, shaking his head vigorously. 'No, sorr. Oi'm not takin' no bus. Dey all has de numbers on 'em. Oh yes, sorr, we wouldn't get a mile before dey had de road blocks up.'

'Just get those rocks from under the wheels.'

Rembrandt rarely looked directly into Terence's face, but he did so now and what he saw wasn't encouraging. He scurried round to the front of the car. 'Oh, oi'll do dat for you all right, sorr, but oi'll not take no bus and dat's a fact.'

He leaned on the bonnet, easing the car back a fraction. While he kicked the nearside rock away, muttering useless obscenities, he gingerly made his way to the front wheel, clinging desperately to the headlamp to stop himself sliding down the incline. Terence walked round in a tight circle as if his ankles were shackled, pondered idly what it was about the Irish that made it logical to risk life and limb scrambling round the front of the car when it would have been much simpler to go round the back. He turned away as his stomach contracted. There was a strangled yelp and he looked round just in time to see Rembrandt fling himself clear as the car rolled down the incline, bouncing slowly at first, then picking up speed as it slewed through the wooden safety fence with an ease that didn't say much for its safety. Rembrandt scrambled to his feet, crossing himself at the same time – it was merely a reflex action. Almost in slow motion, the car tumbled into the gorge. Cartwheeling through the air, it smashed first into one side and a head-lamp flew off. Rocks started to tumble, then in a lazy parabola it careened into the opposite side, gouging a scar. A wheel bounced exuberantly behind it, and finally all the bits and pieces splashed into the tiny stream, followed by a miniature avalanche of rocks, small bushes and anything else that wasn't firmly rooted. Terence was satisfied – nothing at the foot of the gorge bore any resemblance to a car.

Some three hours later the twice daily bus from Blackburn pulled up in front of Grapplewick Town Hall. Rembrandt stepped off with the luggage and stood aside while the conductor gingerly helped Terence onto the pavement. He watched the tall thin man walk stiff-legged, hardly able to put one foot before the other.

'All the best to you, colonel,' he called after him. Terence acknowledged with a slight raise of his hand and shuffled on. The conductor shook his head. The poor devil had had to stand all the way from the Pennine Gorge because of a war wound and, judging from the smell, it was time they changed the dressing.

'Well, we made it, sorr,' said Rembrandt.

Terence didn't reply. He was looking for a gents.

FIVE

And the roof is still leaking?'
Mr Thurk made a note in a little black book and took a sip from his half of bitter. Elsie rang the till and handed out some change to a small, well-dressed man, then came over to Mr Thurk and leaned on the bar. Mr Thurk blushed. Elsie was one of those barmaids that made pubs a viable proposition, and when she leaned over the bar to talk it was a personal favour. She had, without doubt, the finest upper bodywork in Grapplewick, and hindquarters to match.

'Sorry about that, Mr Thurk.'

'That's all right, Elsie. I just made a note that your roof is still leaking.'

Elsie nodded. 'It's worse than ever. We put a bucket under, but when it rains it keeps us awake.'

Mr Thurk had a quick vision of her husband, a strapping lad when he married her not too long ago, now slightly bent with dark rings under eyes that stared out of a white face – it must be a hell of a leak.

'Can you do anything about it? I mean, it's driving my Fred up the wall. When it rains really hard, he's up and down all night.'

I'll bet he is, thought Mr Thurk, then he forced himself to look at her face. 'Pardon?'

Elsie sighed. 'I said, can you do anything about it?'

Mr Thurk took another gulp at his drink. 'Well, it's really not my pigeon, it's more a matter for the Housing Department.'

She pouted. 'Yes, I know, but I thought with you being Mayor and all. . . .

Mr Thurk glanced at his watch. 'All right, Elsie. I'll have a word with Mr Thomas and ask him to pop round and see you.'

Elsie frowned. 'Oh, him . . . he's been to see me . . . tall feller with a big droopy moustache.'

'That's him – what did he say about it?'

'Well, he agreed that it was bad and said there shouldn't be no difficulty in finding alternative accommodation.'

Mr Thurk finished his drink. 'Well, there you are then. . . .'

Elsie plucked his sleeve and drew him closer He gulped and hoped he wouldn't have to agree with anything, because if he nodded his face would go smack into that glorious bosom. Elsie didn't appear to notice. In fact if people didn't stare at her chest she thought they were blind.

'There's just one thing,' she said quietly.

'Yes?' said Mr Thurk. He meant to say yes, but it sounded as if someone had scratched a balloon.

'When he said there'd be no difficulty in finding alternative accommodation, he smiled in a funny way.'

Elsie released his arm and stood back. Mr Thurk straightened. 'Oh come on now, Elsie, he always smiles in a funny way – his teeth don't fit properly.'

Elsie looked slightly disappointed. 'Oh, then you don't think he's expecting a hit of hanky panky, because you know what my Fred's like.'

'Don't worry about that, Elsie. Mr Thomas is a family man, he's chapel.'

'They're the worst,' said Elsie, knowingly.

'No, there's nothing to worry about there,' said Mr Thurk. 'I'll tell him to get on with it as soon as possible.' He buttoned his raincoat.

'Thank you, Mr Thurk.'

'That's all right, Elsie. Give my regards to your Fred.'

And with that he stepped out into the night. Elsie watched him go and wondered idly why he'd never married – although there was a bit of talk about him and Lady Dorothy. Then she thought about her Fred and all those headaches he'd been getting in the last few months. A rapping on the bar snapped her out of her reverie.

'Good evening, miss. A large whisky and a small Guinness for my friend here.'

Rembrandt frowned.

'I'm sorry, sir, it'll have to be a small whisky, I'm afraid. Our stocks aren't back to normal yet, so I usually save it for my regulars.'

Rembrandt cheered up.

'All right, a small whisky then.'

Elsie nodded, already pulling the Guinness. Apparently engrossed, she was well aware that the scruffy little man was standing on tiptoe to get a better view of her superstructure. She placed the two drinks on the bar and looked directly at Rembrandt.

'If you come in here again let me know, and I'll get you a box to stand on.' Then she turned to Terence: 'That'll be two and threepence.'

Terence slapped half a crown on the bar and smiled. 'Keep the change, my dear.'

Elsie put the money in the till and took out threepence, which she tossed into a pint glass behind the bar. 'You're not from round here, are you?' she said.

Terence sipped his whisky. 'That's right,' he smiled. 'No fixed abode, you might say – commercial travellers.'

Elsie stared at him, intrigued by his moustache. One side was all right, but the other half seemed to flap when he talked.

Terence was quick to notice and pressed his hanky to his mouth to repair the damage.

'We're from London,' piped up Rembrandt, addressing Elsie's chest.

Elsie ignored him. 'Commercial traveller, did you say?'

'At the moment, my dear, yes. A bit of this and a bit of that. After six years in the Western Desert and Burma it's rather difficult to adjust to civilian life.' He laughed deprecatingly. 'Still, it's not an uncommon situation these days.'

Elsie nodded sympathetically. 'I know a lot of 'em are finding it hard to settle down.'

Terence tossed back his drink. 'Well, must be off. Have to find a place to get the old head down tonight.'

Elsie took his empty glass. 'Aren't you fixed up anywhere?'

Terence put on his 'don't worry about me' look. 'It's all right, my dear. Had to do a bit of shopping when we arrived – toothbrush, shaving cream.' He shrugged. Rembrandt finished his Guinness. 'And I had to buy a pair of flannels for him.' Terence glared, but it was lost on Elsie.

'Well, you've left it a bit late now,' she said.

'You wouldn't happen to have a first-class hotel in the area?' asked Terence.

Elsie put her hand to her cheek. 'Well, not first-class hotels. But if you're stuck there are usually one or two rooms vacant here.'

Terence brightened. 'That would be excellent, my dear. I don't fancy wandering around on a cold night like this.'

Elsie frowned. 'There hasn't been anybody staying here for ever such a long time, and I don't know if he still lets them.' She thought for a moment. 'Wait here. I'll ask Mr Helliwell to come down.'

Terence's eyes widened and he stared at her without focus. She wondered if he was an epileptic.

'Did you say Helliwell?'

A broad grin spread over Rembrandt's face. 'Oi allus said you were lucky, sort Bulls-eye first time aaargh. . . . .' He finished the sentence with a yelp and hopped round the room.

Terence looked at Elsie. 'He gets it every so often. I think it's the cold weather.'

Rembrandt sat at one of the tables and massaged his shoe. 'You bloody near broke my foot. You do dat again and oi'll, oi'll . . . an' you'll be sorry.'

Elsie smiled uncertainly. 'Mr Helliwell is the landlord.' She edged away to the foot of the stairs and called 'Mr Helliwell'. She put her head on one side and listened, then called again. An unintelligible reply came from upstairs. Elsie looked across at Terence and Rembrandt. 'There's two gentlemen enquiring about rooms.'

Again an undecipherable answer, but Elsie was satisfied and she came back to the bar. 'He'll be down in a minute.'

Terence leaned on the bar, outwardly calm, but his stomach was churning again. He was trying to decide how to handle the situation, but one thing was certain – he'd have this pub for a start. It wouldn't cover the debt Helliwell owed him, but then again there might be more stashed away in a bank or something.

'Another whisky, and make it a large one.'

Elsie was about to say something, but Terence's face didn't encourage a refusal.

Rembrandt limped to the bar. 'And oi'll have a pint of Guinness.'

Terence took the whisky and gulped half of it down. On an empty stomach he was already feeling light-headed. Oh, yes,

Helliwell owed him all right, driving off with the loot while he was only halfway down the ladder. Seven years of his life Helliwell owed him. His heart skipped a beat as he heard footsteps clomping down the stairs. Terence leaned back, elbows on the bar. He intended to turn slowly round and catch the expression on Helliwell's face.

Elsie spoke. 'These two gentlemen wondered if you had any rooms to let.'

Terence turned slowly and his face fell. If this was Helliwell he'd had very poor plastic surgery, and his legs had been amputated at the knees.

Rembrandt stepped into the breach. 'Are you Mr Helliwell?'

'I am.'

The landlord looked at the two of them suspiciously. 'I haven't let rooms for a long time.' He shook his head. 'How long would you be likely to want them for?'

Terence pulled himself together. He should have known there'd be more than one Helliwell. If he'd had any idea just how many, he would have been on his way back to London and Big Alice. 'Shouldn't be more than a few days – all depends on what the business is like.'

Helliwell nodded. 'Two pounds ten a week bed and breakfast . . . each.'

Terence slapped the bar. 'Done!' He pointed to the bags and nodded to Rembrandt to gather them up. Terence smiled at Elsie. 'Oh, put the drinks on my bill will you?'

Helliwell looked sharply at Elsie, then shrugged. 'Follow me, gentlemen.' And they did.

Two weeks later they were still in residence and Elsie had taken to wearing high necked dresses.

SIX

Commander Wilson Brown walked briskly into Helliwell's tobacconist's shop in the High Street.

'Morning, Commander. I haven't seen you for some time.'

'That's true. Been trying to give it up.'

Mr Helliwell sucked in his breath. 'Don't do that, you'll put me out of business . . . the usual?'

Wilson Brown nodded, and the little tobacconist took down a tin of Navy Cut and pushed it across the counter. 'Good film on at the Odeon this week – about a Yankee destroyer. You'd think they won the war without us, wouldn't you? Well made, though – destroyers going in against the Japanese . . .

The Commander pocketed the tin of tobacco. 'Didn't serve in destroyers, I'm afraid. Fleet Air Arm.'

They both turned towards the window when they heard the fire bell, and watched the old engine lumber slowly past. 'Wonder where they're off to?'

The Commander snorted. 'Chip shop, I shouldn't wonder.' Helliwell chuckled and handed over the change. 'Good day to you.'

The Commander touched his cap and left. A grand man, the Commander, thought Mr Helliwell. Didn't go round spouting off about his war experiences like some people, but he'd bet his bottom dollar that the Commander had seen plenty of action. The doorbell tinkled and interrupted his thought. He greeted the tall bearded stranger – the little man he ignored.

'Ten Park Drive and a box of matches.'

He slid them across the counter. 'There you are sir, that'll be twopence ha'penny – anything else?'

'Yes, there is, as a matter of fact. I caught the name "Helliwell" on the window and I wondered if I might have a word with him?'

'You're speaking to him.'

Terence nodded. 'Yes, I'd half gathered that.' He took out his wallet and extracted an old faded newspaper clipping. He proffered it. 'I wonder if you're any relation to this Helliwell?'

The tobacconist pushed his glasses onto his forehead and squinted closely. 'Not very clear, is it?'

He didn't notice Rembrandt edging behind Terence.

'It's about ten years old, taken before the war – Joseph Helliwell.'

The tobacconist handed the clipping back. 'There's some-thing familiar about him, but he's no relation of mine. Mind you, Grapplewick's full of Helliwells.'

Terence put the paper carefully back into his wallet. 'Yes, so I'm beginning to realise. Well, thanks anyway.' He looked round, but Rembrandt had already gone. 'Be seeing you.'

And Terence left. Helliwell rubbed his jaw and pondered for a moment, then, shaking his head, he tossed the coins into the till and slammed the drawer shut. He turned to go back to his fire in the other room, then stopped dead. He whirled back to the till and thumped the key. The drawer flew open, but all it contained was the tall bearded man's twopence ha'penny.

Just around the corner Terence caught sight of Rembrandt shuffling along and hurried to join him. Rembrandt was absorbed, counting out a few one pound notes, and at first didn't notice Terence walking alongside. Terence watched for a moment in amazement, realising where the notes had come from, and then with a snarl he took hold of Rembrandt's lapels and pinned him against the wall. The little Irishman took it stoically – it seemed that never a day went by without Terence hauling him up by his lapels. He once wondered, idly, if he shouldn't cut them off, but he quickly dismissed the idea – it was better than being lifted by the throat. Terence was livid.

'You stupid little Irish git, do you want to get us arrested?'

Rembrandt looked at Terence's adam's apple. 'We can't live widdout money, sorr.'

Terence stared at him for a moment, then released him, snatched the notes from Rembrandt's hand and stuffed them into his own pocket. After a quick glance round, he ripped off his beard and put on a pair of dark glasses.

SEVEN

M r Thurk stood in front of the pot-bellied stove, tapping his empty mug against his leg impatiently. Barmy hopped forward and took it from him, dipping it into the dixie.

'No more, thanks,' said Mr Thurk, and looked at his watch.

Then he walked to the door and gazed over the empty yard. He looked at his watch again and turned to the stove. Barmy pointed to the mug, but Mr Thurk shook his head.

'Didn't they say where they were going?'

Barmy grinned. 'hope,' he said and giggled with delight at being able to help.

Mr Thurk looked at him for a moment, then strode back into the yard, just in time to see the labouring old tender turn into the gates. He walked alongside as Jack turned the engine round in a wide circle. When it came to a stop Ned smiled.

'Morning, Chief. Parky this morning.' He rubbed his hands vigorously together.

Mr Thurk glanced at the red nose shining under the big brass helmet. He noticed too that some of the lads were wearing peaked caps, but this wasn't the moment – he'd get round to that later. He put one foot on the running board. 'Where the devil have you been?'

Jack switched off the engine. 'We ran out of tea.'

Mr Thurk spluttered. 'You ran out of tea . . . there's enough tea on that stove to have a bath in.'

'We ran out of sugar as well.'

Mr Thurk stepped down, raised his arms and let them fall against his sides in exasperation. Ned cleared his throat.

44'It's all right, Chief. We had the grid up in the road and checked the drains while Cyril nipped in like.'

Mr Thurk raised his eyes to heaven and Barmy put his thumb up. 'OK?'

He looked at the faces staring at him with bovine expressions. 'That's all very well,' he said, 'but you can't keep using the tender as a delivery van. I mean, people notice these things.' He paused. 'And look at the time – I'm supposed to be at the Town Hall twenty minutes ago.'

'Sorry, Chief. It won't happen again.'

Ned got down to sit with the lads on the back and Mr Thurk hauled himself up next to the driver. Jim Cork was already cranking the engine. It was still hot and sparked immediately. Jack crashed it into first gear with a noise like a bad train smash. He hauled on the wheel and, as they rolled out of the gates, a tall, middle-aged man with a big parcel under his arm dodged to one side and shouted something. Jack put his foot down and they trundled along Featherstall Road. Mr Thurk leaned over to Jack and yelled in his ear.

'Wasn't that Mr Bottisford's lad?'

Jack didn't take his eyes off the road. 'Who?'

Mr Thurk was about to say something else, but changed his mind, and the lads on the back looked at one another in relief.

The Mayor's Secretary, however, was far from happy. Stoop-shouldered, hands behind his back, he was pacing agitatedly up and down between the pillars on the Town Hall steps. Eyes watering in the wind that had reddened his nose, he looked for all the world like a turkey at the beginning of December. The Mayor was rarely late – and to be so on this day of all days! Three large crates had been delivered first thing, and Councillor Helliwell had had them carried into the Mayor's office. Wilfred followed like a dog watching his breakfast put into the bowl, but Helliwell had told him to leave. It was as if the dog biscuits had been given to the cat – after all, he had been the Secretary when Helliwell was still wetting the bed. Wilfred sniffed in disgust as the thought crossed his mind that by the looks of him he was probably still doing it. He stood behind a pillar to keep out of the wind, when he felt, rather than heard, the rumble of the old fire engine before it came into view in the High Street. He was down at the foot of the steps before Mr Thurk alighted.

'Morning, Your Worship.' He wiped a few drops from the end of his nose with the back of his hand.

Mr Thurk looked at him, then glanced quickly at the Town Hall. 'What's all the panic, Wilfred?'

The Secretary was trying to hurry him up the steps, another droplet appearing on the end of his nose.

Mr Thurk looked away in disgust, and when he looked back it had gone, but another one was forming. He shuddered. If that was blood he'd be dead in ten minutes. They were now striding briskly through the Main Hall.

'What's to do, then, Wilfred?'

Wilfred shook his head. 'Summat's up but I don't know what it is. I was asked to leave.'

Mr Thurk stopped suddenly and Wilfred cannoned into his shoulder.

'They asked you to leave?'

Wilfred looked furtively over his shoulder. 'They did an' all . . . mind you, there was only Councillor Helliwell there at the time, but now Lady Dorothy's in and the Commander and quite a few others. There were these three big boxes delivered about nine o'clock.' He lowered his voice. 'They're in your office.'

'Boxes? What kind of boxes?'

'Big 'uns.' He spread his arms out. 'Any road, we'll soon find out, won't we?'

Mr Thurk nodded and stood aside to allow Wilfred to open the door. They didn't hear him enter because they were crowded round the table giving all their attention to what appeared to be a model of some kind. Wilfred ahemmed 'His Worship the Mayor' and they all whipped round. Mr Thurk surveyed the tableau. It was rather like a headmaster walking in on a dormitory feast. Lady Dorothy smiled uncertainly.

'Good morning, Anthony.'

He looked at her inquiringly. 'Morning, Dorothy.'

Then he approached the table – his apologies for being late forgotten as he saw the model. He took out his specs, which he only used in order to give himself time to think, and surveyed the table. It was a fine-looking effort, no doubt about that. Tiny buildings, large areas of green to represent grass and four high blocks of flats like double-blank dominoes surrounded by tiny trees – it was very impressive. The Members of the Council examined it in silence, or perhaps it was a way of avoiding Mr Thurk's eyes. After what seemed an age, the Mayor took off his glasses.

'Did you know anything about this?' he enquired of Lady Dorothy.

She looked at him sharply. 'I'm afraid I know as much as you do.'

Unaccountable relief flooded through him. He nodded at the model. 'May I enquire what this is?'

Councillor Helliwell rose to his feet and licked his lips. 'I accept that it is highly unorthodox, but I took the liberty of having it constructed, and I may add, at no expense to the Council – that is, after consulting various members . . .

He glanced quickly at Commander Wilson Brown. 'We decided that, er . . .

Mr Thurk broke in. 'Yes, but what is it?'

Helliwell looked at him in amazement. 'It's Grapplewick.'

The Mayor put on his glasses again and bent forward to look closely. 'That's never Grapplewick,' he said. 'Not my Grapplewick – that's more like a Yankee mental home.'

Councillor Helliwell blushed and looked round the table for support. Lady Dorothy put her head on one side. 'I recognise the Town Hall, but it seems to me that this building, here, is situated where the Fire Station now stands.'

Helliwell ran a finger round his collar. 'Yes it does, but then again, something has to go if we are to modernise the town.'

All eyes turned to Mr Thurk's stony face.

Lady Dorothy was aghast. 'But that's the Fire Station! We can't have a town without a Fire Brigade.'

Councillor Wilson Brown smirked. 'Well, my dear lady, that is a matter for debate. With Blackburn and Bolton within close reach and, may I add, better equipped, we may have to disband our Brigade in the interests of economy.'

Mr Thurk looked at the Commander, then at Helliwell. He pointed to another impressive model building. 'And this . . . ?'

Councillor Helliwell wrung his hands together nervously. 'That's the hospital.'

The Mayor's eyes widened.

'The hospital . . . you expecting a plague?'

Helliwell blew his nose, then dabbed his forehead. He'd be cleaning his ears out next unless someone came to his rescue.

Dammit, the Commander was in this too and so were Taylor and Winterbottom – why for God's sake didn't *they* speak up? He glanced at the Commander, who was examining his little finger. He blew his nose again.

'Well, er, naturally . . . this is purely exploratory. The first stage, so to speak.'

'Aaaah,' said Mr Thurk. 'The first stage . . . last night in bed you had this wonderful idea for a new Jerusalem, so you got up early and dashed off this magnificent model before breakfast.'

Lady Dorothy saw the red spots on the Mayor's neck and tried to ease the situation. 'May I ask where all the money for the new development is to come from?'

The Commander looked at Helliwell, and Helliwell stood up as if hypnotised.

'Well, the government are making grants to Town Councils with a view to er. . . .'

The Mayor turned to Lady Dorothy. 'He's a bit of a live-wire, is our Helliwell. He's not only been busy with fret-work, he phoned Mr Attlee in Downing Street this morning and enquired about a state grant.'

Old Crumpshaw missed most of the exchange but he wasn't exactly senile. He waved his hand to encompass the high-rise flats.

'And these skyscrapers, aren't they situated on the area where Coldhurst Street and Sheepfoot Lane are now?' Crumpshaw looked from face to face. There was silence round the table. 'Never mind that,' he said, in case some-body had said anything. 'What's going to happen to all the houses at present in this Ward?'

The Commander decided it was time he took a hand. 'With due respect, Mr Crumpshaw. . . .'

'Eh?'

He sighed and leaned over the table. 'With due respect, Mr Crumpshaw, they're practically slum dwellings and should have been condemned years ago.'

'Condemned!?' Crumpshaw slapped the table. 'Condemned? I live in Coldhurst Street and so did my father before me, and you'll not get a cleaner street in Grapplewick.'

The Mayor nodded. 'I agree. They're not slum dwellings, and they're not exactly palaces either, but they're something that many palaces are not, they're homes.. .. Bricks and mortar don't make homes, it's what goes into them – the loving, the marrying, the children, the dying, a sense of family. Streets where all the doors are open, and troubles and happiness are shared, and at the same time privacy is respected – all this will be destroyed the minute your models become a concrete reality.'

Lady Dorothy fumbled in her handbag. She was moved.

Crumpshaw glared round at his colleagues. 'Every Monday regular as clockwork, the wife black-leads that hob and you can see your face in it, and woe betide anybody who walks in without wiping his feet.'

The Commander smiled. 'That's all very well, but you can't keep Grapplewick in the nineteenth century.'

The Mayor looked at him steadily. 'I'm not against progress, Commander, but above all else it is my wish to keep the people of Grapplewick together, to maintain family unity, to keep their faith in right and wrong and to respect authority which we represent. All this will be turned to rubble when you bulldoze homes and pile them on top of one another in these concrete ghettos.'

Old Crumpshaw tapped the table with a weird bony finger. 'When the wife's finished stoning that front step, you could have your dinner off it.'

The Commander sighed. 'I'm not suggesting that they are dirty – in fact, they are a credit to the householders – but they don't have bathrooms, they don't have indoor toilets . . .'

Mr Thurk leaned forward. 'And those flats of yours won't have fireplaces.'

'Of course not. The flats will be centrally heated.'

'But, no fireplaces.'

A flicker of annoyance crossed the Commander's face. 'Of course not.'

'I've visited that fine house of yours on the Binglewood Estate, Commander, and you have a fireplace – a big 'un too.'

'I fail to see what that has got to do with it.'

'I think you do. The fireplace is the focal point of the home. A cheery glow to greet you when you come in from the cold, where the family can sit and discuss and plan, or just sit, content . . . you can't suddenly uproot them and put them in your buildings. What will they do – arrange the chairs round the radiator?'

Wilson Brown smiled condescendingly. 'With due respect, Mr Mayor, quite a few householders possess television sets, and in a short while most houses will have one, perhaps even two.'

'I'm afraid you're right, Commander, and a sad day that will be. Every television set carries the same picture, but there's a picture in every fire that's different, and it's your own picture, not one that's concocted for mass consumption.'

Mr Thomas got to his feet. 'As one of the Housing Committee, I would like it put on record that although I had some inkling of the proposed plan, I was not aware that it had proceeded to this length and I feel that some Members of this Council are definitely out of order.'

He sat down and made a tick on the notepaper in front of him. Mr Thomas was a great one for sitting on the fence – as more than one Councillor had remarked in the past, he must have a backside like a hot-cross bun.

Wilson Brown rose slowly, as if he was about to announce the end of the world. 'Fellow Councillors, I have not been privileged to sit in these Chambers as long as any of you, and have not yet acclimatised myself to the tempo of the post-war years. Fighting ships at sea is an occupation far removed from discussing the merits of fireplaces – and, incidentally, the only fireplaces on His Majesty's ships are in the boiler rooms, and we had very little time to sit round these discussing the price of meat.'

It was a cheap jibe and only Helliwell started to laugh, which he quickly changed to a cough. Wilson Brown continued.

'Whilst I respect the Mayor's view and his superior knowledge of the town, I feel he must agree that I have seen more of the world and that the world is changing. In fact it has progressed to such a degree that Grapplewick is in danger of being left behind in the great new opportunities that are before us.' He squared his shoulders as if he was addressing the quarter deck. 'I'm not suggesting that we demolish buildings for the sake of erecting new ones, but better ones. The Town Hall with its fine architectural features will remain and so will the church, but why shouldn't we have a modern hospital, a shopping mart, recreational centres? The main road through Grapplewick is hardly a modern highway.'

He paused while Crumpshaw adjusted the whistle on his hearing aid.

'Now I agree that presenting this model before you this morning was unorthodox and a shock tactic, but some of us on this Council have given months of serious thought and discussion to the project. It may appear to some of you to be a rather clandestine mode of conduct, but I think you will concede that, had we pursued the normal channels, we would not have progressed much further than an item on the agenda.'

He looked round the table and, with the knowledge that he had made his point, he sat down. Mr Thurk gazed unseeing at the model. He had had the same cold, sick feeling in his stomach when he realised his father was dying. He felt suddenly weary – he had his finger in the hole but Wilson Brown was hammering away at the dyke. Lady Dorothy slid a note across the table to him. It read, 'It's only the first round'. Without expression he put it in his waistcoat pocket, got to his feet, and addressed himself to Wilson Brown.

'Congratulations on a very fine speech. I think you covered the whole of Grapplewick except for one small item, the one ingredient that makes a town, a village, a country . . . the people.

The Commander fidgeted impatiently.

The Mayor pressed his point. 'Oh yes, the people, the one quantity that appears to be missing from your equation.' He leaned forward. 'Do you know Jimmy Lees?'

The Commander frowned, taken by surprise. 'Jimmy Lees? I don't think I've heard the name.'

Mr Thurk's eyebrows went up a notch. 'Then you're the only one in Grapplewick who hasn't.'

Crumpshaw glared across. 'Jimmy Lees, the bellringer. Everybody knew Jimmy Lees.'

Mr Thurk nodded. 'Before the war we had a peal of bells at St Mary's. Every Wednesday they practised, and they rung them twice on Sundays and at special services. On a fine night people used to stand at their doors and listen. "Jimmy's in fine fettle tonight," or "Jimmy's had a few,' they'd say, and at the end of each peal straight into the Dog and Partridge, regular as clockwork, went Jimmy. Twelve pints of Guinness and in each one he broke a raw egg.'

Crumpshaw chuckled. 'He did an' all, a raw egg – and they were good eggs in them days. Twelve pints, no more no less, and you should have seen him. Six foot four of him striding home with raw egg hanging off his moustache like icicles on a polar bear's belly. A grand lad . . . built like a brick chicken house but wouldn't hurt a fly.'

Wilson Brown sighed impatiently.

Mr Thurk tapped the table. 'One night they were ringing a peal of Grandsire Caters. They got the peal – over six hours – and the conductor called "stand", and it was only then they realised that Jimmy's bell was still going. He was dead as a doornail – eyes wide open, going up and down, up and down, still ringing.'

Crumpshaw shook his head sadly. 'Aye, and to this day nobody knows how long he'd been dead. It took three of them to prise his fingers off that rope.'

Wilson Brown spread his palms. 'Very macabre. But what's the point of the story?'

'The point Commander, is this. The whole of Grapplewick turned out to Jimmy Lees' funeral, and bells all over the North of England were muffled on the Sunday as a token of respect.'

The Commander looked as if he were about to say something.

Mr Thurk held up his hands. 'Just a minute, I haven't finished yet. Since the war the bellringers have disbanded, and we now have a carrillon. Some man presses a button and the bells play. Who is this man? I doubt if anyone in this room knows his name, and when he dies I doubt if there'll be many people of Grapplewick following the cortege.'

The Commander shrugged his shoulders.

'It's people that breath life into a town, Commander – Josh Arkwright . . .'

Crumpshaw knuckled the table. 'Aye, what about Josh Arkwright, then? There's another one – went to London and back in twelve days on his bike.'

Mr Thurk shook his head. 'No, Mr Crumpshaw. He walked to London and back in twelve days with a petition for the cotton workers.'

Crumpshaw nodded. 'That's right. He cycled to London with a petition from the cotton workers. . . .'

The Secretary tugged his sleeve. 'He WALKED to London with a petition.'

Crumpshaw looked blank for a moment, then his face cleared. 'That's right. I tell a lie. He walked to London and handed the petition to Lloyd George.'

The Secretary tapped his arm again. 'You're wrong, Emmanuel. He didn't actually hand it to Lloyd George – Lloyd George was in Scotland at the time – but he did give it to the policeman at the door.'

Crumpshaw nodded. 'Oh, aye, I knew he handed it in.'

'What matters is,' said Mr Thurk, 'that many children born after that were christened "Joshua".'

'That's right,' broke in Crumpshaw. 'And for months afterwards his boots were on display in the Co-op window, worn down to the welt. And I'll tell you something else. There was allus a queue every Saturday, filing past to have a look at 'em . . . there were that.'

Wilson Brown snorted. 'In bygone days every town had its characters. If you go back another fifty years you'll probably be able to dig up a man who walked to Blackpool with a horse under each arm, balancing a barrel of ale on his head.'

Mr Thurk was in quickly. 'All right, then, let's be more recent. What about Mother Nicholson's corner shop on Ripon Street? No child ever leaves empty-handed, nobody goes without. If they don't happen to have any money on them, it'll always do another day. Always a loaf of bread and some dripping for any tramp or down-and-out who happens to pop in. Where's all that going to go when you knock it down and build your shopping mart, or whatever you call it?'

Crumpshaw nodded, but he might have been asleep.

Mr Thurk looked round the table. 'Everybody in Grapplewick knows the lads in the football team, because they work alongside them and pal up with them, see them in the pub after a match. But there'll come a day when that team will be strangers – and that's the black day I'm trying to put off as long as possible. Dr McBride still goes round in a pony and trap – he's brought more than half of Grapplewick into this world, and he's treated more people than you've had hot dinners. He knows everybody's ailments, and in many cases what they're going to get next. Eighty-two years old but they'd rather go to him than the whole of the Royal College of Surgeons. Marty O'Toole, the policeman – every-body knows Matty and the kids love him, except when *they* misbehave, and they only do that once. How can he walk past all the houses chatting to the folks and drinking cups of tea with 'em if they're stacked twenty deep in your wonderful tower blocks?' He wagged his finger at Wilson Brown. 'And make no mistake. Once we get a barrier between the Marty O'Tooles and the people, there'll be locked doors and nobody'll want to venture out at night. Oh yes, Grapplewick is still breathing and we are still a family town.'

Wilson Brown snorted. 'Don't forget the workhouse – old men in one side of the building, and their wives in the other, separated, allowed only to walk out together on Saturday afternoons – children with rickets, consumption, the district nurse visiting the schools every month to de-nit the kids, the means tes . . .'

Mr Thurk slammed the table. 'We also had the gibbet, and we deported men to Australia, and we shoved little boys up chimneys.

Of course it wasn't a perfect system, but the change was gradual. What you are proposing is to change the whole structure of Grapplewick in one clean operation because the means are at your disposal ... a tree takes two hundred years to grow, but you would have it chopped down in order to prove the efficiency of your new machine saw.'

Old Crumpshaw chuckled. 'We used to call her Nitty Nora.'

Mr Thomas rose to his feet. 'If I may intercede ... it seems that neither side has had sufficient time to prepare a case. I suggest that this debate be postponed till some further date.' He sat and began to scribble furiously.

Wilson Brown rose to his feet, but before he could speak there was a discreet knock on the door and Ned Bladdock leaned in, holding out Mr Thurk's white helmet. 'Excuse me,' he said. 'Alarm call, Chief.'

The Mayor rose, and with a final glare at the Commander he was gone.

Wilson Brown sat down and lugged out his pocket watch. 'What a coincidence ... opening time.'

Lady Dorothy slapped the table, and two miniature trees fell over. 'I object in the strongest possible terms to the remarks made by Commander Wilson Brown.'

The Commander was unmoved. 'My dear lady, we have not had a fire in Grapplewick since before the war – fortuitous, perhaps, because I doubt if our illustrious Brigade has the expertise to deal with one.'

Lady Dorothy was on her feet. 'Again I object to these scurrilous and unfounded remarks.' She looked round the table, and her heart sank, for there was no support.

EIGHT

'H ere we are, sorr. Number 26, Waterloo Street.'
Terence nodded and adjusted his eyepatch. It wasn't much of a disguise, but his changing rooms, better known as the gents' toilet at the top of Union Street, were all engaged and he couldn't stand at the urinal forever. The attendant was a doddering old fool, but the less he saw of Terence undisguised the better, so the only change in his appearance was an eyepatch. Still, it wasn't bad. People always remember an eyepatch and ignore the height, weight – or even if the suspect only has one leg. Rembrandt eyed the peeling door and the scuffed window and the half a drab curtain that could have been sacking.

'If he's livin' here, sorr, oi tink he must have spent it all . . . if oi had dat kind o' money he owes you, oi wouldn't be living in dis pigsty.'

Terence was inclined to agree. This was his fifteenth Helliwell. Why couldn't Helliwell have an uncommon name like Joe Aristotle or Joe Archimedes, but then, knowing Helliwell he'd be hiding away in Greece somewhere. If it wasn't for Elsie at the Dog and Partridge he might have given up weeks ago. He brightened at the thought of her. Nothing definite had happened yet, but she was back with her low-cut dresses, and as soon as he entered the bar she poured him a whisky without him having to ask – a large one, too. But he had to find Helliwell first. Then he'd have money and a big car, and he felt sure she wouldn't take much coaxing –

off to Blackburn for a slap-up meal in the best hotel and then . . .
Rembrandt broke the spell with a smart rat-a-tat on the door. The
dingy curtain twitched and a moment later the door opened six
inches and a big woman in curlers peered out.

'Yes?' she asked.

Terence touched his peaked cap. 'We've come to read the gas
meter.'

Curler-face looked from one to the other. 'Again?'

Rembrandt took a notebook from his raincoat and leafed
through a few pages. 'Mrs Helliwell, 26 Waterloo Street?'

She stood there for a moment, undecided, then she opened the
door wide. 'You'd best come in then. It's under the stairs.'

'Tanks very much,' said Rembrandt, and moved along the small
corridor to the meter. Terence followed her into the room. She
turned and stared at him. He smiled – it had once been a winning
smile, but years on a prison diet hadn't done him any favours. She
took a step back.

'Do you want summat, then?' she asked anxiously.

'Well – I was wondering, Mrs Helliwell, if you are related to a
Joseph Helliwell?'

She folded her arms and looked at him suspiciously. 'Yes, he's
my husband.'

Terence's heart sank. He hadn't really wanted to find Helliwell
in a dump like this. He looked round the room and wondered if
they had a dog, because if they did it certainly wasn't house-
trained. The great lump in the torn pinny was waiting for him to
speak. Terence noticed that one of her stockings was down by her
ankles and didn't even match the other one. He almost felt sorry
for Helliwell, but he abandoned the thought quickly. His old
partner had a glib tongue and if Terence didn't watch himself he'd
be lending him money.

Her eyes narrowed. 'You're nowt to do wi' Rugby Club are
you, because if you are you're wastin' yer time. Joe had nuthin'
to do with those funds.'

Terence's heart sank even lower. If Helliwell was down to
fiddling a few bob from the till, he couldn't be sitting on a fortune.
However, he'd come this far and he might as well see it
through. . . .

'No, madam. It's nothing to do with the Rugby Club, but I
would like to see him again.'

She looked at what was left of the carpet. 'Well, I don't know where he'll be now, he's a long-distance lorry driver. 'E could be anywhere, he goes to the docks a lot. . . .

She stopped suddenly and looked at him. 'Again?' she said. 'Have you met him before, then?'

Terence nodded. He didn't believe her for a moment. The thought of Joseph driving a lorry was ludicrous. 'Yes, we met some time ago and I borrowed a fiver off him.'

He took a fiver from his pocket. Her hand almost flashed out, then changed direction and rested on her cheek.

'A fiver from my Joe?'

Terence opened up the crinkly note casually. Her mouth opened and closed, but the fiver was burning her eyeballs.

'Oh, well,' she floundered. ''E might be in the other room. 'E just comes and goes and . . . er . . .' She tailed off and turned her head to call Joe, but her eyes never left the money.

A door opened and a small black man entered the room. 'What's up now, Florrie?'

Terence stared at him, then at the woman. 'Your husband?'

'Yes.' She pointed at the note, which was already disappearing into Terence's pocket. 'This gentleman says 'e borrowed five pounds off you and 'e's come to pay it back,' she added hopefully.

Terence put his hands up to halt her. 'No, madam, there's been a mistake. The, er, Joseph Helliwell I know was . . . er. . . .'

She broke in like a whiplash: 'Was white – that's what you were goin' to say, wasn't it?' She took a step towards him. 'My Joe was born in England, but because 'e's a blackie 'e doesn't count.' Her voice was rising dangerously.

'It's nothing to do with his colour. It's just not the same person.'

'Oh, aye. I've 'eard that one before. If 'e was white you'd 'ave paid up like a man, but because 'e's a blackie it's different.'

She was trembling with self-righteousness, and the other stocking gave up the struggle and sank gratefully over her slipper. The black man put his arm round her shoulders but she shook him off. He smiled at Terence apologetically.

'Don't fret yourself, Florrie. I never lent him any money.'

She was slightly mollified. 'You'd better not, an' all. You're never off your backside long enough to earn any.'

Terence was glad of the change of attack. 'Well, madam . . .'

She whirled back at him. 'Don't you "madam" me. I know your sort, borrowing money all the time an' never paying it back.'

At that moment Rembrandt shuffled in. 'Are you sure you have gas in dis house, missus, 'cos dat machine is empty.'

She looked quickly at her husband and he looked at his feet.

Terence took the opportunity of backing towards the door. He had a feeling that poor black Joe was going to be lifting bales and towing a lot of barges as soon as they'd gone. He was almost at the door when she turned on him.

'Go on – clear off, the pair of you! And if you cut off the gas again, I'll be down at that place of yours and I'll cripple you.' With that she turned suddenly and picked up the poker.

Terence didn't wait to take his leave. He was running up the street with Rembrandt a few paces behind old black Helliwell, and the way he was going he wouldn't slow down till he reached Africa.

NINE

Ordinary folk, wearied by the war, were disillusioned by the peace. The wave of euphoria that seemed to have gripped the rest of the country on the advent of the Labour Government was greeted by a wave of indifference in Grapplewick. Austerity – clothes rationing, food rationing, not even any sweets for the kids – meant they had no desire to be the masters now. They didn't want British Railways. They still thought fondly of the LMS and the LNER and with native shrewdness could not understand the logic of smashing monopolies in order to create a bigger one. They didn't mind the fact that some people were rich – without the rich there'd be no poor, and then where would they be?

Politics had never been a major topic of conversation in Grapplewick, but a couple of years ago men had come to hand out leaflets, and in some cases to speak in the factory yard during the dinner hour. As the older ones used the break to get their heads down and the younger ones kicked a football around, the speakers had never got past 'Comrades' or 'Brothers', and one unfortunate had been used as a goalpost, so the visits ceased. But all the same, the towns-people were unsettled. A herd of wildebeest sensing the approach of lions ... Mr Thurk felt the mood of the town. Grapplewick needed a victory, a shot in the arm, something to unite them. First prize in the brass band competition, or second prize – even getting to Bellevue would be enough. Grapplewick Athletic to win the FA Cup – but no, on second thoughts he had a better chance with the band. The 'Latics had only scored four goals all season – one an own goal and three in a charity match against the scouts (the scouts won ten-three). Mr Thurk was worried, and Lady Dorothy was worried about Mr Thurk. The lads in the Fire Brigade were worried because, although the band was getting stronger, fire equipment was causing a severe shortage of space at Cowell and Bottisford's. It was only due to Mr Thurk's preoccupation with other matters that they'd got away with it so far, and, although they didn't realise it at the time, troubles are like people – it only takes one person to stand outside a closed shop door and in no time at all there's a queue.

It happened one afternoon when they were standing round the fire engine trying to decide which bit should go next, when he swung arrogantly into the yard on a heavy-duty bicycle, rattling on the hard cobbles, which didn't seem to bother him at all. He swung his leg expertly over the saddle and stood on one pedal until he brought his machine to a halt against the wall. The lads watched this display of bikemanship in grudging admiration. He was medium-sized in a brown trilby, scarf, grey-belted raincoat and heavy boots. That was the uniform of rent collectors, debt collectors, bailiffs – in fact, trouble. He carefully took off his gloves, then his bicycle clips, and put them in his raincoat pocket.

'Morning,' he said to everyone in general.

Ned pinched out his Woodbine and put it behind his ear. 'Dost tha want somethin'?'

'Aye,' said the man's back as he unstrapped a thin brief-case from the rack behind the saddle. 'Can we go inside out of this bloody wind?' And without waiting for an invitation he strode into the station.

Cyril tugged Ned's elbow and whispered, 'Shall I go and fetch Mr -Murk?'

Ned thought for a second. 'Nay, it could be about any-thing. Let's find out what's to do first.' Then he looked round at the lads and with a jerk of his head he indicated they should all go inside.

'Right,' said the man as they surrounded him. 'I'm Neville Burtonshaw, Fire Brigade Union North-west Branch.' He paused to let this sink in. 'Now, who's your representative?'

The lads looked at each other and shuffled uneasily. 'Well, come on,' he said testily. 'You must have a representative – it's a Union matter.'

'Oh, aye?' said Ned guardedly. 'What's up then?'

The man looked at them all incredulously. 'What's up?' he repeated. Where've you lot been hidin' for the last fifty years? I'll tell you what's to do.' He spread out the fingers of one hand then started to tick off the items. 'One: you've never paid your Union dues. Two: you've never been represented at any Branch meeting. Three: we've had no reply to any of our directives . . .'

Ned broke in, 'That's because we're not Union members.' Burtonshaw ignored him. 'Shall I go on?'

'No,' said Jack nastily. 'Tha's made thy point. Now if you don't mind, we've work to do.'

'Work?' the man snorted. 'Never mind your bloody work. I've heard about this station. It's organisation you want, not work.'

Ned tried to ease the situation. 'I think you'd better wait till the Chief gets here.'

The man turned on him. 'I'm not 'ere to talk to bosses. I'm talking to you lot as Brothers.'

Jack spat on the hot stove with a sizzling crack. 'If I'd wanted a brother I'd 've picked a better bloody model than thee.' He turned and walked into the cold sunlight. A couple of the lads went with him.

The man pointed after them. 'That's typical, that is! We sweat our guts to get better pay and better working conditions, and that's all the thanks we get.'

We don't do too bad,' said Ned. 'We've always managed.'

Harry Helliwell at the back of the group piped up nervously, 'What if we don't want to join?'

Burtonshaw turned slowly towards him, but Harry had edged behind Lofty Butterworth so he addressed himself to Lofty's collar stud.

'Don't want to join?' he mimicked. He glared round the wall of impassive faces. 'You'll bloody well join all right and there'll be no ifs and buts . . .

The lads shuffled their feet but avoided his eyes. He sensed his advantage and went on. 'Now before I leave 'ere you'll elect a representative. I've not cycled all the way from Black-burn for the good of me health.'

Ned put his hands deep in his trouser pockets, studied his belt buckle for a second and then looked directly at him. 'Oh, aye,' he said, 'and if we do get a representative, what'll his job be, then?'

'His job, Comrade, will be to collect Union dues, list any grievances and complaints, attend Branch meetings and keep you up to date on developments and any instructions the Union might deem it politic to issue.' While he was talking he extracted a sheaf of papers from his briefcase which he now proffered like a conjuror asking someone to take a card. But nobody stepped forward, so he moved to the desk and slapped them down forcefully.

Helliwell had another go. 'There's no law says we have to join. . . .'

Burtonshaw bared his teeth. 'Not yet there isn't, not yet. But there bloody soon will be, Brothers, you mark my words. Our lot are in power – we're the masters now. The bosses 'ave 'ad their day. We're givin' the orders, and the sooner that sinks in the better for all of you.'

Jack Puller appeared at the door, a dark silhouette against the winter sunshine. 'Are you goin' to be at it all day, or is somebody goin' to give us a hand out 'ere?'

The lads turned towards him, uncertain. One or two of them started moving towards the door, then more of them edged away. Burtonshaw worked swiftly round like a sheepdog.

'Where the bloody hell d'you think you're all going? This is an official meeting.'

Jack was incredulous. 'It's 'itler, it is. We've all been thinking 'e's dead and 'ere 'e is as large as life without his 'tache on.'

A couple of lads sniggered and the spell was broken. They started to move positively into the yard. Burtonshaw floundered about, his face a deep red with embarrassment and fury. He turned in time to see Ned stuffing the papers into the pot-bellied stove. He rushed forward and grabbed Ned's arm, but it was too late.

'Right,' he squeaked. 'Right! You've bloody done it now.' He slammed his foot on a chair, his hands shaking with rage as he put his bicycle clips on.

Barmy grinned at him. 'OK?'

'Bugger off, you,' he snarled, pulling on his gloves with trembling hands. Then he pointed a grey woollen finger at Ned. 'Tha's been warned. Make no mistake about it, you'll not get work in any Brigade in the country when I've finished with you.'

Ned observed him calmly. 'So that's the way the wind blows, is it?'

'Aye, that's the way the wind blows.' And with that he hurried out into the yard to where his bike should have been. He looked uncertainly along the wall, then at Jack Puller. Jack was sitting on the running board of the old engine. He squirted a stream of tobacco juice at a pigeon.

''Ave you lost summat?' he asked.

Burtonshaw glared at him. 'You know bloody well what I'm looking for. Where's my hike?'

Jack stood up and looked around the yard. 'Your bike?' Burtonshaw pointed to the ground. 'I left it here against the wall.'

Jack shook his head sadly. 'That was a bloody silly thing to do, wasn't it? Leaving a bike unattended. That's asking for trouble that is, especially in this town. Open your mouth too wide 'ere and they'll 'ave your teeth.'

Burtonshaw was already striding towards the main gate. Jack shouted after him. 'I'll give thee a lift to t'bus stop if you like.'

The tension was gone. The lads jeered and mocked and swaggered behind Jack to the gate. Chadwick lifted his arm in the Nazi salute and shouted, 'Heil Hitler!' Ned watched from the door. He was uneasy and couldn't quite pinpoint the reason, but he knew that somewhere a beetle had entered the woodwork.

Terence and Rembrandt weren't exactly worried, they were just sick of Grapplewick. The pavements were worn and uneven, hardly conducive to Rembrandt's sunsets and landscapes. In any case, Terence had forbidden it and he was tired of being hauled up by the lapels. However, he hadn't been totally frustrated. The walls in his room at the Dog and Partridge were covered with exotic murals – not the usual sea, sand and palm trees that were normally his trade mark, but ladies in all kinds of recumbent postures, all nude. He could never quite get the legs right, but then again he'd only seen Elsie over the top of the bar.

Unfortunately the landlord happened to be passing the room just as Rembrandt was leaving, and caught a glimpse of the exhibition. He pushed the door wide open and strode in, dumbfounded. He didn't recognise Elsie – after all, Rembrandt was only an amateur – but he knew a great pair of bristols when he saw them. After a perfunctory examination he whirled on Rembrandt, white-faced and furious, and told him to pack his things and get out, screaming that Grapplewick was a decent place and that he ran a respectable hostelry. Terence appeared at the door and joined Helliwell in his tirade against Rembrandt, adding that a few years ago he would have had him court-martialled. Rembrandt seemed oblivious, slowly gathering together his meagre possessions, 50 per cent of which appeared to be Guinness. Terence ordered him to clean up the walls before he left, but Helliwell hurriedly overruled him, and moments later Rembrandt found himself on the pavement with his ever-clinking carrier bag. Later that day the landlord moved all his own belongings into Rembrandt's vacant room. Terence stayed on as a guest. A glimpse of those nudes reminded him of Elsie, and his leg twitched most of the morning. He was worried that it was only his leg – had prison life robbed him of his manhood? It would be acutely embarrassing to leap into bed with her, and find only his leg twitching. He couldn't very well put it down to an old war wound, because there'd have to be a mark. He stamped his foot heavily and the twitching ceased, but only until he saw Elise again.

That same evening Rembrandt found himself in the public bar of the Weavers Arms. He was on his second pint when the barman said, 'Go on, 'op it! We don't want you in 'ere.'

He pulled himself out of his glass to ask what he'd done, when he realised the barman was addressing someone over his shoulder.

'Oh? And it's not de loikes of you dat's goin' to stop me.'

Rembrandt brightened. Here was an accent he under-stood. He turned, but the big woman was already alongside him at the bar.

'Go on 'ome, Nellie. We don't want no trouble.'

She leaned over the bar and the man stood back. 'An' who's goin' to put me out, oi'd loike to know? You're not de man to do it. Now are you going to give me a Guinness or not?'

He held his hand up, pleading. 'You know what f boss is like, Nellie. It's not me. 'E says not to serve you.'

'Oi'll buy her a drink. Give her a Guinness and fill me up as well.' Rembrandt surprised himself. He'd never bought anyone a drink in his life. Perhaps it was the sound of the brogue that reminded him of his loneliness, but with the luck of the Irish and that one quixotic gesture he now had accommodation at a reasonable rent, but then a couple of Guinnesses had always been the going rate for Droopy Nellie. Her house, sagging and weary with age, was by the old rubbish tip where the gypsies lived, but it had a roof – well, most of it . . . there was a hole in the bedroom ceiling the size of a football. Rembrandt said he'd mend it, but Nellie said she liked to lie in bed and look at the stars, for which he was grateful, as he had no intention of scrabbling about on top of that house. However, she was delighted when he whitewashed a wall and chalked up a flamboyant sunset over a lagoon with palm trees in the foreground. She stared at it for a long time, and said he was her little genius. She said it was so realistic it made her feel homesick. That flummoxed him for a moment, and he wondered if she was coloured – actually she was quite dark, but that was only lack of soap and water. So he stoically accepted the fact that it wasn't everybody who could appreciate art, and chalked under it 'Dublin Bay'. He was as contented as he'd ever be, if only he didn't have to meet Terence every morning in the gents' lavatory with a fresh list of Helliwells.

They were also worried at the police station. In the past few weeks the crime rate had doubled – all petty theft. The other constables kept clear of Marty O'Toole, who took this thievery as a personal affront. He was sure it wasn't any of the regulars – they, in fact, had complained to him that somebody was giving them a bad name. Also he hadn't seen Droopy Nellie for over a week now, and he wondered if she was ill – however, when he paid her a surprise visit she was having a stand-up wash in an old tin bath. He closed the door hurriedly – he hadn't realised she was that droopy. It wasn't a pretty sight – a weatherbeaten fountain in a garden of empty Guinness bottles. In any case, Droopy Nellie cleaning herself up? She always made a rumpus at the station when a bath was compulsory – Nellie washing herself in her own time didn't make sense. The whole world had gone mad.

It was a worrying time, but the sun still shone on Barmy, the stove glowed and the tea was always hot. Also Jack Puller's father had died, and Jack – more as a joke than anything else – had given Barmy his father's false teeth. It wasn't funny to Barmy, though. He struggled with them for a few days, but they were either upside-down or back to front, or else they simply didn't fit. It didn't bother Barmy – they were now permanently in a glass of water by his bed of sacks. Always cheerful and smiling, hour upon hour Barmy sat facing them, often holding desultory conversations. The teeth just grinned back at him, and eventually Barmy would rise, put up his thumb and say 'OK?'

TEN

I f Terence and Rembrandt were beginning to despair in their search, Ikey the Fixer was frantic. He was not a vindictive man, but could not reasonably accept the fact that he was tightly locked away in a north London prison, while Helliwell was free to enjoy the wealth that had been largely accumulated with Ikey's connivance. He had been transferred from the laundry, even though he was actually in the exercise yard when the head warder inadvertently fell into one of the boilers. After a short spell in the machine shop he was transferred to the hospital, having contracted a mystery virus causing excruciating pain to his bank balance. The treatment prescribed was lots of rest and special food brought in at great expense. The prison doctor, old and wise, diagnosed his condition as a wasting disease, and when Ikey thought of the money he was having to fork out he was inclined to agree. Quite a few bob was outgoing in order to keep the doctor sweet, but the fine balance lay in not overdoing it in case the old fool decided to retire.

Ikey received visits from many doctors, none of whom had been through medical school, although most of them were adept at cutting people up. Everybody knew they were Ikey's mob, but none were brave or foolhardy enough to complain, and today it was the turn of Ballantine, better known to staff and inmates as Jimmy the Hat. A big, florid man, he sported a livid scar down his cheek, the result of a second opinion. He stood at the foot of

Ikey's bed looking down at his feet, so that the brim of his bowler hid most of his face. Ikey, propped up by pillows and smoking a huge cigar, ignored him, apparently engrossed in the *Financial Times*. The door opened and the warder poked his head round. Ikey snatched the cigar from his mouth and said, 'Piss off.'

'Sorry,' said the warder, and withdrew. But the spell was broken and Ikey lowered the paper.

'Well?'

Jimmy the Hat shrugged his shoulders helplessly.

Ikey examined the ash on his cigar. 'You bring me nothing? The money I pay you, and you bring me nothing?'

The big man shrugged again. 'He ain't there, boss ... there's only one Helliwell in Tunbridge Wells, and 'e's not Joe, 'e on'y 'ad one leg.' Ikey looked at him sharply and Jimmy held up his hands. 'It was blown off in the war.'

Ikey nodded for a time, then addressed his cigar. 'Thanks for coming all this way to tell me nothing.' He sank back in the pillows. 'My life, here I am a sick man yet, and all the time you do nothing except steal me blind.'

' 'Ang about,' started the big man.

'Shut up ... eight of the boys I have, and not one of you has come up with something.'

Jimmy fidgeted. 'Joe Helliwell could be dead.'

Ikey slapped his forehead. 'Joe Helliwell could be dead,' he repeated. 'What a brain! He could be dead. Yes, he could be dead. But it would be on a piece of paper. When you are dead, you have to have a piece of paper which says you are dead. When you are born it's a piece of paper. When you are married it's a piece of paper. You cannot have a crap without a piece of paper, eh?' He held out his hands.

Jimmy put his head down again. He had to admit he'd never thought of checking the records – a quick flip through the telephone directory and a few questions – but then thinking wasn't one of his achievements. 'I'll go back and check that out,' he mumbled.

Ikey didn't appear to have heard. He knocked the ash off his cigar and applied a large gold lighter. In between puffs he said, 'Find ... Pillock Brain.'

Jimmy frowned. 'Oo?'

'Terence. He got out a few weeks ago.'

'Oh, 'im. That ponce.'

Ikey blew a cloud of blue smoke upwards. 'That ponce has more brains in his little finger than you got all over your body. And I'll tell you this, he needs Helliwell as much as we do.' He pointed his cigar at Jimmy. 'You find Terence, and Helliwell will not be far away ... you got it?'

Jimmy shuffled uneasily, then nodded. 'OK.'

Ikey's eyes widened. 'Is that all you got to say? You tell me OK ... what is OK? You are some kind of magician that you can pull Terence out of a hat. How you gonna find him? You go out of here and say "OK", then you come back in three weeks later and say where is he.'

'I'll put the word out. If he's in the smoke I'll 'ave 'im.'

Ikey slapped the bed in exasperation. 'If he was in London, I could have him without your help.' He was about to light the cigar again, but stopped as a sudden thought struck him. 'Wait a minute,' he said. 'A piece of paper, you gotta have a piece of paper.' He stared unseeingly at the wall opposite, his brain almost audible.

Jimmy glanced surreptitiously at his watch. He never liked making these visits – he had an uneasy feeling that one day on his way out he would feel a heavy hand on his shoulder, and somebody would be saying, 'Where do you think you're off to, sunshine?'

'Got it!' Ikey applied his lighter and puffed furiously. Jimmy watched him enviously. He was dying for a cigarette but he knew it wasn't allowed. 'That's it,' said Ikey. 'You got a piece of paper ... Helliwell was in the Ministry of Supply in the war.'

Jimmy nodded. 'That's right.'

Ikey spread his arms wide. 'Well,' he said, 'you don't get a job in a government office without a piece of paper. Somewhere there is a piece of paper – Joe Helliwell, when he was born, where he was born.' He leaned forward eagerly. 'Listen, and listen good. There is a man called Thomas Reece – you got it? Thomas Reece, he's in the phone book. You tell him to go through the records, tell him it's for Ikey, he owes me ... you got it?'

Jimmy nodded vigorously. 'Thomas Reece.' He gathered his overcoat round him, eager to be off. 'As good as done, guvnor.' He touched his hat and hurried away.

'Here.' Ikey's voice stopped him as he reached the door. 'You see the screw outside – you tell him I'm ready for my tea.

Jimmy nodded and was gone.

Ikey put his head in his hands, biting viciously on his cigar, angry at not having thought of it before. The money he could have saved! Then he relaxed. A week at most and he would have the information he was after. Sadly, however, it wasn't Ikey's day. He had overestimated Jimmy's capabilities. Thomas Reece was not at the address in the phone book – he had in fact emigrated five months previously – but that wasn't going to stop Jimmy the Hat. He had a job to do and, with the doggedness of a backward pack mule, he booked passage on a flying boat to Australia. Ikey did not see him again for six weeks, when he returned to the prison triumphantly bearing a photostat copy of a piece of paper stating that one Thomas Reece had died in Sydney aged forty-eight.

Later that same day a government office in Whitehall was burgled ... a heavy axe, where Ikey would have preferred a rapier.

ELEVEN

October laid down its burden and November roared in from Siberia, heralding a hard winter to come. For ten days the weather was the main topic of conversation. Winds swirled the smoke back down the chimneys, scattered tiles, rattled the window panes and whistled malevolently through the Grapplewick keyholes.

The eleventh of November blustered over the moors with no respite and a cock, judging it to be dawn, gathered itself to wake the neighbourhood. A sudden gust blew it off the fence before it could open its beak, and another blew it slap against the barn. That was enough. To hell with reveille! It scuttled back inside while it still had feathers.

In the town centre, impervious to the weather, the great clock on the Alliance building disdainfully boomed out the hour, and Grapplewick stirred. Mrs Waterhouse lit the fire and bustled to the stove to prepare Mr Thurk's breakfast. Normally she would have been in an hour later, but today was Remembrance Day, a big day for the Mayor and all the local dignitaries.

'Morning, Mrs Waterhouse.' Mr Thurk padded to the sink in his woolly vest, braces dangling over his striped trousers. 'Don't worry too much about breakfast. I'm not that hungry.'

'You're having breakfast and that's that. It's cold this mornin' and you'll want something 'ot down you.'

Mr Thurk didn't argue – it would be useless anyway. He tucked the towel in the top of his trousers and ran the tap. She elbowed him out of the way and poured some hot water from the kettle.

'Thank you, Mrs Waterhouse.'

'Hark at that wind,' she replied. 'It'll carry a few of 'em off, will that. There'll be some drawn blinds next week.'

He shuddered. Of one thing he was certain – the wind wouldn't shift Mrs Waterhouse. It would take a direct hit from a Junkers 88 to do that. He glanced sideways at her as he lathered his chin, and wondered idly whether a moustache would suit him.

Commander Wilson Brown hadn't slept well. Branches had been flicking the window all night, and he was fearful that the great beech would come crashing down onto the house. He could well do without the day before him. For the last two years he'd enjoyed Remembrance Day. He was proud of his uniform with its gold braid and medal ribbons, a fitting reminder of the debt that the people of Grapplewick owed him. Unfortunately he lived too well and, while his girth had expanded, his uniform hadn't. Glancing furtively towards the bedroom door he unlocked a drawer and took out a brown paper parcel. He quickly shed the wrapping and stared distastefully at the corset, holding it between finger and thumb as if it were a dead cat. In the distance the factory hooter wailed, and he thought of the poor devils who had to be up and about at this time every morning. It was an ordinary working day for the millhands, although the machinery did shut down at two minutes to eleven to observe the silence.

By ten o'clock even the weather seemed to respect the dead. The wind abated in an uneasy truce, helping to swell the congregation in Grapplewick parish church. Lady Dorothy, one of the first to arrive, stood to allow the golf secretary and his wife to pass along the pew. He acknowledged with a slight nod. Remembrance Day for him was an embarrassing reminder of one pitch-black night in 1945. A landmine, jettisoned in panic, had floated gently towards Grapplewick. Luckily it exploded on the golf course and the only casualty was the club secretary's wife, who was found wandering dazed and stark naked. She claimed she was walking the dog before going to bed when the blast blew all her clothes off. It really was a remarkable escape, and, such are the vagaries of explosions, that her clothes were found neatly folded on the second tee. The head greenkeeper, whose trousers had been blown off by the same freak blast, was able to corroborate her statement.

The dog presumably was blown to smithereens, and to this day the club secretary still wonders whose dog it could have been.

The Reverend Leadbetter, carried away by the size of his flock, droned on. He paid tribute to the young men and women who had willingly laid down their lives for King and Country. Mr Thurk squirmed uneasily in his seat. He had a sudden vision of a long queue of khaki-clad men shuffling slowly forward to lay down their lives. It was ludicrous – nobody willingly laid down their life. They kicked and screamed and clawed to hang onto it, no matter what the cause. If the old fool didn't wind it up soon, they'd miss the Last Post round the Cenotaph. Somebody was sobbing quietly, and he turned his head slightly. It was old Mrs Helliwell, and he couldn't help thinking it was always the survivors who suffered. A grand lad, Walter Helliwell, and Grapplewick's first war casualty. Corporal Helliwell, one of the last to be taken off at Dunkirk, had come home on leave. The train pulled into Grapplewick Central in the black of night and, full of navy rum, Walter stepped out of the wrong door. As he was picking himself up, the down train hit him. It took them three days to collect it all together – in fact one of his boots was on the station roof and part of his kitbag was discovered just outside Blackburn. Poor Helliwell!

Noticing a shuffling and uneasy throat clearings the Reverend Leadbetter glanced at his watch, and in almost indecent haste wound up the service. As they moved slowly outside to assemble round the pitiful little Cenotaph Jack Puller, on the battlements of the old church, blew the Last Post. Even Jack's faltering efforts could not conceal its haunting quality. Now, at the eleventh hour of the eleventh day, silence was observed, broken only by the soft keening wind and the church clock striking three. Cold pinched faces looked on – old young faces with new medals, and worn-out faces with medals from earlier campaigns.

Mr Thurk was glad of his thick mayoral robes as the wind freshened. He bowed his head and remembered – he thought of Lady Dorothy and her soft skin, then quickly gathered himself together, staring guiltily at the Cenotaph: SERGEANT W. THURK RAF 1943. Poor Willie! A warm flush of shame passed through him as he recalled the envy he felt for his younger brother when he came home on leave with his three stripes and the magical half brevet of an air gunner on his chest.

Willie had no interest in music and preferred to work in the mill rather than join the Fire Brigade. Yet despite this heresy Father, who was normally a strict disciplinarian, treated him like a puppy dog, always had a toffee for him on Saturday and smiled at his escapades – and there were plenty of them, even the time Willie broke his ankle jumping out of Mrs Tatlock's bedroom window when her husband came home unexpectedly. Mr Tatlock was no fool and guessed immediately who it was, especially as Willie left his trousers on the bedrail.

Twenty minutes later Dr McBride, roused by a frantic knocking, was attending to Willie and listening to his explanation. But Dr McBride wasn't that old – if Willie had fallen off his bike, what was he doing riding round at three in the morning in his shirt and socks? Anyway Willie was Willie, and as he only lived down the street he helped him home. Willie stopped dead when he saw a light on downstairs, and the doctor agreed to come in with him in case of emergency. He hopped pitifully into the room, and had it not been for the doctor blocking his exit he would have hopped out again – to Australia. Mr Tatlock and Father were sitting together in the cold front room drinking whisky. Nobody moved for what seemed an eternity, then Mr Tatlock rose slowly and held Willie's trousers up accusingly. Willie, a pathetic sight in his long shirt, hobbled forward, took them, and then stepped back. It was all done in silence, carried out with a solemnity more fitting to a masonic initiation ceremony. Anthony remembered shivering at the top of the stairs, puzzled by the quiet, his nerves taut, waiting for the inevitable explosion. As the silence lengthened he took a step down, then froze as he heard his father chuckle. Then Dr McBride sniggered, and then the three of them were all laughing like lunatics. Anthony crawled back to bed, glad in a way because he hated violence, but lonely and jealous of Willie. Had the position been reversed he wouldn't have dared to come home at all. Then again, he could never visualise himself with Mrs Tatlock. He shuddered – no wonder Mr Tatlock worked nights. He pretended to be asleep when the three of them helped Willie in to bed beside him, and from under his slitted eyelids he saw his father ruffle Willie's hair.

'You little bugger,' he said, then blew the candle out. As they went downstairs Anthony heard Mr Tatlock asking Dr McBride if he wouldn't mind looking in on his missus on the way back – she'd accidentally walked into a door. And now all that remained of Willie was his name on the Cenotaph. Anthony suddenly loved his brother and tried to visualise what it must have been like on that last fateful raid – enemy shells buffeting the aircraft, searchlights probing and blinding, Willie blazing away with his hot guns, a flash of white light, then oblivion. Anthony fumbled for his handkerchief and hoped it had been quick. Had he known the truth it would have given him little comfort. Willie had never fired his guns in anger. In fact he'd never even seen the enemy coast. His first operational flight was his last. The light flashed from the control tower the pilot released the brakes and G for George was rolling. Willie, sitting dry-mouthed in the rear turret, was mesmerised by the runway unwinding beneath him faster and faster and faster, and his last panic-stricken thought had been, 'Shouldn't we be up in the air by now?'

Anthony remembered when the 'We regret to inform you' telegram arrived. Father read it slowly. Then placed it on the mantelpiece. Then he shook his head sadly and sat down heavily. 'Good job his mother isn't alive, this would've killed her.'

Anthony looked at the poppies, and he was back with Lady Dorothy's lips. He leaned slightly forward to catch a glimpse of her, but she was hidden by Commander Wilson Brown, a very imposing figure in his naval uniform, stiff as a ramrod. But it was his profile that stirred Mr Thurk, the look of anguish on the strong grey face staring unseeingly ahead. Again Mr Thurk felt compassion, and wondered what poignant memories were causing such pain. The Commander, however, was not stirred by memories at all – he was convinced that his corset had drawn blood, and his bowels were moving. If this damned farce didn't end soon, he was going to have a nasty accident. He winced as another spasm gripped him – my kingdom for a nice warm toilet! Lady Dorothy, misreading his inner torment, sympathetically squeezed his arm and he almost lost control. 'Silly bitch,' he thought.

Remembrance was over.

Outside the Gaping Goose, waiting for opening time, Rembrandt replaced his cap. 'Terrible things, wars – oi've been through two of 'em and oi don't want another, and dat's a fact.'

Terence looked at him as one would at a had accident. 'You amaze me, do you know that?'

'No, sorr, oi don't know dat.'

'You've been through two wars?' repeated Terence incredulously.

'Yes, sorr.'

'In the First you were sucking gin at your mother's breast, and you spent the Second World War in southern Ireland making it illegally.'

'Dat's what you tink, isn't it?' Rembrandt jiggled the matches in the tray he was carrying and sniffed. 'Oi would have been in the Commandos but oi didn't have the height.'

'You'll have the height in a minute if I put my toe up your backside.'

Rembrandt edged unobtrusively against the wall, but he wasn't giving up. He pointed with his chin to the impressive row of medals. 'Dey don't give you dem for nothing, sorr.'

Terence looked away, noticing that the crowd around the Cenotaph was beginning to disperse.

'Why don't you shut it, you Irish ratbag. Those medals were attached to the raincoat when you stole it from blind Albert.'

Rembrandt shuffled his feet. 'Oh, dat's what they all say, but there's not a bit of truth in it. Oi never stole it. Blind Albert definitely promised it to me when he'd gone, God rest his soul, and oi was de only one there to hold his hand when he finally passed away.'

Terence fitted the Park Drive to his cigarette holder. Rembrandt struggled to light it, and as he did so Terence looked directly at him and spoke in measured tones. 'Blind Albert died of pneumonia because you nicked his raincoat.'

He was about to refute this when a little old lady fumbled in her purse and put sixpence in the tray. Rembrandt held out a box of matches but she shook her head.

'No, thank you. That sixpence is for you.' And she shuffled away.

'God bless you, mum,' murmured Rembrandt.

Terence looked away. 'Pathetic.'

'Der's a lot of money in selling matches if you go de right ways about it, oh yes, sorr. An iceberg is nine-tenths under the water.'

Terence missed this obscure bit of philosophy as the bolts slid back behind him, and the Gaping Goose opened its doors. With an ingratiating smile he stepped inside. Rembrandt was about to follow when something caught his eye. A large, heavy man stopped in the street, struggling vainly to light his pipe, but what took Rembrandt's eye was a large gold watch chain across his waistcoat. Rembrandt jiggled his matchboxes. The one-tenth of the iceberg was slowly floating towards him.

'Here y'are sorr, take a box wid de compliments of an old soldier.'

The large man stopped. 'Not from an old soldier. I'll take a box but I'll pay for it an all.'

'God bless you, sorr.'

A plane passed overhead and Rembrandt looked up. 'Dat'll be the Dublin plane.'

The man looked up, and it was his undoing. The gold watch was in Rembrandt's pocket. It was a brilliant piece of manipulation, and it subsequently proved to be a costly mistake.

TWELVE

Grapplewick proceeded without incident into the No Man's Land between Remembrance Day and Christmas, but in the Station Yard Fireman Bladdock paced anxiously up and down. Jack Puller was always the last, but he was never this late. Ned lugged out his watch for the umpteenth time and shouted to Helliwell on the gate, 'Any sign of 'im yet?'

Helliwell took his hands out of his trouser pockets long enough to make a 'no' sign at him.

Ned shook his head in exasperation. 'Where the bloody 'ell is 'e, then?'

Barmy held out another pot of tea. 'OK?'

'Not now, Barmy, it's coming out of me ears.'

Jim Cork sauntered over. 'Can't you drive 'er into t'yard?'

'I will if he isn't here in a minute.' He looked at the great old engine and licked his lips. He didn't relish climbing into the driving seat, but if Mr Thurk arrived with Aggie still in bed there'd be hell to pay. He stepped into the yard again, looked towards the gate, and as he did so Helliwell staggered in, half supporting Jack. Ned hurried forward to help, shocked at his appearance. One eye was closed, shot with the colour of the sky before a tropical storm, blood was trickling from his mouth, and there was a nasty cut on his chin trickling onto his torn uniform.

'Bloody 'ell, Jack, did you fall under a train?'

Jack straightened up and brushed the back of his hand gingerly across his chin. 'I'll get the bastard, and when I do I'll wrap that bloody bike round his neck.'

Barmy hurried over with a pot of tea. 'OK?' he grinned. Jack ignored him. 'Four of 'em. Big buggers an' all, but 'e wasn't there himself. They never are – allus get somebody else to do it.'

Barmy edged round the front of him, still proffering the tea.

'Bugger off, Barmy,' snarled Jack.

'OK,' said Barmy, grinning, and went inside to pour it back.

'Who're you talking about, Jack? Who did this?' asked Ned.

Jack winced and felt his eye. 'That union bugger from Blackburn – 'e wasn't there, but they kept calling me scab and blackleg.' He tried to smile. 'Any road, there's one of 'em I'll be on t'operatin' table now, and another bugger won't be havin' any more children.' He walked slowly to the tap in the yard and let the cold water run over his head.

Ned stood at his side. 'We'll report this to Mr Thurk.'

Jack jerked round. 'You bloody well won't,' he hissed. This is nowt to do with Mr Thurk, it's my problem.'

Ned shrugged helplessly. 'Well, you can't let him see thee like this, 'e's bound to ask questions.'

Jack didn't appear to have heard – he was gazing into the distance. Ned followed his gaze but there was nothing to see. It was all in Jack's mind, and Ned wouldn't have been in that union official's shoes for all the brass and medals in the world.

'Burtonshaw, that's the name.'

Ned nodded. 'Aye, that's the name: Neville Burtonshaw.'

Jack pulled himself together. 'Well, I'd best get this bloody engine into t'yard.' He swung himself carefully up into the driving seat. By the time Mr Thurk arrived, Jack had gone home, ostensibly with the flu.

'There's a lot of it about,' said Mr 'Thurk absent-mindedly, and as he didn't trust Ned at the wheel he took the bus to the Town Hall. As soon as he was gone the lads hurried back into the warmth. They stood in a semi-circle round the big pot-bellied stove, and nobody spoke for a time. Then Jim Cork cleared his throat and said, 'Bloody 'ell.'

Barmy dipped a pot into the dixie and offered it, but there were no takers. They needed a good shot of whisky, not stewed tea.

Ned jangled some loose change in his trousers pocket and spoke to the stove. 'Well, that's put t'cat among t'pigeons.'

'It has that,' said Helliwell. 'It could 'ave been any one of us.'

There was another silence, then young Turner fidgeted. He was the newest recruit – tall, red-faced, pimples, and always had a boil going on his neck. 'There's nowt wrong wi' bein' in a Union,' he said.

Ned looked at him. 'No, there's not, but they're not goin' the right way to get new members.'

Turner went even redder. 'What I meant was. . . .'

But Ned cut in. 'What tha meant was, you're scared to bloody death.' He looked round. 'All of you.' Nobody con-tested this, so he went on. 'Well, I tell you this. Nobody from Blackburn's comin' 'ere and duffing up my lads. I don't care 'oo they are.' He looked round the group. 'Now get your helmets on, and climb on that tender. We're going to see this Neville Burtonshaw.'

Nobody moved. They were uneasy.

'What's the matter with you? There'll be no violence. I'm only goin' to have a few well-chosen words with 'im.'

Helliwell coughed. 'It's not that, Ned. 'Ow long is it since you drove that thing? You'd never get it out of t'yard for a start.'

Ned looked at the engine, then back at the lads. He squared his shoulders. 'Listen,' he said, 'I was driving that thing when your mother had to wipe your nose.'

Helliwell came back straight away. 'Aye, I know, but it was easy in them days. You had a man in front with a red flag.'

Nobody laughed – they were still shocked by what had happened to Jack Puller, and had Neville Burtonshaw walked into the yard at that moment they would have been Union members to a man.

Ned, however, was committed. 'Get that crank handle out, and I'll show you whether I can drive or not.' They collected their helmets and wandered unwillingly into the yard. Ned sat high up in the seat, tight-lipped, gripping the wheel as if to hold the whole thing together. Helliwell, red-faced, swung the great handle for the third time, to no effect, and stepped back to catch his breath.

'Give it 'ere,' said Jim Cork, and spat on his hands. 'Right!' And he swung fiercely – but the old engine squatted stubbornly, quietly mocking their efforts. Jim tried again. He swung it round and round in a mad frenzy, but he might as well have been mangling washing. Ned, sitting up in the driving seat, was staring as if mesmerised, and young Helliwell had to tap him twice on the knee.

Ned looked down at him. 'What's up?' he said. 'Is it switched on?'

Ned looked blankly. 'Eh?'

'Switched on.' And Helliwell mimed switching on.

'Oh, aye,' said Ned, embarrassed, and he scanned the dashboard. 'Oh, aye,' and he turned on the ignition.

Jim Cork stood back in disgust. 'That's marvellous, that is! Bloody marvellous! Nearly bloody well ruptured meself.' Barmy sauntered up. 'OK?'

'Bloody marvellous,' said Jim, and gripped the handle tightly. 'Is it switched on now?' he shouted.

Ned put his thumb up.

'Are you sure? Little red light on and everything? I'm not a bloody organ grinder, you know.'

Ned put his thumb up again. 'It's OK now.'

With an ear-splitting roar the engine caught. Everybody ducked instinctively. Pigeons clashed together in a hurry to get out of the way. The engine jerked forward like a cantankerous bullfrog and stalled.

Barmy stepped forward and patted the side. 'Whoa, whoa,' he said. Then, sure that it was calm, he grinned. 'OK.'

Jim wasn't amused. He was flat on his back by the wall, afraid to move in case he couldn't. Some of the lads hurried over to him, but mainly they were concerned for Ned whose head had gone straight through the windscreen. 'Stay still, Ned,' said one of them, while they gingerly picked the shards of glass from the frame. 'Steady, now. Ease back, that's it.' And Ned was free.

He took off his helmet carefully, his face white. 'By the bloody centre,' he said. 'If I hadn't been wearing this.'

Walter Buckley picked a large piece of glass off the bonnet and put it back again. 'I'd just cleaned the bugger, too,' he said, and strolled inside. The rest of the lads joined him, and in no time at all they were back at their favourite positions round the pot-bellied stove, each aware that changes were coming and, whether they liked them or not, they would be forced to accept them. The trip to Blackburn was thankfully postponed.

'Right, lads,' said Ned briskly. 'Who's goin' to nip down to Hepworth's Garage?'

'I'll go,' said Smelly Watkins. 'What do you want?'

Ned raised his eyebrows. He'd rather it hadn't been Smelly. Smelly wasn't too bright – in fact he sometimes made Barmy look like a scholar. 'We'll want a new wind-screen, won't we?' said Ned slowly.

'Oh, aye.' He pondered a moment. 'Will I take the old one with me?'

Ned looked round at the other lads. 'It's like being in a bloody lunatic asylum.'

Smelly came to a decision. 'I'll tell him we want a new one.'

Ned nodded. 'You do that.'

Smelly was about to leave when Ned called after him, 'Oh, and get me five Woodbines while you're at it.'

Smelly took the proffered shilling and shambled off.

Helliwell watched him go. 'You should have written it down for him. He'll never remember that lot. And if he does what's the betting 'e comes back with a Woodbine and five bloody wind-screens.'

Again nobody laughed. They weren't listening – too much had happened and they were all staring fixedly at the stove.

Half to himself, Ned said, 'I'll tek morning off tomorrow and go and see Burtonshaw on't bus.' And there the matter ended.

Surprisingly enough, Jack turned up for band practice that night and seemed in a better frame of mind. Ned marvelled at the way he played the cornet – it wasn't brilliant, but with his cut lip it was downright miraculous. He must have been in agony – but then that was Jack, and Ned felt a great pride in knowing him. Mr Thurk had been so preoccupied that he didn't seem to have noticed the newness of some of the instruments. Ned had taken the precaution of draping an old mac over the big drum to hide the battle honours, but Jim Cork's euphonium, right under his nose, gleamed and glistened like a crystal chandelier. Also the shrinkage in Fire Station property seemed, astonishingly, to have escaped him – after all you'd think he'd have missed the bell by now.

Due to strike action there was no *Grapplewick Chronicle* the following morning, and very few people read the Black-burn paper. Even so they would probably have missed a small item at the bottom of page three, captioned 'Hit and Run': 'Neville Burtonshaw, a Union official, was found in a ditch near his home unconscious, and is suffering from multiple injuries. The police had difficulty in freeing him from the remains of his bicycle, and it is believed he was the victim of a hit and run driver.'

Burtonshaw, lying in the Infirmary, accepted the story, although he couldn't recollect hearing a car, and certainly – if there was a car – it couldn't have had headlights.

Terence took in the three brass balls, then surveyed himself in the pawnshop window. He rather fancied his little moustache and goatee beard, and wondered idly how long it would take him to grow his own. He winked at himself and entered the shop. Almost as soon as the bell tinkled, old Mrs Hellingoe appeared from the inner recesses. Terence raised his homburg. 'Bonjour, Madame.'

She stared at him uncomprehendingly.

Terence smiled apologetically. 'I am vair sorry, Madame, I speak not good ze Anglais.' He lifted his shoulders – it was vintage Charles Boyer. 'Alors, I am desolate. My baggage, vis all my papeurs, my monee, stole . . . how you say? Stole?'

She nodded and spoke to him as if he was deaf. 'STOLEN.'

'Ah so . . . yes, stolen.'

She clucked her tongue. She knew the drill – always a hard luck story, then the stuff that had to be pawned. The better the hard luck, the more they hoped to gain. She leaned towards him. 'HAVE YOU BEEN TO THE POLICE?' When she said 'police', she held her hand up high to depict a tall man.

Terence pretended to be mystified, then his face cleared. 'Ah oui, the police . . . I have been, yes, but, alors, they can do nothing.'

She decided to move things along. 'If everything has been stolen, how can I help you?'

He sighed. 'Not everything, Madame. I have my watch.' He took the heavy gold chain out of his pocket and placed it on the counter. 'I am desperate, compris? But I must be in Paree tomorrow, otherwise I would not part with ziz for a million francs.'

She picked it up and glanced at him sharply, then she took it to the window where there was more light. Terence watched her. 'It was a present for me from an English capitaine, I ide heem from the Germans in the war. Three times the Gestapo question me, but I do not break down, so at the end of the war the capitaine, e say, "Henri . . . you must ave zis." "I do not want it," I say, "as head of the resistance I only do .. '

She broke into his reminiscences. 'I'll see my husband, he'll say how much.' She took the watch into the back room. Terence gave her a Gallic bow. He examined one or two objects in her absence, humming the Marseillaise. With a few pounds in his pocket he might take the bull by the horns and ask Elsie out for a meal tonight. There must be some place in Blackburn and he'd be able to afford a taxi – that would impress her. He wished he'd thought of being a Frenchman long ago, it always got 'em going. 'Darling, je vous aime beaucoup.' He heard the firebell in the distance getting closer, and looked out of the window to watch the old engine lumbering by. It was going so slowly he thought for a moment it was going to stop outside, and he smiled – not a bad idea at that, it must be worth a bob or two on the antique market. He turned just as Mrs Hellingoe sidled up.

She gave him a tight smile. 'My husband,' she pointed to her wedding ring, 'is looking at it now.'

'Merci.' There was a long and awkward pause, and he heard a ring as if the telephone receiver had been replaced. Then a large, heavy man in a velvet smoking jacket came through. Terence smiled and touched his hat, but the man ignored the courtesy and leaned his elbows on the counter while he examined the watch. Terence felt a tickle of cold sweat run from his armpit down his side. Suddenly uneasy, he mumbled, 'In 'all an 'our, I must board on the train . . .'

The man was in no hurry. He looked at Terence. 'The wife tells me you got this during the war.'

Terence nodded quickly. 'Oui, a capitaine.' He wiped the palms of his hands down his overcoat. 'Now I must make haste.'

The large man clicked open the watch. 'It's got his name engraved inside the back.' He tapped the inscription with a finger like a Wall's pork sausage. 'Samuel Hellingoe.'

Terence's lips dried. 'That is correct, Monsieur. Capitaine Sammy, as we used to call him, always he look at the watch and say, "One day the war will be over, Henri, and this will be yours," . . . ha ha.'

The man's eyebrows went up slightly. 'My name also happens to be Samuel Hellingoe.'

Immediately Terence knew the game was up. He snatched forwards, but with amazing speed for such a big man Hellingoe stepped back. His wife yelped. All pretence gone now, Terence glared at him. He should have bolted then, but he wasn't going without the watch or the money. His mind raced – physical violence was out of the question for Hellingoe was all of eighteen stone and the watch was like a penny in a fist that was as big as a sheep's head. Terence put his hand in his overcoat pocket and thrust forward two fingers. 'Hand over the watch or I shoot.'

Hellingoe's face went white, then his eyes flickered over Terence's shoulder and he relaxed. The shop bell jangled and Terence swung round. Marty O'Toole and a much younger constable were blocking his exit.

'He's got a gun,' shrieked Mrs Hellingoe, but Terence quickly held up both arms to show he wasn't armed. He had a feeling that an anti-tank gun wouldn't stop O'Toole.

Hellingoe mopped his brow, and with a malicious little smile he tapped Terence on the elbow. 'Would you like me to contact the French Embassy, Monsieur?'

'Bollocks,' said Terence, and joined the policeman.

THIRTEEN

Every Thursday Mr Thurk arrived at his office early, Thursday being the day the Fire Brigade made their goodwill tour of the farms. As he wasn't supposed to notice where the meat and eggs came from it was his way of turning a blind eye, but in any case there was always plenty for him to do at the Town Hall, and round about half past ten Lady Dorothy called in, and sometimes a few others. If there was a quorum they'd have a meeting, but if not he and Lady Dorothy popped across to Whitehead's cafe, over the billiard hall, to take coffee and biscuits.

The plump little waitress put down the biscuits and asked if there was anything else.

'No thanks, Florrie.' He smiled up at her. 'When's that sister of yours due?'

She blushed. 'Any time now, Mr Thurk. She's at the hospital.'

He patted her hand. 'Well, let me know when it happens and I'll be round to see her.'

Florrie took out a tiny handkerchief, and put it to her nose. 'Thanks,' she said and hurried away.

Lady Dorothy watched her go. 'She doesn't look too happy about it.'

Mr Thurk spooned sugar into his cup. 'She isn't. She's very fond of Emmie, but the trouble is Emmie isn't married. There's been hell to pay ... her father's threatened to chuck her out. It's not just that she's having a baby – she won't tell who's responsible, and that takes a special kind of courage in this town.' He sipped his coffee contemplatively. 'Mind you, if it's black that'll narrow the field. We've only got one blackie here at the moment – Joe Helliwell.'

She looked at him. 'Why should the father be Joe Helliwell?'

He smiled. 'Sorry, my dear. It was a joke in very poor taste. They live next door, you see, in Waterloo Street.' She took a biscuit off the plate. 'Strange, isn't it?' 'Strange?'

'Yes. Well, how did Joe Helliwell come by his name, and how did he come to live here in the first place? I mean, didn't he have a family?'

He chuckled. 'It is strange,' he said. 'They reckon old Fred Helliwell brought him home from the Boer War in his knapsack. I don't know whether that's true or not, but in any case Fred raised him. Anyway, he's married now. He married Florrie Dyson – or rather she married him. I think she wanted him as some kind of ornament.'

Dorothy smiled at him fondly. 'You know, Anthony, that's why it's so right and proper for you to be Mayor. To you Grapplewick isn't just a town, it's your family.'

He nodded absently. 'I suppose so,' he said, 'but for how much longer?'

She looked at him sharply.

'Well, Dorothy, you can see how things are going, how things are changing . . . First the war, then Wilson Brown being elected to the Council – he's the one stirring things up.'

She frowned. 'If only he'd go back to the Navy, or retire or something.'

He looked at her over the rim of his cup. 'Oh, I can get rid of him all right,' he said. 'I could get shot of him tomorrow if I wanted.'

Her eyes widened. 'Well, for goodness sake do it.' She waved her hand searching for words. 'Do it .. . get rid of him before it's too late.'

He shook his head. 'Not yet, Dorothy . . . he's flushing them out for me . . . there are some good Councillors, and some bad ones, and he's pointing them out.'

She put down her cup. 'Yes, young Helliwell's suddenly sprouted wings.'

He nodded. 'Yes . . . I've noticed that too. For years he's been tentative about the Garden of Rest in the town centre – not a bad idea – but now, with Wilson Brown's backing, he wants to uproot the whole of Grapplewick and plant acres and acres of trees . . . shrubs . . . grass . . . flowers.'

Dorothy traced a pattern on the tablecloth. 'He could be sincere,' she said.

'Oh yes, he could be. But there's Ormroyd's Garden Equipment.'

'I know it, yes,' she said, but she wasn't any wiser.

He spoke deliberately. 'Ormroyd's son is married to Helliwell's sister.'

'Aaaah!' She sat back. 'I didn't know that.'

'Oh yes,' he said. 'Before the war they were big. Lawns and stuff on the Binglewood Estate – well, they practically started it. And the park . . . then came the war and the park was used to grow vegetables . . . sectioned off into allotments and so forth . . . and still is. Now the Garden of Rest in the town centre would have helped. In fact Ormroyd came to see me, and dropped the wink that if it went ahead he would as good as finance the band. Young Helliwell doesn't know this, but that's one of the reasons I've been lukewarm to the idea. In any case, if the new Grapplewick project goes ahead that will put old Ormroyd in the big league again, and Helliwell won't go short either.'

Her mouth tightened primly. 'Nor will Commander Wilson Brown.'

He put his cup down. 'No,' he said, 'I don't think so. That's the funny part. I don't think he knows about Ormroyd's. He's never concerned himself with the people of Grapplewick. I don't suppose he'd even recognise one of my lads out of uniform – you see . . .' But he stopped short as she looked over his shoulder. He turned to see Ned Bladdock approaching, helmet under his arm like an emissary bringing the good news from Ghent to Aix.

He bowed to Lady Dorothy, then turned to his Chief. 'Beg to report a fire, sir, at the offices of the *Grapplewick Chronicle*.'

Mr Thurk shot up. 'I'll come at once.'

Ned puffed out his chest. 'It's all taken care of, sir. Everything's under control. His eyes were shining with the story he had to tell – after all this was his first actual fire. He swapped his helmet to his other arm, and Mr Thurk, feeling conspicuous, sat down again. 'You see, sir, apparently the fire had gone out once, before we arrived, and when we dashed in we collared two of 'em sprinkling paraffin over the machinery.'

Mr Thurk was on his feet. 'Paraffin?' he repeated.

Ned calmed him. 'It's all right, sir. The police have them now – two of the printers.' He looked round him, proud of his smoke-blackened face. There hadn't been much smoke at all, but a bit of axle grease had helped.

Mr Thurk sat down again. 'That's all very well, Ned,' he said. 'You've done well, but you know the regulations – on receipt of alarm I am to be informed immediately. I should have been there,' he ended lamely.

'There wasn't time, sir.' Ned leaned one knuckle on the table. This wasn't for public consumption. 'You see, sir, we were on our way to collect the . . . er' he looked round ' .. . the usual Thursday stuff, and we were just passing the *Chronicle* building when one of the pickets outside the gates flagged us down and shouted "Fire!" There was a bit of smoke at one of the windows, then a face appeared and said, "It's gone out again." Then, they tried to stop us goin' in, said it didn't concern us, but Jack Puller takes a bit of stopping. Well, you know Jack . . . any road, that's how we managed to catch 'em red-handed.'

Lady Dorothy looked up at him. 'Did you say pickets?'

Mr Thurk sighed. 'They're on strike.' He stood up wearily. 'Well, Dorothy, if you'll excuse me I'd better be getting along to the Station.'

A flash of alarm crossed Ned's face. 'No, sir. Well, I think it's better if we clear things up first . . . tidy the appliance and that. I'll make out a full report . . . er . . . give us an hour, sir.'

The Mayor looked at him steadily for a moment, then sat down again. 'All right, Ned, I'll be over in an hour'

'Thank you, sir.' Ned bowed slightly to Lady Dorothy, and made for the exit.

Lady Dorothy leaned over. 'He didn't seem too keen to have you back at the Fire Station.'

He smiled. 'I'm not surprised.' He stirred what was left of his coffee absently. 'For some time now they've had a deal going with Cowell and Bottisford's for musical instruments, and, not to put too fine a point on it, the fire engine is somewhat lacking in equipment.' He paused. 'Still, the little episode this morning might give their consciences a bit of a jolt,' he chuckled. 'Mind you, if they'd had a bell it would have given the fire raisers ample warning!'

She didn't appear to have heard him. 'How long have they been on strike?' she asked.

'Eh? . . . Oh, the printers. There's been no *Chronicle* for three days now.' He shook his head sadly. 'I'm afraid it's a sign of the times.'

'Strikes, you mean?'

'No,' he said. 'There's been strikes before, but mainly they were justified and used only as a last resort. Now this one. . . .' He passed his hand wearily over his face. 'What happened was, one of the printers opened a window in the machine shop, said it was too hot. Then the chap who worked under the window said he was in a draught and closed it again. Then the other fellow walks over and opens it again. Then the shop steward was called in, and he suggested they have it half open, but neither of them would agree to that – it had to be fully open or fully closed. Then the man who was working by the window closed it and cut the cord so they couldn't open it at all, by which time a sub-editor walked in and asked what the trouble was, and when they told him he said they were acting like a bunch of kids. That really put the cat among the pigeons. They shut down their machines and walked across to the Star to convene a meeting which went on till closing time. It was too late then to get out next day's edition.'

'And that was three days ago?'

'Yes. They demanded a written apology from the sub-editor which they got, then they immediately convened another meeting to decide whether to accept it, and when they came back it was coupled with a demand for protective clothing and a wage increase. Anyway Arthur Taylor, the owner, said he wasn't going to be blackmailed and threatened to sack the lot of them, and this morning was the result.'

Her eyes widened. 'But this is ridiculous – if they had burned down the building they wouldn't even have a place to work anyway.'

'Ah, yes,' he said. 'But I don't believe that would worry the politically motivated men behind this strike. They'll just move on.'

She looked at him quizzically. 'You're not against Unions, are you, Anthony?'

'Me?' He laughed. 'Before the war, I was one of the most active Union supporters in the North. Speak anywhere, I would, and I still believe that we need good strong Unions. But their main aim should be the welfare of the members, and that's what it was in the old days . . .' He pushed his coffee cup away and leaned forward. 'During the Bolshevik Revolution the mobs were running wild, burning and looting, and Lenin nearly went potty. "Don't burn the palaces, you fools," he said. "If you want to burn something, set fire to your own hovels." '

Dorothy smiled. 'Was it Lenin or was it Marx?'

'Whoever it was, that's what they're doing here now. Well, they're not actually burning palaces, but they're doing their damnedest to tear down existing values and standards.

She looked at him quizzically. 'Yes, but things are vastly different in Russia.'

'For the moment,' he replied darkly, 'a new philosophy is being preached in this country, a philosophy based on dissatisfaction, hate, envy – this in itself is evil.' He leaned forward. 'The only antidote is love.'

Dorothy's eyes flickered but Mr Thurk didn't appear to have noticed.

'Love has no class barriers, and if there was a choice between love and hate I know what most people would choose, and you don't have to be a millionaire to experience it.

This time Dorothy put her head down and busied herself in her handbag. Mr Thurk became suddenly embarrassed as he realised that what he had just said sounded like a proposal. He looked round the cafe, flustered, and his eyes lit on a portrait of the Royal Family. He chuckled. 'Did I ever tell you of the time before the war, when the King and Queen came to Grapplewick?'

Dorothy shook her head and Mr Thurk laughed. What a day that was! The old King George V was due in Grapplewick at eleven thirty. Well, we were all up at five o'clock, Mother fussing around – Dad was Mayor, you see – and it was a beautiful morning, promising to be a scorcher.' He paused. 'We used to have some real hot summers when I were a lad ... Anyway, Mother was arguing with Dad because he wasn't going to wear anything under his robes of office, and she kept saying suppose you get knocked down, and what if a sudden gust of wind springs up. But when Dad made up his mind – that was that.' He leaned back to let the waitress replenish their coffee cups. 'Thank you, Florrie.'

She smiled and teetered off.

'Just after ten Dr McBride called for Dad in his pony and trap and took him to the Town Hall, and we followed on foot. What a sight – flags and bunting everywhere, all the scouts and guides lining the route, St John Ambulance strutting up and down – they had their hands full later on with the heat and everything. And the crowds ... I don't know where they all came from, but they'd been there for hours. Every window was full of faces, every lamp-post was festooned, and the little streets had flags across from window to window.' His eyes narrowed as he looked back over the years. 'When we arrived at the Town Hall a great cheer went up, and I was proud for my father until I saw what had happened ... as he was stepping down from the pony and trap his robe got caught, and of course everybody saw more than they bargained for!' He laughed. 'He was lucky really – if he'd taken one more step forward he'd have walked out of it altogether – my mother didn't speak to him again for a week.'

Dorothy laughed. 'I wish I'd been there,' she said.

'It didn't bother my father. "They cheered, didn't they?" he said. "At least they know they've got one man in the Town Hall." Anyway, the band was playing a selection from something or other – and it was a good band in those days – and Dad was upset because he wanted to conduct them, but it wouldn't have been dignified in his mayoral robes.'

Dorothy chuckled. 'It would have been even more undignified without them.'

He smiled. 'Anyway, the time came nearer to eleven thirty and we all assembled on the Town Hall steps. You could feel the atmosphere ... you could almost reach out and touch it. Everybody was straining to look towards the high point at Pennine Gorge. Arthur Buckley was up there keeping watch, and as soon as the cars came in sight he was to fire a rocket. Then we'd be prepared, you see.'

She nodded.

'Anyway, half past eleven came and went, and no sign of the rocket. Then suddenly we heard cheers at the bottom end by Linney Lane, and we realised that either the rocket hadn't gone off or Arthur was drunk and he'd missed them. As a matter of fact it turned out he was drunk, and as he went to light the rocket the bottle holding it fell over, and the rocket shot through Sag Bottom fields, and what with the drought and everything the crop caught fire, and when the King drove past Arthur was flapping with his coat trying to stop the blaze, so he never got to see the King ...' He laughed. 'Oh, my word! Ten acres and three barns went up. Poor old Arthur. He's dead now, you know ... he had a polypus.' Anthony touched his ear by way of explanation, and she nodded.

'We all saw the smoke, mind you, and as Dad was Fire Chief as well it was his duty to get the Fire Brigade to it. But as he said after, his first duty was to the sovereign. Anyway, the three cars came slowly up Union Street and the crowds were going mad . . . every window in the cotton mills full of waving people, though they couldn't have seen much from where they were. On a signal from my father the band struck up the National Anthem, and as the cars drew level my father took off his hat and the King bowed his head. It was a magic moment. They looked marvellous, just like . . . well, just like a King and Queen. . . .' He took his handkerchief and blew his nose.

Dorothy smiled at him. 'Did they stay long?'

Mr Thurk shook his head. 'Oh, they didn't stop. Straight through and off to Blackburn. But what a day that was . . . the factories closed down at dinner time, the tables were brought into the street, and all afternoon the kids had races and games on Grapplewick Edge. Every door was wide open, and there were great barrels of beer outside every pub, and this town was welded together with such a bond . . .' He leaned back. 'Such a bond. Such love.'

She sighed. 'I wish I'd been there, Anthony.'

He lugged out his watch. 'Bai jingo, look at the time.' He signalled for the bill, and as he turned towards Lady Dorothy a bread roll hit him on the back of the neck. At the same moment a large woman came out of the ladies' toilet and stared, aghast. Then she swept towards a young lad sitting innocently at one of the tables, and gave him such a wallop that his cap went flying.

'That'll teach you,' she said, as she dragged him towards the door. 'That's the Mayor, that is.'

'Well, I didn't know, did I?' he snivelled, and they were gone.

Lady Dorothy pressed the serviette to her mouth to stifle a laugh, but Mr Thurk wasn't too pleased. Then he too began to laugh, brushing the crumbs from the back of his collar. They were still laughing when they walked up the street, in fact tears were streaming down his face and he had to hold onto the bus stop to steady himself.

Lady Dorothy stopped and looked at him seriously for a moment. 'D'you know, Anthony, I can't remember the last time I saw you laugh . . . really laugh.'

'Nor I you.' And they started to giggle again.

FOURTEEN

Commander Wilson Brown had a hangover, and he was trying not to let it interfere with his duty as Magistrate. Normally he enjoyed his days on the bench, and felt that he dispensed justice with a sure, deft touch that roused both respect and even admiration in his colleagues, the police, and even the defendants. The truth, however, was sadly different. The police scornfully referred to him as Admiral Pinhead, and would go to great lengths to avoid having to attend his sessions, while the villains knew they were more likely to be treated leniently in a collar and tie, and a row of medals virtually guaranteed an acquittal. The Commander was blissfully unaware of these sentiments, and was proud of his position. He could be harsh, sometimes witty, even jocular, especially when Droopy Nellie was up before him, but it never occurred to him that nobody ever seemed to laugh. This morning, however, his head was throbbing and three aspirins had made very little difference. He struggled to concentrate – it would hardly be appropriate if the drunks that sagged in the dock realised that, while they were drinking themselves into trouble, the man lecturing them had been dancing on the billiard table in his under-pants. A flush of shame engulfed him as he remembered, but then it wasn't an everyday occurrence to get a hole in one, and it had been a costly affair.

There had only been one or two members at the bar when he had entered the club house, but a hole in one goes round the golf grapevine quicker than greenfly. In no time at all the members' lounge was packed, and half-a-bitter men suddenly developed a taste for scotch, Binglewood golf club being the only place in Grapplewick with an abundant supply. Luckily most of them had left by the time he struggled onto the table to give his impression of a belly dancer, but word would get around.

Lady Dorothy leaned towards him and whispered, 'It's his first offence.'

The Commander tried to collect his scattered thoughts, and looked sternly at the miserable creature in the dock. Then he leaned towards old Brierley on his left. 'What do you think, Walter?'

Walter eased back a little as the stale whisky hit him. 'A caution, I think.'

'Right.' Wilson Brown leaned forward. As this is your first offence, you'll be let off with a caution.'

The little man gave a great sigh of relief. 'Thanks, Your Honour.'

Wilson Brown nodded. 'And next time I suggest you take more water with it.'

The little man looked at the policeman and the PC shrugged. In fact everybody was wondering what taking more water had to do with stealing clothing coupons.

Another sorry creature was hustled into the court, and while the usher was mumbling the formalities Wilson Brown cast a red eye towards the dock, Terence was examining his nails disinterestedly. For some unaccountable reason this nonchalance sent a surge of unease through the Commander. He palmed a couple more aspirins to his mouth, and gulped a tumbler full of water, then looked carefully at the man in the dock. Terence looked up and returned his stare. For a moment it looked as if they were trying desperately to hypnotise each other, then Terence slapped the rail in front of him.

'I don't believe it,' he gasped. 'It's too good to be true. Helliwell!'

The policeman was about to caution him when Wilson Brown gave a large belch and slumped down in a dead faint.

FIFTEEN

The *Grapplewick Chronicle*, now back in uneasy circulation, made it a front-page blockbuster: 'Commander Wilson Brown Has Heart Attack', followed the next day by 'Commander Off Danger List'. This was pure conjecture as the hospital had given them no information, which was hardly surprsing as the Commander hadn't even been there. After being helped from the bench, he'd revived himself with a stiff brandy, and the only visible sign of his heart attack was a plaster on the bridge of his nose where it had come in contact with the bench – but then a bloody nose doesn't sell newspapers. Under normal circumstances the front-page pictures of himself in a naval uniform would have pleased him, and indeed he would have ordered half a dozen, but with the advent of his old partner the charade was over. Terence was relieved. With all the attention focused on the Commander he never even got a mention, and he was having a field day. From his crummy little room at the Dog and Partridge he now had the run of Wilson Brown's magnificent house on the much sought after Binglewood Estate, and he was in no hurry to move on. Actually he'd never been inside a place like this in daylight. He helped himself to a large whisky and settled comfortably in an armchair by the great fireplace. Wilson Brown watched him wearily. 'Suppose I give you £10,000 – and I'll have to struggle to get it, mind you – but would that do?'

Terence raised an eyebrow. 'Do what?' he asked.

Wilson Brown gave a sigh of impatience. 'You know what. Will that settle things?'

Terence pondered a while. 'Moneywise, I suppose it sounds reasonable. But what about my seven years? There must be compensation for that, wouldn't you say?'

'I had no choice.'

Terence swilled his whisky round the glass. 'Perhaps not, dear boy, but to drive off as you did, leaving me halfway down the ladder, was hardly cricket' He paused. 'And with a sackful of goodies over my shoulder; it was difficult to convince the law that I was merely cleaning the windows .. . especially at three in the morning.'

Wilson Brown sprang to his feet. 'Oh, come on now, it wouldn't have helped you if I'd stayed, and there wouldn't be any money, just remember that.' He looked pointedly at Terence to let this sink in.

Terence didn't appear to understand the significance of this – he was idly scratching his crotch. The Commander frowned: after all, they were his trousers. He made a mental note to have them cleaned, or better still his gardener could have them. He'd be overwhelmed, and word would get round ('Always looks after his men, does the Commander'). Then he recalled that the gardener had asked for a raise only last month, and his jaw hardened. That's all everybody wanted nowadays, money money money. Well, OK, but he wasn't having the trousers as well. The bloody cheek of it! It was bad enough having to pay him two pounds twelve and six a week, but he wasn't going to clothe him into the bargain.

'You're right, it wouldn't have helped if you'd stayed.'

The Commander grunted. 'What . . . oh, yes. I'd have been in the same boat as you.' He waved his hand round the room. 'And don't run away with the idea that all this comes from the proceeds. Oh, no. I made most of my money after that, when you were inside.'

Terence smiled. 'Of course you did. Ikey told me about it.' A momentary flash of panic crossed Wilson Brown's face, and he took a gulp from his glass. Terence beamed. 'Incidentally, he sends you his regards . . . he's doing quite well in the laundry.'

Wilson Brown hurried to the sideboard to replenish his drink. 'He's taken care of for a few years anyway,' he muttered.

Terence held out his empty glass. 'His boys aren't. They're sniffing about for you, Joe.'

Wilson Brown poured from a height so that the decanter wouldn't rattle against the glass.

'Nervous, Joe?' asked Terence. 'You know, your best bet is a monastery. Or better still have an operation and be a Mother Superior – you wouldn't be happy as an ordinary nun.' He stood up and sauntered round the room. 'We might get a billiard table in here.'

Wilson Brown's eyebrows went up. 'We?' he said. 'How long do you intend to stay here?'

Terence was examining the ship's bell. 'You seem to be under a misapprehension, old boy. The question is, how long do you intend to stay here?'

Wilson Brown stared at him for a long moment, then dashed off his drink and poured another one.

Terence was now looking closely at a wooden ship's crest. 'Interesting,' he murmured. 'Where did you pick up all this nautical?'

'It was here when I bought the place.'

Terence swung round to him. 'I see ... yes, so you promoted yourself to Commander.' He nodded round the room. The mind boggles, Joe,' he said. 'Had the fixtures and fittings included gothic arches and a picture of the last supper, you might have been a bishop.' He pursed his lips. 'On balance, I think you did well. Commander Wilson Brown sounds right.'

'Wilson Brown is right,' snarled the Commander. 'It happens to be my real name.'

Terence's jaw dropped. 'Well, I'll be damned.' He moved towards him. 'I thought we had no secrets, Joe, and in all those years you never told me.'

There was a discreet tap at the door, and they both turned. 'Yes,' barked the Commander.

His housekeeper peered timidly into the room. 'A gentleman to see you, sir.'

Wilson Brown looked sharply at Terence. 'I'm not expecting anyone ... who is he?'

Mrs Farley flustered. 'He did tell me, but I couldn't quite catch it. It sounded Italian, but I think he's Irish.'

Terence relaxed. 'Ah, yes. Rembrandt. Show him in please, Mrs Farley.'

She looked at her master for confirmation and he nodded. As soon as she'd gone he whirled round to Terence. 'Is he still alive? What's he want?'

Terence shrugged. 'That is something I've never been able to ascertain. However the question is academic . . . I want him here.'

Wilson Brown looked as if he'd just stepped into some-thing nasty. 'Here . . . in this house?'

Before Terence could reply the door opened and Mrs Farley ushered in Rembrandt from a safe distance, then edged round him to escape. Rembrandt's gaze slowly swept round the room. 'Ah, dis is more like it, sorr.' He swaggered over to the fire, his carrier bag jinking and clinking as he walked. 'Oi could settle down here, and dat's a fact.' He took off his cap and stuffed it into the bag, extracting a bottle of Guinness in return. Fascinated, Wilson Brown watched the little Irishman as he fiddled beneath his long dirty raincoat. For one awful moment it looked as if he were undoing his flies, then he brought out a bottle opener attached to a scruffy piece of string.

Wilson Brown sighed audibly. The little ratbag was unpredict-able, and could quite easily have put the fire out as a token gesture.

'Good health . . . here's to the old firm all together again.' As he put the bottle to his lips Wilson Brown was mesmerised by the hairy grey adam's apple bobbing up and down to accommodate the Guinness. Finally Rembrandt took the bottle from his lips and gave a huge belch. 'That'll keep the dust down,' he muttered, and placed the empty on the mantelpiece next to a silver cigarette lighter. Then he wiped his mouth with the back of his hand. 'Oi wouldn't mind a couple of eggs and a bit of bacon, and a sausage if der's one goin'.' As he talked he picked up his bag and made his way to the door.

Terence snapped his fingers, and Rembrandt stopped. 'The lighter.'

Rembrandt made a good attempt at being puzzled for a moment, then he took the lighter from his raincoat pocket. 'Oi was going to light the gas, sorr.'

'Never mind the gas, you stunted peat bog. Put it back.'

'Yes, sorr.' He replaced it on the mantelpiece and shuffled out.

Wilson Brown spread his hands. 'You saw that. He can't stay here . . . I mean, well, he'll attract attention.'

Terence nodded. 'Oh, yes, but he'll attract more attention wandering the streets of Grapplewick. That's why I want him where I can keep an eye on him.'

Wilson Brown tried again. 'You don't understand. If he's seen wandering round the Binglewood Estate he'll be run in purely on suspicion.'

'Oh, I agree,' said Terence. 'So I'll keep him in during the day and exercise him after dark. There's quite a few places on the estate I wouldn't mind seeing myself.' He heaved himself out of the chair. 'You don't have a map of the disposition of the dwellings on the estate, do you?' he asked innocently.

Wilson Brown gazed into his glass. 'There's a map at the gates ... well, there's one at every entrance to the estate and ...' He stopped suddenly, and his eyes widened. 'You're not thinking what I'm thinking, are you?'

Terence looked at him levelly. 'Probably,' he said. Wilson Brown stared at him aghast.

Terence smiled. 'After all, it is my profession, and this is right up my alley. Here I am, a bear in a honey garden.'

Wilson Brown stood back, shaking his head vigorously. 'Oh, no. You're not messing on my front door step. I've finished with all that rubbish. I'm straight now,' he snickered. 'Binglewood Estate – you wouldn't stand a chance. The police aren't all idiots, you know. They'll soon trace you to me. Oh, yes. I stuck my neck out last week when I gave you a suspended sentence. The houses on this estate are pretty well looked after with burglar alarms and dogs. . . .' He trailed off, unable to meet Terence's scornful gaze.

'You know, Joe, you're pathetic. You really are quite pathetic.'

Wilson Brown took the poker and hacked away at the fire. 'It's you who's pathetic. You're the one who got nicked trying to sell a watch back to its owner.' He laughed. 'That's pathetic, isn't it? The great Raffles hauled into a provincial court with cardboard in his shoes and the arse hanging out of his trousers.'

It was Terence's turn to feel embarrassed. He moved away from the fire, for the gum holding his wig was beginning to run down his forehead. 'What about you, Commander? That's a laugh! Commander Wilson Brown – you wouldn't recognise a battleship if one sailed up the drive,' he chuckled. 'Hardly a master stroke, promoting yourself to Commander. I mean it only takes one phone call to the Admiralty and you're up the spout.'

Wilson Brown was unperturbed. 'Really? That's all you know, my friend. I've still got a little bit up here.' He tapped his forehead.

Terence looked at him quizzically, then he shrugged. 'Come off it, you fixed yourself up in the Ministry of Supply during the war.'

'Wrong again. Joe Helliwell worked in the Ministry of Supply.'

Terence felt uneasy. If he wasn't careful he was going to lose game, set and match. Then his brow cleared. 'You still owe society seven years for that abortive little job in £39.'

Wilson Brown turned away. 'You'd still have to prove it,' he said.

'Oh, I've got proof,' said Terence. 'There's no problem there. In any case, all the publicity connected with the trial wouldn't do your career much good.'

Wilson Brown said nothing, but glared at him. Terence relaxed – he was back in the game. He laid his head back and stretched out his legs. The whisky and the fire gave him a marvellous sense of wellbeing, and with so many aces in his hand he almost felt sorry for his old mate. A whiff of frying bacon reminded him he hadn't eaten since breakfast, but his eyes were heavier than his need for food and he dozed.

The slam of the door jerked him upright and Rembrandt glided in with his everlasting carrier bag. Dar's filled a corner up,' he said. 'The sausages could have been done a bit more. Dey take a lot of doing, a good sausage.' He took a half-full bottle of wine from his pocket and took a deep swig.

Wilson Brown winced. Along with the house he'd inherited a very finely stocked wine cellar, and here was this ratbag knocking back a Chateau Lafite as if it was meths – 1933 and all.

Rembrandt put the cork back and stuffed it into his rain-coat pocket. 'Not bad, dat. Oi tink oi put too much sugar in it.' Terence knew Rembrandt was enjoying himself, although one couldn't tell from his expression. He only had two expressions in his repertoire: mouth open and mouth closed. He slapped his cap on his head. 'Where is the car keys?' He held out a greasy hand towards his host.

Wilson Brown stared at him for a moment in astonishment, then his jaw tightened and he started to go red.

Terence saved him from apoplexy. 'All right, you've had your fun and you've been fed. Now shoot upstairs and get your great empty head down for the night.'

'Oi'm goin' into town to see my girlfriend,' said Rembrandt stubbornly.

Terence looked at him steadily. 'If you're not in that pit in ten minutes, I'll cut it off. Then you'll have nothing to play with.'

'Yes, sorr.'

Terence relented a little. 'In any case the car doesn't belong to you. You just can't go round appropriating other people's property like that.'

Rembrandt didn't move. 'Oi was goin' to bring it back. In any case, it's not doin' the car much good sitting der in a damp garage, and nobody's using it tonight.'

'Ah, that's where you're wrong,' said Terence. 'I'm taking it.' He didn't particularly want to go out, but the mention of a girlfriend had twanged a chord, and Elsie would be impressed when she caught sight of the car.

Wilson Brown wasn't giving in that easily. 'Just a minute. I might want to go into town tonight.'

'Splendid,' said Terence. 'I'll give you a lift.'

'You haven't got a licence.'

Terence waved his hand. 'A mere technicality,' he chuckled. 'I'm not sure if I can still drive the damn thing .. . never mind – if anything happens, we can always get another one, eh?' And with that he whistled himself upstairs to select something from Wilson Brown's wardrobe.

Elsie looked bored. It was quiet in the Dog and Partridge – there'd only been one couple in all evening, and when the woman caught sight of Elsie she had her boyfriend out of the bar so fast it was difficult to remember if they'd had anything. Now Elsie surveyed herself in the mirror behind the bar. She prodded her hair, then leaned forwards to examine her lips – satisfied, she turned sideways and tucked her stomach in.

'Aphrodite rising from the water.'

She jerked round at the voice. 'Oh, it's you. Good evening, Major. You're quite a stranger.'

'Yes,' said Terence, inserting a professionally manufactured Player's cigarette into his holder. 'I had to motor down to Manchester, to clinch a deal, and I just thought I'd drop by to say hello.'

Without the asking, Elsie was busy pouring him a large measure of whisky. 'Oh, that's why you're all dressed up to the nines,' she said.

'Thank you,' he smiled at her. He'd always fancied himself in a dark blue pin-striped suit, and this was good material – although the sleeves could have been longer, and he had a choice with the trousers, which either finished four inches above his shoes or else he lengthened the braces, showing a considerable expanse of shirt below the waistcoat. He had opted for the former, since the shortness didn't show behind the bar.

'Where are you staying now?' she said. 'Found somewhere nice?'

He sipped his whisky. 'I'm staying with an old friend of mine . . . met him during the war. Commander Wilson Brown – know him?'

'Oh, yes. Comes in here now and again.'

'Good man,' he said. 'He took me off the beach at Dunkirk.' He looked down at his glass. 'One of the last.'

She looked down in sympathy. 'Nasty, that,' she said, then she brightened. 'Walter Helliwell, he was at Dunkirk,' she said. 'Walter Helliwell used to live in Sheepfoot Lane.'

'Never met him.' He gave a rueful grin. 'Too busy trying to save my batman.' He raised his glass. 'Here's to you, Taffy, wherever you are.'

Elsie frowned. 'I thought the little Irishman was your batman, the one who used to stay here with you.'

'He was, after Taffy bought it . . . four batmen died under me.' He sighed. 'I often wonder why all those good lads went, and an old reprobate like me was spared.'

'Oh, you're not that old,' she said coyly, and poured him another large whisky.

Terence smiled at the compliment. 'Well, that's enough about me. How's that husband of yours?' Her face clouded. 'Oh, Fred.' She began to wipe the bar. 'The doctor's put him on iron jelloids.' She bent forward to rinse the cloth under the bar and his leg twitched. 'There's nothing organically wrong with him,' she went on, 'it's just that he needs a holiday.'

He smiled sympathetically. 'We all need that,' he said. His brain was racing, and he had to make his pitch while the bar was empty. 'I'm thinking about going back into films,' he said.

She stopped rinsing the cloth, and he was sorry. 'Films,' she said. 'Have you been in films?'

'Not *in* them. Before the war I was a producer.' Her face told him that he'd scored. 'I was on the phone to Ronnie yesterday, and he's keen to make a sequel to *Shangri La.*' He drained his whisky and put the glass down, but she was too overawed to fill it again.

'Ronald Coleman?' she said in a hushed voice. 'Did you meet him?'

He laughed. 'Meet him? Ronnie wouldn't move a step without me. "Terence, old boy," he used to say. . . .' As he said this he gave a passable imitation of the Coleman voice. ' "Terence, old boy, if anything happens to me in this picture, you could take over and no one would know the difference." '

Her eyes were wide. 'Have you made any other films?'

'Ooooh . . .' He pursed his lips. '*Life of a Bengal Lancer*, that was one of mine.' He pushed his glass slightly forward and she took the hint. 'Gary Cooper and I,' he went on, 'when we weren't actually shooting the film, we used to go horse riding together.'

She poured the whisky into his glass as if it was communion wine. 'Gary Cooper?'

'Yup,' he said, and laughed. 'Anyway, to change the subject, do you know of any good restaurants in Blackburn? I mean a good one, a really tip-top restaurant?'

'Blackburn,' she said, as if he'd just mentioned Rangoon. 'Well, I don't know offhand, but I could find out for you.'

'No, no,' he said quickly. 'It's just that after all your kindness to me, you know, when I first arrived, I thought perhaps you'd allow me to take you to dinner one evening.'

She stared at him. 'Well,' she said, 'that'll be nice, but I'll have to ask my Fred.'

Bugger Fred, he thought. 'Of course,' he said. 'When are you free?'

She shrugged. 'Well, the evenings are no good. I'm here, you see.'

He brightened. 'Tell you what,' he said, 'it's Saturday tomorrow. Why don't I pick you up after you finish at lunchtime, and we'll go for a spin?'

'Not tomorrow,' she said. 'I go to football on Saturday afternoons.'

'Football,' he said, trying to keep the distaste out of his voice.

'Oh yes, can't miss tomorrow. It's the first round of the FA Cup. . . .' She leaned towards him. 'I've got a good idea. Why don't you come as well?'

The proximity of her chest was too much for him. If she'd said 'Let's jump off the roof with an umbrella,' he'd have been halfway up the stairs with his brolly. 'Right,' he said, and peeled a crispy fiver off a sizeable wad. 'I'll be in tomorrow lunchtime.' He slid off the stool.

'Just a minute,' she said, 'you want some change.' 'Keep it,' he said, 'and buy yourself something nice.'

She stared at the money uncertainly. 'Well, if you're sure . . . that's very nice of you.'

'Nothing, my dear.' He took a couple of steps, then turned. 'Oh, by the way, I'd rather you didn't mention anything about the films – me being a producer and everything.'

She was disappointed, but agreed to say nothing.

'Thank you. Only if it ever got out that I was up here, the press would be on, the film companies would be on, and I wouldn't have a moment's peace.'

'I shan't say nothing,' she replied.

He nodded, then left hurriedly before she caught sight of his too short trousers. A football match was a small price to pay for two hours of her company, and he passed a feverish leg-twitching night.

Grapplewick Athletic, known fondly as t'Latics, weren't brilliant – in fact they were even more widely referred to as 'them clowns'. Nevertheless it was the dream of most young lads one day to don the blue and white shirt, and run out of a little wooden shed every Saturday afternoon. Terence was hardly aware of the stamping supporters. He was content to sit huddled on the cold wooden bench next to Elsie – it purported to be Stand E, although it was the only covered bit on the ground. Fred shivered on the other side of Elsie, but Terence felt no compunction about that. With a bit of luck he'd be dead by half time.

It was easy to spot the home team. They ran onto the field like fathers at the school sports, and two of them didn't join in the kick about because they were too heavily winded and had to put their hands on knees to get their breath back. The star of the 'Latics' was the goalkeeper, which was surprising. He was humpbacked for a start, and scurried from side to side in the goal mouth like a hermit crab. He was dressed all in black, and, unable to afford shinpads, two copies of the *Grapplewick Chronicle* were stuffed down his stockings, giving his legs an odd, misshapen look. The way he crouched it wouldn't have surprised anyone to hear him declaim 'Now is the winter of our discontent . . .' However, appearances were deceptive, and had it not been for his agility Grapplewick would have been considerably more than six down at half time.

Terence enjoyed the first half, or to be more accurate he was fascinated by the goalkeeper and wondered if he was human. He didn't mention this to Elsie, because she obviously thought the whole team was marvellous.

'Do you like it?' she said.

'Very good.' He smiled, and took a flask from his overcoat pocket.

'That's nice,' she said and took it, examining the gold Wilson Brown monogram.

'WB,' she said.

'Warner Brothers,' he whispered.

'Oh.' She hadn't the foggiest idea who Warner Brothers were, but it was obviously expensive.

Terence poured a jigger of whisky into the cap and handed it to her.

'Lovely,' she said, and proffered it to Fred.

He shook his head sullenly and looked away. He wouldn't have minded a drink, but it was too much effort to take his hands out of his pockets.

'Cheers.' Elsie sipped and held it out to Terence.

'No, my dear.' He pushed her hand back gently. 'Get it all down, there's plenty more.'

She knocked it back and gasped.

'That's the style,' said Terence. 'It'll warm you up.' He looked at her rosy face and the smiling lips. God, he thought, I'd warm her up given half the chance. A drum roll broke his thoughts, and he looked towards the field.

Mr Thurk raised his baton, and the band edged into the 'Marche Lorraine'. For football lovers the band was usually the highlight of the match, and for music lovers there was always the second half, and there were the regular wags with raucous, carrying voices: 'Give us "Nellie Dean". . . . When's the last waltz?' And the kids tried to lob pebbles in the bell of Herbert Barlow's double bass, unless Matry O'Toole was on duty – he wasn't today, and Herbert was twitching and ducking, but never missed a note.

Mr Thurk, however, was oblivious, totally absorbed in the music – 'Sons of the Brave', and now 'Three Jolly Sailormen'. He glanced round at the band, and he was proud. Many's the time they'd marched off the pitch bloodied and with lumps caused by flying missiles, but none had ever complained, and no one was absent on Saturday afternoons.

'Pah pah pah pon pom' . . . by jingo, Ned Bladdock was on form today, banging away on the big drum – stalwart Ned in a heavy belted overcoat and a tram conductor's hat. His gaze quickly moved to Cyril Chadwick, the only one to possess a tunic. Cyril loved his tunic, in fact he'd mentioned it several times in his letters to Betty Grable, and he knew that if ever she came to Grapplewick he only had to wear it and she'd spot him at once. He was lucky to inherit the tunic, because his father, being a vindictive man, had told him many times that, when he died, he was to be buried in it, and young Chadwick used to pray every night: 'Please, God, don't let him die.' But God works in mysterious ways, and one warm August night his father fell off the New Brighton ferry and his body was never recovered. The tunic was safe.

There was a smattering of applause, and a few ironic cheers greeted the end of 'Three Jolly Sailormen'. A half-penny fell at Jack Puller's feet. He didn't deign to stoop and pick it up but put his foot on it – he'd have it later when no one was looking.

'Abide with Me,' said Mr Thurk, raising his arms. The lads looked round and shuffled uneasily.

The players were already back on the field, rubbing their hands and jumping up and down to get warm. A whistle blew, and the lads put down their instruments and made to leave the field.

'Stand fast the band,' barked Mr Thurk, and they milled uncertainly, just inside the touchline. The whistle blew again, this time more insistently. Mr Thurk ignored it and raised his baton. The linesmen grabbed at Jack Puller's arm and found himself in the second row of the stand. The crowd cheered.

The referee ran over to Mr Thurk and blew his whistle right into his face. 'Kindly leave the field,' he said.

The crowd were delighted with this. 'Off! off! off!' they chanted, and clapped in time.

' "Abide with Me" is traditional,' said Mr Thurk with dignity.

'Off,' said the referee.

'One more tune isn't going to hurt you, is it?' said Mr Thurk, wildly trying to find a face-saver.

'Very well.' The referee took out his little black notebook. 'Name?'

'One verse.'

'WHAT'S YOUR NAME?'

Over his shoulder Mr Thurk saw the band skulking off towards the exit. 'You know very well what my name is, Norman Taylor. We were in the same class at school.'

'Are you going to leave the field or not?'

Mr Thurk glared at him for a moment, then his resolve weakened. 'All right, I'll go. But you've never really grown up, have you?'

The referee blew a sharp blast at him and pointed to the exit.

'As long as you're in short pants, and sucking something, you're happy.'

The crowd cheered and clapped as he walked to the gate with head held high.

They were not forgotten, however. After Grapplewick went three more goals down, the crowd chanted, 'We want the band! We want the band!' But by this time most of the lads were back home.

Terence watched the performance thoughtfully. An idea was already permeating his mind and he didn't notice the final whistle.

'Enjoy that?' said Elise.

Terence was jolted out of his reverie. 'What? Oh, yes, very much. Where do they practise?'

She laughed. 'Oh, I don't think they practise,' she said. 'They all have jobs to do. The goalkeeper is an undertaker, and Whittaker the right back is a milkman . . .'

'No, no,' he said. 'I mean the band.'

'Oh, they practise every Thursday night over the Fire Station. Mr Thurk, the one who conducts them, is the Mayor.'

'Really?' said Terence, and they turned to shuffle towards the exit.

She stopped suddenly and he bumped into her. It was only her back, but it sent his temperature up several degrees – she put her mouth to his ear and he broke into a sweat. 'I've had a word with Mr Helliwell, and he said he wouldn't mind me having the evening off, as long as I don't make a habit of it.'

Terence shepherded his scattered thoughts. 'This evening?' He remembered he'd offered to take her out to dinner if she was free, but as much as he would have liked, and as much as his leg was twitching, he had other plans. In any case he felt that if they did go to dinner Fred would be sitting there to make up the party, and sod that for a game of shuttle-cock. 'This evening,' he repeated. 'Oh, didn't I mention it? I have an important meeting tonight.'

Her face fell. 'On Saturday,' she said.

'Every day is a business day for me,' he said, but when he looked at her stricken face he was immediately thinking of excuses to get out of the meeting which he had just convened. Then he became resolute. 'I'm sorry, but I've quite a lot of money tied up in this venture.'

She was puzzled for a moment, then she nodded conspiratorially and began to edge along the row again. There'll be another time, thought Terence, but business first. His idea concerning the band was a stroke of genius, and the sooner he got the wheels in motion the better. Like all great inspiration, it was simple.

As Terence was making his thoughtful way home, Wilson Brown sat facing his flickering black and white television set. He'd hardly noticed the sport that afternoon, and he cared even less for the football results. What a way to spend a Saturday afternoon! Television wouldn't last long if that was the best they could do – the highlight was undoubtedly the interlude. Normally he would have spent the day at the Binglewood golf club, but he didn't have a car. Damn Terence, and why his sudden interest in football? Somewhere upstairs a door slammed, and he got up and switched the set off angrily.

Rembrandt came resolutely down the stairs with his ever clinking carrier bag. They were empties, but when he returned from the Weavers Arms the bag would be consider-ably heavier. He was looking forward to seeing Nellie again, and being Saturday there'd be a sing-song in the public bar. He never joined in, but if the Guinness was sitting well inside him he might be persuaded to render a chorus of 'The Wild Colonial Boy'. As he was crossing the hall he yelled, 'Oi'm goin' out, you silly old bag.' He never saw Mrs Farley, but he knew that somewhere she was watching his every move.

The drawing-room door opened and Wilson Brown eyed him with distaste.

Rembrandt stopped. 'Ah, der you are, just de man oi want to see,' and he brushed past him and shuffled to the fire.

Wilson Brown closed the door, waited for a moment, then opened it quickly, and his housekeeper almost fell into his arms. 'Do you want something, Mrs Farley?' he said stiffly.

'No sir, no.' She almost curtseyed in embarrassment, and he closed the door.

Rembrandt pointed to it. 'Dat woman is a menace,' he said.

Wilson Brown ignored him and moved over to the side-board to pour himself a drink.

'Dat woman,' went on Rembrandt, still pointing to the door, 'she took some empty bottles out of my room on Thursday, and der's money on dem.'

Wilson Brown settled down in the armchair and flapped open *The Times*.

Rembrandt came and stood directly in front of him. 'And she wiped off a half finished picture of Winston Churchill – she'd no right to do dat.'

A slight tremor of *The Times* was the only indication that Wilson Brown was listening . . . .

'Also de place stinks of disinfectant. It's worse dan de work-house. It's a better stink in de workhouse, and dat's a fact.'

The paper still obscured Wilson Brown.

'An den dere's my shoes. What about my shoes? My good pair dat used to belong to a vicar – what about dem, eh?' The newspaper didn't move.

'Oi leave dem out one morning to be cleaned, and she's gone and burnt them.'

Wilson Brown lowered the paper in order to take a drink, but his eyes never left the front page.

Rembrandt turned and went back to the fire. 'So on Monday oi'm 'aving a lock put on dat door of mine.'

This had the desired effect, and Wilson Brown looked at him as if he'd suddenly noticed his presence. 'You'll do nothing of the kind.' As soon as he spoke he was angry at himself for having been drawn.

Rembrandt picked up his carrier bag. 'Oh, no? You just watch me, dat's all. Wait till you see dat dirty great padlock oi'm tinking of. Yes, sorr, oi'm not having her pokin' round among my private tings.' He made his way to the door, and was almost knocked flat as Terence entered the room.

'A grand afternoon,' he said to no one in particular, shrugging out of Wilson Brown's black Crombie overcoat. 'And profitable, too. Aah, there's something about a good football match that stirs the blood.' He stood facing the fire and held out his hands to the warmth. 'It was cold, though. By the centre, it was cold. If it had gone on much longer, I'd have been drinking solid whisky.' He shivered and looked over his shoulder at Rembrandt. 'Well, don't just stand there like a badly run jumble sale. A drink, man!'

Rembrandt stood firm, 'Oi'm just on my way out, sorr. Oi'm goin' to see my girlfriend,' he added.

Terence shook his head. 'Not tonight, you're not.'

Rembrandt was immovable. 'Oi promised oi'd see her at the pub and oi'm a man of me word,' he said stoutly. 'Never mind all that sanctimonious twaddle, go and pour me a large one.'

Rembrandt put down his carrier bag and walked over to the decanter. 'Oi'll pour you a drink, an den oi'm off.'

Terence lifted up the back of his jacket and warmed his rear end. 'And what have you been up to today, Joe? Been chasing Mrs Farley round the estate, have you?'

Wilson Brown didn't reply, but he folded his newspaper and laid it aside on the table.

Rembrandt handed Terence his drink. 'On the other hand, sorr, oi wouldn't mind stayin' in tonight. Oi don't mind at all.'

Terence watched him over the rim of his glass.

'Dat's a good idea about stayin' in, sorr. Oi'll just ring de pub and tell her to come up here.'

Wilson Brown slammed the arms of the chair and stood up. 'Oh no, you don't. I'm not having that slag Droopy Nellie in my house.'

Rembrandt turned to him. 'How did you know about Eleanor?' he asked, with much emphasis on the name.

Wilson Brown took his empty glass for a refill. 'There's not a lot goes on in this town that I don't get to hear about.' He looked at the little man in disgust. 'Droopy Nelly – that's about your mark, that is.'

Rembrandt leered knowingly. 'She told me about you, too,' he said. 'Oh, yes. She told me you fancied her. She told me she could have had you at de back of de washhouse once.'

'That'll be the day,' snorted Wilson Brown. 'But one thing is certain – she's not setting one foot on the Binglewood Estate. We don't want an epidemic.'

'She reckons you're a brown hatter.'

118Terence felt it was time to intervene. 'For goodness sake, why don't you toss up for her?'

Wilson Brown shot him a look of annoyance. 'I'm warning you, if that woman comes within a mile of this place I'll have the police up here like a shot.'

Terence smiled indulgently. 'Now, Joe. We know you wouldn't do a silly thing like that. But for old times' sake I'll let him go down to the pub.'

Rembrandt moved to the door again. 'Oi'll give her your love,' he said.

In a flash Terence jerked him on to his toes by his lapels. 'Listen, Clark Gable, I don't want you to breathe a word to anybody about where you're staying. Is that clear?'

Rembrandt could barely speak, but he managed, 'Under-stood, sorr,' and Terence dropped him. 'Oi'll not say nuthin', sorr.' And he scuttled out before Terence changed his mind.

'I'll swing for that little bastard one day,' snarled Wilson Brown. 'He gets on my wick.'

'Yes, but he has his uses. Now sit down and listen to what I have to say.'

Wilson Brown, still seething, slumped into a chair.

Terence watched him for a moment. 'After a week's reconnaissance, and from conversations that have passed between us, I have decided that three houses on this estate deserve my undivided attention.'

Wilson Brown spluttered. 'Three houses?'

'Yes: Holmedene, The Beeches and Woodhaven East.'

Wilson Brown snickered. 'Well, I should forget The Beeches for a start. Burglar alarms, dogs . . . there's no chance. It's sewn up tighter than a Scotsman's purse. I should pick one of the others, if I were you.'

Terence eyed him coolly. 'I intend to visit all three.' Wilson Brown tried to speak, but Terence held up his hand. 'All in one and the same night.'

Wilson Brown hooted. Hah, you've really gone round the twist, haven't you? How can you do them in one night?'

'That part of the plan doesn't concern you. In fact the less you know of it the better.'

The Commander frowned. 'Well, why are you telling me anything at all?'

'Because you can be useful.'

Wilson Brown stumped over to the sideboard and filled his glass. 'I don't like it,' he muttered.

'Well, don't drink it,' said Terence. It was wasted effort. 'I don't like it at all,' repeated Wilson Brown. He began to pace up and down.

'Supposing I just pick up the phone now, and make a clean breast of it to the Inspector – he's a pal of mine.'

'Because,' said Terence, 'we haven't done anything yet. The only thing to suffer would be your reputation, and that, dear Joe, is more precious to you than anything that could happen to me.' He tossed off his drink. 'And besides, you still owe them for the Chelmsford one. They know I didn't pull that job on my own.'

Wilson Brown returned to his chair and stared into his glass, then he tried again. 'Look, Terence, what's your price? How much for you to just pack up and disappear?'

Terence sighed. 'How can I ever make you understand? I'm a professional – I have my reputation to think of. Three houses in one night, and they'll know who's done it. Oh yes – but they won't be able to feel my collar because I'll have a cast iron alibi.'

In spite of himself, Wilson Brown was intrigued. 'I presume you're not telling me all this just to hear your own voice?'

'You presume correctly. Now you are, I believe, acquainted with the occupiers of the three houses?'

'You know I am. You've been asking questions about them all week.'

'Good. Well enough to exchange Christmas gifts?' 'Well, yes. What's wrong with that?'

'It's absolutely splendid, but this year I want you to play cagey. Drop hints that you've organised something rather special for them, a novel gift that you hope will be much appreciated.'

Wilson Brown was more than perplexed. 'Like what?' 'On Christmas Eve, your novel gift will be the Grapplewick Brass Band playing for them personally "Silent Night".' He stood back like a conjuror producing something impossible.

For a moment Wilson Brown stared open-mouthed, then he sprang to his feet. 'That lot couldn't get a tune out of a bloody gramophone.'

Terence smiled. 'As long as they're loud, that's all I care about. Oh – and that they're capable of playing "Silent Night".'

'There won't be much silence with that bunch, I'll tell you that.' He gulped his whisky. 'And why "Silent Night"? What's so special about "Silent Night"?'

'It's the only one I know,' said Terence smoothly, 'and also it runs roughly five minutes, give or take a crochet, and while they're doing their job I'll do mine.'

'Huh.' Wilson Brown was scornful. 'Five minutes isn't long.'

'It's plenty if I know where to look.'

'And how will you get to know that?'

'I'll go through the houses beforehand. How else would I find out – I'm not a bloody clairvoyant.'

Wilson Brown was thinking hard, sizing up the angles and how it could affect him. Finally he shook his head. 'It wouldn't work,' he said.

'Give me one good reason.'

'Well, for a start everyone knows I dislike the band. I've been trying to get it scrapped for the last two years.'

'All the better,' said Terence. 'It will enhance the joke. They'll be laughing about it for months.'

Wilson Brown thought again. 'Ah, yes, but how will you get the band to go up there in the first place?'

'You try and stop 'em when I've finished with 'em.' He chuckled. 'You should have seen them this afternoon – if there hadn't been a football match they'd be playing yet.'

Wilson Brown didn't like it. He didn't like it at all. There were a lot of ifs and buts and snags, but he couldn't think of them at the moment. Nevertheless a warning bell was sounding in the back of his mind. He finished off his drink. 'And when you've done this job you'll leave . . . I mean. . . .' He stopped suddenly as one of the ifs flashed into his mind. It was an enormous if and it staggered him. 'Just hold on a minute,' he said. 'If that damn band plays at these houses, supposedly on my recommendation, while at the same time they're being turned over, I'll be up to my neck in it .. . suspect number one, certainly as an accomplice.'

Terence nodded. 'Yes, I was afraid you'd spot that connection.'

'There you are, then,' said Wilson Brown triumphantly. No way am I getting involved.'

Terence studied him for a moment. 'But you are already involved, dear boy. I'm here, and that alone makes you a fully paid up member.'

Wilson Brown wasn't finished. He adopted a reasonable tone. 'Yes, but why must I inform these houses? Why not just have the band turn up and play?'

Terence shook his head. 'It's too chancy. The occupants wouldn't even get up from the dinner table . . . the butler would be despatched to send them packing the minute they started to blow . . . they'd set the dogs on them . . . or worse, they'd phone the police. No. The band has to be presented as a rather novel Christmas gift.' Wilson Brown snorted, but Terence ignored the interruption. 'Don't you see? People get socks for Christmas, they get ties and handkerchiefs, and they say, "Oh, isn't that lovely. Just what I wanted." And so it will be with the band. Everyone will gather to listen with fixed politeness until the last excruciating bar of music. Then perhaps – who knows – hot punch all round? A discreet fiver stuffed into one of the instruments? Psychology, old boy.'

Wilson Brown was unconvinced. 'It won't work,' he said flatly. 'Oh, I'll grant you there's a certain element of risk in having the band turn up unexpectedly, but I'm afraid that's a chance you'll have to take, because I'm certainly not going to have my name connected in any way.'

There was no reply, and he looked over his shoulder. Terence was at the little escritoire, scribbling on a small message pad. 'Got it,' he said, and tore off the paper, which he took to Wilson Brown. 'There you are. Have that copied on nice greeting cards and sent.'

Wilson Brown studied the text. 'What's this?' he asked.

'Read it,' said Terence.

Wilson Brown flicked open his spectacles with one hand and put them on the end of his nose. 'To the occupants of Holmedene, The Beeches, Woodhaven East and Seven Seas.' Wilson Brown looked at Terence.

'Go on,' urged Terence, 'Read it.'

'At eight o'clock on Christmas Eve you will receive a novel gift, with the season's greetings, from a well-wisher.' He lowered the paper. 'Are you serious?' he asked, incredulous.

'Perfectly serious,' said Terence.

Wilson Brown skimmed the paper across at him. It settled on the rug. 'You don't know the people on this estate,' he said scornfully. 'Get a note like that and they'll tear it up straight away.'

Terence picked up the paper. 'Perhaps,' he said, 'but in any case you'll ring them up and ask if they've also received interesting Christmas cards. Be amused, play on their curiosity, tell them that in a strange way you're rather looking forward to it, whatever it is.' He propped the paper in front of the little clock on the mantelpiece.

'Better still, call round and compare cards. Two sherries and a biscuit, and with your undoubted charm Christmas Eve won't come quick enough.'

Wilson Brown lurched out of the chair and re-read the note. 'Bloody childish. It won't work.'

Terence was unruffled. 'Course it will, dear boy. Simplicity! And its precisely the childishness that will create the intrigue. Imagine it – when Christmas Eve comes, who can fail to be touched by the sound of "Silent Night", played personally by the whole band, in order to wish them the compliments of the season.'

He spread his arms wide. 'The King does it at Buckingham Palace with the whole of the Grenadier Guards band.'

Wilson Brown snorted and moved from the fireplace to the whisky decanter.

Terence relaxed. He noted with satisfaction that Wilson Brown had stuffed the paper surreptitiously into his inside pocket. Bait taken. Terence sauntered over and held out his glass, but it was ignored. He shrugged and helped himself.

'My house is on your list.'

Terence nodded. 'Of course. Easiest way to allay suspicion – makes you one of the victims.'

'I know that,' said Wilson Brown irritably. 'What I would like to know is . . . am I to be turned over as well.'

Terence smiled. 'Would I do that to an old mate?'

Wilson Brown grunted. It was a politician's answer, and he made a mental note to place his valuables in the bank. This last thought brightened him considerably – every item locked away in a safe deposit could be claimed on the insurance as stolen. He began a quick mental assessment of the size of his claim, but his thoughts were interrupted by a discreet tap on the door, and Mrs Farley eased in.

'Ah, Mrs Farley,' said Terence cheerfully.

She ignored him and addressed her master. 'If you don't mind, sir, I'd like to go up to my room now.'

'Not well, Mrs Farley?' he asked solicitously, although he knew the answer. She was suffering from a severe case of Rembrandt.

'Off you go, then, Mrs Farley, and I hope you feel better tomorrow.'

'Thank you, sir. I've left some cold meat and salad in the dining-room.'

'Splendid, Mrs Farley,' said Terence.

He might not have been present. 'Will that be all right, sir?' she asked.

'It'll do, Mrs Farley, thank you. Now off you go and get a good night's rest.'

She bobbed slightly to Wilson Brown and glided out as if on wheels.

Terence squared his shoulders. 'That's the style, Joe,' he said. 'Always look after the lower decks.'

Wilson Brown grunted. 'Nothing wrong with her that your departure won't cure, and that goes for me too.' He settled back in his chair, then suddenly shot bolt upright as if the springs had broken through. 'Wait a minute,' he said. 'Mrs Farley knows you're here. She'll be questioned by the police. She'll have your descriptions, and it won't be too difficult to place two and two together – they'll soon trace the connections.'

Terence had already thought of this. 'She doesn't know who we are, does she?' He spread his arms reasonably. 'And at the time of the, er, incident, we will be in London, so why should we arouse suspicion?'

Wilson Brown's jaw dropped. 'But how will you be in London?' he asked stupidly.

'An express leaves Piccadilly Station, Manchester, about four on Christmas Eve. We'll be on it.' He looked intently into Wilson Brown's face, like a doctor trying to diagnose an ailment. 'Look, Joe, just do as you're told and leave the real thinking to me.'

Wilson Brown looked haggard. He had a feeling that somehow or other he was going to be left holding something nasty. He spoke in a small voice. 'I think I'll go up to my room.'

Terence parted him on the shoulder. 'Cheer up, Joe, there's nothing you can't get over except death.' He laughed. 'Tell you what – why don't you take the car and go into town and have a drink somewhere?'

Wilson Brown gave a mirthless laugh. 'You've had it so bloody often in the last fortnight they'll think I've stolen it.' He made his way slowly towards the door.

Terence called after him: 'Oh, by the way, you haven't got a record of "Silent Night" have you?'

SIXTEEN

K enneth Sagbottom was a happy postman. He enjoyed delivering parcels in his little red van – he was an all-year-round Father Christmas – and when the day came to lay down his sack for the last time he had a pension to look forward to. He whistled as he knocked at number 46. While he waited he read the address on the parcel. Then he looked over his shoulder, but a grimy privet hedge hid his van from sight and he was unable to see the new Vauxhall creeping to a standstill behind it. He knocked again but there was no answer, so he walked round the back and tapped on the window. Old Mrs Buckley waved and got up to open the door.

'Mornin', Mrs Buckley. Parcel for you.'

'For me?' she said.

'Yes.'

'I wonder who it could be from?'

'It's from your son George – look.' He pointed to the sender's address.

She peered at it closely.

Kenneth waited patiently. She got a parcel every week from her son, but there was always the same performance. Once he'd wondered idly what George put in the parcels. Food? Magazines? But then again, knowing what a miser-able devil George was, the most likely bet was his dirty laundry.

It's from my son,' she said. 'He lives in Blackburn.' 'That's right. Would you just sign here, please?'

She did so, and he made his way round to the front, whistling. When he reached the gate his lips remained pursed, but nothing came out ... his van had gone. A knot of panic gripped his stomach. He craned sideways to look round the back of the new Vauxhall, but it wasn't there. He even stopped to look underneath. In a flash he saw his comfortable little world crumbling. The sun came out for a minute when the thought crossed his mind that he couldn't he held responsible if a gang had stolen his van, but the sky quickly darkened again. He was in the wrong for leaving the motor running. A flash of lightning brightened his eyes – it was old Mrs Buckley's fault, he thought childishly. If she had answered the front door like she should, he would have seen it go. But then again, he knew in his heart that she wasn't to blame. He decided to go home and tell his mother – she'd know what to do, she always did. But on this occasion she didn't.

She shook her head worriedly. 'Whatever possessed you to leave it standing in the road like that?'

He wrung his hands. 'I had to. I had to take a parcel round the back, Mam.'

Poor Kenneth, forty-two years old, and in moments of stress he still called her 'Mam'.

She stared into the fire. 'Well, I don't know what we can do. I don't. I mean, did you look properly?'

'Yes, Mam,' he said with a great sigh.

'Oh, Kenneth, you haven't an ounce of grey matter, have you? They'll make you pay for it, you know.'

He was biting his thumbnail. He'd already thought of that, but he still harboured a wild idea that she'd think of something.

'What will we do if you have to pay for it?' she asked petulantly.

He shrugged, his brain racing like an arthritic tortoise.

She tweaked her nose with a corner of her apron. 'I don't know, I don't.' She turned to address the fire: 'You slave and scrimp, to get 'em in the Post Office, and they no sooner get on the vans and they go and lose it.'

'It wasn't my fault, Mam,' he wailed.

She came to a decision. 'Never mind whose fault it is,' she said. 'Fetch me me shawl.'

'Where are we goin', Mam?' he asked anxiously.

'Where are we goin'? I'll tell you where we're goin'. You have while six o'clock before you report back to the Post Office, so we're goin' to look for it.'

He flapped his hands helplessly. 'Where will we look, Mam?' he asked plaintively.

'I don't know,' she said. 'But one thing I'm certain of, we won't find it sittin' on our backsides,' and she snatched the shawl from him.

In fact, the little red post van was chugging up the wide sweeping drive at Holmedene on the Binglewood Estate.

'Here we are, sorr, number one on de hit parade.'

Terence leaned forward in his seat to take in the magnificent old house. All he got was a blurred impression of something huge, but then he was wearing thick pebble glasses, which, with an enormous walrus moustache, completely altered his appearance. He spoke to Rembrandt as he lifted his glasses to examine the facade. 'Right! When we get in there, you keep your thieving hands to yourself, understand? Touch nothing – I don't care if it's a dog drop-ping, you don't touch it, right?'

Rembrandt sat there unmoved. 'Oi wouldn't touch one of dem. Oi don't like dogs, an dat's a fact.'

Terence heaved himself out of the van. 'Good. Get the tools and follow me.'

Rembrandt ignored him. 'Oi'll stay in here if der's a dog. Oi don't want nothin' to do wid a dog.'

Terence opened the door and hauled him outside like a sack of potatoes. 'How should I know if they have a dog?' he hissed. 'That's what we're here to find out. Now get the tools and follow me.'

Rembrandt did so and hurried after him, just in time to prevent Terence walking into an ornamental lily pond. 'The house is over dere, sorr.'

'I know where it is,' said Terence peevishly, and turned to walk towards the house with a confidence he didn't feel.

Rembrandt shuffled to the front door and watched patiently as Terence peremptorily knocked n the garage door.

Lifting his glasses, he glanced round to get his bearings, then joined Rembrandt in the front porch. 'They don't build garages like that any more,' he said in an offhand way.

Rembrandt wasn't fooled for a second. He avoided Terence's groping hand and hammered the door knocker.

Terence wondered whether the glasses were a mistake, but then again, nobody would connect this shortsighted stoop-shouldered menial with Commander Wilson Brown's suave, debonair house guest. Slowly the door opened, and Terence touched the peak of his cap to the tall, blurred shape of the manservant.

'Post Office engineers to check the telephones.'

'Tradesmen round the back,' intoned the dark mass, and closed the door.

'Round-the-back-sort,' said Rembrandt with careful enunciation.

'It's only the glasses. I'm not deaf, you cretinous Guinness bag!'

Raising the glasses, he made his way round the rear of the house, making a careful mental note of the layout.

The manservant took even longer to open the back door. 'Yes?' he inquired.

'Post Office engineers to check the telephones.'

'The apparatus was in use not ten minutes ago, and it appeared perfectly functional then.' The door slammed, almost smashing Terence's brilliant disguise.

They looked at each other, but remained where they were. Terence pretended to examine his fingernails, although he couldn't have seen his hand, while Rembrandt stared at the woodwork. In less than five minutes the door was flung open and the manservant almost knocked them down.

'Ah, there you are,' he said, trying to regain some of his dignity. 'You're quite right, it doesn't appear to be working. Would you follow me?'

They nodded to each other knowingly. It's very difficult for a telephone to work if someone is dastardly enough to cut the wires.

The servant hovered around while they busied themselves. He watched in amazement and wondered how a man so afflicted with blindness could identify a fault in the complicated electrical circuit.

Terence turned in his direction. 'Bai gum. A wouldn't mind a cup of tea, if tha's doin' nowt,' he said in a dreadful parody of a Lancashire accent. He was quite safe: broad Lancashire at Holmedene was as foreign as Swahili.

'I am not the cook,' droned the servant.

'A didn't mean thee. I meant for thee to ask t'cuke.'

'Nor is this a restaurant.' He folded his arms and stood immovable, which was the last thing Terence wanted. 'Ast'a an extension?' He stood up.

'Certainly, they're in the bedrooms,' the man said.

'Well, if you wouldn't mind, like.' Terence gestured for him to show the way, which he reluctantly did, but he watched them even more closely – after all, it was the master's bedroom. Terence groped for the telephone and listened for a moment.

'Robin, lad, will you go t' van and get me t'circuit tester?'

Rembrandt turned to see who the dickens Robin was.

Terence grabbed him by the sleeve. 'I'm waiting, Robin.'

'Ah yes, sorr. Robin, Bat's me. Oi'll go and get dat stuff, sorr.'

'Thank you, Robin. Mind you wipe tha feet, and close t'door after you.'

Rembrandt stood still for a moment, then, in a rare flash of intuition, he knew what was wanted. 'Oi'll close the door all right, sorr.' And he went.

Terence smiled ingratiatingly at where he thought the servant was. ''E's a one, is Robin. He dun't luke much, but e's a wizard with wires.'

There was no reply, and for a moment Terence thought he might be alone and wondered whether to chance taking his glasses off. Then a voice came from somewhere behind him. God – he hoped he hadn't smiled ingratiatingly at the wardrobe. He slowly turned towards the sound.

'How long do you propose to be? I have other duties to attend to.'

Terence pursed his lips. 'Well, if it's a contact tumbler, we have a replacement, but it might be the vibratory coil.' He was about to elaborate but prudence shackled his tongue. Unable to see the effect of his words, he might be digging a pit for himself – he might even be talking to Marconi. 'Ah well,' he said, 'I'll mek a cup o' tea meself if you'll show me wher all t'stuff is.' He didn't expect a reply, but he had to play for time. Where was Rembrandt? Knowing the scrofulous idiot, he was probably scrabbling about in the back of the van searching for a circuit tester – whatever that may be. The silence began to unnerve Terence, but just as he was about to open his mouth to speak four faint thuds came from the bowels of the hall.

'Somebody's at the front door now,' clucked the servant, and Terence felt the whiff of brilliantine as he swept past him.

Quick as a flash Terence had the glasses in his pocket and was at the window behind the curtain, slipping the catch but leaving the window closed – if somebody latched it in the meantime, there were other ways. Then he made a swift inventory of the drawers and cupboards and went on into the next room. A bell sounded below and Terence froze in his tracks. Then he breathed again – full marks to Rembrandt: he'd been to the front, knowing full well he'd be ordered round the back, thus gaining a few more valuable seconds. Perhaps he had underestimated him. He didn't wait to examine the thought, for he had work to do, and by the time Rembrandt and the servant returned he was staring closely at the telephone.

'Oi couldn't find the – er – piece, sorr. Oi tink it's out on another job.'

'I'm not bothered now,' said Terence straightening. 'Ave found t'fault.'

The servant was impressed. 'Is it all right now?'

'Nay, it's not. It's a fault on t'line, I'll have to report it at t'depot.'

The servant's face fell.

'Is der any chance of a cup of tea before we go?' said Rembrandt.

'As I said before, this is not a cafe.' He shepherded them to the back door.

In the next couple of hours three more houses developed inexplicable telephone faults, but with an efficiency remark-able in the Post Office two engineers were on the spot almost immediately – useless, as it turned out, but willing.

Terence, a stickler for details, left the engine running in the little red van and settled himself in the new Vauxhall. 'Home, James, and don't spare the horses.'

Rembrandt released the handbrake, and once again they entered the gates of the Binglewood Estate, but before they put the car in the garage Terence, with the touch of a master, snipped the telephone wires in order to join the victims, and let himself in through the front door. Undoubtedly the covering of his tracks was a stroke of genius.

After finding the little red van exactly where he had left it, poor Kenneth Sagbottom dropped his mother home where she stood on a chair to box his ears. But, as he complained to his teddy that night: it wasn't a joke – some-body had taken it.

SEVENTEEN

D ue to its geographical situation, it was not uncommon for Grapplewick to be covered in a foot of snow while in nearby Blackburn and Bolton an overcoat was unnecessary. Conversely, this year December had slid into the town sunless but mild, and at the same time travellers from Blackburn were alighting at the depot wrapped up like overfed penguins, marvelling at the soft breeze. The workers clockered towards the mills, learning again to walk upright, and pleasant conversation about the weather dominated the morning. It was too good to last, however, and the hardy ones who had gone to work without even scarves scurried home cursing the fickleness of the elements. Most people relaxed in front of their fires that evening, except those living in the vicinity of the Fire Station. It was Thursday – band practice night – and unless you were stone deaf it was a good night for the pictures or the pub.

Mr Thurk surveyed himself in the mirror and adjusted his cap. Then he gave his red sash a tweak – only a fraction, but it mattered. He was about to don his white gloves when there was a knock at the door. A flicker of annoyance crossed over his face, for he was a punctual man and he was already cutting it a bit fine. His brow cleared when he saw his visitor.

'Hello, Dorothy. This is a nice surprise.'

She edged past him towards the fire, and he popped his head out quickly to look up and down the street before closing the door. One or two curtains in the houses opposite fell back into place, and in any case there was Her Lady-ship's unmistakable Daimler parked right outside. They'd all know who the visitor was and how long the visit lasted, but after all he was over twenty-one.

'Anthony, I know it's Thursday, but I have something to tell you and it may be important.'

'Oh?' He motioned to a chair but she shook her head, hardly able to contain herself.

'I went to see Mrs Helliwell this morning.'

He looked puzzled. 'Mrs Helliwell?'

'You know, Walter Helliwell's mother – he was at Dunkirk.'

'Ah yes, he fell under a train on his first leave.' He shuddered.

She allowed a moment's silence in respect, then she continued. 'That's what sparked me off. You see, Mrs Helliwell happened to be reading the press cuttings about it – they're all carefully pasted in a scrapbook. Poor dear, she's finding things very difficult since her husband died.'

He nodded in sympathy. No one realised the effect his son's tragic death had had on old Tommy Helliwell, until one freezing night in the cold winter of 1945 he polished his boots, put on his best suit and left the house. Nobody took much notice of the hole in the ice on the reservoir, and it wasn't until the thaw that they found him. Mr Thurk pulled himself together and glanced involuntarily at the clock.

'I'm sorry,' she said.

'No, no. That's all right, plenty of time.' The lie came easily, but he wished she'd sit down. His feet were killing him.

'I'll be as brief as I can,' she said, 'but I think it's important.'

'Take your time,' he said gently, and settled gratefully into the chair, gesturing towards the other.

'Thank you,' she said. 'After I left the Helliwells I started thinking, and decided to pay the *Grapplewick Chronicle* a visit, or to be more precise, Arthur Taylor. He's a neighbour of mine, as you know, and he kindly put the facilities of the newspaper at my disposal. He didn't ask me why, and I didn't tell him, but together with some of the staff I rummaged through the back numbers of the *Chronicle* covering the war years.' She stopped and looked at him.

'And?' He was beginning to get the drift, but how much had she discovered?

'Your brother,' she went on, 'Sergeant air gunner, quite a hit about him. Helliwell, Buckley, Waterhouse, who was at Arnhem, John Ashton and, er, whatsisname, er, young . . .' She snapped her fingers for whatsisname's name.

'Yes, Dorothy, but I should say that nearly everyone local who was in the forces got in the paper some time, even if it was only for joining up.'

She leaned forward. 'Except Commander Wilson Brown.'

'Ah.' He sat back.

She was triumphant. 'Strange, don't you think?'

'Well, yes,' he said, flicking a speck of something off his trousers. 'But not having resided in Grapplewick for some years before the war, they may have overlooked him.'

She stood up. 'They may, but I'm not satisfied, and tomorrow I'm going to ring a friend of mine in the Admiralty.'

He rose wearily. 'Dorothy, please don't do that.'

Her eyes widened. 'But why not? We must find out.'

He sighed. 'I'll save you the trouble. Sit down.' They settled again. 'There won't be any reference to Commander Wilson Brown in the Navy lists, at least not our Wilson Brown.'

She rose to her feet. 'You mean he was never in the Navy?'

He looked at her. 'That's about the size of it.'

She slumped back in the chair. 'Are you positive about this?'

He spread his hands. 'I'm afraid so, Dorothy. I've known about it ever since he was elected to the Council.'

She stared at him for a moment. 'This is what you meant when you said you could get rid of him tomorrow?'

He nodded.

She looked at him incredulously. 'But why? I don't under-stand. If you've known all this time, why don't you get rid of him? Well, for God's sake, Anthony, you know what he's doing – he's taking Grapplewick away from you.'

He stared into the banked coals. 'I may pull the rug from under him yet.'

She was exasperated. 'It may be too late! Why, oh why, didn't you act when you first found out?'

He shrugged. 'I was intrigued, and in the early days he was like a breath of fresh air in the Town Hall. He wasn't short of ideas. He was a driving force. He put a stiffening into the Council when it was flabby.' He looked down at his hands. 'But I suppose, most of all, I wanted to see where he was going.'

She leaned forward and tapped his knee urgently. 'But now we know where he's going. He wants Grapplewick, not your Grapplewick but a monstrous, soulless concrete desert – and incidentally, he wants to pile up a nice little fortune in the process.'

This time he stood and leaned his forehead on the mantel-piece. 'He has money, Dorothy,' he said to the fire, 'and I don't think his interest is purely financial.'

She sighed heavily. 'For heaven's sake, Anthony, at least go and see him and tell him what you know.'

He turned to face her. 'Dorothy, I couldn't do that. It would be blackmail.'

'I haven't noticed the Commander fighting with kid gloves on,' she said forcefully.

'I know, Dorothy, but to expose him will be a last resort.' He took her by the shoulders. 'Can't you see, Dorothy? We have all the cards, and I don't intend to turn them all face-up at this stage, simply to destroy a man.' She turned away and he gently took her chin until she was facing him again. 'But make no mistake,' he said earnestly, 'if I can be sure that you are right, and that he's using the town simply to fatten his bank account, I'll have him.'

She looked at him for a moment, then her shoulders sagged. 'All right, Anthony. I know that you'll do what's best.' Her eyes glistened. 'You're a good man, d'you know that?' She broke away to fumble in her handbag, and he laughed.

'That's not what the lads'll think when I turn up half an hour late.'

'I'm sorry,' she said. 'I've spent all this time trying to teach my grandmother to suck eggs.' She brightened. 'Come on I'll give you a lift.'

Again the curtains across the street fell back into place as he got in the car.

'They don't miss much round here, do they?' she said switching on the ignition.

'An unhealthy preoccupation,' he said. 'A black car in this street usually means a funeral.'

It was no distance to the fire station, and hardly worth getting into the car, but he enjoyed the luxury of the Daimler, and Dorothy wasn't a bad driver as long as there was little traffic and the road didn't bend. In less than four minutes they were there, and would have arrived sooner had she overtaken the cyclist.

'Well done, Dorothy,' he said, 'and thanks for coming to see me.' He patted her hand on the steering wheel. It was too dark to see her expression, but she suddenly leaned across and kissed him on the cheek. It startled him, and he looked quickly round to see if there was anybody about. But he needn't have bothered – on cold nights Grapplewick was like the inside of a pyramid. 'Well, er, thanks for the lift,' he said lamely, and got out. He bent towards the window to wave, but the car suddenly shot forward, as if Dorothy was embarrassed by her impulsive gesture. Grand girl, that, he thought as he watched the tail lights disappear.

It was then that he noticed the car parked opposite. It looked like Commander Wilson Brown's car, but it couldn't be – Wilson Brown would go a mile out of his way rather than pass the Station, let alone park right outside. He entered the yard and one of the Clydesdales in the stable snickered and stamped a great foot. He sighed: they were planning a new world that had no place for Ajax and Ramillies . . .

He remembered the band practice and strode briskly into the Station. The lights, shining brightly, made the old tender gleam like a precious metal. Then he stopped -good grief, the ladder had gone now! He frowned: there was something else. He walked slowly round the old engine, then it hit him – it was on wood blocks. Right! He'd have it out with them tonight. They meant well, but dammit there were limits. If there was a fire in Grapplewick they'd be about as useful as an ashtray on a motor bike.

He strode over to the stairs leading up to the band room and flicked on the light switch, but there was nothing. He flicked it up and down but there was no light. Good grief – they're not flogging the bulbs as well, are they? At the back of his mind something else bothered him, and in a flash he knew what it was. No music. He should have been able to hear the band streets away, but apart from a desultory mumbling and shuffling from the room above all was quiet. He started up the stairs, but on the second step he stumbled over a helmet that had been strategically placed, and barely seconds after it had rolled to the floor the strains of 'Abide with Me' crashed out from the band room. Good God: they must think he'd fallen off a Christmas tree. When he entered the room there'd be no sign of the cards and football coupons, and music would be covering the magazines. He limped up the stairs trying to decide how to tackle several situations.

Ned Bladdock tapped the conductor's stand and the lads put down their instruments. 'Evening, Chief. It's coming. We've hammered out the passage from letter B, and it's nearly there.'

Mr Thurk nodded. 'I'm sorry I'm late, lads. Something urgent cropped up.' He squared his shoulders and stood resolutely in front of them. 'I've just been examining the tender, and I think I'm due some kind of explanation.'

Ned looked at his Chief and he knew that the kettle was about to boil, so he decided to turn down the gas. He jerked his head to the corner. 'Chief, have you got a minute?'

Mr Thurk followed him out of earshot of the band. 'What is it?' he asked testily.

Ned leaned to him and whispered, 'You've got lipstick on your face.'

Mr Thurk's hand shot to his cheek as if a mosquito had crashed into it. 'Thank you, Ned,' he mumbled. 'Thank you.,

Ned strode back to his place behind the big drum.

Mr Thurk fronted the band again, but he was flustered. His resolution had gone. He spread his hands. 'Lads, lads,' he pleaded. 'You know what I'm on about.'

Ned relaxed. The bomb was defused.

Mr Thurk sighed. 'I'm only going to say one thing to you all. By the weekend I want to see that tender fully equipped again.'

The band eyed him sullenly, then Jack Puller spat into an empty bean can he always brought to rehearsals. 'If we've got to take all these instruments back, that'll be t'end of t'band.'

Mr Thurk shook his head. 'Not necessarily. I'll have a go at the Council again tomorrow.'

Jack spat again. 'That'll be like tryin' to get Ned here to buy a bloody drink,' he said.

Ned ignored him. 'What about allocating something from, say, the housing fund?'

'I'm afraid not,' said Mr Thurk sadly. 'Most of the housing fund goes to the upkeep of the park.'

Ned brightened. 'Well, there's a bandstand in the park. We should be entitled to something out of the park fund.' He looked round, and the band nodded.

'Impossible,' said Mr Thurk. 'The surplus from the park fund was swallowed up decorating the Town Hall.' He tapped his baton on the stand. 'Anyway, let's make the most of the instruments while we've got 'em: "Three Jolly Sailormen".' He raised his arms and waited until they sorted themselves out. 'Right, lads, Briskly now . . . one, two, three.'

The band responded with the briskness of a very old bull elephant making its way to the graveyard.

Terence, huddled in the car outside the Fire Station, winced. He'd never been a music lover, and what he was hearing tonight didn't tempt him to change his mind. He unscrewed the top of his whisky flask and took a deep pull. Oh, God, if only he had Elsie in the car with him. He felt sure her husband wouldn't mind him sharing the load. It was impossible tonight anyway – she fancied the reckless dashing Major Terence, and she would never have recognised the fat, doddering, white-haired old blimp. He considered for a moment nipping into the Dog and Partridge afterwards and giving, himself a build-up, but he dismissed the thought. He wasn't sure that his make-up would stand close scrutiny in the bright lights of the saloon bar.

An hour and twenty minutes later he was about to abandon the evening when in the gloom across the road a man emerged from the yard, and he realised that the band had packed it in some minutes ago. As the figure passed under the street lamp Terence recognised the band leader, who must be Mr Thurk. He struggled out of the car and called, 'Mr Thurk . . . I say, you there, is that Mr Thurk?'

The Mayor stopped and then approached him. 'Yes, I'm Mr Thurk. Can I help you?'

'I hope so, sir, I hope so,' said Terence fervently, in a passable imitation of an alcoholic Colonel in the Indian Army. 'Allow me to introduce myself. My name is Colonel Harper Warburton, ex 47th Punjab Regiment.'

Mr Thurk held out his hand tentatively. 'Pleased to meet you.,

Terence gave his padding an unobtrusive hitch and eased into the deep shadow. 'Firstly, let me congratulate you on your excellent band.'

Mr Thurk beamed. 'Really?' He didn't quite know how to accept the compliment – no one ever enthused about the band. It was as if George Washington's father had said, 'Thank God you got rid of that tree.'

Terence went on, 'I haven't heard music like that since we evacuated Cawnpore.'

'Really?' said Mr Thurk again, and cleared his throat in embarrassment. There must be something else he could say besides 'really'. 'Er, would you like to step into the Station . . .

there's a cup of tea in there.' He made to take the Colonel's arm, but Terence shrank back into the shadows.

'I thank you kindly, sir, but no. I, er, have other rather pressing engagements, so I'll come straight to the point.'

'R . . .' Mr Thurk closed his mouth in time to stop himself saying 'really' again.

'I know that your engagement book must be full, and time is short, but I would like to hire the band.'

Mr Thurk stared at him in amazement. 'Hire the band?' he said in a strangled voice.

'That's the idea,' said Terence briskly. 'I know that it may seem a strange request, but I would like them to play carols on Christmas Eve, or, to be more exact, one carol: "Silent Night".

Mr Thurk was wallowing in uncharted waters. 'We've played carols before, yes, but er. . . .' He trailed off as Terence's shadowy form extracted something from an inside pocket.

'I trust you won't be offended, but I have here an envelope containing one hundred pounds.' Mr Thurk took a step back. 'One hundred pounds!' he gasped.

'I know this may seem to you an unorthodox manner of conducting business, but I'm a man of action . . . objective planning and execution – that's my motto.' He thrust the envelope at Mr Thurk as if it were a declaration of war, and there was little Mr Thurk could do but accept it.

His pride rebelled, however, and he held it out to the Colonel. 'I'm sorry, Colonel er. ..

'Warper Harburton,' beamed Terence.

Mr Thurk didn't notice the slip. 'I'm sorry, Colonel, but a hundred pounds seems a little extravagant for one carol.'

Terence ignored the envelope. 'This, of course, includes your transportation to the Binglewood Estate, plus the fact that I would require you to play the carol exactly at twenty hundred hours on Christmas Eve.'

'Eight o'clock in the evening?'

'Correct,' said Terence. 'Firstly in the driveway outside the house called Holmedene. After finishing the carol, you will proceed to The Beeches, and repeat your performance at Wood-haven East, then finally Seven Seas.'

Mr Thurk became wary. 'Did you say Seven Seas?' he asked.

'Correct,' said the badly stuffed Colonel. 'An old acquaintance of mine – Commander Wilson Brown.'

'Oh,' said Mr Thurk casually. 'Meet him during the war?'

It was too casual, and there were moments when the speed of Terence's brain amazed himself. 'God, no. Met him a couple of years ago in the Army and Navy Club.'

Mr Thurk relaxed visibly, and Terence sensed that he had avoided a rather nasty minefield. 'I must be honest with you,' said Mr Thurk. 'I don't think he'll appreciate us playing outside his house.' He laughed. 'He might even charge us with trespass and disturbing the peace.'

'Nonsense, old boy. I've already warned him I've planned something rather special. He'll be tickled pink . . . no fears on that score. If I know the old curmudgeon he'll accept anything that's free.' He was about to laugh heartily, then thought better of it – he wasn't all that securely put together. He patted his pockets and took out another envelope. 'Ah, here it is. Can't get used to these pockets in mufti, what?'

Mr Thurk, even more mystified, took it.

'In that envelope you'll find all the relevant information, plus a map of the Binglewood Estate.'

Mr Thurk gazed unseeingly at the envelope. 'I don't quite know what to say. I mean, it's all rather unusual.'

'Think nothing of it,' barked Terence. 'They're all acquaintances of mine, and it's a rather novel Christmas present, wouldn't you say?' He laughed heartily and saluted. 'Well, must be off.' He turned, then stopped. 'Oh, and if you wouldn't mind keeping this to yourself. Wouldn't want the surprise to be ruined, what?' And with that he bumbled across the road to the car, the darkness hiding the feathers that were escaping beneath his greatcoat.

Mr Thurk watched the rear lights disappearing round Horsedge Street; then he looked down at the two envelopes in his hands.

The lads sat round the band room. Conversation had been spasmodic since Mr Thurk's departure, and the feeling of discontent was almost tangible.

Jack Puller lifted his head. 'I say bugger 'im, if we hang on to these instruments what can 'e do? Tell me that, what can 'e do?'

Ned shook his head. 'It's no use talking like that, Jack. We've been ordered.'

Jack was unmoved. 'All right, then. What're we goin' to practise on? Band's done for, I'm tellin' you. If we have to wait for a grant from t'town we'll all be too bloody old to blow.'

Nobody had any other suggestions, but they were loath to leave – they needed each other's comfort.

Barmy stood against the wall with his hands behind his back. 'OK,' he grinned.

They ignored him.

He patted his stomach.

'All right,' said Helliwell. 'I'll nip out for some fish and chips.'

But before he reached the door it burst open and Mr Thurk strode in. All heads lifted – he was beaming. 'Don't forget, lads, first thing tomorrow morning I want you at Cowell and Bottisford's to reclaim our stuff.'

The lads moved restlessly. He hadn't come back to rub it in, had he? Mr Thurk strolled over to Ned and chucked the envelope in his lap. 'Any instruments you want, you can pay for out of that.' He smiled. 'Oh, and don't forget the change.' Then he turned and walked back to the door. 'And I'll want a full set of band parts for "Silent Night".' Then he was gone.

Silence followed him, then Ned slit open the envelope with his finger and drew out a wad of crisp fivers. 'Bai the bloody 'ell,' he said, 'he's a bloody miracle worker.'

Ned rose slowly. 'It's always darkest before the dawn.'

Jack grabbed the money. 'Never mind the bloody dawn,' he said gleefully. 'What about a pint before we go?'

Naturally Mr Bottisford was both relieved and delighted to return all the fire equipment. Lack of space had become an embarrassment – he even had parts of the appliance stuffed in his bedroom, and it had become something of an ordeal to make his way up and down stairs, so he hadn't minded being roused in the early hours by a hung-over Fire Brigade to reclaim their equipment under cover of darkness. He was also delighted to put something in the till besides tunic buttons.

Half an hour later Grapplewick stirred itself to face a new day. There was considerably less clockering of the clogs in the direction of the factories – cotton was being manufactured more cheaply in other parts of the world. The Empire was dwindling, countries abroad were now competitors instead of easy markets, resources which were once accessible were now being used against Britain, and more workers were being laid off at the Monarch Mills, while next door at the Rutland they were already on short time. Fortunately the new Welfare State cushioned some of the despair that had gripped them in the thirties, and Christmas was on its way. The first fall of snow dazzled the early risers, but already, with a pale watery sun, the roads were a thin brown slush. It was a significant day, however. The whole Council was meeting to discuss the fate of Grapplewick. At best it would be a stay of execution, but more likely the bull-dozers would be called in – in the warm spaces cold buildings would rise, and the bewildered townspeople would be housed but homeless.

Edward Helliwell made his way slowly up the Town Hall steps. Head down, he almost bumped into Wilson Brown, moving even more slowly.

'Sorry, Commander,' he said lifting a gloved hand to his hat.

Wilson Brown gave him a cursory glance and continued to negotiate the steps.

What's the matter with him these days, thought Helliwell. Probably still suffering from that do in the court room. However the news he had to impart would cheer the old bugger up. 'Oh, Commander . . .'

Wilson Brown stopped and turned slowly, waiting.

'Oh, Commander, before you go in I have a little bit of information that might interest you.' He looked round, but they were alone, and fairly sheltered from the wind. Nevertheless Wilson Brown turned his collar up, bleak eyes staring at the war memorial opposite. 'Information?' he said off-handedly.

Helliwell wasn't put off. Wilson Brown would soon perk up when he heard what he had to say. 'About a week ago I was passing the Fire Station yard, and I noticed something odd.'

Wilson Brown looked down at his feet. 'Oh, yes?'

'Yes, something definitely wrong.' He looked over his shoulder again, and edged close. 'There was no bell, no ladder – in fact it was stripped down.'

The Commander studied him for a moment. 'It could be the equipment was in the Station.'

'Alt,' said Helliwell triumphantly. 'That's what I thought, but then I made some inquiries. I'm not without my sources, you know,' he added smugly.

The Commander surveyed the war memorial again. 'And?'

Helliwell touched his arm. 'The fact of the matter is, they have been trading the equipment to Cowell and Bottisford in return for musical instruments.'

Wilson Brown turned to him slowly. 'That's a very serious accusation.'

'It's true,' beamed Helliwell earnestly.

'Given that you are right, what do you intend to do about it?'

Helliwell was becoming exasperated at the lukewarm reaction. He hadn't expected a bouquet of flowers, but at least a light show of enthusiasm would have been in order. 'Don't you see . . . we've got him . . . the Mayor.'

'Oh.' Wilson Brown's eyebrows went up a shade.

'Well, he may not be directly involved,' went on Helliwell, 'but as Chief he must accept the ultimate responsibility.' He clucked his tongue sanctimoniously. 'If this became known, it could ruin him.'

Wilson Brown turned his head away. 'Is that what you want?'

Helliwell feigned indignation. 'Of course not. Nobody wants that to happen, but in any case nobody need ever know.' He dragged his hanky out and wiped his nose. 'Providing we have his vote for the slum clearance.'

Wilson Brown surveyed him with ill-disguised contempt. In a flash of insight he saw what his mind had been unwilling to accept. Mr Thurk was the only man for Grapplewick – a dedicated man, with no thought of personal gain. He felt a sudden surge of warmth for the man, which surprised him pleasantly. He looked steadily at Helliwell: what a miserable, jumped-up pipsqueak – oh, he'd get on all right, his sort always did. He turned away from the smug white face, hands clenched in his pockets.

Helliwell, misinterpreting the flash of anger in his eyes, nodded complacently. That'll teach him to underestimate me, he thought.

Councillor Pilkington hurried up the steps with a briefcase under his arm. 'Big day, eh?' He touched his hat, not waiting for a reply, and went inside.

Silly sod, always hurrying about with a briefcase under his arm. He'd hurry out of his office and scuttle along, then hurry back to the office to find out where he was supposed to be hurrying to. Never mind, he'd got it right today, and he was pretty certain to vote in the right direction. Helliwell cheered up. If the slum clearance went through, they'd have their high-rise flats, and he'd be out of Waterloo Street and domiciled on the Binglewood Estate before the scaffolding went up.

Across the street a bus pulled into the kerb and old deaf Crumpshaw got off. As usual he immediately began to cross the road, never looking right nor left, and he certainly couldn't hear. Wilson Brown watched, fascinated. How he'd survived so long was a mystery, but then he'd been crossing this road before motor cars were invented, which possibly gave him immunity. Wilson

Brown turned to go inside when a movement caught the corner of his eye. A grocer's van was approaching too fast for comfort on the treacherous surface, and the driver, obviously seeing old Crumpshaw too late, clapped on his brakes. Skidding sideways to the other side of the road, it missed the old fellow by a whisker, to crash sickeningly into a lamp-post. At the same time a Daimler travelling sedately in the opposite direction was forced to swerve, spinning in a complete circle before mounting the kerb in front of the Town Hall.

Oblivious of the chaos behind him, old Crumpshaw wheezed up the steps. He nodded to Wilson Brown. 'Cold this mornin', eh?' Then he disappeared into the big dark doorway.

'Silly old fool,' said Helliwell. 'He'll get himself killed one day.'

Wilson Brown ignored him. A small crowd had gathered round the van, but he noted with relief that the driver was on his feet, although someone was holding a cloth to his head. At the foot of the steps the Daimler eased forward off the kerb, and he heard the rasp of the brake. Lady Dorothy alighted as coolly as if she always parked in this fashion. As she approached, he doffed his hat.

'Good morning, Commander.' She smiled and swept past him in a cloud of expensive perfume.

He followed her with his eyes. Was it his imagination, or had she stressed the word 'Commander'? A cold hand clutched his heart. One way or another his world was falling to bits. He became aware that Helliwell was speaking . . . 'Eh?' he said.

'Could have been nasty, that.'

'Oh yes, but I didn't actually see what happened – I was watching old Crumpshaw.' No way was he getting himself involved as a witness – any publicity at the present time was bad news. He turned to go inside, but Helliwell restrained him with a hand on his arm.

'What about Mr Thurk?'

'Ah . . . yes, Mr Thurk. What are you going to do about it?'

Helliwell was flustered. 'Well, I thought . . .

'Yes?' inquired Wilson Brown in a deceptively calm voice.

Helliwell spread his hands. 'Well, er,' he floundered. 'I rather thought it would carry more weight from you.'

Typical, thought Wilson Brown, they load the gun in secret, then push someone else into the firing line to pull the trigger. He suddenly had an overwhelming urge to smash his fist into the snivelling white face.

Helliwell stepped back. For once he'd read the signs correctly.

The spell was broken by the distant clanging of the fire bell . . . then again, but closer this time. Helliwell gulped – it might be the ambulance for the poor wretch across the road, but a louder clang dashed his hopes. There was only one bell in Grapplewick that sounded like that, and it could only be attached to the fire engine. Ponderously the old juggernaut turned into the High Street and trundled lugubriously towards the Town Hall. Before it had come to a complete stop Mr Thurk relinquished the bell rope and stepped down. Ned Bladdock took his place next to the driver and rubbed his hands vigorously together before grasping the bell rope with joyous anticipation. Mr Thurk said something to the lads, and whatever it was, they laughed. Then with a shuddering roar and a deafening clamour the old engine lurched forward and made its way to wherever it was going.

Mr Thurk watched them for a moment, then turned and made his way up the steps.

'Morning, Helliwell. Morning, Commander.' He saluted as he passed, and disappeared into the Town Hall.

Wilson Brown's eyebrows rose, and he turned to Helliwell. For the first time in weeks he smiled happily. 'Any more bright ideas?'

Helliwell's face was priceless. Somebody had just chopped his Christmas tree down at the very moment he had got the coloured lights to work.

Most of the Councillors were already in the chamber. Some were standing in groups while others were already seated, fumbling with papers. It was going to be a big debate, probably the most important that any of them could remember.

Lady Dorothy was talking to one of the older members when Mr Thurk entered. Her eyes lit up, and she hurried over to meet him. 'Morning, Anthony.'

'Ah, good morning, Dorothy. First snow, eh?' He lugged out his great pocket watch.

She took his arm. 'Anthony, can we go into your room for a minute?'

'We haven't much time.' He smiled apologetically.

'It's important.'

He took out his watch again. 'OK, we have a few minutes.' They made their way along the corridor to the Mayor's Parlour. He closed the door quietly and turned to her. 'Dorothy, I think I know what you're going to say, and the answer is no.'

Her brows came together. 'But Anthony, if Wilson Brown goes against you it could be the end of Grapplewick. He carries a lot of weight.'

'So do I.'

Her mouth tightened in exasperation. 'Anthony, he's an imposter. He has no right to be here at all.'

He shrugged. 'That's my fault. Should have seen him off at the beginning, but now it's gone too far, and perhaps it may be that he's right and I'm wrong.'

Her eyes widened in amazement.

'Dorothy, if I do manage to stop them pulling down Grapplewick, it'll only be a temporary halt. The mills won't last forever, and what happens then? The young people are already drifting away . . . the new generation won't be content to spend their life here. Modern technology will make Australia, America or the Far East as accessible to them as Accrington is to us. The *Grapplewick Chronicle is* just about managing to keep its head above water. Thanks to the new powers granted the Trade Unions, one more strike and this town won't have a newspaper – not because of conditions, but in many cases because of a blind back-lash of revenge for the indignities of the thirties.'

She moved towards him. 'Anthony, I appreciate that you cannot halt progress, but there are still people in Grapplewick – middle-aged people, old people – you must fight for them. Remember the bellringers, the Fire Brigade, the Rose Queen Festival, the Good Friday procession.' She took his hand. 'You are the last of the Thurks – don't you owe it to your family?'

Before he could reply, the Secretary popped his head round the door. 'They're waiting, Mr Mayor.'

'Thank you, Wilfred. Ask the attendant to pop in, will you?'

Dorothy smiled. 'Come on, Mr Mayor. Let t'battle commence.'

He laughed. 'OK, you go ahead. Just got to don my chain and I'll be in there.'

The great debate lived up to all expectations. It was unprecedented even by Grapplewick's unorthodox standards, the great surprise being a change of heart by Commander Wilson Brown, who spoke at length against the motion that he had been largely instrumental in composing. Most of the older Councillors were on the side of the Mayor, while the younger progressives were all geared to follow the Commander's banner, Helliwell, never a good speaker at the best of times, and without the backing of

Wilson Brown quite weightless, babbled inconsequentially about our debt to the young, but floundered when he referred to babies yet unborn (he said 'stillborn'), and the laugh it provoked did nothing to steady him. He was nearing a breakdown. He had already been advanced a considerable sum of money on the understanding that the slum clearance would go through – he could return the diamond ring, his wife's Christmas present, but what about the deposit on White Pines? He'd already sold his own two up, two down. Through dry lips he mouthed meaningless cliches: progress ... debt to society ... he even mentioned the Parthenon. This ended what little support he might have expected. Limply he muttered, 'I beg to move,' and a voice from the public gallery broke the spell: 'Not before bloody time.'

Helliwell slumped back in his seat, acutely aware of the contemptuous gaze of Commander Wilson Brown. No one who valued his position could dare to ally himself with such a travesty of words, and the motion was defeated handsomely. Helliwell, panic-stricken, was frantically trying to find the words to explain to his wife that they might soon have to move back to her mother's house.

Wilson Brown left the chamber feeling better than he had in months, while Lady Dorothy gazed at the Mayor as if he was indeed worshipful. Was it possible that he'd known all along that Wilson Brown would change his attack? And if he didn't know, how infinitely wise of him not to threaten him with blackmail. Mr Thurk sat in the great chair, astonished at his victory, but in his own mind he knew that the reprieve was only temporary. Mercifully he didn't know how brief, but in distant Whitehall, far removed from people, the death of Grapplewick was already on the agenda. He brightened with the thought that there was band practice again this evening: 'Silent Night' was coming along splendidly.

EIGHTEEN

Terence strode out of Heppleworth and Peabody's, one of the more fashionable of Blackburn's dress shops. What with clothes rationing, and a lack of luxury goods, he was pleased and rather surprised at the quality and inexpensiveness of the black silk underwear. At first, when he'd mentioned a present for his wife, a frantic, harassed assistant set out a display of bloomers and camiknickers. The bloomers could only have been Army surplus, dyed to various insipid colours, and the camiknickers looked as if they'd been tried on several times. He eyed them distastefully, and it was only when he mentioned the word 'Duchess' that things had begun to happen. Other shoppers, mostly middle-aged ladies in headscarves, who had been eyeing him with suspicion, stood back a pace in deference to Royalty, and he was received by a servile, dry-hand-washing manager who ushered him into a private room. Over a cup of tea and a cigar he graciously accepted black silk underwear, obviously from a private privileged stock; the price was dismissed with a wave of the hand. As he was escorted to the door he wished he'd opted for a fur coat. He shook hands with the manager, who was looking up and down the street for the arrival of a great crested Rolls. Terence read the signs and was away as doubt began to replace the plastic smile. Once Elsie clapped eyes on the flimsies he'd be home and dry.

He didn't remember the drive back to Grapplewick – he was visualising her posing, showing off to him in the black silk. So vivid was the picture that he had to stop once and adjust himself. He even wound down the window to let the cold air revive him – only for a moment, though: he didn't fancy frostbite. Before he realised it he was back in Grapplewick High Street, bustling now with late shoppers, drifting from temptation to doubt, purses clutched tight – a pair of socks, a pipe, a half-crown Cadbury's selection box, a fountain pen perhaps, coloured lights, Christmas trees. He turned into Featherstall Road, a little darker and with not too many people, and pulled up outside the Fire Station. His brow darkened. All was quiet – he would have bet his bottom dollar they would be practising. Had they taken him for a patsy? He was just beginning to simmer when the opening bars of 'Silent Night' crashed out with such intensity that he flinched. God, he hoped they weren't going to play as loud as that – there'd be no point in making their way from house to house. One rendering, and as far away as Accrington people would be humming it. He decided that Colonel Harper Warburton would have to make a discreet visit, tactfully pointing out the proximity of the houses, and suggesting that a fortissimo rendering would ruin the surprise for the others.

Better still, there was a phone box just across the road and Terence was a man for prompt action. After a brief rehearsal, he dialled 999.

'Fire, Police or Ambulance?' asked the bored female voice.

'Fire, please,' bellowed Colonel Harper Warburton.

'Pardon?' said the voice.

'Fire, dammit. Fire!'

'Well,' said the voice. 'I can try them.' But she didn't sound hopeful.

Happy as always, Barmy slung a shovelful of coke into the red-hot stove. 'OK,' he said, blowing a droplet of sweat from the end of his nose. 'Phew,' he breathed, but it never occurred to him to take off his greatcoat. From the room above the band blasted through 'Silent Night', making a mockery of the title. Barmy nodded, satisfied, and strolled round the tender where it was fractionally cooler.

Deciding that a lie-down for a few minutes wouldn't do him any harm, he stretched himself and was about to yawn when he stopped. Something was different. He cocked his head to one side and there it was – under the crashing sound of the band he discerned a ringing, a tinny peevish insistent ringing. 'What's that?' he inquired to his teeth, but they just grinned back at him from the mug. He looked round him to find out the cause, but avoided the desk. In the deep cavern of his mind he knew it was the telephone, but he was loath to accept it. He could only remember it ringing once before, but then he hadn't been alone. Ned Bladdock had answered it, and even he'd had taken his cap off before speaking. Brrr, brrr. 'OK,' said Barmy, hopping round it, but never looking at it in case it was facing him. Panic-stricken, he skipped to the foot of the stairs and yelled, 'Brrr, brrr.' Hesitatingly the band broke off, and in the silence the telephone screamed. 'OK, OK,' yelled Barmy, petrified.

Mr Thurk hurried down the stairs, followed warily by the band. They bunched behind the tender as Mr Thurk made his way to the desk. Barmy hopped behind him, pointing an accusing finger at the telephone. 'Thank you, Mr Chronicle,' he said, picking up the apparatus. 'Grapplewick Fire Brigade speaking,' he said, but by that time Terence was getting out of the car in front of the Dog and Partridge.

Even before he reached the door of the saloon bar the sound of revelry hit him, and he frowned. In the past it was always a bit quiet at this hour, and he'd visualised strolling to the bar and ordering the usual. Then a little badinage, followed by a casual 'Oh by the way, I've got you a little something for Christmas.' Then perhaps a cigarette while she eagerly tore off the wrapping. But now that was another dream up the spout, he swore to himself as he opened the door.

The cacophony was almost physical – it was a bedlam reeking of sweat, cheap perfume and stale beer. Oh, bollocks! Why tonight of all nights? He stuffed the gift under his overcoat – he couldn't casually stroll to the bar and hand it over with this mob. It's hard to be nonchalant when you're being jostled by drunks. He correctly surmised it to be a Christmas office party – bosses, typists and secretaries all equal today with the levelling effect of alcohol. He decided to stay by the door. He only had to catch Elsie's eye and she'd have a large whisky passed over to him like a shot, then they'd know he was Somebody. He craned and bobbed from side to side to get her attention, but it was hopeless – he could only get fleeting glances of the top of her head as she made her way from the pumps to the till to another cretinous customer. A sweating bore in front of him was in the middle of a story about a prostitute and a vicar. God, not that one. It was years old, and he hadn't thought it particularly funny then, although the prison chaplain wasn't a bad storyteller.

He moved to one side and found himself behind a tall girl. She was really tall -the label sticking out of the back of her blouse was on a level with his nose. He eased back half a pace to see if she was wearing high heels, but his eyes didn't get that far because a thin gnarled hand came round and clutched her backside.

'Don't, Mr Branwood,' she said, but she didn't move.

Terence eased round a little to see who was getting the action. Pathetic – a little old man with watery eyes was smiling up at her. 'Smile' was rather a generous description – it could have been that his feet were hurting.

'Oh, I know I may seem a bit harsh at times.' She cupped her ear with her hand. 'A bit harsh,' he repeated. 'I know I may seem a bit harsh, Doreen, but I've had my eye on you, you know.' He pointed his drink at her face. 'I've had my eye on you.'

She said something in reply that Terence didn't get, but the back of her neck was beginning to redden.

'And less of the "Mr Branwood", Doreen, *mumble mumble mumble* – call me Wilfred.'

She shook her head. 'I couldn't do that, Mr Branwood. It doesn't seem proper.'

He gulped some of his drink – it seemed to come out of his eyes. 'Wilfred,' he insisted.

God help her, thought Terence. If she walked into the office after the holiday and said 'Good morning, Wilfred,' she'd be at the Labour Exchange so fast she wouldn't have time to tuck her label in. He craned to the left and almost caught Elsie's eye, but she couldn't have seen him for she ducked out of sight. At the same time Mr Branwood was telling Doreen she'd been with the firm long enough for a move to the third floor . . . a burst of laughter greeted the prostitute/vicar story – it wasn't all that funny, but perhaps the Managing Director was telling it. He glanced back to the Doreen/Mr Branwood saga. Something was slightly different . . . then it struck him. Branwood was now clutching her with both hands . . . what the hell had happened to his drink? Clever girl, she was holding his glass as well – she'd make the third floor all right. But whether he'd be capable of claiming his prize was doubtful – he didn't look as if he'd see the New Year in.

Again Elsie's face came into view, and Terence stood on tiptoe and snapped his fingers in the air. In that mindless din it had about as much effect as breaking wind under Niagara Falls. A blast of cold air hit the back of his neck as other customers arrived – two large, beefy individuals who surveyed the scene for a moment, then crashed a path steadily through to the bar. There were a few half-hearted protests and drinks were slopped willy-nilly, and the noise subsided, but something about the pair discouraged confrontation. They leaned on the bar and spoke to Elsie, but he couldn't hear what they said – he only saw her head over the crowd make for the stairs and call for Mr Helliwell.

A sudden paralysis gripped Terence. He recognised the black bowler – it was Jimmy the Hat, it had to be. A half-turn and he saw a vivid scar down the left cheek. His worst fears were confirmed. Jimmy the Hat, a monster who'd break your leg just for the exercise. Terence started to shake and the parcel slipped from under his coat. It was unimportant now, and he trampled it in his panic to reach the door and the protection of the night. He flung himself into the car. Thank God he'd left the keys in the ignition – he was in no condition to find the right one, let alone insert it.

The car leaped forward, and a dog crossing the road took immediate evasive action, causing a cyclist to swerve into Buckley's family butchers. A long-dead turkey was dislodged from a hook by the door, and with a reflex action too quick for the eye the dog had it and was halfway up Henshaw Street before Mr Buckley had taken his finger out of his nose.

With a squeal of tyres, Terence swerved left into the blackness of the Binglewood Estate. It was only then that he realised he'd been driving without lights. Quickly glancing in the mirror, he satisfied himself there was no pursuit before he switched them on just in time to prevent himself driving into the ditch. He wrenched the wheel over. How the hell had Jimmy the Hat found his way to Grapplewick? He took momentary comfort in the thought that Jimmy couldn't possibly have seen him, but the fact that he was in the vicinity was enough to double Terence's laundry bill.

By the time he let himself in through the front door he was shaking again. It wouldn't do. He took a few deep breaths to regain his composure. God, what a bombshell he was about to drop . . . he wondered briefly if Wilson Brown's heart would be strong enough to take it. He hung up his coat – a cigarette might help, but as he opened the case his palsied fingers scattered them all over the hall. He flung the case from him and took a few more deep breaths. Then his jaw dropped open – from the drawing-room he heard music: it was 'The Anniversary Waltz'. A wave of revulsion swept over him as he remembered the prison dances when he'd always had to dance 'The Anniversary Waltz' with Billy Big Knuckle. Billy never molested him or anything, he was just mad on dancing – thus Billy became his protector. It had been his own idea to put on scent and wear earrings. He shuddered now at his own sycophancy. He listened to a few bars with something akin to nostalgia. He hated 'La Cucaracha' – they always played that for the tango, and he had a rash on his cheek for three days afterwards. He wondered idly who Billy's partner was now. Then a sudden constriction of the bowels brought Jimmy the Hat back. Holy cow! What was he doing leaning back against the wall humming like a bloody great Deanna Durban?

He strode across the hall and flung open the door. He stopped as if he'd walked into a brick wall, and his mouth fell open. The carpet had been rolled up against the wall, and in the space Rembrandt was slowly gyrating in the arms of a dark-haired woman at least a foot taller. He didn't see Terence at the door – he couldn't see anything, for his face was pressed in between her enormous bosoms giving the impression that he was trying to see right through her. Terence raised his eyes to the ceiling, then crossed over to the radiogram and snatched the needle off the record. The woman stopped and turned her head, but Rembrandt couldn't possibly hear anything, cushioned as he was. Terence guessed rightly that this was Droopy Nellie. She looked at him questioningly, then held Rembrandt away from her. He blinked his eyes as if he'd just had five minutes. What a sight, thought Terence. If Wilson Brown's suits hadn't done a lot for him, they were an absolute travesty on Rembrandt. The shoulders sagged, his hands were invisible, and there was at least eighteen inches of trouser leg concertina-ed on the floor.

Rembrandt smoothed his sparse hair. 'Oh, it's you, sorr. Didn't see you come in.' He pointed to the woman, then looked down in embarrassment. 'We're engaged, sorr.'

Terence, conventionally delighted, was about to step forward and offer his congratulations when Jimmy the Hat sprang sickeningly into his mind. 'Never mind the nuts in May,' he snarled. 'Get rid of her.'

Rembrandt stood his ground. 'We're going to settle down here.'

'I don't care where you settle down – get rid of her. I have to talk to you.'

Nellie eased slightly behind him as he stepped forward and lifted her fiance up by the lapels of Wilson Brown's jacket. Poor Rembrandt nearly slipped through. As it was, only his eyes were visible. Terence glared down at him. 'Now listen to me, Rudolph O'Valentin-bloody-O – .' He didn't get any further. Wallop! An excruciating pain at the back of his head, a blinding flash of white light, the ceiling spun over him, then there was nothing but blackness.

Rembrandt eased his head out of the jacket like a tortoise after a long hibernation. 'Dat'll bring tears to his eyes, oh yes.'

'Is that him?' she asked.

'Oh, dat's him all right. Dat's my partner,' he said proudly.

'Well, he's got a bloody funny way of showing it,' she replied, 'an' that's a fact.' She looked down at Terence and let out a short screech. 'Holy Mother of God, oi've scalped him.'

Rembrandt shook his head. 'Dar's only his wig,' he said, and shuffled over to the cocktail cabinet.

Terence groaned and tried to lift his head, but a sudden stab of pain forced him to abandon the attempt. Slowly he opened his eyes and panicked – he couldn't see. He was blind! His hands flew to his face, and he practically fainted with relief as his fingers touched the wig. Gingerly he lifted it up and squinted into the light. A blurred figure was approaching. He groaned again. Two identical Rembrandts knelt down and, supporting his head, put a glass of brandy to his lips. He gagged on it, but it cleared his vision. His first instinct was to lash out at the dull face above him, but he caught himself in time. Over Rembrandt's shoulder Nellie was hovering, and she was still holding the Guinness bottle. He heaved himself slowly and painfully to a sitting position, and with trembling, anxious fingers he explored the back of his head, but there was no blood – it was just misshapen. He blinked his eyes to eliminate one Rembrandt, and with some slight consolation he noted that they were merging. Lights swept across the room, and he heard the crunch of tyres on the gravel drive as a car pulled up. Rembrandt moved to the window and shaded his eyes, but it was too dark to see Wilson Brown paying off the taxi driver. He turned round but Terence was gone. He looked questioningly at Nellie, and she nodded her head to the bulge behind the trembling curtain.

Wilson Brown closed the front door behind him, and took off his hat. It had been a good day . . . the Grapplewick debate in the morning had given him a certain amount of satisfaction – the surprise on Mr Thurk's face, Lady Dorothy's astonishment (she had even thanked him before she left), and especially the humiliation of Helliwell. He had enjoyed that. The strange part was that, had Helliwell not attempted to co-opt him in that pathetic attempt at black-mail, he might well have gone against Mr Thurk. In the afternoon he'd taken a taxi to Blackburn to get a flight schedule from London Airport, details of sailings from Dover and Southampton and a train timetable (his Christmas present to Grapplewick). He unwound his scarf and was about to hang it up when he sensed that there was somebody in the drawing-room. It was their silence that aroused his curiosity. He made his way to the door and stopped in amazement as he surveyed the scene.

'What the devil's going on?' he asked. Terence's white face appeared round the heavy drapes and Wilson Brown's eyebrows shot up. 'Can anybody play?' he asked.

Terence emerged unsteadily. 'You'll laugh on the other side of your face when you hear what I have to tell you,' he snarled.

Wilson Brown giggled. 'How long has he been looking for you?' he said, jerking his head at Rembrandt. 'And God knows how he managed to count up to a hundred.' Then he noticed Nellie. He hadn't recognised her at first, because she looked different with her black hair in a bun. His face darkened. 'What did I tell you about her?' He took a step forward, but Terence held up his hand.

'That doesn't matter now,' he said. 'Ikey's mob's here.'

Wilson Brown froze, and his face paled like the moon coming out from behind a cloud. Rembrandt stared at Terence disbelievingly, hopping from one foot to the other, while Nellie backed away, startled by the sudden change in the atmosphere. They seemed to stand in silence for ages, broken only by what might have been Wilson Brown's stomach. He shook his head as if to deny what he had heard.

'Ikey's mob? Here?'

Terence nodded vigorously and wished he hadn't. He pointed vaguely. 'In Grapplewick.'

'In Grapplewick?' he echoed stupidly.

Terence was about to nod again but caught himself in time. 'I saw them in the Dog and Partridge.'

Wilson Brown was about to repeat it. Instead he glanced around him wildly, searching for something different to say. It was like a lesson in basic English. 'Oh, my God,' he moaned, and staggered over to the sideboard to pour himself a large scotch. He dashed it down his throat, still holding on to the decanter. Terence snatched it from him, and attended to his own needs. Nellie handed Rembrandt a bottle of Guinness. Wilson Brown turned to Terence and held out his trembling glass for a refill. 'You couldn't be mistaken?' he asked, pleadingly.

Terence gulped down his drink and coughed. 'You can't mistake Jimmy the Hat.'

Wilson Brown stared at him aghast – his face wasn't just pale, it was a whitewashed lavatory wall. Terence topped himself up, then sloshed some to Wilson Brown's glass. He didn't seem to notice, but put it down and turned away. 'Oh, my God. Jimmy the Hat!'

Rembrandt crossed himself, and Nellie followed suit with a quick bob. Neither of them could remember the last time they'd attended mass, but it was insurance and it cost nothing.

Wilson Brown walked slowly across the bare floor and slumped into an armchair, eyes full of naked fear and bowels like a treacle factory. He calmed himself momentarily with the thought that he could always commit suicide – at least it could be quick and painless. He shuddered violently as he thought of one or two unfortunates who had got on the wrong side of Jimmy. Nobody deserved to end up as pig food, or – worse – cemented into the supports of one of those new motorways.

Terence, with the help of Glen Livet (God bless him) had managed to calm down somewhat. Indeed a slight tinge of watery sun was lightening the black cumulonimbus. Ikey had no quarrel with him. Prior to his release he'd handed over his tobacco concession in Block Four – it wasn't a big deal, but Ikey had appreciated it. 'You're a good boy, Raffles,' he had said, slapping him lightly on the cheek. Yes, he was now in possession of himself. He swaggered past a mirror, and shied away from his reflection. Dammit, his wig was on back to front. He looked like an ape badly in need of a haircut. He turned it round and patted it down. It would have to do for the moment.

Nellie put a protesting hand on Rembrandt's shoulder. 'An' what's the old divvil getting you into, my little darlin'?' She looked from one to the other. 'What's goin' on here dat oi don't know about?'

Terence stepped forward. 'Nothing to worry about, my dear. It's just someone who knew the Commander during the war.'

Wilson Brown looked at him sharply.

'Yes, the Commander had him court-martialled and ... well, not to put too fine a point on it, the man don't like the Commander.'

She looked at Rembrandt, who shrugged. 'Not my pigeon. Oi don't know nothin' about de man. Dat man is a complete mystery to me, and dat's a fact.'

Terence nodded. 'Look, why don't you take your girl-friend down to the pub and buy her a drink?' He tried to take Rembrandt's arm, but the little man shrugged him off.

'No, sorr, not me. Oi'm not goin' in dat town on me own. Dat Jimmy is a pig of a man.'

Nellie put her hands on her hips. 'I thought you said you didn't know him?'

Rembrandt shook his head. 'Dar's right, oi don't know de man, but 'e might know me. Oh yes, an' oi wouldn't want to be gettin' into trouble at all.'

'OK,' said Terence. 'Take her up to your room and show her your etchings.'

'Dat's a good idea, sorr. Come on Nellie.' He took her arm, and reluctantly she left.

As soon as the door closed Wilson Brown was on his feet. 'Look, Terence, this isn't any good. I'm going to pack.'

Terence held him back. 'You're not going anywhere, Joe. I need you for Christmas Eve. After that you can dress up and join the *Folies Bergere* for all I care.'

Wilson Brown's mouth dropped open. 'You're not going through with that are you, not now?'

Terence spread his arms. 'Why not? Another day.'

Wilson Brown glared at him. 'Another five minutes is too long with Ikey's mob on our doorstep.'

Terence faced him squarely. 'Listen, I have a job for you on Christmas Eve to establish an alibi. Until then I'm not letting you out of my sight.'

Wilson Brown brushed past him and made for the door.

'Don't be silly, Joe. Come and sit down like a good little boy,' said Terence in a silky voice.

Wilson Brown knew that tone, and he stopped.

'You see,' Terence went on, 'if I don't clap eyes on you at least every five minutes, I'll get worried about you, and I may have to telephone.'

Wilson Brown turned towards him wide-eyed. 'You wouldn't shop an old mate?'

Terence went over to the decanter. 'There's only three places Jimmy the Hat would stay, and if you sloped off somewhere I'd need help.'

Wilson Brown sagged down into a chair. 'God, Terence. Prison's ruined you.'

NINETEEN

There was no stopping it. Once the twenty-third of December was out of the way, it was inevitably Christmas Eve, a day of happy anticipation, all the greater in Grapplewick because of the town's sense of Community. Most of the heavy Christmas shopping had been carried out in Black-burn and Bolton, but it was never quite finished. There were always last-minute additions to the list, knick-knacks that were often better received than more expensive items, oranges for stockings, nuts, a yoyo, coloured pencils. House-wives adopted a harassed, anxious look as they scurried from one place to another, but it was a traditional mask, a badge, and most of them were happy to wear it. A hard frost through the night coated the town and its surroundings with a thin white patina, but the early morning clogs con-verging on the mills were vigorous rather than tentative. It would be an easy, short day – a couple of pints at dinner-time, mince pies, paper hats, jokes and outrageous mimes made necessary by the crashing noise of the machinery. The manager, the mule overlooker, boss of the card room would be all smiles. Who knows? Even they sometimes wore paper hats and traded kisses with the merry knees-up operatives, but this year the festivities would be tempered with unease, not quite a false gaiety, but not as relaxed as when the future, although never bright, was fairly predictable.

While it was not yet light, the cotton workers were already safely inside the great mills and there was peace once more on the white streets, a sheet of newspaper danced along on a sudden gust of wind, pausing at a lamp-post as if for breath. The stillness was shattered by the quavering notes of a cornet playing 'Silent Night'. After a few notes a dog barked and the cornet broke off ... tentatively the comet sounded once more, and the dog immediately joined in. Once again the cornet ceased and a voice shouted: 'Prince, 'old yer bloody noise.' There was a momentary pause, then 'Silent Night' began again. The dog, perhaps not fully understanding what was required, broke into a plaintive howl. The melody increased in volume and the dog, not to be outdone, howled even louder.

Jack Puller snatched the comet away from his lips in exasperation. 'Prince!' he yelled. 'Prince, you great stupid sod ... here, Prince.'

Prince cocked his head on one side, then scratched on the lavatory door.

Jack leaned forward, clicked the latch, and the dog bundled in, tail wagging from the neck down, and nuzzled his bare knees.

'Down, boy ... down.' He lifted the instrument and wet his lips, but before he could take breath the dog yowled again. He lowered the cornet resignedly and broke wind instead. 'Florrie!' he shouted plaintively. It was half-hearted and he knew his wife couldn't hear him. Bloody typical, she wouldn't let him practise in the house, and when he came down here she let the bloody dog out.

Prince sat and watched him earnestly. Jack shook his head and, clutching the cornet and his trousers in one great fist, he took the dog's collar and half dragged the animal up the yard, opened the door and slung it in.

'How long you goin' to be down there?' queried his wife from the gloom within.

'Give us a flippin' chance,' he shouted through the small gap in the door. 'I've only just got sat on.' He eased the door shut, so as not to take off Prince's nose, then made his way carefully back down the yard to his cold brick practice room. . . .

Two doors further up Ned Bladdock heard the strains of the cornet and shook his head sadly. Poor old Jack, he thought. Fancy having to practise in that draught in the middle of winter. He shuddered and settled back in his overstuffed armchair. There was a great similarity between the two – food rationing never bothered him, nor indeed any other member of the brigade. He was full of bacon and eggs – he would in fact have liked two more eggs, but he always felt a little guilty about others who were not so well off. Half an hour yet before he would have to make his way to the Station. He leaned his head back, the heat of the fire stabbing at his moist chins. His eyes wandered over the mantelpiece with its green velvet cloth and watched the fire dancing on the bobbles as they hung down, and had done for many Bladdocks before him. A piece of coal spat, and he moved his eyes to see if a cinder had fallen onto the rug. He couldn't see the rug for the mound of his belly, and he almost raised his head, but the effort was too much, so he made a mental note to have a periodic sniff for the first sign of smouldering.

He felt a draught on his left arm as the door opened, and the windows rattled as his wife padded in from the front room. She knelt in front of the fire to do something to the grate, all the while humming 'Rock of Ages'. He smiled happily to himself. He hoped she'd be pleased – he'd bought her a new carpet sweeper for Christmas and everybody said that Ewbanks were pretty good. The clock wheezed through its chimes and scattered his thoughts.

'Bai heck,' he said to no one in particular. 'I'll be late for band practice.'

'Rock of Ages' stopped immediately and she eased back on her heels. 'Band practice, in t'middle o' t'day?' she said, brushing a wisp of hair from her face with the back of a large red hand.

'Aye,' he said, heaving himself to his feet. 'We've got a show tonight on 't'Binglewood Estate.'

She put down the hand brush. 'Tonight?' she said, watching his retreating back. 'It's Christmas Eve. I told Emmie and Joe we'd meet them at the Star tonight.'

Ned reappeared from the front room, lugging his big drum with him. 'I'll be there as soon as I can.'

'We always go to t'Star on Christmas Eve,' she moaned. Ned didn't appear to have heard – he was shrugging into his overcoat. 'I'll see thee at dinnertime,' he called, and with a swirl of curtains and a gebloom-berdoom he was gone.

Fireman Cyril Chadwick was already at the Station, a glazed look on his face as he rat-tat-a-panned away on his kettle drum. Barmy watched him proudly, eyebrows going up and down every time Cyril lifted his drumsticks on a level with his nose, something he'd been practising ever since he saw the band of the Royal Marines on the newsreel. It was brisk and nothing to do with the carol that evening, but there were no band parts in 'Silent Night' for kettle drums. He stopped suddenly as the thought occurred to him. They didn't really need his drum on the Binglewood Estate tonight, although Mr Thurk had meant it kindly when he'd said: 'Don't look so disappointed, Cyril. Some-body has to carry the lantern.' He perked up, however, at the thought that Betty Grable would have received his Christmas card by now. Then just as quickly he perked down again – just his luck if Betty happened by some gigantic coincidence to be a guest at one of the houses tonight, and him standing there with a candle in a jam jar.

On Featherstall Road some kids caught up with Mr Thurk as he made his way gingerly along the treacherous pavement. From a safe distance they chanted: 'Station's on fire and the band's on parade, send for the Manchester Fire Brigade'. He lurched towards them with a mock ferocity and they scattered, shrieking with delight at their own daring.

Old Norman Winterbottom who was busy putting down salt from his front door to the bus stop glared at him. 'Cheeky young buggers,' he muttered.

Mr Thurk smiled. 'Oh, kids were singing that at my father and his father before him.'

Winterbottom nodded darkly. 'Aye, but thy father would have fetched 'em one.'

'Ah, well,' said Mr Thurk. 'A Merry Christmas.'

He was about to move on when he saw the pony and trap in the distance. Winterbottom turned with him, and they watched its approach. Dr McBride was on his way home, and there was always curiosity to know where he'd been, who he'd been treating and what they'd got. At a steady trot the pony clip-clopped towards them, and as it drew level Mr Thurk smiled.

'Good morning, Dr McBride.'

His greeting was ignored, and the pony continued a further twenty yards or so where it stopped at the doctor's surgery, steam rising from its flank. McBride remained where he was, and the pony looked back and fidgeted.

Winterbottom turned to Mr Thurk. 'Fast asleep, I'll bet. I 'eard 'im leave, just turned five this mornin'.' He sniffed in disapproval. ''E should let young Dr Bedford do them sort of calls.'

A knot of apprehension gripped Mr Thurk. There was some-thing unnatural about the way Dr McBride was sitting. In a flash he knew what it was – one didn't fall asleep with a straight back and head upright. He hurried towards the trap, calling Dr

McBride's name, but now he was sure it was wasted effort. Dr McBride was dead – there was no hurry now. Mr Thurk stared up at the austere face, small icicles hanging from his white moustache, eyes looking out on a Christmas they would never see. Mr Thurk took off his hat, and Winterbottom, who was at his elbow, followed suit. Already there was a knot of people standing round, and doors were opening all the way along the street. Mr Thurk collected himself and stepped up into the trap in order to close the dead eyes, but he would have needed a hammer and chisel. The poor doctor was frozen solid, and they had to carry him into the surgery in a sitting position.

Young Dr Bedford, in an effort to assert himself, smiled cheerfully. 'Ah, well. We all have to go some time.'

Mr Thurk turned slowly away and let himself out.

How trite an epitaph. How shallow a sentiment. But then shallowness was becoming socially acceptable. There wouldn't be any more Dr McBrides. Somewhere in the last few decades they'd lost the mould – integrity was now derided as naivety, dedication was for fools, and truth was to be applied only when advantageous to a lie. Dr McBride had possessed all the qualities of a man, and sadly they would be buried with him. Most of the people of Grapplewick had been brought kicking and scowling into the world by the caring hands of Dr McBride – indeed he was Grapplewick, and now he was gone. Mr Thurk's eyes pricked with tears as he looked at the old, worn trap. He ran his hand lovingly over the cracked leather seat, and he knew in his heart that Grapplewick was sitting up there in place of Dr McBride, but that the end was perilously close.

Barmy greeted him at the Fire Station with a steaming mug of tea. 'OK?' he grinned.

'Yes thanks, Mr Chronicle.' He climbed the stairs heavily and broke the news to the lads. Those with caps took them off, and they all stared at the floor.

It was Jack Puller who broke the spell. He raised his cornet to his lips and started 'Abide with Me'. One by one the band took up their instruments and joined in the hymn. Mr Thurk didn't conduct – for once it was unnecessary. It was as if God had taken over his baton.

By 12.30 the Dog and Partridge was already packed with early Christmas revellers, their babbling voices, laughter and shrieks punctuated by the steady jingling of the till. Helliwell, the proprietor, should have been pleased but he wasn't. He had had to take on three extra staff, but even so his main asset, or rather his two main assets – Elsie – wanted time off. Angrily he pulled a pint of best Threlfall's, shouting over his shoulder to where she was adjusting her little hat in the mirror behind the bar.

'Your mother isn't that poorly that she can't wait while three o'clock.'

'Eh?' said Elsie to the mirror.

He banged the slopping pint on the bar next to the glasses. 'That'll be three and six in all.'

The man screwed up his face to block out the noise. 'Ow much?'

'Three an' six,' yelled Helliwell.

Elsie opened the flap in the bar. 'I'm off,' she mouthed, pointing to herself, then the door.

Helliwell scrabbled in the till for one and six change. 'Don't forget tonight,' he shouted. 'We're open while midnight.' But she was already pushing her way through the leering drinkers.

Old Dobson took off his cap and opened the door of his ancient taxi. Elsie got in, pleased when he spread a plaid rug over her knees. He settled himself in the front seat, and as they pulled away from the kerb he half turned towards her. 'Dr McBride died this morning,' he said over his shoulder. 'Delivered a baby at Sagbottom Farm, got back in 'is cart, and 'e were dead when 'e got back.'

She leaned forward. 'Oh, I am sorry. Me mother 'll be upset.'

'Ay, 'appen.' A couple of miles went by. 'How is your mother?'

Elsie, startled out of a daydream, was about to tell him she was shopping in Accrington but said instead, 'She hasn't been too well lately. Well, she's had a bad leg for about two years now.' He nodded, 'Ay, a know.'

Panic gripped her stomach, then she relaxed. Old Dobson was a teetotaller, so there was very little chance of Helliwell getting to know she was on her way to the Grand Hotel, Manchester. She looked out of the window, but didn't see the sheep-dotted moors flashing past. What a strange man the Major was ... fancy sending a taxi to bring her all the way from Grapplewick just to have a Christmas dinner – she would have walked. She wasn't entirely besotted – more accurately she was flattered by his attention, stimulated by his manner – but having been brought up in an atmosphere of strict North Country orthodoxy bed never entered her thoughts. Well ... fleetingly, but to be dismissed immediately – there was enough guilt in her merely having lunch with him in Manchester, but then how could she refuse? She wasn't, however, so naive as to imagine that he desired her company purely for her mental agility. She'd noticed that, though his eyes were pointing at her face, they were actually looking down the neck of her blouse. But then he was too much of a gentleman for a quick feel and a slobbery kiss – he'd seen too much, done too much ... a film producer, and God! What he must have gone through during the war – dropped at Arnhem, last off the beach at Dunkirk, first on at Normandy, and, according to his scruffy Irish batman, was even awarded the VC but sent it back. The rasp of the brake brought her out of her reverie.

'Here we are, Elsie,' old Dobson wheezed out and opened the door for her.

'Thanks, Mr Dobson,' she said. 'That was quick.' She fiddled in her purse.

'Nay, that's all right, lass ... it's all been taken care of.'

She smiled her thanks.

'Ah well, I'd best be getting back now while it's daylight.'

Gingerly he got back into the driving seat, apprehensive of the traffic, although a Mancunian would have been surprised at the lack of it.

Elsie was even more terrified when she entered the Grand Hotel. She hovered uncertainly by the reception desk, awed by the tired opulence of the foyer and the men and women who looked so self-assured as they made their way in and out.

'Can I help you, miss?' a large man in blue uniform and brass buttons inquired.

'Yes ... er, I'm, er, having lunch with Major ... erm.' She stopped, blushing – she didn't even know the Major's name.

'Oh, yes,' said the large man a trifle coldly, and Elsie blushed again. He must think she was one of those women.

She looked round wildly and was about to dash for the door when she felt a hand on her elbow. She turned, panic-stricken, thinking for one split second that she was about to be forcibly ejected, but it was Terence.

'Ah, my dear. We were beginning to think you'd got lost.'

She smiled feebly, and the commissionaire dry-washed his hands and bowed up and down with a humility that was sickening.

'Thank you and Merry Christmas,' said Terence, and a fiver passed from one hand to the other with a smoothness mastered only by long-serving commissionaires.

If the foyer had unnerved her, the dining-room was a paralysing experience with glittering chandeliers, a steady hubbub of conversation, the rattle of crockery, tailcoated waiters, spotty boy apprentices in short Eton jackets, waitresses in black with white aprons and frilly white caps – all moving purposefully among the tables. Elsie was accustomed to admiring glances, but here she was embarrassed. She was only fractionally relieved at the table when she saw her fellow guests. Commander Wilson Brown rose and held a chair out for her, but the scruffy little Irishman just nodded and continued to stare at the tablecloth. Elsie smiled tentatively at the large woman sitting next to him, and felt slightly more at ease. Droopy Nellie had done her best with make-up, but she was unused to it and the result was a gaudy ship's figurehead. Terence seated himself with a great self-satisfied sigh.

'Pleasant trip?' he asked.

'Yes, thanks. Mr Helliwell wasn't too pleased. I told him ...

Terence leaned back and snapped his fingers. A waiter glided alongside. 'We'll have the wine now.' The waiter bowed and backed off. Terence smiled at Elsie. 'I took the liberty of ordering for you, my dear. Saves time, and we have a train to catch.' He lit a cigarette. . . . 'Oh, so sorry. I interrupted you, my dear.'

She shrugged. 'No, it's all right.'

The Commander raised an eyebrow and glanced disinterestedly round the room.

Elsie looked down at her plate, hands clasped under the table. She could almost feel the hostility round her. Terence, lounging back in his chair, was tapping idly with his fork. From the corner of her eye she noticed that Rembrandt and Nellie were also staring fixedly at the table, although they could have been saying grace.

'What time's your train?' she asked in an effort to break the spell.

'What?' Terence pulled himself back from wherever he was. 'Oh – train,' he sighed. 'Yes, sadly we must get back to London tonight. We were looking forward to spending Christmas in Grapplewick but ... ah.' He broke off as the stooping wine waiter returned.

Elsie watched the Major in admiration as he examined the label on the bottle and nodded. The waiter withdrew the cork, and this too was given close scrutiny. Then the wine – Terence held it up to the light, then he sipped, head to one side as he savoured the bouquet. The wine waiter watched him with a certain amount of trepidation. Finally Terence swallowed and nodded.

'Excellent,' he said.

'Bloody fool,' thought the wine waiter, who was rather good at his job.

When all the glasses were charged Terence raised his; he proposed a toast to Grapplewick and hoped they would return soon. 'To Grapplewick!' They all sipped and pre-tended to enjoy the wine except Rembrandt. He didn't touch it but had a surreptitious swig of Guinness from the bottle he had been holding under the table. The Commander glared at him in disgust, but Rembrandt just grinned back at him and had another swig. The soup arrived to rescue the situation, and conversation was then impossible until Rembrandt had finished. Nellie looked round the guests apologetically but Rembrandt was oblivious. He sighed contentedly and another bottle of Guinness appeared from under the table.

Slices of turkey were carved next and distributed expertly onto the plates. A waitress hovered round with the vegetables, and the various stuffings were delegated to one of the spotty apprentices. This provided the only light relief – so busy was he endeavouring to see down Elsie's blouse that he slammed a large dollop of sage and onion on Rembrandt's lap. The Commander looked away in disgust and when he looked back Rembrandt had eaten it.

Elsie had hardly noticed the meal – in fact she would gladly have got stuck into boiled alligator just to be done with it. The whole group seemed preoccupied and only smiled at the waiters. Why the Major invited her at all was a mystery.

Terence knew, though – her presence was vital, and he complimented himself once again on the brilliance of his plan. He leaned towards her. 'Something else, my dear?' But before she could decline politely, he was already placing five pound notes on top of the bill.

'Thank you, sir,' said the waiter, hesitating just long enough for Terence to wave a deprecating hand to the change.

The Commander rose quickly to his feet. 'Come along, then. We'll see these two off at the station, then I'll take you, er . . . ladies home.' He spoke with false sincerity, like an actor who notices people leaving their seats, but he was acting and he knew roughly what he would have to say during the next hour. Terence noted with satisfaction that London Road Station was crowded, but not too many people had arrived yet for the London train. It was early .. . again it had all been carefully pre-planned. They stood awkwardly at the barrier as people will when goodbyes are in order and there's no common ground. Rembrandt opened a bottle of Guinness and proffered it to Nellie, but she shook her head, unable to speak as black mascara tears flowed through the rouge. Wilson Brown turned away in disgust . . . .

Terence took off his hat carefully – he didn't want his wig to come with it. 'Well, my dear,' he said, 'no point in hanging around.' Elsie looked at the station clock, wondering if he might kiss her. Terence was also wondering whether he should. There was a quick movement by him and Rembrandt was snatched into Nellie's great bosom, black tears splashing his cap.

'Oi'll be waitin' for you, my little darlin', that you are.' Then she released him.

Rembrandt nodded. 'Oi'll be back. Yes, sorr. Don't you worry, oi'll be back.'

Terence smiled at Elsie. 'Don't worry, we'll be back, and if I pull off this deal we may have another lunch at the Grand,' he chuckled. 'Better still, I might buy the hotel for you.' He held out his hand and Elsie shook it, wondering why she'd bothered – bath, hairdo, clean underwear.

'Don't leave it too long.' She smiled and turned to go, but the Commander restrained her.

'Might as well see them safely aboard.'

Terence held out his ticket, and turned back to Elsie. 'Oh, and a Merry Christmas.'

'Same to you,' she called.

'It's in,' grunted the ticket collector.

'Thanks,' said Terence. 'Pity you have to work on Christmas Eve.'

'Oh, it's only the London bound, then I'm finished.'

'Oh well, anyway, have a Christmas drink on me,' and he slipped a fiver into the man's hand.

'Well, that's very nice of you, sir. Thank you.' He hadn't seen what the note was, but by the feel he knew it was a fiver.

Terence raised his hat again so that the man could get a good look at him – it was essential. 'And a Happy New Year.'

'And to you, sir.' By God, he thought, if only there were more like that – this little ratbag holding out his ticket wouldn't give you the end off a cork-tipped cigarette. First-class, too – must have nicked it.

Commander Wilson Brown and the two girls waved. Terence waved back and then pulled up the window and moved down the train.

'Ah, well,' said the Commander, 'let's get you two back.'

They walked slowly towards the exit, Nellie still blubbering. It was embarrassing, to say the least. She'd tried to repair the damage with a minute handkerchief. It would have been better if she hadn't, because she looked like a Black and White Minstrel doing a show in the rain.

'Here we are.' He opened the car door and they got in the back. Elsie was anxious and decided she'd go straight round to her mother's before Fred did. He had still been in bed when she left, and he might not have seen her note about her mother being ill. On the other hand he might have seen the note and gone round to check – he'd do anything rather than cook a meal himself.

'Damn.' Wilson Brown was pressing furiously on the starter but there was no life in the engine. The girls weren't worldly enough to notice that it wasn't even switched on. 'Oh, blast,' he muttered. 'It's broken down again. I'll have to leave it and get Hepworth's to pick it up.' So they all alighted, but before they walked over to the taxi rank he leaned into the car and surreptitiously dropped the keys on the seat.

On platform two the guard held up his flag and blew sharply on his whistle. The last train to London eased out of the station – the big one had gone bang on time. Fifteen minutes later the door to the gents opened, and a hump-backed man with a curly white beard, accompanied by a scruffy little man, made their way cautiously to the exit. The elderly humpback was obviously on the critical list, and the new man at the barrier helped him into his Vauxhall that was parked outside. Five minutes later Terence and Rembrandt were on their way back to Grapplewick, ostensibly speeding towards London – at least four excellent witnesses would testify to this if necessary. Stage one was complete.

At about 6.30 Rembrandt eased the car into Grapplewick High Street.

'Nearly there, sorr,' he called over his shoulder.

There was no reply. Terence was crouched on the floor in the back with a rug over him. Jimmy the Hat was some-where in the vicinity, and he'd be watching the cars. He wasn't sure how well

Jimmy knew Rembrandt, but to be on the safe side he'd lent the scruffy little man a moustache – it was an old one anyway. He lurched as the car turned, and rightly assumed that they were now going up Feathers-tall Road, which, thank God, would be considerably darker than the High Street. Slowly he raised himself and peered furtively out, noticing with satisfaction the lights in the Fire Station and a knot of dark shapes milling in the yard, then blackness as they sped past the gate.

Mr Thurk, happening to glance towards the road at that moment, subconsciously registered what appeared to be Wilson Brown's car, but immediately dismissed the thought – there was a white labrador in the back looking out of the window. Jack Puller went up and down the scale on his cornet, then again, and Mr Thurk turned his attention to the band.

'Once more, lads,' he called. Cigarettes were pinched out. Mr Thurk nodded to the Station. 'Lights, Mr Chronicle,' and Barmy, quivering with self-importance, clicked off the three switches. The sudden darkness was almost tangible. 'Form up on the beacon,' said Mr Thurk smartly but softly. Cyril lifted the jam jar containing the candle high above his head, and the lads scurried into columns, each man holding onto the belt of the man in front of him. When the jostling had ceased Mr Thurk almost whispered, 'By the left, quiiiick march.'

They followed the pathetic pinprick of light to the end of the yard, then round and back, and once again, until Mr Thurk called, 'Baaaand, Halt.' They stopped smartly and there was a shuffling and clink of metal as they adjusted their instruments. A couple of coughs and they were ready. Mr Thurk squeezed Cyril's arm, and the little jam jar waved twice and then was lowered. Mr Thurk called One, two a three,' and they eased into 'Silent Night'.

With head bowed he listened, and it wasn't bad. In fact, considering the short time they'd had to rehearse, it was quite moving. He sighed. Perhaps they were better when he didn't conduct. He squared his shoulders. To hell with it! He was proud of them all. First they'd had to learn it by heart, which not one man had failed to do. Then the practising in the band room, each man blindfolded to accustom him to the dark. Even Barmy had stood to attention with his eyes slightly shut. 'Sleeeep in heavenly peace.' The carol came to an end and all was silent. It was an emotionally charged moment. Mr Thurk, glad of the dark, wiped his nose.

'Lights, Mr Chronicle,' and the Station burst into light, which had them all squinting and turning away. 'Splendid lads, we'll take a fifteen-minute break. Thank you.' The lads jostled about putting down their instruments, and one or two sloped off towards the gate to down a couple of pints before boarding the bus which was to take them to the Binglewood Estate. Some of the lads were disappointed not to be using Aggie, but, as Mr Thurk pointed out, it was really a private engagement and to utilise Corporation trans-port (i.e. the fire engine) without proper authorisation would have been out of order. Hence the hire of a bus – a double-decker to accommodate the smokers.

Unwittingly Lady Dorothy had become an accessory. Anthony had confided in her, apprehensive as to how they would be received, but she assured him that it would be a splendid surprise and the Bendlethorpes would be tickled pink. However, she took the precaution of being at Holmedene at 7.30. Lord Bendlethorpe was a large, self-made man who had risen from a modest tinned meat manufacturer to the nobility, thanks to the healthy appetites of the Allied forces, and was now in the process of buying up large chunks of bombed-out buildings in Manchester. He helped himself to a large whisky and soda.

'Oh, come on, Dorothy,' he said, 'give us a clue.'

She smiled. 'All right, Jack. For a man who's got every-thing, this is something different ... anyway, you'll know in half an hour.'

He looked at her shrewdly, juggling the loose change in his trouser pocket. By jingo, if she only knew – £200,000 tucked away in his wall safe upstairs, a cash deal he would exchange for a large piece of Piccadilly.

His small daughter's eyes widened. 'I know,' she lisped. 'It's somebody going to come down the chimney.'

Lady Dorothy winked at her. 'Who knows?'

The tall manservant circulating with the decanter of sherry glanced at the roaring fire. 'If somebody does,' he thought, 'he'll get his arse burnt.'

Terence and Rembrandt, in black polo neck sweaters, black trousers and plimsolls, crouched in the drainage ditch on the East Road. Terence peered at the fingers on his luminous watch. Dammit, were they going to be late? He rested his forehead on the bank in front of him – he was sweating even thought it was near to freezing. Bile rose in his throat – it had always been thus. He tried not to look at his watch again. It must have been like this during the First World War – Sergeant coming along behind him; 'Steady, lad. You'll 'ear the whistle any minute. Then over over the top, lad.' A soft, cold breeze rustled the trees and the wind died, but the rustling continued. He realised it wasn't the trees – it was Rembrandt having another pee. On a night like this it was enough to waken the dead. He was about to give him a rollicking when he caught sight of the tiny firefly bouncing towards them, then he heard the sound of marching feet.

'Put your cock away,' he hissed. 'They're coming.'

The band approached in good order, and outside the gates of Holmedene the command was given to halt. Terence heard the scrape of a match, and there was a flare of light as someone bent down to examine the name plate. Some-thing was whispered, the great gates squealed open, and the band crunched down the drive to form up in front of the house. The lighted jam jar waved twice, then the band broke into 'Silent Night'. Almost immediately lights went on in the front of the house, and the great oak door opened. Taking advantage of the strident music, Terence and Rembrandt hurried round the back, lugging the ladder between them.

Jack Bendlethorpe didn't know whether to be pleased or disappointed. He dragged on a huge cigar. Ah well, it's different – bloody awful, but different. He leaned towards his manservant scowling in the background.

'Bring out the whisky and some glasses.'

The manservant faded indoors. Lady Dorothy glanced apprehensively at him, but it was a success. His little daughter was standing mesmerised. This would undoubtedly be the highlight of her pampered Christmas.

Terence, knowing exactly where the safe was, couldn't hear the band – a doctor's stethoscope blocked out all the noise except the click of the tumblers. Rembrandt, with one ear on the music, was stuffing anything that sparkled into a black bag. Two very expensive furs went flying out of the window. He glanced at Terence, then stopped. Terence was staring into the safe.

'What's up, sorr?' he said.

There was no need to whisper. Terry whistled and grabbed inside, bringing out wads of new crisp Treasury notes. 'We've come to the wrong place, old fruit. This is bloody Barclay's.'

Quickly they began to transfer the booty, so wrapped up that they didn't notice the band had finished. They need not have worried, however. There was more noise now, as the band enjoyed a Christmas libation with the householders. Finally, all the empty glasses were replaced on the tray, and the band formed up to repeat the performance at the other houses, unnecessary now because Terence was satisfied. As the band marched along towards the Beeches, they followed at a respectable distance carrying the loot between them, Rembrandt loaded with the two fur coats. Any drunk would have sworn that he'd seen a tall man walking down East Road with a polar bear. The band turned left towards The Beeches but Terence and Rembrandt carried on to Seven Seas. They had enough for one night.

Wilson Brown didn't hear them come in, and when they entered the drawing-room he actually shrieked. Terence went quickly to the sideboard – as always the aftermath left him shaking. Wilson Brown was beside him.

'What's happened? Chickened out? Why are you back? Are they still coming here?'

Terence knocked back his drink in one quick gulp, then poured another. 'Is the car in the garage?' he asked.

Wilson Brown nodded.

'All tanked up?'

Wilson Brown nodded again. 'Why are you back so early?' he asked.

Terence jerked his head at Rembrandt. 'Go and get changed. I'll fix the stuff.'

Rembrandt hurried away. He had some Guinness upstairs.

Terence took his glass to a chair and settled down, stretching his legs before him. 'I've only done Holmedene,' he said to the fire, 'so don't go commiserating with the other two houses.'

'What happened?' squeaked Wilson Brown.

'I'm getting old, I think,' he sighed. 'Anyway, it wasn't a bad night's pay. No point in risking the lot.' He sipped his drink. No way was he going to tell his old mate just how successful it had been. He was still in a state of shock himself – good grief, if anybody had any inkling of the size of that wad, they'd all be on his back. He hauled himself to his feet. 'I'm going to get changed.' He put his glass down and left.

Wilson Brown shook his head. Poor old devil, his nerve had gone. All this preparation and planning, and when it finally came to it he hadn't the balls. The noise of the band interrupted his thoughts. Oh God! He had this lot to contend with now.

Mr Thurk was happy. He felt that the evening had been a success, apart from Wilson Brown. The Commander had seemed preoccupied and hadn't even invited them in for a drink afterwards. Still, at least he did hear them out. The bus trundled them back to the Fire Station. One or two of the lads were already a bit over the top and wouldn't see midnight, but as was customary they had a couple in the Star on Christmas Eve, nipping across to the Station every now and again to take Barmy a drink. Barmy just grinned and poured whatever it was into the great dixie of tea.

At Seven Seas Wilson Brown quickly and expertly disarranged his bedroom. He remembered exactly how Terence worked, and this job had to be a replica of the one at Holmedene. He tilted a couple of pictures off-centre, then he took down the reproduction of Constable's *Haywain* and opened the safe, the contents of which were deposited securely at Lloyd's Bank. Lastly he opened one of the windows clumsily with his pocket knife. Satisfied, he picked up the phone.

Detective Inspector Waterhouse was gulping down a mug of sweet black coffee in an effort to steady the room. He wasn't completely drunk, but he'd been working at it. He jammed a battered brown trilby on his head and was about to leave when the phone rang. His wife answered.

'If it's for me tell 'em I left ten minutes ago,' he hissed.

She covered the mouthpiece. 'It's Commander Wilson Brown.'

He frowned, hesitated for a moment, then took the phone from her. 'Hello, Commander. Bill here.'

His wife hovered like a sheepdog waiting for a whistle.

'Another one!' he exploded, but the effect was better than a gallon of black coffee. He turned to his wife and raised his eyes despairingly. 'No, the station's been on to me. I was just about to make my way to Holmedene. There's been a break-in there.' He listened for a while, grunting now and again. Whatever happened, his Christmas was up the spout. He nodded. 'OK, Commander, you know the drill. Don't touch anything, and I'll be up there with a couple of the lads.' He nodded again. 'I'll alert Blackburn, we'll need reinforcements ... well, it's Christmas Eve. I mean it couldn't have happened at a worse time ... OK.' He put the phone down. 'There's been a break-in at the Commander's house as well.'

She put her hand to her mouth in dismay.

'When d'you reckon you'll be back?'

He shrugged. 'God knows.' Then he smiled thinly. 'Anyway, a Merry Christmas.' He kissed her on the cheek and hurried to the door, then he turned. 'God knows,' he repeated. 'But just in case, a Happy New Year.'

Wilson Brown settled himself in a large armchair and stretched his legs towards the fire. At least Terence and that stunted walking peatbog were off his back. He sipped his whisky contentedly – just the one, there'd he plenty more when he'd finished with the police. He laid his head back and stared at the ceiling. The insurance on his valuables alone was worth £25,000, and when that was safely gathered in he knew a fence in the East End who would buy the stuff off him for at least another £15,000. The house was already in the hands of the estate agents, and they'd assured him of a quick sale for this most desirable residence. Yes, in a month or so he could stash it all in a suitcase and head for the Antipodes. He shook his head ruefully, wondering why he hadn't thought of it in the first place instead of burying himself in Grapplewick. A heavy knock on the door scattered his thoughts. He heaved himself out of the chair and hurried towards the hall, composing his face into what he felt to be an expression of perplexed outrage. 'God, Inspector! What do we pay the police for?' He smiled to himself. No, that was a bit strong. No good alienating them. Another heavy knock, and he opened the door.

''Elio, Joe,' leered Jimmy the Hat.

TWENTY

Commander Wilson Brown staggered back a pace, clutching his heart – a mistake: it was the seat of his trousers he should have gone for.

Jimmy the Hat jerked his head and his companion hurried back to the car.

'How did you find me?' he asked stupidly.

Jimmy smiled, but it didn't touch his eyes. 'A bit of paper, Joe. There's always something on a bit of paper. *Grapplewick Chronicle.* Know it, eh? You standing up the Cenotaph there in a sailor suit. Oo's been a naughty boy, eh, eh?'

Wilson Brown struggled to collect himself. He spoke awkwardly because there was no moisture in his mouth. 'Please, Jimmy, we used to meet in the old days. How much? You name it Jimmy. How much?'

The smile left Jimmy's face. 'Ikey wants you,' he snarled, 'and if you don't want to freeze to death, get your coat on.' The other man pushed past and skipped up the stairs two at a time, carrying a five gallon petrol can.

Wilson Brown watched him, then turned to Jimmy. 'What's he up to?' he bleated.

'Don't ask,' said Jimmy, 'and get your coat on. You can walk to the car or you can 'obble with a broken leg.'

Wilson Brown hesitated for a second, then grabbed his overcoat from the hallstand. Out of the corner of his eye he noticed the other guy sloshing petrol on the stairs as he backed down.

'What's the point of that?' he squeaked.

Jimmy nodded. The tall man lit a cigarette and flicked it over the banisters. Wilson Brown finally lost control of his bowels as the stairs exploded in a seething mass of flame.

The new Vauxhall passed smoothly through Royton. In another twenty minutes or so Manchester would be navigated for the second time that day, then south to London. There wasn't much traffic about – in fact they'd only seen two other vehicles mobile; the others were parked every so often outside the noisy watering places a-glitter with lights. Terence glanced sideways at Rembrandt, glugging away at another Guinness bottle. God, not another one. When they stopped for a pee he made a mental note to park on a hill, otherwise they'd be swamped.

Rembrandt belched. 'Dar was a good job we just did. Yes, sorr, dat was class.'

Terence smiled. They were the first words that Rembrandt had uttered since they'd left the Binglewood Estate, and Terence had had a bet with himself that that's exactly what the little ratbag would say. It was just like old times. A cold wind slapped his face as Rembrandt opened the window and jettisoned another dead man. Terence grunted. Bloody fool was laying a fine trail – a smashed Guinness bottle every three miles or so. Hope to God he hadn't got too many left. He pulled up dutifully at the end of the Broadway, then turned right into Oldham Road, and his heart all but stopped. Thirty yards ahead was a police road block, and they were already going past another car which was pulled into the side.

With reflexes too quick for his brain, Terence jammed his foot on the brake, and almost immediately another car ran into him. The back of his head jerked forward, but even as it did he noticed two policemen coming towards him, torches swaying as they ran. Again purely reflex, but when he straightened up – and it couldn't have been more than two seconds – he was wearing a large walrus moustache. As the police reached the car Rembrandt stepped out and leaned into Terence.

'Tanks for de lift, guvnor, oi live just round de corner.' And he was trudging down towards the bright lights of Manchester as if he hadn't seen his old mother for years.

Terence rolled down his window, and one of the policemen stuck his head in. 'You all right, sir?' Terence nodded resignedly.

The other policeman came to the other door, and addressed his companion across Terence. 'The one behind's being sick ... he's drunk as a fiddler's bitch.'

The policeman looked back towards the retching in disgust, then turned back. 'Bit of luck we happened to be on the spot, eh?'

Terence tried to smile – no licence, no insurance: they were about as welcome as piles on a Grand National jockey.

Another car joined the queue, and the policeman straightened. 'Any road, we've got more important things to do.' He flashed his torch over the back seat and the floor. 'Would you mind stepping out and opening the boot, please.'

Terence pulled himself together. Way in the distance he spotted Rembrandt scurrying through the light of a street lamp, and a flush of anger swept over him. 'Constable,' he said in his best browbeating manner, 'at ten o'clock tomorrow I have a very important meeting in London.'

The policemen looked at each other over the top of the car. 'It's Christmas Day tomorrow,' said one of them, then stopped as Terence let himself out of the car. He stepped back a pace as Terence faced him squarely.

'The affairs of the nation do not stop just because it's Christmas,' he said quietly. He took a little black notebook from his inside pocket. 'May I have your name and number, Constable?'

The policeman frowned.

'Nothing to worry about,' Terence assured him. 'I can tell you, however, that the meeting tomorrow is vital, and if I'm late the cabin ...' he pulled himself up, 'er, the people with whom I am meeting will require reasons and corroboration.'

Another car joined the line-up, and the policeman looked anxiously at his watch. His colleague moved to the rear of the car, and while Terence jotted down the particulars he was struggling with the boot. The policeman volunteered his name and number.

'Thank you,' said Terence.

'The boot's jammed,' called the other policeman. They joined him and examined the boot lid.

'May I try the key, sir?'

Terence took his keys from the ignition. 'May I ask why you wish me to open it?'

'Just a routine check, sir.'

'On Christmas Eve?'

'Well, sir, like you we don't stop just because it's Christmas.' He tried to sound jocular, but a glance at Terence unnerved him. 'There's been a series of robberies in the north, and we're stopping all cars.'

Terence was about to insert the key when the other con-stable straightened up. 'You'll never get this open without tools,' he said. 'It's buckled, Jack.' Jack came round and bent down, trying to peer into a one-inch gap. 'Made a bit of a mess of your car, sir.'

Terence smiled. 'There's plenty more in the motor pool.' He walked round and settled down in the driving seat.

The policeman got out his notebook and was about to ask for Terence's licence, etc., when there was a loud groan and the driver in the car behind slid sideways out of his seat and sprawled messily in the road. The policeman stuffed the notebook back in his pocket and moved to the drunk. Grabbing both legs like a wheelbarrow, he started to drag him towards the pavement. The new Vauxhall roared into life, and with a wave Terence was off.

'Hey,' shouted one of the policemen half-heartedly.

'Did you get his number?' said the other one.

'What number?' said his companion, feigning innocence.

'Bloody Lord Fauntleroys . . . that car.'

'I never saw a car,' said the older one, dropping the drunk's legs. 'All I saw was this silly bugger run into a wall.'

Terence watched the receding knot of people in his mirror, then breathed easily. There seemed to be no move to get into the police car and give chase. He made up his mind, however, to switch transport as soon as the opportunity occurred. He was so wrapped up in his thoughts that he almost knocked down the scruffy figure ahead thumbing a lift. He just managed to swerve in time, then pulled up. In his rear view mirror Rembrandt was scuttling towards him, and for one fleeting moment he was tempted to put his foot down and leave the stupid sod to his Guinness.

'Nasty moment that, sort,' puffed Rembrandt, settling back.

'Thanks for your help,' said Terence icily.

'Dar's OK, sorr,' replied Rembrandt, happily taking the top off another bottle. They didn't speak again until after Manchester . . .

'Dey didn't look in the boot, then, sorr?'

Terence glanced at him. 'Why should they look in the boot?'

'Dat's what they're looking for, isn't it?'

'My dear Hibernian dropout, you don't think I'd trust our friend Helliwell to that extent, do you?'

'Oi don't follow dat, sorr.'

Terence shook his head slowly. 'I suspected that he might chicken out, and have a reception committee somewhere along the route.' He chuckled. 'He always did tend to under-estimate me.'

'I taut you said dat de stuff was all packed?'

'I did, but not in the boot. Oh no, my poor leprechaun, the goods are safely locked away in Helliwell's house.'

Rembrandt's mouth fell open in admiration. He took advantage of this to insert the neck of another bottle, then he wiped his lips. 'Dat's good thinkin', sorr. Dat's amazin' thinkin', sorr.' He swigged again. 'Oi wish you'd told me earlier, sorr. Oi've been wetting me pants every time we passed another car, and dat's a fact.'

Terence pulled into the kerb.

'What's up, sorr?'

Terence nodded towards a phone box across the road. 'I'm just going to wish Joe a Happy Christmas, and I suggest you empty your trousers over the hedge now.'

Rembrandt bundled out. 'Does he know dat de stuff's in his house?' he inquired.

Terence shook his head. 'No, but he will.' He was about to add a witty remark but Rembrandt, head down against the hedge, was already enveloped in a cloud of his own steam.

Wilson Brown watched hypnotised as a billow of smoke crept along the ceiling like a malevolent plague. Jimmy the Hat watched as a voyeur might view a stripper, then he pulled himself together. 'Let's go.' He grabbed Wilson Brown's arm and, just as they were about to leave, the telephone rang. They all turned. The bell still had the power to summon people peremptorily.

'Let's go,' said Jimmy again, and as they bustled him up the drive to the car Wilson Brown could still hear the waspish ringing punctuating the crackle and roar of the fire.

Police car Zulu Baker One pulled up outside the Binglewood Estate and a constable nipped smartly out and hauled the big gates shut. His mate pressed his mike: 'Zulu Baker One in position, South Ridge Gate.'

His colleague climbed in and slammed the door. 'Bloody waste of time, this. Talk about locking t'stable bloody door. He pushed his cap back, and was about to light up when he craned forward. ''Elio, 'ello?'

Two pinpoints of light were approaching fast down South Ridge.

Jimmy the Hat peered over the driver's shoulder. 'Wot's the game? They've closed the gates.' The car slowed, and it was then that the police car chose to put on full headlights.

Jimmy, blinded, thumped his mate on the shoulder. 'Quick! Turn left down 'ere.'

The car accelerated, skidding into a left turn down Wimpers Lane, and Wilson Brown caught a fleeting glimpse of a policeman running to open the gate. The car screeched left again at the end just as the tiny beams of the police car bent round into Wimpers Lane behind them.

'Where does this lead?' yelled Jimmy.

'Up to the golf club,' replied Wilson Brown, white-faced and holding tightly onto the strap.

They rounded a curve in the road and drove straight through a large brick gateway. The headlamps swept across the building in front of them, then stabbed out into the darkness. The car followed them over the practice putting green and down the slight bank to the eighteenth green.

'God,' thought Wilson Brown inconsequentially, the secretary won't like this.'

Leaping and bouncing, the car raced along the eighteenth fairway, all three heads banging against the roof of the car. It couldn't be the fairway – the fool was in the rough. Bouncing up and down some way behind them were the beams of the police car, and they seemed to be drawing closer. Wilson Brown didn't care any more. If his spine didn't snap his head would surely go through the roof. The beams of the car behind were flashing up and down, lighting up the driver's back intermittently, getting brighter. Then suddenly all was blackness – there was no pursuit. The driver pulled up slowly and they all looked back. Only Wilson Brown knew that the police car had gone into the deep bunker on the sixteenth. Jimmy tapped the driver on the shoulder, and without lights they cautiously felt their way over the rough ground, still bumping and lurching round the back nine. A clump of trees loomed to the right.

'OK, stop 'ere,' said Jimmy. The driver applied the brake. 'Now get out and 'ave a shufti round, see if you can find a flat bit of somewhere.'

'We're on the practice ground,' said Wilson Brown.

'I'm not asking you,' snarled Jimmy.

About a hundred yards to the left the headlights of a car raced by.

'That's what I want,' said Jimmy, and as he did so the driver returned. 'OK, OK. I saw it,' said Jimmy. 'Give it half an hour and we'll be off.'

He lit a cigarette, then cupped it quickly in his hands as another car flashed by in the opposite direction. Wilson Brown followed it with his eyes. The lights disappeared, leaving a thicker blackness behind, but even so he could just discern the red glow over the tops of the trees.

'Come on,' shouted Jim Cork over the cacophony in the Star. 'Let's have a sing-song.' And in an unsteady voice he began, 'I took my wife for a ramble, a ramble.' He broke off. 'Come on, lads.' He waved his arms: 'Singing High Jig A Jig . . .'

'Give over, Jim,' said Ned Bladdock. 'There's ladies present.'

'Bloody 'ell, Ned, it's Christmas,' he wheedled.

A crash of glass came through from the snug and the noise stopped, then a great cheer went up.

Jim Cork tried again. 'Took my wife for a ramble . . .' But the song degenerated into an incoherent mumble, and he staggered out to the back. As he opened the door he was jostled by PC Jellicoe coming in.

He was a Grapplewick lad, but new to the police. His face puckered as he tried to pierce the heavy, smoke-laden atmosphere. He took a step forward and looked round uncertainly. The noise dribbled away as they became aware of his presence.

The landlord looked up. It's OK, lad. We 'ave an extension while midnight.'

The young constable nodded, embarrassed like a man who has just walked into the ladies by mistake.

'Oh, bless 'im,' said Mrs Dyson, and gave him a smacking kiss. A ragged cheer went up.

Ned Bladdock proffered a glass of rum. 'Get that down you, lad. It'll do you more good than she will.'

Young Jellicoe shook his head. 'Not just now. I'm on duty, thanks.' He craned round the room again. 'You haven't seen Mr Thurk, have you?'

Ned took his arm. 'Chief's over yonder in t'corner.' He pointed his glass across the room, but Mr Thurk was already pushing his way towards him.

'What's up, Constable?' he asked.

Jellicoe pushed back his helmet, relieved. 'Ah, Mr Thurk. I've been looking all over for you. There's a fire.'

Mr Thurk looked at him stupidly. He wasn't a drinking man but it would have been churlish of him to refuse the hospitality of the Binglewood householders, and his eyes and brain were heavy. 'Fire?' he repeated, as if it was a clue in a quiz game.

'Yes. Sorry I couldn't reach you before, sir, but I was on my own at the station. They're all out on the robberies.'

'Robberies?' asked Mr Thurk, although he was still struggling with the word 'fire'.

'I telephoned the Fire Station, but there was no reply,' went on Jellicoe, 'so I nipped over, but I couldn't get any sense out of the man in there.'

'That'll be Barmy,' said Ned, helpfully.

'Well, I couldn't get any information out of him as to your whereabouts. He just handed me a mug of tea.'

Mr Thurk nodded. 'Yes, he would.' Then the full realisation of what the policeman was saying hit him. 'Fire?' he squeaked. He slammed his glass on a table. 'Fire Brigade outside!' he yelled.

'Fire,' shouted Ned. 'Come on. Chop, chop.'

They stared at him for a moment, then drinks were downed quickly and the lads of the Brigade lurched and staggered outside. The wives and some of the more sober customers crowded the door as they watched them stagger up the street towards the Fire Station.

The landlord, stretching to look over their heads, muttered, 'They're in no condition to go to a bloody fire. They're all inflammable as it is.' He laughed at his own joke, but it fell flat.

The wives turned to him. 'It's thanks to our lads you can sleep safe in your bed,' hissed Mrs Bladdock, and wrapping her coat round her she made her way to the gates to watch their departure.

The night was shattered by the roar of the engine, then there was a vigorous clamballang and the old engine trundled towards the gate. PC Jellicoe stood in the middle of the road, hand up to stop all traffic, although there was nothing mobile for miles. He waved them on, but Jack applied the brake. Mr Thurk, adjusting the strap of his helmet, looked at him inquiringly.

Jack shrugged. 'I'm not a bloody mindreader,' he said, 'where's the soddin' fire?'

'Sorry, sir.' He took out his notebook. 'Seven Seas, a house on the Binglewood Estate, it's on the . . .'

'I know where it is,' broke in Mr Thurk. 'Binglewood Estate,' he shouted to Jack, and with a great shuddering roar the engine leaped forward, scattering the onlookers. Fireman Harper fell off, but they couldn't wait for one man, so after being helped to his feet he made his way sheepishly to the bus stop.

Eyes streaming with the wind, Mr Thurk jerked fiercely at the bell. Ned Bladdock, behind him, risking life and limb, leaned over his shoulder to point ahead to the red glow of their destination. Two of the lads were hanging onto Jim Cork, who appeared to have passed out. It was a hairy drive. Jack Puller at the wheel was swerving round objects in the road that only he could see and which in fact were the product of a mind pickled in alcohol.

Tragically he didn't see the car coming towards him at high speed – hardly Jack's fault, because the car was travel-ling on sidelights only. As it closed with the fire engine the driver put on his headlights, blinding them all. Instinctively Jack stamped on the brake, but Lyndhurst Road is narrow, with an abnormally high kerb, and the driver of the oncoming car had no chance. The headlights veered away from them, then suddenly jerked back as the car hit the pavement. The lights swept over them all again at sickening speed, and the rear of the car slammed in to the offside front wheel of the fire tender.

Firemen flew off in all directions, although Jack and Mr Thurk managed to hold on, but the car slid along for thirty yards or more in a shower of sparks, to the scream of tortured metal. Shakily Mr Thurk got down and made his way towards the car. Some of the lads were already struggling with the door, and as he reached them they had extricated the driver, although it was obvious he'd never see the New Year in. The other two were alive, but just how barely it was impossible to tell. Mr Thurk was about to make his way back to the tender when he stopped. God Almighty! It couldn't be – he turned and bent over one of the moaning figures. It was, though, – it was Commander Wilson Brown. Shocked, he tried to identify the others, but they were strangers, one of them with a livid scar on his cheek.

He glanced impatiently towards the red glow in the sky, then at the bodies – he couldn't leave them here. On the other hand he had a duty to the Fire Brigade. Luckily a police car screeched up and matters were taken out of his hands. 'Quick, lads, mount up.'

The lads got shakily onto the engine. They were sober now, but all their guts had been knocked out of them. Jack was heaving at the front mud-guard where it had buckled onto the tyre. He stepped back, wiping his sweating forehead.

'Well, don't just bloody sit there,' he gasped. 'Give us a hand with this.'

Ned and a couple of others got down, but it was hard work. Old Aggie was built like a Sherman tank – thank God, because any other vehicle would have been knocked back into Grapplewick. Mr Thurk fretted. Was it in his imagination, or had the red glow died down? He joggled the bell rope with impatience, and the great juggernaut moved off.

Seven Seas was gutted. The blaze had been so severe and so sudden that it was almost hopeless. By the time the Blackburn Brigade arrived all they could do was contain it, and make sure the woods didn't catch. A tender from Manchester joined them, and together they brought what was left of it under control.

Quite a few sightseers clustered round, huddled in coats and scarves, but now the show was over they were beginning to disperse. Smoke-blackened firemen rolled up the hoses and gathered their equipment together. Some stood in a group having hot tea kindly supplied by one of the neighbours. The two fire chiefs, conspicuous by their white helmets, conferred quietly.

'What a bloody way to spend Christmas Eve,' one of them remarked. His opposite number nodded glumly. Then both their heads turned at the sound of a fire bell. They looked at each other, puzzled, then the Manchester Chief relaxed.

'Well, I'll go to our house and back.'

His colleague shook his head. 'I don't believe it! The Grapplewick lads have arrived – we're saved.'

On approaching, Mr Thurk spotted 'Manchester Fire Brigade' lettered on the side of the sleek gleaming tender. As the weary firemen paused in their duties to greet the new arrival Mr Thurk's head shrank into his collar in embarrassment. This would fuel another generation of derisory stories. They drew up alongside the Blackburn tender and the crowd raised a ragged cheer. One of the Blackburn Brigade sauntered over.

'Don't tell me,' he sniggered, 'one of the 'orses dropped dead.'

The trial was more of local interest than nationwide. Robberies were ten a penny, and too much was happening elsewhere in the world – for which Wilson Brown was grateful. He'd had a remarkable escape in the car smash, suffering mild concussion and a broken ankle. Jimmy the Hat was unfortunately injured rather badly, and as soon as he was able he was transported by ambulance to attend the court, his arm still splinted, one leg shorter than the other, and a heavy bandage round his head. A famous neurologist diagnosed brain damage, which in Jimmy's case was rather complimentary. However, the fates smiled again on Wilson Brown, as Jimmy could recollect nothing of the evening in question, nor, for that matter, the events leading up to it, which left a clear field for Wilson Brown's flights of fancy. Indeed he made a very imposing figure as he hobbled to the witness stand supported by a stout stick. His evidence was lucid and to the point, and the judge was impressed.

It transpired that, after he had reported the robbery, the two villains returned to his house, having inadvertently left some of the stolen goods upstairs. Modestly the Commander went on to describe how he had tackled them, but the odds were too great. Why they fired the house was open to conjecture. Vandalism? Revenge? Still dazed, he had been forced into their car, presumably as a hostage. The court knew the rest. The police were still making inquiries as to the whereabouts of their accomplice, a Colonel Harper Warburton, but so far with little success. It didn't affect the outcome. Jimmy the Hat was ordered to be removed to a prison hospital, and thereafter for several years hard labour – harsh justice, but in his case an occupational hazard.

Some weeks later a popular women's magazine hit on the idea of a series entitled 'Heroes are born, not made'. Commander Wilson Brown was to be the subject of the first article, and a writer was despatched for an interview, but despite all efforts she was unable to trace the whereabouts of the gallant Commander. In the course of her research, however, a number of discrepancies came to light and she notified the police. Inside a week the story was headlined in a national newspaper, but it was a one-day wonder. Thank-fully the *Daily Express* was not delivered in Tocumwal, a small town in New South Wales, Australia.

There weren't many applicants for the post of golf secretary, but as soon as he walked before the committee they knew he was the right man. Two days later Brigadier Wilson Baverstock limped to his desk and took up his post.

Twelve thousand miles away the black police van pulled into the archway of one of His Majesty's prisons. Jimmy the Hat looked out of the little barred window and sighed. His arm was still in splints and he still couldn't understand what he was supposed to have done. His last view of the outside world was a number 11 bus. It pulled up at the stop across the road. A little man in a scruffy raincoat was squatting on the pavement chalking a picture on the pavement.

The bus driver leaned out of his cab. 'I've got a job all planned,' he said.

Rembrandt didn't even look up. 'Oi've retired.'

Terence snarled, 'Next time round you be on this bus or I'll push a bottle of Guinness where it hurts.'

Ting-ting-ting. He glared at the black conductress, then released the brake.

The little man concentrated once again on his masterpiece. With a piece of charcoal he sketched smoke coming out of the two factory chimneys. Then he sat back to survey the scene, and it occurred to him that there hadn't been any smoke coming from the chimneys. To hell with it – artistic licence.

Some years later . . .

Epilogue: The Greater Crime of Grapplewick

Mr Thurk stared out of the window of his sixth-floor flat. The sight of the moors crisscrossed with black dry stone walls still gave him comfort, and the two tall factory chimneys remained, though the mills were derelict now. He leaned his forehead against the cold glass pane and felt the vibration as traffic spiralled round the circular road slightly above his eye level. The road was part of the many complex whorls of the spaghetti junction feeding the industrial towns of the north-west.

When Grapplewick first came to the notice of the planners in Whitehall they found it was ideally suited for their purpose, but the town itself had come as a shock. Research discovered it possessed no parliamentary candidate – not Tory, Labour, Liberal, nor indeed any other. Grapplewick in fact didn't officially exist, but a town in exactly the same location called Gwick did, although forms and letters addressed to it had for years been returned marked 'Not known'. After a humorous debate in cabinet Attlee sarcastically inquired if it was indeed British. Therefore, with no possibility of lost votes, the Town Council and the townsfolk were ignored, and almost before they could grasp the full import of the tragedy the bulldozers were eating into the town. Protests were swept aside, and a delegation to London was shunted from a junior minister to even more junior menials, while all the time concrete was spewing into the town centre.

Now, years later, the Attlee government was gone. Most of the original planners were either dead or else ennobled, diligently scribbling their memoirs to ensure themselves a place in history as the founders of a new, caring society.

Mr Thurk looked over his shoulder at the clock on the wall. In half an hour he would be catching his usual bus to the infirmary in Blackburn. Being a hospital porter didn't carry as much responsibility as his occupations of old had done. It should have been a satisfying vocation, but it wasn't. He could quite easily complete his day's work in one hour, and he was actually embarrassed at the ludicrous overtime, spent mainly in the hospital kitchens drinking tea: skiving was not only acceptable – it was compulsory.

Sadly, the new Gwick didn't warrant a Town Council, nor even a Fire Brigade. His gaze wandered down to the tandoori restaurant where the old Fire Station used to be, and as always he sighed. He remembered how he'd held up the demolition while he and Ned searched for Barmy. It was useless – Barmy had disappeared. Later, when the contractors were clearing the rubble, they found him. The Fire Station had been his home and during the search he had managed to remain hidden somewhere known only to himself. Poor Barmy! A grin had remained on his face even in death, a pair of dentures clutched in his right hand. Some two years later Ned passed away. Jack Puller still worked at Hepworth's Garage, but it wasn't the same Jack. A few years ago half a dozen kids on motorbikes had driven up, squirting petrol from the pumps haphazardly, pulling over the cigarette machine and starting to smash the windows. It was too much for Jack. He went into the garage and came out with a crowbar. Before they realised what was happening he was amongst them, and it was a massacre. Three of the bikes were wrecked, one of the yobbees received a fractured skull and another had his leg broken before the police arrived. The youths were given suspended sentences and ordered to pay for the damage, but Jack was sentenced to six months for assault. He came out a bitter, broken man.

The ghosts of Grapplewick crowded Mr Thurk's mind – the lads in the band, Dr McBride, old deaf Crumpshaw, even the vicar. He looked down at the church. St Mary's had been spared, but he very rarely went in now He couldn't accept a clergyman who wore a pair of blue denims.

The door bell rang. Visitors were rare. He opened the door: 'Ah, it's you, Dorothy.' He stood aside to let her enter.

'I'm off to Blackburn myself,' she said, 'so I thought I'd offer you a lift.'

'Yes, that'll be fine . . . hang on while I get my coat.'

Lady Dorothy walked to the window, as she invariably did. 'If there's a strike next week,' she asked over her shoulder, 'will you come out with them?'

He shrugged into his coat. 'Oh, I don't think there'll be a strike. It's just a lot of hot air.'

She frowned. 'But if they do call a strike, what will happen to the patients?'

He smiled and took her arm. 'Exactly,' he said firmly. For that reason they'll call it off. They wouldn't just drop everything and leave the patients to suffer.' He laughed. 'It's unthinkable.'

They got into the lift, which always embarrassed him. Twice he'd painted it himself, but it was only a fresh back-ground for even more graffiti. He was relieved when they stepped our of the main door. 'Cheer up, Dorothy,' he said. 'There's always a bright side.' He realised that she wasn't listening, and when he followed her gaze his heart sank – all the tyres on her car had been slashed.

SMELLING OF ROSES

ONE

Sergeant Beaconsfield had had a bellyful of the North African desert and, judging by the way it hung over the waistband of his khaki shorts, this was quite something. He took a drag at his cigarette butt and dropped it, scuffing sand over it with his boot. He wasn't a particularly careful man – it was just something to do. He looked around at his gun crew preparing the twenty-five-pounder for action.

'Supercharge?' asked the loader. It was a joke.

'Bloody 'ell, no,' replied the Sergeant. 'Same as last week. It's only five thousand yards, we're not shooting at Berlin.'

He wandered over and checked the angle of sight. He nodded and the crew relaxed.

They were young, tanned, the colour of walnut. He envied them their vigour and enthusiasm as they eagerly exchanged bets on the result of the fall of shot. They'd seen action in the last few months, albeit a retreat. The firing of a few hurried rounds, hitch up and race back a few miles, unlimber, fire a few more rounds over open sights, then back again. They were good lads, he reflected, so it was a relief to be finally posted to this comparative calm. But now, after three weeks, boredom had set in – that is except for Wednesday. This was the shooting match.

'Ten on us, Sergeant?' asked one of the lads.

'You're on,' agreed Beaconsfield without interest.

The ten referred to cigarettes – big deal. But then it was something to relieve the monotony. He scratched the knotted khaki handkerchief on his head, disturbing the flies that were trying to get through to the Brylcream, and gazed towards the distant horizon dancing in the heat haze of the North African desert.

Some three miles ahead on a rocky escarpment the young gunner in the forward observation post shook his head to clear the sweat from his eyes. A droplet splashed the rock in front of him and a lizard skittered over his hand, scaring the living daylights out of both of them. God, what a bloody desolate place to end up in! He would have liked to step back into the shade of an overhang in the rock face but he'd heard too many old sweats' tales of scorpions lurking in the dark places. Once disturbed, they'd be up the leg of his voluminous shorts, and this was one gunner who intended to go home with his dowry intact.

Suddenly he stiffened as he caught a flash from the escarpment some distance away across the flat desert. And then he relaxed. It was his opposite number, the German spotting for his eighty-eights. They sometimes waved to each other. From the corner of his eye, he noticed a movement below and lifted his binoculars. Here we go again, he thought, as an Arab leading his camel came into view. Lowering his glasses, the young gunner turned around and cranked the field telephone. The tinny voice of Sergeant Beaconsfield answered, 'Yes?'

'Arab and camel now approaching target area, Sarge.' He replaced the handset.

At the other end Sergeant Beaconsfield smiled with satisfaction, turned to his gun crew and put up his thumb. The loader rammed home a shell in the breech of the gun and the crew looked around to the Sergeant expectantly. The Sergeant signalled with a curt nod, turned away with eyes closed and fingers in his ears . . . bang! The old artillery piece leapt back startled, bouncing the overhanging camouflage netting, and a crowd of flies rose from a dixie of yesterday's McConochies stew on the trestle table.

In the forward observation post the young gunner was dry-mouthed, apprehensive and fearful of what was to come. A sudden gout of flame and black smoke erupted in the desert well to the left of the target, followed by the dull crack of the twenty-five-pounder.

The camel shied violently, almost lifting the Arab off his feet. With a stream of invective the camel driver jerked savagely at the halter until the beast steadied. He spat, then eased his grip on the camel's rope, and the ludicrous plod continued. He was fatalistic. Soon after, there would be another thundering in the air followed by yet another great bang. Each time he made the journey across this stretch from the oasis to Matruh, he was a target. So be it – he was in the hands of Allah. If it was written, he'd be hurled from this dung heap of a world, so let the accursed infidel do their worst, Allah be praised. He closed his ears to the second rushing in the air coming from the opposite direction. This was followed by another great explosion, closer this time. The sand spattered them and steel fragments shrieked through the air, compliments of Krupps Munition Works, Essen. The camel, unlike his master, having no religious faith, plunged and bellowed swinging his master about like a bundle of rags. Docilely, the camel driver allowed himself to be thrown up and down – a doll in the hands of a demented puppeteer. Eventually the beast wearied of the sport and stood unconcerned awaiting the beating. However, its driver's hands had no feeling and his wrists were too badly chafed, so the pleasure would have to wait. Steadily he settled on his course once more, never deviating by one degree from the track forged by his father, and his father before him back to the days of the Pharaohs, a track now pockmarked by explosions from previous contests.

Each Wednesday the Arab and his camel passed over a certain strip of desert under observation by both British and German gunners. The object of the game was to see which artillery team could bracket the target without actually demolishing it. This was a stand-off period following the short decisive battles of Tobruk and Mersa Matruh, and the first battle of El Alamein, a time when Rommel and his staff were frantically trying to build up their supplies for the final push. The British remained close to their own supplies but did not have enough ordnance to help them regain the initiative.

The field telephone rang again and Sergeant Beaconsfield lifted it from its cradle. 'Yes,' he said, as he flicked the wheel of an enormous lighter and held his head to one side in order to light a fag without scorching his nose, but the cigarette remained unlit. 'Say that again,' he said into the mouthpiece, all attention now. The lads watched him warily. 'OK, if you say so.' Then he replaced the telephone and walked over to check the elevation of the gun.

'Who won that one, then?'

The Sergeant didn't look round. 'Nearly blew the arse off it. Too close for comfort.'

Excitedly, the gun crew was all smiles and a wave of clenched fists but the smiles quickly disappeared when the Sergeant added, 'They were, not us.'

The loader sniffed. 'What chance have we got with this clapped-out drainpipe against their eighty-eights?'

'Hey,' said one of the lads, delighted. 'You owe me ten, Sarge.'

The Sergeant ignored this.

'Up five hundred yards,' he said and watched as the adjustments were made.

The Sergeant was unmoved. It was only cigarettes after all and he was already owed over forty and ten bottles of Stella beer. Some of the lads maintained he dropped the spotter a nice backhander to phone in false reports, and they were not far off the mark.

'Right, lads,' said the Sergeant. 'Eyes down for Round Two.' But the lads, half rising, were gazing over his shoulder to where a fifteen-hundredweight truck was approaching at speed. Beaconsfield turned and shielded his face as the truck screeched to a halt in a swirl of hot white dust.

The young driver sat to attention at the wheel looking sheepish. The thin, slightly built Second Lieutenant adjusted his goggles on to the peak of his cap as he stood up, holding on to the top of the windscreen.

One of the lads nudged his mate. 'It's Rommel, in'it?' he whispered.

The Sergeant eyed him with distaste. 'If that's Rommel, we'll all be back home in a week.'

The young officer stepped down and looked curiously about him before making his way forward. The Sergeant, hands on hips, watched him warily as he approached, noticing the angry redness of his knees. His thin pointed nose was more vivid still and already peeling, and with the large white circles round his eyes where the goggles had been, he looked like an owl that had had a go at the jam pot.

'Who's in charge here?' he piped.

'Captain Brown, sir, but he's in Alexandria.'

Lieutenant Jampton sniffed and sauntered over to where the crew were now pretending to be busy with the twenty-five-pounder. He walked round it and looked down the barrel. The breech was open and the gunner's face at the other end said, 'Hello, sailor.'

Lieutenant Jampton jerked his head back, embarrassed, collected himself and wandered over to the Sergeant. 'Artillery, eh?' he said.

'There's not a lot gets past 'im,' muttered one of the lads, and the others sniggered.

Lieutenant Jampton whirled round with his nose glowing like an inhaled cigarette but before he could convene a court martial Sergeant Beaconsfield spoke. 'Yes, sir, D Battery, 86th Field Artillery.'

'D Battery, eh?' muttered Jampton and marched over to a trestle table where he pushed aside a filthy mess tin and spread out his map. Beaconsfield looked over to the driver, still seated at the wheel of the steaming fifteen-hundredweight, sweat streaming from under the rim of his tin hat. The Sergeant shrugged and strolled over to the table where the Lieutenant was staring earnestly at his map. He was nodding to it, then he consulted a compass strapped to his wrist.

'Ah ha,' he murmured and looked ahead, then back at the map, then he looked behind, and eventually he turned a full circle. 'Right,' he snapped and started to fold the map.

The Sergeant noted idly that it had been upside down.

'Carry on,' said the young officer sternly and, adjusting his goggles, he climbed back into the fifteen-hundredweight.

His driver, anticipating, was already revving the engine awaiting the orders to advance. Jampton pointed ahead and they began to move. Sergeant Beaconsfield was galvanised into action and waved his arms. 'Whoa,' he shouted to the driver, who slammed his foot down on to the brake so hard that his CO almost did a somersault over the windshield on to the bonnet.

Beaconsfield said, 'Sorry, sir,' as the young officer regained his composure, 'but whatever you're looking for it isn't that way.'

He pointed in the direction in which they were facing.

'Ah,' replied Jampton brushing himself down. 'I'm looking for the Special Ordnance Group.'

The Sergeant looked up at him innocently. 'Ours or theirs?'

'Sergeant –' he began, but Beaconsfield cut him short.

'Well the only thing ahead of us here is the Jerries.'

'The enemy?' He stood, raised his binoculars and looked ahead, apprehensive lest he should see the whole of the Afrika Korps bearing down on him. He turned and looked back. 'That way, eh?' he murmured.

'Yes, sir. You'll see plenty of Division signs about six or seven miles back on the coast road.'

'The coast road?'

'Yes, sir, parallel to the sea. You can't miss it – it's full of ships.'

The young Lieutenant leant towards him. 'What's your name?'

'Sergeant Beaconsfield, sir.'

The Lieutenant nodded. 'Well, Sergeant Beaconsfield, I can do without your sarcasm, thank you.'

'Yes, sir.'

The Lieutenant made a rotating sign with his hand and the driver accelerated and screeched round in a full circle, disappearing completely in his own hot dust.

The Sergeant stepped back, expecting to see the vehicle emerge and speed on its way, but it didn't. As the dust settled, the Lieutenant beckoned and he walked forward.

'Sergeant,' he said, 'just before I arrived, you were firing. What was your target?'

The Sergeant looked down at his boots, then over to the gun. He was bored now with this new jumped-up officer, and he didn't like being beckoned. He sprang to attention, sweat flying off him in all directions, looked straight ahead and roared, 'Nothing . . . *sah!*'

The Lieutenant glanced sideways at his driver, triumphant.

'Nothing?' he asked, head to one side.

'No, *sah*, nothing. Time-honoured custom, *sah* . . . that was the noonday gun, *sah*.'

Enlightenment dawned – the noonday gun; he'd heard about that. Of course, he should have known. He pulled himself together. 'Very well. Carry on, Sergeant, and the next time we meet I hope you're properly dressed.'

Fortunately for him the roar of the engine drowned the laughter and as the fifteen-hundredweight shot forward he was jerked back into his seat but he was happy; he was well pleased with his handling of the situation. As the fifteen-hundredweight raced away, he looked back, but anything behind was obscured by the dust of his own passing. He leant across and shouted to his driver, 'Noonday gun . . . it's these traditions that make the British Army the finest in the world.'

Gratwick didn't quite hear what he said and yelled back, 'Thursday, sir.'

Luckily, Jampton didn't hear the reply either. The heat was beginning to bother him. He opened his knees wide to ease the heat rash in his crotch. He desperately wanted to scratch it but not in front of the men.

He made a mental note to write home to his Aunt Dorothy about the noonday gun – she would be thrilled. It wasn't until they had travelled a few miles that it suddenly occurred to him that it wasn't yet eleven o'clock. Could the Sergeant's watch be wrong? He was shaken out of his reverie when Gratwick pulled up by the side of a nest of divisional signs – 1st Armoured, 4th Indian, 151st (Durham) and, almost indecipherable, the Special Ordnance Group, and in brackets (Ladies Welcome). This caused a cluck of disapproval from Jampton and he ordered his driver to follow the arrow. Unfortunately the arrow had pointed towards the desert, and, as every old sweat knew, the desert was a big, unforgiving stretch of nothing – a waste land known as the blue where only the stars or a good compass can guide, and at eleven o'clock in the morning Lieutenant Jampton had neither.

Inevitably, after a couple of hours, they were totally and completely lost. Jampton called a halt and dismounted. He walked around the front of the truck and spread his map on the shimmering bonnet of the fifteen-hundredweight, then yelped and sprang back as his elbows came into contact with the hot metal. Fortuitously for him, Gratwick was gurgling away at his water bottle and hadn't noticed, so he was able to maintain his officer's dignity. He consulted his inadequate compass, then he made his way to the top of a rocky escarpment and surveyed the surrounding desert through his binoculars.

Gratwick watched him dispassionately. He wished he could take his tin hat off in this stifling heat but he had done that once and received a stern rebuke from his CO to be properly dressed at all times. The sun was directly overhead and he'd never known it so hot or so still. He was frightened now and had visions of driving about this desert long after the war was over, missing in action. He saw his father opening the telegram and felt a lump in his throat, then the officer was back.

Jampton eased himself into the seat and pointed vaguely to the left. Gratwick started up and they were bouncing and shuddering over the escarpment and down into the shallow depression.

'Ah,' said Lieutenant Jampton and pointed.

There, over to the left on the shimmering floor, were the burnt-out wrecks of a bygone battle: blackened hulls of tanks, and a couple of burnt-out Bren-carriers.

'Somebody copped it here,' muttered Jampton, with slitted eyes.

Gratwick's heart sank. They had passed this battlefield three hours ago but he wasn't going to let on. He knew then that they had been going round in circles. Several miles later Jampton suddenly looked back, then he glanced sideways at Gratwick.

'We passed that battlefield this morning.'

'Yes, sir,' said Gratwick, trying desperately to miss the potholes.

Jampton spread the map across his knees but the jolting of the wagon made it impossible to read. He shaded his eyes to glance up at the sun.

'Well at least we're travelling east,' he said, and pointed forward. 'The sun sets in the west.'

'Yes, sir,' said Gratwick miserably. Everybody knew that.

They bucketed on for another few miles, when suddenly Gratwick braked hard as they almost ran into a troop of four Crusader tanks. Jampton, although holding on to the windshield, was actually looking the other way at the time and caught his back a tremendous wallop as he was thrown against it.

'Bloody 'ell,' said the tank gunner, a mug of hot tea halfway to his lips. 'I know our camouflage is good but it don't make us invisible.'

Suspicious eyes watched as the Lieutenant dismounted stiffly and walked towards the tanks as easily as he could. By now the chafing of his shorts against his sunburnt knees was agony. His gait was not lost on the deeply tanned men of the Tank Corps. The Lieutenant was either new to Africa or he'd just had an attack of dysentery.

'Who's in charge here?'

Lieutenant Jampton hadn't meant to croak but his water bottle was long since dry. He hadn't expected the desert to be quite so vast or that he would be away from human contact for so long. The tank men looked at one another and shrugged. Jampton's stomach gave a lurch and he took a pace backward. These men were stripped to the waist, showing no insignia or badges of rank; they could be Germans. His eyes flickered uneasily to the camouflaged Crusaders but he was too new to know the difference between a Tiger tank and a water bowser.

Luckily one of the men spoke. 'What d'you want, then?'

The Lieutenant let out a sigh of relief. It could easily have been '*was wollen Sie?*' He smiled – or he tried as much as his lips would allow. 'Oh, er, I'm looking for the Special Ordnance Group.'

The men seated round the brew-up relaxed. For one awful moment they thought he was going to belong to them. The Lieutenant gestured with his map and looked all around him.

'They're in this vicinity somewhere.'

One of the men rose to his feet and sauntered towards him.

'That's where they're supposed to be,' said Jampton, and prodded the map hesitantly. The man studied the map for a few moments, then shook his head.

'That's where we are now.' He pointed. 'You're about ten miles adrift as the crow flies.'

One of the other men had come across and was craning over Jampton's shoulder. 'Yeah, and then some. It all depends how old the crow is.'

The first tank man laughed. 'Take no notice of Lofty, sir. He's bomb happy.' But Jampton wasn't listening.

'Ten miles, eh?' he said almost to himself.

'Well, ten miles or thereabouts. Just keep on a south-southeast bearing.'

'South-southeast?' asked Jampton.

'That's about it,' said the tank man. 'Carry on, south-southeast.'

Jampton looked at his compass, then he gazed in the direction of the Special Ordnance Group, over the limitless stretch of desert. Foreshortening his gaze, he looked at the fifteen-hundredweight and saw that his driver was fast asleep over the wheel. It had been a long day for Gratwick too. Jampton's shoulders slumped. He'd had enough. He was hot and dusty and dried out. Irritation fluttered within him; after all, it was the driver's job to find the location. Why did he have to make all the decisions just because he was an officer? Pettishly, he stamped his foot; he was ready to take his bat and ball and go home.

'Cheer up, sir,' said the tank gunner, and handed him a mug of hot, sweet tea. 'Get that down you,' he said.

Jampton looked blankly at the tall, tanned man and took the proffered mug. 'Thank you,' he muttered, although he would have given his right arm for an ice-cream cornet.

'It'll be sundown in an hour,' said the man. 'No sense in chasing across there in the dark unless there's a flap on.'

'No, there's no rush,' said Jampton, sweating more now because of the hot tea.

In addition, his nostrils had picked up the aroma of frying. He couldn't identify the smell but whatever it was it smelt delicious. Had he had enough juice in him, his mouth would have watered. Jampton was about to ask if he could join them when he realised with a start that he'd already been invited.

'Oh, thanks, thanks, I could do with, er, whatever's going.'

One of the other tank men walked over and shook Gratwick, whose neck was getting the full benefit of the dying sun.

Gratwick's head shot up.

'Yes, sir,' he yelped. 'Coming, sir.'

The tank man patted his shoulder. 'OK, son, relax, you're staying with us tonight. But there's a bit of daylight left so you'd better get some camouflage over your vehicle.'

Gratwick was still disorientated and looked around for a tree or a bush. He realised where he was and his heart sank. The tank man took pity on him.

'Been out long?'

Gratwick stared at this father figure. Here was a real fighting man, and old, too: he must have been about thirty-odd.

'No,' he said. 'Disembarked yesterday and had my orders to be Lieutenant Jampton's driver. We came over on the same boat.'

The old man looked over to Jampton and sighed. They'd be taking them out of the cradle next.

'OK.' He glanced at the fifteen-hundredweight. 'I see you haven't any netting then.'

Gratwick looked back over his shoulder. 'No, they didn't issue us with any. It was a rush job, you see.'

Again the man sighed – it was going to be a long war.

'Right, drive over to that dune and park.' He pointed to a spot some fifty yards distant. 'Shovel some sand over the truck and make it look like a derelict.' He looked over the back. 'They've given you a shovel, I see.'

'Yes, sir.' Gratwick was glad he wouldn't have to drive any more that day.

The man was about to join his comrades when he stopped. 'Oh, by the way, you don't have to call me sir. Corporal Dunnett. I'm just a tank driver.' And with that he strode to the shade.

Gratwick smiled after him; there was a man he could admire. He turned back to the truck and frowned as he humped Jampton's bedroll off the back. He wasn't to know then but that was the first and last time he would have this chore; fate was to take a hand and before he was much older he would never again see Lieutenant Jampton or the Special Ordnance Group. His war would be over.

Some time later Jampton slid gingerly into his sleeping bag and tried to settle down, but it was no use. His knees and arms were burning like the clappers, while the rest of him shivered. The night was black and cold – good grief, was it ever! From the heat of the day to the sheer freezing chill of the night, it was almost impossible for anything to survive. No wonder the desert was arid and desolate. He lay in his blankets in the foetal position with his hands between his thighs for warmth. By jingo, it was cold. The blanket covered his head in the hopes that his breath might add some heat, but it was useless. He snatched the blanket off and the raw night air froze his face.

There were the usual flashes on the horizon but they didn't bother him now. He'd seen all that on the previous night and for a moment he felt good; he felt he could handle the war. A slight snap jerked him up into a sitting position and he held his breath, eyes desperately trying to pierce the blackness. He waited a moment, then slowly he lay back again and drew his blankets close. It could have been one of his knee joints. Then another quiet crack. He was sitting up again. Then an almost inaudible pop. His head swivelled almost three hundred and sixty degrees but there was nothing to see. Panic began to take over. Flashes on the horizon were one thing but these were sounds – and close. Should he waken one of the tank men? Luckily, he dismissed the idea. They wouldn't be too happy being roused to listen to the natural phenomenon of the desert, the creaks and cracks as the earth's crust cooled after the scorching heat of the day. The sounds were benign but Jampton was too fresh and too callow to understand. To him every slight noise was the hobnailed boots of an enemy patrol.

Sleep was impossible now but the cold was forgotten, all his antennae straining for the first signs of disaster. Suddenly in the distance he heard a thin ethereal wailing. He was on his feet now, clutching his blanket. The howl came again. It was inhuman, he thought; and he was right: it happened to be a jackal. It howled again, and why shouldn't it? This was its own back yard; humans were the interlopers. Somewhere closer came the answering call and for the first time in his life Jampton's bowels began to know fear. It was physical and it could have been disastrous had he not been constipated. It might have been the manly thing to wrap himself in his blankets to sleep rough in the open while Gratwick dozed in the cab of the fifteen-hundredweight. But, damn it, after all, he was the superior and this was one of the times when discretion was better than valour. He eased himself in the seat next to his driver and closed the door as softly as he could. This wasn't out of deference for the sleepers round him. In fact they should all be awake after that howling. No, the reason he closed the door with care was purely self-preservation. He wasn't going to give away his position.

He glanced over at the dark shape of Gratwick slumped over the wheel. He was no consolation. Jampton wrapped his sleeping bag around himself and fell into an uneasy shallow doze. Suddenly he was jerked awake by the high-pitched whine of the electric starting motor, then another, then four tank engines roared into life. A few minutes later in the darkness of the pre-dawn he watched with stirring panic as the Crusaders disappeared in line astern. Gratwick, also awake now, watched open-mouthed as the great armoured leviathans rumbled into the darkness. In a few minutes all was silent again. It was as if they had never been – but long after departure the blue diesel fumes that hung in the still night air reminded them that it wasn't a dream. Jampton had never felt so alone in his miserable young life.

After a few moments Gratwick excused himself to answer the call of nature and stumbled out into the black, cold night. And now, to judge from the grunts and gasps coming from the darkness, he hadn't gone far enough. Damn the lower classes: they couldn't even defecate decently. He ground his little teeth in frustration. What was he doing here anyway? Shouldn't he be in Alexandria discussing the state of the war with Uncle Charles?

Somebody somewhere had dropped a monumental clanger.

TWO

B ut there had been no mistake. His movement had been
carefully orchestrated . . . no one could have foreseen the dire
consequences which were to follow.

Whilst Lieutenant Jampton was struggling up the gangplank of
the troopship moored in Southampton water prior to his passage
to North Africa, a letter by diplomatic pouch was delivered to a
large brownstone house in Mina Street, Roushdi, in Alexandria.
A brass plaque to the side of the tall doors proclaimed it to be the
Ministry of Agriculture and Fisheries – it fooled no one. This was
the headquarters of British Military Intelligence.

In a room on the fourth floor, Colonel Charles Brunswick
signed for the letter and passed the clipboard back to the courier.
Ordinary people posted their letters into a pillar box, but then his
wife was Lady Dorothy Belvedere-FitzNorman, her family being
one of the oldest and most powerful in England – certainly
superior to the Royals and only slightly lower than God.
Unfortunately Lieutenant Jampton was also their adopted
nephew, loved and worshipped by Lady Dorothy almost as much
as he loathed the little prat.

The Colonel sighed. He'd come a long way from his humble
origins. Born 1900 in a squalid house in Solihull, Charles
Brunswick and his sister Emily grew apathetically through childhood, measles, whooping cough and mumps, avoiding, by the
grace of God, rickets. Their mother, a shadowy figure, said little

except 'time for bed', or 'eat it up, it's good for you'. Their father was even more obscure. He owned a small carpet shop in the better part of town, which wasn't saying much. And to his credit he was away from home sometimes for a week or so. In fact his visits home became more infrequent as the children grew.

Charles's fourteenth birthday was momentous: World War One was declared – and as if that wasn't enough his mother died. By the time their father had arrived back from wherever he'd been to this time and had heard the news, he'd proclaimed that changes would have to be made. Charles's sister Emily had made up her own mind, however, and was already training to be a nurse. If the war didn't end by Christmas, she'd be somewhere in France and bugger Solihull. Charles was immediately installed in his father's shop in order to learn the wefts and warps of carpet making.

By 1916 his sister was looking after the boys at a field dressing station somewhere in France. And thankfully, two years later, he received his call-up papers. He and the newly formed battalion 'The Midland Pals' no sooner set foot in France than peace was declared.

In 1920, serving in Cologne in the Army of Occupation, Charles received news of his father's death and was granted compassionate leave to attend the funeral. It was a happy affair being reunited with his sister Emily. In all fairness, their father had been away so often they'd never got to know him. And whenever he was at home he wasn't a person you looked at. He rarely spoke and when he did you listened whilst staring at the floor. On the occasions of birthdays and Christmas, you accepted the new penny and thanked his waistcoat buttons. In fact they would have had difficulty in picking him out of an identity parade. Up to this moment, for young Charles and Emily, their lives had been about as colourful as trudging slowly across a rain-sodden slag heap.

But this was all about to change. The summons to a solicitor's office should have alerted them. People of their class didn't make wills. They just died and the relatives came out of obscurity and swept through the rooms like marauding Goths opening drawers and cupboards, looking under cushions and beds as though it were a bargain sale in a second-hand shop, even as the dead lay quietly on a table in the cold front room.

The sunshine bombshell that exploded when the Last Will and Testament was read hit them like a warm wind in winter. It also explained their father's long and mysterious absences . . . He had bequeathed to them a large carpet shop in Bond Street, London, two carpet shops in the expensive part of Birmingham, others in Edinburgh and Glasgow, all these assets exceeding Fifteen Million Pounds . . . It was unbelievable! Incredible! Whichever way you said it Fifteen Million was a foreign language. What kind of a man had their father been? A man with that kind of money in the bank and yet one who would walk a mile rather than pay for a penny tram ride. Emily, white-faced as a piece of foolscap, stared across at her brother. She was afraid to faint in case she came to to find that it had all been a dream . . .

Poor Emily, thought Charles. Only six weeks before, she'd married one of the men she'd nursed in France, a Lance Corporal Jampton, and, apart from having lost a leg on the Somme, he was in fairly good nick. If only she could have waited another month: with her newfound wealth she could have done better – at least have someone with both legs intact.

On the other hand, the born-again Charles Brunswick was footloose and fancy free. He travelled the world first-class, shedding bits of Solihull along the way, but after his third Grand Tour he discovered that England wasn't such a bad place after all. He continued his carousel with the smart sets in Mayfair and when that palled he bought himself a commission in a fashionable cavalry regiment, a change of direction that steered him towards hunt balls, regattas, mentions in the gossip columns of *The Times*, *Punch* and *Tatler*, and he was considered to be the second-most eligible bachelor in England – the Prince of Wales came first.

To be fair, only a small percentage of this popularity was due to Charles Brunswick himself. The great attraction was his large bank account at Coutts and wheels were already beginning to churn. At a mess ball Charles was casually introduced to Lady Dorothy Belvedere-FitzNorman, a debutante of no great beauty and not many offers of matrimony even though she came from one of the oldest, most distinguished families in the land, so powerful they were able to maintain a twenty-bedroom mansion set in thousands of acres of Shropshire countryside, with no money. This lack of funds is not uncommon among the high-bred aristocracy. However, one thing they all have in common, although money is never mentioned, is a nose for it.

So the meeting between the dashing, rich, young subaltern and Lady Dorothy was certainly not by chance. From this came an invitation to a hunt ball – and by chance Lady Dorothy was present – followed by a weekend at a country house, and again by chance another of the guests was Lady Dorothy. His leaves from the regiment became more frequent and in many cases extended. His Commanding Officer began addressing him as 'Charles, old boy'. He was already in the machine and no match for the establishment and inevitably in August 1923, hardly knowing what day it was, Charles found himself walking under the archway of sabres held up by his fellow officers, Lady Dorothy on his arm. And, like it or not, he was now married and the regimental band was playing 'Here Comes The Bride' to prove it.

The only bright spot at the wedding for Charles was again meeting his sister Emily, who was now heavily pregnant. Her husband, ex-Lance Corporal Jampton, seemed jollier than on their last meeting. And so he should. He'd certainly fallen on his feet, or to be more precise his foot. Emily had laughingly pointed to her husband's artificial leg. 'If that bullet had been eight inches higher I wouldn't be having this,' she whispered, patting her extended stomach.

Years later Charles Brunswick was to curse the aim of that unknown German sniper who missed the target by eight inches. It would have saved a lot of heartache.

Colonel Brunswick, white with shock now, read his wife's letter again. 'Dear Brunswick,' it began. She never used the name herself but always addressed him as Brunswick as if he was the boot boy.

Dear Brunswick,
    Wilfred will be arriving, all being well, on or about . . .

She'd told him who the Captain was, the name of the Vice Admiral in overall charge of the convoy – all highly classified information privy only to an exalted few in the Admiralty.

Brunswick slammed the letter on to his desk. Bollocks to all that, he thought. He wasn't going to be saddled with the obnoxious little twat of a nephew. He had enough on his plate being Director of Military Intelligence. The war was going badly enough without the added hassle of having young Jampton under his feet. Brunswick groaned. He, God help him, would be expected to . . . He couldn't think of what he was expected to do but certainly he wouldn't be standing at the foot of the gangplank with a bunch of flowers in his hand and a welcome speech on his lips.

He picked up the letter again. His wife had engineered the posting of Jampton to Alexandria. Why, for God's sake? And a horrible thought struck him. Could his wife and her family be Nazi sympathisers? He shuddered and gulped down his third large whisky of the morning. Then suddenly he was hit by inspiration. No way was he going to be lumbered with the festering presence of his nephew. He smiled as he lifted the telephone and asked to be connected to the Regimental Transport Officer at the docks. Then he poured himself another choda peg. There's more than one way to skin a cat, he thought.

Lieutenant Jampton, the object of this love-and-hate saga, crouched disconsolately in his fifteen-hundredweight. Had it really been only twenty-four hours since he had landed in North Africa? He tried to reconstruct the events as they happened; Aunt Dorothy would want to know every little detail and they were bizarre to say the least.

At two o'clock in the morning the great troop ship had nudged against its berth and even before it was secured he had been tannoyed to report immediately to his disembarkation point on B deck. Jampton remembered the curious stares of other officers as he pushed his way through, feeling a little apprehensive, wondering why he had been picked out to disembark before anybody else, and when he finally came to the top of the gangplank he was reluctant to go any further. He might have been paralysed . . .

He stopped at this point in his recollection.

The bit about being tannoyed would certainly intrigue his Aunt Dorothy. And also his being first off the ship – this would certainly raise her eyebrows. Rapidly in his mind he began to compose his letter. Why not embellish it a little? Why not say that the ship's captain saluted him and the Royal Marine Band played him on to the dock? But as quickly as the thought came, it was cancelled. The Royal Marine Band would not be playing at two o'clock in the morning on the dockside. They were more likely to be playing dance music at a senior officers' club . . . He could imagine his Aunt Dorothy passing his letter around the dinner table with pride and a tearful eye. He went on with his composition. It was all harmless of course, and it was codswallop. In truth, the facts of the matter were slightly different. Indeed there was a vast gulf between the ramblings of Jampton's adolescent mind and what actually happened.

Thousands of eyes watched the young Lieutenant as he stood at the top of the gangplank gazing down at the unknown, blacked-out dockside of Alexandria. Shaded blue torches bobbed and weaved between pools of bright moonlight like heavily sedated fireflies. He might have stood there until the end of the war, when someone remarked, 'What's he waiting for, the National Anthem?'

This caused a roar of laughter and Lieutenant Jampton, relieved that in the darkness they couldn't see his face, struggled down the gangplank dragging his weighty blue suitcase. It was only when he got to the bottom that he realised the rest of his kit was still on board. He turned to make his way back up again, but his path was blocked by a beared sailor who had followed him down.

'It's all right, sir, I've got the rest of your kit here,' he said. Over one shoulder he carried Jampton's bedroll and haversack and under his other arm was the portable, collapsible canvas bath (Officers, For The Use Of), and without stopping he strode purposefully along the dock.

The young officer picked up his suitcase with an almighty effort and scurried to catch up, trying to block his ears to the whistles, jeers and catcalls that came from the massed troops leaning over the rails of the lower decks. The seaman stopped behind a fifteen-hundredweight parked in front of the Regimental Transport Office and dumped his load in the back. Unfortunately, this area was lit by the moon as if from a spotlight in the theatre, and when Jampton staggered out of the blackness with his suitcase the sailor turned towards him and saluted. Jampton put down his suitcase in order to return the salute. A great cheer went up from the ship at this soldierly tableau. The sailor escaped into the obscurity of the dock. Lieutenant Jampton grunted as he picked up his suitcase again and was about to heave it in the back of the wagon when a very young soldier in a too big battledress poured out of the cab.

'Private Gratwick, sir, your driver.' He stamped to attention and snapped up a salute.

Jampton put down his suitcase again and returned the compliment. When the door of the office burst open a red-faced Major wearing an armband identifying him as the Regimental Transport Officer stared unbelievingly at these two idiots facing each other at the salute.

'Never mind all that crap,' he snarled. 'If it's Lieutenant Jampton, get yourself in here pronto.'

Jampton followed him into the little office.

'Right,' said the RTO without preamble. 'Here's your move-ment orders. Special Ordnance Group, about 200 miles in the blue.'

Jampton looked baffled. 'Blue, sir?' he asked.

'Desert to you, laddie,' replied the Major not unkindly. He handed over the movement orders.

A phone rang and the Major lifted the receiver, and whilst he talked into it Jampton read his orders. 'You are to proceed immediately to Special Ordnance Group at the following map reference. Report to Sergeant Major Puller on arrival.' Jampton reread the orders. He was to report to a Sergeant Major whoever he was? It was a mistake surely; an officer shouldn't report to an NCO. He looked over to the Major, who was just putting down the receiver. He turned to Jampton.

'Still here?' he asked.

Jampton proffered him the Movement Orders. 'There must be some mistake, sir. It says here that I'm to report to a Sergeant Major.'

'Well, what's wrong with that?' asked the RTO.

'I'm sorry, sir, but I was under the impression that when an officer joined a new unit, it is customary to report to the CO.'

The RTO snatched the papers and put on his spectacles. Angrily he scanned the papers, then he slapped them triumphantly. Patiently he held the orders out so that Jampton could see them.

'If you read on a litle bit more,' he said as if each utterance gave him pain, 'you'll see that this Sergeant Major Puller will then acquaint you with all the information you require as you take command.'

He thrust the papers back into Jampton's hand. 'And that means you, m'lad. You're it.'

Lieutenant Jampton was dumbstruck. Commanding Officer. He stared unseeing at the paper in his hand. 'Commanding Officer,' he whispered. It took his breath away. First posting, first command.

'It's only an Ordnance mob,' said the Major. 'It's not a post in the Cabinet. Now bugger off, I've got work to do.'

Jampton turned to leave as if in a trance.

'Good luck, lad,' said the RTO. 'You'll find a map amongst those papers.'

'A map?' repeated Jampton, still dazed.

'Yes, but don't worry about that now. I've tacked you on to the back of a convoy of six three-tonners that will take you more than halfway.'

'And what happens then?' asked Jampton fearfully.

The RTO looked at his watch, exasperated. 'Look, sonny,' he said, 'I would love to come with you and show you the way but I've got a bloody big troop ship to unload – preferably,' he added, 'before Rommel gets here.' With this he gave Jampton a push and slammed the door.

Still in another world, Jampton took his seat beside his driver. In front of them was the back end of the last vehicle in the convoy. A Captain walked down the line of trucks and tapped on the window of the fifteen-hundredweight. Gratwick hurriedly wound it down.

'All set?' asked the Captain.

'Yes, sir,' mumbled Gratwick.

'Good. Just keep your distance, but whatever you do don't lose sight of the tail lights of that truck in front. Otherwise you might end up in the Transvaal.'

'Right, sir,' squeaked Gratwick sitting to attention, looking directly ahead.

The Captain nodded and without another word strode up the line of vehicles and climbed into the leading one, and the convoy moved off smoothly; that is, all except for the little fifteen-hundredweight at the rear, which leapt forward in a series of frantic spasmodic jerks as if eager to get at Rommel's jugular. It finally stalled.

Jampton picked his hat up from the floor of the cab and murmured, 'Been in Africa long?'

'No, sir,' mumbled Gratwick, desperately trying to start the motor. 'I came over on the same ship as you.'

Jampton was a little peeved. He hadn't been the first to disembark after all. The motor roared into life and with a better takeoff they found the convoy waiting patiently for them at the dock gates.

A bright flash that lit up the inside of the cab followed by a loud bang suddenly jerked Jampton out of his dockside reverie. It came from the direction the tanks had taken. Had they fired at something? Had they run into a minefield? He wheeled round to the empty driver's seat. Where the dickens was Gratwick? He desperately needed reassurance. He shivered and pulled his sleeping bag tighter around his thin shoulders. What he wouldn't have given for a steaming hot bath. Did it ever get light in this part of the world? he wondered.

Then he remembered that Gratwick was still out there somewhere. Surely he must have finished by now. He thought about his driver for a moment and wasn't terribly encouraged. If the rest of the British Army was like him, it was going to be a long uphill struggle.

A sudden panic gripped him. Had the fool finished his toilet and then walked away in an entirely different direction? His thoughts immediately turned to the gallant Captain Oates in the Scott Expedition. 'I'm going out now, I may be some time,' and with these historic words Oates had left the tent to be lost for ever in the Antarctic wastes.

Had his driver emulated Captain Oates? No, it was unthinkable. In any case 'I'm just whipping out for a crap, sir' wasn't exactly heroic. But then another horrific thought crossed his mind. Could it be that Gratwick had crouched and relieved himself on to an antipersonnel mine? Another flash followed by a bang. Thank God Gratwick was out there somewhere alive and well. After more worrying minutes he decided to parp the horn. But even as he reached out for the wheel second thoughts stopped him. What if the Germans had listening devices in the desert? He had visions of a Panzer Corps homing in on him, and suddenly his bowels weren't exactly secure. Firing a Very pistol was also out of the question. If a battle was being prepared, it might easily start off the attack prematurely.

But how to contact Gratwick? A brilliant idea struck him, and taking a shaded torch from under the dashboard, he climbed out and gave three quick flashes to the north, similarly to the west and south, and shivering he waited and listened. But all he could hear was the thumping of his heart and the chattering of his teeth. Good grief, he'd never been so cold in his life.

Warmth now took precedence over the missing Gratwick. And in a sudden flash of inspiration he thought of his suitcase in the back of the fifteen-hundredweight. Of course, what a fool he'd been, what a ninny. Why hadn't he thought of it before? In the suitcase there were two Fair Isle jumpers, his long trousers and his greatcoat. Oh blessed suitcase! He shuffled round to the back of the truck and clambered in. His groping hands encountered the canvas of his pack, his portable bed. Then he touched what felt like a blanket. He was puzzled. Was it slightly warm? He slid his hand over it and Gratwick sat up with a jerk, startling Jampton, who let out a frightened yelp.

From the darkness came Gratwick's voice, outraged. 'Let's have less of that – I'm not one of them.'

Jampton tried to gain the initiative. 'One of what?' he asked bewildered.

'A brown hatter,' blurted out Gratwick.

The Lieutenant hadn't the foggiest idea what Gratwick was on about, but he most certainly objected to being addressed in this surly manner.

'May I remind you, Gratwick, you are speaking to your superior officer.'

The driver, now fully awake and regretting his outburst, replied, 'I'm sorry, sir, but I thought –'

'Never mind what you thought,' squeaked Jampton. 'You're not paid to think.'

It was a ludicrous exchange, two voices in the middle of nowhere.

'Next time,' went on Jampton, 'when you leave your post to relieve yourself, you will report back to me immediately on completing and not go sneaking into the back of the truck without my permission.'

In the blackness Gratwick listened with tongue out and thumbs against his head while he waggled his fingers.

'Is that clear?' said Jampton.

'Yes, sir.'

'Good.'

Jampton climbed out over the tailgate. 'Now,' he said, 'if you will hand me my suitcase, then return to your post, which is at the wheel . . .'

There was a silence from inside the truck.

'Did you hear what I said?' piped Jampton. 'My suitcase.'

Again there was a pause, then, 'What suitcase, sir?'

'My blue suitcase,' replied Jampton impatiently, 'I left it outside the RTO's office on the dockside.'

'Yes, sir, I remember it,' said Gratwick.

'Well?' asked Jampton, a sickening feeling beginning to stir inside him. He knew how this conversation was going to end.

'Didn't you put it on the back?' he prompted.

'No, sir,' replied Gratwick, 'nobody mentioned it.'

Mercifully, his Commanding Officer's face was indiscernible in the dark. It's not a pretty sight to see a man weep but Jampton was on the verge. His nerves were shredded; he wanted to fling himself down screaming and kick his heels against the hard surface of the desert. But before he could begin his tantrum, a lighter thought saved him. After all, the suitcase had his name and rank stencilled all over it. Surely the RTO would send it on. Of course – that's what would happen. Who knew? It may even be waiting for him at the Special Ordnance Group even before he arrived. With this optimism, he walked round the truck and swung himself into the cab. Gratwick followed and they sat together in surly silence for about ten minutes.

Jampton couldn't rid his mind of 'brown hatter'. What the dickens had Gratwick meant? The only solution he could come up with was that, before his call-up, Gratwick had sat high up on the Twinings tea van whipping up a team of matching horses. Yes, that must be it. They all wore brown bowlers. After satisfying himself with this observation he turned to look out of the side window and noticed that the stars were beginning to lose their glitter and the darkness on the ground seemed to be lightening. The dim shape of the rocks ahead was now faintly recognisable. It was the false dawn but Jampton wasn't to know this. He decided to follow the example of the tanks and move off. He settled in his seat and consulted his wrist compass, shook his arm, peered at it again and ordered the advance. His driver switched on the engine and they moved off in the direction of his CO's pointing finger.

Gratwick was desperate to keep the steering wheel firm so that he might continue in a straight line on a south-southeast bearing. He wasn't unduly worried: his job was to drive. Where they ended up wasn't his pigeon – that was the officer's responsibility.

On the other hand, Lieutenant Jampton was dead worried. It didn't seem to be getting any lighter and he had little faith in his driver, but as the miles went by he was less enthusiastic with the south-southeast direction. It was highly probable they would miss their objective by miles. Further doubts crept into his thoughts. He remembered vividly the tank man saying south-southeast but then had he *meant* south-southeast or did he have a stutter? At least, he thought, trying to cheer himself up, it's getting light.

THREE

At the beginning of the desert campaign in North Africa, the 41st Light Infantry were at the sharp end under the command of General Wavell, and were known as the Cyrenaica Force. They almost succeeded in driving the Italians out of Africa but these heady victories ended when the Afrika Korps under the command of Kesselring and a little-known General called Rommel entered the lists, and this was an entirely different kettle of fish. The British were now forced back, conceding all the ground gained from the Italians. The 41st Light Infanty were fighting a rearguard action, backtracking all the way to Tobruk ... It was their last battle.

When the Stukas peeled out of the dawn skies to begin the attack, it heralded the last rites of the sadly depleted 41st Infantry. The screams and crash of the bombs was augmented by a bombardment from the eighty-eights of the German artillery. Flames and smoke, the bangs of exploding shells, the rattle of small-arms fire, the screams and curses, it was a Dante's *Inferno* and in the midst of this madness the panzer tanks bucked and rocked over the rubble and smoking masonry followed by the infantry divisions of the Afrika Korps.

By the afternoon, Sergeant Major Puller, on the point of exhaustion, found himself in charge of what was left of the 41st, the command post having suffered a direct hit and all of the officers killed or wounded. He made up his mind quickly. Enough was enough – the regiment was finished. He hadn't enough men left to form a decent glee club and he passed the word round they would be pulling out under cover of darkness. But there was an hour of daylight left and as they retreated street by street the Sergeant Major began to wonder how many would be left by the time it got dark.

Mercifully, when night fell, Sergeant Major Puller, commandeering all the serviceable transport he could find, assembled his convoy and travelled as fast as the rubble-strewn streets and the slowest of the vehicles would allow. Fortune was with them. On the outskirts they found gaps in the perimeter wire and, luckiest of all, some white tape had been put down leading them through a heavy minefield, and thence into the blue, where they stopped. Sergeant Major Puller, after a quick check that the convoy was in order, swung himself into the lead truck and followed his compass on an easterly course. His intention was to put as much distance as he could between his pathetic convoy and the blood-red sky, the flashes and the explosions that were once Tobruk.

Some hours later when the sun rose, unconcerned, to light up the desert, Sergeant Major Puller finally called a halt. They'd lost one vehicle when the back axle broke. Now they were six three-tonners, a half-track and a fifteen-hundredweight. The Sergeant Major was the only one to alight; the rest slumped and slept, too weary and dispirited to move. He walked over to the second three-tonner and checked over his supplies, jerry cans of water, thank God, and food packs. But still the situation was critical. He reckoned this sustenance would last three or four days at the most. If they didn't stock up soon, they may as well have stayed in Tobruk. He decided to go at once to Alexandria and seek help. He would take two vehicles and, siphoning the petrol from the other wagons into five-gallon drums, he set out for Alexandria.

Private Dusty Miller was driving the lead truck accompanied by the Sergeant Major, while the second three-tonner was driven by Private Sparks, and his passenger was a girl wrapped in a blanket, white-faced and shell-shocked. There didn't appear to be any superficial damage but God knew what state her innards were in. And besides, she was the only woman and you couldn't leave a woman in the desert. So the Sergeant Major decreed she should go with them and they'd deliver her to the military hospital. Poor little sod, thought Sparks. It was he who had rescued her from the pile of rubble that used to be the Hotel Imperial and it had been a close-run thing.

His mind went back a day. He remembered the heat and the dust and noise as he'd been spread-eagled on a pile of debris, Bren gun levelled at a corner of the street some three hundred yards away awaiting the enemy infantry or, worse, a panzer tank to poke its nose round the corner. Shells had been crashing round him too close for comfort and he had been about to scamper to a better place of concealment when suddenly he froze as something brushed gently against his ankle. He had snatched his leg away with revulsion (he smiled wryly now at the recollection). He'd thought it was a bloody rat, but as he looked round he saw that it was a hand – white, small and human. With a quick glance to the street corner, he'd left his Bren gun and scrabbled away at the rubble. From a doorway opposite, Dusty Miller saw what was happening and dashed over and gave him a hand to free whoever it was. It turned out to be a girl. By the time they'd dug her out, the German infantry were edging round the corner of the street. While Sparks stumbled back carrying the girl, it was Miller who'd covered their retreat.

Sparks paused in his recollections and gave the girl a sidelong glance and offered her his water bottle, but she ignored it, gazing straight ahead with unblinking eyes, and for one frightening moment he thought she was dead. But then she took the bottle from him and he breathed a sigh of relief. Eventually, when they arrived in Alexandria, the Sergeant Major alighted from the truck and brushed some of the sand and dust from his uniform. He made his way to the truck behind and said to Sparks, 'See her to the hospital first and I'll meet you here at eight o'clock sharp tomorrow morning. I'll have something sorted out by then. I've told Miller.' He slapped his hand against the door and Sparks pulled into the traffic while Miller, in the second truck, followed.

The girl riding in the cab with Sparks had still not uttered a word but at least she looked more alive as she pointed out the directions – presumably, Sparks thought, to the hospital. But he began to have doubts when she directed him up a narrow street. This couldn't be the way, surely. Had her experience in Tobruk unhinged her mind? Was he driving around haphazardly with a nutcase? He was almost convinced when after about a hundred yards she made a sign that he stop. He did, and looked out of his side window to see a large shop front and over the top a sign: ABDUL BEN HUSSEIN, IMPORT AND EXPORT. In the window itself was a load of tourist rubbish: brass urns, cheap costume jewellery, ivory and some tatty-looking rugs.

Miller came round to his door and looked up at Sparks. 'Buying her a present, are you?'

But the girl leant across Sparks and pressed the horn several times.

Sparks looked down at Miller's face and raised his eyebrows. 'She's lost her marbles,' he explained, but Miller wasn't listening. He was looking over Sparks's shoulder at something else.

'Bloody hell,' he breathed.

The whole shop front was swinging slowly inward and when it finally stopped the girl motioned for Sparks to drive in. He did so and Miller hauled himself into his own truck and followed. It was a bloody big garage; it was more than that, there was room for a small tank regiment. They were suddenly plunged into darkness as the shop front swung back into place. A light came on – it couldn't have been more than a forty-watt and didn't do much to relieve the gloom. Sparks jumped to the ground and came round the opposite side to lift the girl down. He was intrigued with his surroundings; after all it could be the hospital's back entrance. More light spilled in as a door opened and a fat Egyptian in fez and European suit minced down two steps to greet them. His face lit up when he saw the girl and they embraced each other.

'Yasmin, my little desert flower. I thought you had forgotten your poor old uncle.'

It was then the girl spoke for the first time. 'These are my friends. I think his name is Miller.'

The fat man bowed. This must be Abdul, Sparks thought.

'And this one –' her voice softened '– is Sparks.'

Sparks shuffled his feet and nodded, embarrassed when she added, 'He saved my life.'

Abdul's face brightened. 'Ah then, you will be my honoured guests tonight. My house is your house.' He bowed. 'Come, Yasmin,' he said, 'we have much to talk about.'

Sparks and Miller looked at each other, horrified. They didn't want to spend the night here. They knew a couple of better places in town where they could whoop it up and they wouldn't have to sit cross-legged on a cushion drinking tea.

'Yes, well, er, thanks for the invitation but . . .' He tailed off. The fat man, arm round the girl's shoulder, was going up two steps and through the inner door. Miller shrugged.

'Ten minutes, that's all,' he hissed to his mate, and they followed.

Sergeant Major Puller didn't seem to be having too much luck either. Alexandria was a madhouse; nobody wanted to be bothered with his problems, they had enough of their own, and he was shuttled from one authority to another. They were all too busy burning code books, depositions, unit strengths, movement orders – in fact, almost everything except letters from home ended up in the back of the furnace. The Sergeant Major was now desperate. He had about eighty men way out in the desert with not much food and very little water.

He thought of his options. In the middle of all this disorganisation and muddle, it would have been easy for him to walk into any motor pool and load up at the divisional Quartermaster Stores, but he knew this wouldn't be enough, merely a sticking plaster on an amputation. Then he suddenly remembered his old mate, an RSM of the Royal Army Service Corps. He might not even be in Alex – he might even be dead – but it was a chance the Sergeant Major had to take. It was as he was about to leap into a taxi that he heard his name being called.

'Sergeant Major Puller?' the voice enquired.

He turned curiously and then snapped rigidly to attention and saluted. Colonel Brunswick didn't return the salute, but stuck out his hand.

'Sergeant Major Puller.' He beamed. 'I heard you were in Alex ruffling a few feathers.'

The Sergeant Major shook his hand warmly. 'Good to see you again, sir. Long time.'

'Indeed it is,' replied the Colonel. 'Hyderabad in '38 if I'm not mistaken.'

'Yes, sir, happy days.'

The taxi was still waiting but Colonel Brunswick dismissed it with a peremptory wave. The driver shouted a stream of obscenities in Arabic and sped off.

'And the same to you,' shouted the Colonel after him. Turning back to the Sergeant Major he said, 'Right then, come with me and we'll see if we can't solve some of your problems.'

Reminiscences of old times, large whiskies – then the Sergeant Major poured out his troubles. Colonel Brunswick listened without interruption and then buzzed for his Adjutant and while they waited the Colonel poured a third glass for him. Ten minutes later Sergeant Major Puller had to repeat his problems to the Adjutant, who took notes and finally rose.

'Right, sir, I'll see what I can do.'

Colonel Brunswick looked at him steadily.

'Don't see what you can do, Jimmy, do it. Tomorrow,' he went on, 'Sergeant Major Puller must be on his way across the desert with mission accomplished.'

'Yes, sir,' replied the Adjutant, and left.

Sparks and Miller were still guests of Abdul ben Hussein but they were in a better frame of mind. They were seated at a table smiling at a bottle of Johnny Walker Black Label but this was only the beginning of the joy to come. They had already consumed a magnificent four-course meal and were about to make their excuses and exploit the night life of Alexandria when a small black man in a tuxedo came in and began to pick out a gentle tune on the piano. Abdul followed with a bevy of girls, introducing them all one by one. Beaming, he said, 'Take your pick, you are my guests tonight.' The girls were an international blend of beauty and elegance; these were Abdul's words and he wasn't far out.

The two soldiers couldn't believe their luck. They sat there stunned, then Miller relaxed and his face broke into a broad grin. Immediately all the girls, who had been looking a little apprehensive, smiled back and the ice began to break. They subsequently learned that Abdul not only owned the nightclub they were in but on the floors above were several well-furnished bedrooms. In fact, Abdul also ran the best brothel in North Africa and he wasn't backward in exercising a little trade in hashish ... It was a memorable night.

They didn't see the girl, Yasmin, again until the following morning, and it seemed that a good night's sleep had done the trick – she wasn't half bad. After bidding her uncle farewell she'd climbed up in the cab with Sparks and, strangely enough, it seemed perfectly natural.

'You'll have to show me where the hospital is,' he said.

She looked at him with wide eyes. 'Why do you want the hospital?' she asked. 'Are you not well?'

'There's nothing wrong with me,' said Sparks. 'It's you.'

She smiled. 'I'm fully recovered, thank you.' And she settled back.

'Where to?' he asked.

She shrugged. 'With you,' she said.

Sparks laughed. He hadn't quite sobered up and it didn't seem like such a bad idea.

At five minutes to eight o'clock Sergeant Major Puller waited for his two three-tonners. His hangover hadn't quite caught up with him and he was in a good frame of mind with a pocketful of orders stamped and signed giving him permission to draw this and to draw that from the stores. In fact, he had permission for almost anything that could be put on the truck. Two lorries approached and pulled up in front of him. He noticed the girl in the cab and he strolled over.

'Feeling better?' he asked.

'Yes, thanks,' she replied.

The Sergeant Major looked at her and nodded. There didn't seem to be anything else to say. He clambered up beside Miller and they set off for the Supply Depot.

Two hundred miles away in the desert, somewhere around midnight, Puller's nomads – hungry, thirsty, and still reliving the horrors of Tobruk – huddled over fires or tried desperately to sleep in the back of their three-tonners. It wasn't the best policy to light fires after dark but on this occasion it turned out to be a godsend. Those pinpoints of light were a homing beacon for Sergeant Major Puller's convoy of vital life-support supplies: tents, uniforms, blankets, and so forth, and, even more importantly, food and, best of all, two water bowsers. It was going to be like Christmas. In addition to the necessary supplies, there were plenty of cigarettes, boiled sweets and, for recreation, cricket bats, cricket balls, footballs and pingpong balls. He could have had a full-sized billiards table but transport was the problem. (In any case, the balls for this had been lost in a slight fracas with some American GIs.) And to cater for the less energetic and less erudite minority there were snakes and ladders and ludo. In order to facilitate further supplies, they were given the official title Special Ordnance Group, under the temporary command of Sergeant Major Puller.

And three weeks later they were pretty well organised. For what, it would be anybody's guess – but at least they were fed and watered and receiving regular supplies. A fair description would be that it was the only rest home in the western desert.

* * *

But their days were numbered. Even now an officer was on his way to take overall command, albeit a Second Lieutenant. Even had they been privy to this information they would have greeted the news with a wave of indifference. Little did they know they would have made a grave mistake in being too complacent. This was no ordinary Second Lieutenant: this was Wilfred Ronaldsway Jampton.

The day broke sunnily, as it had done for thousands of years, and the SOG awoke cursing and scratching as Reveille broke the silence. The bandsman blew his bugle from a horizontal position, staying awake just long enough to complete the piece. It was his first duty on awakening, whenever that was. Sometimes he didn't get up until well after midday. In five minutes it was full daylight after the blackness of the African night, but it would be another hour before the sun rose over the horizon to warm the land. Coughing with the cold and 'V' cigarettes, those with appetites shuffled like zombies to the cook's marquee. When the sun rose it would be hot, too hot for comfort, and the flies weren't up yet. In fact, breakfast time would have been the best part of the day if it wasn't for the breakfast. By the time the sun was appearing over the horizon, those who had been filing past the cooks for powdered egg and something else were now forming up outside the latrines.

But all the attention was focused on the marquee that housed the MO and served as a hospital. Nine o'clock was sick parade but it was a joke. If there was anything that bothered anybody, they visited the MO at any time of the day or night, and if he was sober he usually prescribed aspirins, or grazes and desert sores were painted with gentian violet, a blue dye, and as desert sores were commonplace most of the unit looked like an ancient tribe of Iceni with not enough woad to go round.

However, on this momentous morning there was a mob craning and bobbing to see round the man in front into the dim interior of the tent. Only the desperate ones stayed in line for the latrines. Even the Sergeant Major, freshly shaven, strolled across to see what the commotion was about.

'It's Miller, sir,' said one of the spectators helpfully.

The Sergeant Major nodded; he'd had a suspicion it might be. Rifleman Miller had been a good infantryman with the old 41st. He had joined the Army without any feeling of patriotism, King and country. His had been a straight choice. The magistrate had

had enough, either he enlisted or it was prison again. Miller hadn't taken long to make up his mind. Escape from prison was almost impossible but there were no bars round an Army Camp. Now he was up to his old tricks and there weren't many he didn't know.

'Get out,' came the MO's voice from inside the marquee, and the crowd pulled back as Miller was hustled blinking into the harsh sunlight.

The lads nudged one another in delighted anticipation. Most of them, unlike the Sergeant Major, had known Dusty Miller only since Tobruk, but he had established himself as camp comedian. The MO ducked out after him, the effort of being in the bright new sun bringing out pimples of the morning's gin on to his forehead. He belched softly; then, bending again, he scooped up a handful of sand.

'This is sand, see, sand.' A little of it trickled through his fingers.

Miller stared at him uncomprehendingly and looked at the crowd in puzzlement.

A wag at the back shouted, 'Who got you ready then?' and a laugh went up.

Dusty Miller was in full uniform, greatcoat buttoned up to the neck with a blanket round his shoulders and a balaclava underneath his tin helmet. He held his gloved hands to the crowd as if to say 'What's the matter with the MO this morning?'.

The MO struggled to maintain his composure. 'If this was snow I'd be able to make a snowman, wouldn't I?'

The crowd latched on, and there were a few giggles.

'Do you understand, Miller? We are not in the frozen north. This is not snow; this is desert sand, limestone dust and camel droppings.'

This brought a better response from the lads; this gave them the complete picture. Miller was realising that what had once seemed a good idea was dribbling away like the sand in the MO's cupped fists. He cleared his throat and prepared to cut his losses.

'I didn't say it *was* snow, sir. I said it *felt* like snow.' He beamed at the Sergeant Major. 'Oh yes, I can see it's sand now. It's warm. But when I got up I was cold and shivering and the next thing I remember I'm standing at your table.'

The MO wasn't letting him off lightly. 'Yes,' he replied silkily. 'You staggered in and said if they don't find us today we'll have to eat one of the dogs.'

This brought a howl from the crowd. After all, they'd been starved of entertainment and this was better than Flanagan and Allen.

Miller eyed the MO with a puzzled expression. 'I don't remember saying that, sir.'

'Well you did,' yelled the MO, losing his cool. 'And although your memory has been on the blink lately, you always seem to remember where my damn tent is.'

He held on to the guy rope for support; this last effort had brought the sweat pouring down his face. He decided to end the matter, have a large gin and go back to bed.

'Sar'nt Major,' he croaked.

'Sah.' The Sergeant Major sprang to attention.

'This man is malingering. Put him on extra guard duty.'

With that he staggered back into the marquee to leave the rest of the sick to the medical orderly. The Sergeant Major relaxed and stared at Dusty Miller thoughtfully. The crowd, now sensing that the morning's entertainment was over, began to disperse.

The Sergeant Major shook his head in despair. 'Well, my little desert flower, you've done it again, haven't you?'

Miller shuffled his feet and stared off into the far distance; he shrugged and looked back at the Sergeant Major. They had been togther since '36 when the Sergeant Major was a corporal so they had the measure of each other.

The Sergeant Major shook his head again and sighed deeply. 'OK, get your bedding off and relieve Taylor in the Bren pit!'

Miller rallied. 'But, Sar'nt Major, I'm supposed to be off duty.'

The Sergeant Major took a step forward until his nose was within an inch of Miller's. 'Listen, lad, there's no off-duty till the war's over, and with blokes like you around I can't see any possibility of that.'

Miller sulkily took the blanket from his shoulders and was about to unfasten the buttons of his greatcoat. The Sergeant Major was quicker.

'Leave those buttons alone,' he rasped. 'I want you on guard duty properly wrapped up and properly dressed.'

Miller's mouth fell open. 'But, Sar'nt Major, it's hot now and it'll get hotter.'

The Sergeant Major smiled grimly. 'Yes, it will, won't it? But we don't want you catching cold again, do we?'

Miller was about to reply but the Sergeant Major cut him short. 'Ten-*shun* . . . right turn at the double to the Bren pit, eff right, eff right . . .' and Miller doubled off to the jeers of his mates in the sick queue outside the MO's tent.

One wag shouted after him, 'At least you won't get frostbite.' The outpatients laughed good-humouredly and the Sergeant Major whirled angrily towards them.

'If you feel good enough to laugh you don't belong in a sick parade. Do something useful for a change.' And sheepishly they turned away and dispersed.

In the Bren pit Private Sparks eyed his mate Dusty Miller as he joined him and wondered idly why he was well wrapped up. Were they expecting bad weather?

Miller took a swig from his water bottle. What was visible of his face glistened with sweat. He estimated he had already lost half a stone in weight.

Sparks shook his head sadly. 'Do you know,' he said, 'if I was MO I would let you out on the grounds of sheer stupidity.'

'Yes, but this one's never sober,' growled Miller. 'Four days I've been going around in this lot and he didn't take a blind bit of notice.'

'I've watched you,' replied Sparks, 'staggering about, flapping your arms, blowing on your hands: pathetic.'

Miller shrugged and muttered bitterly. 'He used to be a good MO too. I fell at his feet yesterday and he just stepped over me.'

Sparks snorted; even he was beginning to sweat now. Just looking at his mate was enough. Then he laughed. 'You've been in this lot long enough to learn there's no way you can get out on a mental kick. They can see through it a mile off. You'd be better off acting normal – you'd stand a better chance then.'

There was a pause, then Miller spoke defensively. 'It has been done though.'

Sparks's eyebrow went up. 'Oh yes,' he replied, 'but as far as I can recall only once and that was in my old regiment at Catterick, but there wasn't a war then.' He lifted the Bren gun from the sandbags and took out an oily rag.

Miller looked at him quickly. This was Sparks all over. He would start something and then leave it dangling in the air while he went off to do something else. But he wasn't going to get away with it this time. 'What happened?' said Miller.

Sparks looked up. 'Eh?'

Miller looked away in exasperation. 'What happened to the bloke at Catterick?' he said as if talking to a child.

'Oh him,' said Sparks. 'He was really off his rocker, he was. He thought the Adjutant was his mother.'

'Get away,' replied Miller disbelieving.

'He really starved once. He wouldn't eat till the Adjutant fed him with a spoon, and if he had meat the Adjutant had to cut it up for him.'

Miller's heart sank. They didn't have an Adjutant for starters and meat only came out of bully beef tins so what might have been a good idea was a non-starter. He eyed Sparks speculatively. 'Was he really round the twist?'

'Oh yes,' replied Sparks. 'He used to cry every night and wet his bed.'

Miller snorted. Sparks looked directly at him. 'I ought to know,' he said, 'I was in the bunk underneath.'

Miller was intrigued, visualising the scene. Then he pulled himself together. 'Yes, but in the end, this bloke, did he work his ticket?'

Sparks examined the breech of the gun. 'Like I told you,' he said, 'the last I saw of him he was in the back of a three-tonner with the Adjutant reading him *Jack and the Beanstalk*, and they took him to the nuthouse.'

'Was he in there long?' asked Miller after a pause.

'Nah, not long,' said Sparks. 'He was out in a couple of months.' He took a long swig from his water bottle and, slapping back the cork, said, 'They kept the Adjutant though.'

Miller by this time was almost bubbling with heat. Even putting a cigarette to his lips brought another rash of perspiration but his mind was on the Adjutant.

'How long ago was this?' he asked.

But Sparks wasn't listening. He was looking far beyond the opposite end of the camp.

The Sergeant Major, standing outside the mess tent holding a mug full of cold tea, was also watching the approach of the vehicle. The MO emerged from his tent and followed the Sergeant Major's gaze.

'One of ours?' asked the MO dispassionately.

The Sergeant Major nodded. 'Looks like it, sir.' He shaded his eyes.

When it was about two hundred yards away, the vehicle suddenly changed direction and shot behind a rocky escarpment.

The MO, swishing his gin and tonic round his glass, looked quizzically at the Sergeant Major who shrugged back at him. They waited a few moments, then a flash from the top of the small rise told them they were being observed through binoculars.

The MO took a deep swig and murmured, 'Whoever it is, he's very interested in us.'

'Yes,' said the Sergeant Major laconically. The MO glanced down at his glass and found it was empty. 'Let me know what transpires,' he said and ducked back into his tent for a refill.

After what seemed an age, the small truck re-emerged and trundled its way warily forward. The Sergeant Major, identifying it as a fifteen-hundredweight, watched as it groaned up the slight incline towards the camp. Men strolled from the mess tent with bulging mouths to view the arrival; more faces poked around tent flaps and a row of heads appeared above the canvas wall of a latrine looking for all the world like a coconut shy at a vicar's tea party. All silently observed the arrival of the labouring vehicle. Apart from the sound of its approach, the camp was gripped in an unnatural stillness.

The silence was suddenly broken by a shattering, racking early-morning cough as a tall thin figure in a tin hat, khaki vest and boots staggered from his tent in order to shake the detritus of the night from his blanket – sand, dust, cigarette ash. From the Sergeant Major's point of view it looked as if he were flagging the vehicle down. In any event it slowed, whereupon the barely dressed swaddie stepped forward holding the blanket in front of the bonnet of the fifteen-hundredweight and then, in the style of a matador at a bullfight, he whirled the blanket round him executing a passable veronica. '*Olé!*' – the cry went up from a dozen of the lads followed by a laugh. The blanket man turned to them and bowed low to acknowledge the *Olé*s. Then he turned back to the vehicle. As the occupant said something, the matador took a small stub of a cigarette from his lips, bending forward while he had his second rattling cough of the day, and, straightening, returned the stub to his lips and pointed in the direction of the SM.

Jampton looked over to the Sergeant Major and back to the wheezing matador. He wanted to say something else but he couldn't think what. He was outraged! When the pseudo-matador had bowed towards the crowd to acknowledge his applause his vest had ridden up and Jampton had found himself staring at a big, bare, hairy backside. Good grief, the Officers' Training Corps hadn't prepared him for anything like this. Bereft of words, he peremptorily signalled Gratwick to drive on and, in the short stretch to the Sergeant Major, Lieutenant Jampton regained some of his composure.

Sergeant Major Puller watched the fifteen-hundredweight approach with dismay. The driver looked exhausted and certainly scarcely old enough to hold a driver's licence. The officer, standing upright and holding on to the windscreen, was covered in white dust. Even his goggles were coated, so how he managed to see anything was a miracle. The Sergeant Major had a sinking feeling in the pit of his stomach. He knew that this was going to be a memorable day and he'd had enough memorable days in the past not to find them pleasurable.

The first thing Lieutenant Jampton noticed was the leather strap on his left wrist bearing a crown. So this was the legendary Sergeant Major Puller. Secretly he complimented himself on his powers of observation.

'Sar'nt Major,' he croaked.

'Sir?' replied the Sergeant Major.

Jampton was irritated. The man had not come to attention, nor had he saluted. Indeed he was standing easy in a very casual manner, hardly befitting a noncommissioned officer in the presence of his superior, and, what was worse, in full view of the men. Jampton thought for a second whether to take issue but decided there would be time for that later.

'This is the Special Ordnance Group, I take it.'

Puller's heart sank. His worst fears were confirmed: this was the man to be in charge. He shook his head sadly and surveyed this dust-covered apparition from a Dickens novel and knew for a certainty the war was lost.

'Well, sir,' he replied, 'we used to be the 41st Light Infantry. There are only a handful of us left now.' He sighed unhappily and continued. 'What we have now is anybody's guess. It's just a hotchpotch of cooks, drivers, Indians, Foreign Legionnaires; in fact all the last people to get out of Tobruk. So yes, you are right, we are now on record as being the Special Ordnance Group.' He grimaced as he said it.

'Ah ha,' said the dust-covered Lieutenant. 'I thought as much.'

He gazed imperiously round at the camp. His sight was impaired by the dust on his goggles but he wasn't going to let on.

He turned to address the Sergeant Major, who, much to his annoyance, was bending down to pet a flea-bitten mongrel. 'Have you had your breakfast yet?' said the Sergeant Major.

Jampton had a sudden vision of a steaming plate of bacon and eggs with mushrooms. He was about to reply when he realised that the Sergeant Major was talking to the dog.

'Sergeant Major,' Jampton commanded tapping the windshield with impatience.

The Sergeant Major shooed the dog towards the mess tent and shouted after it, 'And don't give it any bacon, he's too fat as it is.' Then, brushing his hands together, he turned to the fifteen-hundredweight. 'Yes, sir?'

'Thank you for your time, Sergeant Major,' said Jampton sarcastically. He would put this man in his place, medal ribbons or no medal ribbons. 'Sergeant Major,' he repeated, 'I am Lieutenant Jampton, your new Commanding Officer.'

He paused to let this sink in. The effect, however, was completely ruined as the dog shot out of the mess tent with a large lump of something in its mouth followed by two pans and an irate cook in a dirty white apron. 'Bloody thief,' he yelled. 'If I catch you in here again it'll be dog pie for supper.' He looked over to the Sergeant Major. 'That bloody dog of yours is a menace.' He stooped to pick up the pans and disappeared back into the shade of his domain. The Lieutenant was aghast. If cooks could yell at the senior NCO, where was the discipline?

The Lieutenant glanced down at Gratwick, who was dozing over the wheel. No moral support there. He addressed the Sergeant Major again.

'I repeat, I am Lieutenant Jampton, your new Commanding Officer.'

The Sergeant Major looked coolly up at him as if to say 'so what?' Jampton ignored this dumb insolence. He went on, 'Why was I not challenged?'

'Challenged, sir?'

'Yes, challenged.'

He decided to remove his goggles to give the Sergeant Major the full benefit of the steely glint in his eyes. Unfortunately as he was lifting the strap he caught the visor of his cap and it fell to the floor. As he bent down to retrieve it, he caught his head a fearsome smack on the corner of the windshield. The Sergeant Major winced and looked away. That was all they were short of, an accident-prone CO. The crowd now had all the information they needed and moved away in order to discuss it.

Lieutenant Jampton, trying desperately not to rub his forehead, eyed the Sergeant Major and the surrounding camp. Now that he could see clearly his worst fears were confirmed – it was like a run-down gypsy encampment. He was about to speak when a voice behind him caused more consternation.

'Care for a drink, old boy?'

Jampton whirled round but before he could disgrace himself further the man spoke. 'Allow me to introduce myself. Captain Witherspoon. I'm the Medical Officer.'

Lieutenant Jampton gazed blankly for a moment and pulled himself together. Another man of breeding; at least he would be someone to talk to in the officers' mess.

'Lieutenant Jampton, your new CO.' He stood to attention and saluted.

'Good ho,' said Captain Witherspoon. 'Follow me and I'll crack open another bottle.' He walked unsteadily towards his tent and disappeared.

Jampton stared blankly after him. Was it his birthday? he wondered. If it was he had a birthday every week.

Captain Witherspoon hadn't been one of the original 41st Light Infantry. He'd been MO to the garrison in Tobruk and after his surgery had gone up in smoke and flames he was the last person to join Sergeant Major Puller's retreat. He was hauled over the tailgate of the last three-tonner and all he had with him was his doctor's Gladstone bag containing not, as expected, medical supplies, but four bottles of Gordon's Gin and two of Scotch.

Standing in the Bren pit, Miller and Sparks watched the young Second Lieutenant. The red, burnt legs, white at the back, did not go unnoticed. Miller winked at his mate and said thoughtfully, 'You know, he'd make a good mother.'

Sparks frowned and they carried on with their game, flipping stones at a passing beetle.

Jampton ordered the Sergeant Major to take him on a tour of inspection around the camp. The Sergeant Major hesitated for a moment. What was there to inspect? The Lieutenant was already four paces ahead tapping the guy ropes of the mess tent with his swagger stick.

'Very sloppy, Sergeant Major. See to it.'

'Yes, sir,' replied the Sergeant Major and immediately forgot about it.

Jampton stopped and gazed around him. 'These are all just tents, Sergeant Major,' he said, waving his arm.

'Yes, sir,' replied the Sergeant Major, baffled. What were they supposed to be, for God's sake? Terraced houses?

Jampton eyed him sternly, slapping his stick into the palm of his hand.

'Well, Sergeant Major?' He waited for a moment and then, exasperated, he followed on. 'Where is the guard tent? Where is the mess tent? The orderly room? My tent? The officers' mess? If you have these locations, why are they not signposted?'

The Sergeant Major was an old soldier, too well trained and too much in command of himself to let his anger show – well, some of it. His mouth set in a grim line and his nostrils went white. These were the only visible signs that Jampton had just avoided hospitalisation.

'With respect, sir,' he started, 'there are no signs because over half this lot don't speak English.' He spread the fingers of his left hand and tapped each point off. This conveyed the impression that he knew what he was talking about and it gave his hands something to do so they didn't stray around the scrawn that joined Jampton's head to his shoulders.

He went on.

'The situation here is that we are only temporary, and any day now –'

'Excuses, excuses,' broke in Jampton snappishly, and suddenly he stopped.

One tent, set apart from the others, intrigued him. He minced across to it and poked in his head. It was crammed full of unused cricket balls, bats, footballs in pristine condition – in fact all the sporting paraphernalia the Sergeant Major had so joyfully brought into camp three weeks ago.

'What's all this?' snapped Jampton, withdrawing his head.

'Give 'em time, sir. They'll come round to it.'

The little Lieutenant was appalled. 'This is supposed to be a military camp on active service,' he yelped, 'not a sports centre. What about a swimming pool?' he asked sarcastically.

'Water's the problem, sir,' replied the SM helpfully.

But the bossy young prat wasn't listening. He turned to carry on the camp inspection only to find his path was blocked by a line of washing strung between tents. A large blanket was being pegged to the line. But it wasn't the laundry that had stopped him dead in his tracks. It was the hands doing the pegging: they were delicate and well shaped. His gaze travelled down the blanket – and the bare legs behind it were not the hairy, thick-type legs that had marched across Africa. These limbs would be more at home in the Folies Bergère.

The young Lieutenant looked enquiringly at the Sergeant Major, who sighed and nodded. Jampton went forward and ducked under the washing line and his suspicions were confirmed. It was not only a girl, it was a beautiful girl with long black hair. That's all he took in – he wasn't old enough to look at the rest of her. Instinctively he made as if to take his cap off, then noticed she was wearing an outsize khaki shirt with two stripes sewn on the arms.

The girl turned and moved towards him and stared into his face. Jampton, disconcerted, realised he was in her way and hurriedly stepped back a pace. This was a mistake: he fell over a bucket. The girl watched him without expression but in that short observation she had taken in the small beak nose, the mouth that looked like the slit in a piggy bank and, more important, the one pip on his shoulder. '*Merci*,' she said tonelessly and jabbed the peg on to the blanket.

Jampton struggled to his feet and in order to regain his composure said 'Carry on, ma'am' and went to tap the peak of his cap with his stick in salute. Unfortunately he was in such a tizzy he missed the peak of his cap altogether and nearly knocked his eye out. The Sergeant Major walked away as if he hadn't seen anything. What a pillock, he thought. With the lump on his forehead getting larger by the minute and a streaming red eye, Jampton was a walking wounded – and nobody had laid a finger on him yet.

Jampton ran after the receding figure and planted himself in front of him so he had to stop. 'Well?' he snapped.

'We call her Corporal Smith, sir. Don't know her real name.'

'A foreigner?' asked Jampton.

'Half Arab, half French, I think,' replied the Sergeant Major.

'But what does she do – come in once a week to do the laundry?' queried Jampton.

The Sergeant Major replied, discomfited, 'Well, no, sir. She's also the camp barber and sometimes helps in the sickbay.'

Jampton digested this and raised his head to look over the Sergeant Major's shoulder to the washing, but the girl had already gone. He cleared his throat and looked the Sergeant Major in the eye.

'I want a straight answer,' he said.

'Of course, sir.'

'Am I to take it that – er – Corporal Smith is on our ration strength?'

'Yes, sir,' replied the Sergeant Major defiantly.

Jampton was astounded. He still couldn't take it all in. He carried on relentlessly. 'And what recruiting office paid her the King's shilling?' he asked sarcastically.

'There are extenuating circumstances, sir,' the Sergeant Major explained patiently. 'Private Sparks found her under a pile of rubble when we were pulling out of Tobruk, and we were moving all the time – never seemed to get a chance to dump her. In any case she wouldn't have gone unless Sparks went too, but we had enough problems on our hands with the Afrika Korps.' He shrugged. 'Eventually we wound up here.'

'And who does she – I mean where does she sleep?' asked Jampton.

'In the back of one of the trucks, sir,' answered the Sergeant Major.

'This is the British Army, Sergeant Major, not a . . .' Jampton struggled to find a suitable comparison. 'Not a Trade Union Congress.'

The Sergeant Major blinked. He couldn't quite make the connection, but then neither could Jampton, who wished he hadn't said it.

'Just look around you, Sergeant Major.' He paused. 'I arrive –'

He suddenly stopped. From the distance came a low growl rapidly reaching a crescendo as, with an ear-splitting roar, a fighter plane buzzed the camp at about thirty feet. Jampton ducked involuntarily and yelped, 'What was that?'

'A sand fly,' murmured a passing soldier. 'Plenty more by the latrines.'

Jampton looked quizzically at the Sergeant Major. The remark was obviously a joke but strangely enough nobody seemed concerned or even curious. Again a scream and a roar and the plane zoomed over, lower this time so that it disturbed a long trail of desert dust.

Suddenly Jampton knew what had niggled him on the first pass. He whirled round to the Sergeant Major. 'That's a German plane,' he gasped.

The Sergeant Major nodded. 'Messerschmitt 109, sir. The lads call him the Red Baron.'

Jampton stared at him perplexed. 'Then why didn't we fire?'

'Well, sir, he comes over every day,' replied the Sergeant Major.

'Every day?' squeaked Jampton, and whirling round he shouted towards the sandbagged Bren-gun pit. 'What's the matter with the Bren? Why don't you shoot?'

Sparks and Miller this time were flipping stones at a passing column of ants. They looked at each other puzzled, and glanced up at the plane, now banking for another run in.

'Shoot, dammit!' screamed Jampton. 'Why don't you shoot?'

Miller shrugged, turned to the gun resting on the sand bags and let off a short burst. He turned towards Jampton and put up his thumb.

Sparks was not best pleased. 'Now what did you want to go and do that for?' he hissed. 'I've just cleaned the bloody thing.'

'Well you heard him,' said Miller.

'Doesn't mean you have to listen to the stupid git, does it?' retorted Sparks, and angrily he whirled on the gun and fired off a long burst.

The Messerschmitt jinked round the upcoming tracer and made height, moving in a graceful arc to set himself up for another approach. By this time there was no lack of interest from the lads in the camp. As soon as the staccato fire burst from the Bren gun, every eye watched fearfully. As the plane approached, the roar of the engine increased and suddenly lights speckled along the leading edge of the wing, spraying bullets and shells. Astonished, everyone flung themselves to the ground. Again the pilot made height in a graceful climbing turn to set himself up for the *coup de grâce*. The lads in the camp watched dry-mouthed, fearful of what was coming next. Some of them rose to their feet and ran madly in every direction.

Sparks and Miller flattened themselves on the floor of the Bren pit. It was three feet deep and comparatively safe. Even so, they would have preferred the Grand Canyon. They listened to the plane for a moment, then Miller muttered, 'Oh Gawd, he's coming round again.'

Jampton, the Sergeant Major and the driver Gratwick lay prone behind the fifteen-hundredweight. The Sergeant Major muttered, 'Gawd, we've upset him now.'

'Upset him?' repeated Jampton.

The Sergeant Major replied, 'He doesn't usually bother us.'

He ducked as the plane, guns blazing, zoomed towards them.

Dusty Miller, in a panic, reached up and without looking fired a short burst from the Bren. It was a token gesture and no one was more astonished than Rifleman Miller when the roar of the departing Messerschmitt suddenly cut out, then it spluttered and coughed. Heads were raised cautiously as the plane struggled to gain height. Black smoke was pouring from it and, as it shrank to a speck in the sky, the faint noise of the engine cut out abruptly. There was a small pinprick of light as if the sun had caught the perspex of the canopy, followed thirty seconds later by a slight crack. Then the plane began the spiralling descent, out of control, black smoke corkscrewing behind it. When it finally crashed into the desert about five hundred yards from the camp, it was almost an anticlimax. There was little left of the plane anyway, just a large smoking black patch.

Dusty Miller couldn't believe his eyes. Sure, he'd fired the Bren many times before with intent when the sky was full of enemy planes, and to his knowledge he'd never hit one yet. But this, this was beyond belief. He'd actually shot one down!

Fifty yards away Lieutenant Jampton stared at the blackened smoking patch of sand. The Sergeant Major eyed the young CO curiously. He was a strange sight, half crouched, holding his shorts away from his crimson, shiny knees, hopping from one foot to the other. God, thought the Sergeant Major, he looks as if he's about to join in a hoedown, poor little bugger.

'Don't let it bother you, sir. There's plenty more where that came from.'

Jampton, encouraged by the SM's support, said eagerly, 'It was either us or him.'

The Sergeant Major shook his head. 'Oh I doubt that, sir. If he'd been serious you'd be writing condolences to a lot of mothers tonight.' He pointed to the vehicle park. 'That's all he took out: the supply wagon. He was teaching us a lesson.'

Jampton looked across at the blazing three-tonner and was galvanised into action.

'Gather the men together, Sergeant Major, and form a bucket chain.'

He took a khaki handkerchief out of his pocket and tied it over his mouth and nostrils before running to the blazing vehicle, but after a few paces he realised he was alone. He turned, but the men and the Sergeant Major hadn't moved. They were standing about watching him curiously.

Jampton tugged the handkerchief down to give his mouth freedom and yelled, 'Didn't you hear me, Sergeant Major. Form a bucket chain.'

But still nobody moved.

Then one of the lads shouted, 'There's ammunition on that truck, sir.'

Jampton turned quickly back to the blazing wreck, then panic-stricken he ran behind his fifteen-hundredweight yelling, 'Stand well back, everybody, there's ammunition on that truck!' And, crouching, he watched wide-eyed as the flames lessened and with a tired lurch the bed of the burning truck collapsed. Then from the dying embers a bright ball shot lazily into the air about fifteen feet, like a very cheap Roman candle, and with a soft bang slowly fell to earth. It was all over.

'Ammunition?' asked Jampton sarcastically.

'I could have sworn we had more than that,' sighed the Sergeant Major, trying hard not to laugh.

The CO rose to his feet, got into the cab and ordered his driver to take him over to the Bren pit.

Dusty Miller was in full flow. 'Ah,' he said modestly, 'it was nothing. He was gettin' on my wick flying over every day showing off.'

'He won't be coming again,' shouted one of the crowd.

Sparks, still in the Bren pit, snorted. Over the last few months he'd seen his mate in action against the Italians and then the Afrika Korps, but what had happened in the last few minutes was straight out of *Comic Cuts*.

The crowd jumped out of the way as the fifteen-hundredweight screeched to a stop. Lieutenant Jampton rose to his feet and rapped on the windshield with his stick to gain attention. He decided this was as good a time as any to introduce himself. It never crossed his mind that the shooting down of the enemy plane was a million-to-one chance, a miracle in his romantic adolescent imagination. He thought that soldiers, especially infantrymen, shot down enemy aeroplanes every day of the week.

'Men,' he began. But he might have been invisible. They were still excited, laughing and chattering with Miller the focus of their admiration.

Jampton clapped his hands and tried again.

'Men,' he screeched.

But Miller had the floor and it was he who shushed the crowd and looked across at the scarecrow of his surrogate mother beating the metal of the windshield in frustration.

Miller raised both arms. 'All right, lads, that's enough,' he bellowed; and the noise of the chattering crowd subsided. He bowed towards Jampton. 'Sorry, sir,' he said humbly. 'Carry on.'

Sergeant Major Puller, arms folded, shook his head sadly at the sheer farcical effrontery of it all. Jampton looked at him enquiringly. 'Private Miller, sir,' muttered the SM.

'Thank you, Sergeant Major,' said the Lieutenant and cleared his throat. 'Men,' he began again, 'now is as good a time as any to introduce myself. I am Lieutenant Jampton, your new Commanding Officer.'

He paused for effect and somebody at the back shouted, 'Speak up!'

'That's enough,' barked the SM, asserting himself, and, turning to his CO, said, 'Carry on, sir.'

'Men,' continued Jampton, this time louder. 'On the first day of my command we have destroyed an enemy plane.'

A match rasped and somebody lit up a fag. Jampton glared at the tall bearded smoker and was about to order the Sergeant Major to take that man's name when a voice bellowed, 'Get on with it, it'll soon be dark.' Jampton was puzzled. What was the man on about, it wasn't yet midday.

'Right,' he continued uncertainly, 'that plane was shot down by whom?'

They all turned their heads to where Miller was standing trying to look modest.

'Yes,' went on Jampton, his voice rising, 'the only man in the camp apart from the Sergeant Major who is properly dressed.

This was greeted with ironic cheers, whistles and 'Good on you, Dusty.'

The young Lieutenant was gratified he'd made his point. When the noise subsided he began to drive his point home.

'The Special Ordnance Group from this day is about to be reborn.'

He wasn't looking at them now. Carried away with his own oratory, he had a vision of his Aunt Dorothy standing, hands clasped in front of her, head tilted slightly to one side. There was a half-smile on her face as she gazed in open admiration at his mastery over this ill-dressed slovenly mob.

His vision faded. Somewhere along the line he'd lost his hold over his new command. They were all looking curiously beyond him where some were pointing. He jerked his head round to see what was the cause of the distraction and saw a figure striding purposefully towards them carrying what appeared to be a bundle of washing; it subsequently turned out to be a parachute.

It was the pilot of the Messerschmitt and from the way he strode purposefully into the camp it was evident that he was not a happy man. He stopped and took in the scene. Then, slinging down his parachute, he made a beeline for Lieutenant Jampton, who was still standing upright in his fifteen-hundredweight.

The pilot spoke through gritted teeth. 'Who is in charge of this –' he gestured disdainfully to the men '– band of gypsies?'

His English was excellent, so much so that Jampton was unsure of himself. He stepped down from his vehicle.

'I am Lieutenant Jampton, the Commanding Officer,' he said shakily. He didn't know whether to salute or offer to shake hands. This man obviously had breeding.

The pilot looked him up and down, then turned to the crowd. 'Which man was responsible for shooting down my plane?'

'You're only required to give your name, rank and number,' squeaked Jampton behind him, trying desperately to regain the initiative.

'I'm waiting,' the pilot said icily.

Some of them turned towards Miller, and the pilot, following their gaze, strode towards the Bren pit as the crowd parted for him to pass.

As he reached Miller he shouted, '*Dumbkof, puta*, cretin, arsehole.' Obviously he was well travelled. To emphasise each word he slapped Miller's face.

Sparks leapt out of the Bren pit, an entrenching tool in his hand and murder in his eyes.

'That's enough, Sparks,' rasped Sergeant Major Puller quickly.

Sparks stopped dead. It was as if he'd walked into a closed door. He didn't look at the SM, his eyes still on the German pilot, who returned his gaze coolly. It was anybody's guess what would happen next; then somebody sneezed and that broke the spell. Sparks' shoulders slumped and he turned away. 'Bollocks to the lot of 'em,' he muttered.

There was a light touch on his arm and he turned to look down into the beautiful dark eyes of Corporal Smith. For a moment it was as if he didn't recognise her. Snatching his arm from her hand he said, 'And bollocks to you, too,' and pushed his way through the crowd.

Lieutenant Jampton watched it all open-mouthed and felt it was time to take charge of the situation. He clapped his hands together like a gym teacher about to call for another game of netball.

'Right,' he squeaked, not quite in control of his voice.

'Why?' barked the pilot.

Jampton stepped back a pace.

'Why,' repeated the pilot, 'did you allow this oaf to open fire?'

The Sergeant Major cleared his throat; he'd heard enough – it was time to end the pantomime.

'All right,' he barked, 'you and you.' He pointed to two of the spellbound audience.

He was about to order them to take charge of the German pilot when Jampton intervened. 'Thank you, Sergeant Major,' he piped. 'I'm in command; I can manage if you don't mind,' he added waspishly.

'*Got in Himmel*,' muttered the pilot. 'When you have quite decided who is in command, I must warn you that you haven't heard the last of this.' He glared at Jampton. 'You, little man,' he said, 'are responsible for a wanton act of destruction contravening the Geneva Convention of War.'

Unsure of the validity of this statement, Jampton replied, 'You are an enemy and it was our duty to shoot you down.'

Ignoring this last fatuous remark, the pilot carried on. 'As you will have no doubt observed, I am too old to fly as a fighter pilot in battle. I am merely a test pilot, a noncombatant.'

Lieutenant Jampton shook his head vigorously, leaving his cap askew.

'Hear me out,' barked the German.

Sergeant Major Puller turned away in disgust. Why didn't the little prat just detail two men to take him prisoner?

The pilot continued, 'For the past days I have entertained this pathetic outpost – aerobatics of daring and brilliance, far in advance of your Spitfires. I was under the impression that you enjoyed these displays of superiority and,' he added modestly, 'appreciated my undoubted skill as a pilot.'

'That's all very well –' broke in Jampton.

'I'm talking,' said the pilot icily, 'and may I remind you my rank is higher than yours.'

'Not in the British Army,' piped Jampton.

Trying desperately to decipher the logic of this last remark, the pilot took in the slight, thin apparition before him. *Mein Got*, if this was the best England could offer, what was taking General Rommel so long? Then he glanced quickly at his wristwatch and, like a businessman dismissing an interviewee, declared, 'Well, it's getting late and I'm hungry for my lunch.' And, whilst everyone was spellbound by this sheer effrontery, he marched over to the fifteen-hundredweight and climbed in beside Gratwick.

'Drive on,' he commanded.

Gratwick looked round to his CO with frightened eyes.

Jampton was flustered. 'What do you think you're doing?' he bleated.

'Isn't it obvious?' replied the German coolly. 'You have destroyed my plane and as I am already overdue I certainly don't intend to walk back.'

Jampton whirled to the Sergeant Major for support but the great man shook his head slightly and nodded towards the fifteen-hundredweight. The German pilot was now holding his service pistol at Gratwick's head.

'Do we go,' he asked calmly, 'or do I blow his head off?'

Jampton remained rooted to the spot.

'Drive on,' said the pilot, and Gratwick, on the verge of filling his pants, put the truck into gear and hurled it into the desert.

Coming to his senses, Jampton sprang into action.

'You there,' Jampton shrieked, pointing at Miller, 'the Bren gun, quick!'

Miller, open-mouthed, looked at the Sergeant Major for confirmation.

'It's no good, sir, you're too late,' said the SM.

But Jampton didn't hear. He was struggling to get his own pistol from its holster. Whilst he hurried forward the fifteen-hundredweight was already five hundred yards away and getting smaller but that didn't deter him.

'Halt or I fire,' he screamed and pulled the trigger.

There was a click. He tried again, and again there was a click. He shook the gun angrily.

Sergeant Major Puller began to turn away wearily. Had nobody told the useless little pillock about the safety catch? As he turned he heard the loud report of the revolver. At last, he thought, he's found out what the safety catch is for. Then he noticed the look of disbelief and incredulity on the lads' faces. Was it possible the young Lieutenant had hit the fleeing truck at what must be half a mile away by now? But as he turned to Jampton he realised what had transpired. The damn fool had inadvertently slipped the safety catch off while returning the pistol to its holster and the bullet was buried deep in the sand, an inch from his foot. Dear God, thought the Sergeant Major, considering seriously a transfer back to an Infantry regiment, Paratroops or Commandos. Any one of these postings would be safer than this.

'Sergeant Major,' yelped the almost hysterical Second Lieutenant, 'he's escaped!'

The Sergeant Major eyed him warily. He didn't like the way Jampton had yelped, 'He's escaped,' as if he, the Sergeant Major, was responsible. He'd been in the Army long enough to step from under this particular can.

'Yes, sir,' he replied, and ever so gently he shifted the ball back into his CO's court with, 'You did what you could, sir.'

Jampton was beside himself. 'Yes, but dammit, man,' he shrieked, 'that truck. All my equipment was on that, my bedding and . . . and . . .' He struggled for words trying to remember what exactly was on the back of the fifteen-hundredweight and what was in his suitcase left on Alexandria docks.

'And,' replied the Sergeant Major smoothly, 'the driver, don't forget the driver, sir. He's in the bag before he's had a chance to get his knees brown.'

Oh God, thought Jampton, of course, Gratwick. He'd have to mention that in his report.

Some of the lads, feeling the excitement was over, drifted back to their tents, some to see if there was any tea going, and quite a few straggled across to the blackened patch of desert looking for souvenirs from what was left of the Messerschmitt. Too much had happened in the last hour – a day that would crop up in conversation when most of the SOG were drawing old-age pensions.

Half an hour later, hunched over the MO's table in the medical tent, Lieutenant Jampton composed his report. It was a slow, laborious, difficult task. After all, to whom did he send the report, it being the Special Ordnance Group? He'd naturally assumed

that the Royal Army Ordnance Corps would be the recipient but
Sergeant Major Puller had been adamant that this might put the
cat amongst the pigeons. He doubted very much that the RAOC
had any record of the Special Ordnance Group and the last thing
the Sergeant Major wanted was to kick the sleeping dog while it
lay. The fewer people who knew about the SOG the better as far
as he was concerned. So, on his advice, Jampton was addressing
his report direct to Colonel Brunswick of Military Intelligence.
This cheered him up a little. Colonel Brunswick was also known
to him as Uncle Charles, his legal guardian. He sighed and began
to write, and two hours later a dispatch rider would be on his way
to add to the confusion in Alexandria.

Lieutenant Jampton sat back wondering what he should do
next. A frown crossed his face. What was it Sergeant Major Puller
had said to him? Suddenly he remembered – a letter of condolence
to Gratwick's parents. Of course, that shouldn't take long and,
after all, it was his duty as Commanding Officer. The grieving
parents would shortly be receiving a telegram from the War Office
informing them that Gratwick was now a prisoner of war. He
reached for the flimsy letter form and unscrewed the cap from his
fountain pen. He began writing.

'Dear Mr and Mrs Gratwick,' he started, and then a thought
struck him. Supposing one of them was dead? It was a tactless
beginning. He screwed the paper up and took another letter form.
This time he'd think it out before committing it to paper. 'Dear
Sir or Madam.' No. No 'Dear'. Best to ignore that. 'I regret to
inform you that your son . . .' Again he stopped. Good grief, he
didn't even know Gratwick's first name.

Private Albert Gratwick, 6120345, of the Base Army Service
Corps, six months ago had been delivering meat on a butcher's
bike in Oldham. Unfortunately it wasn't a reserved occupation
and in any case the size of the meat ration didn't warrant a
delivery boy and so, along with thousands of other eighteen-year-
olds, Gratwick received his call-up papers and reported to the
Army Camp at Catterick. Here he was inoculated, uniformed,
numbered, fed, and on top of all this they gave him a few bob to
spend on himself. Then after a few days the Army taught him to
march, drill, stand still, salute – all under the banner of discipline.
He was given a rifle and taught how to oil the barrel, the use of
a pull-through, how to smack home the magazine containing five

446

bullets; naturally there weren't any bullets – there weren't enough to go round. He was posted to Swaffham in Norfolk, where he drove, reversed, learnt to drive at night with slitted headlamps, and how to move in convoy. But once again, just as he was on the verge of settling in, making friends and finding a girl, he was back in Oldham on embarkation leave. It wasn't a particularly happy homecoming. His parents had let his room and he had to sleep next door at Mrs Taylor's and, what's more, she charged three pounds ten for room and board. All his old mates were either in the Forces or down the coal mines, so it was a great relief to report to Southampton and from there to North Africa, Lieutenant Jampton and the desert.

Gratwick reviewed his first day on the ration strength of the Special Ordnance Group . . . and that was a laugh: he hadn't even had time for a corned-beef sandwich before he was whipped away into the blue, chauffeuring an enemy pilot to God knew where. How would he ever be able to answer 'What did you do in the war, Daddy?'. He resolved never to get married.

For the first hour after leaving the camp, the German pilot and Driver Gratwick hadn't exchanged a word. The pilot, after consulting his wrist compass, silently pointed out directions from time to time. Suddenly he jerked up, alert, and squinted ahead. Approaching was a cloud of dust and Gratwick changed down the gears.

'No, no,' said the pilot. 'Keep going.'

Gratwick did as he was told and, as the oncoming vehicles approached, his spirits jumped – three half-tracks, and, more important, they were British.

'Don't stop,' yelled the pilot over the noise of the engines.

Gratwick was undecided – but only for a moment, until he felt the pressure of the service revolver against his side. When they drew level, the German smiled cheerfully and waved to them and – Bugger me, thought Gratwick incredulously – they waved back. It was hardly surprising, though, as Gratwick was driving a British fifteen-hundredweight.

One hour later, Gratwick – having been stopped twice by enemy patrols, and, after brief exchanges between them and the pilot in rapid German, having been waved on with much merriment – was now a guest of a crack enemy artillery battery.

The first thing he noticed when they entered the German camp was an eighty-eight-millimetre artillery piece. It was awesome.

Surely the British hadn't anything to match one of these. But then Gratwick was hardly in a position to pass judgment. The only British gun he'd seen in his short military career had been the twenty-five-pounder yesterday, and that piece reminded him of the cannon on display in Werneth Park, Oldham, which was supposed to have been captured at Sebastopol. He looked again at the haughty, malevolent barrel of the German artillery piece and wondered if the Special Ordnance Group was within its range. He shuddered. Good grief, it looked so lethal it probably could flatten Cairo.

The pilot ordered Gratwick to stop and eased himself stiffly to the ground and bade Gratwick do the same. He beckoned two of the Wermacht over and spoke swiftly in German, to which one of them clicked his heels and said, '*Jawohl, Herr Hauptman.*'

The pilot turned to Gratwick. 'I'm going over to the officers' mess. These two will take care of you till I get back.'

He spoke again to the two bronzed giants and they pointed him to a small marquee. He nodded. '*Danke,*' he said, and left.

Gratwick looked round furtively. The stares of the soldiers embarrassed him. He felt like a pile of dog droppings in Kew Gardens. He'd never come across a bunch of lads like this. These were real soldiers. If the rest of the Afrika Korps was the same, it was no contest. They had to be the master race.

'Come,' said the fair-haired one and led Gratwick to a trestle table in the shade of a canvas awning. One of them leant across the table. 'I in London . . .' He corrected himself and held up three fingers. 'Tree years past, in town of Canning.'

Gratwick smiled, shaking his head and not understanding. A few yards away a group of the young supermen burst into laughter. Gratwick had a feeling they were laughing at him. It was the last straw. With all that had happened to him it was too much. He laid his head on his folded arms and sobbed himself to sleep. It was the dreamless sleep of the dead; and when a hand shook him awake he blinked and it was several moments before he realised where he was. Somebody slapped down a plate of some kind of processed meat and a tin cup of water.

Good grief, he thought, why for heaven's sake couldn't they let me sleep?

It was only then he noticed that the shadows were long and soon it would be nightfall. He must have slept through the afternoon. Gratefully he gulped the water but ignored the food –

if that's what it was. He looked around and saw the German pilot approaching. He was a changed man, a beatific smile on his face. He slapped one of the men on the back as he passed and threw a gabble of German over his shoulder. Several of them laughed; their morale was high with the prospect of victory.

The pilot looked over to Gratwick. 'Come on, lad. Let's be on our way.' He swung into the fifteen-hundredweight and lit a cigarette. The hospitality in the officers' mess had been more than lavish.

Gratwick stiffly clambered behind the wheel and, to much handclapping and waving, the barbed wire was pulled aside and they trundled off into the blue, heading straight for the setting sun. After a few miles, the yellow sun was now orange and touching the rim of the horizon.

'Stop here,' commanded the pilot. They sat together for a few moments. 'Did you ever see a sunset like that, eh?'

Gratwick didn't reply. 'No' seemed inadequate and he couldn't think of anything else. He was tired and for the first time in his life he was homesick. They sat in silence, then the pilot said, 'By the way, my name is Rudolph and I'd like you to call me Rudy. Everybody does.'

Gratwick, sitting morosely with his hands in his lap, nodded.

'What do they call you then?' asked the pilot. Gratwick muttered his name softly. Rudolph leant towards him. 'Sorry, I didn't catch that.'

Gratwick cleared his throat. 'Gratwick, sir, Albert Gratwick.'

'Albert,' mused the pilot. 'Then I shall call you Albie and less of the "sir", young fella, I'm Rudy. And how are you enjoying the desert, Albie?'

Gratwick looked away, then in a low voice he said, 'I don't know, this is my first day.' After a pause he went on. 'I thought it was going to be all sand.'

He suddenly wanted to cry. 'And now I'm a prisoner of war.' A tear trickled down his cheek, but luckily the light was going and it went unnoticed.

Or perhaps it didn't, because Rudolph spoke softly.

'Come on, Albie, cheer up. For you the war's over. You will be well treated. We're not all barbarians, you know. We have no quarrel with the British. As a matter of fact I once knew a very nice boy at Oxford.'

'I don't want to be a prisoner,' squeaked Gratwick stubbornly.

'Oh come now, Albie. It is only until the war is over and it won't be too long now. Hey, just think of the letters you can write home to your sweetheart. "Hello my darling, I was captured fighting in the Western desert." Yes, she will think you are quite a fellow.' He paused then said, 'Do you have a sweetheart?'

Gratwick, unable to trust himself to speak, shook his head.

'What?' said the pilot laughing. 'A young man like you with no sweetheart.' He clucked his tongue. 'Well perhaps you'll find yourself a nice buxom *fräulein* when you get to Germany.'

Gratwick spoke through his sobs. 'I don't want to go to Germany.' His voice rose to a wail. 'And I don't want a buxom *fräulein*, either.' He sat staring at the last vestige of the sun, blinking back his tears.

The pilot studied him silently for a few moments, then he said quietly, 'You know, Albie, you have very long eyelashes for a boy.'

FOUR

In a cluttered office high in the building that housed British Military Intelligence, Captain Shelley pushed another coloured pin into a large wall map of the streets of Alexandria. For several months now the British Intelligence had been engaged in a joint Anglo-French operation to track down an enemy transmitter sending and receiving information to Rommel's headquarters. The normal transmission times were at 2100 hours. But at that time several rogue transmitters opened up, all in code. It was a system deliberately designed as a smokescreen for the real transmitter and for the intelligence services it was almost an impossible task, like looking for a particular flea in a Marseilles flophouse.

Another night and another fruitless raid on a small café in the native quarter of the city. Four French agents had teamed with six British and taken the place apart, but their only success had been an old Cossor wireless blaring Arabic love songs continuously as a jerky background cacophony. Captain Shelley had been on the raid purely as an observer and once again he had the niggling feeling that the French were just going through the motions as if they knew it was to be a wasted effort. He rubbed his eyes wearily. He was Adjutant to Colonel Brunswick and, having compiled his report on the abortive night's proceedings, he wondered whether or not to acquaint his boss with his foreboding as to French cooperation. But then he rejected the thought. It was only conjecture and he was too tired for a lengthy in-depth discussion. Better he stick to the facts.

The telephone jangled and he picked it up. 'Captain Shelley,' he said tersely. He listened for a time, then said, 'Be right down, sir,' and replaced the earpiece. He sighed. Something was biting his governor and it had little to do with enemy transmissions.

Colonel Brunswick had just received the dispatch from his nephew, Lieutenant Jampton.

'What kind of a bloody report is this?' he said incredulously after reading Jampton's communication for the third time. He gazed round his sparsely furnished office and then looked at the document again – it was incredible, unbelievable. Certainly the correct protocol for submitting reports was obviously of low priority in the present Officers' Training College. It was written more in the style of a chatty newsletter from boarding school. It began 'Dear Uncle'. Dear Uncle, for God's sake. If this report was dispatched in its present form, he'd find himself in charge of the latrines at Aldershot.

There was a knock on the door and his Adjutant entered. 'You sent for me, sir?'

'Yes, Jimmy,' replied the Colonel. He handed over Jampton's report. 'Read that,' he commanded tersely. Then he opened the filing cabinet and took out a bottle of Dimple Haig.

The Adjutant read quickly, then started again in order to give it a more thorough examination. Finally he put the flimsy down on the desk.

'Lieutenant Jampton,' he murmured neutrally.

'My nephew,' replied the Colonel, taking a large swig from his glass. 'I told you about him. He only disembarked two days ago.' He stared morosely into his whisky. 'My wife's family connections – a Brigadier General, a Vice Admiral, a Bishop, two high-ranking members of Parliament, one of them a cabinet minister.' He paused and stared bleakly out of the window. 'With that kind of clout it wasn't difficult to have him posted here, the idea being that I should keep an eye on him.'

His Adjutant nodded understandingly.

The Colonel took another swig. 'I wasn't having him here under my feet – we have enough problems as it is.'

The Adjutant nodded again.

The Colonel went on. 'I arranged with the Regimental Transport Officer on the docks that as soon as he set foot on dry land he was to have him whisked into the blue.'

Enlightenment dawned. 'Ah, yes, sir, he was to report and take charge of the Special Ordnance Group.'

'Yes,' murmured the Colonel, 'a quiet enough billet I would have thought, and far enough to be out of my hair. And on the first day this . . .' He tapped the report angrily.

There was a silence between them, the Colonel back at his window gazing while the Adjutant stared longingly at the half-empty bottle. Finally he broke the silence.

'We can't ignore it, sir.'

'I'm aware of that,' snapped the Colonel testily, 'but if I submitted this to the powers that be, they'd have me certified.'

He snatched up the report again. 'Apart from shooting down a German plane, the rest of it is *Boys Own* paper.' He put on his glasses and read, ' "To my astonishment the German pilot marched into camp, slapped one of my men across the face, the man incidentally who had shot down the plane. NB, the name of the soldier and full particulars are attached to my report, with a strong recommendation for a decoration, also Private Sparks. Details following." '

The Colonel put down the report and took off his glasses. Wearily he put his hand over his eyes. The Adjutant took out his handkerchief to stifle a chuckle. He could picture the scene.

'It's not funny,' barked the Colonel. 'He even goes on to describe in detail how the pilot climbed into the fifteen-hundred-weight and, with a revolver pressed to the driver's head, ordered him to take him back to the German lines and with that was driven off.'

The Colonel stopped reading and lowered the paper. 'Ye Gods,' he muttered, 'this isn't a report: it's straight out of *Woman's Own*. All we're short of is "what's the weather like?" and "wish you were here".'

An idea began to form at the back of the Adjutant's mind. The Colonel looked at him shrewdly. 'Out with it, Jimmy,' he said. 'Have you got the solution?'

The Adjutant pondered for a moment, then nodded slowly. 'I think we can handle this, sir. The German being driven off has just given me an idea. May I, sir?' He held out his hand for the report and Colonel Brunswick passed it over. The Adjutant took it. 'Back as soon as possible, sir,' he said and left the room.

After half an hour or so he returned with his amended version of the report and the first thing he noted was that the bottle of

Dimple Haig was empty. This was going a bit, even for the old man, but he gave him the benefit of the doubt: perhaps he had knocked it over.

Colonel Brunswick chuckled as he perused his Adjutant's work. It was a masterly example of double talk.

'That's great, Jimmy,' he said handing it back. 'You should have been a politician.'

'Thank you, sir,' replied the Adjutant. 'If it hadn't been for the war, I'd have been a politician.'

'Really?' said the Colonel. 'See that it's transmitted immediately. And by the way, Jimmy,' he added in a low voice, 'I never saw this.'

The Adjutant looked at him for a moment and left the office.

Colonel Brunswick stared at the door after he'd gone. Jimmy, lad, he thought, had you been a politician there might not have been a war. And he smiled happily. He rubbed his hands together with satisfaction but his euphoria was premature. If only he'd burnt the report and claimed he'd never received it. That was the best line of approach. If only . . . if only . . . if only people thought before stepping out into the road just as a bus was approaching, there'd be a lot more of us about. In Colonel Brunswick's case, the fuse was lit and the flame started to flicker towards the gunpowder.

There is very little to be read in medical journals regarding morale. But that doesn't mean to say that lack of it shouldn't be classified as an ailment. As one takes two aspirins for a common cold, for low morale a stiff dose of propaganda will do the trick, and sadly it was a time when a low-morale epidemic was sweeping the country and the medicine chest was bare.

Newspaper editors were grasping any straws: eating carrots gives night-fighter pilots better vision . . . Hitler calls in heart specialist . . . Liverpool welcomes GIs . . . pictures of the King and Queen shaking hands with bombed-out Londoners . . . Winston Churchill in blue boiler suit and tin hat shaking his cigar defiantly at the skies.

Fleet Street had rung the changes many times. What was so desperately needed was a victory somewhere, or better still the German High Command signing an unconditional surrender, with the Brandenburg Gate in the background – at least a little stronger medicine than the King and Queen shaking hands with bombed-out Londoners/Churchill/carrots.

It was at this low point that help was mercifully on its way in the form of Lieutenant Jampton's report, or, to be more exact, Captain Shelley's jazzed-up version of it, circulated to the media by the Ministry of Propaganda. A victory at last! Small, yes, but then so is an aspirin. It was a little sunbeam floating through the gloom; that's what it seemed at the time, but it turned out to be more like a cloudburst in the Gobi Desert.

The newspapers couldn't wait to rush it into print, but unfortunately the news would not hit the streets until tomorrow morning. The British Broadcasting Corporation, however, were jubilant. All they had to do was to slip the dispatch in front of the newsreader and the radio would scoop the tabloids by at least twelve hours. The editors in Fleet Street were undismayed, however. Already the teleprinters were busy alerting journalists and photographers on the spot in Alexandria. The nine o'clock news broadcast would merely be the appetiser. The roast beef and two veg would be served up by the national newspapers – pictures, in-depth interviews, a rundown of the young Second Lieutenant perhaps.

The first domino, given a gentle nudge, was already wobbling.

Colonel Brunswick was standing at a corner of the bar in the officers' mess nursing a glass of whisky. He was tired. Until an hour ago he'd been closeted with his French counterparts in Intelligence, a meeting soured by acrimony, each side endeavouring to shift the blame for the abortive raid on the café. Pressure from both Intelligence Services was being brought to bear. The enemy transmitter had to be found but, more importantly, the codes broken. It was vital for the survival of North Africa. Captain Shelley broke into his thoughts by handing him another Scotch. The mess was half full, the usual collection of worried-looking base wallahs, all the life and jollity coming from a group of young tank officers, easily identified by their light cavalry-twill trousers, brown suede shoes and silk neckwear, enjoying a few hours' relaxation. But their noisy antics were enough to keep the Colonel's conversation private.

'I think you're right, Jimmy,' said the Colonel. 'I have a feeling the Frogs are holding something back.' He looked at his whisky. 'I feel it in my guts. There's something they're not telling us.'

He gulped down half his drink, then he gazed around the room. 'What's the latest from the cypher johnnies?'

The Adjutant shook his head. 'Nothing new I'm afraid, sir.' The Colonel nodded morosely. 'In fact they're now of the opinion that the transmitters that don't matter are sending out Mickey Mouse stuff . . .'

He left the sentence unfinished.

'Yes,' said the Colonel. 'Until we find the one transmitting the real information, we're up a gum tree.'

The Corporal behind the bar turned up the volume of the wireless on the shelf. It was time for the nine o'clock news. The noise in the club subsided as they gave it all their attention.

'. . . And this is Alvar Liddell reading it.' There was a faint rustle of paper, then the newsreader continued. 'In the Western desert a small unit of British soldiers under the command of a Second Lieutenant were attacked from the air. The unit, not yet up to operational strength, returned the fire, and one of the enemy aircraft, a Messerschmitt, was shot down in flames. The enemy broke through the perimeter, engaged in hand-to-hand fighting and after a short skirmish the enemy was driven off. Our casualties were light: one man was taken prisoner and two of our vehicles were destroyed.'

The second item announced by Alvar Liddell was drowned by the ironic cheers of the tank men. The Corporal behind the bar switched off the set. It would have been impossible to hear in any case. Colonel Brunswick stared at the now silent wireless. His mouth was open. Could he possibly have heard Alvar Liddell announcing Jampton's report? He turned incredulously to his Adjutant who, anticipating his question, nodded. He was equally amazed. Then the Colonel found his voice.

'How the bloody hell did the BBC get hold of it? It's classified information.'

The Adjutant shrugged and took a large gulp of whisky to avoid a reply. He didn't know the answer either.

The Adjutant leant towards him. 'Try to look happy, sir. You're attracting some very curious stares,' he said in a low voice. The Colonel screwed his face into a fatuous grin and beamed round the room.

'Don't worry, sir. It's just a one-off. By this time tomorrow it'll all be forgotten.'

Colonel Brunswick nodded gloomily. Oh yes, it would be forgotten all right, provided something bigger came along, like two divisions of German paratroops dropping on to Hyde Park;

or perhaps the King and Ivor Novello could sing 'Hitler Has Only Got One Ball', at a charity concert. Another large whisky appeared before him and he began to cheer up. What the hell! Jimmy was right: it was a one-day wonder. It would all be forgotten by tomorrow. In a much lighter mood he drained his glass.

'Must be off, Jimmy. Sign the chit, will you?' And he made his way unsteadily towards the exit. His *joie de vivre*, however, was premature. He of all people should have known the folly of lowering one's guard.

Life may be a bowl of cherries but in every cherry there's a stone. In this case the long fuse which had been lit by Jampton's report was now dangerously close to the powder barrel.

The explosion came with the strident tones of the bedside telephone rousing Colonel Brunswick from his happy stupor. He groped for the handset and by the illuminated fingers on his watch he noted that it was only 2 a.m. Good grief, only a few hours ago he'd been in the mess getting rid of the stock of whisky so that it wouldn't fall into enemy hands.

'Colonel Brunswick,' he muttered into the telephone, then, 'Jimmy, do you know what time it is?'

He listened for a few moments, then he shot upright into a sitting position; he was wide awake now.

'Good God,' he murmured, 'sweet merciful saviour. Where the bloody hell did the press get their permits from?' he asked.

He listened again. 'But how did the Ministry of Information know? Only a few of us were privy to the exact location of the Special Ordnance Group.'

The Colonel groaned. Of course, the Regimental Transport Officer would have a record of the map reference.

'Listen Jimmy,' he barked, 'we've got to head off the press before they reach the camp. If they start to question Jampton, we're all up the creek without a canoe. Be round at the factory soonest. I'll see you there. And I trust,' he said coldly, 'that you come up with something better for this one.'

He slammed down the receiver and staggered over to his trousers, which were still warm.

The Adjutant put down his end more thoughtfully. He understood his Colonel. The wily old bastard was beginning his retreat, dumping the whole shoddy mess on to yours truly.

He remembered the Colonel's last words when he had left the office to tart up Jampton's original dispatch: 'And by the way, Jimmy, I never saw this.' In his mind's eye he visualised the Colonel in full dress uniform, stiff as a ramrod facing the Courts Martial reporting in a clear military voice that up to the unfortunate incident appertaining to Second Lieutenant Jampton's report, Captain Shelley had carried out his duties as an Adjutant in an exemplary military fashion. Jimmy shrugged. After all, he wasn't a regular. It just meant his demob would come up that much sooner.

There was little to be done about the press, however. They were already well into the blue and by early morning reporters, war correspondents and photographers would be all over the Special Ordnance Group. He groaned inwardly. God help us when they besiege Lieutenant Jampton, he thought. Naively, the stupid little twit will stick to his original story of the farcical happenings.

His thoughts were scattered by the door bursting open.

'Transport, Jimmy.'

'Yes sir, but –'

'I know, I know, they've got a head start. Our mission will be damage-limitational if that bloody nephew of mine has blown the gaff. And to make no mistake, Jimmy, if he does you'll be better off driving straight on to surrender yourself to the nearest German outpost.'

The Adjutant accepted this and hurried out to organise things.

When he'd gone the Colonel paced up and down. Damn the war, damn his wife Dorothy for sending out the little prat. Suddenly a happy thought unexpectedly came to mind. When the German pilot made his own report, it wasn't without the bounds of possibility that there would follow a reprisal air raid. He visualised the Stukas screaming down to go into the attack and with any luck the first bomb would land plumb on top of Jampton. As quickly as these thoughts appeared he dismissed them, ashamed and a little frightened by how desperate he'd become.

At about 9 a.m. the first truckload bearing the press correspondents entered the camp of the Special Ordnance Group. Stiff and weary they jumped down with cameras, microphones, and other paraphernalia, and looked around, feeling slightly embarrassed at the curious vacant stares of the soldiers.

Sergeant Major Puller walked from the mess tent wiping his lips with the back of his hand. He looked at the new arrivals, noting their press arm bands, and slowly approached the group.

'What's all this about?' he enquired.

'Press,' said one of them, and some of them nodded, holding up identification.

After a pause the Sergeant Major asked, 'Are you lost or something?'

One of them laughed easily. 'Come off it, Sergeant Major, you know why we're here; that little to-do you had yesterday morning.'

The Sergeant Major was still puzzled. The to-do the man referred to was the Messerschmitt and loss of Gratwick. But that was nothing, certainly not enough to bring a posse of newshounds this far into the blue. They all looked round as another press vehicle arrived, a square of cardboard behind the windscreen identifying it as BBC.

The Sergeant Major made up his mind.

'Right then,' he said. 'You'll be tired and hungry so if you'll make your way into the mess tent –' he pointed '– get yourself a brew-up and a plate of powdered egg.'

As they made their way over, the Sergeant Major caught hold of one of them by the arm.

'Just a minute, lad,' he said when the others were safely out of earshot. 'What's all this about?' he asked quietly.

'You're the flavour of the month,' he said. 'Didn't you hear the nine o'clock news last night?'

The Sergeant Major was intrigued; he shook his head. 'No. Nine o'clock news?'

'Everybody else did,' said the reporter, and showed a page of his notebook to the Sergeant Major.

It was a transcript of the news bulletin read by Alvar Liddell. When he'd finished reading, Puller's eyebrows went up. He whistled softly to himself. That report must have been a master-piece of overstatement. He gazed towards the CO's tent. Maybe I've misjudged the little fella after all, he thought.

He shoved the pressman towards the mess tent. 'Better get your breakfast while there's any left,' he said, and he made his way over to his CO's tent.

The little fellow in question hadn't heard the arrival of the press. He was looking over a manuscript of military tactics, which he was in the process of writing. He heard the rap on the tent pole.

'Sergeant Major Puller, sir.'

Jampton's head jerked up. 'What is it, Sergeant Major?'

'The press are here, sir.'

'Press?' Jampton was puzzled. He turned down a corner of the page he'd been writing headed 'Hannibal's First Mistake', put it to one side and unfastened the tent flap.

'Come in, Sergeant Major.' He stepped back. 'What's all this about the press?'

'A pack of 'em, sir.' He smiled. 'Something to do with that report you sent in yesterday. Apparently it was given first priority on the nine o'clock news last night.'

'Gosh,' said Jampton and immediately regretted it. He should have said something like 'Really?' but he couldn't contain his excitement. Aunt Dorothy was bound to have been listening. She never missed the nine o'clock news. Then with a slight frown he remembered the events of yesterday morning's sad affair. Apart from shooting down the Messerschmitt, there was nothing to be proud of. The German pilot being driven off, with Gratwick at the point of a gun. Surely that hadn't been broadcast on the nine o'clock news.

'Have you any idea what exactly was said?' asked Jampton fearfully.

'I've just been talking to one of 'em, sir, and I don't know what you put in your report but whatever it was it seems to have done the trick.'

Jampton looked at him blankly. 'What I put in my report to Colonel Brunswick,' he said tartly, 'was classified and confidential. I put down the events exactly as they happened. Yes, even to the German pilot holding a pistol to my driver's head and making his way into the desert in my fifteen-hundredweight.'

The Sergeant Major stared at him incredulously. Then it came to him in a flash. Of course, he could imagine his old Colonel reading the report and could well understand the reaction it would provoke. No way would that report in its original form be sent to London.

'Right,' snapped Jampton. 'I think the time has come to meet the press.' He began to button his shirt.

Sergeant Major Puller was aghast. He visualised the pompous little prat holding court telling them exactly what had happened.

It didn't bear thinking about. That would certainly put the cat amongst the pigeons. He made a quick decision: whatever happened, Second Lieutenant Jampton must be kept away from the media. He was used to making quick decisions – they had saved his life on more than one occasion.

'With due respect, sir,' he began, 'the press are out in force and in my experience when interviewed on occasions like this, an officer or noncommissioned officer must be properly dressed.'

Lieutenant Jampton looked at him sternly, then decided that the Sergeant Major was only trying to be helpful.

'I agree with you, Sergeant Major, but war is a mitigating circumstance and in any case all I own at present is what I stand up in.'

He smirked in what he thought was a comradely 'Jack the Lad' attitude.

'Don't worry, Sergeant Major,' he went on. 'I'll explain it to the press people how all my kit was on the fifteen-hundredweight. They'll understand. It may even raise a laugh.'

'Yes,' replied the Sergeant Major desperately, 'but will the mandarins, the brass hats in Whitehall, take a lenient view when they see your picture all over the front page of the *Daily Mail*?'

Jampton gulped. He could see his Aunt Dorothy staring at his picture on the front page, and him hardly distinguishable from the men, especially if the Sergeant Major took it in his head to change into his ceremonial dress . . . It wasn't fair. All his possessions had been on the fifteen-hundredweight when Gratwick had driven the German officer away. In any case his dress uniform, complete with his sword, had been packed away in the suitcase that was still lying on the docks at Alexandria.

'I've got nothing else to wear apart from what I stand up in,' he bleated.

The Sergeant Major sighed sympathetically. 'Well it looks like you'll have to wear that then.'

'I've got no alternative, Sergeant Major,' snapped Jampton stamping his foot.

Then the Sergeant Major smiled suddenly, as if hit with a brilliant idea.

'Well, what is it?' squeaked Jampton.

'Give me your uniform, sir, and I'll nip smartly over to Corporal Smith and we'll have it back to you clean and crisp like it's just come out of Burton's window.'

The CO was undecided for a moment, then he quickly began to unbutton his shirt. The Sergeant Major watched him fascinated. That chest reminded him of the half-carved chicken at the Christmas dinner – not a pretty sight. He watched as the CO started to unfasten the top button on his shorts. This could be interesting, he thought. At least he'd know if Jampton had joined the right branch of the service.

Jampton stopped suddenly.

'Do you mind waiting outside, Sergeant Major?' he said coldly.

'Sorry, sir.' He ducked out through the tent flap.

He was over the first hurdle. A few moments later a thin white stick of an arm, red from the elbow down, poked through a gap in the tent flap and the Sergeant Major took the pathetic bundle of soiled khaki clothing over to Corporal Smith.

'Yes?' she asked.

The Sergeant Major handed over Jampton's uniform. His instructions were short and quiet and to the casual observer he might have been saying 'and not too much starch on the collar'. Whatever he did say, Corporal Smith nodded and carried the stuff away.

He watched her go, then shook his head. She was unflappable. Since knowing her he'd never ever seen a flicker of emotion cross her face, even when she looked at Sparks, and everyone in camp knew that she was his bint. Like an icicle on a drainpipe, that one. He shrugged. He had more important matters to attend to inside the mess tent.

The Press Corps had bolted down their powdered egg and were gathering their equipment together when the Sergeant Major strode in. He went to the head of the trestle table and rapped on it with his knuckles.

'Gentlemen, my name is Sergeant Major Puller and I'm in charge of this operation.'

Conversation died as they turned expectantly towards him.

'Gentlemen,' he repeated, 'in order to save time I'll take you over to the Bren-gun pit where most of the action took place . . . and I'll arrange for Privates Miller and Sparks to be present and you can interview them there.'

'Who're Miller and Sparks?'

'Ah yes,' said the Sergeant Major. 'Private Miller is the one who actually brought down the Messerschmitt. Sparks was number two on the gun.'

A ripple of excitement went through the group. Some of them jotted down notes and one or two rose from their seats.

The Sergeant Major raised his hand.

'I must ask you all to remain here till I organise things. This will be the quickest way as I know you'll all be in a rush to get back with your interviews and stuff. For those with cameras, what's left of the plane is about five hundred yards away and you might like to get some shots of our burnt-out supply wagon.'

'Can we do that now?' asked one elderly gentleman picking up his camera.

'Why not?' replied the Sergeant Major. 'Get your stuff together and Hardesty here will take you.'

The photographers began to gather up their equipment while the Sergeant Major drew Hardesty to one side.

'They're not to speak to anybody, understand?' he hissed.

'Why me?' objected Hardesty. 'I'm the bloody cook.'

'Yes,' replied the Sergeant Major. 'Well for the next hour you're excused potato peeling. Just make sure they take pictures but on no account must they talk to anybody.'

Then he turned back to the table.

'Right then, gentlemen, if you'll just hang on here for a minute, I'll assemble the lads. OK?'

They murmured their assent and off went the Sergeant Major to brief Miller and Sparks. He ducked into their tent, pleasantly surprised to find them up and dressed – it was only half past nine.

'Want a beer, sir?' asked Miller.

'Later,' replied the Sergeant Major. 'I haven't got much time so listen and listen good.'

They both looked up at him from where they sat on their blankets. The Sergeant Major squatted on his haunches – this was confidential.

'Whether you like it or not, you're heroes,' he began.

Miller raised his eyebrows and looked at Sparks, who shrugged.

'That little upset we had yesterday, it seems the powers that be have blown it up into a second Battle of Waterloo.'

They looked at him uncomprehendingly.

'Never mind why,' went on the Sergeant Major, 'the press is here to interview you. Right now, pay attention. I'll give you the gen.'

They leant forward and the Sergeant Major explained about the enemy aircraft . . . how they shot one down . . . the hand-to-hand fighting . . .

Miller broke in. 'I never laid a finger on him.'

'Don't interrupt,' snapped the Sergeant Major.

When he'd finished, Dusty Miller nodded. 'Oh yes, I remember now. I saw the film – Errol Flynn, wasn't it?'

'Never mind the funnies, Miller, this is serious. Get your tin hats on, button up your shirts and get yourselves over to the Bren pit. Move!'

He didn't wait to see them go; they'd been in the 41st Light Infantry together in the old India days when he was a Corporal. They wouldn't let him down. But all the same, he'd be on hand to make sure they didn't say anything stupid. Partly satisfied, he strode over to the mess tent to collect the eyes and ears of the world.

The press interview with Miller and Sparks was music hall with a dash of party political broadcast.

'How many planes were there?'

'Don't ask me,' said Miller. 'I only had eyes for this one.'

The Sergeant Major breathed a sigh of relief; straight back into their court.

'Was this your first action?'

Miller gazed at the reporter then nudged his oppo. 'Here, Sparks, did you hear that?'

He turned back to the reporter. 'Listen, son,' he said, 'we were in the old 41st Light Infantry and the Sergeant Major and one or two of the other lads there were pulled out of line at Tobruk.' He paused and leant forward. 'At Rommel's personal request.'

Some of the lads sniggered. Another reporter put up his hand. 'What is your full name?' he asked.

'Dusty Miller.'

'That's just a nickname. What's your real name?'

'Ribbentrop,' yelled a wag.

And the cook laughed so much his upper dentures flew out and plopped into the dixie from which he was ladling out the dinner. He fiddled around in the lukewarm stew, and with a grunt of satisfaction popped them back into his mouth. He sucked for a minute then, satisfied, he murmured, 'Mm, it's good today.' Wiping his hand on his apron he found the queue had gone. He shrugged. It was all the same to him: they'd get it warmed up tomorrow.

Sparks took no interest at all in the interview. He just stood in the Bren pit waiting for the fantasy to end. He answered only one question. It came from an elderly war correspondent.

'Being number two on the gun, would you have taken over had Miller been hit?'

Sparks turned away in disgust but another reporter persisted.

'Would you have taken over if Miller caught a packet?'

Sparks cleared his throat and they all waited, pencils poised.

'The only packet he's likely to catch will have twenty fags in it.'

With that he climbed out of the trench and strode away.

The Sergeant Major didn't try to stop him. Sparks was highly flammable and he wasn't about to light the blue touchpaper. They'd got enough, anyway, and some of them were already sidling away towards their trucks for the mad race to the teleprinters in Alexandria. They had enough information, especially with the research that would be carried out on the old 41st Infantry. That alone should be enough to fill the front page.

While all this was going on, in the tent marked CO Jampton was going spare. Almost an hour had elapsed and still no sign of his uniform. What was happening? He certainly couldn't meet the press draped only in an Army blanket. What the dickens was going on out there? Over and over in his mind he'd gone through the interview, how he'd ordered his men to open fire on the German plane and – he was proud of this bit – the fracas with the enemy pilot and his subsequent defection in the fifteen-hundred-weight driven by his own driver. He would skip lightly over this, treat it as a joke. It had to be told but they'd understand. We all make mistakes and it's a big man who'll admit them.

For goodness' sake! Corporal Smith should be here by now. Some time ago he'd put his mouth to a gap in the tent flap to order a passing soldier to send her to him immediately. The man hadn't replied, but had signified that he would be back in two minutes. He'd done this by raising two fingers. Then a thought struck Jampton. Good grief, he couldn't possibly have meant two hours!

Not until the second vehicle was a speck on the horizon did the Sergeant Major rap on the tailgate of Corporal Smith's workshop. She opened the canvas flap to see who it was and five minutes later Lieutenant Jampton received his freshly laundered uniform.

Meanwhile Colonel Brunswick and his Adjutant, having missed the press trucks – which wasn't difficult in a thousand square miles of desert – were approaching the camp from a slightly different direction. Lurching and bumping across the waste land they finally arrived at the Special Ordnance Group in time to see the whole of the camp personnel lined up in front of Second Lieutenant Jampton, who was obviously berating them, tapping his swagger stick on to his hand to emphasise each point. Colonel Brunswick noticed his pressed, clean uniform in direct contrast to those of his charges: some were stripped to the waist, others wore dirty singlets, one of them wore a striped football jersey. It looked more like a badly run prisoner-of-war camp.

The Colonel and his Adjutant got slowly out of the car. Sergeant Major Puller, recognising them, called out 'Parade, atten-*shun*!'. The lads behind him shuffled their feet together in their own time, some of them having a quick drag at cigarettes. The Sergeant Major hadn't missed the blue cloud that had hung over the gathering. It had been the same all through the lecture. Every time the CO looked down for further inspiration many cupped hands went to mouths for quick drags in perfect unison. If this had been a drill movement, it would have shamed the Coldstream Guards.

Second Lieutenant Jampton turned to see what the interruption was, and, seeing his uncle, bounded towards him. Then collecting himself, he marched smartly back to the Sergeant Major.

'You may dismiss the men, Sergeant Major,' he said in a voice he hoped would carry to his uncle.

'Sah!' replied the Sergeant Major, snapping up another salute. He about turned to dismiss the parade but most of them had already gone.

'How are you, Uncle?'

'Dammit, Lieutenant, for as long as this war lasts I'm *not* your uncle. I'm *Colonel* Brunswick.'

Jampton's smile left his face. He stamped to attention and saluted.

'Oh, for God's sake,' said the Colonel, touching the peak of his cap in acknowledgment. Then, slightly ashamed of himself, he said gruffly, 'By the way, this is my Adjutant, Captain Shelley.' This caused another salute from Jampton. The Colonel raised his eyes to heaven.

'You look very well, Uncle,' said Jampton.

The Colonel gave up. His nephew had a skin as thick as a pub doormat.

'The press have been rampaging all over the camp, Uncle.'

Colonel Brunswick suppressed his rage. God almighty, he thought, it's still 'Uncle'. Can't the little bastard see the badges of rank on my shoulder?

The Adjutant stepped in quickly. 'What did they want?'

'Apparently they were here to get first-hand knowledge of the Messerschmitt affair.'

'Apparently?' pressed the Adjutant.

'Yes,' replied Jampton. 'I didn't actually speak to them myself. The Sergeant Major took away my uniform to be cleaned and by the time I got it back they'd gone.'

Colonel Brunswick brightened. 'So you didn't actually speak to them yourself?' he asked hopefully.

'No, sir,' replied Jampton. 'But needless to say I had some harsh words with the Sergeant Major and when you arrived I was laying down the law to the men. In future they will not – I repeat, will *not* . . .' He smiled. 'I actually said that to them, sir.'

'Yes, yes,' interrupted the Colonel, not interested in what would be or would not be done. 'Excuse me, I must have a word with Sergeant Major Puller.'

'I'll come with you,' said Jampton.

'I'm afraid not. My Adjutant would like to have a few words with you privately. Nothing serious, just how to make out military reports. A general talk on the responsibilities of command, et cetera.'

And with this he went in search of the Sergeant Major.

Jampton looked after his uncle wistfully, then turned back to the Captain. He cleared his throat and said proudly, 'I'm the Commanding Officer here and Colonel Brunswick is my uncle.'

'So I gathered,' remarked the Adjutant dryly.

'I don't suppose you've met Colonel Brunswick's wife, Aunt Dorothy. She's absolutely wizard. She's the real boss, you know.'

'Really?' said the Adjutant. He didn't want to get involved in domestic issues. 'Now, with regard to your military reports . . .'

'Ah yes,' replied Jampton and they began to walk up and down as they talked.

It was heavy going. Everything that the Adjutant said was interrupted by 'Ah yes, but you don't quite understand . . .' or 'I appreciate what you're saying but . . .' and at one time 'Could it be, Captain, that you're out of touch in Alexandria?'.

The Adjutant gave up. He finished his uphill struggle with 'Please, Lieutenant, please, I beg of you . . .' He paused searching for the right words. 'Just relax and enjoy the sun. Don't start anything until we're *all* ready.'

'Don't worry, sir,' said Jampton, his head wobbling with

self-righteousness. 'The next time you visit us you'll find a fighting unit well drilled and eager to go into action.'

The Adjutant sighed. He might just as well have saved his breath. It was like talking to a sand dune. He gazed round and was heartily relieved to see his Colonel approaching.

Again Jampton saluted. Brunswick acknowledged with a nod – he was in a benevolent mood.

'Would you like a pot of tea and something?' asked Jampton.

'No,' replied the Adjutant a shade too quickly. 'I really think we should be making tracks, sir,' he said to the Colonel.

'Oh, aren't you stopping for a while, Uncle? We could have a drink together in the officers' mess.'

'Officers' mess?' enquired the Colonel.

'It's that tent over there,' said Jampton as he pointed.

'No,' replied the Colonel. 'Some other time.' And he made his way towards the car.

Lieutenant Jampton watched as the driver opened the rear door and suddenly remembered he'd meant to ask his Uncle about the blue suitcase he'd left outside the RTO's office on the docks and to remind him that his name 'Lieutenant Jampton' was stencilled on both sides. But it was too late. When the car moved off the Colonel swivelled round to see his nephew standing rigidly at the salute.

'God,' he muttered, 'I wonder who winds him up every morning.'

But it was said in a jocular mood. His conversation with Sergeant Major Puller had been a great relief. Perhaps now the whole petty incident could be put to bed, filed away somewhere deep in Whitehall, forgotten, buried, ciao, finito. He tapped his knee as he hummed a catchy little bit from *The Chocolate Soldier*.

His Adjutant mopped his forehead. 'I think I now understand your antipathy towards Lieutenant Jampton.'

Colonel Brunswick's face clouded. He was silent for a moment, then he said, 'Did I ever tell you about him?'

'No, sir,' replied the Adjutant. It would help to pass the journey.

'Jampton,' began the Colonel, 'is my sister's only child.' He paused to get his words together.

'Poor Emily,' he said. 'You can't imagine what her life must have been like being the mother of that . . .' He jerked his thumb over his shoulder. 'She had two nervous breakdowns, eventually a divorce, and then do you know what she did, Jimmy?' The

Adjutant shook his head. 'She got into her car and drove up to Beachy Head, then she got out, locked it, walked smartly to the edge of the cliff, and jumped over.'

The Adjutant whistled sympathetically.

'All from eyewitnesses, you understand, but it's the sort of thing my sister would have done. And the following day young Jampton, only eight mind you, presents himself at my home. And when the butler took him to Her Ladyship she was overjoyed, and she more or less adopted him on the spot.'

He looked out of the car window at a laager of heavy tanks.

'You see, Jimmy,' he went on, 'for a lady in my wife's position her most important function in life is to produce a male heir to carry on the line – and unfortunately she couldn't have children of her own.'

He looked across at his Adjutant, who was fast asleep, and shrugged. He was glad that Captain Shelley hadn't heard the last bit – it wasn't strictly true. He shuddered as he remembered the disastrous coupling on his honeymoon night after which embarrassing episode he'd never insisted on his conjugal rights. She was even uglier with nothing on. For her own part she had been sickened by the whole sordid, disgusting act of copulation. No wonder the poor people did it at the weekend. And so young Wilfred Jampton became the heir apparent, and also, when he was older, he would inherit his own mother's fortune – a little matter that hadn't gone unnoticed.

'Go on, sir,' said the Adjutant.

'Oh, I thought you were asleep, Jimmy.'

'No, sir, I was listening with my eyes closed,' he lied. 'You were telling me how your sister was on holiday at Beachy Head.'

The Colonel stared at him in amusement. 'It's nothing, Jimmy,' he said after a time, all his good humour restored.

In other words he was wide open for the sucker punch that was to be delivered with all the might and power of the press. The battle of the Special Ordnance Group, as it was already being dubbed by headline writers, was beginning to take shape. From the little acorn of Jampton's report, a mighty forest was already begining to bloom, a gem that the media were going to polish far beyond its value. If ever a news item like this was desperately needed, it was now.

In the propaganda war the enemy were having it all their own way. The Germans and Italians were over the moon and they didn't even have to lie about events. In a home movie Eva Braun filmed a jubilant Adolf, a happy smile on his face, doing a Bavarian jig at Berchesgarten. And at a secret indoor riding school just outside Rome, Mussolini, on a heavily sedated white horse, was being led round and round as he prepared to lead the victory parade through Alexandria, and probably Cairo, too, unless he fell off. While in the North African desert, Rommel's High Command excitedly pored over street maps of Alexandria with gleeful anticipation that the battle after next would be over who got the best billet.

So it was hardly surprising that a fracas between the little Special Ordnance Group and the might of the German Afrika Korps was a heaven-sent opportunity in the propaganda war.

The snippet on the nine o'clock news broadcast might have turned out to be a one-day wonder, as Colonel Brunswick fervently hoped, but the press interviews with Sparks and Miller put paid to his optimism. On every front page of every broadsheet and tabloid was a huge picture of Private Sparks glowering over his shoulder at the camera, and Miller, a fatuous grin on his face as he held up his thumb.

Most of the articles were devoted to eulogies – how they were oppos, had served in a front-line infantry regiment in India, and after Dunkirk and their subsequent posting to North Africa had chased the Italians out of the fight, then the rearguard against Rommel and his Afrika Korps, finally ending in Tobruk.

Reading the more colourful writings, it would seem they hadn't had a day off since 1937. It was stirring stuff and it grabbed the nation. Volunteers besieged the recruiting offices; an amateur songwriter came up with a bit of silly doggerel:

You may have had Attilla
But now we've got Sparks and Miller.

It swept the country, it was whistled, sung and hummed in factories all over Britain. Huge sacks of fan mail simply addressed to Sparks and Miller were collected at the sorting offices. There was no possibility of sending them overseas – shipping space to North Africa was too tight for that. But all the letters were answered by a staff of civil servants in Shepherds Bush.

Even the politicians jumped on the bandwagon. In Parliament

one faction led by the Home Secretary was strongly in favour of bringing Sparks and Miller over to England for a morale-boosting tour of munition factories, training establishments and the like. This proposal, however, was quickly quashed by the Ministry of Production, being of the opinion that, should Sparks and Miller be unleashed on the British public, production could be adversely affected.

Such was their lionisation that munition factories, plants and other industries could shut down as hero-worshippers travelled miles in order to catch a glimpse and perhaps even to touch 'those two brave lads from over there.'

It was resolved, therefore, to keep them where they were, metaphorically patted on the head, and given a toffee sweet. In official parlance they were both awarded the Military Medal and Jampton, as the Commanding Officer, was promoted from Second Lieutenant to First.

In British Military Intelligence Colonel Brunswick was also invited to step up on to the podium. It was hardly surprising: having formed the Special Ordnance Group in the first place he had been commended for his initiative and foresight, so it seemed only natural to award him the OBE. Unfortunately, two weeks later in a directive from the War Office, it was deemed only fitting that he should travel to the camp in order that Sparks and Miller should receive their Military Medals from his own hands.

His first reaction was to refuse on the grounds of urgent intelligence work but on reflection, much as he detested this chore, it was vital that he, and only he, should present the medals. After all, should Winston Churchill, the King or anybody else for that matter take it upon themselves to present the awards personally, the fat would surely be in the fire. God knew what Jampton might come out with.

'Best get it over, Jimmy,' he said. 'Quick trip, in and out, no messing about, back in time for tea.'

And now, once again, they were approaching the Special Ordnance Group. Within five hundred yards of the camp the Adjutant leant forward to look over the driver's shoulder.

'What's up, Jimmy?' asked the Colonel.

The Adjutant pointed. Right across the track and barring their way was a red-and-white-striped pole and from holes in the ground on either side of it four heads popped up.

'What the bloody hell's going on?' muttered the Colonel.

One of the soldiers put his head through the driver's open window, turned back to his mates with his thumb up, and they raised the pole in order to let the car move on.

'I don't believe it,' said the Colonel. 'Fifty miles of nothing and he has a striped pole across the entrance.'

Just before they drove into the camp a notice by the track informed them that all visitors must report to the guard tent. And they couldn't miss it: it was neatly bordered by stones. God knew where the little prat had got the stuff from but each stone was painted a glaring white. Looking round him, he noticed that, instead of the one Bren pit where the famous battle of the erroneous Qatari Depression had taken place, there were now four Bren pits, one at each cardinal point round the camp. All were manned but there was, as far as he could see, still only one Bren gun. The rest of the poor sods had to make do with sticks.

Sergeant Major Puller was drilling a squad more or less uniformed, but it was clear his heart wasn't in it. On seeing the Colonel, however, he slammed to attention, called his motley crew to a halt, and saluted. This brought Jampton's head out of the tent and, seeing his distinguished visitors, he leapt forward.

The Colonel half edged behind the Adjutant. From the look on his nephew's face he couldn't be certain the prat wasn't about to embrace him.

After the obligatory salute Jampton said, 'Good to see you, Unc– Colonel.'

The Colonel heaved a sigh of relief. At least Jampton had learnt something. He turned suddenly and said, 'Excuse me, isn't that Sarn't Major Puller over there?'

It wasn't but it didn't matter. He had to get away from this pompous little twat of a nephew before he drew his service revolver and ended Jampton's military career and his own.

Five minutes later he was sitting in the Sergeant Major's tent pouring two healthy libations of Scotch from his hip flask into the two enamel mugs provided by the SM. Puller had reported briefly on events at the camp since Colonel Brunswick's last visit. It was like reading the script of a George Formby film.

'Go on,' said the Colonel.

'Well, and then two days ago one of our three-tonners disappeared.'

The Colonel frowned. 'Disappeared?' he echoed.

'Yes, sir, and so did the two French Legionnaires and six other bods.' The Colonel looked at him searchingly. 'They weren't happy, sir.'

'Did they tell you that, Sergeant Major?'

The Sergeant Major was uneasy. He looked away, stroking his blue chin.

'Come on, man,' snapped the Colonel. 'Why didn't you put a guard on the transport?'

The Sergeant Major straightened. 'I did so, sir – two guards.'

'And I suppose they were both asleep?'

'Oh no, sir,' replied the Sergeant Major. 'They went with 'em. Officially,' he went on, 'we have no jurisdiction over the Legionnaires. They are French nationals. Three of the others are RAF personnel, and the rest . . .' He shrugged. 'Civvies.'

The Colonel nodded. 'And how many of the old 41st Light Infantry are left?'

'Eight, sir, including me.'

The Colonel looked up at the sky, then shook his head sadly. 'Eight,' he mused. Poor bloody infantry, the old 41st. All they wanted was hot food whenever possible, fags, letters from home, but most important, a damn good Commanding Officer. And he had lumbered them with his nephew . . . Poor bloody infantry.

Finally he said, 'I appreciate your difficulty, Sergeant Major. But don't worry. I'll have a word with your CO.'

But even as he said it he knew he wouldn't, and despised himself for his cowardice, but, good grief, every man was entitled to his Achilles heel and Jampton was a whole foot.

Later, in the screened-off portion of the medical marquee marked OFFICERS' MESS, the Colonel listened morosely while his Adjutant related his exchange with his nephew.

'Any other requirements?' asked the Colonel.

'Quite a few, sir, but his next item was a padre.'

The Colonel's eyebrows shot up.

'Isn't he well?' he asked hopefully.

His Adjutant smiled. 'It's not that, sir. As from next Sunday he's instigated church parades.'

'Good grief,' exploded the Colonel. 'I hope you told him that padres had better things to do than officiate at church parades.' Unaware of the irony of his remarks, he continued. 'Jampton'll want a military band to go with it, I suppose.'

'Don't worry, sir, I quashed that one. I reminded him that there was a war on.'

'And what did he say to that?'

The Adjutant shrugged. 'He took it well enough, said he understood and would settle for fife and drums.'

The Colonel stared at him for a moment. 'And?' he said finally.

'I told him he could have the drums but Fife was in Scotland.'

The Colonel chuckled and slapped his thigh. 'Did he laugh?'

'No, sir. He stared at me in a peculiar way, than made a note on his pad.'

'What about the medals and stuff?' interrupted the Colonel.

'Ah yes,' replied his Adjutant. 'I've arranged that handing the citations to Sparks and Miller take place in the orderly tent.'

'Good for you, Jimmy,' the Colonel chuckled. 'I'll bet that didn't go down too well.'

'No, sir.' The Adjutant shuddered. 'He was all for a full dress parade formed up in a square with the Sergeant Major in full dress uniform handing you both medals on a cushion.' The Colonel's eyebrows shot up. 'Yes sir,' said the Adjutant. 'I asked him where he was going to get a cushion from and he told me he'd had a pillow dyed purple.'

Brunswick stared at him in disbelief. Jampton was his sister's child and a frightening thought crossed his mind. Could it be that there was insanity in his family?

'Oh don't worry, sir,' went on the Adjutant. 'Like I said, no fuss, and a quick handover in the orderly tent.'

'Brilliant,' said the Colonel. 'A register office as opposed to Westminster Abbey.'

'He took it rather well, sir.'

'Right,' said the Colonel briskly. 'Let's get it over with and then back to Alex. Somebody's got to be there to show Rommel where everything is.'

FIVE

The following Monday Sergeant Major Puller strode across to the CO's tent. In the last few days there had been six more desertions but it was the two that had gone over the hill this morning that disturbed him most. There was no reply to his knock on the tent pole, so he tentatively pulled back the flap to find that the CO was not at home. He was about to duck out when he caught sight of the manuscript on the table. It was headed 'MILITARY TACTICS' BY WILFRED RONALDSAY JAMPTON. He was intrigued. Curiously, he flipped through it. CHAPTER 6: HOW TO SALUTE FROM A MOVING VEHICLE. CHAPTER 7: CLAUSEWITZ WAS WRONG, and then BISMARK'S FOLLY. What a load of balls, he thought. How had he managed to get himself lumbered with Lieutenant Wilfred Ronaldsway Jampton, who wasn't old enough to be mad but was certainly retarded? He'd have to be to write this crap.

He turned as the author ducked in through the tent flap. On seeing the Sergeant Major, he looked quickly round to see if he was in the right tent. On being assured that he was, he spoke.

'Been waiting long?' he asked sarcastically.

The Sergeant Major eyed him coolly, not deigning to reply.

Jampton walked round his desk and sat on the chair. 'What's the problem, Sarn't Major?' he asked.

'It's Sparks and Miller, sir.' He paused.

'What about Sparks and Miller?' asked Jampton.

'They've deserted, sir.'

He waited for Jampton's reaction, but he couldn't quite make it out. The CO was smiling with what looked like amusement, the way a man will look after his opponent has just moved a piece on the chessboard that will cost him the game.

'And what makes you think they've deserted?' he asked smoothly.

The Sergeant Major found his anger was rising, but he managed to bring himself under control.

'Because, sir,' he said through gritted teeth, 'they're not here any more. They've gone over the hill, done a bunk.'

He drew a breath; he was sailing dangerously close to the line of insolence and was too well trained to step over it.

'They've taken their small kit with them and one of the wagons is missing,' he added.

The CO regarded him with an enigmatic smile.

'And where d'you think they've deserted to?' he asked.

Good Christ, help me, thought Sergeant Major Puller. Much more of this and I swear I'll bury him up to his neck in sand and let the ants have him.

Jampton leant forward over the table.

'Let me put you out of your misery, Sarn't Major.' He looked at his wristwatch. 'By now they should be halfway to Alexandria.'

The Sergeant Major stared blankly at the pompous little ferret-eyed face.

'Oh yes,' went on Jampton. 'I detailed them to take the three-tonner into Alex to pick up supplies.'

The Sergeant Major couldn't believe his ears. It was as if the prison warden had sent a lifer up to London for a packet of his favourite cigarettes.

'Something troubling you, Sergeant Major?' asked Jampton silkily.

'Yes, sir,' he said resignedly. 'That's the last we'll see of Sparks and Miller and the three-tonner . . .'

Jampton raised his hands and stopped him.

'You're still convinced they've deserted, Sarn't Major?'

'I know these men, sir.'

'You knew these men, Sarn't Major, but this was before they were awarded the Military Medal. If my judgment of human nature is anything to go by, they'll be back in three days, and with more supplies than we indented for, eh?' He winked conspiratorially. But the SM wasn't about to join the conspiracy.

Jampton leant back confidently.

'Listen, Sergeant Major, I'm not a betting man, but I'll wager my wristwatch against your cap badge that I'm right and they'll be back here in three days.'

The Sergeant Major shook his head. 'Right,' he said sadly, 'it's your wristwatch.'

Jampton was flustered. After four more days, sadly, reluctantly and inevitably, he came around to the conclusion that the Sergeant Major was right. Sparks and Miller, military medals and all, were gone for good. The realisation made Jampton cross; he was too young and pampered to understand anger. Whenever something nasty had happened to him in the past it had been swiftly dealt with by his loving, doting and formidable aunt. Even when the young horror set fire to the gardener's cottage there'd been no reprimand, and the old gardener had been dismissed for being stupid enough to leave a box of matches on a shelf by the gas stove, even though young Jampton had had to climb up on a chair to get them.

Sparks and Miller would not have dared to desert if his Aunt Dorothy was here. It wasn't just the actual crime of desertion that bothered him, but he'd given them specific instructions where to find his blue suitcase, its dimensions, and the fact that his name was stencilled all over it; he'd even mentioned the torn label in the bottom corner from a hotel in Eastbourne. He glanced at his wrist and saw only a white band where his watch had been. Exasperated, he threw his copy of *Military Tactics* to the floor and stamped on it.

Seated in the front of the bumping, lurching three-tonner, Sergeant Major Puller dozed. Up to now the journey had been uneventful. It wasn't a safe run, and for that reason the first half was completed under the cover of darkness. This wasn't entirely risk-free. There was always the danger of running into an enemy patrol, or a minefield, but at least there was safety from air attacks.

Now it was beginning to get light and the Sergeant Major yawned and stretched. He was an infantryman and if he wished to sleep he closed his eyes and it was so. He could sleep deeply and quietly until something unusual aroused him – the click of a rifle bolt, the distant soft squeal of heavy tank tracks, or, as it was in this case, first light. He lit two cigarettes and handed one to the driver. They hadn't exchanged much conversation during the journey.

'Want to stop for a minute?' asked the SM.

'No, sir, I'm all right for a bit.'

And as the heat in the cab began to rise, the driver took off his tin hat. Puller looked across at him with interest. The back of his driver's head was flat. It was exraordinarily flat. It reminded the SM of an Easter Island statue. Perhaps he had been born like that, but more than likely his father had fetched him a sharp blow to the back of his head with a shovel during his formative years. He was about to ask idly if this was so but decided against it.

They rumbled on and as the sun began to float from beyond the horizon they noticed a few signs of activity – not very close and most likely to be British now that they were on the last leg. The Sergeant Major glanced at his watch, and this reminded him. He took the CO's wristwatch from his shirt pocket and examined it. He turned it over and engraved on the back was 'From Aunt Dorothy to Her Little Soldier'. He shuddered. God, he'd have that taken off sharpish. If he caught a packet it wouldn't do to have that on his wrist.

'Got a file?' he asked the driver.

'One in the toolbox, sir. I'll get it out when we stop.'

The Sergeant Major nodded and put the watch on the floor of the cab. The danger now would be from the air. Some lone, predatory Luftwaffe pilot might fancy a bit of target practice and Jampton's wristwatch would be the first thing out of the window.

Suddenly the Sergeant Major leant forward. Ahead of them and to one side of the track were the burnt-out remains of a vehicle. This was not unusual in itself – the desert was littered with sights like this – but something else had caught the SM's eye.

'Pull up,' he ordered.

Then the driver noticed it too, a poignant reminder of the war. Two small, rough crosses topped by two British tin hats. There were no markings but hanging by their string were two identifica-tion discs. Slowly the SM bent and took one of them: 'Miller, M. C of E'. The other one was stamped 'Sparks, Agnostic'.

The driver took off his own tin hat in respect. 'Poor bastards,' he muttered.

The Sergeant Major was thoughtful. He wandered over to the burnt-out vehicle. There wasn't too much left of it. He bent to brush the sand from the blackened piece of what was once a radiator, then quickly he straightened.

'In you get, laddie,' he said briskly. 'You'll get your evening in Alex, have no fear.'

The driver was staggered.

'But, sir –' he pointed at the crosses '– what about Sparks and Miller?'

'We're going to pick 'em up.'

The driver stared again at the two crosses, not understanding.

'Oh don't worry about that little bit of pantomime. They're not due for their eternal rest yet, lad. They're in Alex.' The driver wasn't convinced. 'You see that?' The SM pointed to the burnt-out wreck.

'The supply wagon,' said the driver mechanically.

The Sergeant Major snorted. 'And since when have we been driving Mercedes?'

The Sergeant Major had been correct in his assumption. Sparks and Miller had indeed arrived in Alexandria four days ago. It had been just after midnight when they had pulled up behind a line of Bren carriers. As they sat smoking in the cab of their three-tonner they quietly discussed their next move. The first job was to get rid of the truck. This didn't pose much of a problem: they already had a buyer in mind. With this money they would bribe one of the boatmen to take them up the Nile to wherever it took them.

It was a simple strategy and about as watertight as a string vest. Obstacles and unforeseen events were to see to that. However, they settled themselves down for a few hours' sleep with the intention of being on the road at first light. But as sleep was always a luxury to an infantryman, the sun was already halfway up the sky when they finally awoke. But they weren't unduly worried – they felt they had plenty of time in hand. What they hadn't put into their equation was their new-found fame and notoriety.

The *Daily Express* had been first off the mark. Bales of the flimsy overseas editions were flown out to Alexandria and Cairo on the direct orders of the Minister of Propaganda. It was a morale booster to lift up the flagging spirits of the British and Allied Forces, a desperate attempt to stiffen up the blood in a last-ditch effort to save North Africa. So the privilege of English newspapers, hitherto afforded to only high-ranking officers' messes, was now extended to anybody who could read. And for those who couldn't, there were always the large pictures of Sparks and Miller. In fact, since the newspapers had arrived their faces had become more familiar than Clark Gable and Carole Lombard.

Sparks, who was not driving, was the first to notice the curious stares every time they were forced to slow down in the volume of traffic. A small group of Australians were the first to confirm his fears that, for some unaccountable reason, they were attracting attention. One of the Aussies pointed and yelled, 'Good on ya, Sparks,' and together they whistled, yahooed and waved their one-sided, pinned-up hats.

'Take the next left,' yelled Sparks and they shot down a less-populated side street, and after a few more detours Miller pulled up and stared at Sparks.

'What the bloody hell's going on?'

'Don't ask me,' snapped Sparks.

'I didn't know you knew any Aussies,' said Miller.

'It's not just them,' said Sparks. 'Everybody's been staring at us . . .'

He was about to continue when a well-dressed Egyptian in a linen suit and a fez tapped his fly whisk against Miller's door.

'Yes?' said Miller suspiciously.

The Egyptian looked up at him. 'Welcome to Alexandria, Mr Miller,' he said. Then he craned to one side, standing on tiptoes. 'And Mr Sparks too, I see.'

They looked at each other, baffled.

'Would you do me the greatest honour and sign my newspaper?'

He held up a copy of the *Daily Express* and a pen. Miller snatched the newspaper from him but ignored the pen. Quickly he unfolded the paper.

'Jesus,' he breathed and held the thing across to his oppo.

'Shit and derision,' said Sparks as he glanced at his picture on the front page of the newspaper.

By now a small crowd was beginning to collect.

'It's us,' murmured Miller.

'I know who it is,' snapped Sparks. 'Get this bloody truck moving, now, quick for Christ's sake!'

Miller gunned the engine and the crowd fell back.

'Bloody hell,' said Sparks once they were moving again. 'Have you got any more bright ideas?'

'Me?' protested Miller.

'Let's go up to Alex, you said, and disappear.'

'Well I didn't know, did I?' bleated Miller.

'Look at 'em all staring.'

'Yeh,' said Sparks, 'and these are friendly. They're on our side. What happens when Rommel gets a copy of the *Daily Express*?'

Miller didn't connect for a moment. 'Bloody 'ell,' he shouted slapping the wheel. 'I hope we haven't upset him. One Stuka and half a dozen Hitler youth, that's all he'd need and the camp would be a black patch in the desert. We're better off out of it. Potbelly's place can't be far now.' And his foot went down on the accelerator.

'It's around here some place,' said Sparks, ducking and bobbing his head trying to recognise a landmark. 'Got it!' he shouted slapping his thigh. 'Turn right into that street up there.'

'Which one?'

'By the sign. I'm sure that's Potbelly's place.'

A Sergeant and a Lance Corporal of the Military Police were standing stiffly against a wall, only their eyes moving under the low peaks of their red caps. But they didn't miss much and registered mentally the erratic progress of the three-ton truck speeding dangerously in and out of the traffic.

'Mad bastard,' said the Sergeant out of the corner of his mouth, eyes swivelling to follow its wild dash.

Everybody was in a hurry these days – roll on demob. It was only when the truck, heeling over, took a suicidal dive up one of the side streets that they became animated. That street was out of bounds.

'Come on,' said the Sergeant and together they pushed their way through the strolling mob, most of whom made way, especially anybody in uniform. When redcaps moved quickly it was best to be somewhere else.

Miller swung hard across the road and into the narrow street. The sign read OUT OF BOUNDS TO ALL MILITARY PERSONNEL.

'I've never noticed that before,' said Miller.

'That's because you never bloody well looked where you were going,' yelled Sparks.

The locals were scattering on all sides, cursing and hawking. The lorry wasn't going to slow down and kismet was one thing and 'what is to be will be' was another, but Allah couldn't be every place at once.

'This is it,' shouted Miller and jabbed his foot on the brake.

Sparks lunged across to hammer on the horn. The hostile mob surged round the truck, some beating the canvas side with sticks and screaming in a frenzy of hate. Miller sat petrified while Sparks beat frantically on the horn. A rock splintered the windscreen.

'Come on, come on,' muttered Sparks frantically.

And slowly – bloody hell was it ever slow – the whole shop front swung inward. Panic-stricken, in a series of jerks, Miller turned into the blackness of the car park and immediately behind them the shop front creaked back into place. It was only then that Miller switched off the engine and the two of them sat shakily in the darkness.

By the time the Military Police reached the end of the street they were already too late. The Lance Corporal was about to rush up the street and the Sergeant restrained him. There was a mass of people as far as the eye could see but no truck. Faces cold and hostile turned towards the two military policemen.

'What's happened to the truck, Sarge?'

'What truck?'

The Lance Jack looked at him in amazement.

'The three-tonner.'

'I never saw a three-tonner,' muttered the Sergeant, never taking his eyes off the crowd.

The bustle and anger that had erupted a few minutes ago subsided into a malevolent silence, their attention now directed at the two policemen. It was a page out of the Old Testament.

'Come on, lad.'

The Sergeant was backing slowly towards the main street again. The Lance Corporal was undecided.

'We can make enquiries, Sarge. The truck couldn't have reached the other end, that's for sure.'

He turned to see the Sergeant already rounding the corner into the main drag. Still the locals hadn't moved. He cleared his throat about to speak but his courage left him as a stone whistled past his ear. He turned and ran to catch up with his Sergeant, who was now back in his own patch demanding to see a small soldier's pay book and, while he flicked unseeingly through the pages, the Lance Corporal joined him.

'What about that truck, Sarge?'

The Sergeant handed back the pay book and when the little man had left them he said, out of the corner of his mouth, 'I didn't see any truck, lad. And if you did you should lay off the old . . .' He mimed drinking. Then he added, 'Listen, son, that street is dangerous. I wouldn't go up there in an armoured car with an escort of Royal Marines. I wouldn't even send the missus up there.'

He looked beyond the Lance Corporal. 'Where's your cap, soldier?' he barked at a passing soldier.

'Bollocks,' replied the soldier and moved on.

The Sergeant shrugged. 'You can't win 'em all,' he muttered philosophically.

In the cab of their three-tonner Sparks and Miller sat in silence while they collected their jangling nerves.

'What a bastard,' whispered Dusty Miller. He applied a match to his cigarette and the way the flame jumped about and the glowing end of the cigarette trembled it was clear that he still hadn't got over the last half-hour. He took the cigarette from his lips.

'What a bastard,' he muttered again. 'What a lousy, jumped-up, never-come-down bastard.'

There was a silence. Then, 'What if Potbelly won't buy the truck?' asked Sparks.

Miller digested this for a moment. 'He'll have it, don't you worry.'

'He'd better,' replied Sparks. 'I'm not going out there again in this. And he opened the door and jumped down to wait for Abdul. They had a long wait, at least half an hour, but then time wasn't on a watch in this part of the world.

A tiny bulb was switched on and Abdul came mincing down the two steps. Sparks and Miller quietly smoked as they watched him approach.

'My house is yours,' he began, and they all bowed. 'We've been expecting you.'

They looked at each other in astonishment. 'Expecting us?' said Miller. 'How did you know we were coming?'

'Ah,' smiled Abdul coquettishly, 'a little bird, eh? Yes, my friends, a little bird. Now, how can I help you?'

Miller shook himself out of his puzzlement. 'How much?' he said and gestured to the back of the truck.

Abdul peered over the tailgate and shrugged. 'What is this, a joke?'

'No,' replied Miller. 'It's all yours.'

'But there's nothing here.' And he peered over the tailgate again and struck a match in case there was something he had missed.

'The truck, it's all yours, all three tons of it – wheels, good tyres, radiator, the lot; low mileage and the tank's practically full.'

Abdul sucked in his breath and stepped back. 'Oh no, no, no, no, no – is too dangerous.'

Sparks ground out his cigarette. 'Oh come on, Dusty, I told you we should have taken it to One-eyed Ahmed.'

Miller looked at his oppo in amazement. What the hell was he on about? He'd never heard of One-eyed Ahmed.

Abdul was unmoved. 'No, no. A truck is different.'

Sparks snorted. 'Well, that's it then,' he said. 'Come on, Dusty, we'll get a better price from One-eyed Ahmed anyway.' He made to open the passenger door.

'Wait, wait,' implored Abdul. 'Come upstairs. We have a drink and talk, yes?'

Sparks looked to Miller and winked. 'OK, let's hear what he has to say.'

Abdul moved round the bar on the edge of the small dance floor. The place was empty apart from the three of them, which was hardly surprising. It was a nightclub and they didn't do afternoon tea dancing. Miller was satisfied Abdul wanted the truck. All that remained was the price. An hour and three-quarters of a bottle of Scotch later, price was still the only obstacle. Abdul was impassive. He'd kept up, drink for drink, which was hardly surprising as he was only on lemonade.

'All right, then,' said Miller, 'and this is our last offer.'

It was the fourth time it had been his last offer, but he was in the big league and Abdul was a past master.

'I'm listening,' he said quietly.

'Right,' said Miller. 'Two hundred pounds cash, plus room and board for three months.'

Abdul reached for a small bell and shook it delicately, and before he put it down a huge black fella eased from the shadows and bowed. They stared at him. Without a doubt he was the biggest, widest man they'd ever seen. What a monster! The door was easily four feet wide and he still had to come in sideways. His bare arms were bigger than Miller's thighs.

A shiver of fear went through him. Had he blown it? They were up a one-way street. To the military they'd already disappeared and the bits of them floating down the Nile wouldn't be enough to identify. Bloody stupid to leave their rifles in the cab. In any case you'd need an antitank gun to make an impression on this one.

His relief was equalled only by the deep sigh from Sparks as Abdul said, 'Mohammed, my pills.' He leant back, clutching his heart.

'Ain't it marvellous?' breathed Sparks. 'They always have to throw a Sarah Bernhardt.'

Miller looked at him in amazement. Would his oppo realise how close they'd been to the knacker's yard?

Sparks half rose. 'I told you,' he said, 'we should have taken it to One-eyed Ahmed's.'

Miller was puzzled. He dragged his mate back into his chair and, whilst Abdul was washing the pills down with a glass of water, hissed low into Sparks's ear.

'Who the bloody hell is One-eyed Ahmed?'

Sparks shrugged in return; it was enough.

'My friends.' Abdul smiled, spreading his arms. 'My good friends ... I always help my friends, especially the soldiers who protect us from harm.' He shook his head. 'But three months' room and board, it's impossible.'

Miller knew why three months was too long. The old bastard was expecting Rommel and the Afrika Korps. The last thing he wanted was to be caught harbouring two British soldiers.

But the penny didn't seem to have dropped with Sparks. 'Ah, give him a kick up the arse and let's go.'

But again Miller waved him down. 'Two months then,' he said.

'Two months?' wailed Abdul. 'Two hours you have been here and already one bottle of finest Scotch whisky, zut, gone.' He shook his head sadly. 'My good friends,' he went on. 'Look around you. Am I flocking with customers?' He gestured round the room. 'Nobody ... How can I pay my poor girls? All they do is eat, sleep and get fat. And who has to feed them? I'm a poor man.'

Miller snorted. 'You're breaking my heart,' he said. 'In a couple of hours this place'll be jam-packed and you know it. You had this place put out of bounds 'cos there's more money in civilians, right?'

'Two weeks,' said Abdul suddenly raising his hands in surrender.

Miller looked at Sparks, who yawned. 'Suits me,' he said. He was bored with all the palaver. One week in this place would be more than enough.

'Well, that's settled then,' said Miller. 'Now the money.'

Sparks stood up. 'Sort that out between you. I'm going to get my head down.' He turned to Abdul. 'Which room am I in? Just give me the key and I'll find it.'

'A key?' asked Abdul. A laugh started deep in the fat belly, all the flab quivering like a blancmange in a high wind. 'A key?' he said. 'Yes, my lord, and what time would you like breakfast, my lord?'

Sparks stared down at the man. Miller grabbed the whisky bottle and made to fill his glass. Nobody laughed at Sparks. The bottle was the only weapon within reach.

It didn't seem to bother Abdul. He was wiping tears from his eyes. 'Show Milord to his room,' he ordered. 'But in my humble establishment we cannot afford the luxury of keys.'

This diffused the situation; well that, and the massive Mr Universe standing behind his chair. The enormous monster of a man beckoned and Sparks followed.

Miller relaxed. That could have been nasty. He gulped down his Scotch. Had it been true to its Johnny Walker label he would have been under the table by now, but we all had to make a crust and each bottle was mainly cold tea. At least it was better than gin: half that came straight out of the Nile.

Upstairs Sparks took off his shirt and poured some water out of a cracked jug into the basin. Then he fiddled around in his small kit for a sliver of soap. He worked hard for some lather and finally he managed enough for a wash. The cold water against his face was exhilarating, the best thing that had happened all day. He felt for the jug and poured the rest of the water over his head, then he scooped more water from the basin and repeated the action. He straightened and only then realised there was no towel. He wouldn't open his eyes – his bit of soap had been thinner than a communion wafer but was enough to blind him.

'There's never a bloody towel when you want one,' he muttered stupidly.

'Oh yes there is.'

He stopped dead in his tracks, feeling the roughness of a towel draped over his hands. He liked the sound of that voice. 'Ello,

'ello, he thought, my ship's come in. But when he cleared his vision his face dropped.

'Not you again,' he said. 'How did you know I'd be here?'

'Where else?' said Yasmin.

In the camp it was Corporal Smith and he suspected that Yasmin wasn't her real name, but what the hell! She'd told him that she was half French, half Arab. In any case he called her Yasmin; it wasn't too hard to remember. Up to now he'd only seen her in oversized khaki shirt and shorts, and a few times out of them, but she'd never worn a dress before and he had to admit that the red shoes with high heels did a lot more for her than a pair of Army boots. She sat on the bed and crossed her legs, and, bloody 'ell, they weren't bad either.

He stared at her, perplexed. What kind of a woman was this? She was always several jumps ahead; no wonder Abdul had opened the shop entrance so promptly: they'd been expected. Also, their accommodation was arranged. In all his experience he'd never come across a woman like Yasmin before. Hitherto his women had fallen into two categories – those who would and those who wouldn't. He fancied her but the warning bell in the back of his head jangled. He was the original chauvinist; it was time to lay down a few ground rules.

'You didn't walk here,' asked Sparks, but it wasn't a query.

She smiled. 'No, I've been here for a few days. I got a lift from ... the other people – the two Legionnaires. We had a very nice journey.'

Sparks was about to remind her that the two Legionnaires had not only stolen a truck but they had deserted. His mouth was open ready to speak when he remembered that that was exactly what he and Miller had done.

She might have been reading his mind.

'I've bought for you a nice shirt and tie and a light suit.'

While she talked she moved over to the old wardrobe and opened the door.

'*Voilà*,' she said with a gesture towards a white suit on a hanger.

He stared in amazement, water dripping off his chin. It wasn't so much the suit – it was the dresses on several other hangers, her dresses. He glanced down at the bed. It would be a tight squeeze. Then he frowned – it was all too organised.

'Listen, Yasmin,' he started. 'How did you know I'd be in this room, this particular one?'

Again she smiled and it made him uneasy. He didn't like being manipulated.

'I told you, Sparks, but you don't listen. Abdul is my uncle. How you say, from far away.'

'Distant,' said Sparks.

'Yes, distant uncle. If it was not for me you would not have been welcome. And even if you come in, you would never have got out again.'

He nodded, then remembered her dresses in the wardrobe.

'Yes, OK, OK,' he said. 'Now listen, Yasmin. It's time we had a talk – let's get it all out in the open.'

He turned to look out of the window, which faced the high whitewashed wall of the building opposite. He wasn't a man of words, and why the hell did she just sit there with that superior smile on her face as if she knew what he was going to say? The wall opposite was easier than having to face her.

'You can't just move in. It's too much like being married.'

She remained silent.

'I told you in the beginning I have to be free.'

Still no response.

'I like you. Yes, I like you a lot, but if I'd known you were going to stick to me like a mustard plaster I would have left you under that pile of rocks back in Tobruk.'

This time she spoke. 'Oh no, you could not do that, it was fate.'

'My eye,' replied Sparks. 'I make my own fate.'

He turned to face her and stopped in surprise. She'd taken off her shoes and was lying, hands behind her head, smiling again. He'd never seen her smile before today.

He went on reasonably. 'Now you're a nice bit. I'll give you that, but British blokes are not like other men. They like to be on their tod sometimes. You know, Tod Sloane, alone, by themselves. They like their women . . . well, somewhere else – waiting, like the Arabs. They do it all the time. You ought to understand that, being half Arab.'

Yasmin was angry. 'I am not an Arab. I am French,' she snapped.

'OK, OK,' said Sparks. 'How come old Potbelly's your uncle?'

She snorted derisively. 'Abdul is not my uncle, not a real uncle. It's a courtesy title. I used to work here.'

Sparks's eyebrows went up.

'No, it's not what you're thinking. I wasn't one of the girls. I was the madame, and being Abdul's niece I was under his protection.' Sparks opened his mouth to speak but Yasmin went on. 'And the answer to that is no. Abdul prefers little boys.'

Sparks couldn't help the feeling of relief, but another question entered his mind.

'And Tobruk?'

She waved a hand deprecatingly. 'I was a receptionist at the Hotel Imperial. That's where I was when the roof fell in.'

Sparks nodded. 'You don't half pick some nice places to work.'

He looked down at the towel in his hands, then remembered her dresses in the wardrobe and the way she had taken control of the conversation, the possessiveness of her attitude as if she belonged. He screwed up the towel and flung it into the wash basin.

'As if I haven't got enough problems,' he muttered.

Behind him, swinging her legs off the bed, she began to put her shoes back on, then she stood and made for the door.

'Where you off to?' Sparks said uncertainly.

'What should that matter to you?' she snapped, opening the door.

'Hang on, hang on,' pleaded Sparks. Quickly coming over to her, he closed the door and turned her towards him. They stood for a moment looking into each other's face.

'I love you, Sparks,' she said softly.

'Yeah, yeah,' he replied huskily, and then, with a desperate attempt to regain the high ground, he said, 'All right, then, just this once,' and led her back to the bed.

The following day Sparks and Yasmin were sitting in companionable silence at a table on the pavement in front of Le Chat Noir, a popular restaurant at the corner of Saad Zaghioul Street. They were idly watching the colourful panorama of many different races passing up and down – Egyptians in djellabas, uniforms of many nations, black-robed, masked ladies carrying baskets, pots, suitcases on their heads. Some of the tenseness was leaving Sparks. Passers-by had looked towards them but without recognition. Most of the military ignored him altogether and had eyes only for Yasmin. It was hardly surprising. His off-white suit wasn't a bad fit and his light hair dyed black was now supplemented by a Ronald Colman moustache. He was satisfied his disguise had passed the test. In fact, when he had seen himself in the fly-specked mirror over the wash basin, he'd half ducked, wondering who the bloody hell it was. He smiled at the recollection and beckoned a waiter over. 'Two beers,' he said.

'*Bien.*' The waiter bowed and was about to leave when Yasmin spoke to him in French.

'My friend is a joker. Cancel the two beers and make it two pastis.'

'*Bien, madame.*' The waiter bowed again and left.

Sparks watched him go then turned to Yasmin. 'What was all that about?' he hissed.

Yasmin leant towards him and said softly, 'A rich young Egyptian does not order beer, and most certainly not for his girlfriend.'

Sparks was about to argue, then realised the logic in this and decided to ignore the girlfriend bit.

'*Voilà,*' said the waiter placing the two glasses and a jug of water on the table.

'*Merci,*' replied Yasmin dismissively.

And the waiter bowed and left, disappointed not to have poured the water, which would have given him a bird's-eye view down her cleavage. Yasmin did the honours, turning the yellow liquid into a milky whiteness.

'What's this?' asked Sparks dubiously.

'Pernod,' she said, and added mischievously, 'It's good for your sex life.'

Clinking her glass with his, they drank. Sparks nodded appreciatively and relaxed even more. He was about to take out a packet of cigarettes when suddenly he stiffened. Yasmin followed his gaze quickly. Two military policemen, redcaps, blancoed webbing, boots that shone like a new gramophone record, were about twenty yards away, walking in step unhurriedly. But surely they would pass the table. Yasmin squeezed his hand but it didn't reassure him. He appreciated all the work she'd done on dying his hair and stuff but these bastards had X-ray eyes.

He looked round him searching frantically for a quick exit when his eyes fell on a newspaper discarded on the next table. Snatching it up, he held it open to hide his face. It looked for all the world as if he was reading the bottom line on one of the centre pages, but in reality he was watching the black shiny boots and white gaiters approaching from underneath the paper. Slowly and inevitably they drew level, then they stopped and moved towards the table. Sparks's heart was beating faster than it had ever done, even before an attack. At least in battle he knew what to expect.

He closed his eyes, desperately trying to stop his hands from shaking, when one of the redcaps spoke.

'That one's Sparks isn't it, the light-haired geezer?'

Sparks was baffled. Could they see through the newspaper? Then Yasmin leant forward and looked at the front page of the old edition of the *Daily Express*.

'Ah yes,' she said, 'and the other one is Miller, yes?'

'Yes,' said one of them, and the boots turned away from the table and the voice spoke again to his mate. 'I've seen those two somewhere.'

There was a pause and then the other voice replied, 'I think everybody in the world has seen them two. I wouldn't be surprised if they were on the front of *Time* magazine.'

Again there was a pause and the first voice spoke. 'I can't help feeling I've seen them recently, here in Alexandria.'

There was a silence once more. 'It'll come to me,' said the voice. And the boots moved off.

Yasmin took the newspaper from Sparks's trembling fingers and turned it round to show him the front page and the photos of himself and Dusty Miller.

Sparks sagged back in his chair, sweat pouring down his face. He pushed his glass away.

'Bugger that for a lark. I need a proper drink.' And he sent the waiter inside for a large Scotch.

Yasmin patted his hand. 'Relax,' she whispered. 'You are not Sparks now. You look more like an unsuccessful Egyptian tax collector.'

A tumbler full of doubtful whisky was set before him and he was about to drink when he felt a tug on his sleeve. His nerves were still ragged and he yelped, throwing most of his drink over the table. He turned his head to see an Egyptian wearing dark glasses, fez and striped djellaba.

'You buy postcard, yes?'

Ignoring the singsong sales pitch, he turned back to his reading.

'Hello, sir, you like dirty postcard?'

'Piss off,' he muttered out of the corner of his mouth.

'Many positions, yes?'

Sparks's fists bunched on the table. The Arab leant forward quickly and whispered in his ear. 'It's me, you pillock.'

Sparks was dumbstruck. It was Miller all right and he really had some postcards.

'Pretend to be going through 'em,' he hissed.

Sparks took the pictures. They weren't dirty postcards, just the crap tourists bought showing 'Pompeii's Pillar', 'The Catacombs of Kom al-Shqafa' and other places to visit in Alexandria.

Yasmin turned away in disgust. An unsuccessful Egyptian tax collector would certainly not be buying dirty postcards at the corner of Saad Zaghioul Street. An unsuccessful Egyptian tax collector would most likely be selling them himself.

Miller, who had nodded to Yasmin, whispered in Sparks's ear pointing to the postcards as he did so. 'Some time next week a felucca going up the Nile. Cost a bit but it's the best I can do. OK?'

'Your Gestapo is back,' whispered Yasmin, and Sparks looked up to see the two military policemen returning along their beat. Miller snatched the photographs and disappeared. But the military policemen, showing no interest at all, carried on past the table.

Sparks drained what was left of his whisky. His nerves couldn't stand much more of this but the news from Dusty Miller was good. In a few days they'd be on a boat going up the Nile, and then what? He didn't care. Any boat, anywhere, as long as they didn't end up in a convoy to Russia.

Three days later another one of the Special Ordnance vehicles pulled up in the commercial part of the city on Salah Salem Street and Sergeant Major Puller jumped down. Turning, he looked up at the driver. 'I'll see you at the Allied Services Club at nine o'clock.'

'Where's that, sir?'

'It's two blocks up from here.' He turned and pointed. 'You can't miss it. It's opposite the Egyptian Officers' Club.'

'OK, sir, I'll find it.' He put the lorry into gear and was gone.

Sergeant Major Puller watched as the Bedford rejoined the disorderly stream of traffic, then he made his way into the building marked MINISTRY OF AG & FISH. He asked a Corporal at the enquiry desk for Colonel Brunswick and within ten minutes, a tumbler of Dimple Haig in his hand, he sat facing his old CO.

'You're quite right,' said Colonel Brunswick softly. 'They're in Alex – but God knows where. But they're here all right. You can't plaster their ugly mugs all over the front pages of the newspaper without some bright Charlie recognising them.'

The Sergeant Major nodded into his whisky. 'In that case, they shouldn't be too hard to find, sir.'

'Don't be too sure,' said the Colonel. 'I've had several eyewitness reports. On Monday they were seen driving along the main boulevard then they turned up a side street, and that's it, bingo. According to the Military Police, they just disappeared up their own exhaust pipe. I don't know how they do it,' he went on, 'but they're going the right way to be bigger than Lawrence of Arabia.'

The Sergeant Major nodded. 'Well me and my driver will be doing the rounds tonight, sir, all the usual watering places.'

'That's no good, old friend. They won't be there. They'd be recognised.'

'I agree, sir. But if I ask a few questions, somebody may come up with something.'

Colonel Brunswick shook his head sadly.

'You'll have to tread warily, Sergeant Major,' he said. 'If this ever gets out that they've done a bunk, my head will be on the block. You can't paint them up one minute to be the lily-white saviours of our civilisation, and the next as common deserters. It wouldn't look good and you know the form as well as I do. It doesn't matter how tall the pile of crap is as long as it doesn't fall on you.'

He poured them another drink and his next question was right off at a tangent.

'How many other desertions did you say you'd had?' asked the Colonel looking out of the window.

'Eighteen, counting Sparks and Miller, sir,' replied the Sergeant Major.

There was a pause.

'Eighteen,' murmured the Colonel, 'and all of them since Lieutenant Jampton took command?'

Sergeant Major Puller squirmed uneasily in his chair but before he could speak the Colonel swivelled back to the desk.

'I'm sorry, Sergeant Major. I shouldn't have asked you that.'

The Colonel was embarrassed. It was a tactless question and he was out of order. God Almighty, Puller was the glue that had held the SOG together, but he wasn't there now: he was here, in Alex, while his nephew Jampton was loose in the camp. Christopher Columbus! There could be a mass breakout and when the Sergeant Major returned he could find all the men and vehicles gone while that young pillock of a First Lieutenant was marching up and down by himself. It would have been funny if they weren't related.

The Sergeant Major finished his drink and rose from his seat. 'Well, the sooner I get started the better, sir.'

'Good man,' said Colonel Brunswick and led him to the door. 'You know where I am if anything turns up. Good luck,' he said, extending his hand.

'Thank you, sir, I'll be in touch.' And with that he left the office.

The Colonel closed the door softly. He was on the horns of a dilemma; in fact, one of the points was in a very uncomfortable place. All the trouble had started since he'd appointed Lieutenant Jampton to take command of the Special Ordnance Group.

Had it been any other young officer, the answer would be simple: a quick posting to one of the farthest corners of the Empire where he could parade, salute and march to his heart's content. But unfortunately Lieutenant Jampton was not just any other officer: he was his nephew, and it was his wife Dorothy who had engineered his posting. If the truth be known, he feared Dorothy more than all the brass hats in Whitehall, and didn't those mandarins look upon Jampton as some sort of a hero? And hadn't the Colonel himself been honoured with the OBE for appointing Lieutenant Jampton to the command of the Special Ordnance Group?

A huge sigh escaped him. Damn and blast, he'd had enough of his nephew, Sparks and Miller. Fur was going to fly when he got his hands on them; they'd disappear all right and so would Lieutenant Jampton. And they'd be heroes again and decorated no doubt, but posthumously this time – he'd see to that. There were ways and means – having them parachuted behind the German lines was the first idea that sprang to mind. They wouldn't walk away from that, even if he had to pack the parachutes himself. There was a war on, goddammit!

Three minutes after nine o'clock that evening Sergeant Major Puller arrived at the Allied Forces Club ignoring the curious hostile stares as he entered. It was understandable – it wasn't the place for officers and senior NCOs. To his left a great mob shuffled round the dance floor paying no attention to the efforts of the sweating musicians. It was too hot for dancing anyway but this wasn't dancing: this was mobile coupling. Those that weren't part of the slow gyrations on the dance floor were eyeing the crumpet from the sidelines.

The Sergeant Major looked across to where the tables were; most of them were unoccupied. But one table was busy: a soldier with his back to him. It was his driver all right – he'd recognise that flat head anywhere. Seated opposite him were three girls hanging on to his every word. Whatever he was saying must be a great line. One of the girls turned towards the door, catching sight of the Sergeant Major. The SM pointed to the soldier at the table and the girl patted his arm. He looked over his shoulder, then stood up and hurried across.

'Any luck?' asked the Sergeant Major.

'Yeah,' said his driver. 'That one in the green dress, she's panting for it.'

The Sergeant Major passed his hand across his eyes in exasperation. 'I'm sure she is,' he said, 'but what about our lads?'

The driver was puzzled for a moment. 'Oh,' he said, 'Sparks and Miller.' He became confidential. 'Tell you what, Sergeant Major. I only had to mention they were mates of mine and the birds are round me like flies round a corned-beef tin.'

The Sergeant Major glanced over the driver's shoulder at the girls, heads together and now in animated, excited conversation.

'So it's obvious that Sparks and Miller aren't here.'

'No, sir. Bloody hell, if they were here nobody else would get a look-in. They could have their pick.'

'Right lad,' said the Sergeant Major, 'we'll go somewhere else.'

The driver was stricken. 'What about the birds, sir?'

'Say goodnight,' said the Sergeant Major gently, 'and I'll see you outside in one minute.'

'But, sir,' wailed the driver to the disappearing Sergeant Major. He turned to the table but the girls were still wrapped up in each other.

'Ah bollocks,' he muttered and went out to join his governor.

They visited two more places but, like the first, they were hopeless. Sergeant Major Puller came to the conclusion that there was no way Sparks and Miller would flaunt themselves in public but he felt in his bones they were still hidden away in deep cover somewhere in Alexandria. He dismissed his driver, who couldn't believe his luck and hurried back to the Allied Forces' dance to rejoin his fan club. Sergeant Major Puller smiled and made steps to the senior NCOs' mess for some serious drinking.

In Abdul's nightclub the volume of noise was lower than in the dancing places of the Allied troops. But there was the same frenetic atmosphere, that undercurrent of excitement that presages a typhoon, a plague of locusts, or imminent takeover by Rommel and his Afrika Korps. In one corner of the room a grand piano was played softly by the usual black man, strikingly handsome with a smile that flashed round the room like a second-hand lighthouse. Four drinks were lined up on the piano before him, testimony to his expertise and popularity.

On a table by the small dance floor Sparks and Yasmin faced each other. He ran his finger round his collar. The shirt seemed fine that morning but the heat must have shrunk it, he thought. He was still wearing the cheap off-white linen suit.

Most of the other tables were occupied, but because it was out of bounds to all troops there were no uniforms and probably no wives. It wasn't that kind of a place. There were enough girls to go round and, being professionals, they were wearing happy smiling faces behind which mental tills were pinging softly.

Dances had always fascinated Sparks: a herd of wildebeest scenting lion; too far away for immediate concern but close enough to stop them eating. He watched the dancers. No room for actual dancing, just enough for moving slowly in a one-way shuffle. It would be easier to make the floor go round and save everybody the trouble of having to move at all.

Yasmin looked at Sparks, thoughtfully twiddling the stem of her glass. 'What do you mean when you say "over the wall"?'

Sparks shrugged. 'Take off, disappear, scarper.'

'You mean desert?' asked Yasmin.

'If you like,' he said.

She was silent for a moment, then: 'Don't they shoot you for that?'

'They'll have to catch me first,' he added sardonically. It was time to change tack. 'How the hell did we get on to this subject anyway?' But she wouldn't let go.

'But you're not a coward, *mon cher*.'

He flinched at the endearment – it was getting too cosy.

'Don't you believe it, gel,' he said. 'I don't want to go home on a stretcher with a fag in me mouth and me thumb in the air. I'm a coward all right. Most of the heroes I knew are six feet under in a war grave.'

She reached across the table and put her hand in his. He thought for a second, then his hand stayed where it was. Bloody hell, what was happening to him? He'd been running off at the mouth like a lovesick teenager. He'd said more in the last few hours than he'd said all year and it was July, for God's sake. He could feel the shackles going on, and worse, he didn't dislike the sensation. It must be the Scotch. He looked into her eyes, though, and he knew it wasn't.

A well-dressed European approached their table and, ignoring Sparks, he addressed the girl.

'May I introduce myself? I am Hans Gruber. Good evening,' he said with a slight foreign accent. 'I am sure we have met,' he said, 'but the place eludes me.'

'I live in Paris,' replied Yasmin coolly.

'Ah Paris,' he said softly. 'I know it well.'

Sparks was getting restless, his fingers drummed on the table but the man went on as if he wasn't there.

'And that is where we have met; the George Cinq perhaps.'

Yasmin didn't reply. The man held out a gold cigarette case. She shook her head and he took one for himself and lit it. He blew smoke to the ceiling, then asked.

'And what brought you to Alexandria?'

Sparks had had a bellyful. 'Look, mate,' he said softly, 'that's enough questions for one night. Go and drink your sherbet.'

The man looked at him disdainfully. 'I'm sorry, forgive me.' He bowed stiffly and walked away.

Yasmin followed his departure with cold eyes, then turned to Sparks. 'I know that one,' she said. 'He claims to be Dutch but he's German.'

Sparks raised his eyebrows. 'Probably doing a bunk, same as me. Still, if we all did that there wouldn't be a war, eh?'

The pianist arpeggioed into a popular hit tune and couples started to gyrate slowly around the floor again. Yasmin smiled at Sparks, rose and pulled him to his feet. Good grief, he hadn't been on a dance floor since before the war and now here he was shuffling round like the rest of 'em.

Christ, he thought, better go easy on the Johnny Walker.

Yasmin was talking. 'Pardon?' he said.

'But you are a regular soldier, you enlisted.' She was back on that tack again.

'Yeah, that's right,' he said. 'Back in 1936 I was out of work and I was waiting in the pouring rain for a bus when I saw this poster. "Join the Army" it said and underneath it showed a laughing great pillock by a palm tree with a tennis racket in his hand. Well that was it. I always fancied meself at Wimbledon; I signed up the next day, but I didn't know there was going to be a war, did I?'

'But surely the Army fed you and clothed you; surely you mustn't complain if they ask you to fight in return.'

'I've been fighting,' said Sparks, bored with the topic now. 'They've had their four pennyworth out of me. Listen,' he went on, 'I'm starting to hate our officers now more than I do the Germans so I think it's time to move on.'

'But you can't beat the Army, Sparks. It's too big, too powerful.'

'I know,' he said, 'but you have to try, don't you?' He took her hand. 'Come on, let's sit down. I'm thirsty.'

As they came back to their table Abdul was waiting for them. Dry-washing his hands, he was in a bit of a state. Next to him was the tall German who claimed to be Dutch and knew Paris. Sparks pulled out the chair for Yasmin, then moved round and sat opposite. It was his turn to ignore the visitors.

'What'll you have to drink?' he asked Yasmin. She shook her head. Sparks snapped his fingers at Abdul. 'I'll have a large Scotch,' he said.

Abdul was unhappy and worried. 'Please,' he said, 'this gentleman here would like to buy the lady a drink.'

'She doesn't want a drink but I'll have a large Scotch, OK?'

'Please,' wailed Abdul bouncing from one foot to the other, 'this gentleman is an old and valued customer.'

'What about me?' said Sparks. 'I'm a founder member.'

The German broke in swiftly and smoothly. 'In that case you must be aware that it is against the rules to monopolise one of the girls unless, of course, you are willing to pay for the pleasure.'

'Are you willing to pay for the pleasure?' asked Sparks, matching the German's even tones.

'But of course,' said the German, bowing to Yasmin.

Sparks stood. 'As you wish,' he said and hit the German full in the face, knocking him arse over tit across the next two tables, scattering glasses and ashtrays. He was out cold. For a second there was a stunned silence, then pandemonium broke out as dancers surged round the table to see what was going on. Some people stood on chairs to get a better view and the pianist thumped into 'An Apple for the Teacher'. Waiters pushed their way through to clean up the broken glass and bits of food.

Abdul gazed horrified at the slack form of his old and valued customer.

'He's paid for it,' said Sparks coolly, then behind him he heard an urgent tinkling. 'Hurry it up,' he said to Yasmin. 'Abdul's little bell is a direct line to his muscle-bound minder and this room isn't big enough for both of us; it's hardly big enough for him.' He took her arm.

Yasmin was white and trembling. 'You said that nothing was ever settled by force.'

'Who says it's settled?' replied Sparks drily. 'He and I might get together again one day.' And with that he hustled her through the bead curtains, took hold of her hand and dragged her upstairs to their room. He stopped outside the door, listening.

'For God's sake, Sparks,' began Yasmin, but he silenced her with a finger to his lips. Cautiously he looked over the balustrade but there was no sign of pursuit. Satisfied, he entered his room quickly and quietly.

Yasmin shrugged and, as she was about to follow him, he returned to the door with a bundle of silk.

'Take your nightie somewhere else,' he whispered urgently. 'I'm expecting company.'

Before she could speak he pushed her into the corridor and slammed the door shut. Once inside he jammed a chair under the door handle. It was pathetic. Sickeningly, he thought of Abdul's great monster of a minder, those huge hands that could easily strangle a water buffalo, making his way purposefully up the stairs.

In a panic he dragged the chest of drawers behind the chair. It wasn't much but at least he'd have fair warning. Taking his rifle from the top of the wardrobe, he slapped in a magazine and pushed the bolt, levering a bullet up the spout. Fear gripped him as he thought of the monster again.

It was in this ready position that he awoke with a start. Sunlight was streaming through the window, so at least he'd got through the night. Quickly he looked to the door, but the chair and dresser were still in place. He stretched and smiled ruefully about his fears the night before. They had been unfounded.

This was what he thought and he couldn't have been more wrong. This was just a reprieve.

After another fruitless day of search, Sergeant Major Puller decided it would be easier to find a wandering yeti than Sparks and Miller. It was hopeless, and now, after a shower and a quick shave, he was in the senior NCOs' mess seated comfortably at a brass table littered with bottles of Stella beer, the chasers. It was the hard stuff in Dimple Haig bottles that did the damage. He was in the company of his old mate, Quartermaster Sergeant Docherty.

It was his last night in Alex and he was determined to hang one on. Soon he'd be back with the Special Ordnance Group, and, if there was anybody left, they would be short on water now. He cleared his throat.

'My driver will be round at your place at first light for supplies, Doc,' he said.

'Aye, that's OK, Sam, just take what you want. I'll not be there myself but Sergeant Cockerell will attend to you.'

'Thanks, Doc.'

They downed two shorts, then reached for the Stella. It was a grand life. After a time the Quartermaster leant forward and tapped the Sergeant Major's knee.

'Any luck with that blue suitcase you were enquiring about?'

'Nah,' replied Puller. 'I've seen the RTO and he reckons that if it was left on the dockside it would probably be loaded back on the ship. He says my best bet is to write to Southampton – but bugger that for a lark. I have enough trouble just writing home.'

They sat together for another few minutes smoking quietly; it was good to be with your mates. A mess Corporal came up to the table. 'Sergeant Major Puller?' he enquired.

'That's me, laddie,' said Puller.

He took a folded note. It was a memo – he was to report soonest to Military Police barracks; information received regarding two lost lambs. He stood wearily. It always bloody happens when you're having fun.

'Problems?' asked the Quartermaster.

'Could be. If I'm not back in an hour, there're problems.'

He gulped down one of the glasses of Scotch. 'Well, if I don't see you again this time, I'll be back.'

'Sure you will, Sam.'

Puller took a deep breath to get himself in order. 'Just starting to hang one on, too.'

'Always the same,' said Doc. 'Be seeing you, so long.'

'Yes,' said Puller making his way to the door.

In the Military Police barracks an incident room had been set up and three Sergeants and an officer were poring over a street map when Sergeant Major Puller walked in. They turned and nodded a greeting. The Captain beamed.

'That was quick, Sergeant Major. Thanks for letting us know where you would be.'

Sergeant Major Puller nodded. Even he was not quite at ease in a Military Police barracks.

The Captain went on. 'The situation is this. We've had an anonymous telephone call and we think it's genuine. Sergeant Bailey here reports that he identified a three-ton Bedford truck turn into this street.' He tapped the map with a pencil. 'This street, by the way, is out of bounds to all military personnel. That's why it stuck in Bailey's mind. Somewhere up this street the truck vanished and as you can see it's a helluva long street. If we started a house-to-house search it would take forever and our birds would certainly get wind of it and fly the coop.'

Puller waited. It sounded good so far.

'Right, then,' said the Captain briskly. 'We make a dawn raid. Not too many people about and light enough to see what we're doing, OK?' He looked at the Sergeant Major.

'Sounds all right to me, sir, but which house are we raiding?'

'Ah well,' said the Captain shaking his head, 'that's where we have to rely on our mystery phone caller. If he's genuine, he'll be in the street and will point us to our objective.'

'What if he's not there, sir?'

The Captain shrugged. 'In that case we carry on up the street and come out the other end.'

Sergeant Major Puller nodded. Under the influence of the whisky, he thought this seemed a reasonable assumption.

The Captain went on. 'But from that moment both ends of the street will be kept under a strict surveillance. If they're there, they'll have to come out sometime. And make no mistake – once they've got wind of our slow patrol up the street they'll be spooked all right. They'll try to break cover sooner rather than later.'

'Right, sir. When do you want me at the start line?'

The Captain looked at his watch. 'Let's say four thirty a.m. That'll give us time for a final briefing and a cup of black coffee, I hope.' He laughed loudly. Who said a policeman's lot was not a happy one?

Some hours later as the streets were beginning to lighten, Sergeant Major Puller was sitting alongside the Captain in the lead jeep.

He shivered from the cold of the morning air. A shower and several mugs of black coffee were clearing the whisky fumes from his brain and, with the adrenalin coursing through his blood, he was almost at maximum readiness.

Stealthily the six vehicles crawled up the deserted street. They hadn't gone more than eighty yards when a white-sleeved arm shot out from a dark doorway pointing across the street. This done, the arm disappeared just as quickly. The Captain and Sergeant Major Puller looked curiously at each other and back to the doorway. This time a man emerged and repeated his pointing to an import-and-export firm. He was uneasy at being out in the open and, having pointed again, hurried back into the shadow of his doorway.

The redcaps alighted and looked blankly at the shutters and then at the Captain. How the bloody hell were they going to get in? There was no entrance, a real weird setup. They turned to look for their informant and one of the Sergeants went across to the doorway and dragged out the man, who shook off the Sergeant's hand and hissed, 'I thought you would come in the dark.'

He wasn't a pretty sight: he had two enormous black eyes and a plaster over the bridge of his nose. Then quickly he looked sharply up and down the street, and reached up to press a part of the wood surrounding the shutters. Immediately the façade began slowly to move inwards and, as it did so, Hans Gruber scuttled back to the opposite dark doorway. The dark-haired Englishman would be paid in full for his moment of brutality.

Some of the redcaps remained outside to apprehend anybody making a bolt for it. But the main body entered the cavernous maw quickly and by the light of their torches they picked out the three-ton Bedford.

'Bull's-eye,' whispered the Captain and swiftly they moved up the two steps that led to the empty nightclub and above that the bedrooms. Whistles shrilled and they fanned out along the corridors. There was no need for stealth now. The idea was to create bedlam and panic and they certainly achieved this. Doors opened and worried faces peered out. Somewhere a woman screamed. But not having the full layout, the MPs had under-estimated the extent of the honeycombed building. It sprawled out from the original façade over several shops on either side and they would have needed three times the manpower to cover the place.

The Captain came to a quick decision: search from the lower floor up making sure that nobody slipped through the net. This afforded rooms on the top floor breathing space.

And the rooms upstairs, being the smallest and cheapest, were where Sparks and Miller were billeted. Yasmin, organised and cool, pushed into Miller's room and shook him awake.

'Put this on,' she said and thrust a long black wig in his hands.

'What's up?' he said. 'What's all the racket?'

'Just put this on,' she spat. 'Ali will join you in a minute. He knows what to do.' And she was gone.

On the floor beneath, the redcaps systematically entered and searched every room. It was quite an experience. In one room a woman crouched on the floor, mother-naked, while behind her a tall man in white tuxedo jacket and holding an enormous feather looked round dispassionately as the Military Police hurried in, opening the wardrobe, looking under the bed, then, apparently satisfied, hurrying out and closing the door behind them. One of them, a Sergeant, let out a great breath.

'By the balls of St George,' he exclaimed, 'it takes all sorts.'

'I know, Sarge,' said his colleague still in a state of shock. 'But what does he do with the feather?'

The Sergeant looked at him in astonishment. 'I'll have a fatherly talk to you later,' he said, and they pushed into the next room.

A fat woman lay alone in bed. 'Get out of here, you pigs,' she said. 'Is my day off.' And when they looked under the bed she said, 'Is not there; there's one at little door at the end of corridor.' Then she heaved herself over and before they'd left she was snoring.

On the top floor now Yasmin hurried along the corridor followed by Sparks.

'In here, quickly.' There was one door that had a keyhole and Yasmin had the key. Quickly she opened the door and pushed Sparks into the room, slipping in behind him and locking the door.

'Bloody hell,' said Sparks. 'This room's a bit of all right.'

'Yes,' said Yasmin quickly. 'This is Hans Gruber's room, the man you hit in the face. Luckily he's away tonight.'

She hurried over to a large wardrobe. 'Quickly now,' she said, 'help me push this.' And between them they manoeuvred the piece out of the way. Behind it was a narrow opening and, squeezing through, Yasmin held out her hand to Sparks.

'*Vite, vite,*' she hissed, 'in here.'

With a little more difficulty he was through. What met his gaze stopped him dead in his tracks. The whole room was a mass of electrical equipment. On one side a huge wireless transmitter occupied the entire wall and smaller sets stood on a bench at the back.

'Blimey,' he muttered, completely awestruck. 'Well I'm damn sure this isn't just for *Forces Favourites.*'

He turned to Yasmin but she wasn't there. From the other room came a gasp and a strangled '*Merde*!'. Quickly he stepped through the narrow opening and saw her struggling to move the heavy wardrobe back into place. He pushed her away but before he could get his shoulder behind it Yasmin dragged him away and hissed, 'Don't be such a fool.' She tugged him to one side and pushed him back into the wireless room. 'I'm as big a fool as you,' she gabbled hurriedly. 'It was my intention to hide you in here. I'd forgotten the weight of the wardrobe.'

A whistle pierced the silence. Yasmin bit her lip in frustration – she had to think faster than she'd ever done in her life. Sparks took a step towards her but she angrily waved him away. Then suddenly she snapped her fingers. 'We have about three minutes so listen and do not interrupt.' She motioned towards the huge wireless transmitter. 'This is the centre of espionage of German Intelligence.'

Sparks was about to speak.

'Shut up and listen,' she said. 'This is what you will do.' And quickly she explained the plan.

In the corridor below Sergeant Major Puller flung open a door of the last room on that floor. Two redcaps followed him. In the bed a woman lay with her back towards them. Facing her, leaning on one elbow with his other arm round her, lay a middle-aged Egyptian. He was angry and hurled abuse at them in some language or other, but his meaning was clear.

'Won't be a minute,' said the Sergeant Major. 'Keep your hair on.'

They'd done under the bed and the wardrobe and as they made to leave the SM turned. 'Carry on smoking,' he said and closed the door behind him.

The 'woman' on the bed turned and breathed a sigh of relief. It was Dusty Miller in a wig. 'Cor, that was close,' he whispered. 'Thanks, mate.'

He turned to the man, who was looking at him in a strange way. Enlightenment dawned. He was out of bed like a flash, backing away clad only in his khaki underpants.

'Let's not get carried away, mister,' he said shakily.

The man fluttered his eyelashes. 'I help you, now you help me, yes? We can be nice to each other,' he simpered. 'I show you ecstasy, yes.'

Miller backed away. 'Don't let's be hasty. I'm warning you, mate.'

Outside in the corridor the Sergeant Major stopped as he heard the commotion, then with an almighty crash the Arab came flying through the closed door, wood and plaster flying everywhere. The Sergeant Major advanced cautiously. Stepping over the prostrate body, he stared through the hovering dust and the splintered remains of the door. A broad smile creased his face as he gazed upon Dusty Miller, still wearing the wig.

'Well, I didn't know he was ginger,' said Miller.

Puller pushed open what was left of the shattered door and beamed at him. 'You know,' he said, 'in that wig I could fancy you myself.'

Miller snatched off the wig and slung it on to the bed.

'Now come on, lad,' said the SM gently. 'Where's your mate?'

'Isn't he with you?' said Miller all innocent. 'I thought he was with you lot back at the camp.'

The MP slipped on the handcuffs, one round Miller's wrist and the other he snapped round the bed rail. They still had one more room to search. The MP gave a blast on his whistle. It was the signal that one of them was in the bag. More MPs dashed up the stairs led by the Sergeant Major, who tried the handle of the first door they came to.

'This looks interesting,' he said, 'the only door that's locked.'

The MP, a sturdy lad from Newcastle, stood back and with one mighty thrust of his size twelves the door crashed open and in ten seconds the room was full of redcaps.

The Military Police Captain pushed his way through and stared at Sparks and Yasmin seated at the console.

'What's all this then?' he asked.

Sparks flung down a pencil in disgust. 'You've really messed it up this time,' he said. 'Another day and I'd have had the lot of 'em.'

* * *

On being taken to the Military Police barracks, Sparks, still feigning anger and frustration, insisted on making a statement. Miller looked on in disbelief. He had never heard his mate speak for so long nor with such fluency, calling into question the legitimate births of all Military Police, General Auchinleck and the Army and insisting that, given another two days, he would, without a doubt, have rounded up all the German agents in Alexandria, Cairo and possibly Lisbon. All this would not now be accomplished because of the bumbling of the British Army machine. This done, they were marched into a cell in the Military Police barracks, given a huge breakfast of bacon and eggs, and for the rest of the day nobody came near them.

It was a mistake. This gave them more than enough time to cobble up a plausible story. The reason they'd been left alone was a typical Army balls-up. Nobody knew who was to press charges. The MPs had a strong case: Sparks and Miller had been picked up in an out-of-bounds area. But the Special Ordnance Group wanted to charge them as deserters.

Colonel Brunswick arrived and questioned Sparks and Miller in one of the debriefing rooms. They were questioned separately but by now had had plenty of time to get their stories together on what had transpired. This time they both made and signed statements. But after perusing them the Military Police were reluctant to charge them at all. Naturally, they didn't want to put themselves in the firing line by accusing two legends who quite possibly were sincere in their assertion that they were following a lead that had uncovered the German espionage network.

But Colonel Brunswick was also in a quandary. After all the adulation and canonisation of our two heroes, it wouldn't do. He, himself, had joined in the applause so now it was incongruous that he should denounce them as common deserters.

As for Sergeant Major Puller, he could see which way the wind was blowing. 'I knew it,' he muttered to himself. 'It's all going to end up smelling of bloody roses again.' And he left the building to get some fresh air.

Back at the Special Ordnance Group, it hadn't been a good day for Lieutenant Jampton either. For a start, the man he'd assigned as his batman forgot to wake him with an early-morning cup of tea, the result being he'd slept in till the sun was well into the sky. He hurriedly dressed and stepped out of his tent – and his heart nearly stopped. The place was deserted. Surely they hadn't all decamped during the night. He glanced at his wrist and realisation hit him. His watch wasn't there. He remembered he had lost it in a foolish bet with Sergeant Major Puller. He shaded his eyes and looked towards the sun, but he was no nearer judging the time. His only conclusion was that it was daylight. Carefully, heart in his mouth, he approached the first tent and was greatly relieved when he heard steady snoring. He poked his head through the tent flap. The two lads were blissfully sleeping and, judging from the smiles on their faces, in a better world. Jampton's little mouth tightened and he kicked one of them not too gently. The sleeper came from wherever he'd been and rubbed his eyes.

' 'Ere, what's goin' on?' he said.

Jampton was beside himself. 'D'you know what time it is?' he snapped. It was meant as a rebuke but by now the whole camp knew about the CO's watch.

'Hang on a minute, sir,' said the man, helpfully fiddling in a boot for his watch. He stared at it, not fully awake yet, and said, 'It's a quarter past nine, sir.' Then he smiled and settled back in his blankets again.

For a moment Jampton was spellbound and then he found his voice. 'Get up! Get up, the pair of you!' he shrieked.

'Yes, sir,' they mumbled and scrambled to their feet.

Jampton was about to speak again when he noticed that one of them wore only a short singlet and socks. But Jampton's horrified stare was taken by the man's wherewithal: it was enormous. He seemed to recognise the scruffy short singlet. Could it be the pseudo-matador who'd greeted him on his first arrival at the camp? He'd been shocked then by the white hairy backside, but this was worse: it was a frontal view. Embarrassed, Jampton tore his eyes away and staggered outside into the hot sun. Good grief! Was the man deformed? Or perhaps it was some tropical disease. He didn't enter any other tents but strode back to his own for his swagger stick. From there he went from tent to tent, banging on the canvas, shouting, 'Out you get, rise and shine!' The cook hadn't even started breakfast.

'It's after nine o'clock, man,' shouted Jampton.

'I'm sorry, sir, I thought it was Sunday.'

It was three tents further on before the inanity of that remark hit Jampton. Sunday was a day like all the rest – the war didn't stop on the Sabbath. The camp was now crawling back to life but even so it was half past eleven before he mustered them all for roll call. When the Sergeant Major was here this was all taken care of and out of the way by eight o'clock. But dammit, wasn't he the Commanding Officer? He'd show them. And as a punishment, before they entered the mess tent for breakfast, he'd have them jogging around the camp perimeter three times. Oh yes, he'd show them who was boss all right.

Having explained all this to them he gave the order to 'Right turn' and smiled pompously as he watched them double out of the camp. This done, he strode over to the mess tent for a steaming mug of tea but when he entered it was deserted. 'Good Christmas,' he muttered. The cook was sweating round the perimeter with the rest of 'em.

Someone else came in behind him. He whirled in relief, but it was only Captain Witherspoon, the MO, holding a large mugful of gin. 'I saw all that,' he said. 'You're a hard man. Yes, sir. They'll know better next time.' And he strolled back to his own little world leaving Jampton mollified. And yes, the MO was right: he did have a way with the men.

Time passed and still no sign of his joggers. A new fear gripped him. Suppose they kept on running till they reached Alexandria? It was a stupid thought but then thinking wasn't his strong point. He heaved a sigh of relief when they finally appeared, still jogging. It never occurred to him they were returning the same way they had left; nor that the escarpment on the side of the camp could conceal so many men. Had he decided to take a stroll round the rocks, he might have wondered where all the cigarette butts had come from. He waved his hands above his head. 'All right,' he yelled, 'that's enough.' And gratefully they wheeled abruptly and trotted sweating into the mess tent.

As they passed him he spotted Jackson, his new batman.

'Jackson,' he squeaked, 'fall out and come here.'

Jackson did as he was told and stood to attention.

'What happened to my early-morning cup of tea?' asked Jampton wishing he'd chosen a smaller batman. It wasn't dignified to have to look upward every time he gave him an order, even less dignified to carry a box round with him. He wished he still had his fifteen-hundredweight. That was always a good platform. He realised that Jackson hadn't replied.

'All right, then, I'll let it go this time but any more of it and you're on a charge.'

'Yes, sir,' replied Jackson stiffly.

'Good. Now a cup of tea and whatever else is going, in my tent, now! Is that clear?' And before Jackson could reply he swung on his heel and marched to his tent. Suddenly he stopped and turned again.

'Jackson,' he yelled.

'Sir,' Jackson yelled back.

'What time is it?'

Jackson looked at his wrist watch. 'Ten past twelve, sir.'

'Thank you,' replied Jampton, and ducked into his tent.

The first thing he noticed was the letter he'd been writing the night before. He sat down and picked it up.

Regimental Transport Officer
c/o Alexandria Docks.

Dear Sir,

We met some time ago in your office where you handed me my movement orders. I was the first to disembark and I would like to thank you for the help you gave me with directions to this location, etc.

I am now here – but unfortunately my suitcase is not. It was inadvertently left just outside your office – a large blue suitcase – and my name, rank and number is stencilled on both back and front . . .

An idea struck him. It might be easier if the RTO delivered it to his uncle, and, yes, Colonel Brunswick would carry some weight. After all, he did outrank the man. His thoughts were interrupted when Jackson bowed into the tent with a mug of lukewarm tea and a mess tin full of hard biscuits. Jampton's face fell.

'I'm sorry, sir, but that's what we're down to until Sparks and Miller get back with the rations.'

Jampton stared at him and what added insult to injury was the great blob of powdered egg on Jackson's chin.

'Well,' said Jampton, 'let me know the minute they get back.'

'Very good, sir.' And, pushing the tent flap to one side, Jackson ducked out.

Sparks and Miller spent their eighth day under close arrest in the Military Police barracks. Close arrest is probably too harsh a term. Eight days in a five-star luxury hotel would have been more appropriate, and they enjoyed their holiday. Too many people knew who they were and inevitably tongues were beginning to wag. Fan letters started to arrive at the barracks, boxes of chocolates, books, Havana cigars, and hundreds of cigarettes, all of which Sparks and Miller were happy to share with their gaolers who, in return, put carpets and white linen sheets in the cell and served breakfast in bed. They were even provided with a wireless so they could listen to Vera Lynn – they were exemplary prisoners.

However, investigations and discussions were still flying backward and forward between Whitehall and North Africa in an effort to decide what should be done with them.

Colonel Brunswick was summoned to the British Consulate and was immediately shown into the large ornate office of the Consul.

'Ah, Colonel Brunswick.' A tall, smartly dressed, grey-haired man rose from his chair and extended a hand across the desk.

The Colonel shook it, then placed his hat and baton on the desk before settling himself in a black leather chair. Then he noticed the bleak stare of the Consul and realised he hadn't been invited to sit. Surely he hadn't been expected to stand to attention throughout the interview. After all, he was a Colonel. He returned the baleful look and tried to regain some composure.

The Consul sat and cleared his throat. 'Tell me, Colonel Brunswick,' he began, 'Sparks and Miller.' He leant back in his chair and looked keenly at the Colonel, awaiting an answer.

Brunswick stared back. What was he supposed to say, and why had he been summoned so peremptorily? Sparks and Miller were strictly military, so why was he in the Consulate? His first thought had been wildly exciting. Was he to be asked to consider the acceptance of a knighthood? But the frostiness of his reception kicked this heady thought well over the grandstand.

'Sparks and Miller,' he returned as if he wasn't quite sure he should be discussing the matter.

The man leant his elbows on the desk and thrust his head forward. 'Colonel Brunswick, I would like you to understand that I am speaking on behalf of the Government at the very highest level . . .'

The Colonel felt a cold trickle of sweat from his armpit. He didn't like what he was hearing, nor the tone with which it was delivered. He could definitely forget his knighthood for a start. They might even ask him to return his OBE.

'Now,' went on the Consul, 'having cleared the decks as it were, I am authorised to acquaint you with a few details.' He looked steadily at the Colonel as if expecting a reply.

'May I smoke?' he said, and before the man could respond he was already patting his pockets, only to find he'd forgotten his pipe and cigarettes. He had only matches and he could hardly smoke one of them.

The Consul coolly pushed over a silver cigarette box and Colonel Brunswick gratefully helped himself. They were Turkish, cork-tipped, and in his confusion he lit the wrong end. Doggedly he drew on the cigarette hoping his clumsiness had gone unnoticed, which was highly improbable. Sparks were flying all over the place and he was frantically patting his thighs to avoid going up in flames.

The Consul rose diplomatically and walked over to the window. 'Colonel Brunswick,' he said to the view outside, 'your two heroes claim that owing to overhearing a suspicious conversation they followed a man to a notorious night spot and stumbled inadvertently upon the centre of German Espionage.' He turned from the window. 'Those are the facts?'

The Colonel, having stubbed out his flaming cigarette, nodded weakly. 'Broadly speaking, yes,' he coughed.

The Consul smiled sardonically and resumed his seat.

'Bullshit,' he snapped explosively.

The Colonel jerked bolt upright in his chair. Coming so unexpectedly from the lips of this cultured, sophisticated man, it was as if he had suddenly dropped his trousers and shouted, 'Anyone for tennis?' Pulling himself together, the Colonel replied.

'I tend to agree, sir,' he said lamely. 'I must admit, some of their testimony is extraordinarily coincidental and, er, fanciful.' He broke off as a pinprick of pain stabbed his thigh, and he thought he smelt burning.

'My dear Colonel,' said the Consul silkily, 'you don't believe their story any more than I do, and neither do my superiors in Whitehall.'

The Colonel bristled. He wasn't some day boy being carpeted by his form master: he was the Director of Military Intelligence, for God's sake. But even as the thought crossed his mind he dismissed it. He might be one of the bigger fish in Alex but in the corridors of Westminster he wasn't even plankton bait and the Consul was merely voicing the instructions of the War Cabinet. But then again, wasn't this purely a military matter?

As if reading his thoughts the Consul went on. 'In the normal course of events it would be dealt with summarily by one of your courts martial, but I'm afraid the whole situation has now become political dynamite between us and the French.'

'Us and the French?' repeated the Colonel stupidly.

'Yes,' replied the Consul. 'The search for the enemy transmitter was a joint Anglo-French operation, was it not?'

Brunswick nodded, then enlightenment dawned. 'I see it all now, sir. Typical French. They're squealing like stuck pigs because we got there first.'

'Hardly,' said the Consul, 'the French apparently uncovered the transmitter seven months ago.'

Brunswick's mouth fell open in astonishment. He was absolutely dumbfounded. How could this be? He and his French counterpart held meetings at least once a week to compare notes. He stared incredulously at the Consul. 'Seven months?' he gasped.

'I'm afraid so,' said the Consul.

Colonel Brunswick rose slowly to his feet and began pacing thoughtfully up and down the carpet. It was all becoming clear now – the number of abortive raids based mainly on French Intelligence, and the number of times he'd been assured that the area around Abdul ben Hussein's establishment had been swept clean by French agents.

'The bastards,' he muttered.

'I tend to agree with you, Colonel,' said the Consul. 'Churchill and de Gaulle have been at each other's throats and the entente cordiale is in a very parlous state.'

Colonel Brunswick stopped his walkabout and slumped back in his chair. He shook his head disbelievingly, still unable to take it in. 'But the transmitter was in operation right up to the time we closed it down last week.'

'Of course,' said the Consul, 'when the French agent penetrated their source of transmission, the code books were photographed.' He shrugged his shoulders. 'Naturally this enabled the French to decipher all communications between Rommel's Headquarters and the Abwehr.'

Brunswick screwed up his eyes. While his backroom boys were going spare trying desperately to break the code, their French counterparts had been going through the motions. 'But goddammit,' he blurted, 'why didn't they let us know?'

The Consul smiled wryly and spread his hands. 'They didn't trust us not to blow the whistle and have the station shut down.' He paused. 'Exactly as you did. However, the good news is that the French double-cross in withholding information is Winston's strong card and de Gaulle will have to climb down and toe the line.'

After a time the Colonel rose. 'And what about Sparks and Miller?' he asked.

'Ah yes,' said the Consul, 'Sparks and Miller.' He cleared his throat. 'We come now to the crux of the matter and the reason for our meeting.'

Colonel Brunswick sighed. He'd already had the crux. Was there more, for God's sake?'

The Consul cleared his throat. 'The popularity of Sparks and Miller is such that Whitehall was about to have them taken out of the battle zone for a personal tour of the British Isles.' He paused. 'However, this latest escapade has put the tin lid firmly on their triumphal tour of Blighty, and this is the scenario I am instructed to pass on to you.'

The Colonel craned forward eagerly.

'First of all,' said the Consul, 'it must be fully understood that no meeting at any level has been convened to discuss this matter. In fact, the whole of this suggestion is entirely your own idea.'

Brunswick nodded weakly. He knew the form. If it all went wrong he'd be the one with the black hood over his head standing on the trapdoor.

The Consul continued. 'On your own initiative you approached Sparks and Miller with a proposal and on acceptance you clandestinely enrolled them in the Intelligence Service.'

Colonel Brunswick's eyes widened in disbelief.

The Consul nodded. 'I know,' he said, 'but this is what I am instructed to pass on to you. I am merely the messenger.'

He went on: 'As their superior you ordered them to make their way to Alexandria and thence to the address of Abdul ben Hussein and see what they could uncover.' He looked directly at the Colonel. 'Are you with me so far?'

Brunswick nodded. It was getting better by the minute. After all, it had had a successful outcome; why shouldn't he be the instigator? He decided to elaborate a little. 'Ah yes, the reason we couldn't send in any of our regular agents –' he shrugged and spread his hands '– it would have created a breach of confidence with our French allies.'

The Consul couldn't believe his ears. After all, he was merely passing on a face-saving formula cobbled up in London and this idiot sounded like he was starting to believe it. 'Yes, well,' he said, 'be that as it may . . .'

He desperately wanted to terminate this interview. 'Naturally,' he went on, 'none of this will reach the news media. The discovery of this transmitter is classified material and in this case *especially* classified.'

'I understand,' agreed the Colonel.

'I believe,' concluded the Consul, 'I have passed on all the information supplied to me by my superiors, and I do not have to tell you that this conversation never took place.' He looked for a moment at the Colonel and sighed. 'Have I made myself clear or is there anything you would like me to clarify?'

The Colonel, recognising the bum's rush, rose to his feet with dignity. 'As this conversation never took place,' he said coldly, 'I would like to remind you that I am not a fool and I resent your treating me as one.'

The Consul regarded him steadily while he digested the outburst. The first part was debatable, and as for the second half, how else did you treat a man who believed the trumped-up poppycock constructed in this elaborate cover-up? Not only that, he'd almost set fire to himself before this conversation never took place.

Colonel Brunswick wriggled uneasily in the silence. Had he said too much? Ah well, bugger the knighthood and roll on peacetime, when he could carry on his soldiering in a more leisurely fashion.

The Consul rose to terminate the meeting.

'Incidentally,' he said, 'you are to promote Sparks and Miller to the rank of Sergeant. After all, they are to be rewarded for their services to British Military Intelligence and are to be returned to their unit forthwith and with God's help that will be the end of the matter.'

'Very good,' muttered the Colonel looking as if he had been hit by a steam hammer. 'I'll inform Lieutenant Jampton.'

'Ah yes,' said the Consul, 'Lieutenant Jampton . . . would naturally have to be a party to this. He is upgraded to the rank of Captain.'

Brunswick reeled back. What comic opera was he in? At this rate in a few months he'd be standing before Jampton's desk calling *him* sir. He waited for a moment or two, hoping to hear some good news about his own career prospects, but then as the Consul took some papers from a drawer in his desk he realised this was a sign of dismissal. So he picked up his cap and baton and made his way towards the door.

The Consul spoke. 'By the way, Colonel, did you ever come across a French woman by the name of Estelle Chambertin?'

Brunswick looked at the floor. 'Estelle Chambertin?' he repeated.

'A young society beauty in Alexandria before the war.'

'Ah,' said Brunswick, straightening his shoulders, 'before the war I was a serving officer in India.' Then as an afterthought he asked, 'Should I have known her, sir?'

'It's of no importance,' said the Consul. 'Only she was one of the best agents in French intelligence. It was she who cracked the location of the enemy transmitter and who photographed the code books.'

The Colonel whistled softly. 'Estelle Chambertin,' he muttered.

The Consul nodded. 'Her cover name, however, was Yasmin.'

The Colonel nodded again. 'I'd like to meet her one day,' he said and opened the door.

'That won't be possible,' said the Consul. 'According to the French Intelligence she was killed in Tobruk when the Germans took it.'

'I'm sorry,' said the Colonel, and let himself out.

As soon as he left the building he let out a long sigh of relief, recollecting the interview as he pushed his way through the crowded thoroughfare. Well, interview wasn't exactly the right word – it was more of a bollocking, really. This thought rushed to the surface of his mind, dragging anger with it. Sparks and Miller would pay for this, by God they would. It was obvious their main objective had been to desert and in defending their attempt to cover up, he'd been made to look a right nana. The passers-by parted to give him passage when they saw the look on his face. It was the same look in any language – 'Get out of my way or I'll kill you.'

He almost broke into a run but stopped himself just in time. Colonels didn't run, they had other ranks to do that for them. Slowing his pace had a calming effect on him and by the time he'd reached the Ministry of Ag and Fish he was in a more rational frame of mind.

SIX

When Sergeant Major Puller and his flat-headed driver rolled into camp followed by the second three-tonner and two water bowsers, Lieutenant Jampton shot out of his tent as if he'd been spat out of a peashooter and he could hardly conceal his relief when Sparks and Miller alighted and stopped before him bringing up two fine military salutes. But there was something different about them and it wasn't just Miller's haircut. Then he suddenly tumbled: they both sported the white chevrons of Sergeants so whatever they'd been up to in Alex had been successful enough to gain them promotion. Then an awful thought struck him. If they had made Sergeant, what heights must Sergeant Major Puller have reached? He hoped to God he still outranked him.

The Sergeant Major jumped down from the cab wearily and saluted his Commanding Officer. Thank God, thought Jampton, I'm still in charge.

As the trucks were unloaded, Jampton's eyes gleamed with suppressed excitement – crates of rifles and light machine guns were offloaded. He hadn't expected to receive these, but the truth of the matter was that the RAOC in Alexandria would have supplied anybody with whole arsenals of bombs, land mines, high-explosive shells – in fact anything to clear the decks before Rommel could get his hands on them.

For the young Lieutenant it was Christmas morning, especially when the Sergeant Major handed him a package marked 'Private and Confidential'. He slit it open and a handful of cloth pips fell out on to the ground and, reaching in, he pulled out the citation informing him that he was now promoted to the rank of Captain.

Sergeant Major Puller couldn't believe his eyes as he looked round the camp. Small changes had been made during their adventures in Alexandria. The guy ropes on the CO's tent had been painted white, many new stones had been found and painted white also and these formed dinky little paths criss-crossing the camp. All they were short of was a wishing well, half a dozen donkeys and a model railway and they could have run day trips for the poor kids of Alexandria.

Besides all this reorganisation, Jampton had been working on a scheme for a night exercise. It was brilliant in its simplicity – a convoy of trucks with himself at the head. They would travel fifteen miles southeast under cover of darkness, returning to encircle the camp. They would then break into two sections just before first light and with a pincer movement execute a mock attack from two sides. Umpires with white armbands stationed at various points around the perimeter would judge the successes. He couldn't wait to pass on his plan to his three senior NCOs – but first things first. He had to get his extra pips sewn on to his epaulettes.

The lads would be pleased. He felt that he was making great progress with them. As two of the lads had walked past his tent one night he'd heard himself referred to as 'Hugh'. It wasn't a bad nickname. It had a warm familiarity about it and he was not displeased.

If only he had known that Hampton Wick was Cockney rhyming slang alluding to a man's anatomy and Hugh Jampton denoted one of great size.

On 7 August the brand-new Captain Jampton was strutting busily inspecting various parts of his camp, head swinging from side to side, eyes down in order to keep them on his new Captain's pips. He hadn't the foggiest idea how he'd come by this promotion. Naturally he'd interrogated the Sergeant Major and Sergeants Sparks and Miller but to his every question they had replied 'Classified'. They were as close-mouthed as a suffragette on a hunger strike.

He had acquainted the three of them of his night exercise and they hadn't exactly demurred. However, he wasn't taking any chances and for the last two evenings had had the rotor arms from all the vehicles brought to him. So if they wanted to desert again, they were welcome to walk.

It was an uncomfortably hot morning and he decided that a lemonade was in order, so he made his way back to his tent, and while he sat sipping his drink his heart beat fast with excitement as he thought of this evening's exercise. What fun! Quickly he erased this last thought from his mind. It wasn't fun, it was war. His jaw set firmly and he had a steely glint in his eye; to be more exact he thought he had. He decided to check this out. Rising quickly from his chair he stepped towards the mirror but as he bent to look into it he recoiled in horror: a large squashed fly was smeared over the glass.

At that moment his batman, Jackson, entered with Jampton's afternoon tea. Jackson put the cup and saucer down reverently. Only the common soldier drank out of enamel mugs. He was about to leave when his CO called him back. Jackson turned with a sigh of exasperation.

'Yes, sir?'

Jampton eyed him coldly. 'Your job,' he said in biting tones, 'is to keep my billet clean and tidy.'

Jackson frowned. 'Well with due respect, sir, it's not in bad shape for a tent in the desert.'

'Oh really?' replied his CO. 'Then may I ask what that fly is doing on my shaving mirror?'

Jackson craned his head round the tent pole, then he looked across at Jampton. 'Not a lot, sir. He's dead.'

'I can see that,' snapped Jampton waspishly. 'I am a soldier.' He said this with heavy sarcasm, although it was the first dead thing he'd seen in his short military career. Then even he realised the stupidity of his remark. 'Clean it up at once.'

Jackson took a dirty khaki handkerchief from his pocket and spat on the mirror. Jampton's stomach lurched. 'Not in here, man, take it to the mess tent and wash it thoroughly in boiling water and disinfectant.'

Jackson lifted the small round mirror from its nail, and as he was about to leave the tent Jampton called after him, 'And kindly inform Sergeants Sparks and Miller I'm ready for them now.'

'Yes, sir,' replied Jackson, and when he was outside he turned back towards the tent and curtsied.

In a tent marked SENIOR NCOs Sergeants Sparks and Miller sat cross-legged on a blanket facing each other. 'Yours and up twenty,' said Sparks and pushed a pile of matches into the centre. Miller looked at his cards, panic-stricken. He wasn't a good poker player – if he was dealt a handful of rubbish he'd groan and moan, and if ever he was dealt a full house or a royal flush he'd most likely faint. Sparks took a long swig from a bottle of Stella. He was unconcerned; they were only playing for matches, for God's sake. Still it passed the time.

Miller, in an agony of indecision, glared at his cards. At that moment Jackson stuck his head through the tent flap. 'Hugh wants to see you pronto,' he said.

Sparks and Miller ignored him and after a couple of minutes Miller tore his eyes from the cards and spoke to Jackson, who was still there. 'All right,' he said, 'we got the message.'

Jackson didn't move. He was probably hoping to be offered a bottle of beer, but Miller wasn't having any. 'What are you waiting for,' he said, 'a twenty-one-gun salute?'

Jackson withdrew his head.

Throwing down his hand, Sparks said, 'Come on, let's make tracks.'

Greatly relieved, Miller threw his own hand down and rose.

'I hope it's not tonight,' muttered Sparks.

'What's wrong with tonight?' asked Miller.

'Have you seen the weather?'

'Yeah,' replied Miller enthusiastically and ducked out of the tent.

Sparks stood thoughtfully for a moment. He knew his oppo and he didn't trust the eager way he'd said yeah. Hurriedly he ducked out into the hot furnace of the afternoon. There was no sun, however, just a brassy sky. He caught up with Miller and grabbed his arm.

'All right, arsehole,' he said. 'What d'you have in mind?'

'Me?' asked Miller, innocent as a first-year choirboy.

And before Sparks could tap him further they were joined by Sergeant Major Puller and wordlessly they made their way on to the CO's tent and ducked inside.

'Make yourselves comfortable, gentlemen,' said Jampton, gesturing to the three upturned beer crates.

When they'd entered his head was bent over the maps on the table so he couldn't be sure if they'd saluted. No matter – there were more important things to discuss. He glanced round at the blank respectful faces.

'It's tonight gentlemen,' he said dramatically and waited eagerly for their reaction.

It wasn't exactly exuberant. To be more accurate it was received with bored indifference, so he pressed on. He turned towards the blackboard, on which was pinned a large map of the North African Desert. Over this large yellow area Jampton had pencilled lots of circles, triangles and thousands of arrows pointing every which way, rather reminiscent of the Bayeux Tapestries depicting the Battle of Hastings. With his pointer he rapped on the map to emphasise his words – speed of the convoy, supplies, the blackening of faces, passwords, and general tactics. After twenty minutes he turned from his blackboard to his audience.

'Any questions?' he beamed.

Sergeant Major Puller, who had been sitting with his arms on his knees, head down, eyes closed, raised his head wearily and said, 'Pardon, sir?'

Jampton, brought down to earth, repeated lamely, 'Any questions?'

They looked at one another, then after a time Miller put up his hand and asked, 'Any mail for us while we were away?'

Jampton sighed in exasperation. 'Let me reiterate,' he said, 'and go over the salient points again. The convoy will consist of eight three-tonners. I will be leading in my fifteen-hundredweight; you Sergeant Major, in the fourth vehicle and Sergeants Sparks and Miller in the second fifteen-hundredweight will take up the rear. Questions, gentlemen?'

Sergeant Major Puller looked across at Miller, who returned the stare with an expression too innocent to be honest. Puller turned towards the CO.

'You did say Sergeants Sparks and Miller would take up the rear, sir?' he asked.

'I did, Sergeant Major.' He shrugged his thin shoulders. 'I had no choice; Sergeant Miller volunteered.'

Half to himself, the Sergeant Major muttered, 'Yes, I'd a feeling he might.'

God almighty, placing these two at the rear of the convoy was like putting juicy beefsteak in front of a hungry dog and telling it to sit.

Miller jumped in. 'I know it's a risky placement, sir,' he said earnestly in his best Errol Flynn impersonation, 'but the lads would feel easier knowing we were backup.'

'Jesus,' breathed Sparks and turned away, only to find himself staring at a portrait of the King and Queen hanging from the ridge pole. It's a madhouse, he thought. His gaze swept over the neatly folded blankets on the bed. A bed, for God's sake. Where the hell had Hugh come by that? He craned slowly forward to see if there was a pisspot underneath.

'Well, the order of march is settled then,' chirped Jampton.

'It seems to me,' said the Sergeant Major, 'this is all academic. We won't be going out tonight, sir.'

Jampton was thunderstruck. This sounded dangerously like mutiny. 'May I ask why not?' He must remember this for the court martial.

'Weather conditions,' replied the Sergeant Major.

Jampton relaxed. 'The weather,' he snorted. 'I know it's hot now, of course it's hot.' He leant forward. 'But you seem to have forgotten that this is a night exercise. It'll be bl–' He stopped himself. He almost said bloody cold but not in front of the men. Next thing they'd be calling him Wilfred.

The Sergeant Major sighed. 'I don't think you quite understood, sir. There's a dark band along the horizon on the south, sir, a khamsin, and if my guess is right, it's going to be the daddy of all sandstorms and it's heading our way.'

Jampton's mouth opened and his eyes stared ahead as if trying to see through the canvas to the south. He gulped noisily. 'A sandstorm,' he muttered stupidly.

'Yes, sir,' said Puller relentlessly. 'And in a sandstorm nothing moves except the desert. Even the camels hunker down until it's blown itself out.'

Jampton looked as if he would burst into tears. It wasn't fair. He couldn't go out to bat because it had started to rain. He was saved, however, when Sergeant Miller intervened.

'With due respect to Sarn't Major Puller, sir,' he began, 'we're a fighting unit and war does not wait for weather conditions. This would be a test of our combat efficiency in the worst of all climatic conditions.'

Jampton brightened and metaphorically he put his pads back on.

Miller continued: 'And to go out on this night we will be stretched to the limits of our endurance.'

With this, he leant back, remembering just in time that he was seated on an upturned beer crate and to topple to the floor would have taken the gloss from his morale-boosting speech.

Sparks stared aghast, especially when he saw the relief on Jampton's face.

'My thoughts entirely,' snapped the little CO, jabbing the point of a pair of compasses into the map so hard that when he tried to pull them out the table rose slightly and his cup of tea slid gently to the edge and crashed to the floor.

Sparks gazed down at the smashed crockery and watched the tea disappearing down a crack in the floorboards. Good Christmas, he thought. Floorboards, for God's sake! I wonder what the bathroom's like.

The meeting lasted another two hours, during which Jampton lectured on the history of the British Army going back to Henry V, Part II, through the Crimea and up to the present day. Sergeant Major Puller, watching him with glazed eyes, hadn't uttered a word and Sparks had slowly fallen sideways off his packing case fast asleep. Miller sprang forward, helped him to his feet and explained to his Commanding Officer it was a recurring bout of malaria and Sparks had obviously forgotten to take his medication. And with that he helped Sparks out of the tent, presumably to visit the MO.

As soon as they left, Sergeant Major Puller deemed it a good opportunity to change Jampton's mind. Deep African darkness had fallen outside and outriders of the khamsin were beginning to cause the tent to billow and wriggle. Vainly, Sergeant Major Puller tried to point out the dangers of the coming exercise. In weather like this they could drive blindly into an enemy stronghold, drive arse over tit into a deep wadi, get bogged down in the Qatari Depression.

'That's fifty miles off our course,' Jampton replied.

The Sergeant Major shook his head. Fifty miles off track was quite likely with Jampton navigating. The Sergeant Major had then persevered. There were also the marshlands, and he had to explain that marshland was the desert jargon for minefield.

But no matter what objections the Sergeant Major had come up with, they fell on deaf ears. The little prat jocularly enquired if the Sergeant Major was getting cold feet. Jampton seemed to revel in the elements. Mind you, he didn't look so cocksure when he stepped out of the tent and the wind blew him back in again. The Sergeant Major gave it up as a bad job. It was like talking to a deaf camel. Disgustedly he made his way back to his own billet.

At 2300 hours the convoy was lined up rocking furiously under the onslaught of shrieking sand. All the crews were aboard and waiting patiently for their Commanding Officer. An ironic cheer went up as Jampton emerged from his tent. Sergeant Major Puller, from the cab of his three-tonner, watched the dim figure approaching. He was no match for the wind. It was like watching a wounded dung beetle struggling to its last resting place, one step forward and two steps back. Exasperated, the Sergeant Major heaved the door of the cab open and let himself down to assist the pathetic figure. Grabbing his arm, he dragged him to the lee of the nearest vehicle. It wasn't much better but at least they could stand, provided they held on to the tailgate.

Puller made a last plea for common sense. Putting his mouth to Jampton's ear he shouted, 'Abort this exercise, sir. Tomorrow night will be better.'

Jampton could see that this was the only sensible course and was about to agree when, with some odd freak of nature, the ferocity of the storm lessened as if the wind itself wanted to hear the verdict.

Jampton's head came up as he noticed the lull and he had a vision of his Aunt Dorothy at the dinner table: 'Wilfred may not look as strong as other boys but he has a backbone of pure British steel.'

It was enough. Jampton straightened. 'The exercise will proceed as planned,' he piped, and with that he left the shelter of the wagon.

It was a mistake. The desert storm, angry at his decision, picked him up and hurled him backwards into the arms of the Sergeant Major. But the die was cast – Puller struggled with him and with the help of the driver managed to manhandle him into his fifteen-hundredweight at the head of the column.

Once inside the security of the cab, protected against the maniacal screaming of the khamsin, Jampton felt better. He'd show his men that he wasn't just their Commanding Officer, he was a leader. Hadn't they all laughed at Hannibal when he took his elephants over the Alps. He gazed along the faint beams of the headlights as the bits of sand and grit flew towards him, glistening as they hurled themselves at the windscreen at fantastic speed. Shaking himself out of his hypnosis, he picked up his handset.

'Point to rear, do you read me? Over.'

He waited a moment. Through the static he faintly heard Miller's voice. 'Rear to point, Strength two. Out.'

Jampton flicked his switch again. 'Point to all vehicles,

advance.' And the convoy lurched slowly into the teeth of one of the worst storms in living memory.

The Sergeant Major, in the passenger seat of his three-ton Bedford, swayed as the vehicle lurched over the uneven terrain. He was an angry man. He'd served under many useless officers during his military career but Jampton took first prize. The sheer arrogance and stupidity of the little prat beggared belief. The Sergeant Major regretted the promise he'd made to Colonel Brunswick, a promise that he would keep an eye on his nephew and guide him in the hopes that one day he may prove himself. It was becoming an impossible task – like trying to train a tsetse fly to be a vegetarian. And like tonight's lunatic episode the tsetse fly had the capacity to kill.

The convoy struggled into the storm. They were grinding into the teeth of it and it was awe-inspiring. Jampton, in the lead vehicle, was scared out of his wits. He'd had the headlight covers removed in order to give him better night vision, but all he had was about three yards. A normal CO would have aborted the exercise, but this was Jampton, and wasn't he at the front?

Sergeant Major Puller, only a yard or so from the vehicle they were following, glanced across at the dark figure of his driver, Old Flathead, who was desperately trying to keep in view the two faint rear lights of the vehicle in front.

'Bloody 'ell,' he said, 'we want our 'eads examined. I wouldn't send 'Itler out on a night like this.'

It was horrendous. The winscreen wipers were useless, smearing the glass in the all-too-infrequent lulls. It was so bad that some of the lads had left letters with their mates at the camp to be posted in case they didn't return.

Jampton's voice crackled over the intercom. 'Point to rear, everything all right?' There was a rush of static, then a faint voice: 'OK, sir. No problem. Over and out.'

Sergeant Major Puller listened to this exchange, as did all the convoy. His mouth was gritted with sand. It was sheer lunacy.

Another burst of static and the CO's piping voice enquiring as to the welfare of the convoy. The Sergeant Major groaned. He had a feeling the CO was enjoying the challenge. The radio squawked again. 'God blimey,' ejaculated the Sergeant Major. If the prat had a gramophone in his cab, he'd be playing record requests.

Slowly and ponderously the convoy forced its cumbersome trek through the howling sand. Every five minutes or so point-to-rear communications were issued. The Sergeant Major smiled grimly. At least the little arsehole was now beginning to have doubts as to the wisdom of having Sparks and Miller at the back end.

At the rear end of the convoy Sparks and Miller were in the middle of a heated argument.

'Major Crawley?' exploded Sparks.

'Yes, Major Crawley. He was the best officer we ever had.'

'Bollocks.'

'It's not bollocks,' yelled Miller. His voice was raised not so much in anger, but rather to make himself audible above the shrieking madness of the storm.

'Creepy Crawley was an arsehole,' insisted Sparks. 'He was a forty-year-old Jampton.'

'Jampton wasn't killed at Tobruk, was he?'

Sparks looked across at the dark, hunched shape of his passenger.

'What are you on about?' he said finally. 'Neither was Creepy Crawley.'

'Course he was, I'm telling you he was.'

'Well, you're bloody wrong, mate.'

Sparks slapped the wheel in exasperation. 'A week before Tobruk he went up to Alex for a conference.'

It slowly sunk into Miller's mind that Sparks was right. Major Crawley had been at a high-level conference in Alexandria but he wasn't going to admit he was wrong.

'All right,' he said. 'He may have left for Alex but nobody's seen him since.'

Sparks slapped his forehead in exasperation. 'He's in the base hospital at Alexandria, you great steaming pillock.'

There was silence for quite a few moments, then Miller said, 'Where was he wounded?'

'He wasn't wounded, either,' said Sparks, beating the wheel to emphasise each word. 'He went to a high-level conference and pissed as a fart he fell out of a gharry and broke his leg.'

Sparks waited for a reply but there wasn't one.

Miller was hunched forward, nose to the windscreen.

'What've you seen?' asked Sparks.

'Nothing,' said Miller.

Sparks relaxed, then Miller thumped him on the arm. 'Didn't you hear me?' he yelled. 'Where's the bloody rear lights?'

Instantly Sparks put his foot down and the fifteen-hundredweight shot forward, but, strain as they might, there were no two red pinpricks of light ahead.

'Get on the blower to Hugh.'

Miller took up the microphone. 'What shall I tell him?'

'Just contact him, you useless pillock. Tell him we've got a puncture, the engine's packed in ... I dunno ... We've stopped for a picnic.'

Miller was already trying to raise the convoy but it was hopeless and with a sickening feeling they realised that they were utterly lost in a wild, screaming frenzy of a world gone mad.

Sparks eased up on the accelerator.

'Go on, go on!' urged Miller.

And so they bumped, lurched and lolloped into the ever-increasing maelstrom. But they had no chance of catching up with the convoy – they might just as well have tried to cross the Atlantic on foot.

Miles ahead, Sergeant Major Puller groaned as the wireless clicked again.

Jampton's voice squeaked through but this time it wasn't the usual enquiry about his rear guard. 'Point to all transport, ten minutes' halt. Out.'

Thank God and little apples for that, thought the Sergeant Major. Now was the time to have a word in private with his CO. The amount of wireless traffic emanating from his fifteen-hundredweight during the journey would have been picked up by every listening post within a twenty-five-mile radius, and could have been interpreted as anything from the convoy they were to a tank battalion moving to their start lines in preparation for a full-scale attack. Even in this weather German units could already be standing to on red alert.

He struggled to force his door open. The strength and scream of the wind fought him as he pulled himself alongside the vehicles to Jampton's fifteen-hundredweight. The twenty yards or so by the side of the dim line of vehicles was the longest twenty yards of his life.

He clambered into the back breathing as if he had run all the way from Cairo. He tapped his CO on the shoulder. Jampton gave a startled yelp and whirled to the dark hulk leaning over him. The Sergeant Major put his mouth to the CO's ear. 'Your wireless transmissions, sir.'

'Pardon?' yelled Jampton.

'Cut down on your wireless transmission – easy for an enemy to pinpoint.'

'Oh,' shouted Jampton, 'transmission.' He snatched up the mouthpiece and put it to his lips. 'Point to rear. Over.'

Puller shook his head, exasperated. He was about to repeat his warning when he stopped suddenly. On the wireless there was only static. Jampton was unperturbed, however, and again he pressed his transmit button. 'Point to rear, I say again, do you read me? Over.' And once more there was no reply.

After a few moments the Sergeant Major shook his head, and then: 'The crafty bastards,' he muttered. They'd hopped it again. He was sure, now, and reluctantly he had to admire their single-mindedness. This time they'd get away with it. The stupidity of a night exercise with conditions like this . . . They'd be lucky if the whole convoy didn't disappear as well.

Jampton pressed the transmit button again, but the Sergeant Major gently took the instrument from him. 'May I suggest something, sir?'

Jampton nodded eagerly. He was near to panic. It was enough that he'd lost Sparks and Miller again and any help from whatever quarter was more than welcome.

The Sergeant Major continued. 'I suggest, sir, we head back for camp,' he shouted, and paused as the demoniacal wind rose to a shriek. When the screaming died to an acceptable level he pressed on: 'This way we have every chance of running into Sparks and Miller if they've broken down somewhere, in which case –'

But here Jampton interrupted. 'I've got a better idea,' he shouted. 'We'll make our way back to camp and with any luck we may come across Sparks and Miller.'

The Sergeant Major added sarcastically, 'I was about to suggest something like that.'

He turned to leave Jampton's fifteen-hundredweight when a hand restrained him. He looked back to the shape of his CO.

'Sergeant Major,' shouted Jampton, 'I want you to lead us back to camp.'

Puller eyed him suspiciously.

Jampton craned towards his ear. 'It'll be good experience for you and should anything happen to me in actual combat it would be your responsibility anyway.' And before the Sergeant Major could reply, he'd forced himself out of the door in order to make his way to the Sergeant Major's vehicle in the middle of the convoy.

The Sergeant Major clambered over and took the CO's vacant seat. But before he'd settled the radio crackled and he heard the tinny voice of his CO: 'Wagons Roll!' There was a click as communication was broken off.

'Bloody 'ell,' breathed the Sergeant Major, 'that was quick.'

Jampton had obviously been blown four vehicles' length in three seconds. He nodded to the driver, who turned his ignition key, and after some heart-stopping moments the engine roared into life.

The journey back was a doddle; the storm was now at their backs and, sensing victory, eased, finally dying out. And when the convoy arrived back at base, the desert several miles north of its previous location had rearranged itself and lay, docile, to greet the sun appearing over the eastern rim.

Sergeant Major Puller sighed with relief as his battered convoy halted at the storm-vandalised camp that was once the Special Ordnance Group. Hardly surprisingly, there was no one to greet them. Wisely, as the last red tail-lights had disappeared into the gloom at 23.00 hours, there had been a concerted rush – defence force, umpires alike – to the safety of the mess tent, which was shielded by an escarpment of rock.

It hadn't been a holiday for them either. Several of the tents had been blown away and were conceivably swinging gently from some lamppost or other in Alexandria's main street. The white stones were in disarray all over the place and from the air it must have looked like a poison toadstool.

The lads who'd been out all night in the convoy dropped red-eyed and bone-weary out of their trucks and made their way to the mess tent, striding over the sleeping defence force for a mug of char and something solid. Others, too far gone to eat, moved like zombies to some of the tents left standing and fell into a deep sleep, too tired even to snore.

Captain Jampton, however, sat proudly at his table. He wasn't too tired, having slept most of the way back. Now refreshed, he was mentally composing a letter to his Aunt Dorothy. After all, his convoy was probably the only living thing that had moved last night. Even the war had come to a standstill whilst friend and foe alike cowered hugging themselves while the storm raged. But hadn't he led them through the worst of the elements? It was leadership above and beyond the call of duty equalling Scott's expedition to the Antarctic. Still fantasising, he reached for an airmail form, but his train of thought was broken as Sergeant Major Puller entered the tent.

Jampton looked up at the weary figure and his thoughts of the gallant Captain Oates sprang to mind, the only difference being that Captain Oates was leaving the tent whilst Puller was coming in.

The Sergeant Major, eyes red-rimmed, spoke through dry cracked lips. 'I've checked the men and equipment, sir. All present and correct.' He paused for a moment, then added with relish, 'Except the loss of Sergeants Sparks and Miller and one fifteen-hundredweight vehicle.'

Jampton's heart sank. He'd almost forgotten about those two. 'Tell me, Sergeant Major, is it your belief they've deserted?'

Puller shrugged. Good grief, thought Jampton, what is the Army coming to when in answer to a question from the Commanding Officer an NCO, a senior one at that, just shrugs? And come to think of it, when he entered the tent he'd omitted to salute. Wisely he ignored the lack of discipline. There'd be time for a quiet reprimand later. Finally he said, 'Thank you, Sergeant Major, that will be all.'

'Just one more thing, sir. We've lost another three-tonner and eight men.'

Jampton stared at him aghast. 'But you said apart from Sergeants Sparks and Miller all the convoy was present and correct.'

'This three-tonner wasn't in the convoy, sir. At first light this morning they left camp.'

Jampton was stricken. On the verge of panic he could see his command crumbling and being decimated and the only German he'd seen so far was the pilot of the Messerschmitt. Not a lot for his future memoirs.

'Didn't anyone try to stop them?' he blurted. 'The guards?'

Again the SM shrugged. How could he explain to this incompetent that the guards, like any other sensible human beings, had hunkered down and in all probability were fast asleep when the truck left? In fact, the truck had been dispatched with a rousing send-off, some of the lads handing letters over the tailgate to be posted in Alexandria.

Captain Jampton stared up at his Sergeant Major, aghast. Then after a moment he remembered who he was, sprang to his feet and snapped, 'Right, Sergeant Major, I want everybody on parade in ten minutes.' But as he looked into Puller's face, a shiver ran through him. Had he had a few more marbles he would have recognised Puller's expression as that of a man about to commit murder. Involuntarily he took a step back, his chair crashing to the floor, and hurriedly cancelled his last order.

'I'd forgotten about the convoy, Sergeant Major. Let the men sleep for a while.'

The Sergeant Major nodded and let the anger flow out of him as he left the tent.

When he'd gone, Captain Jampton shakily poured himself a glass of lemonade. God, how he needed that! He righted his chair and sat down to compose a report to his uncle, but what could he say? He pushed the paper to one side. Sparks and Miller wouldn't have deserted; it was unbelievable. No, they'd walk into camp in the next few days, sand-encrusted and sheep-faced at having lost the end of the convoy. If only he could have realised how near he was to the truth.

Sergeant Sparks struggled to open his eyes. It wasn't easy – sweat and sand made it difficult. He tried to lick his lips but there was no moisture. As he gradually came to his senses his first impression was that he was being roasted. Through half-open eyelids he tried to identify his surroundings. Everything was bathed in a sickly yellow light. It was only when he saw the dashboard that he realised he was in the cab of his fifteen-hundredweight. The windscreen and side windows had been blasted with sand and the truck itself was listing at an alarming angle. With an effort he managed to haul himself behind the steering wheel.

He looked across to his left and saw that his mate was sleeping like a pig in a rubbish tip, his sandy and sweat-plastered face poking out from a balaclava – not a pretty sight. Stale ciagarette smoke, the stink of sweat and the odour of rotting feet pervaded the atmosphere.

The door swung slowly open letting in a shaft of bright sunlight. Sparks heaved himself out on to the soft sand and yawned. He stretched his arms above his head. The heat was ferocious but infinitely more enjoyable than the malodorous atmosphere inside the cab. He fiddled for his fly buttons and faced the truck – when it hit him like a sackful of All Bran. He hadn't touched the door and it hadn't opened by itself. He whirled round to see an Arab woman in the traditional black chador, one arm holding the material to cover her nose and mouth. Sparks stared at her for a moment, then gazed all around him. Nothing but the high mounds of the sand dunes. He turned back to the woman. Where the hell had she come from? The woman bowed.

'Good morning, my heroic Sergeant Sparks. I hope you slept well.'

Sparks was dumbfounded. 'Yasmin,' he croaked.

'Of course,' she said calmly.

Sparks was baffled. 'Yes, but how did you . . .' He stopped. 'Oh bloody 'ell, you were in the back.' She nodded. 'I might have known,' he said. He slapped the top of the cab in exasperation, then yelped as the hot metal burnt his palm.

Yasmin lowered her head to hide her laughter. Sparks whirled round but the head of Miller came between them as he sought to disembark.

'What's all this bloody racket?' he demanded peevishly. 'I was having a lovely dream then – I was a chicken and the cook was just taking me out of the oven.'

He turned to Yasmin. 'Good trip?' he asked.

Sparks's eyes blazed, 'You knew she was in the back?' he hissed incredulously.

'Well, yeh,' said Miller easing himself out of arm's reach. He wasn't afraid of his oppo but neither was he in the mood for a punch-up, not before breakfast.

'Listen, old son,' he said. 'If I'd told you she was on board, I know you. In that bloody awful sandstorm you would have turned round and dropped her back at the camp.'

Sparks snorted. 'That's where you're wrong. I would have turfed her out and let her walk back.'

Yasmin's eyes flashed but she said nothing.

'All right,' said Miller, 'let me ask you something. Where are we? Go on, answer me that. Where are we?'

'How the hell should I know?' blurted Sparks. They glared at each other, fists clenched, but just as the bell was about to go for Round One Yasmin spoke. 'Would anyone like a grape?'

Quarrel forgotten for the moment, they stared at her in bewilderment. Slowly, from the folds of her chador, she drew out a bunch of luscious green grapes. She broke the bunch into two halves, handed one to Miller and tossed the other contemptuously to Sparks. He grabbed them clumsily and several fell to the ground. Miller was stuffing his face with a look of rapture, juice rolling down his chin.

Sparks tossed his lot disdainfully on to his seat in the cab. 'Where did you get these?' he asked quietly.

'From the oasis,' replied Yasmin coolly.

Miller, sucking juice from his hand, looked at the grapes on the seat. 'They'll dry out there,' he said and scooped them up to his joyful mouth.

Ignoring him, Sparks continued. 'So you know where we are?' he said.

'Yes, I do.' Then with some asperity, she added, 'You are both like children. This isn't your East End of London. This is the desert and without me you would not last a week.'

Sparks looked down as he scuffed sand over the grapes. 'OK, OK, I'm sorry. It's just that . . .' He stopped and looked at her. 'Oh bollocks.'

Yasmin smiled. She was happy again. 'Bollocks' was Sparks's way of making an apology.

Miller smiled too. 'See what I mean? She knows the desert, speaks Arabic like a native, and she's got you taped.'

Sparks wasn't listening. He was leaning in the cab for his water bottle. Miller turned to Yasmin and winked at her with a thumbs-up sign. Sparks guzzled the tepid water, swilled it around his mouth, then he had a proper drink and snapped back the cork.

'OK,' he said, 'let's get mobile. It'll take us half an hour to dig this heap out of the sand.'

Miller looked at Yasmin. 'How far is this oasis then?'

Yasmin smiled. 'Not very far. As I said I was there first thing. That's where I got the grapes.' She paused then, coyly: 'I hope you don't mind, Mr Miller. To get the grapes I traded your spare shirt.'

Miller pretended to be aghast. 'Bloody 'ell, I was saving that for church parade.'

Sparks was already busy with a spade. The wheels on one side of the truck were axle-deep in sand.

'Never mind that,' said Miller. 'If she can walk it, so can we.'

'Oh yes,' said Yasmin. 'Just over this large dune and you can see the oasis.'

Miller snatched off his balaclava and combed his hair. 'Must make a good impression,' he said and started off up the dune.

Sparks eyed the large humped sand hill and watched his mate scrabbling up to the top. He squinted as Miller reached his point of vantage. Miller, a small figure now, stood for a moment, then in a panic-stricken rush tumbled and rolled, slithering back to Sparks's feet. He grabbed Sparks's leg, then hauled himself up, struggling to regain his breath.

'It's an oasis all right,' he panted, 'but it's full of troops.'

'Ours?' asked Sparks urgently.

'I don't think so. They've got a flag up but it's not the Union Jack.'

They both looked questioningly at the girl. 'Oh yes,' she said, 'it's an Italian base . . . but it's up to you.' She shrugged. 'The next oasis on this track is two hundred kilometres away.'

Sparks grunted as he resumed his digging. 'I knew there'd be a catch in it somewhere.'

Miller grabbed a second shovel and was already furiously trying to extricate the other wheel.

Yasmin spoke softly. 'I do not think you have much choice.'

They both stopped attacking the sand and followed her gaze. A line of dots shimmering in the heat was approaching slowly.

'What is it?' asked Miller.

No one answered; they watched in silence as the shapes shimmered into recognition. Twenty or thirty Arabs mounted on camels, in line, plodded towards them.

'Friendly?' asked Sparks.

There was a pause, then Yasmin said, 'If they continue as now towards us they may be friendly, but on the other hand if they stop . . .'

It was at that moment the cavalcade stopped. They were about two hundred yards away. Two other riders jogged up to join the leader.

'The rifles,' hissed Sparks.

Yasmin steadied him. 'Do not move suddenly. They will be upon you before you can open the cab door.'

Miller gulped. His bowels were turning to water and it wasn't just the grapes. He muttered, 'God Almighty! They stake you out naked, cut your balls off and stuff 'em in your mouth.'

'Yea?' said Sparks quietly. 'They wouldn't get all yours in.'

Yasmin spoke softly. 'They are undecided. Walk up the dune and surrender to the Italians.'

Miller wasn't so sure. 'They'll pick us off before we get halfway up.'

'I do not think so,' said Yasmin. 'I think they are more interested in your vehicle. They will be puzzled as to why you walk away and leave it and while they make up their minds you will be over the top and protected by the Italians.'

The two Sergeants looked at each other, then dropping their spades moved as casually as they could up the treacherous sliding sand. Halfway up, without stopping, Miller clasped his hands over his head.

'What's that for?' gasped Sparks.

'We're surrendering. When we get to the top we'll be in full view of the Itis and I don't want to be shot by them either.'

Sparks said nothing but slowly raised his hands to clasp them as Miller had done. Only a few more yards. It was heavy going and not easy with hands clasped over their heads. They daren't look down to see what the Arabs were up to. Each slithering step was a nightmare. Any moment could bring that sledgehammer blow from a bullet between the shoulder blades. Only the lucky ones heard the crack of a rifle that followed.

They hadn't much further to go when a strange thing happened. From the opposite side of the dune a white topi came into view over a red face, then the rest of whoever it was appeared as he breasted the rise, sun sparkling on his bemedalled chest. He was obviously an officer of some nationality or other. The two soldiers' eyebrows shot up in unison as a long line of men came into view following him. But the strangest thing of all was that every man had his hands clasped firmly on top of his head.

Sparks and Miller, hands clasped over their heads, stared uncomprehendingly as the General, or whatever he was, stopped a pace in front of them. He was a pathetic figure for all his medals and highly polished boots with his hands clasped over his topi showing the black sweat patches under his armpits. For a few seconds they stood facing each other and Miller began to see the ludicrousness of the situation. Here in an unmapped piece of desert in North Africa, this hands-on-head charade was at an impasse. Ships were being torpedoed and sunk off the west coast of Africa; the Luftwaffe patrolled the skies with the arrogance of victors; tank battles were being fought; men were dying on the hot dusty desert; and whilst all this carnage was going on, this ludicrous comedy was taking place on top of a sand dune.

Miller felt an urge to giggle; it was on the tip of his tongue to blurt out, 'O'Grady says hands down', an old childhood game. But then some soldiers never really grew up.

The 'General' was the first to speak. '*Bon Giorno*,' he said, 'I am Capitano Carlo Abruzzi and I have the honour to surrender my command.'

Sparks and Miller stared at him in complete bafflement and, fearing he had not been understood, the Italian went on. 'We are your prisoners.' He gestured to his troops with his elbows.

The two Sergeants looked at each other. 'No, no,' said Miller, '*niente*. We are *your* prisoners.' He smiled ingratiatingly, pointing in turn to the officer with his elbow.

Sparks was fed up with the whole thing. 'Listen, Capitano,' he muttered, 'I don't know how many lads you have, but there's only two of us.'

The Italian Officer eyed him suspiciously. 'Then you are not forward reconnaissance for more British troops?' he asked.

'You must be joking.' Sparks unclasped his hands and fished a cigarette out of his shirt pocket and lit it, blowing a plume of blue smoke into the hot still air.

The spell was broken. The Italian troops were already scrambling back down their side of the dune. Some then shouted back in a tone that didn't sound exactly complimentary. Their officer shrugged and took his hands from his head. He gestured at his disappearing troops.

'You must understand. We have been here for a long, long time and they are a little sand crazy, *comprendi*?' He turned and followed his command down to the oasis.

'Got any more bright ideas?' asked Sparks when the officer had gone.

Miller shrugged. 'We'll see what Yasmin says.'

Sparks thought for a moment, then nodded, and they made their way back across the dune. As they neared the edge they looked down on to the fifteen-hundredweight, but there was no sign of Yasmin.

After a moment's silence Miller glanced at his mate. 'Where is she?' he whispered.

Sparks indicated her tracks in the direction of and around the side of another large pile of sand. Miller nodded and was about to slither down the dune to the truck when Sparks restrained him. Miller looked up enquiringly but Sparks was looking past him and down the track. Two hundred yards to their right the Arabs were exactly as they had been, still and motionless high on their camel saddles.

Miller came to a sudden decision. 'Sod this for a game of skittles,' he said. 'I'm going to collect my gear and follow Yasmin's trail.'

He was about to move forward when he noticed that Sparks had turned and was walking in the opposite direction in the wake of the Italians. Miller struggled after him and caught his arm. 'What about our gear?' he asked.

Sparks eyed him curiously for a moment. 'If you make a move to that truck, I wouldn't bet a penny on you coming back alive.'

Miller scoffed. 'You're getting jumpy in your old age.'

Sparks nodded. 'You go if you want. I can just see you at the Pearly Gates and when St Peter says "Who're you?" you won't be able to tell him because you'll have a mouth full of bollocks.'

He turned and strode away and, after a moment's hesitation, Miller scrambled after him – he was convinced.

The oasis was a pleasant surprise. When they first caught sight of it below them they stopped dead in their tracks and gazed in wonderment at the spectacle. They weren't the first people to be enchanted at their first view of the El Waddim Oasis.

Before the war the El Waddim Oasis was described in Thomas Cook's travel book as 'The Jewel in the North African Desert' and visitors to Alexandria were urged to take advantage of a three-day trip to where native caravans from the four corners of Africa exchanged goods, craftware and gossip. For tourists in Alexandria it was a visit not to be missed. Accommodation was available at the El Waddim Hotel and the cuisine was European under the direction of a French chef.

Sparks and Miller would have agreed wholeheartedly with this description. They could hardly believe their eyes. Below them was a wonderland, palm trees fringing a glittering lake surrounded by a sprawl of whitewashed huts. Some of them were two-storeyed and, like a duck shepherding its brood to the water, there was a larger building which could have been a picture palace or a mosque but was, in fact, a hotel or, to be more exact, a hotel in happier, more tranquil days.

After a time Miller turned to Sparks and asked in a hushed voice, 'Is this for real or are they making a film?'

Sparks didn't reply but Miller could see that he was impressed. In a sort of daze they made their way towards a trestle table in the shade of a copse of palm trees.

'Please be seated,' welcomed the Capitano, and a white-coated steward placed a large jug of beer before them and two glasses.

Miller filled his glass and raised it to the Italian in a toast of comradeship. Then he glanced around him and sighed happily. If this was being a prisoner of war so be it – he could put up with the hardships.

After a few more bottles of beer the stiffness and formality of the occasion disappeared and euphoria began to take its place.

The Capitano was now relaxed, his tunic unbuttoned and a soft damp cloth on his head. His white topi had been removed by his batman and placed reverently in a hatbox.

'Nice place you have here, Capitano.'

The Italian waved his hand deprecatingly. 'Please not to call me Capitano – I am not a soldier and I'll be happy for you to call me Carlo.'

'Thank you,' said Miller, 'and you can call me Dusty if you like.'

They shook hands solemnly and then clinked glasses as they toasted each other, and they sat together in easy silence for a few moments. Then Miller shaded his eyes.

'What's all that lot down there?' he asked, indicating a cluster of native tents shimmering in the heat about a half mile away. There were camels, goats and lots of tiny children running around.

'Ach,' said Carlo, 'that is the native Bedouin encampment. They were all the staff at this hotel before the war. They were moved out to accommodate us, but obviously they didn't go far.'

Miller sighed, taking in the general scene. 'This is better than Blackpool,' he muttered.

Sparks smiled sardonically. 'All we need is a few fish-and-chip shops. I can live without the candy floss.' And feeling that he'd already said too much for one day he downed another bottle of Stella.

Carlo nodded. 'It's not too bad for a week or two,' he said, 'but we are here more than one year. We are a little *fou*, you understand. How you say, sand crazy?' He belched softly. 'I think Il Duce has forgotten us. When Hitler beckoned, Mussolini rolled over on his back to have his belly tickled – and *phutt* – we are in the big war.' He slapped his biceps and gave an impressive uppercut in the air in an Italian gesture of contempt.

'Tough tits,' muttered Sparks, but nobody seemed to have heard.

Carlo took a sip of wine and continued. 'Straight away I am constipated into the Army.'

Miller choked on his beer.

'This isa notta fonni,' snapped the Italian.

Miller held up his hands placatingly. 'No, no,' he said, 'I think you mean conscripted into the Army.'

'I said that,' snapped the Italian.

'No,' said Miller, 'you said constipated into the Army.'

Carlo looked puzzled. 'What is constipated?'

'Well, it's, er, it's when you can't go.'

'Go where?' asked Carlo.

'Leave it,' said Sparks. 'Don't take any notice of him.' He nodded at his mate. 'He's been out here too long as well.'

Carlo recovered his good humour. 'I will never understand your English language.' He laughed and Miller joined him and they toasted each other again.

Sparks leant across the table. 'You sound as if you don't like the Army,' he said.

Carlo snorted. 'I hate the Army. I am not a soldier. I am the best head waiter in Roma.' He stared gloomily into his glass for a moment, then struck the table with his fist. 'Everybody who was anybody dined at the Hotel Excelsior on the beautiful Via Vittorio Veneto to sample the magnificent cuisine – and to see me.' He thumped his chest and coughed slightly.

He smiled sadly at his reminiscences.

'Once we were patronised by Mussolini's son, Count Ciano, a party of six. What beauty, aah!' He kissed his fingers. 'That lunch went on for three days.'

'I'll bet that cost a packet,' said Miller enviously.

Carlo stared at him for a moment, then his face cleared and his hand waved dismissively. 'We did not speak of money – it was Mussolini's son.' It was said casually but it was obvious that it hurt.

'Not even a tip?' asked Miller guilelessly.

Immediately Carlo's mood changed. 'Oh yes, I get a tip. Do you know what it was?'

They both shook their heads dutifully.

Carlo continued, 'A week later an envelope is coming from the Ministry of War, and me –' he thumped his chest, '– the greatest head waiter in Italy, instructed to pack and report to the Stazione Centrale Roma Termini immediately and shortly after I become

Capitano Carlo Abruzzi in this godforsaken place. That was my tip.'

A mess waiter in a shabby off-white jacket brought two more jugs to the table. Miller smiled his thanks and gazed round with a sigh of satisfaction.

'Where is everybody?' he asked.

'Everybody?' asked Carlo, puzzled.

'The troops, you know, soldiers.'

'Ah,' Carlo said, dismissing them contemptuously. 'As I told you before, they are not soldiers, they are waiters, fruit sellers, wine producers. Soldiers!' He sniffed. 'We are not fighting men, we are supply and catering.'

'Oh,' said Miller, not quite understanding.

At that moment Yasmin joined them. She sat next to Sparks and an agitated Italian followed her, gesticulating but not brave enough to touch her. He bowed to his CO and in a flood of Italian apologised for the intrusion of the Arab woman. The CO dismissed him with a wave of his hand and stared coldly at Yasmin. Coolly she removed her head covering and the change in the Italian was electric. This was no Arab woman. Suddenly he was the head waiter again. Rising with supreme politeness, he leant over the table, took her hand and kissed it. She bowed her head graciously and in fluent Italian proceeded to introduce herself.

Sparks and Miller listened open-mouthed. They heard her mention their names and when she had finished Carlo beamed at Sparks. 'You are a very lucky man indeed.'

'Yeh,' said Sparks and took a long pull at his beer.

Miller was lost in admiration. 'She's full of surprises,' he said. 'She's got Italian as well.'

Carlo clapped his hands and his batman emerged from the large building with the hatbox. The Capitano glared at it, then rattled off in Italian sending the man back inside to return with another wineglass. After it was filled, Carlo stood, raising his own glass. He bowed to Sparks. 'A toast to your beautiful signorina.'

Yasmin looked at Sparks with a half-smile on her face. Sparks hesitated for a moment, then raised his glass of Stella and drank.

'Lovely here, isn't it?' said Miller, making an all-round gesture with his glass. He stopped as two men approached, hand in hand, dressed in long flowing djellabas and obviously enjoying each other's company. They sat down at the table and nodded to the company, eyeing the two Sergeants curiously. Performing his duty as the host, Carlo introduced the new arrivals as Eeny and Meany. The slighter of the two, in a broad Lancashire accent, said, 'I'm Eeny.' Then with a giggle said, 'He's the Meany.'

Miller stood up, bowed his head and offered his hand, which they shook delicately. 'I'm Dusty Miller and this is my friend and comrade, Sergeant Sparks.'

He clicked his heels and sat. Already he was under the Italian influence. Sparks looked away in disgust; he wasn't fully reconciled to the ludicrous situation. Any minute now, he thought, I'm going to wake up in an Army mental section.

Carlo rose. 'If you will excuse me, I have some work to do.' He bowed to the table and was gone.

A soldier with a serviette over his arm brought fresh glasses and poured the wine for Eeny and Meany and discreetly backed away. Miller took a long swig of his beer while Eeny and Meany clinked glasses and sipped.

'This is the life.' Miller smiled expansively, and then said pensively, 'I wonder if they sell postcards.'

'Just arrived?' asked Meany.

'A couple of hours ago,' said Miller.

'You'll like it here,' said the other one and added, 'How did you find this place?'

Miller chuckled. 'We were on a night exercise in all that bloody muck and sand and somehow we got detached from the others and ended up here.'

'What mob are you with?' asked Eeny.

'Special Ordnance Group,' said Miller.

Meany stiffened and Eeny spluttered in his wineglass. They all looked at each other, all joy gone now.

'Did I say something wrong?' asked Miller. He looked at Sparks, who burst out laughing.

Miller was shocked. He hadn't seen Sparks laugh like that since the cook backed on to the stove and set his trousers on fire.

'What's so funny?' asked Miller.

Sparks wiped his eyes. 'Have another look,' he said. 'It's that bloody Jerry pilot you shot down and the little fella's Hugh's driver.'

Miller was still perplexed.

'You shot him down,' said Sparks. 'He forced what's his name to drive him back to his unit.'

'Oh yeah,' gasped Miller as enlightenment dawned. Then he brightened and a broad grin spread across his face. 'How are you both?' He reached over the table with his hand outstretched.

For a moment the German pilot stared at him, then he also laughed and eagerly shook Miller's hand. 'Allow me to introduce myself – I am der Fliegerhauptmann Rudolph von Bosch. You may call me Rudy.'

The slight man leant forward. 'And I'm Driver Gratwick.'

'And how is Deadshot Dick?' Rudy asked laughing. 'I didn't recognise you at first because when we had our little contretemps your face was covered with a balaclava helmet.'

For the next few minutes they toasted one another, then Carlo, then the British and the Germans, and for some obscure reason Tito got a mention.

Rudy filled them in on how he had known of this oasis having overflown it as a test pilot and how Carlo had welcomed them with open arms, thirsty for news of the outside world and the state of the war. He went on to explain that, although Carlo had a highly functional wireless transmitter/receiver, the news in both Italian and German was heavily biased.

'Where's your transport?' asked Gratwick.

'It's over the other side of that dune,' said Miller pointing. There was a moment's silence while Rudy and Gratwick stared at him aghast. Miller looked from face to face. 'What's up?' he asked finally.

'You left your truck unguarded?' gasped Rudy and they both rose and hurried towards the dune, Miller trying to keep up with them, wondering what all the fuss was about. Perhaps he was in Carlo's parking space. They wallowed frantically up the soft sand of the dune and with sweat pouring down their faces they finally staggered across the top and gazed down the other side. The German pilot wiped the sweat away with the back of his hand and shrugged.

'The bastards,' gasped Miller.

He couldn't believe his eyes. The fifteen-hundredweight had been there – a patch of oil testified to that – and the truck hadn't been driven away. The tyre tracks stopped at the patch of oil. The pilot pointed along the scuffed tracks of the camels, leading straight and inexorably into the distance. Miller shook his head in bewilderment. He'd served long enough in India to have witnessed and heard tales of events that bore no rational explanation. And here in the Middle East, set an Arab down anywhere in the desert and he would unerringly make his way to Cairo, Alexandria, or anywhere he decided to go.

As if reading his thoughts, Gratwick chimed, 'I suppose they dismantle the truck, distribute the load and just carry on.'

Sparks nodded and squinted towards the sun. 'They'd had a few hours' start,' he murmured.

Miller was still mystified, unable to grasp the situation. 'Blimey,' he burst out. 'I must remember to write to the motor-racing authorities. Those lads would be a godsend in the pits at Brooklands.'

'Our truck went like that,' said Gratwick as they started back to the oasis. 'Parked outside our hut it was and when we got up in the morning – *phhhh* – it had vanished into the air.' He paused, then after a moment: 'I've still got the rotor arm.'

'We're not the only victims,' said Rudy. 'What about poor old Carlo?'

'What about him?' asked Miller.

'When he first arrived here he had a half-track and eight Dovunque 35 trucks. After only two days the half-track was gone. The rest soon followed.'

'Yes,' Gratwick broke in. 'And can you imagine how much one of them would weigh? This wasn't like one of our Bren carriers. This was more like a medium-sized tank.'

'Bloody hell,' said Miller automatically. It was scorching hot now and he didn't want to hang about chitchatting. He began to move forward to the distant shade of the oasis.

'No, wait,' chuckled Rudy. 'You haven't heard the best bit.'

Miller groaned inwardly and blew a bead of sweat off the end of his nose.

'The following night,' the pilot went on, 'Carlo mounted a four-man guard but of course not being soldiers they climbed into the back of one of the trucks with a few bottles of wine and a pack of cards.'

Miller laughed. 'I get it, and in the morning all the other trucks had gone.' It was a good yarn but not worth getting sunstroke for.

'No, no, you're wrong,' put in Gratwick. 'That's what we thought at first.' He nudged his companion. 'Go on, Rudy,' he whispered.

Rudy smiled fondly at him and continued. 'The funny part was, well not funny really, but the trucks were still there in the morning except for the one containing the guards that had completely disappeared. How do you like that? A truck and four guards vanished into thin air.'

Miller stopped, now intrigued. 'How d'you know they were in the back playing cards?'

'Ah,' he said, 'that is the interesting part.'

Now Miller was hooked and even Sparks, who had been a short distance away, came to join the group.

'Go on,' he said. 'I've been listening.'

'Well,' continued Rudy, 'Carlo naturally took a patrol down to the native village to search for clues and just outside the Bedouin tents they found the Four of Hearts half buried in the sand.'

'So that's how you know they're the villains?' Sparks nodded to the distant sprawl of the native camp.

'Yes,' said Gratwick, 'but you haven't heard the best bit.' He glanced shyly at his companion. 'You tell it best, Rudy.'

The German pilot smiled and stroked the back of his fingers down the boy's cheek. Behind them Miller looked quickly at Sparks and blew him a kiss. Sparks glowered, then addressed the German. 'Go on, then,' he said. 'What's the best bit?'

Tearing his gaze from Gratwick's face, Rudy turned to them. 'Naturally,' he began, 'Carlo reported the loss and within a few hours a Fiat G12 transport plane landed and a company from a crack Italian regiment entered the camp and began to search with probing rods. They had the Arabs digging all over the place. Mine detectors were used. But after two days of turning the place upside down, nix.' He made a sweeping gesture with his hands to emphasise the nix. 'It was only when the elite force was boarding the plane to return that one of them discovered his wristwatch had gone, then another looked at the white band on his wrist where *his* watch should have been.

'Frantically the troops checked their personal belongings – five wristwatches, three wallets and even two of the mine detectors. They were angry and it was all their CO could do to shepherd them into the plane. No way were they going to enter that camp again. He couldn't afford to lose a dozen members of a crack Italian regiment.'

At the end of the anecdote, Rudy and Gratwick laughed uproariously. Miller laughed with them, although he thought the story about as funny as an amputation. Still chuckling he led the slither down the soft sand of the dune. At the bottom his good humour returned. 'Well, we're stuck here now. We'll have to make the best of it,' he chirped.

His euphoria was short-lived. When they arrived at the table under the palms, Carlo greeted them morosely. He rose from his chair and as he turned to go he looked over his shoulder and growled, 'The Germans are coming.' Then he entered the shadowy doorway of the hotel.

Miller stared after him, unable to digest the words; the scent of roses was fading fast. 'The Germans are coming,' he muttered to himself in a strangled voice. He'd heard these words many times as an infantryman but this time it didn't seem fair. He jerked his head round to Sparks, who merely shrugged.

'Did you hear that?' gasped Miller.

Sparks nodded and straddled a chair. 'You didn't expect it to last for ever, did you?' he said laconically, helping himself to a bottle of Stella.

Miller turned to Rudy and Gratwick for enlightenment but they didn't seem to be too bothered. He knew they were good mates but then so were he and Sparks, but they didn't sit leaning towards each other like that, foreheads touching while they looked into each other's eyes. You might do that with a bird, but not two men.

But there were more immediate matters on his mind and whirling around he made his way to the hotel to seek clarification from Carlo. He'd never been in the hotel and as he reached the door it was as if he'd stepped out of the war into the Grand Hotel, Bournemouth. He was dumbstruck. In the middle of the floor, Carlo was supervising his staff while they busied themselves spreading table cloths and arranging cutlery, candlesticks, wineglasses and ice buckets. Miller was flabbergasted. This had nothing to do with the Army: this was a poncy hotel and he was suitably impressed.

He wandered over to Carlo. 'Got a wedding this afternoon, have you?' he asked, gesturing towards the tables. Carlo ignored him as he straightened a napkin.

Miller stared round him. What was going on? His brain would accommodate only so much and he'd had enough input for one day. He was about to speak when he heard the sound of a piano coming from the gallery and he looked up to see a string quartet tuning their instruments. He cleared his throat.

'Is this all for the Germans?'

Carlo nodded abstractedly while he studied a menu. The quartet broke into 'The Merry Widow Waltz'.

Miller shook his head in disbelief. 'Will there be dancing as well?'

Carlo handed the menu to one of his staff, then turned towards the chubby, sweating Britisher. He sighed. 'Let me explain, my friend,' he began. 'Twice a week a German supply plane flies in with our rations. They arrive after dark and return before first light – a pilot, a navigator and a Feldwebel.' He drew his thumb down his cheek and blew a soft raspberry. 'A pig of a man, even for a German.'

Miller nodded sagely. 'All this for the German flight crew?'

Carlo shook his head and tapped his finger along the side of his nose and quietly he said, 'Sometimes they bring with them besides a ration a Very Important Person ... We are not told, you understand, the name of our guest but at the end of the message informing us of the arrival of the supply plane there are the words "Grade I". And so tonight we are expecting a Very Important Person, whoever it may be.'

'Ah,' said Miller, but although he could not for the life of him comprehend any of it, and more for the want of something to say, he asked, 'What table am I on?'

The Commandant placed a hand on his shoulder in fatherly fashion and said, 'You, my friend, along with your comrades will be locked away in your hut until they have gone.'

Then his manner changed abruptly. 'Do you play chess?' he said.

'No,' replied Miller.

'Pity,' sighed Carlo. 'Then you'll have to find something else to do, won't you, because I'm busy.' And with that he disappeared into the kitchen.

SEVEN

The letter, as usual, came via diplomatic pouch, delivered by dispatch rider to the Ministry of Ag and Fish, to be accepted and signed for by Colonel Brunswick. He sighed, not for the first time, at all this official rigmarole for what was, after all, only a letter from his wife. But then for people in the stratospheric heights of the Social Register, objects such as postboxes were for ordinary people. In any event they could hardly be termed letters. A more accurate description would be documents containing vital information. In fact, had they been intercepted by the enemy intelligence service, Hitler would most certainly have his feet up in Buckingham Palace by now.

He read on:

> At dinner the other night Winston, looking remarkably fit after his trip to Cairo, was scathing (as only he can be) when he referred to General Auchinleck, and by the time you receive this Auchinleck will be on his way to India under a cloud.

Colonel Brunswick put the letter down and sat back in his chair, took off his glasses, and pinched the bridge of his nose to digest this. He wasn't totally surprised at Auchinleck getting the boot, but shouldn't he, as Director of British Military Intelligence, have been privy to this information before now? He hadn't even been aware of Churchill's visit to Cairo, and that was only up the road, for God's sake. Shaking his head, he readjusted his glasses and continued to read:

> His replacement is almost certain to be a General Bernard Montgomery – a bit of a dark horse. But Max (Lord Beaverbrook) was in favour, saying Montgomery may yet surprise everybody. If it is to be Montgomery, your assessment of him would be appreciated.
> As ever –
> D.
> P.S. I understand the pressures of your work but it seems that you have made no headway at all in the matter of Wilfred's missing suitcase. Surely in your position you have agents in the dock area. It does not appear to me to be an insurmountable task to recover it. After all it is a fairly large blue suitcase with 'Jampton' stencilled all over it.

Exactly as his wife had forecast, seven days later, on 18 August, General Bernard Montgomery took over command of the Eighth Army.

Colonel Brunswick was neither elated nor depressed by the news. Morale was low and it seemed obvious that the new Commander had only been appointed to hand over Alexandria to the Afrika Korps. However, he would present his credentials. It never occurred to him that General Montgomery was himself planning to visit the headquarters of British Intelligence, and soon – the following day to be exact.

The headquarters of British Miliary Intelligence in Alexandria bustled with frenzied activity. Every day brought its new crisis and this Wednesday was no exception. Colonel Brunswick paced up and down in a muck sweat. At 1800 hours precisely General Montgomery would walk through the door. Ordinarily this would not have thrown him in such a panic. At worst he would have been mildly apprehensive. But the General had engineered the meeting for the express purpose of making the aquaintance of Sergeants Sparks and Miller. It was a get-together that must be avoided at all costs – but his options were few. He couldn't think. Short of blowing up the building, there didn't seem a way out.

The General had even dispatched a light plane to the Special Ordnance Group to bring them in – a plane, for God's sake. They were only Sergeants, whilst he, a Colonel, had to make trips out there in a clapped-out staff car, the only consolation being that had the General taken it into his head to fly down to meet them, it would be catastrophic – 'goodnight Vienna'.

In five minutes he would realise that his heroes, and his nephew, were only human. At least Sparks and Miller were. He groaned. Jampton would surely blow the gaff on what really happened during his battle with the Messerschmitt and that would trigger off a chain reaction that would end up with him running a recruiting office in Outer Mongolia.

'Bloody Montgomery,' he muttered, 'he's only arrived in the country five minutes ago, hasn't even had time to get his knees brown, and his first priority is to meet Sparks and Miller. You'd think he'd have more important things on his mind.'

Brunswick poured himself a large whisky, downing it in one. He was about to replenish his drink when suddenly he slammed the bottle down on his desk as if it had burnt his hand. From all he'd heard, General Montgomery was a strict teetotaller and could smell alcohol across the length of a moderately sized parade ground.

Hurriedly the Colonel locked the bottle in a drawer and searched around frantically for his bag of Mint Imperials. In his panic he didn't hear the knock on the door but couldn't stifle a yelp as he saw his Adjutant standing before the desk.

'Bloody hell, Jimmy,' he gasped. 'Must you creep around like the Holy Ghost? And whatever happened to knocking?'

Captain Shelley was unflustered as he handed over a large bag of mints. 'Managed to locate some from one of the cypher clerks.'

The Colonel looked at him in amazement.

'You asked me some time ago, sir, and *voilà*.' He put the paper bag on the desk.

'Ah yes, I remember,' said the Colonel, helping himself to a sizable handful.

Captain Shelley coughed discreetly and was about to speak when the Colonel raised his hand. Whatever his Adjutant had to say would have to wait until he finished the burning mess of mint in his mouth, which was bringing tears to his eyes. He was chomping hurriedly like a man eating hot chips on a cold night.

Finally with a great gulp he belched softly and began. 'First of all, Jimmy,' he started, pausing while his tongue cleared the last remnants from his teeth.

Again the Adjutant cleared his throat.

'No, hear me out first, Jimmy,' said the Colonel. 'When Sergeants Sparks and Miller get here I want you to spirit them away and brief them before they meet the General.'

This time Captain Shelley didn't bother to clear his throat. He leapt straight in: 'But, sir –'

'Don't interrupt me,' snapped the Colonel, slamming his fist on the desk. 'In an hour or two they will be here. It doesn't take that long by air.'

Judging his moment, the Adjutant said softly, 'Sergeants Sparks and Miller aren't coming, sir.'

Brunswick's jaw fell open, his expression that of a man just discovering he's incontinent. The Adjutant watched him curiously; the healthy brown tan of the Colonel's face changed to a sickly yellow, then, like the sun going down over Mandalay, it became bright red.

'Go on,' said Colonel Brunswick in a small clenched voice.

'The plane returned empty-handed, sir, and according to the pilot the two Sergeants are missing.'

'Missing?' echoed the Colonel reaching for the keys that opened the drawer to his Dimple Haig.

'Yes, sir,' said the Adjutant. 'Apparently they were all out on a night exercise when they became detached from the convoy, which is hardly surprising in that sandstorm.'

The Colonel stared at his Adjutant. Then with trembling hands he unlocked the drawer and slammed the bottle of whisky on the desk. Out of the heap of garbage that raced in his head, he came up with a question. 'Why weren't we informed immediately?' he snapped.

The Adjutant shrugged. 'The pilot said that a Sergeant Major told him that Captain Jampton has held up his report in the hope that Sergeants Sparks and Miller would return to camp in the next day or so and no harm would be done.'

He swivelled his chair viciously. What a king-sized cock-up, attaching Jampton to the Special Ordnance Group. Why the hell hadn't he posted him to set up a listening post or something in the back end of Sudan? He thought about this for a moment and then he brightened. Yes, why not? Yes, why bloody not? He had only to sign the movement order and his nephew would be out of his hair for good.

He stood up. 'Let's go to the wireless room, Jimmy,' he hissed. 'I want to speak personally to that jumped-up, never-come-down arsehole of a nephew of mine.'

The Adjutant didn't move and the Colonel looked at him enquiringly, feeling that his crisis hadn't quite come to the boil.

'It's no good contacting the Special Ordnance Group, sir,' he said. 'I did that half an hour ago and Captain Jampton has just left, leading a patrol to search for the two Sergeants.' The Colonel dropped back into his seat. There was only so much a man could take. He poured himself a large drink. There wasn't going to be a meeting anyway, so first things first.

'Jimmy,' he said, 'I want you to put me in contact with General Montgomery in person. There's no point in meeting now, right?'

'Have you any idea where I might locate him, sir?'

Brunswick lost control for a moment. 'How the hell should I know? I'm not Nostradamus – I'm just the poor humble Director of British Military Intelligence.'

The Adjutant turned to leave but the Colonel hadn't quite finished. 'Get in touch with my wife in England,' he said. 'She's the most likely person to know the whereabouts of Montgomery. Pass on my regards and while you're at it ask her how Rommel is.' He chuckled at his last sally.

The Adjutant smiled briefly and the Colonel, now restored to good humour, relaxed. 'Now seriously, Jimmy,' he went on, 'let's find a way out of this present disaster.' He poured himself a large whisky and invited his Adjutant to pull up a chair and join him. For a time they sipped and thought, staring down at the carpet. Finally the Colonel broke the silence.

'Whatever possessed that stupid nephew of mine to take his men out on a night exercise in a sandstorm?'

His Adjutant nodded slowly. 'Not just a sandstorm, sir, the worst in living memory. A large chunk of South Africa is now in the war zone.'

The Colonel stared at him, then after a time he said, 'Hardly a night for deserting.'

The Adjutant shrugged. 'I wouldn't put anything past Sparks and Miller, sir, but to break off from the convoy would have been sheer lunacy. It certainly couldn't have been premeditated.' He went on: 'No, sir, if you want my opinion I believe Sparks and Miller genuinely lost contact with the convoy.'

Colonel Brunswick swivelled in his chair and stared out of the window. 'Let's hope they have enough fuel and water to find their way back.' He raised his glass. He'd had just enough to make him maudlin. He took a large drink and added, 'Poor sods.'

EIGHT

The poor sods at that precise moment were enjoying a glass of after-lunch Courvoisier at the table under the shade of the palms. 'I could put up with this life for ever.' Miller beamed expansively, drumming his hands on his tight belly.

Carlo nodded sadly. 'And I, my friends, would gladly exchange this life for a daily bowl of watery soup in a POW camp.'

Miller's eyes widened. 'You're joking,' he said.

Rudy smiled sadly from the other side of the table. 'I fear the good Commandant is quite serious,' he said. 'You are ex-Infantry men, you live rough, share hardship and danger, and to be alive at the end of each day is a bonus. So to you, this oasis is a bed of roses.' He looked into his glass and sighed. 'For myself, after only a few weeks here sometimes I yearn to be back in the sky.' He turned towards Gratwick and patted his hand. 'It is only you, *mein schatz*, who keeps me sane and happy.'

A gloom settled over the assembly and after a few moments Carlo drained his glass, rose and said, '*Scusi*, but I have to look after the arrangements to receive our guests.'

They watched as he disappeared into the hotel. 'Ah well,' sighed Miller, 'I hope somebody turns up this time. He ponced the place up on Tuesday but nobody important arrived – just the flight crews. I'll bet they thought it was Carlo's birthday or something.'

'It must be somebody very special,' said Gratwick nodding towards the hotel. 'They've been at it since dawn.' He shook his head and smiled. 'You should have seen Carlo in his dressing gown, strutting about, clicking his fingers, tasting the wine, and the flowers.' He held up his hands. 'It looks like Lenin's funeral in there.'

Two Italians, soaked to the skin, emerged from the hotel carrying buckets.

'Any luck?' shouted Gratwick.

One of the Italians stopped. '*Si, signor*,' he said. '*Manifico!*'

'*Bene*,' replied Gratwick and the two Italians bowed and hurried off.

Miller stared at Gratwick in amazement. 'Where did you learn to speak Italian?' he said. Gratwick bowed his head modestly. 'Well go on,' said Miller, 'what was that all about?'

Gratwick giggled. 'You're not going to believe this,' he said, 'but they're rigging up a fountain in the middle of the floor.'

'Blimey,' whispered Miller. 'Who're they expecting, Reich Marschall Goering?'

Rudy sipped his wine. 'Hardly,' he said. 'Not fat Hermann. He wouldn't come this close to the fighting and if he did he'd have two Staffels of Messerschmitts escorting him.'

He was interrupted by the reappearance of Carlo, uniform sodden, lank black hair plastered over his face. 'Is not quite right, this fountain. One time little water.' He held forward his thumb and forefinger to indicate a two-inch jet. 'I go to look, and whoosh!' He made an extravagant gesture with his arms. 'Water everywhere, all the candles phutt.' He shrugged. 'Ah,' he said philosophically, 'there is still time.' He sat there, a forlorn heap of Italiano, then two tears ran down his already wet face.

'Don't let it get you down,' said Miller. 'If you haven't got it fixed by the time they arrive, how about a regatta?' It was a vain attempt to lighten the atmosphere.

'*Scusi*,' said Carlo wiping his eyes. 'This place makes me unhappy.' He dragged out a handkerchief as more tears poured down his face. Then he raised his head to the sky and wailed, 'I want to go home.'

There was an embarrassed silence round the table, as all tried to avoid looking at him. The moment was so tinged with sadness that even Sparks began to feel homesick, although he could never remember having had a home.

Gratwick broke the gloomy silence. 'Cheer up, Carlo, it'll soon be over.' There was a pause, then he added, 'One way or another.'

He glanced covertly at Rudy and immediately tears welled in his eyes. Rudy put a protective arm round him, too full to speak.

Miller looked round the table. 'Bloody hell,' he said, 'what time is the reading of the will?' He turned to Carlo. 'Look, mate, if it's that bad why don't you form up your lads and march out into the blue and give yourselves up to the first patrol you come across?'

'Oh yes,' replied Carlo. 'I'm not a lucky man. The first patrol will be German and what then?'

'Well,' replied Miller with a shrug, but that was all. He couldn't answer that.

In the silence that followed Yasmin moved round the table and poured Carlo a glass of wine. He didn't seem to notice.

Then Sparks with a sardonic grin said, 'There's a camp maybe ten to fifteen miles from here, northwest. They're British. They'll be glad to have you.'

Miller looked at him, puzzled. Then his face cleared. 'Yes,' he said, 'the Special Ordnance Group. We know the CO very well: Captain Jampton.'

Then suddenly he stopped as if hit by a tube train, realising with horror the consequences of what was being proposed. It was all very well to walk into camp with a bunch of Italian prisoners – they'd be heroes again – but the prospect of giving up this life of Reilly to return to the ramblings of the asylum didn't bear thinking about.

'Well, I'm not going for one,' snapped Gratwick in a voice they hadn't heard before. 'I'd sooner take my chance with Rudy and his mob.'

Carlo looked from one to the other. 'What is this Special Ordnance Group?' he asked.

Miller shook his head. 'No, Grat's right. It wouldn't work. Captain Jampton, the CO, is a funny bloke. He'll most likely lock all your lads up in a wire cage. And, blimey, he'd peg you out in the desert somewhere and let the ants have breakfast.'

Carlo shuddered. 'There is the Geneva Convention,' he muttered.

'Jampton won't give a bugger about that,' said Miller. 'He's a hard man.'

He was desperately trying to think of something to put the cork back in the bottle of the SOG when inspiration struck him. He slapped the table, eyes wide. They all turned towards him curiously. 'How's this for a top-of-me-head suggestion?'

They were all expectant now. Miller leant forward conspiratorially, glancing over his shoulder to assure himself there was no one within earshot. 'That supply plane, when it lands, why don't we commandeer it? We'll all nip on board and in a few hours we'll be in Alexandria.'

'*Mio dio*,' exploded Carlo in disgust and made to rise.

'No, hear me out,' said Miller tugging him back into his chair. But Carlo snorted derisively. 'I see it now. Sixty or seventy of us crammed into the plane, some more on the wing and the rest strapped to the tail.' He looked sternly at Miller. 'If I were you, my friend, I'd take more water with it.'

Miller stared at him, his brain racing like a tortoise with a bad leg. 'We can't take everybody on one flight,' he said. 'That stands to reason. We just take a plane load to Alexandria, then we come back and take some more of them, like a bus service.'

He knew he was babbling a load of rubbish but it was necessary; anything to divert Carlo's happy thoughts of sanctuary with the Special Ordnance Group.

Carlo rose, shaking his head. 'I think is better we forget it. I apologise for my weakness and is good of you all for your kind suggestions.' With that he went back into the hotel.

Instantly Miller whirled round at Sparks. 'Why don't you keep your big mouth shut?'

Sparks lit a cigarette. 'What's the matter?' he said. 'Can't you take a joke?'

'A joke?' spluttered Miller. 'Didn't you see his eyes light up for a minute? Ten-mile march. Good Christ, he was thinking about it. If I hadn't stepped in they'd be getting their small kit together now ready for off.'

Gratwick shook his head. 'Carlo would be mad to give all this up,' he said.

'No, *leibchen*, you do not understand,' said Rudy. 'This, to them, is a prison without bars and they have served a sentence of more than a year; same sun, same faces, every day the same. At least as prisoners of war there would be other Italians. Probably they would meet old friends.'

Gratwick looked at him sadly. 'You want to be flying again, don't you, Rudy?'

Rudy laughed. 'Of course I do, but here I am enjoying a wonderful holiday. No, not holiday – what was the word you used?'

Gratwick blushed. 'Honeymoon,' he whispered softly.

There was a moment's silence. Then Sparks rose and stretched. 'Come on, Yasmin,' he said. 'It's time for my Italian lesson.'

Yasmin stared at him, puzzled.

Sparks shrugged. 'Forget it,' he said and started towards the huts.

He hadn't gone more than a few paces when Carlo hurried out to the table and called him back. And when he had their full attention he said, 'As Commandant I couldn't possibly go on that plane. It would not be honourable.'

They looked at each other with 'what's he on about?' expressions. 'The German plane,' said Carlo, as if this explained everything. 'I have spoken with my second in command and two senior members of my staff.'

Miller made to speak but the Italian waved him to silence.

Carlo chuckled. 'It would appear that such a plan as yours has been discussed many times but they were afraid to speak with me, uncertain of my, er, et . . .' He struggled but the word 'reaction' escaped him. So he ended lamely, 'They do not trust how I will feel.'

He rang a small bell on the table and immediately from the shaded doorway of the hotel three figures joined them – presumably the second in command and two of the seniors. Carlo didn't bother with introductions.

'Now, gentlemen, we have only about four hours before Junkers lands.'

Miller gulped and thought, Is the man serious? But a look at the four earnest Italian faces convinced him that the plan was not only afoot but was at the eight-furlong marker.

Carlo gestured for his second in command to take the floor.

'My English very bad, *capiche*?' They nodded, wondering what was to come. 'It lands, yes,' started the man, demonstrating his words with a motion of his hand descending slowly on to the table, even to the bumps as it landed. ' "Allo," says Fat Fritz.' He spat and flicked his thumbnail against his front teeth. ' "Come," we say, "we have girl for you in hut." And when in, *poof*.' He made a motion turning a key in a lock. And to make sure he'd been understood he added, 'We make prisoner, yes?'

And making the identical mime he locked up one of the officers. 'We all on plane, yes?' Two of the Italians nodded eagerly and the second carried on. 'We keep pilot, yes?' He struggled for the words and pointed two fingers saying, 'Bam bam.'

'Gun?' said Miller helpfully.

'*Si*, gun to pilot head and we say "Alexandria, *subito*".' He sat back exhausted.

It was all too simple. It was more than that – it was lunacy! Several moments passed in appalled silence then all the 'buts' came tumbling out.

The Luftwaffe wouldn't just sit back when their supply plane failed to return.

Did they intend to shoot the two Germans locked in the huts?

Would the pilot know where Alexandria was? After all, it wasn't signposted; and four hours was hardly enough time to make preparations. And wouldn't it be wiser to leave this until the next trip?

At this the second in command shook his head violently and slapped the table. 'No! No! No!' he said. 'It must be tonight. We wait next trip, then next trip, and next trip, another year has gone.'

Carlo sadly nodded his head. 'He is right, of course. After all, what is there to do? The Germans are taken prisoner and that is all. My second in command has explained to me that the plane will not leave before one o'clock in the morning. So they fly through the darkness for protection and arrive in Alexandria at first light. Simple, no?' But it was far from that.

There were enough doubts and questions to fill the *Encyclopaedia Britannica*. But after another half-hour of discussion two things became clear: one, come hell or high water they were going tonight; and two, Sergeants Sparks and Miller were to deliver them to the provos in Alexandria. Miller added a silent codicil to this – at a price.

Sparks shook his head in disbelief. The enormity of the enterprise was beyond credulity. It was outrageous, fraught with booby traps, and he knew for a certainty that he, for one, would not be going – but a glance at his oppo's face was enough. With a sinking heart he knew he would be on that plane.

Inside the hotel preparations for the enterprise were already well in hand. Weeks ago a list of aspiring POWs had been drawn up and the second in command was already apprising the lucky few of their good fortune.

Carlo was back in command but with more urgency. He was beginning to believe that the plan was his own. There was no doubt that it was common knowledge. He had to remonstrate with some of the men who began singing as they worked, and with a final look around he ordered his second in command to oversee the preparations whilst he went to his hut to arrange the seating plan.

Everyone nodded happily; it was a well-known fact that the seating plan was an excuse – it was time for the siesta of Capitano Carlo Abruzzi and nothing short of the Armistice was going to deprive him of his happy hour.

Yasmin rose from the table and made her way to her billet. She entered swiftly, locking the door behind her. Then she took down a piece of paper and wrote out a message. Thankfully, it was short and the encoding of it didn't take too long. In fact, in less than ten minutes she was making her way round the back of another larger hut and, looking round to make sure she was unobserved, she raised her hand to knock quietly.

Inside Carlo was about to climb into bed when he was interrupted by the discreet knock at the door.

'*Prego! Comme esta?*' he shouted peevishly.

'Yasmin,' came a small voice.

'*Momento,*' he called, but it was five minutes before he opened the door letting out a cloud of expensive perfume.

Quickly she slipped inside.

'This is indeed a pleasure,' said Carlo, gallantly. He was glad he'd had time to snatch off his hairnet and put in his teeth. 'Would you like a glass of wine?' he asked.

'Thank you, no,' she replied. 'This is not a social visit. It concerns the plane going to Alexandria.'

Carlo's smile vanished when he took in the serious look on Yasmin's face. He was surprised to realise that, from their very first meeting when her beauty had lit up the future, he hadn't seen much of her. She'd become almost invisible in the anonymity of her black Arab chador. And now as she turned back her headscarf he was startled with a realisation that he'd almost forgotten her as a woman.

'Capitano Abruzzi,' she began urgently, 'you must stop this madness. You must not let this nonsense take place.'

Carlo was speechless. The whole enormity of the exploit flooded him with instant panic. If his second in command or even one of his men uttered these words he would have agreed at once. But the enthusiasm, and the speed at which all the discussions had taken place, had taken the matter out of his hands. He'd been swept along like a cigarette butt in the Tiber.

'One word from you,' she urged.

'You don't understand,' he said helplessly.

But he knew she did. He was weak. He wasn't Capitano Abruzzi – he was Carlo, a head waiter. *Mamma mia*, what could he do? The express was already racing towards the buffers without brakes.

Yasmin regarded him helplessly with those soulful dark eyes.

Immediately he stiffened. Like all good Italians he became a man again. 'You are right, my dear,' he said in a commanding voice. 'It is madness.'

But even as he took down the hanger containing his tunic his shoulders slumped. He turned slowly to face her, raising his arms aside in a useless gesture of defeat. With his tunic on the hanger he could have been a matador, apologising to the bull for what he was about to do.

Yasmin knew in that moment that further appeals would be a waste of time. She sighed. 'As the outcome appears to be inevitable, Carlo, I would ask you to do one thing for me.'

Carlo returned his tunic to the wardrobe and walked towards her. 'What would you have me do?' he said.

'Listen to me carefully,' she said. 'What I have to say is official.'

He straightened and his eyes took on a new wariness, 'official' being the trigger word. 'I am listening,' he said and eyed her gravely.

Yasmin handed him the sheet of paper consisting of five figure cyphers. He glanced at it, then looked at her enquiringly.

Yasmin went on. 'I want you to instruct your wireless operator to send this message.' She paused. 'Below I have put in the frequency he must use.'

He stared at her for a moment, then said, 'Am I permitted to ask what the message is and to whom it is addressed?'

'It's addressed to British Military Intelligence and it gives the ETA of the plane that is to leave tonight.'

Carlo stared at her, a million questions roaring inside his head. 'But this is impossible, my dear,' he spluttered. 'The success of the flight is totally dependent on secrecy.'

She smiled. 'What is secret about an unarmed enemy plane flying over British airspace? It would be an easy target for every anti-aircraft battery within fifty miles of Alexandria, not to mention the fighter planes of the Royal Air Force.'

Carlo nodded slowly. They had naturally discussed this possibility, but it had been glossed over as one of the hazards of war.

But now, in the cold light of reason, Carlo had to accept that it would indeed be suicide.

As if reading his thoughts, Yasmin continued. 'This message will guarantee safe passage and a landing at Aboukir.'

Carlo pondered this at length and after a time he nodded again. 'Yes, I see.' He rose and paced the room as if measuring it for a carpet.

'Who are you?' he finally asked.

'Yasmin.'

He came over to the table and leant towards her.

'And who is Yasmin?' His face was a few inches from hers.

'That is information you do not need to know,' she replied coolly.

'Are you with British Military Intelligence?'

'No, I am not connected in any way with British Military Intelligence. I can only repeat that unless you send the message you will be responsible for the deaths of many of your compatriots, not to mention the British contingent.'

They looked at each other, then after a time Carlo capitulated. 'Very well, I will see that this is transmitted.'

'Thank you,' said Yasmin. 'This message must be sent immediately and repeated until an acknowledgement is received.'

He turned to take his topi from its hatbox and when he looked round she was gone. She was halfway across the compound as he raced towards the wireless hut. Yasmin let out a sigh of relief and walked over to rejoin the rest of the company, stopping suddenly when she caught sight of Sparks and Miller. A smile of amusement crossed her face and she shook her head in reluctant admiration.

Dusty Miller never missed a trick! 'All aboard for the *Skylark*,' he greeted her. And she smiled again at the neat stack of papers and the large empty biscuit tin. This mystified her and Miller winked. It had been a hard wrangle with the second in command but Miller had finally won the day. First, they required paper and a rubber stamp. These requests didn't create any difficulty but the sticking point had been when Miller insisted that all the would-be prisoners would have to pay their fare with gold wristwatches, bangles or money if there was any. This was when tempers flared.

Sparks stepped forward and was about to hang one on the second in command, who stepped back quickly, but there was a knife in his hand. Miller jumped between them and calmed matters down with a soothing, brilliant explanation. There had been a misunderstanding. The fares charged to the prisoners would be needed to grease the palms of the British authorities in Alexandria in order to ensure special treatment for the POWs. It seemed reasonable enough to the Italian way of life and with acquiescent nods they all shook hands and the day was saved.

The Italians wouldn't have capitulated so easily had they known the truth. No British official was going to get his hot, sticky little hands on this pile of joy. It would barely cover the expenses of a safe passage down the Nile. Disappearing from the airfield was the hard part; they already knew of a boat.

Yasmin was intrigued as a straggling line of POWs approached the table. Miller put out his hand to receive a gold wristwatch from the first man in the queue and after a cursory examination he put it into the biscuit tin. The man then passed on to Sparks, who briskly banged down a rubber stamp on to a piece of paper, which he solemnly handed over. The man stared joyfully at his boarding pass and the date, 23 December. He didn't mind. He'd worked in the office and 23 December was the only date on the rubber stamp.

The next in line took his place in front of Miller with his worldly goods, and so on until all the passengers had been booked in. Miller's eyes gleamed as he looked into the biscuit tin. He could hardly get the lid on. To hell with the boat – there was enough here to hire a light plane.

In the rest of the camp, excitement was now at fever pitch. Letters were being written hurriedly to be posted in Alexandria and for some unknown reason everybody seemed to be talking in whispers. The lucky prisoners of war were embraced many times and tears were shed all over the place. The tension was unbearable and when the African night came down like a heavy velvet curtain whisked over a lighted window, hearts were beating faster and mouths were becoming drier – they were committed.

In the blackness of the night the side of the runway was seething with watchers, but nobody spoke. Eyes scanned the dark sky as if they were waiting for the end of the world, ears straining for the uneven beat of the approaching supply plane. Way over in the Bedouin encampment a camel coughed and all heads jerked in that direction, but on identifying the sound there was a general relaxation. It broke the almost unbearable suspense.

But the quiet mutterings ceased immediately when in the distance came the sound they had all been waiting for: badly synchronised engines getting louder as the plane neared its destination. As if this was a signal, the dark shapes awaiting its arrival evaporated into their huts. It was vital that this was to be a normal, ordinary, scheduled flight. A command was issued and the kerosene lamps on either side of the runway were lit as the plane made its final approach. It wasn't a bad landing considering the unevenness of the flight path.

When the plane came to a final stop Carlo minced nervously forward, resplendent in his full dress uniform, complete with medals, just in time to reach the plane as der Oberst der Luftwaffe ducked out of the door. Carlo saluted and then escorted him towards the hotel. During the fifty yards of darkness Carlo was proud of himself – cool, urbane and gracious – but immediately they stepped into the lights of the hotel his bottle went. Sweat poured from his face and he was trembling so violently he had to explain to his honoured guest that it was an illness which ran in the family.

He turned to summon the wine waiter. He snapped his fingers but they didn't seem to work, so he clapped his hands. And at the signal one of his minions hurried over with a glass of champagne on a silver salver. Unfortunately he, too, was gripped by nerves and by the time he reached der Oberst, there wasn't much champagne in the glass but his tray was awash.

The situation was saved at that moment when a huge jet of water erupted from the rockery in the centre of the floor, drenching both Carlo and his honoured guest. Carlo was mortified, ineffectively dabbing der Oberst der Luftwaffe's uniform with his handkerchief and babbling apologies. Der Oberst, however, seemed to take it all in good part. In fact, he was envisaging a humorous anecdote at the dinner table when he returned to his mess. Carlo's second in command, assessing the situation at a glance, came forward and ushered the great man to his suite on the first floor . . .

And Phase I of Plan Junkers was already in operation.

The plane itself was still on the runway and in the back the Feldwebel, a large, pimply faced Bavarian, sat on a crate watching the Italians at work, but he was uneasy. He wasn't too thick to notice that as the Italians carried the supplies down the ramp they seemed to be avoiding looking at him. Something was afoot, but when another Italian sidled up to him with a much-thumbed, creased photo of an undressed female, he relaxed, feeling that this must be the reason for their unusual behaviour.

He waved the man away scornfully. But the man was persistent. He pointed at the picture and then towards a camp. The Feldwebel took the picture from him and had another look. He hoped it wasn't *this* woman – if the photo was anything to go by she must be over eighty by now.

The Italian, sensing interest, sketched the shape of the woman with his hands, pointed at the German and said 'jigga-jig'. He stepped back out of the plane and beckoned to him. The German was intrigued; at least it was a change from the dull routine of his flight. Looking round he ascertained that he could safely leave the unloading to the Italians and jumped down to follow the pimp.

When they reached a hut the Italian knocked lightly on the door and cooed softly, 'Here is Fritz.' Then, pushing the door open, he stood aside to let the German enter. Immediately the door slammed shut, Fritz whirled round to hear a heavy key turning in the lock. Wildly he looked round him but there were no windows at all, no furniture either. He wasn't very bright but he had sense enough not to hammer on the door with his fists. Shrugging his shoulders he sat on the floor and waited for developments.

The German navigator was as easy as his comrade. Going through the hotel he went to the washrooms at the back and stripped off for his customary shower before the return trip. Refreshed and cleansed, he donned his uniform, but when he tried the door handle he found he was locked in. Puzzled and angered, he hammered on the door. Somebody was going to suffer for this! It never occurred to him that it might be himself.

The pilot was a different matter altogether. Sometimes he would go into the hotel for a shower but this could not be guaranteed. More often than not he stayed with the plane until it was time to take off. This was one of those occasions. He was sitting in his seat making routine checks and as he bent over his instruments he felt the cold muzzle of a revolver against his neck. Two Italians sprang forward, pinning his arms while they tied his wrists behind his back. It was all done so expertly and so quickly he hadn't even time to say "Gott in Himmel". The pressure of the revolver eased and Miller said, 'That didn't hurt, did it?'

The pilot was bewildered. He couldn't understand English, far less the situation he was in. He only knew that something was definitely wrong. He was escorted to the rear of the plane and forced to sit on the floor. Miller strode over and crouched before him. He was about to speak, but instead he rose and staggered back a pace, holding a handkerchief to his face. 'Bloody hell,' he muttered, 'he's crapped himself.' At least this one wasn't going to be a problem. '*Sprecken sie* English?' he said.

'*Ja*,' squeaked the man, frightened now.

'Good,' said Miller. 'Well, just sit quietly while I collect the rest of your mates . . . *comprendez*?'

The young pilot nodded quickly and Miller signalled to a couple of the Italians to keep their eye on him. He backed away and jumped down from the plane where the air was fresher.

At the same time in the VIP suite at the hotel, der Oberst der Luftwaffe was a happy man. It was his first visit and tales of this fabulous oasis had not been exaggerated. This suite would not have disgraced the Adler Hotel in the Wilhelmstrasse.

Clouds of steam emanated from the bathroom as the General, wrapping a towel round his waist, walked into the bedroom and felt the softness of the bed, marvelling at the clean white sheets and the soft eiderdown. It was tempting but there would be plenty of time for a good night's sleep when he had eaten. And again, tales of the fabulous chef were already making his mouth water.

He frowned as his eye fell upon his discarded uniform on the floor. It was where he had left it on the understanding that, by the time he had bathed, it would be pressed and ironed for the banquet. Anger began to replace his euphoria. He snatched up the soiled garments, then whirled as a voice from the doorway said quietly, 'Get dressed.' Der Oberst der Luftwaffe was at first startled, then bewildered. Surely his eyes were playing him tricks. It was a British Sergeant pointing a Luger pistol at him.

Sparks strode forward, snatched the uniform from the General and flung it back at him. 'Put it on!' snapped Sparks, cocking the pistol.

And Phase I of the plan was complete.

Outside the plane the Italian prisoners waited nervously for their orders to board. It had all seemed rosy during the planning stages of the day but now when all was inevitable the future didn't look too bright. The German flight crew were already sitting dejectedly at the back end of the plane while Miller, standing at the door screwing up his eyes, peered hard into the blackness, wondering what had happened to Sparks and der Oberst der Luftwaffe and his part in the exercise. Impatiently he was about to jump down and investigate when out of the gloom stepped his last passenger, followed by Sparks.

'Where the hell have you been?' snapped Miller. 'It'll soon be daylight.' And he wasn't far wrong, it was now nearly 3 a.m.

Sparks didn't reply but ushered der Oberst der Luftwaffe to sit on the floor with his colleagues. They all sat at attention looking straight ahead in deference to the high rank of their senior officer. And then Sparks noticed the fat Feldwebel who sat glowering, his eyes a purplish black and closed, and there was an ugly bruise on his cheek. Sparks looked at him, then turned to Miller. 'Walk into the propeller did he?'

Miller replied, 'Nah, he was going to board the plane and on the top step he suddenly turns and shouts "*Heil* Hitler".'

Sparks smiled.

Miller went on. 'Well, I was on the bottom step and the only place I could reach was his bollocks so I gave him an uppercut and as he doubled forward his face caught my knee. He's a lucky man. If I hadn't been there, he would have had a very nasty fall.'

The Feldwebel lowered his head and stared at the floor, watching the droplets of bright-red blood that leaked from his nose. He wasn't happy. He'd only shouted '*Heil* Hitler' to impress his senior officer. Well bugger him, bugger all officers and bugger the German military, and as this was only a thought he added, and bugger Hitler too.

As soon as the Italians were settled comfortably the door was closed and Rudy started the engines – only he wasn't Rudy the German pilot. He now wore Gratwick's identity discs round his neck and in his battledress pocket he had Gratwick's paybook. The uniform was almost tight enough to be ludicrous but then not many of these uniforms were made to fit.

'Where the hell is that woman?' shouted Sparks leaning out the door. 'Yasmin,' he yelled at the top of his voice.

But she couldn't hear him. She was in the hotel seeking Carlo. Her eyes quickly scanned the room, and she found him sitting at a corner table hunched over a glass of red wine. Quickly she hurried over and sat down opposite. He lifted his bleary eyes, then sat bolt upright in alarm.

'Is something wrong?' he asked.

'No, no, Carlo. It's just something I'd like to know.' She looked round quickly to make sure there was no one to overhear. 'Tell me, Carlo,' she said, 'when you originally moved in here, did you have girls?'

'Girls?' he said, not understanding.

'Yes, girls. This was meant to be a place for senior Italian officers to relax, yes?'

He nodded, then the lira dropped. 'Ah, girls. What a difference they would have made.' He smiled dreamily. 'Oh yes, they were promised – beautiful girls of all nations. They were promised but they never came. Every day I say "Where are the girls?". "They are coming," I'm told. But, no, and the war goes badly for us.' He shrugged expressively. 'So we never got the girls.'

'Thanks, Carlo,' she said, and patting his hand she hurried out, leaving Carlo with a dreamy smile on his face, remembering what might have been.

Suddenly he stiffened and slapped his forehead. '*Mama mia*,' he ejaculated. 'I did not wish them good luck.' And his chair toppled backward in his haste to get out.

Yasmin settled into the seat next to Rudy, who buckled her into the straps. Behind them Sparks and Miller sat on the floor behind each seat. There was an air of apprehension as Rudy revved up the engines. As they reached maximum revs, he released the brakes and the plane rolled forward, bumping at first, then picking up speed, and as he eased back on the stick the motion became smooth and they were airborne. The Italians broke into spontaneous applause.

As the plane disappeared into the blackness, Carlo arrived breathless to meet Gratwick at the end of the runway, a heavy blanket round his thin shoulders, and they waved until the sound of the engines died away. Together they made their way to the hotel. Perhaps a bottle of brandy would ease the pain.

Squatting on the floor of the vibrating aircraft, Sergeant Sparks blew into his cold hands. Why the bloody hell did he let Miller talk him into these messes? He stuffed his hands under his armpits for warmth and tried to sleep. It was a black night and a new moon was obscured from time to time by clouds casting a veil over the stars.

But there was a good pyrotechnical display several miles off the port side, and to the north flashes lit the horizon. After the first half-hour the happy murmurs of the Italians interspersed with snatches of arias gradually died away and the only sound was the monotonous drone of the three engines.

It's bloody freezing, thought Miller. If I'd known it was going to be this cold I'd have walked. If things didn't warm up soon, they'd have to be lifted out of the plane like carcasses at Smithfield.

Yasmin drowsed in the navigator's seat and suddenly was aware that something was different. The plane was banking gently towards the rising sun. She put her hand up to shield her eyes from the glare and when she felt a tap on her arm she turned to Rudy, who handed her a pair of earphones. She clamped them over her head and Rudy spoke into his mouthpiece.

'We should be there in an hour or so.'

Yasmin looked at her watch incredulously.

'Surely we're not that far from Alexandria?' she asked. But he had to reach out and flick her speak button. She repeated her question.

'No,' he replied, 'we're not going to Alexandria. It's too dangerous. We've got away with it so far but now it is light . . . I don't fancy my chances with the English fighters.' She stared at him blankly. He shrugged. 'It was Sergeant Miller's suggestion and I'm inclined to agree with him.'

Yasmin groaned inwardly. Did not the poor fool realise the only reason they'd had a peaceful passage was that they were expected? Outwardly calm, she asked, 'If we're not going to Alexandria, what is our new destination?'

'It is a little place about sixty miles away called Alam Farâfa, and I know a little airstrip there. It is not a very large . . .' But the rest of his words were drowned by a loud roar and a plane flashed over the perspex of the cockpit and dwindled into the distance ahead.

Sparks and Miller clawed themselves to their feet.

'What the bloody 'ell was that?' shouted Miller over the pilot's shoulder but Rudy was struggling with the controls as the Junkers wallowed in the backwash.

Rudy leant his head back. 'A Spitfire,' he yelled.

'Oh, no,' groaned Miller. 'I knew it wouldn't last.' He ducked instinctively as they were buzzed again by another Spitfire. Rudy tried to keep the plane straight and level. There was no evasive action he could take short of diving into the ground.

In the back of the plane the prisoners were on the verge of panic and the smell of fear was almost tangible – or it might have been something more basic.

Miller grabbed Sparks's arm. 'Why don't they get it over with?' he yelled, and without waiting for a reply he shook Rudy's shoulder. But Rudy waved him away. He was busy twiddling a knob on his radio, listening intently.

A voice came through his headphones. 'This is Red Leader to Bandit. Are you receiving me now? Over.'

Rudy's adjustment to a new frequency was spot-on. 'Loud and clear. Over,' he replied.

'Red Leader to Bandit. You are veering off course. Reset your heading to one six eight. We will escort you on to the airfield. Out.'

Rudy eased off his headphones. 'They're not hostile,' he said. 'We have an escort into Alex.' And with that he banked the plane gently round on to its original setting.

Yasmin breathed a sigh of relief. At least the wireless message had got through.

Thirty minutes later as they approached the airstrip the Spitfires peeled away with a final 'Good Luck' and, as Rudy lowered the flaps, he couldn't help feeling they were going to need all the good fortune they could handle, and more.

Miller's nose was crushed against the perspex of the side window as he gazed down on the welcoming committee. The whole place was seething with Military Police. Redcaps were everywhere. It was like landing in a poppy field. Miller's stomach churned. But what had he been expecting – a band playing 'Rule Britannia'?

Rudy was about to put the plane down gently, like a butterfly with burnt feet, when he suddenly remembered just in time that he wasn't der Fliegerhauptmann von Bosch: he was Driver Gratwick, a rusty prewar pilot taking holidaymakers on trips round the Island of Jersey. He slammed the plane down on to the runway and bounced several times before it came to rest skewwhiff at the end of the runway. It must have been a bad landing, even had Albie been a pilot and not just a cover story . . .

As the Junkers came to a halt Miller opened the door and pushed out the steps, but before he could alight a Squadron Leader shoved him back, pulled up the steps and slammed the door.

'Squadron Leader Dankworth,' he said by way of introduction. Then he leant over Rudy, giving him instructions to follow the truck that had pulled in front of them. Rudy released the brakes and they were guided to a remote part of the airfield into a heavily guarded hanger. From there the Italians and the German aircrew disembarked and were helped into three-ton Bedfords and taken away with an escort of Military Police motorcycles.

Der Oberst der Luftwaffe, being of importance, was ushered into a staff car with cool formality and whisked off to a safe house for interrogation. Sparks and Miller and the ersatz Gratwick were kept under close guard aboard the aircraft. They watched curiously as Yasmin was allowed to leave the plane in order to speak quietly to Squadron Leader Dankworth, who saluted and escorted her out into the bright sunlight.

Miller looked at Sparks. 'What did she say to him?'

Sparks shrugged. 'How the hell should I know?' he snarled, angry at his weakness in the feeling of jealousy that swept through him.

Miller turned away dejected. This was hardly the conquering heroes' welcome he'd envisaged – cheering crowds, a military band, flashbulbs, a short speech, tea with the Air Marshal's wife, a ride round the city in an open car and dinner at Government House. 'Bugger this for a game of skittles,' he said out loud and ducked through the doorway. But immediately he was facing a large Military Police Captain.

'I'm sorry, Sergeant,' he said officially. 'No one else is to leave the plane.' Then with a surreptitious glance over his shoulder he took his pay book from his tunic pocket and unclipped a pen. Thrusting these towards Miller he whispered, 'Could you sign this "To Len. With Best Wishes"?'

Colonel Brunswick sat at his desk wondering what fairy story they'd concocted this time. Sergeants Sparks and Miller were under heavy guard at the airfield and would stay there until he sent for them, and this might not be until the war was over. If General Montgomery insisted on meeting them during the next six months he'd know exactly where to find them. They'd be in that hanger at the end of the airfield. He pulled himself together; there were more important things to see to. He took a batch of intelligence reports from a drawer and began to peruse them.

There was a discreet knock on the door and his Adjutant entered.

'Not now, Jimmy,' he growled. 'I'm busy.'

'There's an Estelle Chambertin to see you, sir.'

Colonel Brunswick stared at him. 'A woman?' he asked stupidly.

The Adjutant was unmoved. 'Yes, sir.'

Brunswick exploded. 'What's the matter with you, Captain?' he yelled. 'Here I am, saddled with probably the greatest crisis of my military career and you come in here, trying to organise my sex life.'

'No, sir,' replied the Adjutant. 'Her code name is Yasmin.'

'Yasmin!' breathed the Colonel. Then he rose, all businesslike. He donned his tunic and smoothed his hair back. 'Send her in immediately, Jimmy. If anybody can pick the bones out of all this, she can.'

A few minutes later the girl was ushered in. She was still clad in the black chador of the desert.

'Yasmin, I presume,' said the Colonel with outstretched hand.

She ignored it. When she bared her head and face he was staggered by her beauty.

'I understood you were dead,' he spluttered, off his guard.

'Then you have been misinformed,' she replied, and looked over pointedly at the Adjutant.

'Ah yes,' said Colonel Brunswick. 'This is my Adjutant, Captain Shelley.'

There was an awkward pause, then, after a moment, the Colonel got the message. He coughed. 'Perhaps, Jimmy, it would be better if you left us alone for a while.

Without a word the Adjutant left quietly.

When he'd gone Colonel Brunswick said, 'Will you have a seat?' And when they were settled he became businesslike again. 'And to what do we owe the pleasure of this visit?'

Yasmin didn't waste any time. Quickly she explained the history and present activities of the Italian camp at the El Waddim Oasis; the twice-weekly visits of the German supply plane and the lack of morale leading up to the flight of the Junkers. It was precise and detailed as one would expect from a highly trained operative.

Brunswick nodded. He had the picture and was wondering what was coming next.

'As we are both aware,' she went on, 'the Germans are not a benevolent society. They do not send a supply plane in twice a week out of the goodness of their hearts just to feed their Italian allies.'

Colonel Brunswick stared at her fixedly, still waiting for the punchline. This wasn't the big picture – it was only the trailer. 'Please go on, mam'selle,' he said.

She leant forward. 'I think the supplies the Germans fly in is merely a smokescreen. It is what they take back with them that's important.'

After a moment Colonel Brunswick asked, 'And what would that be?'

She shrugged. 'What indeed? It is my intention to find out but I know in my bones that with the tight secrecy that surrounds it, it could be something extremely important.'

The Colonel swivelled his chair and looked out of the window. He wished to God he hadn't dismissed his Adjutant. His usual 'What do you think, Jimmy?' had seen him out of many tight corners in the past. After a time he swung round to face her.

'If this information is as important as you say, how do we acquire it?'

She seemed puzzled by the question. 'By returning to El Waddim Oasis, of course.'

'And how do you propose to return?'

'By the Junkers, naturally.'

Brunswick pondered her answer. This was not as simple as it sounded. He could authorise many things but to send her back in the Junkers was beyond even his capacity. He would have to go through all the official rigmarole again with the Air Force for fighter protection and with the Artillery to alert their batteries along the route.

'And Sergeants Sparks and Miller?' he asked, more for something to say than anything else.

Yasmin raised her eyebrows. 'Well naturally they will return with me. Everything must appear to be normal. If we did not return the Italians would be suspicious and the whole operation would be a nonstarter.'

Colonel Brunswick sighed and began to write hurriedly on his pad. And when he had jabbed the paper with a full stop he threw down his pencil. 'You realise, of course, that what you are proposing is beyond my authority and I will have to get clearance from higher up.'

She nodded quickly. 'I understand,' she said, 'but it is imperative that we return tonight.'

Colonel Brunswick sat bolt upright. 'Tonight?' he spluttered . . . he iffed and butted and supposed and finally snatched up the telephone. 'I want you in here, Jimmy, a.s.a.p.' He slammed the phone down.

All the intricate planning and arrangements would have to be done in any case by his Adjutant. It didn't appear to be too difficult and, with this highly trained intelligence agent, the pickings might be enormous.

'Come in,' he said in response to the familiar knock. And when the Adjutant was seated, pencil and pad in hand, Brunswick explained briefly what had to be done.

It didn't take long, and when the Adjutant rose to set the wheels in motion, Yasmin said, 'There is something more I would ask.'

The Colonel and his Adjutant froze, and she went on.

'I have explained to you, Colonel Brunswick, the purpose of the El Waddim Oasis and the original intention as to the activities that would be carried out there.'

The Colonel nodded. 'Yes, I understand it was to be a holiday camp for top-ranking Italian officers – in other words a high-class brothel.'

She nodded. 'And if it was restored it would attract many high-ranking officers, only this time they would be German.'

The Adjutant caught on at once. 'It's an idea, sir,' he said.

But it was well beyond Brunswick's comprehension. 'Are you suggesting,' he said, outraged, 'that we set up a brothel for German officers?'

Yasmin was unabashed. 'That is exactly what I am suggesting, Colonel. The oasis could be one of the most important centres of intelligence gathering in the Middle East. Take it from me, Colonel, when I was working on the German transmitter case at Abdul's, his girls were my best sources of information. Be assured, Colonel, brains are useless when the cock does the thinking.'

Brunswick harrumphed at this crudity, but he let it pass.

'Are there girls there already?' asked the Adjutant.

'No,' replied Yasmin coolly. 'But since you closed Abdul's place I know where to recruit some. I know where they live and three of them speak German fluently. And believe me, Colonel, they could use the work.'

Colonel Brunswick was almost at panic stations. He was out of his depth – more than that, he was in mid-Atlantic with a hole in his waterwings. He could imagine the faces of the men in Whitehall when he put forward the proposal to airlift eight girls to a remote part of the desert to set up a brothel. He would certainly be sent for a medical and, even if the transportation of the girls was successful, the Germans would certainly be extremely suspicious of eight beauties suddenly appearing from nowhere. On the plus side, if they did take the bait, he recognised the importance of the intelligence that could be passed on.

He looked hopefully at his Adjutant, who turned away and looked out of the window. There was no help from that quarter.

As if reading his mind, Yasmin went on. 'I fully understand your worries regarding the eight girls but I have considered this very carefully and with a proper cover story it should not be too difficult.'

They listened intently while she outlined her plan and when she'd finished it not only seemed logical, but, better than that, it looked like a brilliant idea. Even Colonel Brunswick was impressed, so much so that he couldn't wait to expound the theory to his superiors as his own idea.

Yasmin rose and said, 'If that is all, Colonel, I'll get back to the airfield to await your decision.'

And before Colonel Brunswick could say 'Well goodbye, then', she was gone.

'Well, Jimmy,' said the Colonel briskly, 'you know what the situation is.'

'Yes, sir, we haven't much time.' And he hurried down the corridor to his own office in order to set the wheels in motion for an emergency high-level meeting. It was urgent, top-priority, most immediate, and within half an hour dispatch riders roared madly from one office block to another, telephone operators had no time for tea breaks, and the teleprinter machines clacked frantically and incessantly between Whitehall and Alexandria. There was no time for long discussion – it was either yes or no and it was the reputation of Sergeants Sparks and Miller that won the day.

Even as the Junkers rose into the dark African night on its way back to El Waddim Oasis, there were still final arrangements to be made and okayed.

The Germans, alerted by all this increased activity, dispatched half a dozen more agents into Alexandria to find out what was going on – they didn't have long to wait.

The following day all the British newspapers flooded the streets with glaring headlines such as

EIGHT DANCING GIRLS LOST IN DESERT
ENSA ANGRY AT DANCING TROOP
THEY WENT WITHOUT PERMISSION,
SAYS UNION OFFICIAL
WHERE ARE THEY?

The stories were similar: 'The girls, called "The Tip Top Eight", had gone into the desert to entertain the troops, the last reported sightings being twelve miles out from Alexandria.' To all intents and purposes they'd disappeared into the blue, but the German Intelligence were not impressed. The story of the eight girls was obviously a fabrication to divert the minds of the British people from the ultimate loss of Africa. The Tip Top Eight were a fantasy dreamt up by the Propaganda Ministry. They didn't even exist. Even so, along with British patrols, the Germans had also sent out search parties for the missing girls.

On 19 August the nonexistent girls were enjoying a hearty breakfast at the El Waddim Oasis. On the plane over they had been in trepidation and even scared of what they'd let themselves in for. By the airstrip about sixty Italians had cheered as the plane had come in to land and when it finally came to a stop they all surged forward. But when the cabin door opened the Italians were cut off in mid-cheer and stared in astonishment as a beautiful girl appeared. Then after a moment's stunned silence pandemonium broke out, wolf whistles, whoops and applause. Then, incredibly, another girl appeared, followed by another.

Eyes on stalks the Italians tried to take it all in. Perhaps there would be one for each of them. But when Miller was next to show his face, they realised the parade was over. The girls felt like film stars; they'd never had so much attention in the whole of their lives and all their past fears on the journey were a distant memory.

Miller, still framed in the doorway, watched happily. He'd already picked his girl. Then Sparks nudged him in the back with a suitcase and he became all business again.

'Oi,' he shouted after the Italians, 'what about giving us a hand with this luggage?'

There was still much to do – the plane had to be towed off the runway to a spot some distance into the desert, then blanketed with several tons of sand until it became just another dune. The wheel tracks had to be obliterated and Junkers 498 cease to exist until the next trip.

Carlo was overjoyed when the girls trooped in. He couldn't believe it. With tears streaming down his face, he embraced them all in turn and afterwards looked round for Yasmin. This time it was an embrace and a kiss on both cheeks. 'You are my Mother Christmas,' he said embracing her again.

And while her cheek was next to his she spoke into his ear, 'Carlo, we have to talk.'

'Later,' he said happily. 'Now we drink champagne.'

'We have to talk now, Carlo. It's important.'

Carlo looked at her and his face went serious. 'Come with me,' he said and led her into a side room.

Yasmin quickly filled him in with the girls' cover story. It didn't take long and Carlo got it in one.

'I understand,' he said quietly.

'This cover story must be drilled into every member of your staff. There must be no slip-ups when the German investigation team arrive.'

Carlo's eyes panicked for a second.

'Oh yes, they'll come,' insisted Yasmin. 'They're not going to let a plane disappear without a thorough investigation.'

'Yes, I was forgetting them.' His face fell. 'The Germans are not fools – I think the story of the lost dancing girls will not convince them.'

Yasmin smiled. 'It will, Carlo, it will; I can promise you that. By now it will be in all the English papers.'

A howl of laughter came through from the dining room and Carlo straightened his tunic. 'The sooner they all know of the situation the better.' He opened the door and strode into the happy crowd clapping his hands for attention. He stood on a chair and addressed the assembly. 'You must treat these girls with care and courtesy.' They cheered and whooped but he silenced them as he continued gravely. 'These poor girls, the Tip Top Eight, came into the desert to entertain the troops when, *zump*, the bus on which they travel breaks down and they are stranded.'

Murmurs of condolence went round the room.

'Three days,' went on Carlo, 'they wander through the vast unforgiving desert and with only a half-litre of water between them, they found this camp.'

He bowed as if he'd just recited 'To be or not to be', and dutifully they applauded. When the clapping had died down one of the Italians raised his hand and said, 'Capitano Abruzzi, this cannot be true. Did we not help them down from the plane ten minutes ago?'

There was a stunned silence and they looked towards Carlo to see how he would get out of this. They need not have worried, he was equal to the occasion.

'My friend,' he said laughing, 'you must remember in future to put your hat on when you go out into the sun. What plane did you help them down from? I have seen no plane.' He looked innocently round at all the faces. 'Did anyone here see a plane arrive ten minutes ago? And if a plane landed, where is it now?'

This was the trigger and someone started to laugh and say 'Yes, where is it now?'. Others joined in the laughter and Carlo went on. 'And when the Germans come to ask you about their missing supply plane, what do we say?' The reply came with a unanimous roar. '*What supply plane?*' they yelled and the moment was saved.

Carlo gazed down. His wireless operator was tugging at his trouser leg and holding out a sheet of paper. He took the message and read it carefully. The happy sound of laughter and ribaldry tailed off as they watched their *Commandante* anxiously. He cleared his throat.

'My friends,' he said, 'I have just received a wireless message.' He paused to let this sink in and then went on. 'Tomorrow night a German plane will arrive carrying members of the Military Police, and a man from the Gestapo. They are here from die Luftwaffepolizei to investigate the loss of Junkers 498.'

That killed the celebrations like a bucket of cold spaghetti. The Germans weren't wasting much time.

The investigating officers from die Luftwaffepolizei arrived by plane the following night and Carlo was there to greet them as they disembarked. He led them towards the hotel with a torch, talking ten to the dozen – commiserations for the missing flight crew, assuring them over and over that no one was more surprised when it didn't arrive. And just before they entered the hotel he halted and turned towards them.

'And, gentlemen,' he said in a conspiratorial voice, 'I have a very pleasant surprise for you. Eight little angels who dropped in out of heaven a few days ago! You like surprises, yes?' he asked.

The man in civilian clothes growled, 'Anything is better than standing out here in the freezing cold.'

'*Si, si,*' said Carlo, and ushered them into the light and warmth of the hotel.

As they stepped inside they screwed up their eyes to adjust to the bright lights. All sound died away leaving only the click-click of the gramophone as the record reached its end. With a sudden screech someone lifted the needle.

At a bar in the corner eight girls and their attendants stared at the newcomers. Carlo wished desperately they hadn't removed the fountain – the trickle of water might have soothed the moment. Suddenly the stalemate was broken when one of the Germans yelped excitedly and pointed to the girls.

'Tip Top Eight!' He whirled to his comrades. 'Haven't you heard? These are the eight dancing girls that were missing in the desert.'

The girls had been well briefed. They looked at one another. They were good actresses. Being on the game, they had to be. One of them slid from her stool and took a pace towards the men.

'Yes,' she said in a small voice, 'we are the Tip Top Girls.'

There was a moment's silence. Then the German who had spoken said, 'I knew it.' He laughed. 'Everyone in North Africa is searching for you, even from our base. Planes have been sent out to reconnoitre.' He laughed again. 'And here you are.'

The girls still pretended to look frightened and it did not take much effort.

The man chuckled. 'As we have found you, do not we deserve a prize?' He shrugged out of his greatcoat and rubbing his hands walked confidently to the bar. 'At least we can have a drink together.' His comrade, now following his example, joined him.

Carlo was in his element – he clapped his hands. 'What will you have to drink, gentlemen? My men will serve you whatever you like.'

The girls began to smile tentatively. 'Come now, girls,' said Carlo heartily. 'They will not bite you – make them welcome.'

And the ice was broken – almost.

Carlo noticed that the man in a leather top coat, the standard Gestapo uniform, had taken a bottle and a glass to a side table; he was sitting there alone. Capitano Abruzzi, once more the head waiter, wandered over genially.

'Why not join the party?' He gestured towards the bar.

The man stared up at him coldly and in a quiet voice replied, 'They look in remarkably good condition.'

Carlo's smile froze but he recovered quickly and laughed, 'Ah yes, they look very well, but,' he said, leaning forward confidentially, 'when they arrived four days ago, oh what a mess.' He shrugged. 'But they are young and what different girls they are now after sleep, good food, wine.' He laughed again.

'They didn't walk from Alexandria,' said the man.

Carlo feigned surprise but had his answer ready. Yasmin had rehearsed him. 'No, no, no, it is impossible – they came in a bus.' And remembered in time, 'A yellow one.'

The man poured himself another glass and drank. Carlo watched him uneasily; he knew what the next question would be.

'And where is the yellow bus now?'

As per script, thought Carlo smugly, and replied, face darkening, 'The girls leave it just over the hill.' He pointed. 'Not two hundred metres from here and – *ecco*! – in the morning it is gone, disappeared. I know where it will be.' He pointed in another direction. 'Down there in that stinking Arab village are thieves, villains, criminals.' He leant over the table. 'While you are here, I implore you and your comrades to search that encampment and should you come across eight Dovunque 35 trucks they are mine. But you must take care when entering: they will have your boots while you're walking.' He laughed at his little joke and was about to return to the bar when the man spoke again.

'And what happened to the driver?'

'The driver?' asked Carlo, his composure gone. Yasmin hadn't mentioned a driver at the briefing. Then inspiration hit him. 'Ah, the driver,' he repeated, 'he was an Arab.' And in order to hammer this one down tight he nodded. 'That place down there –' he pointed in the direction of the Arab camp '– is very likely his village. They're all related – husbands, brothers, wives. Even camels.'

'Do you have schnapps?' interrupted the man.

Carlo bowed with a sigh of relief. The act was over and he was secretly pleased with his performance. He hadn't had a standing ovation but on the other hand no one had asked for his money back.

When he returned from the bar with the schnapps he was also escorting a buxom blonde. 'Sir,' said Carlo, 'a little surprise.'

He ushered the girl forward. 'This is Inga.'

The German did not rise. He looked up at the girl. 'You are German?' he asked.

'*Ja*,' she said with a quick curtsey. 'I am from Flensburg.'

'Won't you sit down?'

'Thank you,' she said demurely, and with a shy smile took the seat opposite him.

Carlo bowed to both of them and moved away. She wouldn't be a problem. She had been well rehearsed with her cover story. He heard her begin the tale of her life but winced when he heard her say they'd emigrated to England in 1938 when she was just fifteen. Silly cow. She was thirty-five if she was a day.

Looking back at the Gestapo man over his shoulder, Carlo relaxed. The Gestapo man wasn't listening too hard. He was gazing at the two large breasts resting docilely on the table. It was going to be a long night.

Carlo joined the group at the bar, smiling happily. The party was already up and running. One of die Luftwaffepolizei with head tilted back was balancing a glass of beer on his forehead.

The investigators stayed for three days but there was very little investigation. In fact, they didn't really question the Italians at all. The Germans believed that the supply plane had crashed or been shot down somewhere on the way. After all, if it had landed yesterday the girls would have noticed. Little did the Germans realise that in giving the Italians a clean bill of health, they had saved their own lives. Had their suspicions been aroused they would never have survived the flight back. Carlo had one or two men on his staff who knew how to tinker with aero engines.

Two hours after the German plane had taken off, the first intelligence report from El Waddim Oasis was on Colonel Brunswick's desk – alongside a memo from his nephew requesting immediate dispatch of three dozen pairs of Indian clubs.

Captain Jampton looked forward to his PT sessions. Although he directed them wearing singlet and shorts, he never joined in – he wouldn't have lasted a day.

'Hup two three! Down two three! Hup two three!'

The lads were doing press-ups but in that heat it would have been frowned upon in the toughest glasshouse.

'Hup two three! Hup two three and stop!' As a body they collapsed on the sand but on a sharp, peremptory blast of the whistle they sprang to their feet, or to be more exact they got up; some of them couldn't and just lay there, gathering their strength. Jampton blew his whistle again and clapped his hands as well.

Sergeant Major Puller winced as the men struggled upright. One man, however, remained flat on his face. Sergeant Major Puller's fists clenched. He recognised Jim Butterworth, who was nearly fifty, for God's sake, and he wasn't even military. Settling in Tobruk after World War One, he was the owner of the antique shop. But he wasn't there when one of the first bombs from the Stukas had flattened it. Unfortunately his wife and two children were still in bed when it happened. This was how he'd come to join Sergeant Major Puller's convoy into the blue.

'That man there,' squeaked Jampton, 'on your feet!'

The man lay prone, gasping for breath. He got slowly on to his hands and knees.

The Sergeant Major tensed. As the man was still in a kneeling position, his hand closed over a large stone. He rose slowly and took a step towards the CO.

'Butterworth!'

Puller's voice could be heard half a mile away. Butterworth stopped but his eyes never left Jampton.

'Drop it, lad,' said the Sergeant Major quietly.

Butterworth didn't move, then with a quick motion he flung down the stone and staggered off the parade ground.

Jampton was paralysed but quickly recovered himself enough to shout, 'Sergeant Major! Take that man's name!'

Puller stared back at him, white-faced with anger. You could have cut the tension with a butter knife. The whole scene was a still photograph – everyone frozen in a grand tableau. Even Prince, the flea-bitten mongrel, stood motionless by the side of the Sergeant Major with the hairs on his back stiffly upright. God knows what might have happened next.

But suddenly the spell was broken. Approaching the camp in a large cloud of dust were two heavily armed 30-cwt Chevrolet trucks. Sergeant Major Puller recognised them as a long-range desert group patrol.

Jampton hadn't a clue who they were. They could have been collecting the dustbins for all he knew. However, he swelled with pride as the guard in tin helmet and heavily blancoed webbing ran out of the guard tent. From the distance his tinny voice rang out, 'Halt, who goes there?'

Jampton swelled with outrage as the two vehicles ignored the challenge, swept slowly past the guard and ground to a halt by the mess tent. Jampton clucked his tongue in annoyance. This wouldn't have happened had the red-striped pole been in place.

Sergeant Major Puller, all his black thoughts of the past few moments gone, chuckled softly. He, too, was thinking of the large red-and-white guard pole which had mysteriously disappeared one night. There had been one helluva flap over that, and Jampton had been beside himself with rage. In truth it was too juvenile to describe his behaviour as angry. It was more of a childish tantrum, akin to refusing to eat his prunes at teatime.

The whole of the Special Ordnance Group had been paraded

while he began a tent search, although how in God's name anyone could hide a fifteen-foot pole in a two-man tent was beyond comprehension. The Sergeant Major smiled at the recollection as he made his way over to meet the visitors.

They were bone weary, alighting from their battle wagons like old men. He was only twenty yards away when the guard rushed past him breathing hard. He levelled his rifle. 'Halt! Who goes there?' he croaked.

Again he was ignored. The Sergeant Major patted him on the shoulder and said soothingly, 'You did your best, lad.' Mollified, the guard returned to his post.

The SM followed the visitors into the mess tent but Captain Jampton was there before him. He wasn't an impressive sight: his shorts and singlet had been a goodbye present from the last batch of deserters. The man had been taller and three stone heavier than Jampton, which didn't make for a perfect fit, and for the first time Sergeant Major Puller felt embarrassed in the company of these hard-fighting men.

'Who's in charge here?' piped up Jampton.

One of them stepped forward, still sipping a mug of hot sweet tea.

'What's the problem, mate?' he said in a nasal Australian accent.

Jampton squared his shoulders. 'I am Captain Jampton, Commanding Officer.'

The man blowing on his steaming brew eyed him over the rim of his mug, then his face broke into a tired smile. 'Where the hell did you get those rompers from?' he said.

The others now turned to join the fun. Jampton drew himself up to his full five foot eight inches and eyed the man coldly. 'If it's not too much trouble,' he asked sarcastically, 'would you mind telling me who you are?'

The man didn't hesitate. 'Captain White, Long Range Desert Group.'

Immediately Jampton's manner changed. He knew of the LRDG. Stories of them and their exploits were a big part of his boyhood dreams. He put out his hand. 'Make yourself at home,' he said and shouted across to the sweating cook, 'Look after them.' Whirling round so quickly that his baggy shorts had difficulty keeping up and facing the Sergeant Major, he snapped, 'See to it.' After which he completed a full circle to face the

Australian again. 'Come over to my tent when you're rested.' And he added manfully, 'We can have a tot and a yarn.' With that he marched out of the tent, back straight, a military man to his fingertips, he thought, although his large flapping shorts rather let him down.

Some hours later Captain Jampton sat at the table in his tent. He was looking forward to meeting Captain White. Before him was spread out the inevitable map. It was his way of appearing to be busy. When his guest arrived he'd fling down his dividers and mutter something like 'What a stinking mess', or, better still, 'Roll on peace'.

There was a knock on the tent pole. 'Come in,' he said and without looking up muttered, 'I'll take a patrol out tonight,' and flung his pencil down. As he looked up he frowned. It wasn't the Australian Captain: it was Jackson, his batman.

'Yes, what is it?' snapped Jampton, wishing he hadn't muttered that bit about the patrol. It would be all over the camp in less than five minutes and the MOs tent would be heaving with mystery ailments.

'Captain White's compliments, sir, and he'll be right over.'

Jampton perked up. 'Thank you, Jackson,' he said. 'Lay out a bottle of whisky and two glasses.'

Jackson stared at the little prat, dumbfounded. 'Sir?' he croaked.

'You heard me, Jackson. Surely you know what whisky is.'

'Yes, sir,' and he hurried from the tent to spread the tale of his CO's conversion to the hard stuff. He was back in five minutes with a bottle and two glasses. 'Got the whisky from the MO, sir. Said he might join you later – and he'll bring his own glass.'

Jampton shuddered. The last thing he wanted was the company of Captain Witherspoon. When Jackson had gone he examined the bottle and, taking the cork out gingerly, he sniffed at its contents, staggering back as if somebody had hit him. It was awful! He pushed the cork back in and was wiping his eyes when, without ceremony, Captain White entered, looking rested and younger.

'This is mighty nice of you,' he said, 'but I can't stay long. We're off in half an hour.'

'Time for a quick one, then,' said Jampton manfully. He sloshed half a tumblerful and handed it over, then attended to his own, pouring barely enough to cover the bottom of the glass.

'This is better than Horlicks,' he said and put the glass to his lips although he didn't open his mouth. The Australian didn't seem to notice as he took a large gulp from his own.

'Jesus,' he breathed, 'a drop of good stuff you've got here, mate.' And he sat in the chair facing the table.

Jampton sat himself down opposite, eager to get this man talking. What a letter to Aunt Dorothy! He kicked off with: 'Was it rough last night?'

The Captain took another drink. 'Average,' he said laconically, then: 'You know, I have a confession to make.' He looked down at his glass. Jampton was all ears. 'We didn't drop in on you accidentally, like.' Jampton's eyebrows went up. 'We were on our way back to base and we made a detour of ten miles for this.'

Jampton was beside himself with pride and joy. He knocked back his teaspoon of whisky to hide his pleasure. And when he managed to control his coughing he noticed that his glass had been replenished. He waved a casual hand. 'Yes I suppose word gets around.' Then added modestly, 'Like you, we're just doing our job.'

The Captain eyed him curiously. 'This is the Special Ordnance Group, isn't it?'

Even that small sip of whisky was beginning to affect Jampton. 'Right on the button,' he said, laughing, and took a large drink. This seemed to go down much easier.

There was a long pause. The Captain was puzzled. From the stories he'd heard Captain Jampton was the guiding light behind the exploits of Sergeants Sparks and Miller. He didn't look like a hero, more like a trainee bus conductor. But then this could only be a façade, a front behind which lurked a brain cool, determined and razor sharp. He decided to give Jampton the benefit of the doubt. After all, Lawrence of Arabia was no great shakes in a civvy suit. And noticing his host's glass was empty he took the bottle and said, 'Let me top you up, sir.'

'Why not?' said Jampton grandly, contentment seeping through him. 'No need to call me "sir",' he said expansively. 'My name is Wilfred.'

Captain White raised his glass. 'Well thank you, Wilf,' he said.

Jampton winced. He wasn't all that drunk but recovering himself with gay abandon he gulped down a mouthful and almost fell over the back of his chair. This time it took him a little longer to recover but he was game. 'First today,' he gasped, smiling through his tears.

The Australian nodded sympathetically. It was obvious the lad wasn't used to it. This was probably the first ever. What must he have been through in his short military career? He coughed, embarrassed. 'Besides yourself, the two drongos the lads would really like to meet are your two Sergeants.'

Jampton eyed the two waving images in the chair opposite.

'You know, Sparks and Miller.' White's voice was getting quieter.

Jampton pulled himself together with a monumental effort. 'Ah,' he said, 'Sergeants Sparks and Miller.' He struggled to control his diction. 'I'm sorry to disappoint you, Captain,' he said slowly, 'but you can't. They've disappeared.' He waved his now empty glass into the air and crooned: 'Gone . . . over the hills and far away.' Then the glass fell from his hand and he slumped face down on to the map of Africa – Abyssinia to be exact.

Captain White rose and looked down at one of his heroes. 'Sod the bloody war. This poor bastard's coming apart at the seams.' And he dragged Jampton over to his bed and laid him out gently.'

As he ducked out of the tent he almost ran into Sergeant Major Puller. The man made a drinking gesture with his hand and shrugged. 'Poor sod.'

The Sergeant Major's eyebrows went up in amazement and, gazing towards the CO's tent, he whistled softly. The little man was human after all.

'Well,' he said, 'your lads are ready and waiting.'

'Thanks.' The Captain nodded. 'Oh, and by the way, I'm sorry to hear about Sergeants Sparks and Miller.'

'What?' said Puller.

'I gather they've bought it.'

Puller jerked his thumb over his shoulder. 'Is that what he's been telling you?'

The Captain replied, 'Well that's what I gathered from his conversation.'

'Take my word, sir, I'll bet my last pay parade they're living it up somewhere, maybe Alex for all I know.'

The Captain was intrigued as Puller filled him in briefly about the night of the great sandstorm, and when he had finished the Australian thought for a moment. Then: 'Southwest?' he said.

Puller nodded. And after a time the Captain rubbed his chin. 'There's nothing down there for most of three hundred kilometres – well there is. There's an oasis, about fifteen miles in that direction – El something or other . . . never been there meself. It's a little off the beaten track. Well,' he finished, 'we'll be off. Thank him for all his hospitality when he wakes up.' And with a flip of his hand he hurried over to his own mob.

Puller waved them off into the blue, then he gazed over to the southwest. It's worth a try, he mused. Yes, just the place that might appeal to those two bastards. And with mind made up he strode into the CO's tent.

But when he stuck his head through the flap he almost gagged. Not only had Jampton been sick all over himself, but also the bed and a large part of the floor as well. The Sergeant Major didn't envy Jackson having to clean this lot up. The uniform was only fit for burning, but that wasn't an option. It was all Jampton had to stand up in until his suitcase turned up. There'd be no chance of putting forward his idea today, probably not for three days at least.

He moved over to the table and lifted the bottle of whisky and shook his head. Then, taking the cork out, he helped himself to a fair swig. He belched pleasurably and put the bottle back on the table and left the tent.

The first intelligence report from the El Waddim Oasis was dynamite. Colonel Brunswick could hardly believe his luck when he read through it. It was brief and to the point as one would expect from a highly trained intelligence agent, albeit French. The girls had passed on pillow talk, everything they could remember, to Yasmin but the Colonel was spared banalities such as 'After the war I am going to marry you' and 'You are more beautiful than the moon over Wilhelmstrasse'.

Even so it was a long report, but after half an hour Brunswick felt he had struck the Mother Lode. 'I'll take you back to Alexandria.' 'When?' 'It won't be long – only a few more days.' And, more importantly, 'The Tommies will not be searching for you on Friday – they will have other things to worry about.'

From these and other drunken boasts, a pattern began to emerge – Rommel was up to something, something big in the next few days – and it could only be Alexandria. And in order to gain this objective the British defence line would have to be breached at Alam el Halfa Ridge.

Colonel Brunswick, eyes gleaming with excitement, reached for the telephone. It was the vital information that General Montgomery's headquarters had been waiting for and the action taken was immediate. The weak gaps in the defence line were strengthened by New Zealand and Indian divisions. Tanks moved into position, antitank guns were dug in and, most important of all, the minefields on the approach to Alam el Halfa were heavily reinforced. General Montgomery was facing the bowling and this was his first ball but now he knew which side of the wicket it would break.

On 31 August the Germans rolled into the attack but it was against an infinitely superior force to what their intelligence had led them to believe. From the beginning of the battle when their panzer tanks foundered in a bigger minefield than they had expected, holding up their advances, it was a series of disasters for the vaunted Afrika Korps. After five days Rommel, battered, bruised and bewildered, was forced to retreat. It was General Montgomery's first victory. It wasn't the match, but it was at least a boundary. Perhaps he was the right man even if he was a teetotaller, didn't smoke and wore two cap badges.

From this victory tiny seeds of optimism began to grow. Plans were now being discussed, not for the defence of Alexandria, but for an all-out offensive. To the troops of the Eighth Army, General Montgomery, or Monty as he was popularly known, was welcomed wherever he went. He was here, there and everywhere seemingly in several different locations at the same time. It was rumoured that the General had four lookalikes.

On the other hand, the newly promoted Field Marshal Rommel, frustrated and angry, could only wait, hamstrung by his lack of fuel. If supplies didn't get through the British sea blockade, his panzer tanks would have to go into battle pushed by the infantry.

Colonel Brunswick was revitalised and his meetings with General Montgomery became more frequent. It wasn't exactly 'Charles' and 'Monty' yet but they were shaking hands now. On their last meeting in Monty's caravan, much to his astonishment the General asked him if he would like a glass of whisky and Brunswick astonished himself even more by turning it down; they discussed further stratagems over two glasses of lemonade.

September stepped back in order to give October a chance. During the last few weeks there hadn't been much intelligence from El Waddim Oasis but what little snippets arrived at British Military Intelligence were encouraging.

The girls reported to Yasmin that their high-ranking German clients were becoming a bit heavy and not much fun. Their bombast and arrogance were now replaced by gloom and probably apprehension and their visits were less frequent. In fact, the cup presented to the girl pulling the highest-ranking officer had lost its flavour. All this information gathered together in a bundle was invaluable to the British, direct proof of the low morale pervading the enemy forces.

The Tip Top Eight, however, were glad to see the backs of the master race. What the hell – the Italians were better lovers anyway, and some of the girls quite enjoyed the change; not only that, it was a great improvement on Abdul's lousy setup. Here they were coining it and, more important, engaged in vital war work. They just lay back and thought of England, Germany, Poland and Lithuania, and the other three with no homeland thought of their old-age pension.

This turn of events didn't suit Miller at all. No one was volunteering for the next flight to Alexandria. They were having too much of a good time with the girls and you didn't get that in a prisoner-of-war camp. Miller fretted; if he didn't get back to Alexandria his biscuit tin full of valuables was useless.

Colonel Brunswick waited eagerly for Yasmin's report regarding the German supply plane. It could be of low priority, or it could be of vital importance. Whichever way the ball bounced, Charles Brunswick was a born-again Colonel in British Military Intelligence. Oh yes, there had been those foolish enough to snigger behind his back when he'd mooted his idea to plant eight girls in the oasis, but those unbelievers were now hailing it as a stroke of genius. He rang down to the canteen and asked for a cup of tea to be sent up. His sun was shining and there wasn't a cloud in the sky.

Little did he know that, somewhere out in the desert, the lid was off a tin of ointment and a small fly was already buzzing around.

Captain Jampton stumbled through the soft sand. The night was black and any sound was too far away to cause concern. It was Jampton's third night patrol, or Exercise Spiller 3, a clever composition of the names of his missing Sergeants with the number 3 denoting his number of previous missions. Sergeant Major Puller, next in line behind his Commanding Officer, eyed Jampton's crouching, weaving shape. He shook his head; the little pillock was also holding his pistol. He hoped to God it wasn't loaded.

Suddenly he froze and cocked his head to one side. It was the sound of an approaching aircraft and, from the uneven throb of its engines, it certainly wasn't British. The sound of the engines got louder as if it was above them. It was certainly close, and then to their right the sky was lit by a faint gleam of light. With a final crescendo the plane's engines cut abruptly, and the lights were extinguished, leaving the night blacker and more fearful.

Jampton's mouth was dry. 'Sar'nt Major,' he hissed.

But the Sergeant Major wasn't there. Louder this time he repeated it, then anxiety began to crawl up his legs. Where the dickens was the patrol? It was a simple explanation. When the column halted on hearing the plane, Jampton hadn't. He'd been wrapped in his own fantasy world and it had been the gleam of the flare path that had brought him back to earth. He was well ahead of the patrol, that was all. But then rationality had never been one of Jampton's strong points. He turned full circle in an attempt to pierce the night, and then something sprang into his mind, something he'd read in a book by Baden-Powell – 'When separated from your comrades on a dark night, drop instantly to a prone position. The sky with stars is lighter than the ground and against this backcloth silhouettes may be discerned.' Jampton got down on his belly and was searching fiercely in the darkness when somebody tripped over him.

'Ouch!' he yelped as the man stumbled.

'Bloody 'ell,' said Private Summerskill, 'who's that?'

'It's me, Captain Jampton,' muttered the CO, brushing sand from himself as he rose to his feet.

'Sorry, sir,' mumbled Summerskill. 'I hope I didn't wake you.'

The Sergeant Major, guided by the prattle of their exchange, joined them. 'Keep your voices down,' he hissed. 'Sound travels a long way in the desert.'

Jampton was about to reply sternly to this usurping of his command but the Sergeant Major was already addressing the man. 'Go on, lad,' he whispered.

Summerskill had been scouting well ahead of the column when the plane approached. In fact he had actually been in the oasis when the kerosene lamps of the flare path were lit and as shapes had hurried towards the plane when it had finally braked to a stop. As he made his report he became more excited.

'You're not going to believe this,' he said, 'but I swear I could hear dance music coming from one of the buildings and women laughing.'

'Guards?' snapped Jampton regaining his superiority. 'I didn't see anybody – nobody challenged me.'

'Did you see the plane?' asked Puller.

'Yes, sir. It was German all right. Bloody great swastikas on it.'

Eagerly Jampton chipped in. 'Then if Sergeants Sparks and Miller are here, they are being held prisoner.'

Jampton swung round, staring in the direction of the oasis. His heart was beating faster as heroic thoughts sprang to mind. According to Summerskill it was very sloppily defended, if at all. And what a feather in his cap if he were to lead his patrol in and free the two Sergeants. He whirled towards Puller and Summerskill but now there were more dark shapes. The patrol wanted to know what was in the wind.

'We're going in,' he hissed. He wished it was light so he could see their faces as he uttered these momentous words. Luckily for him, though, it was dark and he couldn't see them edging surreptitiously away.

'Right Sar'nt Major,' he said. 'Take six men and deploy round that side of the camp.' His pointing finger was invisible in the darkness.

The Sergeant Major interrupted the half-baked diatribe. 'Sir,' he said patiently, 'with due respect, from Summerskill's report this could be a German camp and I wouldn't give much for our chances – twenty rifles against God knows what.'

'Under cover of darkness?' said Jampton. 'And with the element of surprise?'

'It may be dark now, sir, but it won't be for long.'

'We need only reconnoitre,' pleaded Jampton, modifying his plan somewhat.

'Believe me, sir, it's not our bag. This is a job for three companies of light infantry.'

In any case the discussion was academic; the patrol were well on their way back to the vehicles.

At first light Alexandria began to wake up. Traffic became heavier, noises increased and somewhere a cock crowed. Colonel Brunswick lay in bed listening to Bing Crosby on his shortwave wireless. He harmonised a little, softly so as not to blot out the Master's voice. He was a happy man.

The phone rang and, switching off the set, he lifted the receiver and rapped in a brisk voice, 'Brunswick.' He'd learnt his lesson –

he'd once picked up the phone and yelled 'What the hell d'you want now, Agnes!'. It was a mistake – it turned out to be the Minister of War.

'Message from the oasis, sir.' It was his Adjutant.

'Well,' snapped Brunswick, 'what's it say?'

'I'd rather not over the telephone, sir, but I think you'll like it.'

The Colonel sat up. 'Quite right, Jimmy. I was out of order there. Have my car here in ten minutes – coffee and toast.' He slammed down the receiver and jumped out of bed. He was intrigued and a feeling of happiness swept over him – this was going to be a good day. He switched on the wireless to continue hearing the voice of Bing while he dressed, but a slow, ponderous voice assured him that carrots are good to eat and the nutritional val–

'Bollocks,' he said and switched it off. He padded into his bathroom and stood under the shower – but not for the first time there was no water. However, his mind was elsewhere. He stepped out of the nonexistent shower and from force of habit towelled himself briskly.

Captain Shelley was his usual urbane, unflappable self when his superior strode in, flung his cap on the desk and lifted his coffee cup, which was still tolerably warm. First he sniffed at it, then swallowed a large mouthful, sighing with satisfaction. His Adjutant didn't forget a thing. It had been laced with Dimple Haig; pity about the coffee. Then he sat in his chair and looked up expectantly.

'Well, come on, Jimmy, let's have it,' he said.

'Well, sir,' he began. 'It would appear that Yasmin has struck oil – literally.'

Colonel Brunswick frowned as the report was placed before him. He put on his glasses and began to read. He read for only a short time, then he looked up. 'I don't understand,' he said. 'Supply plane arrives with rations, they load it up with oil for the trip back.'

His Adjutant pointed to the report. 'That's only the first paragraph, sir.'

'I'm aware of that, but the amount of oil taken away is hardly enough to service Rommel's car, let alone ultimate victory.'

'It's a little more than that, sir,' said the Adjutant, twisting his body to look over the desk at the message. 'According to this a Junkers 52 carries a payload of –' he tilted his head further '–

approximately three thousand nine hundred kilos and with two trips a week that makes seven thousand eight hundred kilos, and that's enough to keep a flight of Focke Wolf 190s in the air.'

Brunswick stared at him. 'Then why isn't the oil going to Rommel? It's the only thing that's holding him back.'

'The only explanation I can think of,' replied the Adjutant, 'is that Rommel isn't aware of what's going on. After all, there's no love lost between the Luftwaffe and the Afrika Korps. The Wermacht being the star of the show, the flying men are not too happy as the supporting cast.'

Brunswick nodded and went on with his reading – it was a long, detailed report. Captain Shelley watched him patiently. It wasn't long in coming.

Brunswick's face broke into a smile. 'Ah,' he said and jabbed his finger down on the paper. 'That's more like it,' he said. 'By God, Jimmy, that girl Yasmin is worth a squadron of tanks.'

He'd every reason to be pleased. According to the report, the oil taken away by the Junkers was only the tip of the iceberg. Yasmin had discovered several more camouflage dunes under which lay a vastly greater amount of oil and most likely ammunition as well. Naturally this was only a calculated guess but the enormity of the dump was not in question – it was more than enough to take Rommel's troops into Alexandria and beyond.

Colonel Brunswick rubbed his hands together with a feeling of excitement and chuckled. News of the oil would certainly send his stock soaring in the War Cabinet. He might even get a pat on the head from Winston himself. Yes sir, the war was looking up!

The intelligence report arrived in Whitehall like warm sunshine in the middle of December. Its impact was electrifying. It couldn't have had more of an effect if Hitler had applied for political asylum. It was obvious that the Luftwaffe had no knowledge of the immense reserves of fuel at their disposal, otherwise they would have passed on the information to Field Marshal Rommel and more than likely Rommel and his headquarters staff would be whooping it up in Cairo by now. It was imperative that the British take possession without delay. Whichever side had use of this gigantic oil supply would be two goals up at half-time.

The stratagem concocted by the brass hats in Whitehall was put at the top of the priority list.

Object: oil from El Waddim Oasis to be transferred to Alexandria, British War Effort, for the use of. This was passed down to the planners, the outcome being that twelve Dakotas carrying paratroops would make their way to El Waddim Oasis, the airborne soldiers would be dropped and, after securing their objective, a Dakota would land to be loaded with oil for Alexandria followed by a second Dakota to repeat this action, and subsequently until all twelve had completed the operation.

Further trips to El Waddim Oasis would depend on the quantity of oil. This was then passed down the ladder for the more mundane operating details to be worked out. The stumbling block that took up most of the time was the selection of a code name for the operation. It was finally decided to call it Operation Jupiter. Having accomplished this it was rushed back to the top of the heap and Winston Churchill, peering through his cigar smoke, grunted and wrote across the bottom of the message 'Action This Day'.

Every contingency had been gone over thoroughly. It wasn't a difficult operation and nothing had been overlooked. However, there was a snag that not even the sharpest brains in Whitehall could have foreseen. It was another assault on El Waddim Oasis but this one was code named Exercise Spiller 4.

NINE

The Special Ordnance Group led by the indomitable Captain Jampton were back among the dunes surrounding the oasis. But this time it was midday and a full turnout, nearly sixty men, carried rifles and some of the more experienced of the old 41st Infantry were equipped with light machine guns.

They were on the brink of exhaustion when they reached the start point. It had been a torturous trek through the soft sand in a temperature over a hundred degrees. The high-noon strategy had been Jampton's idea – hit them when they were at their most vulnerable during their siesta, sleeping and dozing in the midday heat. It had never occurred to him that his own troops would also be suffering and certainly no match for an enemy refreshed by sleep under some shade or other.

Now Captain Jampton, face red as a turkey cock and shirt black with sweat, was reluctantly coming to the conclusion that his idea wasn't a good one after all. He ordered a halt and assembled his men in a long line on either side of him and passed the order for a ten-minute break. They were now only six or seven hundred yards from their objective.

Sergeant Major Puller struggled wearily through the treacherous sand towards him. Thinking back, he decided that the horrendous convoy through the sandstorm was infinitely better than today. How the hell were they supposed to take this camp was beyond him. By the time they reached the oasis the lads wouldn't have the strength to lift their arms in surrender and he was damn certain it wasn't worth all this effort just to free Sergeants Sparks and Miller. As far as he was concerned he was glad to be shot of them.

He watched as Jampton sat on the sand, immediately springing back on to his feet as if he'd bounced off a trampoline and patting his backside.

Sergeant Major Puller was too far gone to smile. The little pillock hadn't even got the sense to realise the sand would be like a hotplate. He slithered over to where his CO was still patting his backside.

'It's no good, sir,' he said, 'the lads are knackered. In their condition they couldn't beat a junior girls' netball team.'

There was a silence between them then Jampton said in a dry voice, 'What are you trying to say, Sar'nt Major?'

The Sergeant Major said it and Jampton was off the hook.

'All right,' he sighed. 'At the end of the break, pass the word along to make tracks for the vehicles.'

When the order was passed on that they were returning to camp it was a shot in the arm. Several of them rose to their feet, brushing sand from their uniforms. They didn't want a break: they wanted to be off. They were rejuvenated like school boys at the end of term. The whitewashed stones and the replacement red-and-white pole of the Special Ordnance Group had never been more appreciated.

But, sadly, many of them would never see the camp again. That break of ten minutes was to be the last they would ever enjoy. For those who survived, it would haunt them for the rest of their lives.

It all began at the far end of the extended skirmishing line. Nobby Clark stared around him through a pair of binoculars, twiddling the focusing wheel. 'Where'd you get these from?' he asked his mate, who winked and patted them. 'Zeiss,' he said, and made to take them back.

'Hang on,' said Nobby, jerking his arm away. He started to slither and stagger to the top of a high dune. When he reached the summit he couldn't get his breath and had to take the cigarette out of his mouth in order to cough. This done he replaced the cigarette and raised the binoculars to his eyes and stared into the distance. Then he swivelled to the right and as he did so he had a feeling that something was wrong. He looked down at his feet and then moved to one side, and looked again. It wasn't sand – it looked like canvas or tarpaulin. He took the cigarette from his lips and shouted, 'Hey Jacko, there's something funny about this lot . . .' He never finished his sentence. There was a ripping noise and with a yelp Nobby disappeared from view.

Jacko looked up, perplexed. It was the last thing he ever saw. A burning cigarette and high-octane fuel are a lethal mix – the explosion was horrendous.

The dune was ripped apart by a second, louder, explosion as burning fuel shot hundreds of feet into the air. The sun was blotted out by the oily black smoke. All the men unfortunate enough to be in the vicinity were never seen again. Others were screaming and writhing in the sand in a vain attempt to put out the flames engulfing them.

Jampton stared in horrified fascination. Some of the soldiers ran for protection behind the next dune but it was a mistake. Burning fuel from the first silo was already eating through the thin covering of sand, and with another shattering explosion the second dune erupted taking all the men with it.

The Sergeant Major, face blackened with smoke, realised the situation at once. They were trapped in a blazing oil dump. From another dune a further explosion, and this was accompanied by flying tracer bullets. 'God Almighty!' he breathed. 'That's ammo.' He grabbed Jampton's arm. They had to get out of the valley. Every dune was suspect. God only knew how much stuff was hidden away here and with the domino effect as other dunes went up, death was creeping towards them.

He tried to drag Jampton away but the little man had found some strength from somewhere. He wouldn't budge and was staring at the carnage, eyes like headlamps. Puller grabbed his arm again. The heat was now unbearable and Puller's eyebrows were singed and his hair was beginning to crackle. He dragged Jampton a yard or two but the little bastard shook himself free and began to run towards the inferno.

Another explosion ripped the air, slamming him back, and something rolled towards him. He didn't move as it came to rest at his feet but when he saw what it was he began screaming like a young girl on the big dipper. Puller looked down. It was a man's head, blackened out of recognition.

Jampton was still screaming at the top of his voice and when the Sergeant Major grabbed his arm again he fought himself free and, still screaming, he scrabbled for his pistol. But the Sergeant

Major had had enough. He smashed his fist into Jampton's face, caught the sagging body and humped it over his shoulder, staggering off to God knew where, any place to get out of this blistering deathtrap. 'You stupid bastard,' he yelled at the top of his voice. 'You wanted to see action,' he screamed, tears rolling down his face. 'I hope you're satisfied, you useless pillock.'

Jampton, lolling over the Sergeant Major's shoulder, didn't mind. He was out to the wide.

The shock of the first explosion jerked the Italians in the oasis out of sleep. Sparks and Miller, who had been dozing at the table in the shade of the palm, sprang instantly to their feet as the blast shredded all the leaves from the tops of the trees, exposing them both to bright sunlight.

Italians in various stages of undress ran from their billets in a mad stampede. There was another, louder, explosion and immediately the whole mass of them veered in a different direction.

Sparks and Miller ran round the corner of the hotel as another explosion hurled Sparks against the wall. Miller hauled him to his feet, scanning the sky for the bombers. In complete disorientation they ran to a corner of the building and immediately stopped dead in their tracks, frozen with horror – the whole desert was ablaze and creeping towards them was a burning river of oil. They were transfixed, too paralysed with the enormity of the scene to move, when out of the smoke staggered someone carrying what looked like a sack of potatoes over his shoulders. He almost collapsed in front of them and Miller grabbed his burden. It was a man, and, laying him gently on the ground, he wiped some of the grime from the man's face and then stopped and jerked back.

'What's up?' said Sparks.

Miller didn't look around. 'Take a look for yourself. You're not going to believe this. It's Hugh.' And on hearing his voice Captain Jampton sat up and wiped his eyes.

'I thought it might be,' said Sparks. 'This one's the Sergeant Major.'

'Can you walk, sir?' asked Miller.

Jampton turned towards him with vacant eyes and a beatific smile on his face but he didn't say anything. Miller didn't like the look of him at all. He held up his hand in front of Jampton's face. 'How many fingers have I got up?' he said. But Jampton stared at him with eyes that didn't look as if they could see. A rivulet of burning oil crept round the corner. It was enough. Miller picked up his CO and slung him over his shoulder and the three of them began to run towards the comparative safety of the lake.

At 2300 hours the first Dakota took off from Aboukir and when all twelve planes were airborne, they set course for El Waddim Oasis under an umbrella of night fighters equipped with extra fuel tanks. Operation Jupiter was well into Phase One. The two companies of paratroops occupied the first four Dakotas. They had been well briefed. It should be a soft landing and opposition was likely to be nonexistent. Some of them, those who'd seen action in the past, weren't convinced – they'd heard it all before.

Apart from a hairy five minutes from a hostile anti-aircraft battery, probably British, the flight was uneventful. The Squadron Leader at the controls in the leading Dakota with thirty-five minutes to his ETA was puzzled. What had seemed to be a red glare ahead in the far distance was confirmed. The glare was getting brighter and, whatever it was, it was something immense. After a few more minutes' flying his worst fear became a certainty. It could only be El Waddim Oasis – what the hell was going on?

The Paratroop Captain was leaning over his shoulder. Bloody hell, he thought. It's a bit too big for a barbecue. In another fifteen minutes they were right over the target; at 2,000 feet they circled the conflagration. The pilot was thinking hard – his orders had been clear. The only word to be transmitted would be 'Bingo' and only then on completion of a successful mission. The wireless operator came forward and looked down – even at this height his horror-stricken face was lit by the flames.

The skipper decided to break radio silence and instructed his operator to inform base of the situation. Target in flames – landing impossible – await further orders.

On the ground it could only be assumed that the last of the deadly silos had been detonated. There had not been an explosion for some time. Most of the survivors were on the other side of the lake in comparative safety. Shocked, blackened and dishevelled, they stood apathetically amidst the groans and screams of the badly burnt survivors. Several men and some of the girls did their utmost to comfort them but with few supplies of medicine and certainly no morphine they could do little to alleviate the suffering. They didn't even bother to look up as the Dakotas thundered overhead.

At first light the paratroopers jumped out of the Dakotas, parachutes blossoming as they floated down some miles to the north of the oasis, the Dakotas peeling away to make their way to Alexandria, one Dakota remaining to circle the oasis in order to maintain wireless contact with the paratroopers when they hit the ground.

Colonel Brunswick was apprised of the situation as he was rushed to Aboukir and inside ten minutes he was airborne in a Lysander. At the oasis the paratroopers had taken command of the situation and were doing all they could for the survivors, but it was a hopeless task. Although they had two medical orderlies and supplies of morphine, there was little they could do. Even so, their presence was a comfort.

At ten o'clock the light plane was circling the oasis and Colonel Brunswick stared down, white-faced. The whole area was decimated. Fires still blazing here and there, it was like looking down into the gaping mouth of an active volcano. The pilot tapped him on the shoulder. 'It's OK to land, sir. They've cleared the strip.'

Ten minutes later Colonel Brunswick took in the scene from ground level. He was appalled as he walked slowly through the blanket-covered bodies arranged in neat rows by the lake. The carnage about him was indescribable.

'Sir.' He whirled round. Staring into the blackened, exhausted face of Sergeant Major Puller, he wasn't even surprised to see him there. In some strange way he'd known all along. He couldn't bring himself to speak. He waved his arms ineffectually at the carnage around him and shook his head.

'How did it happen?' he asked finally in a low voice.

Briefly Puller explained about Exercise Spiller, how Captain Jampton had passed on orders to abort the operation when the first dune went up. He couldn't explain why or how.

The Colonel sighed heavily and looked round at the devastation. At least, he thought, it'll deny Rommel the use of it. Then, turning to the Sergeant Major, he asked, 'And how is my nephew?'

'Captain Jampton, sir . . .' Puller was uncomfortable. 'I'm afraid they'll send him home, sir.'

Brunswick looked at him sharply.

'Oh he's not wounded, sir. Not physically that is, but, er, mentally I'm afraid he's . . .'

Again the Colonel said nothing.

'I'm sorry, sir,' added the Sergeant Major. 'I think he felt responsible and it was all too much for him.' His voice tailed off.

'Thank you, Sar'nt Major. I understand.'

He understood all too well. It had been his brilliant idea to form the Special Ordnance Group, and an even brighter one to place it under the command of his nephew. The blame rested squarely on his own shoulders. The responsibility for this tragedy was his alone and he knew the guilt would trouble him for the rest of his life.

The Colonel glanced down at the blackened and burned hands and arms, then up into the Sergeant Major's tired face.

'I think it's time you got yourself some medical attention,' he said gruffly.

'Yes, sir,' snapped Puller. 'Just as soon as some more medical supplies come in.' He saluted wearily and made his way towards the huts. The Colonel watched him go then turned to survey the long rows of blanket-covered bodies. God what a mess. The roar of a landing Dakota caused him to look towards the air strip and at the pathetic line of stretcher cases and walking wounded, some assisted by the girls, patiently waiting to board the planes. When this plane was loaded, another would take its place, and then another, until the evacuation was complete.

Colonel Brunswick lit a cigarette. It wasn't easy. He hoped no one noticed his trembling hand. As a Director of British Intelligence he know that in the next few days there would be many more deaths. The war in North Africa was about to explode and every war threw up its casualties – but then, did there really have to be wars? He shook his head sadly. He thought of his wife, Lady Dorothy, and her high-born relations, and the power they wielded behind the scene – unelected, unaccountable and yet influencing the tide of history with aristocratic disdain for all those beneath them. No one had asked the Gallant Six Hundred if they wanted to ride into the cannons of the Turks, or the 60,000 casualties on the Somme as they marched with their rifles at high port across no man's land to be cut down row upon row by the German machine guns. These mass suicides had been approved and in many cases instigated over vintage claret in cut-crystal glasses. Whoever carried the can, the aristocracy always survived.

Yet again, was the alternative any better? The French revolution had been a disaster. In Russia, Stalin was infinitely more dangerous than the Tzar and his relations. Hitler wasn't far behind him, either. The Colonel winced as the cigarette burned his fingers. It had burned right down without him even taking a drag. The Dakota lumbered into the air and another was already in the circuit waiting to land. This broke his train of thought. He took out his handkerchief and blew his nose, then shrugged. Politics and philosophising weren't his pigeon. He had a war to run . . . and where the hell were Sparks and Miller?

Sparks and Miller went to find Carlo. He was in the hotel, or what was left of it. There was just enough roof left to provide the shade under which Carlo sat at a table staring morosely into a glass of wine. They stood awkwardly in front of him. He looked up.

'My dear friends, you have come to say goodbye.' He shook his head. 'I see you have still got your biscuit tin.'

Miller, embarrassed, shuffled uneasily. 'Yes, sir, er, and I'm sorry about, er, what's happened and that.'

'Ach,' said Carlo. 'Is not your fault. And since you two arrive we have fun, yes? And excitement and what about the girls? The last few weeks have been happy. At last the El Waddim Oasis became what it was originally designed to be.' A tired smile crossed his face. 'What did you call it once? The best little knocking shop in Africa?'

The Sergeant Major walked in and broke up the party, saluting Carlo smartly.

'Colonel Brunswick's compliments, sir. And would you get your lads assembled, taking only what they can carry. It's an hour or two's march to the truck line.'

Carlo thanked him, and came round the table to embrace Sparks and Miller. 'If you are ever in Roma,' he said, 'ask for Carlo and I will give you the best table.'

Two hours later, the long line of three-ton Bedfords, packed with Italians, rolled out along the flat stony surface towards Alexandria. Then the Sergeant Major turned back to his own convoy for the survivors of Special Ordnance – just two trucks, and these half empty. Forty-seven dead and injured was a helluva price to pay. Sparks and Miller were about to clamber aboard when Puller stopped them.

'Not you lads. They've laid on a special treat for you.'

The two Sergeants looked at each other.

'Like what, sir?' asked Miller, but the Sergeant Major didn't reply. He shaded his eyes at a small speck in the distance, creating a very impressive dust trail. As it got nearer they could see it was an open touring car. When it drew up in a cloud of dust, Miller whistled softly.

'Blimey,' he said. 'Where're we off to?'

The Sergeant Major thrust an envelope at Miller. 'There's your marching orders,' he said. He turned towards his own truck, then stopped and turned back again. 'By the way,' he asked in a curious voice, 'what have you got in the biscuit tin?'

Miller didn't look up. 'Ginger nuts,' he said, struggling to open the envelope.

Sparks took it from him and proceeded to read: '. . . to make all speed to General Montgomery's caravan, reference 607982. As from 22nd you are promoted to the rank of Warrant Officer and will be attached to General Montgomery's personal staff.'

Sergeant Major Puller looked away disgustedly. 'If you two fell head first down a Whitechapel sewer, you'd come up smelling of roses.'

He watched as they made themselves comfortable in the back seats. Miller leant forward and tapped the driver on the shoulder. 'Who's this General Montgomery?' he said.

Before the driver could reply, the Sergeant Major strolled over and leant on the door. 'General Montgomery?' he asked. 'Oh yes, you don't know him yet, do you? He came over when you were on your holidays.'

Miller leant forward to the driver and said, 'Do you know where this reference place is?'

'Yes, sir,' replied the driver.

'Well then, let's go,' said Miller and waved grandly at the Sergeant Major as he passed him in a cloud of dust. 'This is the life,' said Miller, beaming all over his face.

Sparks didn't reply.

'Warrant Officers, eh?' went on Miller proudly. 'Next thing you know we'll be Brigadier Generals.'

They'd been travelling for half an hour when Sparks leant forward and, tapping the driver on his shoulder, said, 'Stop here, mate.'

The driver pulled up and Sparks got out. Miller looked at him curiously. 'You should have gone before we set out,' he said, but he didn't like the way his oppo was smiling at him.

'What's up?' he asked.

Sparks sighed. 'This is as far as I go, Dusty. It's been nice knowing you.'

Miller stared at him uncomprehendingly. 'What the bloody hell are you on about?'

Sparks looked at him for a minute. 'I don't want to join General Montgomery's staff. I don't want to be a Warrant Officer, and I've got enough medals.'

Miller looked at him and then noticed a movement on top of a ridge behind his mate. He squinted – it was an Arab woman in the black robes of the desert. 'Yasmin?' he asked softly.

Sparks shrugged.

Miller was worried. 'What shall I tell the General?' he asked.

'You'll think of something,' said Sparks and turning on his heel he walked away.

'Oi,' shouted Miller half-heartedly as Sparks continued.

Miller watched him join the Arab woman, who turned and waved. Miller waved back and they drove on.

The car trundled on. Miller was deep in thought. He was miserable and panic surged through him at the vision of life without Sparks.

'Ah well,' he muttered, 'I'll miss him, you know.'

The driver looked at him through the mirror. 'Yes, Sergeant,' he replied in a neutral voice.

It was going to be a long trip and he didn't want to be involved in a maudlin diatribe about comradeship and brotherly love. The car lurched up a slight rise and before them stretched a flat bit of the Sahara. This made driving easier and they increased speed. The driver squinted his eyes as in the distance he saw indistinct shapes coming slowly towards them. Miller had also spotted them and craned forward over the back of the front seat. Then as the figures became recognisable he relaxed and flopped back against the leather upholstery.

'Bloody Arab and his camel,' he said with a smile. 'He doesn't have to worry about who's winning as long as he can sell his fruit.'

The driver smiled, then Miller tapped him eagerly on his shoulder. 'Here,' he said, 'fancy a melon?' And before the driver had time to decide whether he fancied a melon there came a loud whooshing of air and a twenty-five-pound shell blew the car and its occupants to a better place.

The Arab, never deviating, continued his regular journey passing the burning wreck with hardly a glance. The date was 23 October and when darkness fell the greatest artillery barrage in military history was unleashed at a little town called Alamein, heralding the beginning of the end.

EPILOGUE

OCTOBER 1947

Five years after the decisive battle of Alamein, the North African desert, having staged this devastating extravaganza, settled itself back into its thousands of years of anonymity.

The camel and its driver plod through the desert skirting the detritus of war, rusting hulks of tanks, burnt out wagons, ugly, spent scrap metal ...

Sir Charles Brunswick now serves as Governor of a little island in the South Seas, one of the last outposts of the Empire. Not a fitting promotion perhaps, but then anything was better than pushing his nephew's wheelchair through the leafy lanes of Shropshire ...

At the Aeolian Hall in Bond Street, London, where the BBC records many shows, a commissionaire will open the door for you. Two rows of medal ribbons brighten the breast of his black uniform. He has only one arm, having been one of the first casualties of Sword Beach during the D-Day Landings in Normandy. Most of the employees hurry past him into the building with scarcely a nod, medal ribbons mean nothing to them and amongst themselves they refer to him as Granddad. Ex Sergeant Major Puller is not yet forty ...

The camel perks up as it reaches the soft sand now on home territory the journey almost at an end ...

Albert Gratwick and Rudolph Borsch run a children's book shop in Amsterdam ... they were married in August 1946 ...

The camel, led by its driver, entered the El Waddim Oasis with a look of smug satisfaction on its face. It's mission was once more complete. A goat came out of the front door of the ramshackle hotel and surveyed the camel with arrogant eyes and a hen fussed around it, clucking and whinging at some imagined outrage. From one of the huts, a handful of small children ran, skipped and stumbled, joyously surrounding the man, holding on to his legs and laughing. He bent to pick up the smallest toddler, lifting him high on the camel's saddle, then, taking down the cloth that protected his mouth and nose he smiled. He turned towards the building – 'Yasmin!' he yelled. 'Where's my bloody tea?'